Charles Bertram Black

The South of France

east half - including the valleys of the Rhône, Drôme and Durance, the baths of

Vichy, Royat, Aix, Mont-Dore and Bourboule, the whole of the Riviera from Cette to

Leghorn with the inland towns of Turin, Bologna, Parma, Florence

Charles Bertram Black

The South of France
east half - including the valleys of the Rhône, Drôme and Durance, the baths of Vichy, Royat, Aix, Mont-Dore and Bourboule, the whole of the Riviera from Cette to Leghorn with the inland towns of Turin, Bologna, Parma, Florence

ISBN/EAN: 9783337382827

Printed in Europe, USA, Canada, Australia, Japan

Cover: Foto ©Andreas Hilbeck / pixelio.de

More available books at **www.hansebooks.com**

THE

SOUTH OF FRANCE

EAST HALF

INCLUDING THE VALLEYS OF

THE RHÔNE, DRÔME AND DURANCE

THE BATHS OF

VICHY, ROYAT, AIX, MONT-DORE AND BOURBOULE

THE WHOLE OF THE

RIVIERA FROM CETTE TO LEGHORN

WITH THE INLAND TOWNS OF

TURIN, BOLOGNA, PARMA, FLORENCE AND PISA

AND

THE PASSES BETWEEN FRANCE AND ITALY

Illustrated with Maps and Plans

FOURTH EDITION

C. B. BLACK

EDINBURGH: ADAM AND CHARLES BLACK
1885

PREFACE.

THIS Guide-book consists of *Routes* which follow the course of the main Railways. To adapt these Routes as far as possible to the requirements of every one the Branch Lines are also pointed out, together with the stations from which the Coaches run, in connection with the trains, to towns distant from the railway. The description of the places on these branch lines is printed either in a closer or in a smaller letter than that of the towns on the main lines.

Each Route has the *Map* indicated on which it is to be found. By aid of these maps the traveller can easily discover his exact situation, and either form new routes for himself, or follow those given.

The *Arrangement* of the Routes is such that they may be taken either from the commencement to the end, or from the end to the commencement. The Route from Paris to Marseilles, for example, does equally well for Marseilles to Paris.

The *Distance* of towns from the place of starting to the terminus is expressed by the figures which accompany them on each side of the margin ; while the distance of any two towns on the same route from each other is found by subtracting their marginal figures on either side from each other.

In the *Description* of towns the places of interest have been taken in the order of their position, so that, if a cab be engaged, all that is necessary is to mention to the driver their names in succession. Cabs on such occasions should be hired by the hour. To guard against omission, the traveller should underline the names of the places to be visited before commencing the round. In France the Churches are open all the day. In Italy they close at 12 ; but most of them reopen at 2 P.M. All the

Picture-Galleries are open on Sundays, and very many also on Thursdays. When not open to the public, admission is generally granted on payment of a franc.

In "Table of Contents" the Routes are classified and explained. For the Time-tables recommended, and for the mode of procedure on the Continental Railways, see "Preliminary Information."

Before commencing our description of the Winter Resorts on the Mediterranean, with the best routes towards them, let it be clearly understood that not even in the very mildest of these stations is it safe for the invalid to venture out either in the early morning or after sunset without being well protected with warm clothing ; and that, even with this precaution, the risk run of counteracting the beneficial influences of a sojourn in these regions is so great as to render it prudent to determine from the first to spend those hours always within doors. On the other hand, it is most conducive to health, during the sunny hours of the day, to remain as much as possible in the open air, walking and driving along the many beautiful terraces and roads with which these places abound ; and if the day be well employed in such exercise, it will be no great hardship to rest at home in the evening. Nor is it necessary to remain in the same town during the entire season ; indeed a change of scene is generally most beneficial, for which the railway as well as the steamers affords every facility. "I would strongly advise every person who goes abroad for the recovery of his health, whatever may be his disease or to what climate soever he may go, to consider the change as placing him merely in a more favourable situation for the removal of his disease ; in fact, to bear constantly in mind that the beneficial influence of travelling, of sailing, and of climate requires to be aided by such dietetic regimen and general mode of living, and by such remedial measures as would have been requisite in his case had he remained in his own country. All the circumstances requiring attention from the invalid at home should be equally attended to abroad. If in some things greater latitude may be permitted, others will demand even a more rigid attention. It is, in truth, only by a due regard to all these circumstances that the powers of the constitution can be enabled to throw off, or even materially mitigate, in the best climate, a disease of long standing.

"It may appear strange that I should think it requisite to insist so strongly on the necessity of attention to these directions; but I have witnessed the injurious effects of a neglect of them too often not to deem such remarks called for in this place. It was, indeed, matter of surprise to me, during my residence abroad, to observe the manner in which many invalids seemed to lose sight of the object for which they left their own country —the recovery of their health. This appeared to arise chiefly from too much being expected from climate.

"The more common and more injurious deviations from that system of living which an invalid ought to adopt, consist in errors of diet, exposure to cold, over-fatigue, and excitement in what is called 'sight-seeing,' frequenting crowded and over-heated rooms, and keeping late hours. Many cases fell under my observation in which climate promised the greatest advantage, but where its beneficial influence was counteracted by the operation of these causes."—*Sir James Clark on the Sanative Influence of Climate.*

SEE MAP PAGE 27, AND MAP ON FLY-LEAF.

Many after leaving the Riviera are the better of making a short stay at some of the baths, such as Vichy (p. 359), Vals (p. 93), Mont-Dore (p. 378), Bourboule (p. 383), Aix-les-Bains (p. 283), Bourbon-l'Archambault (p. 357), or Bourbon-Lancy (p. 358). If at the eastern end of the Riviera, the nearest way to them is by rail from Savona (pp. 209 and 183), or from Genoa (pp. 212 and 279) to Turin (p. 292). From Turin a short branch line extends to Torre-Pèllice (p. 305), situated in one of the most beautiful of the Waldensian valleys.

If the journey from Turin to Aix-les-Bains, 128 miles, be too long, a halt may be made for the night at Modane (p. 290); where, however, on account of the elevation, 3445 ft., the air is generally rather sharp and bracing.

From the western end of the Riviera the best way north and to the baths is by the valley of the Rhône (map, p. 27), in which there are many places of great interest, such as Arles (p. 68), Avignon (p. 58), Orange (p. 51), and Lyons (p. 29). From Lyons take the western branch by Montbrison (p. 349) for Vichy, Mont-Dore, and Bourboule. For Aix-les-Bains take the eastern by Ambérieux (p. 281) and Culoz (p. 282). From Avignon, Carpentras (p. 54), Pont-St. Esprit (p. 98), Montélimart (p. 48), La Voulte (p. 82), Crest (p. 46) and Grenoble (p. 324), interesting and picturesque excursions are made. From Carpentras Mont Ventoux (p. 56) is visited. From La Voulte, Ardeche (p. 45) is entered. From Crest diligences run to the towns and villages between it and Aspres (pp. 47 and 345). From Grenoble the roads and railways diverge which lead to the lofty peaks of the western Alps and to the mountain passes between France and Italy.

None should go abroad without a passport. Even where several are travelling together in one party, each should have his own passport. They are easily procured and easily carried, and may be of great use.

The best hotels in the places frequented by the Americans and English cost per day from 12 to 22 frs., and the pensions from 9 to 15 frs., including wine (often sour) in both. The general charge in the hotels of the other towns throughout France is from 8 to 9 frs. per day. Meat breakfast, 2 to 3 frs.; dinner, 3 to 4 frs.; service, $\frac{1}{2}$ fr.; "café au lait," with bread and butter, $1\frac{1}{2}$ fr. The omnibus between the hotel and the station costs each from 6 to 10 sous. The driver in most cases loads and unloads the luggage himself at the station, when he expects a small gratuity from 2 to 10 sous, according to the quantity of bags and trunks. The omnibuses of the Riviera hotels cost from $1\frac{1}{2}$ to 2 frs. each, and although the conductor does not unload the luggage he expects a gratuity.

Neither jewellery nor money should be carried in portmanteaus. When a stay of merely a day or two is intended, the bulky and heavy luggage should be left in depôt at the station. Some companies charge 1, others 2 sous for each article (colis) per day. See "Railways" in "Preliminary Information."

C. B. B.

PRELIMINARY INFORMATION.

THE LANDING-PLACES ON THE FRENCH SIDE OF THE CHANNEL.

THE six principal ports on the French side of the English Channel connected by railroad with Paris are :—

Dieppe—distant from Paris 125 miles ; passing Clères Junction, 100 m. ; Rouen, 85 m. ; Gaillon, 58 m. ; Mantes Junction, 36 m. ; and Poissy, 17 m. from Paris. Arrives at the station of the Chemins de Fer de l'Ouest, Saint Lazare. Time, 4½ hours. Fares—1st class, 25 frs. ; 2d cl. 19 frs. ; 3d cl. 14 frs.

London to Paris *via* Newhaven and Dieppe (240 miles) :—tidal ; daily, except Sunday, from Victoria Station and London Bridge Station. Fare —1st class, 31s. ; 2d cl. 23s. ; 3d cl. 16s. 6d. Sea journey, 60 miles ; time, 8 hours. Time for entire journey, 16 hours. For tickets, etc., in Paris apply to Chemin de Fer de l'Ouest, Gare St. Lazare, Rue St. Lazare 110, ancien 124. Bureau spécial, agent, M. Marcillet, Rue de la Paix, 7. A. Collin et Cie, 20 Boulevard Saint Denis.

From Dieppe another line goes to Paris by Arques, Neufchâtel, Serqueux, Forges-les-Eaux, Gournay, Gisors, and Pontoise. Distance, 105 miles. Time by ordinary trains, 5 hours 10 minutes. Fares—1st class, 21 frs. ; 2d, 15½ frs. ; 3d, 11¼ frs. Arrives at the St. Lazare station of the Chemins de Fer de l'Ouest.

From Tréport a railway extends to Paris by Eu, Gamaches, Aumale, Abancourt, Beauvais, and Creil. Distance, 119¼ miles. Time, 8 hours 40 minutes. Fares, 1st class, 24 frs. ; 2d, 18 frs. ; 3d, 13 frs. Arrives at the station of the Chemin de Fer du Nord. There are few through trains by this line.

BOULOGNE—distant 158 miles from Paris ; passing Montreuil, 134 m. ; Abbeville, 109 m. ; Amiens, 82 m. ; Clermont, 41 m. ; and Creil, 32 m. from Paris. Arrives at the station of the Chemin de Fer du Nord, No. 18 Place Roubaix. Time by express, 4½ hours. Fares—1st class, 31 frs. 25 c. ; 2d cl. 23 frs. 45 c. ; 3d cl. 17 frs. 20 c.

London to Paris, *via* Folkestone and Boulogne (255 miles) :—tidal route ; from Charing Cross, Cannon Street, or London Bridge. Express trains daily to Folkestone, and from Boulogne, first and second class. Sea journey, 27 miles ; time of crossing, 1 hour 40 minutes. Fares from London to Paris by Boulogne—1st class, 56s. ; 2d cl. 42s. Time for the entire journey, 10 hours. For tickets, etc., in Paris apply to the railway station of the Chemin de Fer du Nord.

CALAIS—185 miles from Paris; by Boulogne, 158 m.; Montreuil, 134 m.; Abbeville, 109 m.; Amiens, 82 m.; Clermont, 41 m.; and Creil, 32 m. from Paris. Arrives at the station of the Chemin de Fer du Nord, No. 18 Place Roubaix. Time by express, 5½ hours. Fares—1st class, 36 frs. 55 c.; 2d cl. 27 frs. 40 c.

London to Paris, *via* Dover and Calais (mail route, distance 283 miles); —departing from Charing Cross, Cannon Street, or London Bridge. Sea journey, 21 miles; time about 80 minutes. First and second class, express. Fares—60s.; 2d cl. 45s. Total time, London to Paris, 10 hours. Luggage is registered throughout from London, and examined in Paris. Only 60 lbs. free. For tickets, etc., in Paris apply at the railway station of the Chemins de Fer du Nord.

CALAIS—204 miles from Paris; by Saint Omer, 177 m.; Hazebrouck, 165 m.; Arras, 119 m.; Amiens, 82 m.; Clermont, 41 m.; and Creil, 32 m. Arrives at the station, No. 18 Place Roubaix. Time, 7 hours 40 minutes. Fares—1st class, 36 frs. 55 c.; 2d cl. 27 frs. 40 c.; 3d. cl. 20 frs. 10 c.

DUNKERQUE—190 miles from Paris; by Bergues, 185 miles; Hazebrouck, 165 m., where it joins the line from Calais; Arras, 119 m.; Amiens, 81 m.; Clermont, 41 m.; and Creil, 32 m. Arrives at the station, No. 18 Place Roubaix. Time, 10½ hours. Fares—1st class, 37 frs. 55 c.; 2d cl. 28 frs. 15 c.

England and Channel, *via* Thames and Dunkirk (screw):—tidal; three times a week from Fenning's Wharf. Also from Leith, in 48 to 54 hours.

LE HAVRE—142 miles from Paris; by Harfleur, 138 m.; Beuzeville Junction, 126 miles; Bolbec-Nointot, 123 m.; Yvetot, 111 m.; Rouen, 87 m.; Gaillon, 58 m.; Mantes Junction, 36 m.; and Poissy, 17 m. from Paris. Arrives, as from Dieppe and Cherbourg, at the station of the Chemin de Fer de l'Ouest, No. 124 Rue St. Lazare. Fares—1st class, 28 frs. 10 c.; 2d cl. 21 frs. 5 c.; 3d cl. 15 frs. 45 c. Time by express, 4 hours 50 minutes, and nearly 3 hours longer by the ordinary trains.

London and Channel, *via* Southampton and Le Havre:—Monday, Wednesday, and Friday, 9 P.M. from Waterloo Station, leaving Southampton 11.45 P.M. Sea journey, 80 m.; time, 8 hours.

CHERBOURG—231 miles from Paris; by Lison, 184 m.; Bayeux, 167 m.; Caen, 149 m.; Mezidon Junction, 134 m.; Lisieux, 119 m.; Serquigny Junction, 93 m.; Evreux, 67 m.; Mantes Junction, 36 m.; and Poissy, 17 m. from Paris. Time by express, 8½ hours; slow trains, nearly 13 hours.

FRENCH, BELGIAN, AND GERMAN RAILWAYS.

On these railways the rate of travelling is slower than in England, but the time is more accurately kept.

To each passenger is allowed 30 kilogrammes, or 66 lbs. weight of luggage free.

Railway Time-Tables.

Time-tables or Indicateurs. For France the most useful and only official time-tables are those published by Chaix and Cie, and sold at all the railway stations. Of these excellent publications there are various kinds. The most complete and most expensive is the "Livret-Chaix Continental," which, besides the time-tables of the French railways, gives those also of the whole Continent, and is furnished with a complete index; size 18mo, with about 800 pages. The "Livret-Chaix Continental" is sold at the station bookstalls. Price 2 frs.

Next in importance is the "Indicateur des Chemins de Fer," sold at every station; size 128 small folio pages, price 60 c. It contains the time-tables of the French railways alone, and an index and railway map.

The great French lines of the "Chemins de Fer de l'Ouest," of the "Chemins de Fer d'Orleans," of the "Chemins de Fer de Paris à Lyon et à la Méditerranée," of the "Chemins de Fer du Nord," and of the "Chemins de Fer de l'Est," have each time-tables of their own, sold at all their stations. Price 40 c. Size 18me. With good index.

For Belgium, the best time-tables are in the "Guide Officiel sur tous les Chemins de Fer de Belgique." Sold at the Belgian railway stations. Size 18me. Price 30 c. It contains a good railway map of Belgium.

For Italy, use "L'Indicatore Ufficiale delle Strade Ferrate d'Italia." Containing excellent maps illustrating their circular tours. Price 1 fr.

In Spain use the "Indicador de los Ferro-Carriles," sold at the stations. The distances are, as in the French tables, in kilometres, of which 8 make 5 miles. *Lleg.* or *Llegada* means "arrival"; *Salida*, "departure."

In England consult the "Continental Time-tables of the London, Chatham, and Dover Railway," sold at the Victoria Station, Pimlico, price 2d.; or those of the London and South-Eastern, 1d.

In the Railway Station.

Before going to the station, it is a good plan to turn up in the index of the "Livret-Chaix Continental" the place required, to ascertain the fare and the time of starting, which stations are supplied with refreshment rooms (marked B), and the time the train halts at each on its way.

On arriving at the station join the single file (queue) of people before the small window (guichet), where the tickets (billets) are sold. Your turn having arrived, and having procured your ticket, proceed to the luggage department, where deposit your baggage and deliver your ticket to be stamped. The luggage tickets are called also "bulletins."

After your articles have been weighed, your ticket, along with a luggage receipt, is handed you from the "guichet" of the luggage office, where, if your baggage is not overweight, you pay 10 c. or 2 sous. Before pocketing the luggage ticket, just run your eye down the column headed "Nombre de Colis," and see that the exact number of your articles has been given. The French have a strange way of making the figures 3, 5, and 7. Whatever is overweight is paid for at this office ; but remember, when two or more are travelling together, to present the tickets of the whole party at the luggage department, otherwise the luggage will be treated as belonging to one person, and thus it will probably be overweight. Another advantage of having the entire number of the party on the "Billet de Bagage" is that, in case of one or other losing their carriage tickets, this will prove the accident to the stationmaster (chef-de-Gare) and satisfy him. If, after having purchased a ticket, the train is missed, that ticket, to be available for the next train, must be presented again to the ticket office, to be re-stamped (être visé).

The traveller, on arriving at his destination, will frequently find it more convenient not to take his luggage away with him ; in which case, having seen it brought from the train to the station, he should tell the porter that he wishes it left there. He retains, however, his luggage ticket, which he only presents when he desires his luggage again.

On the Railway.

In the carriage cast the eye over the line as given in our railway map, and note the junctions ; for at many of these—such as Amiens, Rouen, Culoz, Macon, etc. etc.—the passengers are frequently discharged from the carriages and sent into the waiting-rooms to await other trains. On such occasions great attention must be paid to the names the porter calls out when he opens the door of the waiting-room, otherwise the wrong train may be taken. To avoid this, observe on our railway map what are the principal towns along the line in the direction required to go ; so that when, for example, he calls out, "Voyageurs du Côté de Lyon !" and we be going to Marseilles from Macon, we may, with confidence, enter the train, because, by reference to the map, we see we must pass Lyon to reach Marseilles. The little railway map will be found very useful, and ought always to be kept in readiness for reference.

Buffet means "refreshment-room" ; and *Salle d'Attente*, "waiting-room."

There are separate first, second, and third class carriages for ladies.

Express trains have third class carriages for long distances.

Railway Omnibuses.

At the stations of the largest and wealthiest towns three kinds of omnibuses await the arrival of passengers. They may be distinguished by the names of the General Omnibus, the Hotel Omnibus, and the Private Omnibus. The general omnibus takes passengers to all parts of the town for a fixed sum, rarely above half a franc ; so that, should the omnibus be full, it is some time till the last passenger gets put down at his destination. The hotel omnibus takes passengers only to the hotel or hotels whose name or names it bears.

CONTENTS.

THE RIVIERA.

MAPS AND PLANS.

CARTE DU JOUR.

THE following List contains the explanation of the technical terms of some of the most useful dishes mentioned in the "Cartes du Jour" of the restaurants. Fancy names cannot be translated.

SOUPS.

Consommé, beef-tea.
Bouillon, broth.
Potage, soup.
Julienne, vegetable soups.
Purée, pease-soup.
  Purée, when qualifying a noun, means "mashed," as—
Purée de pommes, mashed potatoes.
  „ „ *marron*, mashed chestnuts.

BEEF.

Bœuf au naturel, or simply "nature," plain boiled beef.
  Naturel in cookery means "plain."
Bœuf à la mode, beef stewed with carrots. Nearly the same as the next.
Bœuf à la jardinière, beef with vegetables.
Aloyau, a sirloin of beef.

Aloyau à la jardinière, sirloin with vegetables.
Aloyau sauté, sirloin in slices.
  Sauté in cookery means "sliced."
Rosbif aux pommes, roast beef with potatoes.
  In these lists the words *de terre* are rarely affixed to *pommes*.
Bifteck au naturel, plain beefsteak.
  „ *aux pommes*, with potatoes.
  „ *aux pommes sautées*, with sliced potatoes.
  „ *aux haricots*, with kidney beans.
  „ *bien cuit*, well done.
  „ *saignant*, under done.
Palais de Bœuf au gratin, broiled ox palate.
  Au gratin in cookery means "baked" or "broiled"; when applied to potatoes it means "browned."

MUTTON.

Côtelettes de mouton au naturel, plain
mutton chops.

" " " *panées*, mutton
chops fried with crumbs.

" " " *aux pointes d'as-
perge*, mutton chops with asparagus
tops.

" " " *à la purée de
pommes*, mutton chops with mashed
potatoes.

Gigot roti, a roast leg of mutton.
Pieds de mouton, sheep's trotters.
Gigot d'agneau, a leg of lamb.
Blanquette d'agneau, hashed stewed lamb.
Rognons à la brochette, broiled kidneys.

" *sautés*, sliced kidneys.
Etuvé, stewed.

VEAL.

Côtelette de veau, veal cutlet.
Tête de veau en vinaigrette, calf's head
with oil and vinegar.
Oreille de veau en marinade, pickled calf's
ear.
Ris de veau, sweetbread.
Foie de veau, calf's liver.
Blanquette de veau, hashed stewed veal.
Fricandeau au jus, Scotch collops with
gravy.
Jus, gravy.

VEGETABLES.

Pommes de terre, potatoes.
Legumes et fruits primeurs, early vege-
tables and fruits.
Asperges à la sauce, asparagus with sauce.
Chou, cabbage.
Champignons, mushrooms.
Epinards, spinage.
Fèves de marais, garden beans.
Haricots verts, green kidney beans.
Oseille, sorrel.
Petits pois, green peas.
Jardinière means "dressed with vege-
tables."

POULTRY AND GAME.

Poularde, fowl.
Poulet, chicken.
Chapon, capon.
Cuisse de poulet, leg of a chicken.

Des œufs à la coque, boiled eggs.
Dindonneau, young turkey.
Canard, duck.
Perdreau, partridge.
Mauviettes, field-larks.
Alouettes, larks.
Grives, thrushes.
Becasse, woodcock.
Becassine, snipe.
Chevreuil, venison.
Caille, quail.

FISH.

Anguille, eel.
Eperlans, smelts ; or, as the Scotch call
them, sperlings.
Homard, lobster.
Huitres, oysters.
Merlans, whitings.
Morue, cod.
Raie, skate.
Saumon, salmon.
Sole, sole.
Turbot, turbot.
Frit, fried.
Grillé, done on the gridiron.

DESSERT.

Compote, applied to fruits, means
"stewed."

" *de pommes*, stewed apples.

" *de pruneaux*, stewed prunes.
Beignets de pommes, apple fritters.

" " *soufflés*, puffed apple
fritters.
Mendiants, raisins, nuts and almonds.

DRINK.

Vin de Bordeaux, claret.
A bottle of soda - water is called a
siphon. The cheap wines ought
always to be drunk with it, or with
common water.
At even the cheap restaurants palatable
wine may be had by paying a little
extra.
Frappé, applied to liquids, means "iced."
Caraffe frappé, iced water.
Vin frappé, iced wine.
The litre of beer is called a *canette*, and
the half-litre a *choppe*.
The fifth part of a litre of wine is called
a *carafon*, a word often used in the
cheap restaurants.

THE DIRECT ROAD TO THE RIVIERA.

Paris to Lyons, Marseilles, Hyères, Cannes, Nice, Monaco and Menton, 692 miles.

PART I.—PARIS TO MARSEILLES.

By Sens, Dijon, Lyons, and Avignon, 537 miles.

Best resting-places, Sens, Dijon, Macon, Lyons, and Avignon. For "London to Marseilles," see under that head in the "Continental Time-tables of the London, Chatham, and Dover Railway." Through tickets sold at their London office.

PARIS   MARSEILLES
MILES FROM   MILES TO
                                                                          537

PARIS. Start from the station of the Chemin de Fer de Paris à Lyon, No. 20 Boulevard Mazas, where purchase one of the Time-tables, 8 sous or 40 cents, the only absolutely trustworthy tables respecting the prices, distances, and movements of the trains. Good restaurant at station. Opposite the station is the H. de l'Univers, and a little farther off the H. Jules César.

Maps.—For the general route, consult map on fly-leaf; for the details as far as Macon, map page 1; and for the remainder of the journey, map page 26. The fare, third class, from London to Paris by Dieppe, by the London, Brighton, and South Coast Railway, is 17s. From Paris to Marseilles, by the Paris and Lyons Railway, it is £2 : 7s., time 23 hours ; starting from the station of the Chemin de Fer de Lyon at 6.30 A.M., and arriving next day at 5.33 A.M. From Marseilles a train starts at 6.35 A.M. for Toulon, where it arrives at 9 A.M. From Toulon a train starts for Hyères at 9.32 A.M., and arrives at 10.13 A.M. The third-class carriages between Paris and

B

Marseilles are provided with separate compartments for ladies, and with warming-pans. For those going to Hyères, the nearest of the winter-stations, it is better, if possible, not to break the journey, but to take a through ticket from Paris to Hyères (£2 : 12s.), as every break adds considerably to the expense ; moreover, the train passes the most suitable resting-places at a most inconvenient hour in the night. By the first class the whole journey from Paris to Hyères can be done in 18¼ hours for £4 : 13 : 6.

The train, after leaving the station, skirts the S.W. corner of the Bois de Vincennes at Charenton and St. Maurice, both upon the Marne, which here joins the Seine. **Charenton**, 4 m. from Paris, pop. 9000, has a large lunatic asylum founded in 1644. Boarders pay £60 the year. **St. Maurice**, pop. 4300, has in the Château d'Alfort a veterinary college with an hospital for animals, which takes horses for 2s. per day. It contains a library, museum, and laboratory ; and possesses a nursery for the cultivation of grasses. Immediately beyond Fort Charenton are the **Maisons-Alfort**, pop. 8000, on the Seine. Diana of Poitiers and Robespierre resided here some time.

9½ m. S. from Paris is the pretty town of Villeneuve St. George, pop. 1500, on the Seine, where it unites with the Yères, a deep river flowing through a verdant valley. 3¼ m. farther is **Montgeron** on the Yères, pop. 1300, with the castle which belonged to Sillery, chancellor of Henri IV. On the other side of the river is the village of **Crosne** ; where on the 1st November 1636 was born, in the house No. 3 Rue Simon, Nicolas Boileau Despréaux, died 13th March 1711. He was a great critic, and the first to introduce French versification to rule. Through Pope and his contemporaries he had also a strong influence on English literature.

13¾ m. from Paris is **Brunoy**, pop. 1550, an ancient town, which was inhabited by the earliest kings of France. Louis XVIII. created the Duke of Wellington Marquis of Brunoy. The train now traverses the Yères viaduct, 1235 ft. long, on 28 arches 104½ ft. high. 28 m. S. from Paris is the prettily situated town of **MELUN**, pop. 12,000. *Inns :* Grand Monarque ; Commerce ; both near each other, and near St. Aspais. Between them is the omnibus office. Église Protestante. Melun, the Melodunum of Julius Cæsar, occupies both banks of the Seine, and the island in the centre, as well as both sides of the Almont, which here enters the Seine. One long, nearly straight road, under the names of the Avenue de Thiers, Rue St. Ambroise, Rue St. Etienne, Rue St. Aspais, and the Rue du Palais de Justice, extends from the railway station to the northmost limit of the town. In the part of Melun on the left or south bank are large cavalry barracks. On the island is the church of Notre Dame, 11th cent., restored ; with a neat 2 storied tower over each transept, 10th cent. The large building behind the church is the principal prison. Very near the church, in the Rue Notre Dame, is the Eglise Protestante, a small chapel. Off the main street, in the part of the town on the right or north bank, is St. Aspais, an elegant church of the 14th cent. surrounded by crocketed gabled chapels. By the side of the main entrance rises a buttressed square tower, terminating in a high peaked roof prolonged into a short spire. In the interior are some delicately sculptured canopy work and 8 windows with valuable old glass. A few yards off the main street is the Hotel de Ville with a round attached turret in each corner ; and in the centre of the court a marble statue to Jacques Amyot, born in 1514, "Un des Grandes Reformateurs de la langue française au 16me siècle." Behind are the public gardens containing some capitals of ancient columns. Near it is the Place St. Jean, with a handsome fountain. North-west from St. Aspais are the Prefecture and the belfry St. Barthélemy, restored in 1858. The Palais de Justice, the theatre, the Gendarmerie, and another of the prisons, are all together at the north end of the town. The gardens of Melun produce excellent pears —some are very large. Hardly 4 m. N.E. from Melun is the Chateau of Vaux-Praslin, containing paintings by Lebrun and Mignard. From Melun the line continues by the side of the Seine till Bois-le-Roi, where it enters the forest of Fontainebleau.

37
500
FONTAINEBLEAU pop. 9200, about 2 miles from the Seine, and one from the station ; but omnibuses await passengers for the hotels. Fare, 30 c. For the Cour du Cheval Blanc of the Chateau, 50 c. The most expensive hotels front the Chateau. The Londres ; Europe ; France et Angleterre ; Ville de Lyon ; Aigle Noir ; Lion d'Or. At the end of the main street, No. 9 Rue Grande, is the Cadran Bleu. In the Rue de la Chancellerie, near the Cour des Offices or east end of the Chateau, is the H. de la Chancellerie. In the Rue de France, the H. de la Sirène. The last 4 hotels are the most moderate in their charges. Situated among the large hotels facing the Cour du Cheval Blanc is the Pension Launoy ; 1st storey, 13 frs., 2d, 11 frs. per day. For those who come for one day, the best plan is to enter at the station any of the Chateau omnibuses. Alight at the end of the Rue Grande, where there is a square with a garden surrounded with good shops—a bookseller's with maps, plans, and photographs—souvenirs made from wood of the forest ; a good confectioner's shop and some restaurants, where refreshments can be had either before or after visiting the chateau. Those afraid of losing the train, should, however, rather take their refreshments at some of the restaurants opposite the station. From the end of the Rue Grande, the Cour du Cheval Blanc is about 5 minutes' walk.

Temple Protestant, in which an English service is also held.

Coach Tariff.—The principal cab-stand is at the end of the Rue Grande at the square. Before starting procure a plan, 1½ fr., of the forest in the shop opposite.

A four-wheeled carriage for 5 persons, with 2 horses, 20 frs. for the day, with a gratuity to the coachman. For 4 persons, with 1 horse, 10 frs. for the day.

Carriages may also be engaged by the hour at the following prices:—
A four-wheeled carriage for 5 persons, with 2 horses, 4 frs. for the first hour, and 3 frs. for each succeeding hour.

A four-wheeled carriage for 4 persons, with 1 horse, for the first hour 3 frs., and each succeeding hour 2 frs. 25 c.

A two-wheeled carriage for 4 persons, with 1 horse, 2 frs. an hour.

Donkeys and mules may be hired at 3 frs. a day.

Fontainebleau deserves a visit, not only to see the Chateau, but to enjoy the delightful air and walks in the gardens and woods, which cover an area of 18,740 acres, intersected by 12,000 m. of roads and footpaths. The palace consists of square towers linked together by congeries of low brick buildings, enclosing spacious courts, each bearing some suggestive name. The roofing is said to occupy 14 acres. The palace is open from 11 to 4. The men who show it attend in one of the rooms on the left side of the "Cour des Adieux," or "du Cheval Blanc," which court forms the *main entrance.* A small fee is expected ; but as the Palace belongs to the State, it is not obligatory.

To see the "appartements reservés" an especial order is requisite, procured by letter addressed to "M. Le Commandant des Chateaux." The "appartements reservés" comprehend sometimes a greater, and sometimes a smaller number of rooms, according to the requirements of the household, but never any of the splendid halls. The order observed in showing the Palace is constantly changed, yet the itinerary we give will be found in the main correct. It is sometimes reversed.

The Chateau of Fontainebleau, as it now stands, was founded by Francis I., who commenced by demolishing the whole of the former edifice, excepting the pavilion of St. Louis, which still exists. Henri IV., who spent £100,000 upon it, doubled the area of the buildings and gardens, and added, among other portions, the gallery of Diana and the gallery des Cerfs. Napoleon I. expended £250,000 upon it, and Louis XVIII. and Louis Philippe contributed also large sums.

The principal entrance is at the west end by the Cour du CHEVAL BLANC, the largest of all the courts, measuring 498 ft. by 368. It is also called the Cour des Adieux, because here Napoleon I., forsaken by nearly all his generals, took leave, on the 20th of April 1814, of the ever-faithful soldiers of his Old Guard, from whom he tore himself away amidst sobs and tears, and threw himself into his carriage. On the 19th of March 1815 he was back again in this palace from the island of Elba, wandering with almost infantine joy through the splendid apartments which had witnessed his glory and his wretchedness.

As very little time is given to inspect the different articles, the following abridged list should be read before entering.

The visitor enters by the door under the Horseshoe staircase, which has 46 steps on each side. To the right, the longer of the 2 iron bars in the wall represents the height of Francis I. The first place entered is the Chapelle de la Trinité, built by Francis I. in 1529, and largely decorated by Henri IV. in consequence of the Spanish ambassador having remarked that "the palace would be more beautiful if the Almighty were as well housed as his majesty." Louis XI. was married in this chapel. The divorce between Napoleon and Josephine was pronounced in it; and here, in 1810, Napoleon III. was baptized. The paintings are by Fréminet, made during the reigns of Henri IV. and Marie de Médicis and Louis XIII. The high altar was finished in the reign of Louis XIII. by Bordogni. The reredos is by Jean Dubois. The statues on each side of the altar, representing Charlemagne and St. Louis, are by G. Pilon. The magnificent angels, which support the escutcheons of France and Navarre, are by Jean Goujon. The 4 bronze angels are by G. Pilon.

Ascend staircase to the **APARTMENTS OF NAPOLEON.** The first room is the Antichambre des **Huissiers** (ushers), painting by Brenet, 1785. Cabinet des **Secretaires**, paintings by Vanloo, Doyen, and Hallé. Pass now through a small passage, painted with flowers by Spraendonck, to the most charming **Salle des Bains**. The walls are of plate glass, on which are painted, in graceful forms and lovely colours, cupids, birds, and flowers. The bath-room opens into the **Abdication Room**, containing the famous mahogany table, about a yard in diameter, on which Napoleon signed his abdication, 5th April 1814. Walls hung with rich embroidered satin from Lyons. **Cabinet de Travail** (study) of the Emperor. Beautiful writing desk by Jakob. Painting on ceiling represents law and justice. **Bedroom of Napoleon** I. and III. Bed restored under Louis Philippe, and hung with silk velvet from Lyons. Round the wall grisaille paintings of cupids, admirable imitations of relief, by Sauvage. Clock, present from Pio VII. to Napoleon. **Salon de Famille** or Salle du Conseil; dates from François I. and Henri IV., and made by Louis XV. his study. In centre of room mahogany table, 6 yards in circumference, one piece. The 20 red and blue symbolical paintings round wall are by the two Vanloos. On ceiling arms of France on gold ground. Furniture covered with Beauvais tapestry of time of Louis XV. Clock of Louis XIV. **Throne-room.** Built by Charles IX., ornamented by Louis XIII. and XIV., to which Napoleon I. added the throne. In this room the marshals of France used to take their oath of allegiance. The ceiling magnificently gilt and painted, and chimney-piece in same style. Over it portrait of Louis XIII. The lustre of rock crystal is valued at £2000.

APARTMENTS OF MARIE ANTOINETTE and of the Empress Eugenie. Aurora on ceiling by Barthélemy. Arabesques of the panels on green ground. On console tables by Coindrel, 2 ivory vases presented to Napoleon I by the Emp. of Austria. This room was fitted up for Marie Antoinette by Louis XVI., who forged, but did not finish, the window bolts (espagnolettes). **The Bedroom.** Occupied successively by Marie de Medicis, Maria Theresa of Austria, Marie Antoinette, Marie-Amélie, wife of Louis Philippe, and the Empress Eugenie. The gorgeous drapery and curtains of the bed were presented to Marie Antoinette by the city of Lyons on the occasion of her marriage.

SALONS DE FRANCOIS I. AND LOUIS XIII.

Wall hung with the richest satin, hand embroidered. Two wardrobes by Riésener. Clock of Louis XVI. **Salon de Musique.** Ceiling, Minerva and the Muses by Barthélemy, 1786. Over door the Muses painted in grisaille by Sauvage. Porcelain table by Georget, 1806. Petit Salon, from which a door opens into the

GALERIE DE DIANE or Bibliothèque, built in 1600. The ceiling, divided into compartments, is painted by Pujol and Blondel, representing mythological scenes. In front of one of the windows are suspended the sword and coat of mail worn by Monaldeschi, when he was assassinated on the 15th of October 1657 by order of Christina of Sweden, second daughter of Gustavus Adolphus. The atrocious deed took place in the room immediately below, in the Galerie des Cerfs. The unfortunate man, in parrying the first thrust, had 3 of his fingers cut off. He then fell on his knees before his confessor Father Le Bel, sent him by Christina, and, while praying God for pardon of his sins, one of the murderers thrust his sword into his face; while the other first cut off the crown of his skull, and then pierced his throat, which made him fall to the ground, where he lay breathing for quarter of an hour. Throughout all this terrible scene the kind priest kept bawling aloud with all his might consolation to the dying man. That same evening he was buried, near the holy water basin, in the church of Avon, 1 m. E. from the chateau, at the extremity of the park. Monaldeschi was Queen Christina's chamberlain, and is supposed to have betrayed some of her secrets. The Marquis begged most piteously Father Le Bel to implore the Queen to spare his life; but when the confessor went to her and beseeched her, in the name of Our Blessed Lord, to have mercy on the unhappy man, she replied with petulance, "that she could not, and that many had been condemned to the wheel who did not deserve it so much as this coward."

At the extremity of the gallery of Diana is the Salon de Diane, with indifferent modern paintings by Blondel, representing the story of the goddess Diana.

We now enter the Escalier de la Reine, ornamented with hunting scenes by C. Parocel, 1688-1782; Oudry, 1686-1755; and F. Desportes, 1661-1743. The door to the left opens into the Galerie des Chasses, not shown (see page 8). The other leads into

LES GRANDS APPARTEMENTS. The Antechamber. Ceiling of pinewood in gilt compartments. Walls hung with ancient Gobelins tapestry. **Salon des Tapisseries** hung with beautiful tapestry, representing the loves of Psyche. Sevres porcelain vase worth £600, gift to the Empress Eugenie. **Salon de François I.** Napoleon I. and Charles X. used it as their dining-room. Louis Philippe restored the ceiling. The Flemish tapestry represents royal hunting scenes. In the centre of chimney-piece fresco by Primaticcio, Mars and Venus. The ebony cabinets are of the 15 and 16 cents. Furniture covered with very remarkable Beauvais tapestry. **Salon de Louis XIII.** The small Venetian looking-glass, one of the earliest manufactured, and the first that came to France, indicates the place where the bed of Marie de

SALLES ST. LOUIS AND DES GARDES.

Médicis stood when Louis XIII. was born. The paintings on the ceiling and on the walls represent the story of Theagenes and Charicles, which had been translated from the Greek by Jacques Amyot, and dedicated to Francis I. Beautiful marble chimney-piece. Salle de Saint Louis. Over chimney-piece equestrian statue in relief of Henri IV. by Jacquet. Salon des Aides-de-Camp. Portraits in Gobelins tapestry of Henri IV. and Louis XV., 1773-1777. Salle des Gardes, principally by Charles IX., but restored by Louis Philippe. In the medallions above the five real and mock doors are portraits of Francis I., with the allegorical figures of Might and the Fine Arts ; Henri II., with figures of Diana and Liberality ; Antoine Bourbon (father of Henri IV., with figures of Hope and Abundance ; Henri IV., with figures of Peace and Glory ; and Louis XIII., with figures of Religion and Justice. Beautiful chimney-piece by Jacquet, 1590, 17 ft. high and 13 wide. In centre bust of Henri IV., and at each side statues of Might and Peace by Francarville. A very pretty little room, with floor of inlaid wood, corresponding in design with the ceiling, leads to the
    ESCALIER DU ROI. The top part of this staircase, built by Louis XV., was originally the Chambre de la Duchesse d'Etampes. The frescoes, representing scenes in the life of Alexander, are chiefly by Niccolo dell' Abate, indifferently restored in 1836 by Abel Pujol.
    GALERIE DE HENRI II., or Salle des Fêtes. The most magnificent hall in the palace, shining with gold, 90 ft. long by 30 wide, lighted on one side by 5 windows looking into the Cour Ovale, and on the other by the same number looking to the gardens. It was built by François I., and decorated by Henri II. for his favourite Diane de Poitiers. The walls are covered with frescoes between gilt coupled columns by Primaticcio, Rosso, and Abate, restored in 1864 by Alaux. The ceiling, of walnut, is divided into 27 compartments, elaborately ornamented with scrolls, mouldings, and friezes, all richly gilt, and enclosing the ciphers of Henri II. and of Diana. The chimney-piece, of rare marbles, covered with fleurs-de-lis, is by Rondelet. At the end of this gallery is one of the entrances into the chapel of St. Saturnin, generally closed (see page 8). We return now to the Escalier du Roi, where we enter the
    GALERIE DE FRANÇOIS I., parallel to the apartments of Napoleon, 210 ft. long by 20 wide. It was built by Francis to serve as a communication between the Courts of the Cheval Blanc and of St. Louis. Ceiling in variously shaped gilt panels, producing a curious effect. The frescoes, representing mythological scenes, are chiefly by Rosso, but a few are by Primaticcio, restored by Condere. Bust of François I. From the vestibule of the Horseshoe staircase we enter the
    APPARTEMENTS DES REINES MERES et du Pape Pie VII. They were inhabited by Catherine de Médicis and Anne of Austria (mother of Louis XIV.), whose portraits hang opposite each other in the bedroom ; and also by Pope Pius VII., more, however, as a prisoner than a guest of Napoleon I. The magnificent bedstead was put up by Napoleon III. for Queen Victoria and Prince Albert, when they were expected to have visited Fontainebleau. The tapestry is of the finest

quality from the Gobelins manufactory, and the paintings are by Coypel, Mignard, and other French masters. **Antechamber.** Portrait of Diana de Poitiers as the goddess of the chase, one of Primaticcio's best works. Cabinet (Bahut) of time of Louis XIII. Walls hung with embossed leather. Furniture covered with Cordova leather. **Salles des Officers.** Hung with Gobelins tapestry, representing the story of Esther. **Salon.** Walls hung with beautiful coloured Gobelins. Furniture covered with Beauvais tapestry. Elegant ceiling, divided into compartments bearing the initials of Anne of Austria and of Louis XIII. The **Old Bedroom** (see above). Modern furniture in style of Louis XIII. Table in mosaic given by Pio IX., bearing his signature. Very beautiful ceiling by Cotelle de Meaux. Study of Pio VII.—portrait of him by David. **Dressing-room**—wardrobe of inlaid wood by Riésener, one of the finest in France. Bust of Louis XV. by Lemoyne, 1751. **New Bedroom**—bedstead of time of Louis XIV., enlarged in reign of Louis Philippe. **Salon de Reception**—Gobelins tapestry—furniture of time of Louis XV. Bust of Napoleon by Canova. **Waiting-room** or Salle d'Attente. Gobelins dating from the time of Louis XV. Beautiful clock of Louis XVI. **Antechamber.** 4 pictures by Breughel, of which one is on wood. Vestibule of the Galerie des Fresques.

GALERIE DES FRESQUES or Des Assiettes. All the pictures in this gallery were painted in fresco in the reign of Henri IV. by Ambroise Dubois on the gallery of Diana, whence they were removed in 1805, and some of them put on canvas. In addition Louis Philippe placed on the walls 128 plates, with views of the royal residences in France, and incidents connected with Fontainebleau. We now enter the gallery leading to the

SALLE DE SPECTACLE or theatre, built by Napoleon III., and seated for 400. Visitors now leave the palace by the staircase of Charles VIII., adorned with a statue of him in stucco.

LES APPARTEMENTS RESERVES.

Chapelle Basse de St. Saturnin, built by Louis VII. after his return from Palestine, and consecrated by Thomas à Becket in 1169. The painted glass of the windows was manufactured at Sevres from designs by the Princess Marie, 1836, daughter of Louis Philippe; and the altar is the same at which Pope Pius VII. performed mass during his stay at Fontainebleau from 1812 to 1814. The lower chapel was reconstructed in 1545 by Francis I., upon which he built the **Upper Chapel.** It was ornamented with charming frescoes, in the reign of Henri IV., about the year 1608. Napoleon III. commenced the restoration.

Adjoining the lower chapel a corridor leads to the Ancienne Salle à Manger de Louis Philippe, or the Galerie des Colonnes, of the same dimensions as the Galerie de Henri II. immediately over it. To the right is the old spiral staircase of Francis I.

Galerie des Cerfs, built by Henri IV., under the Galerie de Diane, ornamented with views of the royal residences, indifferently executed. It was here Monaldeschi was murdered (see p. 6).

Appartements des Chasses, consisting of two rooms, hung round with pictures representing dogs, game, and hunting scenes. The best by J. B. Oudry.

Appartements de Madame de Maintenon, consisting of an ante-chamber, saloon, boudoir, and toilet-room. They are of no interest further than that it was in one of them, it is said, that Louis XIV. signed the revocation of the Edict of Nantes in 1685, which led to such cruelties. The embroidery on the furniture and screen is by the noble pupils of St. Cyr. Adjoining is the Galerie de Henri II. (see p. 7).

The **Musée Chinois**, consisting of a valuable and interesting collection of articles from China, cannot be seen without especial permission.

THE COURTS.

From the Cour du Cheval Blanc an arched way, near the Horseshoe staircase, leads through to the **Cour de la Fontaine**. In the side facing the lake is the Galerie de François I. Having passed through the porch in the N.E. corner of the Cour de la Fontaine, we have before us the gardens and forests of Fontainebleau, and immediately to the left the **Porte Dorée**, one of the gates that opens into the Cour Ovale. It is generally closed. On the soffit and sides are frescoes on a gold ground by Primaticcio, restored in 1835 by Picot. The subjects are mythological. Charles V. entered by this gateway in 1539. And by this portal the Duchesse d'Etampes fled from Fontainebleau, driven from it by the haughty and jealous Diana. Eastward to the left we pass the apsidal portion of St. Saturnin, supported by narrow buttresses, faced with pillars and pilasters. Both here and on the Porte Dorée is the device of Francis I., a salamander. The principal entrance to the Cour Ovale faces the Cour des Offices.

At the east end of the palace, fronting the Place d'Armes, connected with the Rue Grande by the Rue de la Chancellerie, is the Cour de Henri IV. or Des Offices, 285 ft. long by 255 wide, occupied by the artillery college, formerly at Metz. The course lasts 2 years. The gateway is grand, but heavy ; the buildings contain nothing particular.

Excursions into the forest. Those wishing to walk should provide themselves with a pocket compass and a copy of the plan of the Forêt de Fontainebleau, 1½ fr. In the forest the posts painted red indicate the way back to the town ; the black posts lead in the other direction. The coachmen are acquainted with all the roads. The artistic part of the forest comprises only 3719 acres. The following are the three principal drives, each requiring 6 hours :—

1. Croix du Grand Veneur par la Tillaie—Point de vue du camp de Chailly par la Table du Grand Maître et le carrefour de Belle Vue—Barbison par le Bas Bréau—Gorges d'Apremont et Franchard.

2. Vallée du Nid de l'Aigle—Mont Ussy—Caverne d'Augas—Vue sur le champ de Courses et Mont Chauvet—Gorges et Rochers de la Solle—Rocher St. Germain—Bocages des Ecouettes—Fort l'Empereur —Calvaire—Roche Eponge et Point de vue de Nemorosa.

3. Rocher Bouligny—Rocher des Demoiselles—Gorge aux Loups

et Mare aux Fées—Long Rocher et Arcades de la Vanne par la Croix du Gd. Maitre.

The most picturesque parts of the first drive, or perhaps in the whole forest, are the ravines of Apremont, about 3 m. N. W. from Fontainebleau ; and Franchard, about 2½ m. W. The second contains the best places for obtaining good general views of the forest, such as from the Croix du Calvaire, near the railway station, but especially from the Fort de l'Empereur, about 2½ m. N. The Gorge aux Loups in the 3d drive, 3½ m. S., leads to a very picturesque part called the Long Rocher. If only one drive can be taken, take the first, 3¼ m. by rail from Fontainebleau.

After Fontainebleau is Thomery. *Inn :* Popardin, where the famous grape, the Chasselas de Fontainebleau, is grown extensively on walls and trellis-work.

$\frac{42}{}$ MORET, pop. 2000. *Inn :* Écu de France. An ancient town $\frac{495}{}$ on the Loing, with remains of fortifications, 15th cent., and the two old city gates Paris and Bourgogne. The church, containing some curious woodwork, is principally of the 12th cent. The portal and organ are of the 15th. 7½ m. farther S. E. is Montereau junction, where the Chemins de Fer of the Paris and Lyons system unite with those of the Eastern system.

Montereau-faut-Yonne, pop. 7000 ; station about a mile from the town. *Inn :* Grand Monarque, where the omnibus stops, near the post office. Those who may require to wait for a train at this junction, should, if time permit, drive up in the omnibus to the town and visit the parish church, with its handsome columns gracefully ramifying into the groining of the roof of the aisles. Suspended to the right of the high altar is the sword of Jean Sans Peur. Beyond this church a fine stone bridge, or rather two continuous bridges, cross the Seine and the Yonne, which here unite. On the tongue of land between them is an equestrian statue of Napoleon I. ; and on the bridge over the Yonne a marble slab indicates the spot where Jean Sans Peur was murdered in 1419. On the steep hill overlooking the town is the handsome modern castle of Surville. Montereau has important potteries.

$\frac{71}{}$ SENS on the Yonne, pop. 12,400. *Inns :* Paris ; Écu. The best $\frac{466}{}$ street, the Rue Royale, extends from north to south. At the north end is the promenade, and going southwards up the street, we have first the statue of the chemist Thénard, and then the cathedral. At the end of the street is the arch erected in honour of the Duchess of Angoulême, when she visited this city in 1828. Behind are spacious boulevards, which, together with the promenade, form agreeable walks.

The **Cathedral of St. Etienne** was commenced in 972, but nearly rebuilt two centuries afterwards. The façade, though not without beauty, is heavy and massive. The south tower, 240 feet high, has a belfry attached to it. In the interior, coupled columns, alternating with massive piers, run down each side of the nave, supporting pointed arches, over which runs a triforium of round arches on clustered colonnettes. Against the 5th pier left is a reredos, with sculptured canopies. In the chapel immediately behind the high altar is a beautiful relief in marble, representing the death of St. Savinien, first bishop of Sens, who suffered martyrdom in 240. In the adjoining chapel is the mausoleum of the Dauphin, brother of Louis XVI., by G. Coustou, and statues of Archbishop Duperron and his nephew. In the next or 3d chapel, Becket used to officiate. The picture on the wall by Bouchet, 1846, represents his assassination. He stayed, 1166, in the abbey of St. Columba, 1 m. from the cathedral. It is now occupied by the Sœurs de l'Enfance de Jesus. The transepts are lighted by superb glass ; but the best window is the second to the right on entering from the façade, painted in 1530 by Jean Cousin. In a glass case in the treasury are the mitre, albe, chasuble, stole, and maniple worn by Thomas à Becket ; discovered in 1523 in an old house adjoining the cathedral ; yet there does not exist sufficient evidence to prove that they are genuine. In the same case is an ivory crucifix by Girardon. In the case behind are enamels from Limoges, 15th century, and two small paintings on marble by A. del Sarto. Next them is valuable old tapestry. Near two shrines is a deed signed by St. Vincent de Paul. In one of the shrines is a bone of the arm of Simeon. Adjoining the cathedral is the hall, called the Officialité, restored by Violet le Duc. The convent of St. Colombes is about 1 m. from the church, and to the left of the high road. The only portion of the present buildings that existed in Becket's time is the piece parallel to the Abbey Church. When in France, he lived chiefly in the Cistercian Abbey of Pontigny, 7 m. S. from St. Florentin, page 16, and 13 m. N.E. from Auxerre, page 14. Becket was assassinated at the foot of the altar of St. Benedict in Canterbury cathedral in 1170, and canonised two years afterwards. Down to the Reformation pilgrimages were made to his shrine by devotees from every corner of Christendom. Every 50th year a jubilee was celebrated in his honour.

41 m. E. from Sens by the Chemin de Fer de l'Etat is **TROYES**, pop. 39,000. *Hotels :* At the station, the Grand Mulet. In the principal street, the Rue Notre Dame, the hotels Saint Laurent, Commerce. In the Rue Hôtel de Ville, the Hôtel des Couriers.

Troyes, the former capital of Champagne, is situate on the Seine, canalised in the 12th century by Theobald IV. These canals move the machinery of numerous manufactories of hosiery, paper, and linen, which produce an annual average value of about two million pounds sterling. Troyes is famous for the number and beauty of its churches, of which the most important is the **Cathedral of St. Pierre et St. Paul**, situated at the eastern side of the town, the railway station being on the western or opposite side. This edifice, among the most beautiful in France, was commenced in 1208, but as it was not finished till the end of the 16th century, represents the different styles of these intermediate epochs. The fine western façade belongs to the 16th century, while the portal of the N. transept belongs to the 13th. Three hundred and seventy-eight steps lead to the top of the tower rising above the western façade. The building is 352 feet long, and the transept 154 feet. Two spacious aisles run up each side of the nave, separated by clustered columns supporting pointed arches, the front row being surmounted by a narrow mullioned triforium and a lofty clerestory, both lighted by beautifully-painted glass windows. The height of the roof of the nave is 92 feet, and of the cupola 192. The glass of the windows of the choir, of the roses in the transepts, and over the western entrance behind the organ, is of the 13th cent. The marble statues of Jesus and Mary in the first chapel, N. side of choir, are of the 16th cent., and the altar piece, with reliefs in wood, of the 17th cent. Before the high altar in this church Henry V. of England was affianced to the Princess Catherine, daughter of Charles VI. of France, on the 20th May 1420. Next day the famous treaty was signed, which secured the crown of France to Henry by the exclusion of the dauphin Charles, whenever the poor mad Charles VI. should cease to live. Behind the high altar in the Lady chapel is a Madonna by Simard, and the window containing the oldest glass in the church. A stair to the right of the high altar leads to the treasury, of no great interest. It contains croziers of the 13th century, reliquaries of St. Loup and St. Bernard, with enamels of the 12th century, a tooth of St. Peter in a small gold box, etc. In the reliquary of St. Bernard is a bit of the skull of an Irish primate, St. Malachie, who lived between the 11th and 12th centuries. A few yards to the N. of the cathedral is the building containing the *Library*, open from 10 to 3, with 125,000 volumes and 3600 MSS., in a large hall, with windows composed of curiously-painted panelled panes. Among the illuminated books are a Bible of St. Bernard and St. Paul's Epistles, 12th century. In the same building are the **Museum**, or picture gallery, with paintings by Watteau, Coypel, Mignard, etc. ; and the *Salle Simard*, containing a valuable collection of the **Models made by** Simard for his statues and works in relief. Also some statuary by Girardon, and other French sculptors. The museum is open to the public on Sundays and feast-days from 1 to 4. On other occasions a small fee is expected. A short distance eastward from the cathedral is the Hospice, and a little beyond St. Nizier, with painted panel panes in the window of the sacristy. The glass in the windows of the church is of the 16th century. Westward, in Rue Urbain IV., is a gem of Gothic architecture, the church of St. Urbain, built by that Pope towards the end of the 13th century. The high altar occupies the place where his father used to sit in the exercise of his calling, which was that of a cobbler. A short way N. is St. Remi, 14th century, with a bronze crucifix over the altar by Girardon. Directly W. from St. Urbain, by the Rue de l'Hotel de Ville, is the *Hotel de Ville*, built according to the plans of Mansard, commenced in 1624, and finished in

TROYES

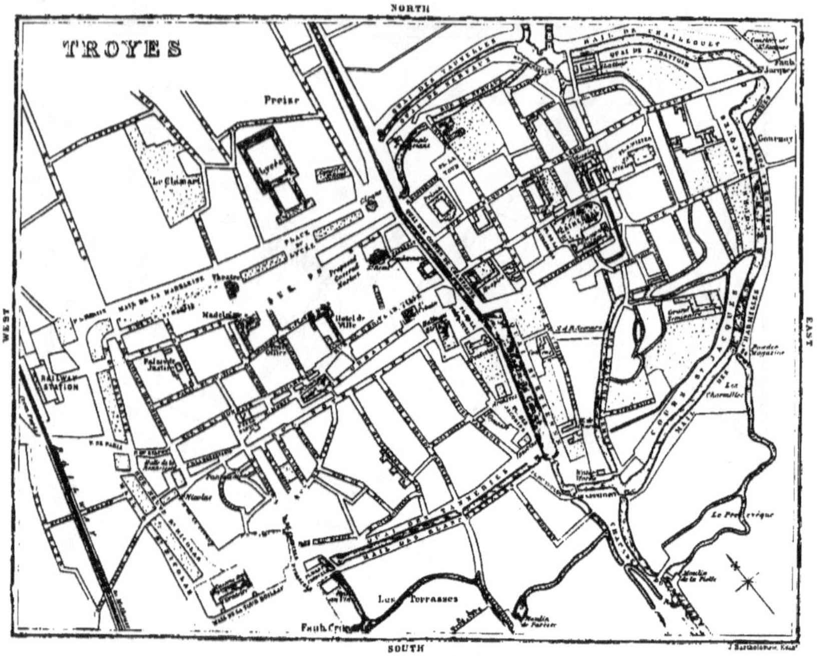
NORTH
TROYES
Preize
Le Clamart
Lycée
RAILWAY STATION
Theatre
Madeleine
Hotel de Ville
Palais de Justice
Les Terrasses
Gournay
Grand Seminaire
Powder Magazine
Les Charmilles
Le Pré l'évêque
Moulin de la Pielle
WEST
EAST
SOUTH
J. Bartholomew, Edin.

1670. Beyond is St. Jean, 14th century. The high altar was sculptured by Girardon, while the painting of the Baptism of our Lord, forming the reredos of the altar, is by Mignard. Behind, in the chapel "O Sacrum Convivium," are some good relief sculptures. From St. Jean, pass up northwards by the Rue de Montabert. At the N. corner of the first division is the Post Office; and at the end of the next division is **La Madeleine**, commenced in the 12th century, and remarkable for its magnificent jubé, or rood-loft, constructed by Jean de Gualde in 1508. The beautiful windows behind the altar belong to the same period. The nearly flat roof might have been called an achievement in Gothic architecture, if the vaulting did not show signs of weakness. West from St. Jean is St. Nicolas, 16th century, near the Hôtel Mulet. To the right of the entrance a broad staircase leads up to a Calvary containing a colossal statue of Christ. In the chapel below is a statue of our Saviour by Gentil, representing him as rising from the dead.

Near St. Nicolas is St. Pantaleon, 16th century. To the right on entering is a Calvary by Gentil. On the panels of the pulpit are beautiful reliefs in bronze by Simard. Behind the pulpit is the chapel of St. Crispin, the patron of shoemakers, containing curious groups. The glass of the windows is rich, while the numerous statues on consoles give the church the appearance of a statue gallery.

South from the church St. Pantaleon by the Rue de Croncels, and its continuation the Faubourg de Croncels, is the small chapel of St. Gilles. In this neighbourhood, 1½ mile northwards from the barracks of the Oratoire, by a road through gardens and fields, are the village and church of St. André, of which the principal feature is the west portal, constructed at the expense of the inhabitants in 1549, and ornamented by Gentil.

Those who prefer to drive through the town should follow the order we have adopted. A cab for four costs 3 frs. per hour; and for two, 2 frs. However, before entering request to see the tariff.

The weight known by the name of the Troy weight was brought from Cairo during the time of the crusades, and first adopted in this city. Troyes was the headquarters of Napoleon I. during his struggles in 1814.

79   458

VILLENEUVE-SUR-YONNE, pop. 5100. *Hotel :* Dauphin. In the old castle here of Pulteau the man "au masque de Fer" spent some days while on his way to the Bastile (p. 158). Villeneuve is joined to its suburb, Saint Laurent, by a bridge 700 ft. long. 5 m. beyond, or 84 m. from Paris, is St. Julien du Sault, pop. 1500. *Hotel :* Des Bons Enfants. A poor town, nearly a mile from the station, but possessing a fine church, of which the greater part of the choir, as well as the S. and N. porches, belong to the 13th cent., and the remainder of the edifice to the 14th-16th cents. Overlooking the town, and distinctly seen from the station, is a ruined chapel belonging to the 13th cent.

JOIGNY, pop. 7000. A good resting-place. *Hotels:* The Poste, between the station and the bridge ; the *Bourgogne, on the quay on the right bank of the Yonne, which is the principal promenade. The most important part of the town occupies the hill rising from the promenade, in which are situated St. André, the most prominent of all ; St. Jean, 16th cent.; and St. Thibault, 15th cent.

LA ROCHE, on the Canal de Bourgogne, at the confluence of the Armançon and the Yonne. Large refreshment-rooms. Junction with branch line to Les Laumes, 79½ m. southwards, passing by Auxerre, Cravant, Sermizelles, Vezelay, Avallon, and Semur. (See map on p. 1.)

LA ROCHE TO AUXERRE, VEZELAY, AND LES LAUMES.

12½ m. S. from La Roche is Auxerre, pop. 16,500, on the Yonne and the hill rising from the river ; Hôtel Laspard. Seen from the station, the most prominent object is the Cathedral, to the right is St. Germain, to the left St. Pierre, and, above St. Pierre, the Tour Guillarde or Clock Tower, at the market-place. The Cathedral, St. Etienne, was rebuilt in the 13th cent., over a crypt of the 11th. The tower over the western entrance is 230 feet high. The north and south portals are crowded with statues. The entire length of the church is 332 feet, and of the transepts 128 feet. 110 feet intervene between the floor and the vaulted roof of the nave and choir, and the pillars are 79 feet high. The great western window, and the end windows of the N. and S. transepts, contain superb glass set in light flamboyant tracery. Adjoining is the Préfecture, formerly the Episcopal Palace, built in the 13th cent. Near the Cathedral is the hospital and the church of St. Germain, with a curious crypt of the 9th cent., but restored in the 17th. Apply to the concierge at the gate beside the now isolated tower, 173 feet high, built in the 11th cent. St. Pierre, begun in the 16th and finished in the 17th cent., is in Italian-Gothic.

Near the Hôtel de l'Épé is the church of St. Eusebe, founded in the 12th cent. The most remarkable parts of the church are the tower, the capitals of the fascicled columns, and the glass of the windows around the chapel of the Virgin behind the high altar. In the principal walk is a statue of Maréchal Davoust. Coach from Auxerre to Pontigny and Chablis. (For Pontigny, see page 16.)

13 miles east from Auxerre is Chablis, pop. 3000, Hôtel Lion d'Or, on the Serein. The vineyards, occupying 30,000 acres, produce the well-known white wine, of which the best growths are those of Val Mur, Vauxdésir, Grenouille, Blanchot, and Mont de Milieu. When the quality of the vintage is good, the wines are dry, diuretic, and of a flinty flavour.

Cravant, pop. 1000, *Inn:* Hôtel de l'Espérance, on the Yonne, nearly a mile from the station, owing its importance to its position at the junction of the branch to Clamecy, 22 miles S., with the line to Les Laumes, 56 miles S.E. Cravant is 85 miles from Nevers by Clamecy, and 116 miles from Paris by La Roche. (See map, page 1.)

37¼ miles from La Roche, 14¼ miles from Cravant, and 42½ miles from Les Laumes is Sermizelles, the station for Vezelay (6¼ miles distant), for which a coach awaits passengers. Fare, 1½ fr. At the station there is a comfortable little inn, the Hôtel de la Gare, where a private vehicle can be had (20 frs.) for visiting Vezelay, Pont Pierre-Perthuis (for the view), 2 miles distant, and St. Père ; then back to Sermizelles Station. See also p. 354.

Vezelay, pop. 1300. *Inn:* Hôtel de la Poste. An ancient and decayed town on the top of a hill, possessing one of the finest ecclesiastical edifices in France, the Church of the Madeleine ; restored by Violet le Duc. The narthex belongs to the 12th cent., the nave and aisles to the 11th, and the choir and transept to the 12th and 13th. The length of the building is 404, and the height of the roof 70 feet. The exterior is unadorned, and supported by plain receding flying buttresses. The doors and tympanum of the western entrance are enclosed by a wide expanding circular arch with four sculptured ribs. Above rises a large window with boldly sculptured mullions. Within the doorway is a spacious narthex, of which the triforium is filled with antiquities connected with the monastery which adjoined the church. To appreciate the noble proportions, simplicity, and harmony of this vast edifice it is necessary to have the door between this narthex and the nave opened. The nave and aisles are lighted by forty small round-headed windows, and their roofs rest on forty semicircular arches springing from massive piers, with attached columns ornamented with the peculiar capitals of their period. A triforium runs round the transept and choir. Eleven circular columns, of one stone each, support the arches which enclose the sanctuary. From the S. side of the choir a door opens into what was formerly the "salle capitulaire," built in the 12th cent. The cloister is a modern addition by Violet le Duc, who also constructed the altar in the beautiful crypt below the choir. Near the abbey church is St. Martin's, 12th cent., and St. Etienne, now used as a storehouse. The Port St. Croix (15th cent.), as well as parts of the fortifications, still remain. Thomas à Becket celebrated mass in the Madeleine on the 15th May 1166 ; when also, with the awful forms provided by the Roman ritual, he pronounced sentence of excommunication against John of Oxford and others, and would have included Henri II. himself, had he not been informed that the King at that time was seriously ill. At Vezelay, in 1190, the crusaders under Richard Cœur-de-Lion joined those under Philippe-Auguste to set out on the third crusade. Vezelay is the birthplace of Theodore Beza (June 24, 1519), one of the pillars of the Reformed Church. In his arms Calvin expired.

1¼ m. from Vezelay is St. Père, pop. 2000, with a beautiful church of the 14th cent., but the elegant steeple is of the 13th. 5 m. from St. Père is the Château Baroche, which belonged to Marshal Vauban.

PARIS
MILES FROM
    SEMUR. SAINT FLORENTIN.
    MARSEILLES
MILES TO

9½ m. E. from Sermizelles by rail is **Avallon**, pop. 6000, on the Cousin. *Hotels:* Chapeau Rouge ; Poste. The parish church of St. Lazare, 12th cent., is a beautiful but somewhat peculiar specimen of Burgundian architecture. Coach awaits passengers at the station for Saulieu, 17 miles distant, pop. 4000. Hôtel de la Poste. An interesting town with a church, St. Andoche, 12th cent. The vineyards of Avallon produce good wine. The best keeps well in bottle from fifteen to twenty years. 10 miles S.W. from Avallon is the Forêt de Morvan, whence Paris receives firewood, sent down the Yonne and Seine in rafts.

After Avallon comes Rouvray, with vineyards producing good wine, and then, 20 miles from Avallon and 12½ from Les Laumes, is Semur, pop. 4150. *Hotels:* Côte d'Or ; Commerce. Picturesquely situated on the Armançon, about a mile from the station. The parish church of Notre Dame was founded in 1065 by Robert I., Duke of Burgundy, rebuilt in the 13th cent., and repaired in 1450. The entrance is provided with a sculptured porch. The windows of the N. aisle contain fine old glass ; the subjects are portrayed with great expression and quaintness. In this part is a beautifully wrought tabernacle of one stone 16½ feet high. At each transept is a small cloister. There are some pleasant walks around and about the town. The dungeon tower and part of the ramparts still remain. 12½ miles N.E. this branch line joins the main line at Les Laumes, 160 miles from Paris. (See page 19, and map page 1.)

107½   429½

~~ SAINT FLORENTIN, pop. 3000. *Inns:* At station, H. de la ~~ Gare. In town, H. Porte Dilo. Pilgrims to Pontigny alight here, whence a coach starts in the afternoon for Chablis and Ligny, passing within a mile of Pontigny. There is a small inn at the part where the Pontigny road separates from the Chablis road.

Saint Florentin is on an eminence more than a mile from the station. The parish church, 12th to 15th cents., is small, but interesting. The windows contain 15th and 16th cent. glass, repaired with modern pieces. The sanctuary is surrounded by a screen composed of slender colonnettes standing diagonally, and is shut off from the nave by a beautiful rood-loft. Behind the high altar, which is elaborately sculptured, is a relief, 1548, sadly mutilated, representing the death and resurrection of Jesus Christ.

At Pontigny there is a small but comfortable inn, the Hôtel St. Éloi, but pilgrims to the shrine of St. Edmund are generally lodged in the abbey buildings. From Pontigny a coach runs every other day to Auxerre, 13 m. S.W., stopping at a café near the station. The greater part of the church of Pontigny was built in 1150. It is a plain vast edifice with narthex and round turret at main entrance. The interior, which is grand and imposing, is 355 ft. from W. to E., 72 ft.

wide, and 72 high, and is upheld by 30 arches springing from lofty massive piers. There are 11 chapels in the choir, but none in the nave. A row of small round-headed windows extends round the church below the arches, and another, exactly similar, above them. In a shrine, 18th cent., behind the high altar are the bones of St. Edmund, Archbishop of Canterbury, who died in 1243 at a village in the neighbourhood. The original shrine, a plain wooden coffin, is upstairs in the cloister. The view of the interior of the building is spoilt by an ugly screen, rendered necessary to shut off the sanctuary from the rest of the church to make it more comfortable for the villagers, whose parish church it has now become. The abbey buildings, of which parts still remain in good condition, were inhabited by Becket. In the treasury is the black strip of a stole he used to wear, sewed on to another stole. Also relics of St. Edmund, and curious deeds connected with him and others, who had retired to this, then an austere Cistercian monastery. The walls of the cloister are hung with engravings representing scenes in the life of St. Edmund.

Becket arrived at this abbey on the 29th of November 1164, and remained till Easter 1166. From Pontigny he went to Vezelay, and from Vezelay to Sens.

123   **414**
TONNERRE, pop. 6000, on the Armançon. *Inns:* Lion d'Or ; Courriers—both near each other. The street St. Pierre, to the left of the Lion d'Or, leads past the church of Notre Dame (now condemned) up to the cemetery, and to the church of St. Pierre, situated on a terrace right above the town. At the foot of this hill is a beautiful spring of water, enclosed in a circular basin about 40 feet in diameter, called the Fosse Dionne ; but it is in a dirty part of the town, and used by the washerwomen. A straight street to the right of the Lion d'Or leads down to the hospital, built in 1834, the original part of which, built by Marguerite de Bourgogne in 1293, is now the church of the hospital. Her remains repose under a beautiful mausoleum in front of the high altar (died September 4, 1308). To the left is the mausoleum of the Marquis de Louvois (died 1691). The arrondissement of Tonnerre produces some excellent wine.

127½   **409½**
TANLAY, pop. 1000, on the Armançon. A small village with a handsome castle in an extensive park. The oldest part was built by Guillaume de Montmorenci, in 1520, but by far the largest portion by a brother of Admiral Coligny, in 1559. The vast façade is flanked by two wings. The principal court is 79 feet by 36. In a

C

room in the second story of the Tour de la Ligue the leaders of the
Protestant party used to meet under the presidency of Admiral Coligny.
A fresco on the ceiling represents, under the disguise of the gods of
Olympus, the persons who took the most prominent part in the
political and religious events of that period.   Catherine de Médicis is
portrayed as Juno, Charles IX. as Pluto, and the Condé as Mars.
Round the room are a series of curiously-constructed recesses, communicating with each other in the walls.   The largest of the splendid
chimney-pieces is 12½ feet high by 7 wide.   Beyond the grounds are
the ruins of the abbey of de Quincy, and the well of St. Gaultier,
both of the 13th cent.   At this station is a coach for Cruzy-le-Chatel,
pop. 1000, time 1 hour 45 minutes, among forests, and famous for
truffles.

136   401
⤳ ANCY-LE-FRANC, pop. 2000.   The fine castle here was ⤳
commenced in 1545, and built according to the plans of Primaticcio.

142   395
⤳NUITS-SOUS-RAVIERES, pop. 700.   Important junction ⤳
with the Paris and Bâle line, by Troyes (see page 11), by a branch
extending 72 miles north-east to Bricon, passing Châtillon, 22 miles
north-east from Nuits.   In the environs of Nuits-sur-Armençon are
the ruins of the castle of Rochefort, 17th and 18th cents.

151   386
⤳ MONTBARD, pop. 3000, on the Canal de Bourgogne.   *Inn:* ⤳
Hôtel de la Poste.   Buffon, the celebrated naturalist, was born in this
small village on the 7th of September 1707.   His château, a plain large
house, is entered from the extremity of the main street farthest from
the station.   The grounds are extensive, and laid out in terraces.   On
the western front of the terrace is the small square house, with three
windows and one door, into which he retired at five in the morning to
pursue his studies.   In another building he kept his manuscripts.   In
the grounds of the château, on the walk below the dungeon tower of
the castle of the Dukes of Bourgogne, is the small column erected to
his memory by his son, who fell a victim to the tyranny of Robespierre,
only fifteen days before the downfall of that monster.   Situated on a
terrace at the entrance of the grounds is the parish church, containing
the tomb of Buffon.   A black stone slab over the door bears the
following inscription :—

BUFFON
A été inhumé dans le
Caveau de cette chapelle
Le 20 Avril 1788.

There is also a bronze statue of him here. 3½ miles from Montbard is the abbey of Fontenay, founded in 1118 ; now a paper mill.

160 LES LAUMES. *Inn:* H. Duvernet. Overlooking the station **377** is Mount Auxois, 1370 ft. above the sea. Near the top, and about 1½ mile from the station, is the ancient Alesia (Alise-Sainte-Reine, pop. 900. *Inn:* H. du Cheval Blanc), where Cæsar, B.C. 50, defeated the Gauls under Vercingetorix, whose statue by Millet, pedestal by V. le Duc, stands just above the hospital. The church of St. Thibault (14th cent.) has some curious sculpture. It is visited by pilgrims on the 7th of September. Four miles from Les Laumes is the Château Bussy Rabutin, in a beautiful park of 84 acres, built by Renaudin, one of the benefactors of the abbey of Fontenay, about the year 1150. It contains a valuable collection of portraits of historical personages by eminent artists. (See page 14.)

165 DARCEY, pop. 850, 2 miles from its station, at the foot of **372** steep mountains 1315 ft. high. *Inn:* Hôtel Guyot. Near the village are curious caves, and a subterranean lake, the source of the Douix. Omnibus at station for **Flavigny,** 1½ mile distant, pop. 1300, on a hill 1390 ft. above the Lozerain. Remains of fine old walls. Church 13th cent., with rood-loft 16th cent. Houses of 13th, 14th, and 15th cents. Convent of the Ursulines, with splendid view.

171½ VERREY, pop. 900. *Inns:* Hôtel de la Gare ; Bourbogne. **365½** Station for the Source of the Seine, 6¼ miles S. by the path over the hill through the woods, but 9¼ by the carriage-road, which follows the railway till the village of Villotte, pop. 800, where it ascends the hill towards Bligny-le-Sec, pop. 700, 5 miles from Verrey, and after passing the farmhouse Bonne Rencontre joins the Dijon road. Then turn to the left and follow the Dijon road to a few yards beyond the 33 kilomètre (Côte d'Or) stone, where take the narrow road to the left, which passes first the farmhouse Vergerois and then descends to the source of the Seine (1545 feet above the sea), under an artistic grotto in the midst of a little garden enclosed by a railing. The keeper lives in the house beyond. The tiny infant stream issues forth under the protection of a recumbent statue of the river divinity. Coach there and back 10 frs., or guide 5 frs. It is not necessary to return to Verrey. Those who please can go back by the Dijon road to St. Seine, on the Cressonne, 5 miles south, pop. 1000. *Inns:* Mack ; Soleil d'Or. With a 14th cent. church. A diligence runs between it and Dijon. The railway station for St. Seine is Blaizy-Bas, 7½ m. distant.

179 / **358**
BLAIZY-BAS, situated at the commencement of the tunnel which pierces through the basin of the Seine to that of the Rhône. It is 13,440 feet long, and 1330 feet above the sea.

190 / **347**
VELARS, pop. 1400. After the preceding station of Malain, and before reaching the next station, Plombières-sur-Ouche, there is some bold railway engineering. The viaduct of the Combe-Bouchard is on two tiers of arches and is 492 feet long, while that of Neuvon is 774 feet long. From Velars commences the branch to Nevers by Autun, 74½ miles from Nevers. (For Autun, see page 24.)

196 / **341**
DIJON, pop. 48,000. Good refreshment-rooms at the station. *Hotels:* La Cloche, in the Rue Guillaume; and the Jura, near the station. Near the Cloche is the Galère. Just outside the arch, the Bourgogne and the Nord. In the Rue Bossuet, the Genève. Dijon is famous for mustard, gingerbread, and the liqueur Cassis.

Cabs, 1 fr. 75 c. the first hour, and 1 fr. 50 c. every succeeding hour. Coaches daily to Ancey, Fleury-sur-Ouche, La Cude, Cissey, and St. Seine. The St. Seine dil. starts daily from the inn, Hôtel du Commerce, 82 Rue Godrans, and takes about 3½ hours. From St. Seine an excellent road leads to the source of the Seine, 5 m. distant. (See page 19.)

The most interesting buildings in Dijon are near the palace, which was inhabited by Jean Sans Peur, Philippe le Bon, and Charles le Temeraire; but of that ancient building there remain only the Tour de Brancion, the Salle des Gardes, the kitchens and vaulted rooms on the ground-floor, and the Tour de la Terrasse, 152 feet high, ascended by 323 steps, and commanding a bird's-eye view of the whole town. The rest is modern, and is occupied by the Hôtel de Ville, the Post Office, the École des Beaux Arts, the Museums, and the Protestant church. The museum is on the right side of the great court, and is open to the public on Sundays. Other days a fee of 1 fr. is expected. In the Salle des Gardes are the magnificent mausoleums of Philippe le Hardi, 1342-1404, and of his son Jean Sans Peur, 1371-1419, with his consort Margaret of Bavaria. Of the two, the first is the more elaborate. It is in pure black and white marble, set round with a delicate frieze, and adorned with forty statuettes representing his most famous contemporaries. Among the articles which belonged to them in this room are three beautifully-carved folding altar-screens for private chapel service; and, under a glass case, the ducal crown, the cup of St. Bernard, and the crozier of St. Robert, first abbot of the Cistercian order, died 1098.

THE principal street is the Rue Guillaume. To the left is the Castle built by Louis XI., now the Gendarmerie. Beyond, at No. 1, are the Place and Statue of St. Bernard. No. 2 is the Préfecture. That large building at the foot of the Rue Condé, Nos. 4 and 5, is the ancient Palace of the Dukes of Burgundy, containing the Hôtel de Ville, the Museums, and the Post Office. No. 3 is the Church of Notre Dame; No. 6 St. Michel; and No. 7 the Theatre. Opposite the Palace, at No. 9, is the Palais de Justice. The church near the station (No. 8) is St. Bénigne, easily recognised by its lofty needle spire. Close to it is St. Jean, the church of Bossuet.

The chimney-piece in this hall is 30 feet high and 20 wide. Two statues of mail-clad knights stand on it, apparently a yard high each, but in reality 6 feet 2 inches. The picture-gallery contains a few choice paintings, and some good statuary. No. 402, St. Jerome, is considered one of the best. Down stairs is the Musée Archéologique, and the kitchen, nearly 50 feet square, and provided with 6 chimneys. Fronting the Palais is the Place d'Armes, with its shops and houses arranged in a kind of horse-shoe curve. Behind the palace runs the Rue des Forges. Nos. 34 and 36 is the Maison Richard, formerly the residence of the British Embassy to the Court of Burgundy. At the top of the spiral staircase is the "Homme au panier," a statue 4 feet 6 inches in height, on a pedestal at the topmost step, representing a manciple or serving-man bearing a basket on his right shoulder, out of which spring, like so many stems of wheat, nearly a score of vaulting ribs for the roof that closes in the staircase. No. 38, the Maison Milsand has a fine Renaissance façade, also some sculpture in the court. On No. 52 and 54 of this same street is exhibited a reproduction of that kind of double arch seen in the Hotel de Ville. Close to the Rue des Forges is Notre Dame, consecrated in 1331, a very beautiful and interesting specimen of Burgundian architecture. At the east end is the house Vogue, in the Renaissance style, and farther east, in the Rue Chaudronnière, the Maison des Cariatides. A short distance from the front of the Hotel de Ville is the Palais de Justice, formerly the palace of the Parliament of Burgundy. The ceiling of the Cour d'Assises is of massive carved chestnut, 17th cent. The crucifixion in the same room is by Belle. At the end of the Salle des Pas Perdus is the pretty little chapel which belonged to the parliament house. Near the theatre is St. Etienne, founded in the 10th cent., and partly rebuilt in the 18th, but now the corn-market. At the end of this same street, R. Vaillan, is St. Michel, rebuilt in the 16th cent., with a few curious frescoes. Standing at the Arc de Triomphe, looking down the Rue Guillaume, we have, towards the left, the chateau built by Louis XI. in 1478, or rather what remains of it, converted into the Gendarmerie ; and a little to the N.E. by a wide Boulevard, the Place and statue of St. Bernard, who was born (1091) at Fontaine Lez-Dijon, in the chateau beside the curious little church, 2 miles N.W. by the road of that name. Towards the right is St. Benigne, easily recognised by its slightly twisted needle spire, built in 1742, 300 feet high, and a little inclined by the tempest of 1805. The crypt and the porch belong to the 11th cent., the remainder to the 13th. In the south aisle is the slab tomb of Ladislaus Czartoryski (1388), and adjoining the beautiful mausoleum of Joannes Berbisey. In the N. aisle, in the baptistery chapel, are deposited the remains of Jean sans Peur. Near St. Benigne is St. Philibert, 12th cent., with a narthex and a beautiful crocketed spire. It is now used as an artillery store. From this the narrow street, Rue des Novices, leads to St. Jean, founded, as the tablet in the church states, in the 2d cent., rebuilt in 1458, and restored in 1866. The vault of the roof is bold, the tracery of the windows nearly rectilinear, and the mural paintings not without merit. Bossuet was baptised in this church, and born in No. 10 of this "Place," 27th September 1627. Among the writings of this eloquent and illustrious prelate the finest is the funeral oration on the death of Henrietta Anne, the daughter of our Charles I., and wife of the Duke of Orleans. Southwards is St. Anne, 1690. At the Octroi gate, beside the railway, is the entrance into the Asile des Aliénés, formerly the Chartreuse, founded by Philippe le Hardi in 1379. Fee, 1 fr. On the portal (14th cent.) of the chapel are the kneeling effigies of Philippe and his spouse Marguerite, accompanied by Sts. Antoine and Catherine, whose figures are portrayed in the beautiful glass (15th cent.) of the chancel windows. The visitor is next taken to the well called Le Puits de Moise, 22½ feet in diameter, consisting of a hexagonal pedestal, having on each side a statue of one of the prophets, by Claux Sluter in the 14th cent., the sculptor of the ducal monuments in the Palais des Etats. The statue of Moses is the least successful, and that of Zachariah the most expressive. The house contains on an average 500 patients. Dijon is not a town for sightseers, but an admirable town for resting during a long journey. The Cloche and Jura are comfortable houses, and although La Galère is less so, its charges are more moderate, while its fare is better. There are a number of pleasant walks. Just beyond the arch is the Promenade du Chateau d'eau, and at the foot of the railway station the Botanic Gardens. Towards the extremity of the gardens is a black poplar 490 years old. The southern continuation of the Place de St. Etienne leads by the Rue Chabot Charny, the Place St. Pierre, and the Cours du Pari (1465 yards long), to the public park. From Dijon the rail runs southwards parallel to the slopes of the famous wine producing hills of the Côte d'Or, extending from N.E. to S.W., and attaining an elevation of 324 feet. Behind them rises another range, reaching the height of 1315 feet, and sheltering the lower range from the cold winds. Between Dijon and Meursault grow the first-class Burgundy wines ; while south from Meursault follow the

Macon wines. First-class Burgundy is at its best after having been ten years in bottle. The inferior classes can hardly stand three years.

203
GEVREY-CHAMBERTIN, 1¼ mile from station, pop. 2000. **334** Famous for their first-class growths, of which the best are the red and white Chambertin. Bèze, St. Jacques, Mazy, and Vèroilles, in the commune of Gevrey, produce also first-class Burgundies.

206½
VOUGEOT, on the Vouge, pop. 500, ¾-mile from station. **330¾**
Inn: Groffier. Here there are above 125 acres of vineyards producing first-class Burgundies. Among the most distinguished are the Romanée St. Vivant, Romanée Conti, Richebourg, and La Tache.

209½
NUITS, pop. 4000. *Inn:* Trois Maures. Omnibus awaits **327½** passengers. The best vineyard here is the St. George, which produces a wine of an exquisite flavour and a delicate and delicious bouquet. The church, St. Symphorien, belongs to the 13th cent., and St. Denis to the 14th. 8 miles from Nuits is the abbey of Citeaux, now used as a house of detention for youthful criminals, who are trained here to be agricultural labourers. This abbey, founded by Robert de Molesme in 1098, had at one time 3600 dependent convents of the Cistercian order, and from it went forth four of its abbots, to assume the keys of St. Peter. The greater part of the buildings was rebuilt in 1798.

219
BEAUNE, pop. 12,000. *Hotels:* Chevreuil; France. On **318** the stream Buzoise. This town is the headquarters of the merchants who deal in Burgundy wines, as Bordeaux is that of the claret merchants. Around it are the first-class vineyards of Beaune Pommard, Volnay, and Romanée. Of these the Volnay vineyards, extending over 532 acres, produce the most valuable wine, under the names of Bouche d'Or and Caillerets, and the Pommard under that of Commarine. The town is of poor appearance. The principal church, Notre Dame, founded in the 12th cent., contains semicircular and equilateral-triangled arches and cusped and Corinthian capitals.

In the Place Monge, off the street de l'Ile, is a bronze statue to Gaspard Monge, the inventor of descriptive geometry, born at Beaune in 1746. To him France is indebted for the establishment of the Polytechnic School. Contiguous to the Chevreuil Inn is the hospital, built in the 15th cent.—a curious and interesting building. The Salle de Conseil upstairs is hung with Aubusson tapestry, and contains also a painting of the Last Judgment by Roger van der Weyden.

Near Beaune is Savigny, with a château built in 1672 ; in the neighbourhood are the Fontaine Froide, the ruins of the abbey of St. Marguerite, and the Roche Percée.

223½ ↷↷ MEURSAULT, pop. 3000, 1½ m. from the station. Omni- **313½** ↷↷ bus awaits passengers for the Inn. The most distinguished wines produced here are the Goutte d'Or, a golden-coloured wine, and the Perrières, a dry white wine of a slightly sulphureous taste. In the neighbourhood is Puligny, where the delicious sparkling white wine called Montrachet is grown.

228 ↷↷ CHAGNY, pop. 4200. *Inn :* Commerce. Junction with **309** line to Nevers 102 m. W., passing Nolay 5 m. W., Autun 26 m. W., Montchanin 18 m. W., and Le Creusot 22 m. W. (see page 25, and map page 1). From Chagny southwards commence the Macon wines, of which the vineyards around Chagny produce a first-class quality.

Nolay, pop. 5000. *Inns :* Cheval Blanc, La St. Marie. The vineyards in this neighbourhood produce a good white Macon. A few miles distant is the Vallon de Vaux-Chignon, below cliffs 200 ft. high. In a deep fissure is the source of the Cusane. 3¼ m. E. are the ruins of the castle Rochepot, 15th cent. In the church of the village is a remarkable echo. 8 m. beyond is Epinac, pop. 5000, with coal mines.

26 m. W. from Chagny is **Autun**, pop. 13,000. *Hotels :* Poste ; Cloche. This modernised little town, the ancient Bibracte, claims with Trèves the honour of having been built before the Roman invasion. Cæsar spent a winter in this city with two Roman legions ; and at a later period, when the Emperor Augustus went to Gaul, he made Bibracte his headquarters, and erected so many magnificent public buildings that the name of the town was changed to Augustodonum, modernised into Autun. Napoleon III., in his "History of Cæsar," considers, however, that the site of Bibracte was on the summit of Mount Beauvray, 14 miles westwards, where coins of Gaul, mosaic pavements, fragments of pottery, and an enormous number of amphoræ, have been discovered. The walls of Autun were 10,000 feet in circumference and 8 feet thick, and were garnished with 40 towers, and pierced with four large gates, of which two—the Porte d'Arroux, 55 feet high, and the Porte St. André, lately restored—still remain. The Porte d'Arroux and the temple of Janus (a plain square tower) are behind the railway station. But the Porte St. André, adjoining an ancient church, is on the town side of the line at the Faubourg St. Jean. The **Cathedral**, which commands the entire city, was completed in 1178. The architecture of the modern portions is Gothic, but the more ancient is Romanesque. The two towers have been restored and adorned with Gothic spires. The interior contains several windows of painted glass. The entrance is by a handsome open portico with sculptured arches and columns. From the Porte St.

Blaise (straight up from the cathedral) a cross road leads to the Pierre Couchard (Coarre), a pyramidal monument of great antiquity.

In the College is the Public Library, with 12,000 volumes ; and the Picture Gallery, containing paintings by Horace Vernet. In 1789 Talleyrand, afterwards Prince Talleyrand, was Bishop of Autun.

73 m. E. from Moulins, 86 m. E. from Nevers, 18 m. W. from Chagny, is **Montchanin**, pop. 2500. *Inn :* H. des Minis ; its omnibus awaits passengers. The town, nearly a mile from the station, consists chiefly of the houses of the workmen employed in the surrounding coal-pits, foundries, and large artistic brick and tile works. Outside the town is the Étang Berthaud, the reservoir of the Canal du Centre, which connects the Saône with the Loire, between Chalon and Digoin.

78¼ m. E. from Nevers, 7¾ m. W. from Montchanin, and 26 m. W. from Chagny, is **Le Creusot**, pop. 25,000, of whom 6300 are employed in the ironworks. *Hotels :* Commerce ; Rodrigue, near each other in the principal street, the Rue d'Autun. Their coaches await passengers. Le Creusot is on the southern slope of one of the wooded hills which enclose this valley, 1¼ mile long and ½ mile wide, occupied by the coal-pits, forges, and foundries of Schneider et Cie, bought by them from the former owners, Manby, Wilson, and Co. Detached straggling suburbs occupy the other slopes of the hills. In all the general feature is the same, rather untidy streets and houses, with parks, shops, and cafés to suit. The streets are full of children, but few priests, policemen, and beggars. In the principal square, near the two hotels, is a statue by H. Chapu of Eugene Schneider, erected in 1878 by the workmen and inhabitants. The view of the works from the road is imposing, and, although they contain a forest of chimneys and all manner of powerful machinery, there is no noise.

West from Le Creusot, and 65¼ m. E. from Nevers, is Etang, with an ancient castle. 51½ m. E. from Nevers is Luzy, pop. 3000, on the Alène. *Inn :* H. Delaigue, close to station. Coach 12 m. to St. Honoré-Les-Bains, with alkaline sulphureous springs, 90° Fahr. 33 m. E. from Nevers is Cercy-la-Tour, on the Aron, 53 m. south from Clamecy by the rail, skirting the Canal Nivernais. *Inn :* H. de la Croix, close to station. 23½ m. E. from Nevers is Decize, pop. 4800. *Inns :* Paris ; Commerce. Omnibus awaits passengers. Situated on an island in the Loire, at its junction with the Aron and the Canal Nivernais, which commences here and flows into the Yonne at Auxerre. The parish church has a choir of the 11th, nave of the 16th, and crypt of the 10th cent., containing the tomb of St. Aré. Foundries, glass bottle works, and coal-mines. Coach from Decize to La Machine 80 minutes.

235 CHALON - SUR - SAÔNE, pop. 21,000. *Hotels:* at the **302** station, Hôtel Bourgogne ; in the town, Chevreuil ; Commerce ; Trois Faissans. Steamer to Macon and Lyons. Chalon is a quiet town situated on an extensive plain on the Saône, at the mouth of the Canal du Centre, both lined with good quays. The chief structures are—St. Vincent, a Gothic edifice of the latter part of the 13th cent., occupying the site of a church founded in 532 ; St. Peter, 1713, with two lofty steeples ; and the hospitals of St. Laurent and St. Louis. Chalon has two stations—one in the town, and another at St. Come, where the express trains halt. 2 miles from Chalon is St. Marcel, where Abélard died 1142. The church still remains, but the monastery has disappeared. A few miles west by coach is Givry, pop. 3200, with first-class vineyards. Rail to

243 VARENNES. South from this station the train passes before **294** the abbey of St. Ambreuil.

254 TOURNUS, on the Saône, pop. 6200. *Inn:* Hôtel Sauvage, **283** not clean. An untidy town on the Saône, with remains of Roman fortifications. In the Place de l'Hôtel de Ville is a marble statue of Greuze, erected by the citizens in 1868. Jean Baptiste Greuze, some of whose works are among the finest paintings of the French school in the Louvre, was born here on August 21, 1725. The parish church, St. Philibert, is an interesting Gothic monument, of which the earliest portions belong to the 9th and the latest to the 16th cent. The interior is ornamented with mosaics. The Hôtel Dieu was founded in 1674, the Hospice de la Charité in 1718, and the Hôtel de Ville more recently. The vineyards of Tournus produce good wines.

274 MACON, pop. 20,000. At station, large refreshment-rooms. **263** Junction with line to Bourg, 41 m. E. *Hotels.*—Near the station, H. Étrangers. In town the Europe, on the Quai du Nord, near the landing-place from the steamers, which sail daily up and down the Saône; between Chalons, Macon, and Lyons. In the centre of the town are the hotels Champs Elysées and Sauvage. Macon is the great dépôt of the Macon wines, an inferior Burgundy. The finest part of the town extends along the quays which line the right side of the Saône, crossed by a stone bridge of 12 arches, uniting Macon with its suburb Saint Laurent on the left side of the river. The oldest edifice is the Cathedral of St. Vincent, built in the 12th cent. The arches are stilted, the columns Romanesque, and the porch arcaded. Next to it is the Préfecture, formerly the Episcopal palace. In this neighbour-

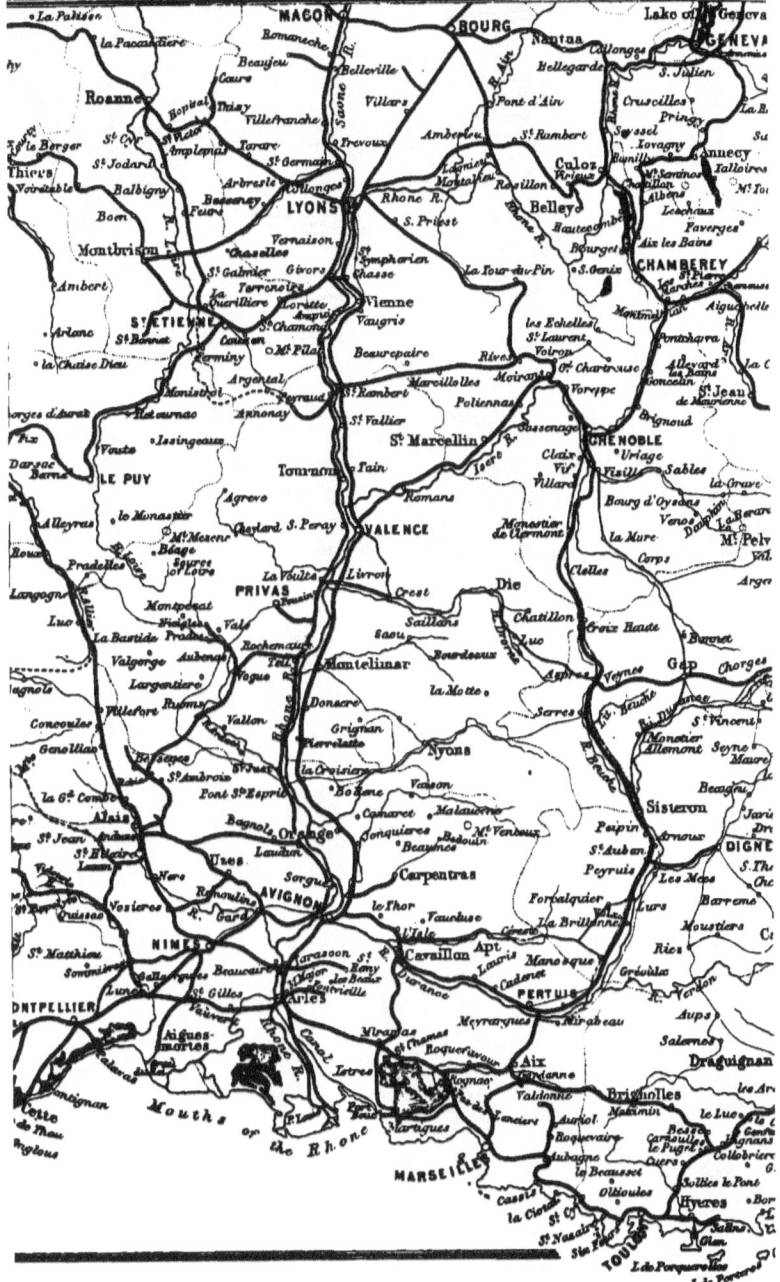

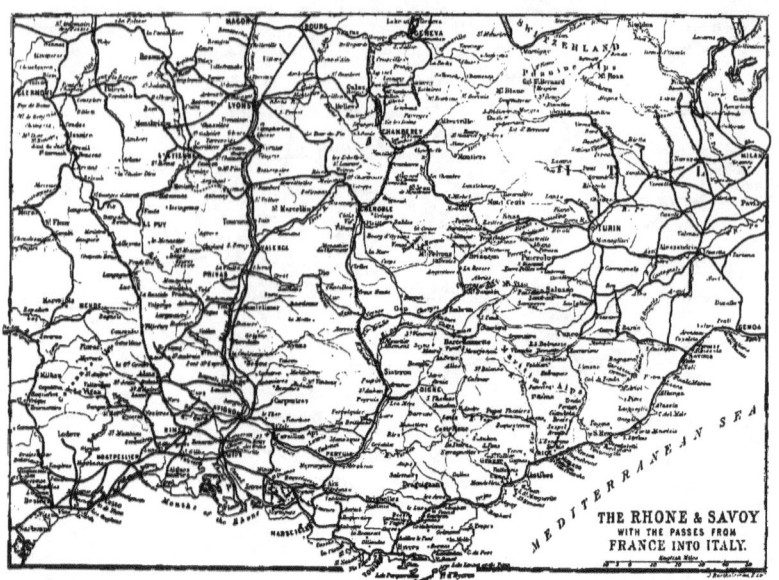

THE RHONE & SAVOY
WITH THE PASSES FROM
FRANCE INTO ITALY.

hood, at No. 21 Rue des Ursulines, is the house where Lamartine was born. On a black marble slab over the door are the words :—Ici est né Alphonse-Marie-Louis De Lamartine, le 21 Octobre 1790.

In the Rue Dombey is an old timber house, and towards the station, the beautiful church of St. Pierre, built in 1865, in the Romanesque style, and decorated with frescoes. Opposite is the Hôtel de Ville.

From Macon a branch line extends 48 miles westward to Paray-le-Monial, passing Cluny, 15 miles from Macon. From Macon a line extends to Geneva 74 m. E., by Bourg 13½ m. E., Nantua and Belle-gards 39¾ m. E. (See Black's *France*, North Half, and map page 1.)

Cluny, pop. 5000. In the valley of the Grosne. *Hotels :* Bourgogne ; Pavillons—both near each other. This is the place where Guillaume-le-Pieux founded in the 10th cent. the famous abbey of Cluny. The abbey buildings are now used as a school. Of the abbey church an insignificant portion alone remains, and of it the most interesting part is the spire. In the Chapelle des Bourbons (15th cent.) are enormous corbels under the empty niches. About 300 yards distant is the Maison Abbatiale, 15th cent., with flattened elliptical-headed windows and ogee arches over the doors. At the entrance is a collection of columns, capitals, etc., from the first church founded in the 10th cent. Upstairs there is a small museum ; entrance, ½-franc each.

41½ m. E. from Moulins and 33 m. from Montchanin is Paray-le-Monial, pop. 3700, on the Bourbince. *Inns :* The Poste, the best ; across the bridge, the Lion d'Or ; at the head of the principal street, near the Palais de Justice, the Trois Pigeons and the Commerce ; opposite the Chapelle de la Visitation, the Inn H. des Pelerins. The Palais de Justice, with the clock tower, occupies the remains of an edifice built in the 16th cent., to which date belongs also the house close to it, occupied by the Mairie and the Post Office.

A little way down the Bourbince is the formerly abbey, now the parish church, founded in the 11th cent., but nearly rebuilt in the 12th cent. Over the façade rise two elegant square towers with pyramidal roofs, 11th cent. ; while from the centre of the transepts rises an octagonal tower in 2 stages, surmounted by a tapering 8-sided slated spire. From the apse radiate chapels adorned with dental friezes and short attached columns.

From this church, the narrow street, the Rue de la Visitation, leads up to the nunnery of the Visitation, an order instituted in 1620, and established in Paray on the 4th September 1626 by 8 nuns from the monastery of Bellecour at Lyons. In 1633 they commenced to build their chapel, which was repaired in 1823, and restored and beautified in 1854. To this chapel the order attach great importance, as it was in this building that Marguerite-Marie Alacoque had most of her interviews with J. C. In the interior the walls and roof are painted light brown, with frescoes and marguerites or daisies, but so hung with banners and votive offerings, chiefly hearts, that little of them is seen. The first picture, right hand, represents J. C. and 3 angels before Marguerite. The 2d, J. C., with flowing yellow hair and dressed in white, stoops to touch with his heart (which is very red and outside his garment) the head of the kneeling Marguerite, who holds her hands up near to her neck. The 3d is a full-length portrait of her. To the left of entrance the pictures are—1st, a Vision; 2d, Mary, sitting on a cloud, has put the child Jesus into the arms of Marguerite; 3d, life-size statues of J. C. and Marguerite. The picture over the high altar represents the interview in this place, when J. C. is said to have declared to Margaret: "I have chosen and sanctified this chapel, that my eyes and my heart may remain here for ever." On the 2d July 1688 Mary, in great pomp and majesty, accompanied by numerous angels, appeared to Marguerite, and told her that the orders of the "Visitation" and of "Jesus" (the Jesuits) were to have the special charge of the worship of the sacred heart. For this worship there is a regular litany, containing 31 invocations to the heart of J. C. In many of the Romanist churches is a picture representing one of the above incidents.

The bones of Marguerite, covered with flesh-like wax, and attired in the habit of the order, recline on a silver embroidered cloth in a coffin-like shrine of richly-gilt, tiny glazed arches set with rock-crystal. The face and hands are uncovered. The body is 5 ft. long. On her feast day the shrine is placed beside the Communion rail; at other times it is kept within the very beautiful altar-table, made of one piece of pure white marble. Marguerite-Marie Alacoque was born 22d July 1647, in the village of Versovres, near Autun, entered the convent of the Visitation in Paray on the 25th May 1671, and took the vows on the 6th November 1672. On the day when J. C. told her she had been chosen by him to propagate the worship of his heart, she was seized with a pain in her own heart, which continued throughout her life. She met at first with great opposition in her endeavours to institute the worship of the heart, and her sister nuns treated her as a visionary till 1675, when the R. P. de la Colombière, superior of the Jesuit establishment at Paray, became her convert. In her last illness she said: "I shall die in peace, because the heart of my Saviour commences to be known." She died in October 1690, and was canonised by Pio IX. on the 14th October 1864. Since the institution of N. D. de Lourdes and de la Salette the number of pilgrims has decreased. In Paray there are 3 nunneries and a vast building belonging to the Jesuits.

From Macon the railway continues its course by the side of the Saône, whose banks become now more picturesque. From Macon use map on page 26.

283   **254**

~ ROMANECHE, pop. 3000. *Inn:* Commerce. Produces a ~ delicate light wine, with a pleasant flavour and bouquet, called Moulin-a-Vent, which should be drunk in the second year from the vintage.

288½ BELLEVILLE, pop. 4000. The first part of the town is St. **248½**
Jean, and the next Belleville, 1¼ m. from the station, with a comfortable little inn, the H. Jambon. Omnibus at station. The church,
12th cent., has small round-headed and pointed windows, with some
good glass, especially in those of the square towers at the end of the
transept, and the small circular window over the west portal. This
is the headquarters of the Beaujolais wines. From Belleville a branch
line extends 10 m. W. to Beaujeu, pop. 4000, on the Ardière. Church,
13th cent., and some curious houses. (Map, page 26.)

297 VILLEFRANCHE-sur-saône, pop. 12,600, on the river **240**
Morgan, near the Saône. *Hotels:* Provence ; Europe. Containing
important linen manufactories, and vineyards producing a good white
wine. The parish church, N. D. des Marais, was commenced in the
14th cent. 5½ m. S. is Trévoux station, 1½ m. from the town, pop.
3000, on the E. bank of the Saône. *Inns:* Terrasse ; France. The
Jesuits compiled and printed in this town the *Journal de Trévoux* in
1701, and the *Dictionnaire de Trévoux* in 1704.

306 ST. GERMAIN au-mont-d'or, junction with line from Paris **231**
to Lyons, by Roanne and Tarare.

318 LYONS, pop. 343,000. The Perrache railway station is **219**
218 m. from Paris, 219 m. from Marseilles, 78 m. from Aix-les-Bains,
36½ m. from Bourg, 104 m. from Geneva, 36 m. from St. Etienne, 56
m. from Roanne, 100 from Vichy, and 214 m. from Turin.

Hotels (first-class).—H. de l'Europe, admirably situated, with one
side to the Saône and the Tilsit bridge, and the other to the Place
Bellecour, the terminus of some of the best trams. In the Rue de la
République are the H. Collet and the H. de Lyon. H. Bellecour in
the Place Bellecour. H. des Beaux Arts in the R. de l'Hôtel de Ville,
also well situated. In the Place Perrache, below the station, are the
hotels Univers, Angleterre, Bordeaux et du Parc.

Less expensive Hotels. — The H. du Globe ; and the Havre et du
Luxemburg — both near the Place Bellecour. Near the Place des
Terreaux in the R. Platière, the H. de Paris et du Nord. Near the
Bourse, the H. des Négociants, a large house frequented chiefly by
commercial men. Near the Négociants, at No. 47 Rue de l'Hôtel de
Ville, the H. Bayard. Hôtel des Étrangers, Place de la République.
Hôtel de Toulouse et de Strasbourg, 8 frs., in the Place Perrache, opposite
the station. Hôtel National, opposite the theatre. On the Quai de
la Charité, near the General Hospital, the H. Bourne. A great

many diligences start from this neighbourhood.   Hôtel de France et des 4 Nations, 9 Rue St. Catherine, close to the Place des Terreaux, one of the cheapest.   Among the best cafés are the Café Anglais, opposite the Bourse ; Casati, No. 8 ; Café Neuf, No. 7 ; and Maderni, No. 19 R. de la République ; Café du Rhône, Place Bellecour.   They have English newspapers.   In Lyons the term Comptoir is applied to bars where wines, cordials, and brandies are sold.

Post Office.—Head Post Office in the Place de la Charité, at the south end of the Place Bellecour.   Branch Post Offices in the arcade of the Place des Terreaux and 39 Cours Morand.

Telegraph.—Head office, No. 53 Place de la République.   Branch offices—Perrache station, St. Paul station, and No. 38 Cours Morand.

Railway Stations.—The great and central station is the **Gare de Perrache,** in the centre of the tongue of land between the Rhône and the Saône.   From it passengers can reach any place, excepting those on the railway to Bourg.   The **Bourg or Satonay** railway station is at the top of the Rue Terme, a street commencing near the N.E. corner of the Place des Terreaux.   From the Rue Terme the train is pulled up the hill by a rope in the same way as at Fourvière.   The gradient is 16 per 100, and the distance 547 yards.   At the top station, in the Boulevard de la Croix Rousse, passengers for Bourg enter the ordinary railway carriages.   The rope railway runs every 5 minutes, fare 1d., and forms a convenient way of escaping from the damp foggy atmosphere of Lyons.   The Dombes or **St. Paul's** railway station is for Montbrison, 40 m. S.W.   The Vaise and Brotteaux stations are auxiliaries of the Perrache station.   The Brotteaux station, situated on the confines of the Parc de la Tête d'Or, is the terminus of the best of the trams.

CAB FARES

KIND OF CAB.	DE 7 H. DU MATIN À MINUIT.			DE MINUIT À 7 H. DU MAT.	
	LA course.	LA 1re heure.	LES H. suiv.	LA course.	l'heure.
A 2 places (coupés).............	1 25	1 50	1 25	1 65	2 50
A 4 places (berlines).............	1 50	2	1 50	2	3
Voitures découvertes { à 2 places	1 75	2	1 75	2 15	3
à 4 places	2	2 50	2	2 50	3 50

The "coupés" are cabs with a seat for two.   The "berlines" are cabs with 2 seats for four.   Each portmanteau 25 c.   At the railway stations the omnibuses from the hotels await passengers.

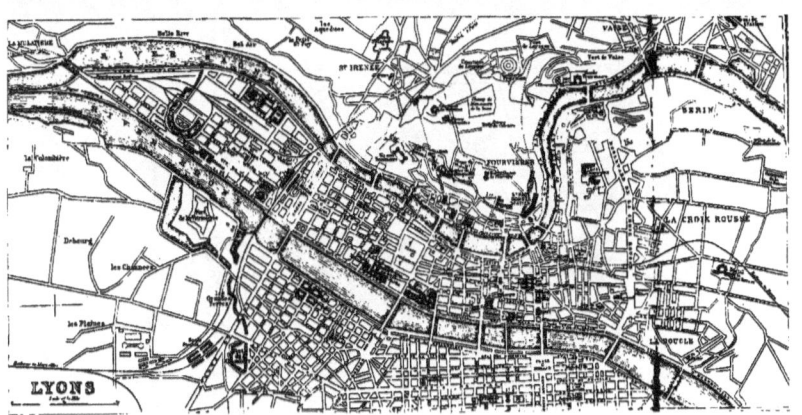

LYONS

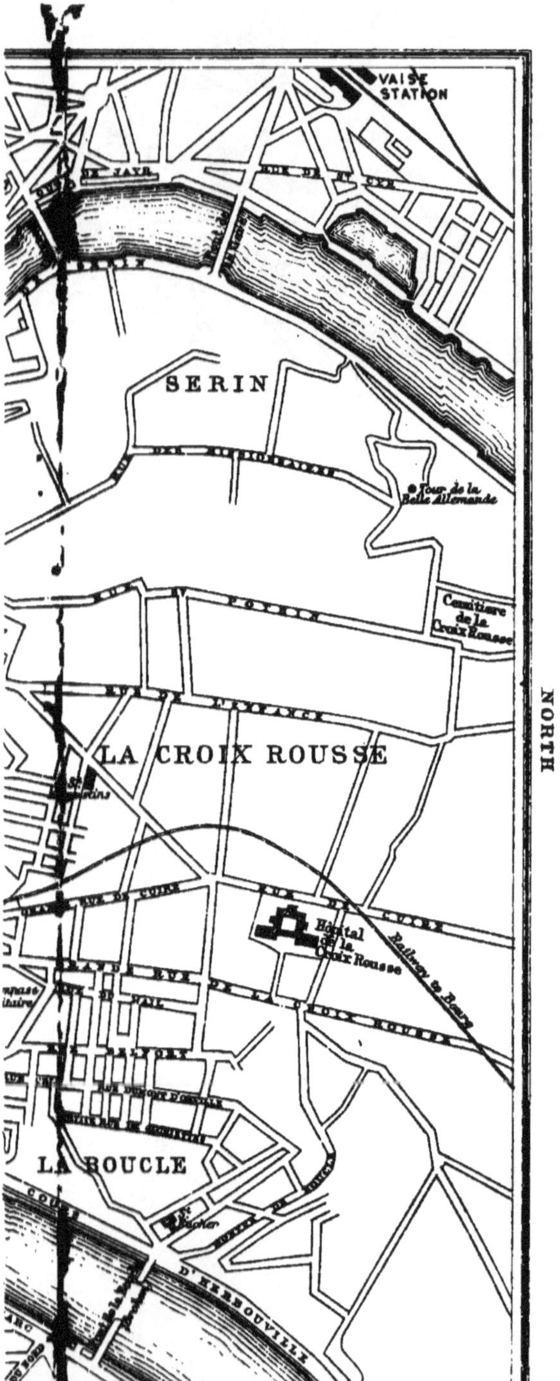

VAISE STATION

SERIN

Tour de la
Belle Allemande

Cimetière
de la
Croix Rousse

LA CROIX ROUSSE

Hôpital
de la
Croix Rousse

Railway to Paris

LA BOUCLE

D'HERBOUVILLE

NORTH

J. Bartholomew, Edin.

Tramways.—The fares are moderate, and most of the cars comfortable. The best to take to see the principal parts of the town is the large roomy car running between the Perrache railway station and the Brotteaux railway station, passing through the P. Perrache, P. Henri IV., Rue Bourbon, P. Bellecour, R. and P. de la République between the Hôtel de Ville and the Grand Theatre, across the bridge Morand, and up the Cour Morand to the terminus at the Brotteaux railway station. At the Brotteaux terminus the road by the side of the fort "des Charpennes" leads in 5 minutes into the Parc de la Tête d'Or (see page 40), which having visited, return either by the same car, starting every 10 minutes, or by the other, whose terminus is in the Quai de la Charité. The outside of the cars, taken also by ladies, costs 3 sous ; inside, 4. The two most important places to visit on the return journey are the Palais des Arts (page 35), and the silk museum in the Bourse (page 38). Tram between the Place de la Charité and Oullins every 15 minutes ; fare outside, 3 sous. To visit the meeting-place of the two rivers, come out at the bridge before crossing the Saône. Oullins, 3¼ m. .from Lyons, pop. 4000, is approached also by rail from Lyons.

Theatres.—The **Grand Théâtre**, between the Hôtel de Ville and the Rhône. Boxes and front stalls, 6 frs. The Théâtre des Célestins, between the Rue St. Dominique and the Saône. Boxes, 6 frs. ; stalls, 4 frs. **Théâtre Bellecour**, No. 85 Rue de la République, quite a new theatre, with all the modern comforts and appliances, and seated for 3000. The prices vary according to the subject. . For an opera the stalls cost 7 frs. each ; for a play, 4 frs. There are also the Théâtre des Variétés, Cours de Morand ; Théâtre du Gymnase, 30 Quai St. Antoine ; and the Théâtre de l'Elysée, 3 Place de la Victoire.

Steamers on the Saône (Les Guèpes).—Sail between the Quai St. Antoine (to the north of the Bourse) and Collonges, calling at the Ile Barbe. In summer 5 departures daily.

Les Mouches, or penny boats, sail from the quay near the Place Perrache, by the side of the Pont du Midi, to the Pont du Port Mouton on the Quai de Vaise, calling on the way at numerous stations. From the Pont du Port another set of penny boats ascend to St. Rambert, calling likewise at numerous stations on the way. Opposite St. Rambert is Cuire, and between them in the centre of the river is the Ile Barbe.

The large steamers Parisiens sail in summer between the Quai St. Claire on the Rhône and Aix-les-Bains on Tuesdays, Thursdays, and

Saturdays.   Fare, 9 frs.   Another line sails between Lyons and Avignon, calling at the principal towns on the way, but chiefly for the landing and shipping of cargo.

Sights.—Notre-Dame-de-Fourvière (see below).   Drive in tram car, outside if possible, between the Place Perrache and the Brotteaux railway station, page 31.   The Parc de la Tête d'Or, page 40.   The galleries in the Palais des Arts, page 35.   The museum of silk manufacture, page 38.

Lyons is a strongly-fortified city, intersected by two of the largest rivers in France, the Rhône and the Saône, which form as they approach each other the isthmus, 545 ft. above the sea, on which the finest part of the city is built.   This portion is traversed by three great streets, the Rue de la République, the R. de l'Hôtel de Ville, and the R. Centrale, and contains the three most important and beautiful squares, the Places Perrache, Bellecour, and Des Terreaux.   The Place Perrache, in front of the station, was planted with trees in 1851. In the centre was a bronze statue of Napoleon I. by Nieuwerkerke, which was taken down in 1870 and afterwards destroyed by order of the municipality.   In its place is a fountain.   The Place Bellecour (Bella-Curia), 339 yards long and 328 yards wide, is also planted with trees.   In the centre is an equestrian statue of Louis XIV. by Lemot, which occupies the place of a former one by Desjardins, destroyed in 1793.   Trams to all the important parts of the city run through these two squares.   The Place des Terreaux, flooded with human blood in 1794, during the reign of terror, has on the south side the Palais des Arts, on the east the Hôtel de Ville, and on the west a block of buildings pierced by an arcade decorated by P. Delorme and Maupin (see page 37).

The Rhône is crossed by 9 bridges, and the Saône by 13.   The extent of substantial and spacious quays on both sides of these rivers measures 24 miles.   For sailing on the Rhône the best steamers are the Bateaux Parisiens, starting from the quay in front of the Place Tholozan behind the Hôtel de Ville, and plying between Lyons and Avignon.   For short sails on the Saône the Bateaux Mouches are very convenient, page 31.

The most prominent building in Lyons is the church of **Notre-Dame-de-Fourvière**, standing on the site of the forum erected by Trajan, the Forum Vetus or Foro Vetere ; whence the term Fourvière is supposed to be derived.   It ought to be visited as early as possible, even should there be no time for anything else, on account of the excellent bird's-eye view of the city obtained from it and its terraces.   At the west end of the bridge of Tilsitt across the Saône, at the upper side of

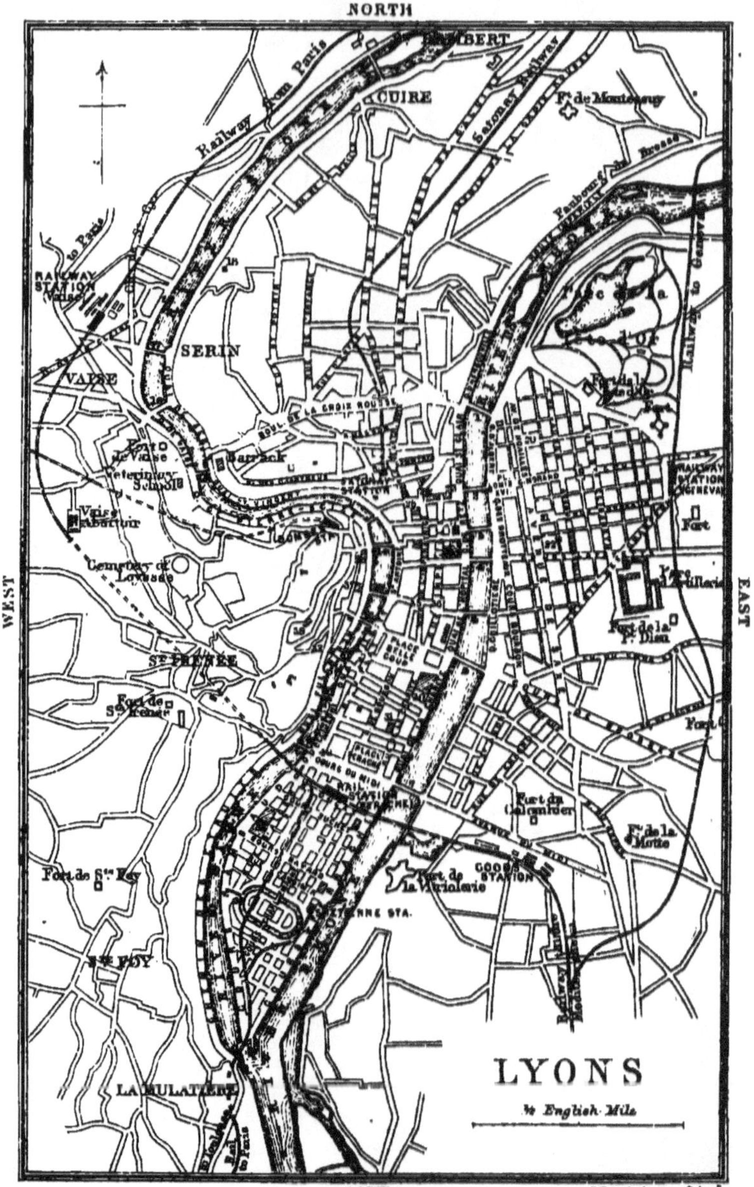

NORTH

LAMBERT

CUIRE

Ft de Montessuy

Railway from Paris

Saone Railway

to Paris

RAILWAY
STATION
(Vaise)

SERIN

VAISE

Port
de Vaise

Veterinary
School

Barrack

RAILWAY
STATION
(Brotteaux)

Fort

WEST   EAST

Veter.
Abattoir

Cemetery of
Loyasse

St IRENEE

Fort de
St Irenee

PLACE
BELLECOUR

Fort Tête d'Or

Fort de la
Pt Bleu

Fort

Fort de
Catherine

Ft de la
Motte

Fort de St Foy

GARE DU MIDI

Port de
la Varioleric

GOODS
STATION

PERRACHE STA.

Ste FOY

LA MULATIERE

<big>LYONS</big>

¼ English Mile

SOUTH   J. Bartholomew Edin.ʳ the "Place," is the rope railway, which ascends through tunnels the hill of Fourvière, the length of the Place des Minimes about ¾ of the way up the hill. Fare, 5 sous. From the station walk up, right hand, by the broad road, l'Antiquaille. At the highest part of this road is a large ugly edifice, the Hôpital de l'Antiquaille, especially devoted to the treatment of insanity and of cutaneous diseases. It has accommodation for 600 patients, and occupies the site of the Roman palace in which Claudius and Caligula were born. From in front of this hospital commences a narrow steep road called the Montée de Fourvière, lined nearly all the way with little shops stocked with wares for the pilgrims and devotees, such as images, crucifixes, amulets, chaplets, medals, photographs, and books. At the top are restaurants and hotels.

On the summit, 1206 feet above the sea and 410 feet above the Saône, is the chapel of the "miraculous" image of Notre-Dame-de-Fourvière, from which rises a domed tower crowned with a gilt image of Mary 6½ ft. high. This tower is ascended by 200 steps, fee 25 c., and commands a superb view of the city and environs. Lyons and its two great rivers are immediately below, while in the distance, if the weather be clear, Mont Blanc is distinctly seen. As for the sacred image itself, in the church below, it is about the size of a big doll, and the child rather less. The number of worshippers having become so great, the adjoining church, which is more elegant and much more commodious, was constructed in 1884. It stands on the very brow of the hill, and is the most prominent object in Lyons. In shape it is rectangular, with at the eastern termination an octagonal tower 115 ft. high, which forms the chancel. At each of the four corners is a similar tower, and in each of the two sides are three large windows separated by buttresses like square towers. Round the top of the building as well as of the towers extends a balustrade of stiff sculpture resembling acanthus leaves. The large buildings in the neighbourhood are convents. A little eastward is the "Observatoire Gay," from which a steep path, the Montée des Carmes Déchaussées, 536 yards long, descends to the city, reaching it by the side of the station of the Chemin de Fer des Dombes (page 30). Near this station is the church of St. Paul, all modern excepting the beautiful N. portal, the handsome octagonal lantern resting on pendentive arches, a few of the windows, and part of the walls which belonged to the original church of the 11th cent. The old walls which remain in all the early churches of Lyons are characterised by the enormous size of the stones of which they are composed. Beyond is the bridge of St. Vincent.

D

St. Irénée. Cathedral of St. Jean.

The Terminus of the rope railway from the Pont Tilsit is at No. 42 Rue Trion, higher and to the N.W. of Fourvière and within a very short distance of the church of St. Irénée, on the summit of a hill in the suburb of St. Just. On the terrace at the east end of St. Irénée are a Via Crucis and Calvary, commanding a superb view of the plain watered by the Rhône and the Saône. By the N. side of the church is the entrance into the crypt. The first flight consists of 25 steps; and the second, which terminates in the crypt, of eight. On the first arch across the first flight an inscription states : "Cette crypte fut construite par St. Patient evéque de Lyon au V siècle sur l'emplacement du lieu ou St. Pothin et St. Irénée, envoyés a Lyon par Polycarpe disciple de l'apôtre St. Jean, reunissaient les premiers chretiens. De nombreux martyrs y furent ensevelis." On the second arch another inscription states that in 1562 the Calvinists having injured the crypt and thrown the bones of animals among those of the saints, Grolier, Prior of St. Irénée, restored the building, separated the bones, and placed those of the saints in that small vault to the right, at the foot of the first flight. In the centre of the crypt is a now covered up well, the original resting-place of the martyrs, down which their bodies were thrown till it overflowed with blood, in the reign of Septimius Severus, A.D. 202. To visit the calvary and crypt apply to the concierge, 50 c. The church of St. Irénée has nothing particular. To the west, in the parish of Ste. Foy, are the remains of the Roman aqueduct which brought water to the city from Mont Pilat. It was 52 miles long, and capable of supplying 11,000,000 gallons per day. At present the water-supply of Lyons is obtained from the Rhône.

Opposite the commencement of the rope railway, and close to the Tilsit bridge, is the Cathedral of Saint Jean, founded in the 8th cent., repaired by Archbishop Leydrade, friend of Charlemagne, and reconstructed almost entirely three centuries later. The chancel dates from the end of the 12th cent., the lower part of the façade from the 13th, and the upper from the 14th cent. The exterior is chastely decorated, but the four towers are too low. The interior, 259 ft. from W. to E. and 108 ft. high, contains some brilliant 13th, 14th, and 15th cent. glass. The wheel window at the west end resembles a fully-blown flower. The clerestory windows are majestic and graceful. First, right hand, is the chapel built by the Cardinal de Bourbon and his brother Pierre, son-in-law of Louis XI. The two windows bearing their portraits, and the curious wheel window at the end, are admirable. The soffits of the arches and the vault of the roof are richly decorated.   In the N. transept is the now useless clock made by Nicholas Lippeus of Basel in 1508.   The founder of the See of Lyons was St. Pothinus, an Asiatic Greek, who preached in this city A.D. 177, and sealed his doctrines with his blood.   Adjoining the S. aisle is the Manécanterie, 11th cent., formerly the bishop's place, now the music school for the choristers.

A little farther down the river is the church of St. George (rebuilt) occupied in the 13th cent. by the Knight Templars.   Above the cathedral is the Palais de Justice, planned by Baltard, the architect of the large market, the Halles Centrales of Paris.   In front is a colonnade of 24 Corinthian columns.   The hall is spacious and elegant, but the court rooms around it are too small.   The bridge higher up— the Pont de Nemours—leads directly to the church of Saint Nizier, with the façade towards the bridge and the chancel towards the Rue de l'Hôtel de Ville.   The handsome portal surmounted by twin spires is by Philibert Delorme, a native of Lyons, and dates from the 16th cent.   The rest of the building belongs to the 15th cent.   In the interior a broad triforium with heavily-canopied window-openings surrounds the church.   The vaulting shafts expand in a curious way over the roof.   In the chapel of the south transept is a statue of Mary by Coysvox.   At the foot of the pier in this transept a trap-door opens into the crypt, 10th cent.   At the south side of the Palais des Arts is St. Pierre, a modern edifice, with a beautiful portal of the 11th cent., all that remains of the original church.

On the south side of the Place des Terreaux is the **Palais des Beaux-Arts**, built in 1667, formerly a convent of the Dames Bénédictines de Saint-Pierre.   It contains the picture galleries and the museums.   Open to the public on Sundays, Thursdays, and feast-days, from 11 to 4, and to strangers daily.

Admirably arranged under a wide corridor round the great court are the ancient marbles or **Musée Lapidaire**, one of the best in Europe.   The sepulchral inscriptions form a most interesting series of epitaphs, in many instances most tender and affecting.   Indeed, reading these records of the love of kindred among the ancient heathen, from the Augustan age upwards, one would incline to believe that the Romans of that day were already "feeling after" Christianity.   In the left corner of the court on entering is the stair which leads up to the Archæological Museum and the Picture Gallery, both on the first floor.   Up on the second floor is the collection of paintings by the "peintres lyonnais."

MUSÉE ARCHÉOLOGIQUE. GALERIE CHENAVARD.

The Musée Archéologique is well arranged and carefully labelled. The only object we would indicate, as it is apt to be overlooked, is the bronze table, A.D. 48, in the second room left hand, with inscribed portions of the harangue of Claudius before he became emperor, imploring the senate to grant to Lyons, his native city, the title of a Roman colony. The letters are beautifully cut and easily legible. This table was discovered in 1528 on the heights of Saint Sébastien. Germanicus, and the Emperors Claudius, Marcus Aurelius, and Cara-calla, were also born in Lyons. The father of St. Ambrose was for some time prefect of Lyons. In the same room is a decree of the Egyptian pontiffs in hieroglyphics. There is a good collection of seals, coins, enamels, armour, carved work, and bronzes, as well as some necklaces, bracelets, rings, and coins, part of a treasure buried during the Roman period on the Fourvière heights, and discovered in 1811. The numismatic collection, 30,000 pieces, includes a series of the coins struck at Lyons from 43 B.C. to 1857. Adjoining and on the same floor is the Picture Gallery, contained in six small rooms, of which the first three contain the Flemish and Dutch schools, the next two the Italian and Spanish schools, and the sixth the French school. They are all carefully labelled. Among the pictures which represent the Flemish school are works by Rembrandt, Rubens, Teniers, Van Dyck, Holbein, Stein, Dietrich, Breughel, Wouvermans, and Ruys-dael. The Italian and Spanish schools are represented by Canaletto, Sasso Ferrati, Guercino, Zucharo, Murillo, Ribera, Zurbaran, etc. On the floor of the fourth room is a remarkably perfect mosaic pavement, 5½ yards by 3, representing chariot races in the Circus. It was dis-covered near the church of Ainay.

In the S.E. corner a handsome staircase leads up to the Galerie Chenavard on the first floor, containing large cartoons drawn by him illustrative of the scenes which accompanied the introduction of Christianity into France. They were intended for the Pantheon of Paris, but, the age of reason supervening, they were not sent. On the floors are three beautiful mosaic pavements found at Lyons. In the room above are the best pictures—J. F. Barbieri, 1590-1661; Bol, Breughel, P. Caliari, 1530-1588 ; A. Carracci, 1557-1602 ; L. Carracci, 1555-1619 ; P. Champaigne, Crayer, Greuze, 1721-1805 ; E. L. David, 1748-1825 ; Desportes, 1661-1742 ; Cuyp, Van Dyck, Heem, 1604-1674 ; Jordaens, Jouvenet, 1644-1717 ; Largillière, M. Mierveld, Murillo, 1618-1682 ; J. Palma, 1544-1628 ; Pietro Perugino, 1446-1524 ; an Ascension of Christ, considered the gem of the collection.   This picture, originally in the church of San Pietro at Perugia, was presented by Pope Pio VII. "in attestato del suo affetto é della grata sua rimembranza per la citta di Lione."   The lower part of the picture is by far the best, the figures in the air are too massive, and the posture of J. C. is stiff.   J. Ribera, 1584-1656 ; H. Rigaud, 1552-1745 ; Robusti, 1512-1594 ; Rubens, Ruysdael, A. del Sarto, 1488-1530 ; Sasso Ferrati, 1605 - 1685; Schorreel, 1495 - 1565 ; Sueur, 1617-1656 ; Sneyders, Teniers, Terburg, Zampieri, and Zurbaran.

The Palais des Arts contains also the Natural History Museum, the **Mineralogical Collection**, in which are represented the characteristic rocks and fossils of every department of France, and the copper ores from the mine of Chessy, near Arbrèsle ; and a library containing 40,000'engravings and drawings, and 650 volumes treating principally on the arts and sciences.   There are likewise 6 municipal libraries, open every evening from 7 to 10, and the Bibliothèque de la Ville.

On the north side of the Place des Terreaux is the Hôtel de Ville, built in 1665 by Maupin, at the cost of £320,000.   The façade, flanked by domed square pavilions, is 160 ft. wide, while the building itself is 1150 ft. long.   The back part, fronting the theatre, is the Préfecture. From the centre rises the clock-tower, 157 ft. high.   On the façade over the entrance is an equestrian statue of Henri IV. in bold relief.   Within the vestibule, to the right and left, are colossal bronze groups, by the brothers Coustou, representing the Rhône and the Saône. They stood originally under the statue of Louis XIV. in the Place Bellecour.

In 1642 Cinq Mars and De Thou were executed, by order of Richelieu, in the Place des Terreaux.   In 1794 the revolutionary tribunal, sitting in the Hôtel de Ville, guillotined so many people in this square that it became so flooded with blood as to render it necessary to send the executioners to Brotteaux, near the present railway station, to finish this wholesale slaughter of Frenchmen by Frenchmen.

Behind the Hôtel de Ville, up the Rue de St. Polycarpe, house No. 7, is the establishment of the **Condition des Soies**, where the bales of silk brought to Lyons are sent to be dried.   They are placed on an iron grating, and subjected for twenty-four hours to a temperature of from 64° to 72° Fahr., and are weighed both before and after this operation. The same is done to the wool. The sample drying room is in the first story, left hand.   Any one may visit it.   A little higher up are St. Polycarpe built in 1760, and St. Bruno built in 1688.   At the opposite end of the bridge of St. Clair is the English church.

Lyons. Library. Bourse. Silk Museum.

In the Rue de la République is the **Bourse**, a profusely ornamented edifice inaugurated in 1860. At the south end is St. Bonaventure, built in the 14th cent., and recently restored. At the north end is the Lycée with the public library, containing the great terrestrial globe made at Lyons in 1701, indicating the great African lakes, the rediscovery of which has been one of the events of the present century. There are 160,000 volumes and 2500 manuscripts,—about 600 of the printed works being incunabula, and 25 of the MSS. belonging to the Carlovingian period.

In the second story of the Bourse is the museum of the **Art and Manufacture** of silk. Open to the public on Sundays and Thursdays between 11 and 4. The great hall contains, in high glass cases, specimens of silk, satin, velvet, crape, and lace, arranged according to centuries from the 13th and 14th to the 19th. The 19th, which is by far the richest and most beautiful, is in two cases, representing the first and the latter half of the century. This collection is choice and highly artistic, displaying miniature portraits, superb embroidery, and lovely designs in charming colours, woven in the loom. At the entrance to the hall is a portrait (about 13 in. by 10) of Jacquard, in a sitting posture, woven in white and black silk, like those at St. Etienne. Also the Will of Louis XVI. In the next room are looms and models of looms from the time of Louis XI. The models are so perfect that each contains part of a web woven in it. Among them is the model of the famous loom made by Jacquard in 1804, by which a single workman was enabled to produce elaborate fabrics as easily as the plainest web, and by merely changing the "cartoons" to make the most different textures on the same loom. Near the loom is the first **sewing machine**. The inventor was B. Thimonier of Lyons in 1829, from which those now in use are improved copies.

The cases round the inmost room are devoted to the natural history of silk—displaying every variety of the silk butterfly, Bombyx mori, as well as of the allied species ; cocoons of every kind and in every condition ; eggs and caterpillars at every stage of their existence ; and hanks of raw silk from every part of the world where it is produced. Adjoining is a room with drawings, many by the great masters.

Formerly Lyons manufactured only high-class silks, but the demand for these having been for some years on the decrease, the manufacturers, to hold their place in the market against especially their Créfeld rivals, have had to turn their attention to cheaper stuffs. This in some measure is owing to the rapid and violent changes of fashion, which makes a silk dress good only for a few months, whereas formerly, with an occasional alteration, it was worn for years.

In the street behind the east side of the Bourse are the large covered markets ; where many of the fishes of the Rhône may be seen alive in tanks, and good Mont d'Or cheese be bought. It makes capital railway travelling provision. (See page 42.)

Farther down the street, with the principal façade to the Rhône, and the other, containing the entrance, to the Rue de l'Hôpital, is the Hôtel Dieu, or general hospital, with 1500 beds, founded in the 6th cent. by Childebert and Ultrogotha his queen. The present building is principally the work of Soufflet, the architect of the Pantheon in Paris. Of the beds, about 1300 are free, the remainder pay from 1¼ fr. to 12 frs. per day. The rooms are lofty and well ventilated. The principal female wards are arranged in the form of a cross, with an altar in the centre under the small dome, in such a position that all the patients can see it from their beds. From the large dome extends the principal ward of the men, containing 100 beds, and a smaller one on the other side. The sick are tended by nuns. The hospital has a house on the heights of the Croix-Rousse, near the terminus of the rope railway, and another at Oullins for incurables.

In the first court left of the large court, Dr. Young buried Mrs. Temple, the Narcissa of his *Night Thoughts*, who died in 1730 at Montpellier, but was there refused burial. At that time what is now a built-up court was a cemetery. Fifty years ago it was a garden, now it is covered with buildings. All trace of the grave has disappeared.

Near the entrance to the hospital is the church, 18th cent., richly decorated. In a chapel, left, is the enormous gilt shrine, in 5 stages, of Sainte Valentine.

Farther down the Rhône is the Hospice de la Charité, founded in 1531, on the occasion of a great famine. It receives the poor of both sexes who have reached 70 ; sick children under 15, and young women about to be mothers. The church was built in 1617.

North from the hospice or workhouse, near the bridge of Ainay across the Saône, is the church of St. Martin d'Ainay, which, with the monastery, was founded by St. Badulph during the reign of Constantine, on the site of a temple erected by the sixty nations of Gaul in honour of Cæsar Augustus. The first church having been destroyed by the Saracens, in the 8th cent., it was rebuilt in 1070, and consecrated in 1106 by Pope Pascal II. Since then it has been frequently repaired and altered. The style belongs to what is called modern

St. Martin d'Ainay.   Parc de la Tête-d'Or.

Greek, introduced into France under Charlemagne. The cupola of the chancel rests on circular pendentive arches springing from four granite columns which stood formerly in the temple of Augustus. They were originally 2, but were cut into 4. The fresco paintings in the apsidal chapels are by H. Flandrin, a native of Lyons. To the right is the sacristy or chapel of Saint Blandina, in which a short stair leads down to the crypt and the dungeons, one on each side, where Pothinus, first bishop of Lyons, and Blandina, a converted slave, were kept before being tortured and put to death in A.D. 177, during the persecution under Marcus Antoninus, the implacable enemy of Christianity. The crypt, about 12 ft. square, was, as well as the dungeons, about 10 feet deeper, but on account of the overflowing of the river the floors were filled up to their present level.

The Parc de la Tête-d'Or, or park of Lyons, is situated at the N.E. extremity of the city, between the Brotteaux railway station and the left bank of the Rhône. It measures 282 acres, and contains, besides an abundant supply of varied walks, a large and excellent botanic garden with hothouses, a lake with islands inhabited by aquatic birds, and a dairy farm, whose produce is sent every morning into town for sale. Adjoining the park are the rifle-butts and the racecourse. In the Boulevard du Nord is the Guimet Museum, containing a collection of objects from the extreme east, to facilitate the study of the history, religions, and customs of the inhabitants of that part of the world. The institution publishes essays and translations.

By the western side of the Brotteaux railway station are the large barracks of the Part-Dieu and the Fort des Brotteaux.

Lyons employs 70,000 looms and 140,000 weavers in the manufacture of silk ; and here, as at St. Etienne, the work is principally performed on the domestic system in the dwellings of the master weavers, each of whom has usually from two to six or eight looms, which, with their fittings, are generally his own property. Himself and as many of his family as can work are employed on these looms, aided frequently by one or more *compagnons*, or journeymen, who inhabit chiefly the suburb of La Croix Rousse, to the north of the town, and that of Fourvières, on the Saône. The silk merchants supply the silk and patterns to the owners of looms, who are entrusted with the task of producing the web in a finished state. The mean annual value of the silk goods manufactured is estimated at £15,000,000.

The dyeing of the silk is also an important branch of manufacture. Many experiments had been made to bring this art to perfection, and in particular to discover a dye of perfect black that would retain its colour. This a common dyer of Lyons at last invented, for which he received a pension, besides being made a member of the Legion of Honour. Prior to this the black dye which was used changed in a few days to a brown, and came off the stuff when it was hard pressed by the hand. Another improvement which was made consisted in procuring a silk of a permanent white colour. The eggs of the worm which produced this silk were brought from China, not, however, with the desired success. The worm was afterwards purchased from a merchant of Alais, and distributed in the southern departments of the country, where now a large number of persons are engaged in silkworm hatcheries. The produce of white silk is now very considerable and of great importance in the manufacture of gauzes, crapes, and tulles. Extensive chemical works, breweries, foundries, potteries, engineering works, printing establishments, and hat factories represent the secondary industries of Lyons. A large trade is carried on in chestnuts brought from the neighbouring departments, and known as *marrons de Lyon*.

The earliest Gallic occupants of the territory at the confluence of the Rhône and the Saône were the Segusians. In 590 B.C. some Greek refugees from the banks of the Hérault, having obtained permission of the natives to establish themselves on the Croix Rousse, called their new town by the Gallic name Lugdunum; and in 43 B.C. Munatius Plancus brought a Roman colony to Fourvières from Vienne. This settlement soon acquired importance, and was made by Agrippa the starting-point of four great roads. Augustus, besides building aqueducts, temples, and a theatre, gave it a senate and made it the seat of an annual assembly of deputies from the sixty cities of Gallia Comata. Under the emperors the colony of Forum Vetus and the municipium of Lugdunum were united, receiving the *jus senatus*. The town, burnt by Nero in 59 A.D., was rebuilt by him in a much finer style, and adorned by Trajan, Adrian, and Antoninus.

Among the most interesting, and at the same time easiest excursions from Lyons is to Mont Ceindre, 4 m. from Lyons. Take the omnibus starting from the Rue de la Platière to the village of St. Cyr-au-Mont-d'Or, 3¼ m., time 1½ hr., by a road always ascending. Fare, ½ fr. The omnibus office at St. Cyr, the inn, and the café, are on a wide terrace commanding an extensive view. The village, pop. 2000, is poor and dirty, and built on the side of the hill. To ascend Mont Ceindre walk from the omnibus office up to the new church, whence ascend by the telegraph posts, and then turn to the right. The ascent

42

PARIS
MILES FROM Mont-d'Or. Cheese. Vienne. MARSEILLES
MILES TO

and descent can be done easily in 80 minutes, in time to go back to Lyons by the returning coach. On the top of Mont Ceindre are some houses, an old hermitage, and a chapel surmounted with a statue of Mary. The view is grand, embracing the valleys of the Rhône and the Saône, the towns of Bugey and Beaujolais, the mountains of the Forez, the Dauphiné, and the Alps. Mont Ceindre, 1532 ft. above the sea ; Mont Verdun, 2020 ft. ; and Mont Houx, 2008 ft., form together **Mont-d'Or**, a group of mountains covered with vineyards and meadows. The wine is thin, but the cheese is one of the best and most celebrated in France. They are soft, round, and flat, about 5 inches in diameter and half an inch thick, like round pancakes. They are made from a mixture of cow and goat's milk, and are said to derive their peculiar flavour from the vine leaves on which the goats feed during a considerable portion of the year. The cheeses of Mont Dore (likewise famous) are thicker and smaller in diameter, and sold in small boxes. The coach, on its way from Lyons to St. Cyr, passes by Roche-Cardon, a favourite retreat of J. J. Rousseau. Another easy excursion is to the Ile Barbe. Take any of the mouches (penny boats) going up the Saône to Vaise station. Here change into the penny boat going to St. Rambert, a rather dirty little town on the right bank, 1½ m. above Vaise. Opposite, and connected by a bridge, is the town of Cuire. In the centre of the river is the Ile Barbe, across which the bridge passes. On the island there are a few uninviting country-houses, and the tower of a chapel (private property) of the 12th cent. The sail is the best part of the excursion, not the island.

For Lyons to Nîmes, by rail 172 m. south by the west bank of the Rhône, see p. 81 ; Paris to Lyons by Roanne and St. Etienne, p. 346 ; Paris to Lyons by Tarare, p. 348 ; Lyons to Clermont-Ferrand by St. Etienne, Montbrison, and Thiers, see p. 349, and map p. 27.

338   199

〜〜 VIENNE, pop. 27,000. *Hotels :* Nord ; Poste ; Jacquet. In 〜〜 this, the capital of the first kingdom of Burgundy, there exist remains of important edifices, which indicate that the citizens inhabiting it in the days of Cicero were no strangers to the luxury and wealth preceding the Augustan age. The most interesting of these is the **Maison Carrée**, an oblong temple of the Corinthian order, dedicated to Augustus and his wife Livia, 55 ft. high, 88 long, and 80 broad, situated a litle way north from the cathedral by the Rue St. Clementine. On a terrace fronting the chain bridge is **St. Maurice**, a beautiful Gothic cathedral commenced in the 12th cent., 315 ft. long, and the roof of the nave 88 ft. high. It contains some fine glass, and near the altar the skilfully-sculptured mausoleum of Cardinal Montmorin, who died in 1723. At the main entrance are two ancient sarcophagi. At the other end of the chain bridge is the Tour St. Colombe, built by Philippe Valois. Up the Rhône, on the east side, at the top of the Quai Pajot, near a stair leading down to the river, stood the Tour de Mauconseil, where Pontius Pilate, who had been banished to Vienne by Tiberius, ended his life (it is said) by throwing himself into the Rhône. About ¼ m. down the Rhône from the railway station, by the Marseilles road, is the Pyramide de l'Aiguille, called also the tomb of Pilate. It is 52 feet high, and rises from four arches resting on a square basement. Columns with cushioned capitals ornament the four corners, which cannot date earlier than the 4th cent. Vienne is a busy commercial town, with important woollen manufactories. 3¼ m. S. by rail is Vaugris, pop. 250. On the other side of the Rhône is Ampuis (p. 81). 6 m. farther S. by rail is Le Péage-de-Roussillon. Roussillon, pop. 1500, is a straggling village among vineyards, less than a mile E. from the station. From the Château de Roussillon Charles IX. issued, in 1564, the decree that in future the year was to commence with the first of January.

356¼
180¼
ST. RAMBERT-D'ALBON, junction with line to Grenoble 57½ m. E., by Rives 35 m., and Voiron 42 m. E. Junction by bridge with Peyraud, 3¾ m. W., on the opposite side of the Rhône, whence rail to Annonay (see page 81, and map pages 26 and 46).

5 m. S. by rail from St. Rambert is St. Vallier, pop. 4000. *Inn:* Merle. On the junction of the Galaure with the Rhône. In the town is the restored castle of Anne de Poitiers, and up the valley of the Galaure are the pass of the Roche Taillée, the ruins of a château of the Dauphins, and the chapel of N. D. de Vals (see map, page 46).

368
169
TAIN, pop. 3000. *Inns:* H. Europe ; Midi. A pleasant town on the Rhône, immediately opposite Tournon (page 82), and at the foot of the hill, whose vineyards produce the Hermitage wines. The red variety has a fine perfume, and is gratefully stomachic. The white is a luxurious wine, and will keep for a century, but the produce is small. Omnibus at station for Romans, 13 m. on the rail between Valence and Voiron (see map page 46), pop. 13,000. *Inns:* Europe ; Midi. Situated at the confluence of the Isère with the Savasse, crossed by a bridge of 4 arches which unites it with Bourg-du-Péage, pop. 5000.

~~ VALENCE, pop. 24,000. *Hotels:* Louvre ; Croix d'Or ; ~~
France. The first the most expensive. Commodious Temple Protestant. Good Protestant schools. Suspension bridge across the Rhône.
Omnibus to St. Péray, 2½ m. west. Coaches daily to Ardèche.
Valence is a pleasant town on an eminence rising from the Rhône,
surrounded by broad boulevards on the site of the old fortifications.
The most handsome is the Place Championnet, on the site of the
citadel, commenced by François. It commands an excellent view of
the river and of the hills beyond. In the distance, to the right, on an
arid rock, is the castle of Crussol. In this Place is the statue "au
General Championnet, sorti des rangs du peuple. Hommage public de
sa ville natale." Died at Antibes 1800.

To the left of the statue is the cathedral St. Apollinaire, built
in 1095, and restored in 1604 and 1730. The west portal and tower
were rebuilt in 1880. The other parts of the exterior have a venerable
appearance. The buttresses are shallow, and do not reach the eaves.
A delicate dentil cornice runs round the building, bending over the
round-headed windows and across the buttresses. Within, the church
by restoration looks as if it were modern. Tall piers, with attached
Corinthian columns and vaulting shafts, run up to the commencement
of the arches of the aisles and of the vault of the roof, all of stone.
From the semicircular chancel radiate 4 semicircular chapels, one
being occupied by the organ. At the right or S. side of the altar is
the bust by Canova of Pope Pius VI., who died at Valence in 1799.
His remains were removed to Rome.

Outside, opposite the N. transept, is Le Pendentif, a sepulchral
chapel (22 ft. square and 25 ft. high) of the Mistral family, built in
1548. On each side is a large round arch, over which rises a remarkably flat dome. Close to the "Place des Clercs" is the Maison des
Têtes, built in 1531, covered with mutilated statues and medallions
under canopy work. The medallions, bosses, and groining in the
passage leading into the court are in a much better state of preservation. The windows in the court are square-headed, but most have
lost their transoms. Among the other buildings are a Temple Protestant, 18th cent., and a picture gallery.

Rail to Grenoble, 62 m. N.E., and to Chambery, 40 m. farther.
Omnibus daily to St. Péray (p. 82). Coach by St. Péray to Vernoux,
18 m. W. Vernoux, 1920 ft. above the sea, pop. 3100. *Inns:* Nord ;
Verd. Temple Protestant. One of the nicest towns in Ardèche,
situated in the midst of carefully-cultivated mountains and valleys.
A large proportion of the inhabitants are Protestants.

Valence is one of the most convenient places for entering the Ardèche. Diligences from Valence to St. Laurent-du-Pape, St. Fortunat, Les Ollières, St. Sauveur, St. Pierreville, and Le Cheilard (see page 83). The diligences from Valence, Soyons, Charmes, Beauchastel, and La Voulte to St. Pierreville and Le Cheilard meet at St. Laurent-du-Pape ; whence the passengers are conveyed in two diligences the length of St. Sauveur, by St. Fortunat and Ollières. At Ollières, H. du Pont, they meet and correspond with the diligence from Privas. From St. Sauveur one diligence runs westward by the Glaire to St. Pierreville and Marcols, the other northwards to Le Cheilard. Valence is 5 hrs. from St. Sauveur. Beauchastel and La Voulte, 4 hrs. St. Sauveur to Pierreville, 2½ hrs. ; and to Le Cheilard, 3½ hrs. (see also pages 93 and 94). Coach from Valence to La Mastre, 21¼ m. W., passing by Champis, pop. 3380, at the foot of a mountain, which during a part of the day intercepts the rays of the sun.

ARDÈCHE.
(See Map, page 46).

Ardèche should not be visited till June, and not later than September. In the villages and hamlets in the pastoral districts most of the best houses are inns or auberges, where a bed can be had, and abundance of fare, in the shape of fried potatoes, butter, milk, eggs, coffee, bread often of rye, and hard salt pork sausages. The national dish is potatoes sliced very thin and fried with butter. They make also a pleasant soup of herbs mixed with potatoes. The numerous inns are required for the accommodation of guests during the fairs, of which each hamlet has at least 2, while the larger villages and towns have from 4 to 8, besides market-days. One of the prettiest sights in Ardèche is to see the people flocking from every direction along the winding mountain roads to the village where the fair is being held—many on foot driving small parcels of pigs, sheep, goats, or cattle, or carrying baskets full of eggs, cheese, and butter, and often an old hen ; others with carts loaded with potatoes ; others travelling comfortably in their char-à-bancs ; and others on horseback, the women as well as the men being astride.

Many of the inns, and even of the owners, are at first sight forbidding, but after a little kindly conversation the aspect of things improves rapidly. In the higher regions the agricultural products are potatoes and hay. In the next zone are wheat, chestnut, walnut, apple, pear, and cherry trees, cultivated on terraces supported by low stone walls of rough unhewn stones. Vineyards are in the lowest zone, on the sunny side of the mountains. The cattle are of a goodly size, mostly cream-coloured and light brown, with large bones and white horns generally tipped with black.

At the fairs, besides every kind of country produce, girls and grown-up women offer their hair for sale. The best do not yield above 8s., and many only 2s. 6d. or 3s. When the bargain is made a woman shears it off in the same way as sheep are shorn, leaving only a little in front. It is all over in two minutes, twisted into a hank, and thrust into a sack. Instead of receiving money, they usually take the value in cloth and ribbons. The standard occupation of the females during their long winters is lace-making.

Among the remarkable sights in Ardèche are the volcanic rocks, Mont Mezenc and the Gerbier-de-Joncs, above the source of the Loire. The most central station of the diligences is Le Cheilard (see page 83).

After Valence the railway traverses some of the most picturesque parts of the valley of the Rhône. At Mornas, 44½ m. S. from Valence and 23½ m. N. from Avignon, begins the region of the olives.

395   LIVRON, pop. 4500, on the Drôme, at some distance from **142** the station. Restaurants at station. Inns in the town. On the other side of the Rhône, connected by railway bridge, is La Voulte, 1¼ m. W. (see p. 82). A highway, partly by rail and partly by diligence, extends from Livron, 68 m. east, to Aspres on the line between Grenoble and Marseilles. As far as the Pass de Cabres the road ascends the picturesque and well-cultivated valley of the Drôme, where there is a large Protestant population, nearly every village having its Temple Protestant (see maps, pages 26, 46, and 56).

11 miles E. from Livron by rail is Crest, pop. 6000. *Hotels :* Bonsans-Reboul, the best ; opposite the France ; and on the promenade, by the side of the river and the bridge, the inn Pont de la Drôme. The omnibuses of the two hotels await passengers. Crest is situated partly on the Drôme and partly on the steep sides of a high hill. At the foot, in the market-place, are the parish church and the Bibliothèque. Straight up from the bridge by the R. des Cordeliers, and a flight of 116 steps, is the entrance to the poor church of N. D. de la Garde, attached to the "Asile" for young children. A little higher up are the hospital and church. Above the "Asile" is the entrance to the enclosure, on which stands a huge structure, partly Roman and partly the remains of a castle which was added to it in the 13th cent. The highest side is 170 ft. above the ground, and the other three 148 ft., ascended by 260 steps. Although so high, the view is limited by the high side, into which visitors are not admitted. The concierge lives below in the town, near the hotel. The best way up the hill is by the first narrow street, left from the hotel, the Rue de la Carrière, which continue to a stone lettered "limite de l'Octroi," whence ascend by the path, right, to the Calvary, where there is a splendid view of the valley of the Drôme.

Coaches daily from Crest to Montelimart, 22½ m. S.W. (see Index) ; also to Beaufort, 12 m. N.E., on the Geroanne. From the copious source of the Geroanne are occasionally thrown up blind trout. 3 miles from Beaufort is the picturesque gorge of Ombléze. Coach also to Bourdeaux, 16 m. S., passing Saou, 9 m. S. from Crest (see map, p. 56). Saou, pronounced Sou, pop. 1200, is a poor dirty village on the Vebre. *Inn :* H. Lattard. Mixed up with and built into the surrounding squalid houses are the remains of the abbey church and

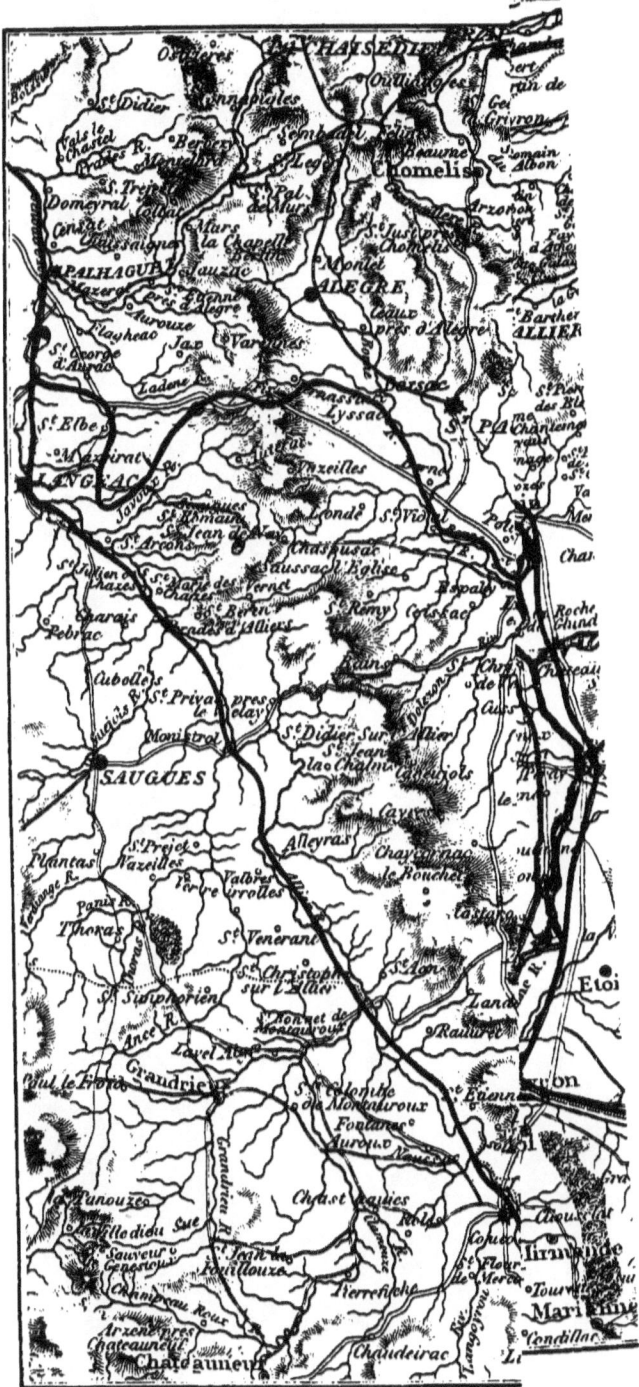

ARDECHE
ITS VINEYARDS AND
EXTINCT VOLCANOES.

buildings of Saint Tiers, founded in the 9th cent. The best parts are the wall and square tower near the Mairie. The remains of the church are within the court of a stable. Near it is the little parish church, 12th and 13th cents. Saou is visited principally on account of the beauty of the narrow valley of the Vebre, between two ranges of wooded mountains, from 4000 to 5000 ft. above the sea, with sand and limestone strata piled up into vertical cliffs and twisted into strange fantastic forms. It is 8 m. long, and from a few yards to 2 m. wide. At the commencement or west end, and on the right or N. side of the stream, is the Roche Colombe, 4595 feet above the sea, and opposite, on the other side, is the Roc, an isolated cliff like the shaft of a column. Mt. Colombe has also a columnar cliff, and at the base a house called the Donjon de Lastic, 14th cent., and a little farther down a square house, with two round turrets, called the Château d'Eurre. The best parts of the valley are this entrance and the east end, or its termination, where the Roche Courbe or Veillou rises to the height of 5324 ft. above the sea, and on which is the source of the Vebre. At the foot of Mt. Pomeyrol, about a mile from the entrance, the valley becomes so narrow that there is scarcely sufficient room for the stream to pass through. 2¼ m. farther up is the villa of Tibur, and, a little beyond, the terminus of the valley.

Coach from Saou to Bourdeaux, 7 m. S. Bourdeaux, pop. 1800. *Inns:* Blanc ; Petit; Temple Protestant. On both sides of the Roubion, 8 m. N. from Dieulefit. On the left side of the river is the old town, composed of squalid houses and execrably paved steep lanes, creeping up the hill, crowned with the ruins of a large castle founded in the 8th cent. Agriculture and the rearing of silkworms are the chief industries. Although Bourdeaux is hardly 8 m. from Dieulefit the courrier requires 2 hours to perform the journey, as a high mountain ridge, the Dieu-Grace, intervenes between the two places.

Dieulefit, pop. 5000. *Inns:* H. du Levant ; Temple Protestant. On the Jabron at the foot of Mont de Dieu-Grace, 17½ m. E. from Montelimart, between which two towns several coaches run daily. In the town are silk, cotton, and cloth mills, and in the suburbs potteries where a coarse kitchen ware is made. The principal towns passed on the road to Montelimart are Poët-Lavat, 3¼ m. ; La Begude, 7½ m. ; under Châteauneuf-de-Mazenc and Montboucher, situated on eminences at a considerable distance from the road (see map, page 56).

CREST TO ASPRES (Maps, pp. 46 and 56).

Crest to Aspres, 57 miles east by Die.—The road as far as the Pass de Cabres follows the course of the Drôme. The first town passed is Saillans, 9½ m. E. from Crest, pop. 1800. *Inns:* Lambert; Latour. In a ravine of the Drôme, 6½ m. farther, is Pontaix, similarly situated. 23 m. L. from Crest, and 34 m. W. from Aspres, is Die, pop. 4000, the principal town in the valley of the Drôme, which here receives the Mérosse. *Inns:* St. Dominique ; Alpes—the coach stops between them ; Église Protestante. The Clairette de Die is a thin white wine, drank during its first year ;

in the second it is apt to deteriorate. Coach to Châtillon, 12 m. S. E. Die, on the Drôme, is in a small plain surrounded by mountains, of which the most remarkable is Mont Glandaz, 6648 ft. above the sea, flanked by great buttress cliffs. On the top is an undulating plateau, covered with *small* stones and grass ; 5 hrs. required for the ascent. At the foot of the mountain is the rustic but not uncomfortable establishment of Sallières-les-Bains ; pension per day, with baths, 9 frs. The treatment is called "Sudations résineuses." The bath resembles a large oven, in which, after having been heated with resinous fir-wood, the patients sit as in a Turkish bath. Open from 15th June to 15th September. The landlord is likewise proprietor of a large part of Mt. Glandaz, whence he receives his supplies of fir-wood. On the top of a hill on the other side of the Drôme is a similar establishment, called the Martouret, pension 12 frs. The way to it strikes off the main road opposite the eminence, on which is the chapel of Notre Dame, commanding a very good view of the valley. At the entrance into Die from Crest, at one of the old gateways, a road strikes off to the left, which makes the tour of the ruins of the castle, amidst vines and mulberry trees. At the other end of the town, near the viaduct, is a much better gateway or Roman triumphal arch, fronting the " Place " St. Marcel. The parish church has been rebuilt, excepting the narthex.

From Die the road to Aspres is continued by another diligence, which changes horses at LUC en Diois, pop. 940. *Inn :* Du Levant ; Église Protestante, 10½ m. S. from Die, or 23½ N.W. from Aspres. A poor town, among vineyards and walnut trees, on the Drôme, at the foot of high mountains. Nearly a mile up the river the narrow gorge becomes almost closed by huge fantastic masses of conglomerate which have fallen from the adjoining cliffs. 9½ m. farther up the valley is the village of Beaurières (*Inn*, where the coach changes horses). The ascent is now commenced by a beautiful and excellent road, of the Col de Cabres, 15 m. S. from Luc, and 4923 ft. high. On the pass, 2 m. from Beaurières, is La Baume, with the cave of Baumette, and a waterfall 195 ft. high. 4½ miles from Baume, and 3 from Aspres, is St. Pierre d'Argenson, with a sparkling acidulous chalybeate spring, grateful to the palate and invigorating to the system, and forming a refreshing mixture with the wine of Aspres, which is thin, and is at its best when 2 years old. Aspres, pop. 800, is situated on the railway, 126½ m. N. from Marseilles, and 77½ m. S. from Grenoble. The coach sets down passengers either at the station or at the inn H. Ferdinand. The church has been rebuilt, excepting the portal, which has on the tympanum a curious representation of the Trinity.

412   125
⌒ MONTÉLIMART, pop. 12,000, situated at the confluence of ⌒ the Roubion and Jabron with the Rhône. *Hotels :* near the station, the France ; in the town the Poste ; the Princes. The office of the coaches for Le Teil, on the W. side of the Rhône ; for Grignan, p. 49 ; Dieulefit, p. 47 ; Bourdeaux, p. 47 ; and Nyons, p. 50 ; is near the hotels Poste and Princes. Up the Grande Rue is the principal

church. On the opposite side of it is the Place d'Armes, with the Post Office, the Palais de Justice, and the Hôtel de Ville. At the top of the first flight of steps in the Hôtel de Ville is a marble slab 1 yard long and 2 ft. wide, bearing in Latin a charter of the town engraved in 1198. At the end of the street, the Rue Porte-Neuve, off the "Place," is the Temple Protestant. Montelimart is famous for white almond-cake, "Nougat," of which the best is in the shops in the Grande Rue. On· an eminence on the side of the town farthest from the station are the ancient citadel and the tour de Narbonne, 11th cent. Montelimart, originally a city of the Seglauni, became a Roman settlement under the name of Montilium, which was changed afterwards into Monteil-d'Adhemar by a powerful family, who came into possession of it in the days of Charlemagne. To the same family belonged also Rochemaure, on the opposite side of the Rhône (see page 92, and map page 56).

Omnibuses to the sparkling chalybeate spring of Bondonneau, 2½ m. S.E. Two coaches daily to Grignan, 15 m. S.E. from Montelimart; one by Alan and Reauville, the other goes round by Donzère, 4½ m. longer. (See map, page 56.)

According to Mr. Murray (p. 109) in the village of Alan, half-way between Montelimart and Grignan, "there existed down to 1802 the first white mulberry tree planted in France. It was brought from Naples by Guy Pope de St. Auban, seigneur of Alan, one of the soldiers who accompanied Charles VIII. on his Italian campaign, in 1494." The mulberry tree occupies a much wider zone in the south of France than the olive (see map, page 56).

Grignan, pop. 1900; *Inn*: Sévigné, is built on the slopes of a hill on the top of which, 100 ft. above the "Place," are the gardens and ugly half-ruined and half-inhabited castle where Mme. Sévigné died. The former Salle du Roi has been converted into a picture-gallery, containing upwards of 300 paintings, among which the most interesting are—the portraits of Madame and her daughter, by Mignard. About half-way up the hill is the church, commenced in the 12th cent. In front of the altar a white marble slab, 2½ ft. long by 1½ wide, bears the following inscription:—"Cy Git Marie de Rabutin Chantal, Marquise de Sévigné. Décédé le 18 Avril 1696." Above the well, in the "Place," is a bronze statue of her with corkscrew curls. About ½ m. from the town is what was one of her favourite walks to an overhanging ledge of sandstone called the Grotte de Roche-Courbière. To visit it, descend from the inn, then take the first byeroad right, by a row of poplars to a short stair. A coach runs from Grignan to Nyons, 20½ m. S.E. by Valréas and Taulignan. **Valréas** (pronounce the "s"), 8¼ m. from Nyons and 22 from Orange, pop. 950; *Inn:* H. du Nord, is partly surrounded with its old walls, garnished with square towers and pierced by narrow gateways. Taulignan, 17 m. N.W.

E

from Nyons by Valréas and 11¼ m. by Rousset, *Inn:* H. du Commerce, pop. 1200, is also partly surrounded with its old walls.

420 — DONZERE. H. du Commerce. Romanesque church with **117** — handsome spire. Four and a half miles south is **Pierrelatte** station, and the terminus of the unfinished railway to Nyons, 15 miles from Grignan. Coach from Pierrelatte to St. Paul-Trois-Châteaux, fare 6 sous, time 45 minutes. This, the Roman Augusta-Tricastinorum, contains an interesting cathedral of the 12th cent., restored. Many Roman relics have been found in the neighbourhood.

432 — LA CROISIERE. Two small inns at station. **105** — Omnibus awaits passengers for Pont Saint-Esprit, H. de l'Europe, 3⅛ m. W. on the other side of the Rhône by an avenue of poplars. Fare, 40 c. The bridge is 2756 ft. long, has 20 arches, was commenced in 1265 and finished in 1309. Till 1865 it had 21 arches, when the two at the W. end were demolished and converted into one large iron arch for the convenience of the steamboat to pass through. (For Pont Saint-Esprit, see page 98).

Diligence at La Croisiere station for Nyons, 29½ m. E. by the valleys of the Lez and the Aigues, and the town of Bollène, pop. 6000. *Inn:* Croix Blanche, on the Lez, 4½ m. E. Manufactures of fire-bricks and clay-tubing. 7½ m. E., Suze-le-Rousse, pop. 2200. Coach here to Mansis. 12 m. E., Tulette, pop. 1300 ; *Inn:* Vigne. Horses changed here. 15¾ m. E., St. Maurice, pop. 1000 ; *Inn:* Lion d'Or. Near the village of Vinsobres a cross-road leads to the highway between Nyons and Vaison. At Nyons the coach stops in the "Place" in front of the H. du Louvre ; whence the diligences start for Grignan and Montelimart (see map, page 56).

NYONS, on the Aigues, pop. 4000. *Hotels:* Louvre, in the Place ; Voyageurs, in a corner. Temple Protestant next the hospital. Nyons, surrounded by high mountains, is famous for its mild springs, and therefore eminently fitted for those returning from the Riviera. The orange and palm do not grow here, but abundance of mulberry, almond, fig, peach, and pear trees. In the oak forests are remarkably fine truffles. Silk mills and the preserving of fruit and truffles supply the principal industries. The old town, called Les Forts, is built on an eminence partly surrounded with its old walls garnished with square towers, 14th cent. The vieux château, or centre tower, has been converted by the curate into a chapel surmounted with an image of the "immaculately conceived." The part of the town below is called Les Halles, whose dirty streets are bordered with thick heavy arches. The rest of the town, extending to the Aigues, is called the Bourg. The bridge, built in 1341, is of one arch and considerably higher in the centre than at the ends.

Behind the old town is the ridge called the Col-du-Divès, on which is the cavern, or rather hole, whence it is reported (most absurdly) that the night-breeze called the Pontias issues. In winter this wind is very cold, and blows from 5 P.M. to 9 A.M.   In summer it is pleasant, and blows from 9 P.M. to 7 A.M.   The peculiarity is, that the degree of force is constant, and never breaks out into gusts.   To go to the cave, commence from the foot of the tower of the church and ascend by the Rue Pousterle, having on the left the old town-walls.   Beyond the last tower a path strikes off to the right, which take, and ascend to a small chapel on the top of the ridge, passing at about half-way a pavilion.   Or, if preferred, continue the road from the tower to the part of the ridge where there is a gap; whence take the path at the back of the ridge leading to the chapel.   Those who have ascended by this latter way retrace their steps from the chapel by the same path for 116 yards; while those who have come by the other go 116 yards beyond the chapel.   Then about 30 yards to the left of the path will be observed the thin ledge of a rock overlying a small cavity, which is the entrance to the Pontias hole, of great depth, but otherwise of insignificant dimension.   Among the neighbouring calcareous strata are several crevices.   The view of the valley of the Aigues from this hill is very beautiful.   The ascent takes 35 minutes.

NYONS TO SERRES.

Nyons to Serres (see map, p. 56), 41 miles east by the valleys of the Aigues and Blème, bounded on both sides by high mountains. Time, 7 to 8 hours.   Fare, 7½ frs.   Most of the towns passed are at a considerable height above the road, and sometimes on account of the steepness of the banks cannot be seen from it.   The first village passed is Les Piles, situated on the road 3¾ m. from Nyons, and 3½ m. from the gorge "Des 30 Pas," one of the excursions from Nyons.   A little farther E. is Curnier, on a hill on the S. side of the river, here crossed by a bridge.   Then follows Sahune, also on a hill on the S. side of the river. The gorge now becomes very narrow and the mountains precipitous, and, having passed under Villeperdrix, the road crosses to the S. side of the river and arrives at the station for St. May, where there is an inn, H. Marius.   St. May itself is high up on the opposite side of the river. The cemetery is on the point of a lofty precipitous rock.   After St. May the diligence crosses the river to the village of Rémusat, 17 m. E. from Nyons on the Oule, at its junction with the Aigues.   The diligence now returns to the S. side of the river, which it crosses for the last time at Verclause, 22 m. from Nyons, and then proceeds to Rosans, 3½ m. farther or 15½ m. from Serres.   From Rosans commences the ascent of the low Col of Ribeyret, whence the road descends to Serres by the N. side of the Blème, passing the villages of Epine and Montclus.   Serres, pop. 1200.   *Inns:* Voyageurs; Alpes.   On the railway, 112½ m. N. from Marseilles and 77½ S. from Grenoble (see p. 340).

444   **93**
⌣⌣ ORANGE, pop. 10,300.   *Inn:* H. de la Poste et des Princes. ⌣⌣
This, the Arausio of the Romans, is situated on the slowly-running Meine.   Close to the hotel is the Triumphal Arch supposed to have been erected in honour of Tiberius for his victory over Sacrovir and

PRINCE OF ORANGE AND ORANGEMEN.

Florus, A.D. 21. It stands E. and W., is of a yellowish sandstone, 75 ft. high, 64 wide, 27½ deep, and consists of 3 arches, of which the centre one has a span of 17 ft. and each of the other two a span of 10 ft. The soffits are ornamented with six-sided sculptured panels. By the side of each arch is a grooved Corinthian column. Over the small arches are sculptured trophies in the shape of shields, boars, bulls, rostra, ropes, masts, dolphins, arrows, etc. Over the main arch, on each side, is a group representing a combat.

At the other end of the town are the cathedral and the Roman theatre at the foot of the hill, crowned with an image of Mary. The Cathedral of Notre Dame, 12th cent., is small, and resembles in style the churches of the S.W. of France, of which the cathedral of Perpignan is the great type. No transepts nor triforia. Lofty chapels between the buttresses, and over the arches diminutive clerestory windows. A plain and ugly square tower, in this case, at the east end. Adjoining is the Place de l'Hôtel de Ville, with a statue to "Raimbaud II., Comte d'Orange, vainqueur à Antioche et à Jérusalem en MXCIX." In the promenade of the town, the Cours St. Martin, is a statue to the Comte de Gasparin, a writer on agriculture, and a native of Orange; where also he died in 1862. At the foot of the hill, overlooking the town, are the grand and imposing ruins of one of the most perfect Roman theatres. It is built in a semicircular form, has a façade 118 ft. high and 384 ft. wide. The wall is 13 ft. thick, composed of huge blocks of stone. The semicircular wall consists of five stages, and included accommodation for 6500 spectators. The building has recently been repaired and cleared of a quantity of rubbish.

In the 11th cent. Orange became an independent countship, probably under Raimbaud I., whose successor, Raimbaud II., has just been noticed. On the death of Philibert of Châlons, last of the third line of princes, the inheritance fell to his sister's son Count René (Renatus) of Nassau-Dillenburg, who remaining childless chose as his successor his cousin William I., stadtholder of the United Netherlands. The title "Prince of Orange" was consequently borne by the stadtholders Maurice, Frederick-Henry, William I., William II., and William III. After the Revolution in Ireland of 1688, the English-Protestant party were designated Orangemen, from the title of their leader, William III., Prince of Orange. Louis XIV. seized the principality of Orange in 1672, but lost it by the peace of Ryswick. On the death of William III. there were two claimants—John William Friso of Nassau-Dietz, designated by William's will, and Frederick I., King of

Prussia, who claimed to be nearer of kin, and to have been appointed by the will of Frederick-Henry. Thereupon Louis XIV. declared the principality a forfeited fief of the French crown, and assigned it to the Prince of Conti. The Parliament of Paris decided that this last prince should have the *dominium utile;* and its finding was confirmed by the treaty of Utrecht (1713), which, however, left the title and coat of arms to the King of Prussia, who is still styled Prince of Orange (Prinz von Oranien). John William Friso, however, also took the title, and his successors the stadtholders and kings of the Netherlands have all been designated princes of Orange-Nassau. Vast numbers of silkworms are reared at Orange. Coach daily to Valréas 22 m. E., p. 49, and to Vaison 17½ m. N.E. (Map p. 56.)

Vaison, pop. 3400. *Inn:* H. du Commerce. 5 m. N. from Malaucene, 17½ m. N. from Carpentras, 11¼ m. S. from Nyons, 13½ m. W. from Le Buis, and 4 m. S. from Villedieu. Old or high Vaison is on the left side of the Ouvèze, and new Vaison on the right. Both are connected by a Roman bridge of one arch of 48 ft. span, having at the left side a more elongated curve than at the right. The old town, with its squalid streets and poor houses, covers the sides of a hill crowned with the ruins of a castle built by Raymond VI., Count of Toulouse, in 1195. It is a plain rectangular edifice, 20 yards square, with a small square tower at one of the angles. A little below is the parish church with round and early pointed arches and square tower at S.E. end. The view from the terrace is beautiful.

The most ancient and most interesting buildings are in new Vaison, and very near each other. Take the Villedieu road to just without the town, where a byeway on the right leaves the main road at an acute angle. Continue this byeway to two arches, which indicate the site of the Roman theatre. The chapel seen to the N.W. is St. Quenin, while a little beyond is the cathedral. The amphitheatre, or "les arènes" as they call it, is built on the same plan, and in a similar position, as the theatre of Orange, but far less perfect. Besides the two arches, there exist still five tiers, but all the stone seats are gone, excepting those on the lowest stage. Now it has become a vineyard and an orchard. Beyond, by a narrow road, is St. Quenin, of which the east end is Roman, and may date from the 4th cent., but the rest belongs to the 10th. The east end, or apsidal termination, is in the form of an equilateral triangle, with an attached fluted Corinthian column at the apex, and also at each of the angles of the base. One of the pillars has figures on the capital. The neat little round-headed window on each side of the triangle is evidently a later addition. Bishop Quenin died in 578.

Of the **Cathedral** the best part is also the outside. Under the eaves of the roof of the nave run a dentil moulding, and a frieze of medallions connected by an undulating line of foliage. The walls are pierced by small round-headed windows resting on spiral colonnettes.

The frieze of the aisles is plainer.   In the interior, early pointed
arches of great span, rising from four massive piers of clustered pilasters
on each side of the nave, support a narrow-vaulted roof, also pointed.
This part of the church dates from the 12th or 13th cent. ; but the
chancel, with its two Roman pillars, and arcade of blank arches on colonnettes, is much earlier.   Over the little chapel, at the N.E. side, rises
an elegant square tower.   Next the tower is a very beautiful cloister,
11th cent., bearing some resemblance to the cloister of St. Michel in
Brittany.   It is 22 yards square, surrounded by an arcade of 13 arches
on colonnettes in couples 3½ ft. high.   At the corners is either a massive
stone pier, or the stone hewn into 5 colonnettes.   All the Roman
antiquities Vaison has retained for itself are under this corridor.
The most perfect piece of sculpture is a skull.   On the top of the hill
opposite the castle stands an image of the "Immaculée" on the
capital and part of the shaft of a Roman column.   (Map p. 56.)

455   82
~~ SORGUES, pop. 4000, on the Sorgues, which rises at Vaucluse.~~
Junction with line to Carpentras, 10½ m. eastwards.   **Carpentras**,
pop. 10,500, on an eminence surrounded by avenues, rising from the
Auzon.   *Hotels :* Universe ; Orient, both good, and in the large
" Place " opposite, the Hôtel-Dieu, built in 1760 by Bishop Malachie.
In the Hôtel-Dieu are a portrait by Rigaud of the Abbot Rancé,
and a handsome staircase.   In the centre of the Place is a bronze
statue of the benevolent Malachie d'Inguimbert.   From this "Place,"
up the narrow street, the first public building is the church of St.
Siffrein, dating from 1405.   The square tower, with octangular cupola,
attached to the north side of the chancel, was part of a former church
constructed in the time of Charlemagne.   The stair (89 steps) up to
the roof, whence there is a pleasing view, commences at the south side
of the chancel, outside.   Among the pictures in the interior of the
church, the best is a " Salutation " by the Flemish painter Andreas
Schoonjans.   Behind the pulpit is a picture by Mignard representing
Mary giving some of her milk to St. Bernard.   At the commencement
of the chancel, near the cupola, is the chapel in which the reliquaries
are kept.   Among them are the 'skull and bones of St. Siffrein, and
the nail that pierced the right hand of J. C. on the Cross.   In the
chancel is a " Coronation" of Mary painted on wood, 15th cent., and
behind the altar another "Coronation" by P. Veronese.   In the fore-
ground are Saints Laurence and Siffrein.   Adjoining is the Palais de
Justice, 1640, with frescoes and a crucifix in the " salle des assises."
Within the court, right hand, is a Triumphal arch, erected by Diocletian
between 284 and 305, 30 ft. high (but originally higher), 25½ ft. wide,
14½ ft. deep, and 10 ft. span.   On the N. side, between two attached
fluted columns, is, in bold relief, a Latin cross with the arms at obtuse
angles.   On each side stands a prisoner, with his hands behind him,
chained loosely to the cross.   From the cross are suspended swords,
horns, and pouches.   On the south side is a similar cross, but not in

such a good state of preservation. The main beam resembles more the stem of a tree. From the top hangs the dress of a warrior.

The continuation of the street from the church leads to the Porte d'Orange, surmounted by a square tower 120 ft. high, of which only three sides exist. It was built by Innocent VI., who also surrounded the town with the ramparts, which now form beautiful Boulevards. From the boulevard in front of the gate are seen to the left the canal aqueduct, to the right the town water aqueduct, and in the distance, between the two, beyond a smaller ridge, Mont Ventoux, extending from N.W. to S.E., with a slight bend. The aqueduct which brings water to Carpentras crosses the valley of the Auzon by 48 massive arches. The canal, which by irrigation fertilises the surrounding country, extends from the Durance to the Ouvèze, a distance of 43 miles, and cost £90,000. In the principal Boulevard, nearly opposite the manufactory of preserved fruits of Eysseric, is the building containing the library and museum. The library contains a valuable collection of manuscripts, explained in a printed 4to volume, several rare incunables, and above 4000 vols., for which there is not sufficient accommodation. In the "Musée" are a few good pictures, and Roman statuettes in bronze and marble, all from Vaison, excepting a small Apollo found at Carpentras. The gem of the antiquities is an Egyptian-Aramaic limestone slab, 4th or 3d cent. B.C., $19\frac{3}{4}$ in. long by $13\frac{1}{2}$ wide and 1 thick, divided into three compartments by narrow borders. In the principal compartment stands a young woman with uplifted hands before Osiris, who is seated in front of a table on which are sacrifices. Behind Osiris stands Isis. Below, in the second compartment, is the embalmed body of the deceased, attended by the jackal-headed Anubis and the hawk-headed Horus. Below the body are the four customary funeral vases. Below this, in the third compartment, is an Aramaic inscription in four lines, of which the last two are injured. The first French opera was written in Carpentras by the Abbot Mailly in 1646. Truffles or tuberous mushrooms are black, dark gray, violet-coloured, or white. The last variety, principally found in the N. of Italy, has the smell of garlic. About Carpentras, and in the department of Vaucluse, they are black, and are found from 4 inches to 1 foot below the ground, at the extremities of the fibrous roots, both of the common and of the evergreen oak. The season for gathering them is from November to the end of March, after which those which remain become soft and decompose. They are at their best in January, when the rind is black, hard, and rough, and the inside mottled black and white. In size and shape the best resemble small round potatoes, of which the largest may weigh $\frac{1}{2}$ lb., although few are of that size. They are sought by means of dogs and swine, both of a peculiar breed ; the sow being the more dexterous of the two, and continues efficient for its duty for upwards of 21 years. It scoops out the earth with its powerful snout in a masterly manner faster than any dog can do. When just about to seize the truffle, the attendant thrusts a stick between its jaws, picks up the truffle himself, and throws to the sow instead two acorns. Without this reward each time, the sow would not continue the search. Till the truffles are ripe, they have no odour.

The ortolans, which breed about the hills and woods of Carpentras, migrate in autumn. While on the wing they are allured down to nets laid for them by ortolans singing in cages. Those caught are put into dark rooms, where they are fattened. In about a month's time they become so plump as hardly to be able to fly, when they are killed and sold, excepting a few kept for alluring the others next year. The singing time of these is transferred from spring to August, by pulling out the large feathers of the tail and wings in April, and keeping them in a dark apartment till August.

Carpentras is also famous for its preserved fruits and "berlingots," a sweetmeat made of the syrup of a mixture of fruits, not unlike barley sugar, but cut into pieces 1 in. square. The best maker is Eysseric.

Carpentras is a good halting-place for delicate people returning from the Riviera—the hotels are comfortable and the prices moderate— excellent public library, pleasant walks, and in the vicinity of many interesting places connected by roomy diligences.

Coach daily from Carpentras to Nyons 28½ m. N., by Vacqueyras 6½ m., and Vaison 17½ m. Also to Nyons 26 m., by Malaucene 10 m. N.E., and Vaison 15 m. by this way. Coach to Buis-les-Baronnies 23 m. N.E., passing through Malaucene. Coach from Buis to Nyons 19 m. N.W. by Mollans. Courrier from Vaison to Buisson 7½ m. N. on the Aigues. Coach to Sault 28½ m. E.

Omnibus several times daily to St. Didier 4½ m. S.E. Coach daily to L'Ile 10¼ m. S., convenient for visiting the fountain of Vaucluse. Coach on market-days from Carpentras to Apt 28½ m. S.E., by Venasque 7¼ m. S.E. (For these places see Index, and maps pages 56 and 66.)

Coach daily to Bedoin 8¾ m. N.E., 900 ft. above the sea, pop. 1300. *Inn:* Hôtel de Mont Ventoux. Station to ascend Mont Ventoux, 6274 ft., by a good road from the south end of the ridge. The base is about 2 m. from the village and the top 10 m. by the easy southern slope. Time to ascend, from 5 to 6 hours. Mule, 10 frs. No guide necessary. Before commencing the ascent, go to the top of the hill by the side of the church and take a general survey of the land. The road extending to the right, under those mulberry trees, is the one to take. A little distance along it, at a well with a cistern, a narrow road strikes off to the left and ascends the mountain by a steeper and shorter way. The mountain offers a splendid field for botanists. To see the sun rise from the top, travellers generally start at 11 P.M., and await the appearance of the glorious luminary in the chapel of Ste. Croix, on the summit. Mont Ventoux is the culminating point of the Lure range, an offshoot from the Alps. Among the minerals it has quartz in every form and colour, in nodules and in strata. Also beautiful jasper and fossils such as ammonites and belemnites. The kaoline clay, "terre de Bedouin," is found in the plain between Bedoin and Crillon, a village 2¾ m. N.E. At different parts in this

For continuation northwards see map, page 46. For continuation northwards see map, page 36.

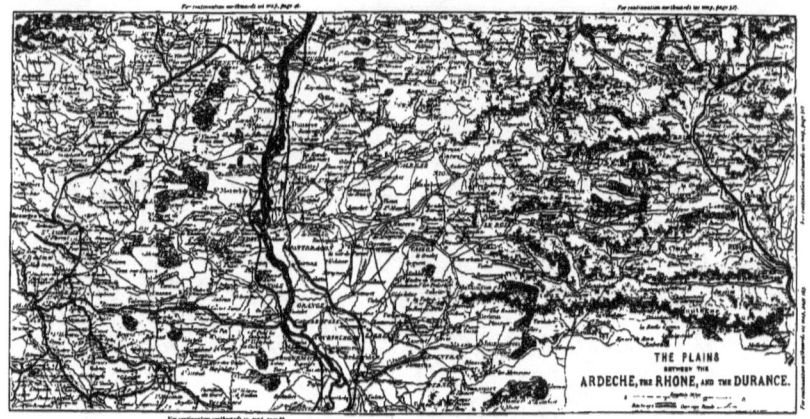

THE PLAINS
BETWEEN THE
ARDECHE, THE RHONE, AND THE DURANCE.

For continuation southwards see map, near 68.

neighbourhood are strata of sandstone with fossils, overlying beds of sand. These strata crop up at different parts of the department.

Four and a half m. S. by omnibus from Carpentras is the village of St. Didier, with a good hydropathic establishment in an old château. Rooms from 1½ fr. to 3 frs. Servants' rooms, 1 fr. Meat, breakfast and dinner, both with wine, 5 frs. Coffee in the mornings, ½ fr. Meat, breakfast and dinner, for children and servants, 3 frs. Service, ½ fr. First consultation, 10 frs. Every other consultation in the study gratis ; but in the guests' room 1 fr. each time. The baths are in the style of the Turkish baths, with the addition that the heated air is impregnated with resin or is turpentinised (*térébenthiné*). It has a beneficial effect on the lungs and muscular rheumatism. St. Didier is 2¾ m. W. from Venasque and 2 m. from Le Beaucet (map p. 56).

Two coaches daily from Carpentras to Buis-les-Baronnies, 23 m. N.E., by Malaucene 10 m. N.E. The road from Carpentras, in crossing the N.W. extremity of the Ventoux chain, passes by the village of Le Barroux on a hill crowned with the ruins of a castle, 15th cent. At the foot of Mont Ventoux, 5 m. S. from Vaison and 13 m. S.W. from Buis, is **Malaucene**, 1000 ft. above the sea, pop. 3000. *Inn :* Hôtel de Cours, in a picturesque neighbourhood, of which there is a good view from the calvary on an eminence in the town. At about ½ m. from the inn is the spring Groseau, gushing forth from the base of a lofty calcareous cliff, crowned with the ruins of the chapel of Groseaux, 11th cent. The stream that issues from the spring is soon strong enough to set in motion the machinery of paper, silk, and flour mills. Any one may visit the silk mills. In 1345 Petrarch ascended Mont Ventoux from Malaucene. The ascent from this place is more difficult, but more picturesque than from Bedoin and requires 2 hours more. On the side of the mountain are the springs—Angel, 3826 ft. ; Puits de Mont-Serein, 4774 ft. ; and Font Filiole, 5866 ft.

The road from Malaucene to Buis follows the picturesque valley of the Ouvèze. The most important village passed on the way is Mollans, with, in the neighbourhood, a great cave, beyond which is a deep lake. Shortly before arriving at Le Buis are seen, on an eminence, the bronze statue of Bishop Trophime, and beyond, the cliff of St. Julien. No public vehicle goes farther than Le Buis, although the road is good the length of the railway between Marseilles and Grenoble, passing St. Euphemie 7 m. E., St. Auban 10 m. E., Montguers 11¼ m. E., Lacombe 13¼ m. E., and Laborel 27 m. E., after which the road descends to the railway by the valley of the Céans.

LE BUIS, pop. 2000 ; *Inns :* Luxembourg ; Commerce ; is situated in a hollow on the Ouvèze surrounded by mountains covered with olive, mulberry, fig, peach, and cherry trees. Schistose and shingle strata cover some parts ; at others there are calcareous rocks in every form, either in gigantic cliffs or in countless strata of various thickness and at different angles. To go to the statue of St. Trophime and to the top of St. Julien, having crossed the bridge, ascend by the winding road to the valley, right hand, which continue to the next bridge. For the statue cross the bridge and go directly to the right: for the cliffs, ascend by the back of St. Julien by the path on the left, just before reaching the bridge.

461 AVIGNON, pop. 39,000, surrounded with strong embrasured **76** walls, garnished with 39 towers, and pierced with 9 gates, is situated on the Rhône, 2 m. above its junction with the Durance, and 20 m. N.E. from Nîmes by the railway passing the Pont d'Avignon and Remoulins. *Hotels:* * Europe, near the Pont; * Luxembourg ; Louvre; St. Yves, in the centre of the town, near the Place Pie, the great market-place. Temple Protestant in the R. Dorée, near the Préfecture. Cabstands at station and in the Place de l'Hôtel de Ville, 2 frs. per hour. From the station, a beautiful avenue, the Cours de la République, leads up to the Place de l'Hôtel de Ville, with statue "au brave Crillon," the friend of Henri IV., "Louis des Balbes-Berton duc de Crillon et Lieutenant-colonel de l'infanterie française," died at Avignon in 1615. To the right is the road leading up to the *Palace of the Popes, the church of *N. D. des Domes, and the promenade, *"au Rochers des Doms ;" which, with the ramparts, compose the principal sights of Avignon. The concierge of the palace lives just within the entrance. Fee for party, 1 fr. Opposite gate is the Conservatoire de Musique, built in 1610 for a mint. The churches are closed between 12 and 2. The Musées are open to the public on Sundays between 12 and 4.

The present **Palace**, commenced by Benedict XII. in 1336, and finished by Gregory XI. in 1370, is an ugly huge structure, consisting of plain walls 100 ft. high and 14 thick, strengthened by long ungainly buttresses. Above the entrance, composed of a low archway, are the arms of Clement VI. ; and higher up, on two oriel turrets, the balcony from which the Popes blessed the people. Within the gate is the Cour d'Honneur, a vast quadrangular space between flat walls, pierced by from 3 to 4 stories of windows, not on the same level nor of the same size. From the court ascend the Escalier d'Honneur, a groined staircase, of which the steps were formerly of marble, to the Salle Consistoriale d'Hiver, with an elegantly-groined roof. Before this hall was divided into two, it was 52 ft. high, 65½ wide, and 170 long. From it we enter the Salle d'Armes, with mural paintings by Simone Memmi of Sienna. Ascending higher the grand staircase, we pass on the left the small window for the Spies, and then go along a narrow lobby tunnelled in the wall, to a succession of large bare halls, the Galerie de Conclave, the Salle des Gardes, the Salle de Reception, and then enter the Tour St. Jean, containing the Chapelle du Saint-Office,

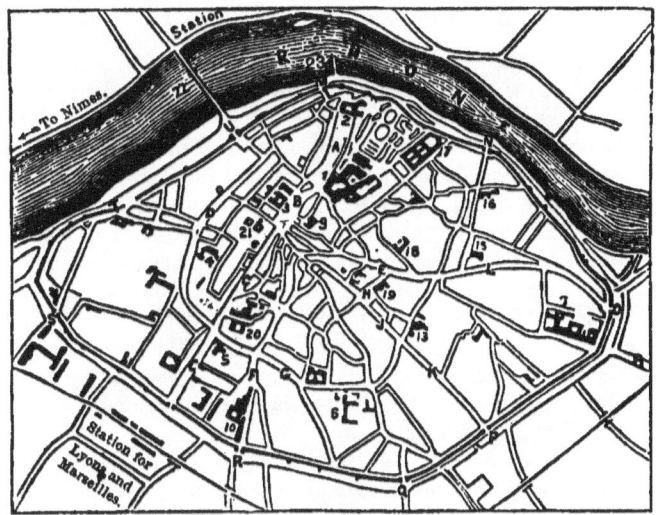

SKETCH PLAN OF AVIGNON.

1. Palace of the Popes : the small building opposite is the Consistoire de Musique ; by the side of the palace is the church of Notre-Dame Des Doms, and by the
side of the church, on the top of the hill, the beautiful promenade des Doms ;
whence a stair leads down to the Rhone, near 23, the old bridge Bénézet. Below
the promenade is, 2, formerly an archbishop's palace, now a seminary. Below the
Pope's Palace is B, the Place de l'Hotel de Ville, with the H. de Ville and theatre.
The street C C, extending southward to the principal station, is called the R. de
la Republique or Rue Petrarque, its original name. Just behind, 3, the Hotel de
Ville is the church of St. Agricol, and a little farther S.W. is the Rue Calade, with,
at 4, the Musée Calvet, and at 5, across the Rue de la Republique, the Musée
Requien, a museum of natural history. Farther east is, 6, St. Joseph's College,
with all that remains of the Church of the Cordeliers, where Laura was buried.
That large building at the east corner of the town, 7, is the Hotel-Dieu or hospital ;
the gate, O, beside it, is the Porte St. Lazare ; while 8 indicates the road to the
cemetery. A short way E. from the Place de l'Hotel de Ville is, 9, the church of
St. Pierre. No. 10, not far from the station, is the Penitentiary, formerly the
Convent of the Celestins, founded by Clement VII. in 1879 ; entrance from the
Place du Corps-Saint. No. 13, Convent du St. Sacrement. 14. Chapel Bénézet on
bridge. 15. St. Symphorien. 16. Sacré-Cœur. 17. Prison. 18. Mont-de-Piété.
19. Court-house. 20. Lyceum. 21. Prefecture. 22. Suspension Bridge. 23. Béné-
zet Bridge. A, Place du Palais. B, Place de l'Hôtel de Ville. C, Rue de la
République. D, Rue Calade. F, Place du Corps Saint. G, Rue des Lices. H,
Place Pie. J, Vieux Septier. K, Rue du Saule. L, Rue Carréterie. M, Porte
du Rhône. N, Porte de la Ligne. O, Porte St. Lazarus. Q, Porte L'Imbert.
R, Porte St. Michael. S, Porte St. Roche. T, Porte de l'Oulle.

or the chapel of the Inquisition, with mural paintings.   In the story immediately below is the chapel of the Popes.   From the Tour St. Jean, after passing through a large hall, we enter an octagonal room, gradually narrowing towards the centre, till it forms a chimney-tower, called the Tour Strapade.   Some say this was the torture room ; but it is evidently more suited for a kitchen, which in all probability it was. Adjoining is the Glacière, into whose underground cellars, now built up, the democrats of 1791 flung the bodies of 60 men and women they had murdered.   From this we enter again the Place d'Honneur by the Tour Trouillas, in which Rienzi was imprisoned five years, bound to a chain fixed to the roof of his cell.   During the time of the Popes, from 1305 to 1234, and till 1793, the half of Avignon was occupied by ecclesiastical edifices, which tolled daily 300 bells, and had among them a daily succession of religious processions.

From the palace the road leads up to the highest part of the town, the **Rocher des Doms** ; commanding a magnificent view, and laid out as a public garden, with in the centre a statue of Jean Althen, who introduced, in 1766, the culture of the "garance," the *Rubia tinctoria*, now superseded, for the dyeing of red.   From this terrace a stair leads down to the Rhône near the Bridge Bénézet (see page 63).   In the middle of the river is the Ile de Barthelasse, and on the other side are the Tour de Philippe le Bel, the town of Villeneuve, and above it the Fort St. André.   On the promenade is the Cathedral **Notre-Dame-des-Doms**, 194 feet above the Rhône, approached by a stair called the Pater, because originally it had as many steps as there are words in the Lord's Prayer.   This church has undergone many changes, and belongs to various periods.   The portal and lower part of the tower are of the 10th cent., and are due to Fulcherius.   The nave is two centuries later.   The apse was added in 1671.   The most remarkable part of the structure is the cupola, terminating in an octagonal lantern, and supported on pendentive arches. It bears traces of frescoes painted in 1672.   In the sanctuary is the marble throne used by the Popes, in the sacristy the Gothic mausoleum of Jean XXII., and in one of the side chapels the tomb of Benoit XII.   In the third chapel (right hand) is a Madonna in white marble, by Pradier.   The sacristan is generally in the small room next the main entrance.   Fee, $\frac{1}{2}$ fr. for showing the church and the tomb.

Now return to the Place de l'Hôtel de Ville.   At the foot or south end a tram-car leaves every $\frac{1}{4}$ to the Pont d'Avignon station on the other side of the Rhône, 2 sous ; and another to St. Lazare at the

St. Agricol.   Musée Calvet.

eastern end of the town near the cemetery, 2 sous.   An omnibus starts every hour from the corner of the theatre for Villeneuve, where it stops at the east end of the church.   Fare both ways, 4 sous.

In the "Place" the principal edifice is the **Hôtel de Ville**, built in 1862, on the site of the Palais Colonna, 14th cent., of which all that remains is the handsome belfry called Jacquemard and his wife, from the two figures which strike the hours.   Next the Hôtel de Ville is the theatre, built in 1847.   Behind is the church of **St. Agricol**, 1340, the patron saint of Avignon.   To the right on entering is the tomb of the painter Pierre Mignard, d. 4th April 1725, aged 86, and third chapel on same side is a virgin and child in wood by Coysevox. To the left of the entrance is an ancient and elegant marble baptismal font.   At the foot of the short street St. Agricol, in the Rue Calade, is the Oratoire, built in 1730.   At No. 65 of the Rue Calade is the **Musée Calvet**, containing a valuable collection of art treasures open to the public on Sundays from 12 to 4, and a library and reading-room open every day except Sunday.   Against the wall of the inner court is the tomb of the donor of this museum, Claud François Calvet, d. 25th July 1810, in his 82d year.   On the right is the monument erected by Sir Charles Kelsall in 1823 to Laura de Sade, dead of small-pox in 1348, and buried in the church of the Cordeliers (see p. 62). On the other side is the tomb of the military strategist Folard, a native of Avignon.   In the outer court, and in the rooms and passages on the ground-floor, are Roman altars, monuments, milestones, torses, amphoræ, and 170 Latin inscriptions, found in the neighbourhood, but chiefly from Orange and Vaison (p. 53).   Among the sculptures in relief, one represents a Roman chariot drawn by two horses with their hoofs shod.   There are 27 Greek inscriptions, 3d or 4th cent., from Venice.   The statuary and sculpture of the Middle Ages and the Renaissance have been gathered principally from the suppressed churches and convents.   The most noticeable are : the mausoleums of Pope Urban V., of Cardinals Lagrange and Brancas, and of Marshal Palice.   Within railings are : Cassandra by Pradier, a faun by Brian, and a bather by Esparcieux, all in the finest white marble. Upstairs is a valuable collection of Roman glass and bronzes, and 20,000 coins and medals, including a complete set of the seals and medals of the Popes during their residence at Avignon, and the seal used by the Inquisition while here.   There are nearly 500 pictures, and a collection of drawings, including the original sketches of Horace Vernet.   Most of the pictures have the artists' names affixed.   Those

62

AVIGNON. MUSÉES CALVET AND REQUIEN.

in the great hall are by Albano, Bassano, Berghem, Blœmen, Bourdon,
Canaletto, A. Carracci, Caravaggio, Châlons, Coypel, Credi, David,
*Eckout (crucifixion), Sasso Ferrati, F. Floris, Gericault, Girodet,
Gros, Holbein, Lomi, Meel, P. and N. Mignard, J. and P. Parrocel,
Poussin, Ruysdael, Salvator Rosa, Teniers jun., Veronese, Vigée-
Lebrun, and Zurbaran. In the small room are the paintings by
Claude-Joseph, Horace and Carle Vernet, with a few by Paul Huet.
The marble busts of Horace and Carle are by Thorwaldsen. In the
centre of an inner room, containing the medals and engravings, is the
famous ivory crucifixion, 27 inches long, of one piece, excepting the
arms, a chef-d'œuvre of the sculptor Guillermin in 1659. It is said
that Canova stood in ecstasy over this delicate achievement in art.
Continuing down the R. Calade to the other side of the R. Petrarque
or de la République, we have on the right the Museum of Natural
History in the church St. Martial, 15th cent. The greater part of the
specimens were bequeathed by M. Requien, d. 1851, and of them the
most interesting are those connected with the neighbourhood, such as
the flamingo and beaver of the Rhône, and the fossils from 'Aix. In
the eastern continuation of the R. Calade, at No. 62 R. des Lices, is
the Collége Saint Joseph, containing within its grounds all that
remains (the belfry and piece of the north aisle) of the church of the
Cordeliers ; in which Laura was buried. The aisle has been repaired,
and is now used as a chapel. Visitors are freely admitted. It is to
the left of the entrance. Of the tomb there are no vestiges, having
been destroyed along with the church by an infuriated mob in 1791.
On the E. side of the R. Petrarque, by the narrow R. Prévot, is the
church of St. Dedier, 1355, containing, in first chapel right from
entrance, a relief in marble representing Christ bearing his cross,
executed by Francesco in 1481 at the request of King René. Opposite,
over second arch, 36 ft. above the floor, is a stone pulpit with a
sculptured pendant. The grave of St. Bénézet is under a plain slab
in the middle of the nave, in front of the high altar. Near St. Dedier
is the Hôtel Crillon, 17th cent. ; and to the east of the Place de l'Hôtel
de Ville is the church of St. Pierre(9 in plan), 1520, with an elaborately-
sculptured door and pulpit. The pictures about the high altar are by
N. Mignard, J. and P. Parrocel, and Simon de Châlons. From the
S.E. corner of the Place de l'Hôtel de Ville, the R. des Marchands
and its continuation the Rues Saunerie and Carréterie, lead to the
Porte St. Lazare, with, to the right, the town hospital (7 in plan),
having a frontage of 192 yards, built in the last century on the site of

the hospital of St. Martha, founded in 1354.   Here, outside the town-walls to the right, then by a broad road to the left, is the Cemetery. The Protestant division is on the right side of the entrance.   In a corner at the end of a short avenue of pine trees is the white marble monument to John Stuart Mill, b. 20th May 1806, d. 7th May 1873. In the same grave is interred Harriet Mill, his beloved wife, who died at Avignon in the Hôtel de l'Europe, Nov. 3, 1858.   A touching epitaph, recounting her virtues, occupies the whole surface of the top slab. From the Porte St. Lazare, a walk may be taken between the ram-parts and the Rhône down to the bridge built in 1184, partly in the style of the Pont-du-Gard, by the shepherd, saint, and architect, Bénézet, who before had constructed one over the Durance at Maupas. This bridge, which stood 100 years, was 2952 ft. long and 13 wide, on 19 arches, of which four still remain.   On the second arch is the chapel of St. Nicolas, in which the relics of St. Bénézet were kept till removed to the church of St. Dedier.

Avignon to Villeneuve.

Every ¼, a tram crosses the bridge for the Pont d'Avignon station, while every hour an omnibus crosses for Villeneuve-les-Avignon, pop. 3100, 2½ m. from the "Place," or 1¼ m. from the Pont station. Near the parish church, 14th cent., is the Hospital, containing, in the chapel to the left, the mausoleum of Innocent VI., under a lofty elaborately-sculptured canopy, rising in pinnacles to the roof.   Up-stairs is the picture gallery, in two rooms.   The most remarkable picture belongs to the 15th or 16th cent., painted on wood, and re-presents two subjects, Purgatory and the Judgment Day, apparently by two different artists.   Although stiff, the design is admirable, and all the heads, even the smallest, are carefully executed.   But the gem is the most charming and bewitching portrait by Mignard of Mme. de Ganges attired as a nun.   She was born at Avignon in 1636, and when only 13 married the Marquis de Castellane, with whom she frequented the court of Louis XIV., where she was called La Belle Provençale.   After her husband's death she married the Marquis de Ganges, with whom she returned to Avignon, where her sorrows com-menced, caused by the conduct of her two brothers-in-law, the Abbot and the Chevalier de Ganges, whose unlawful passion she steadfastly resisted.   At last the exasperated abbot having made her drink poison, she threw herself out of the window, and while lying on the ground in the agony of death, the chevalier pierced her seven times with his sword.   These two monsters were condemned by the parliament to be

broken alive on the wheel. The other pictures in the collection by
Mignard are : Jesus before the Doctors, an Annunciation, and a St.
Bruno. Fee, 1 fr., given to the hospital. In the parish church, built
in the 14th cent. by Cardinal Arnaud de Via, there is nothing extraordinary. Near it are the ruins of the Chartreuse-du-Val-de-
Bénédiction, and on an eminence Fort André, now inhabited as a
walled village. The omnibus for Avignon starts every hour at the
hour, from the apsidal end of the parish church of Villeneuve.

Avignon is very much exposed to different winds, especially the
Mistral, yet perhaps they are necessary, for, according to the adage,
"Avenio ventosa, cum vento fastidiosa, sine vento venenosa," the
odours from the drains in some of the streets being very offensive.

Till July 26, 1793, Avignon belonged to the Papal See, when it
was forcibly taken possession of by the Republican army under General
Cartaux, who owed his victory to the skill of his captain of artillery,
the young commandant Napoleon, who afterwards remained nearly a
month in this town for the establishment of his health, in No. 65 Rue
Calade, opposite the Musée Calvet, where he wrote "Le Souper de
Beaucaire."

Avignon to Nîmes.

Avignon is 1½ hour or 15½ miles N.E. from Nîmes by rail, starting
from the Pont-d'Avignon station on the west side of the Rhône. Those
wishing to visit the Pont-du-Gard on the way should take their tickets
for the Pont-du-Gard station, changing carriages at Remoulins. If
with luggage, it is better to take the tickets only to Remoulins ; where,
without loss of time on arriving, take other tickets to the Pont-du-Gard,
leaving the luggage behind. Time will generally be saved by returning from the Pont to Remoulins on foot, about 3 m. by the road, but
5 m. by the rail. See Map, p. 56. For Nîmes see p. 110, and for
the Pont-du-Gard see p. 114. Consult the "Indicateur des Chemins
de Fer du Lyon" before starting.

Avignon to Vaucluse by L'Isle.

From Avignon the Fontaine de Vaucluse is 18 m. eastward, by
the village of Isle, on the line to Cavaillon. L'Isle, pop. 7000,
a village on the Sorgues, with decorated church rebuilt in the 17th
cent. Handsome reredos over high altar and several good paintings.
The Tour d'Argent dates from the 11th cent. At the station the
omnibuses of the Isle hotels, Petrarque et Laure and St. Martin, await
passengers and take them to Vaucluse and back for 4 frs. each. From
the village of Vaucluse, pop. 600, take for the fountain the road on

the right bank of stream, but for the house and garden of Petrarch take the left side, crossing the bridge. On the left side, against a cliff near the cloth mill, is a small house on the site of Petrarch's, of which it is a copy. Before it, is still a piece of what was Petrarch's garden. On the other side of the Sorgue is a cigar-paper mill. There is a little hotel at Vaucluse, the Hôtel Petrarch et Laure. Under a stupendous cliff 1148 feet high is the source of the river Sorgue, the placid **Fontaine de Vaucluse**, about 30 yards in diameter—"a mirror of blue-black water, so pure, so still, that where it laps the pebbles you can scarcely say where air begins and water ends." During floods, however, the cavern being no longer able to contain the increased volume, the water rushes over in a cascade into the bed below. The poet's modest house stood at the foot of the rock crowned by the ruins of the castle in which lived his friend Cardinal Philippe de Cabasole. Petrarch himself gives the following description of the site :—"On one side my garden is bounded by a deep river ; on another by a rugged mountain, a barrier against the noon-day heats, and which never refuses, not even at mid-day, to lend me its friendly shade ; but the sweet air reaches me through all obstacles. In the distance a surly wall makes me inaccessible to both man and beast. Figs, grapes, walnuts, almonds—these are my delights. My table is also graced with the fish that abound in my river ; and it is one of my greatest pleasures to watch the fishermen draw their nets, and to draw them myself. All about me is changed. I once used to dress myself with care ; now you would believe me a labourer or a shepherd. My house resembles that of Fabius or Cato. I have but a valet and a dog. The house of my servant adjoins my own. I call him when I want him, and when I have no more need of him he returns home."

On the 6th of April 1327 Francesco Petrarca saw in a church of Avignon Laura the daughter of Audibert de Noves, for whom he conceived a romantic but hopeless attachment. Incessantly haunted with the beautiful vision of the fair Laura, he visited in succession the south of France, Paris, and the Netherlands, and after an exile of eight months returned to bury himself in the solitude of Vaucluse.

Vehicles are also hired at Avignon. Fare to Vaucluse and back, 12 to 18 frs. ; time, 8 hours. Also for the Pont du Gard, same price.

20½ m. from Avignon by rail is Cavaillon (p. 66), whence a branch line extends 20 m. E. to Apt, another line 27 m. S.E. to Pertuis on the Marseilles and Grenoble line, and another 22½ m. S. to Miramas (p. 76), between Arles and Marseilles. (See map, p. 66.)

AVIGNON TO MANOSQUE BY APT.

40½ m. E. by rail from Avignon, by Cavaillon, is **Apt,** pop. 7000, on the torrent Calavon, in a sheltered hollow surrounded by mountains and calcareous cliffs. *Hotels:* The *Louvre ; des Alpes. The principal industries are agriculture, pottery, and the making of preserved fruits. Fruit to be glazed with sugar, as well as that on which the sugar is to be crystallised, is allowed to soak from 2 to 8 months in a strong solution of white sugar, in uncovered "terrines," like small basins. Fruits with thick rinds, such as oranges, are pricked before being immersed. The best pottery (Bernard Croix) is near the station, to the left on descending the hill. The clay, gray and reddish, is in thick beds close to the establishment, and resembles that of Vallauris, near Cannes, in its power of resisting fire, and is therefore principally used for the manufacture of kitchen pottery. M. Croix has added artistic pottery and dinner and tea services, of which the prices are extremely low. Opposite is the establishment of L. A. Esbérard, who confines himself almost exclusively to kitchen pottery.

The parish church of St. Anne dates from the 11th cent. To the left on entering is the chapel of St. Anne, under a low octagonal domed tower. Below the altar is a crypt, 10th cent., said to contain the bones of the mother of Mary. Round about the town are pleasant walks, of which many are shaded with Oriental plane trees. Coach daily to Manosque (*Hotel :* Eymon), 26 m. E., passing Céreste, 5¼ m. E., and Reillanne, on the top of a hill, 5 m. farther. Manosque is on the rail between Marseilles and Grenoble. (See maps, pages 26 and 66.)

Cavaillon to Miramas, 22½ m. S. (see map, p. 66), across a fertile plain, with vineyards and groves of olive, almond, and apricot trees. **Cavaillon** (pop. 8000). *Inns:* Parrocel ; Teston. Omnibus at station. Cavaillon is a pleasant town, intersected by avenues, and situated on the Durance at the base of great limestone cliffs. It possesses an ancient triumphal arch and a cathedral dating from the 12th and 13th cents., with a cloister of the 12th. Excellent melons are grown in the neighbourhood. 4¼ m. S. from Cavaillon is **Orgon** (pop. 3000. *Inns:* Paris ; Poste), on the Durance. 11 m. farther S. is **Salon** (pop. 7100. *Inns:* Poste ; Croix de Malte), on the canal Craponne. This town, dealing largely in first-class olive oil, has still remnants of its old ramparts : a church, St. Michel, of the 13th cent., another, St. Laurent, of the 14th, and a castle of the same date. In the town is a fountain to the memory of Adam de Craponne, the engineer of the canal. (For Miramas, see p. 75.)

474 TARASCON, pop. 11,000. *Hotels :* At the foot of the sta- **63** tion stairs, the Luxembourg ; in the town, the Empereurs. Junction with branch to Nîmes, 17 m. W., and 31 m. farther Montpellier. Below the station is a large hospital for old men and orphans, founded in 1761 by Clerc Molière. Tarascon is an unimportant town on the Rhône, opposite Beaucaire, and connected with it by a chain bridge

THE MOUTHS OF TH[

For continuation see map, page 107.

English Miles

Railways ▬▬▬ Carriage Roads ≈≈

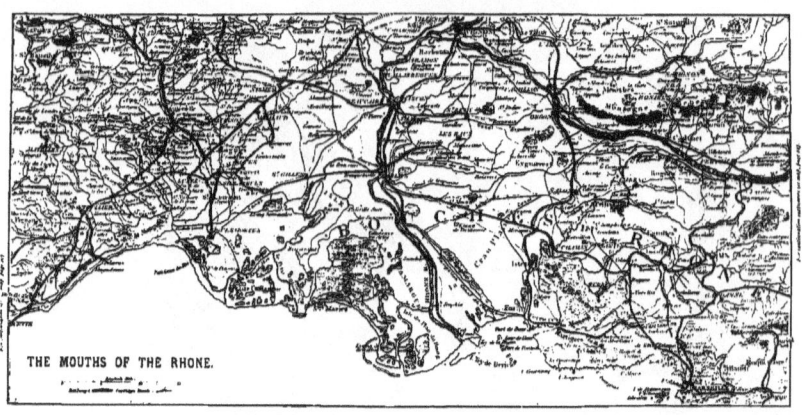

THE MOUTHS OF THE RHONE.

1450 feet long. In the church of St. Martha, built in the 12th cent., is an ancient crypt, just under the spire, with the tomb of Martha, the sister of Lazarus, whose mortal remains are said to repose here under the peaceful-looking marble effigy which marks the spot. The tradition of the place says she had come with her maid from Aix, at the request of the inhabitants, to kill a terrible dragon with a body as thick as a bull's, and having succeeded, the inhabitants, out of gratitude to her, after her death buried her in this place. A few steps from the church, by the side of the river, rises the massive strong square castle, begun in 1400 and finished by the Roi René, now used as a prison. On the opposite side of the river, overlooking Beaucaire, are the more picturesque ruins of the castle of Montmorency, whose adjoining garden forms one of the many promenades of the people of Beaucaire. Beaucaire is a poor town with poor houses. The formerly famous fair, commencing on July 1, has become now of little importance. It is held in the broad avenue between the castle and the Rhône.

9½ m. east from Tarascon by rail is **St. Remy**, pop. 6800. *Inn:* Hôtel du Cheval Blanc, a comfortable house, where carriages can be hired for Les Baux, 6 m. S.W., 10 frs. Also for Arles by Les Baux and Mont-Majour, 19 m. distant, 24 frs. A mile from the Hôtel Cheval Blanc, by the high road, stood the ancient Glanum, one of the commercial stations of the Phœnician traders from Marseilles, before it fell into the possession of the Romans, who have left here two remarkable monuments, of which the more perfect consists of an open square tower standing on a massive pedestal, and surmounted by a peristyle of ten columns surrounding two statues representing the parents of Sextus and Marius, of the family of the Julii, by whom it was erected. It is 50 ft. high ; the faces of the statues look to the north. The sculpture on the north side of the pedestal represents a cavalry fight ; the south, "sacrificing ;" the west, a combat between infantry ; and the east, which is the most dilapidated, "Victory crowning a wounded soldier." Alongside stands a triumphal arch, of which the most perfect portions are the coffered panellings of the soffit.

6 m. S.W. from St. Remy is **Les Baux**, the ancient Castrum de Baucis, pop. 100. *Inn:* Monte Carlo. The castle town of Les Baux, commenced in 485, occupies a naked mountain of yellow sandstone, worn away by nature into bastions and buttresses, and coigns of vantage, sculptured by ancient art into palaces and chapels, battlements and dungeons. Now art and nature are confounded in one ruin. Blocks of masonry lie cheek-by-jowl with masses of the rough-hewn

rock ; fallen cavern vaults are heaped round fragments of fan-shaped spandrel and clustered column shaft ; the doors and windows of old pleasure rooms are hung with ivy and wild fig tapestry ; while winding staircases start midway upon the cliff and lead to vacancy. High overhead, suspended in mid-air, hang chambers—lady's bower or poet's singing room—now inaccessible, the haunt of hawks and swallows. Within this rocky honeycomb—"cette ville en monolithe," as it has been aptly called, for it is literally scooped out of one mountain block —live a few poor people, foddering their wretched goats at carved piscina and stately sideboards, erecting their mud-beplastered hovels in the halls of feudal princes. From Les Baux road to Fontvieille, 7 m. ; whence rail to Mont-Majour and Arles (see map, page 66).

483　**54**

ARLES, pop. 26,000. *Hotels :* Nord ; Forum ; near each other in the Place du Forum. Arles is situated on the Rhône, near the Camargue, in a marshy place, as its original name, Arelas, from the Celtic words, "Ar lach," damp place, indicates. It is said to have been founded 900 years before Marseilles, 700 years before Rome, and 1500 before the birth of Christ. The ramparts and walls rising from the public gardens and the Boulevard des Aliscamps are chiefly the work of the Emperor Constantine, who came to Arles with his family and mother, Saint Helena. He built by the side of the Rhône a superb palace, called afterwards "de la Trouille," because opposite a ferry-boat, which was pulled or dragged from one side of the river to the other. Of this palace little more remains than the attached tower La Trouille, constructed of alternate layers of brick and stone. On the 7th August 312 his wife Faustina presented him with a son, Constantine II., who succeeded his father in May 357. He commenced the Forum, but was shortly after killed in battle defending himself against his brother Constance, who usurped the throne and finished the Forum. All that remains of this formerly splendid edifice are the two Corinthian columns, with part of the pediment encrusted into the wall of the Hôtel du Nord. It occupied the site of the Place du Forum, called also the Place des Hommes, because labourers and men-servants used to be hired in this "Place."

In the Place de la République is the Hôtel de Ville, built in 1675 on the site of the Roman baths constructed by the Emperor Augustus. The spacious vaults under the Hôtel du Nord formed probably a part of these baths, although in later times they seem to have been used as an ossuary.

Almost adjoining the Hôtel de Ville is the church of St. Anne,

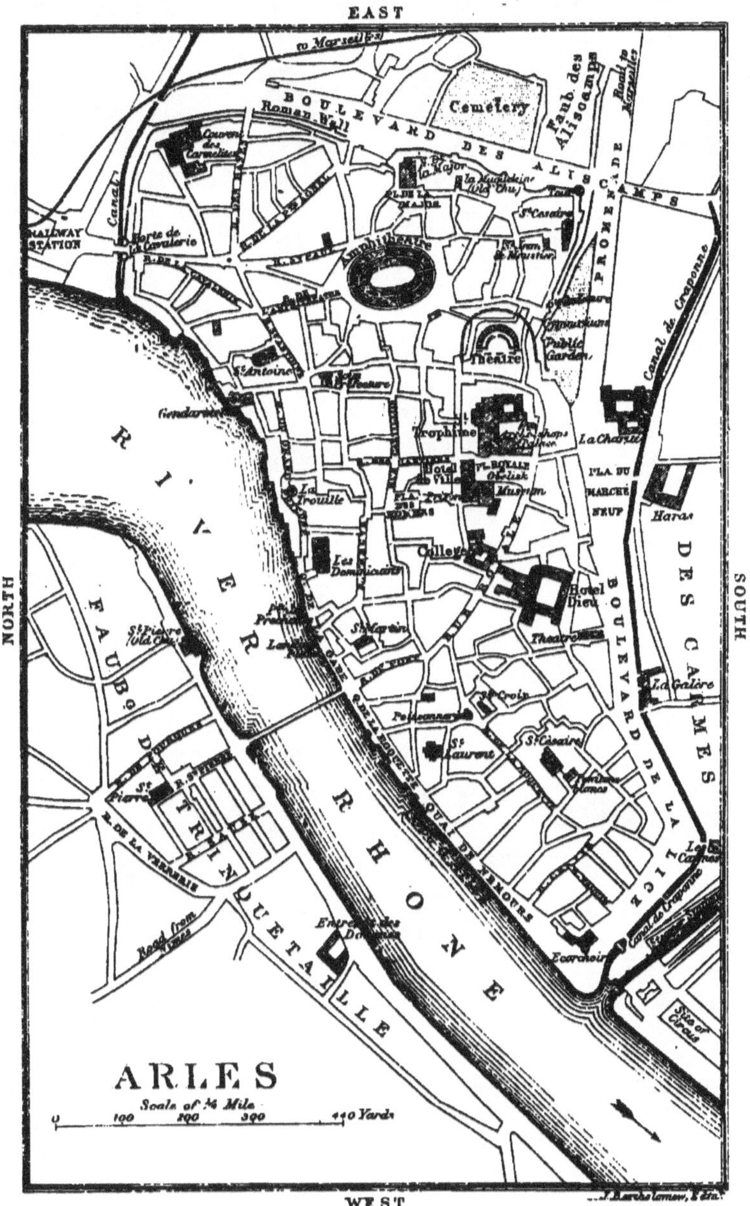
EAST
WEST
NORTH
SOUTH
ARLES
Scale of ¼ Mile
0 100 200 300 440 Yards
to Marseilles
Cemetery
Faub. des Alisoamps
Road to Marseilles
BOULEVARD DES ALISCAMPS
Roman Wall
Couvent des Carmelites
Canal
RAILWAY STATION
Porte de la Cavalerie
Amphitheatre
Theatre
Public Garden
Canal de Craponne
St. Antoine
Gendarmerie
RIVER RHONE
Trophime
La Charité
PLA DU MARCHÉ NEUF
Haras
Museum
Obelisk
Hotel de Ville
La Trouille
Les Dominicains
College
Hotel Dieu
BOULEVARD DE LA LICE
DES CARMES
St. Martin
Theatre
St. Pierre (Old Chu.)
FAUBG. DE TRINQUETAILLE
La Galère
Ste. Croix
St. Laurent
St. Césaire
QUAI DE NEMOURS
St. Pierre
R. DE LA VERRERIE
Road from Nimes
Les Carmes
Canal de Craponne
Ecarchoir
Site of Circus
J. Bartholomew, Edin.

now the Archæological Museum, with a collection of inscriptions, sarcophagi, urns, statues, columns, friezes, altars, and tombstones, those
of the Pagans having the letters D.M., *Diis manibus.* Also some of
the long lead pipes, with the name of the plumber, "C. Canthius
Porthinus fac.," which helped to bring water from the fountain at the
foot of the hill on which Baux stands. At the inner end, right hand,
is a torse of Mithras of white Pharos marble, 3 ft. 2 inches high, found
in 1598 on the site of the Roman Circus. A serpent is coiled round
the body, and between the coils are the signs of the Zodiac. In the
opposite corner is an altar in Carrara marble to the good goddess
"Bonae-Deae," found under the church La Major. On the front face
is a garland of oak leaves and acorns, and 7 inches distant from each
other two human ears. Near it is a good head of Augustus, and a
mutilated one of Diana. About the centre of the room is a recumbent
figure of Silenus, with a wine skin under his arm.

In the centre of the "Place" is the monolith obelisk, 49 ft. high,
hewn by the Romans from the quarries of Esterel. It stood originally
in the Circus at the S.W. corner of the town; but of it no vestiges remain.

Opposite St. Anne is the cathedral of St. Trophime, consecrated on
the 17th May 626, and rebuilt in the 9th cent. The portal, erected
in 1221, consists of a semicircular arch resting on six columns, behind
which are statues of apostles and saints separated by pilasters. In
the tympanum is Christ, the judge of the world, with the symbols of
the Evangelists. In the interior the door on the S. side of the choir
leads out to the cloister, of which the N. side belongs to the 9th, the
south to the 16th, the east to the 13th, and the west to the 14th cent.

Passing from the cloister into the street, and turning to the left,
we arrive at the Theatre, commenced during the dominion of the
Greeks, and finished before the Christian era. In the centre of this
grand ruin, originally 335 ft. in its greatest diameter, stand two
Corinthian columns 30 ft. high, and the base of other two, which
formed part of the proscenium. Opposite them is the semicircular space
for the spectators, with still many of the stone seats. The Venus of
Arles, one of the most valuable statues in the Louvre, was found here.
The theatre is open to the public, but the keeper endeavours to attach
himself to strangers.

A short way N.E. is the far grander and more imposing **Amphitheatre** or Les Arènes, said to have been commenced by the father of
Tiberius Nero, B.C. 46. It is elliptic, 459 ft. long and 132 wide,
surrounded by a double wall 60 ft. high, each with two stages of

arches, and in each stage 60 arches. From around the arena rise 43 tiers of stone seats, capable of containing 23,438 spectators. The stone steps leading up to them were 1½ ft. high and 2 ft. 3 inches long. There were besides above 150 rooms for the gladiators and men connected with the theatre, and 100 dens for wild beasts. The three towers were added by the Saracens in the 8th cent. Bull-fights are given in the building, when a multitude of spectators, as in the time of the Romans, fill the galleries. A splendid view of the amphitheatre, the city, and of the commencement of the delta of the Rhône, is had from the western tower. The entrance into the amphitheatre is by the north gate. The doorkeeper lives in a house a little to the left of the gate. This grand ruin should, if possible, be visited by moonlight; yet during the day the beautiful masonry is more easily examined. It is the great sight in Arles, and it is better to omit all the others than to do this one hurriedly.

The Camargue or Delta of the Rhône, commencing at the outskirts of Arles, is a triangular plain of 180,000 acres extending to the Mediterranean, bounded on the west by the Petit Rhône, and on the east by the Grand Rhône. It contains small villages and large farms, with extensive vineyards and grazing ground for cattle, sheep, and horses. It is best visited by the steamboat sailing between Arles and Port St. Louis on the mouth of the great Rhône. (See p. 72, and map, p. 66.)

S. E. above the Promenade is the church of St. Cesaire, 9th cent., on the site of a temple of Jupiter. From this to go to Alyscamps, walk down the Boulevard Alyscamps to the canal Craponne, where turn to the left. The first ruin passed is an old entrance into what was the domain of the monastery of St. Cesaire. The Avenue of Alyscamps is lined on each side by 33 large stone coffins with lids, and 120 smaller coffins without lids. This, the Elysei Campi, an ancient Roman cemetery, is now divested of all its valuables and statues, of which a few are in the museum. As J. C. Himself is said to have appeared during the consecration of the cemetery, it was believed that at the resurrection it would be especially favoured by Him; hence the efforts made by so many to bury their friends here. It is said that up to the 12th cent. coffins with their dead, and money for the funeral expenses, floated down the Rhône, of their own accord, to be buried in this privileged spot. At the end of the avenue is the church of St. Honorat, on the site of the chapel founded by Trophimus the Ephesian, one of St. Paul's converts, who was sent to Arles to preach the gospel and to put an end to human sacrifices. Among the first things he is said to have done was to consecrate the Alyscamps and transform it thus from a heathen into a Christian burial-place, and add to it a little chapel.   An old Arles writer alleges on his own authority that Trophimus dedicated this chapel to Mary, who was then alive.   After labouring 36 years in this diocese he died on the 29th of November 94, and was buried in the little chapel he himself had built.   Among the successors of Trophimus were Ambrose in 160, who remained here 20 years ; Augustine in 220, who died 10 years afterwards ; Jerome in 230, who also died 10 years afterwards ; Marcien in 252, the originator of the Novatien sect; and St. Cyprien in 253.   Saint Virgil, one of the successors, founded in 601 the church of St. Honorat beside the chapel of Trophimus.   The present church dates only from the 12th to the 14th cent.   The best and oldest part, excepting the foundations, is the apsidal termination, which is semicircular, with 4 pilasters and a small window in the centre to give light to the officiating priest.   Over it rises a neat octagonal belfry in two arcaded stages.   Under the chancel is a small crypt.   The keeper calls a small chapel at the left hand corner of the chancel, the chapel of Trophimus.

The Picture Gallery, or the Musée Reattu, is at No. 11 R. Grand Prieure, near the Tour Trouille.   The house and pictures were bequeathed to the town by a cousin of the painter Reattu, b. at Arles 1760, d. 1833. On picture 119 are portraits of himself, wife, and two cousins.   Next the picture gallery is the school of design.

Branch line from Arles to Fontvieille, 7 m. E., passing Mont-Majour 4 m. E.   Fontvieille is 7 m. S.W. from Les Baux by a good road. Junction at Arles with line to Aigues-Mortes, 36 m. S.W., and to Montpellier, 58 m. S.W. ; Cette is 17 m. farther.   (See map, p. 66.)

4 m. eastwards by rail from Arles are the ruins of the castle and abbey of Mont-Majour, all in a good state of preservation, excepting the domestic buildings, constructed in 1786.   The concierge lives in a house near the station.   Fee, 1 fr.   He generally shows first the church, 11th cent., and the spacious crypt below, 9th cent.   Adjoining the church are the cloisters, 11th cent., of the same kind as those of St. Trophime, but more interesting and more perfect, and containing the tombs of some of the counts of Anjou.   Next is the beautiful square dungeon tower, nearly as perfect as when erected in 1374.   It is 262 ft. high, is ascended by 137 steps, and commands a wide prospect.   From this, a stair leads down the face of the hill to the chapel and cell of St. Trophimus, principally hewn in the soft limestone cliff. Standing apart at the base of the hill is St. Croix, dedicated in 1019,

consisting of four semicircular sides, crowned with semidomes projecting from a square tower crowned with a kind of pyramid spire. At
Fontvieille (Hôtel du Commerce) are important quarries of soft calcareous sandstone.

Arles to Port Saint Louis, at the mouth of the Great Rhône,
25 m. S. by steamer on the Great Rhône. Time, 5 hrs. Fare, 2 frs.
Railway unfinished (see map, p. 66). The steamboat passes by an important part of the Camargue with large vineyards, rendered very
fertile by irrigation, the water being forced up from the river by steam
engines. Cattle, sheep, and horses are reared on the tufts of coarse
grass which cover the more arid portions. The population is so sparse
that not a village is seen during the whole journey. (See also p. 70.)

Port Saint Louis (Hôtel Saint Louis), 6½ m. W. from Port Bouc,
consists of a straggling village between the Rhône and the basin of the
canal constructed to enable vessels to avoid the bar of the Rhône.
This canal is 2½ m. long, 196 ft. wide, and 22 ft. deep. To understand the geography of this desolate flat region of land and water, exposed to every wind, it is necessary to ascend the "tour Saint Louis,"
whence the plain, intersected by the Rhône and numerous canals,
appears literally like a map. The only villages seen in the vast
expanse are Fos, on a hill, and near it the Port Bouc.

Great expense has been incurred to make Port St. Louis a convenient place for shipping, and attract to it some of the commerce
from Marseilles.

23 m. S.W. from Arles, and separated from Port St. Louis by the
great Étang Valcarès, is the port called Les Saintes-Maries-de-la-Mer,
or simply Les Saintes. The parish church, 12th cent., surrounded by
fortifications, contains the tombs of the Maries and some good sculpture.

For **Arles to Port Bouc,** 29 m. S., see p. 76. The steamer sails
from the S.W. corner of Arles (see map, page 66).

11¼ m. W. by rail from Arles is St. Gilles, pop. 7000. Hôtel du
Cheval-Blanc. A poor and ancient town on the canal of Aigues-
Mortes, near the Petit Rhône. The abbey church, founded in 1116,
is considered a good specimen of Byzantine architecture. The façade
consists of a bald wall with a plain tower on each side. Between these
towers are three semicircular recessed portals, below an entablature
resting on two single and two double columns. The capitals are
Corinthian, but the pedestals (considerably effaced) consist of lions and
grotesque animals in uncouth positions. Behind them, on the piers
of the arches of the portals, stand in bold relief statues of apostles
and saints, separated from each other by pilasters. The interior, consisting of a nave and two aisles, is 290 ft. long, 88 wide, and 62 high.
In the N. aisle a stair of 33 steps leads down to the lower church,
with semicircular arches on short massive piers. From the centre 7
more steps descend to the tomb of St. Gilles. All the characteristics
of this church are equally well represented in St. Trophime of Arles.

16¾ m. farther W., or 28 m. from Arles by rail, is **Lunel,** pop.

7300. *Inns:* Palais; Nord; Tapis-verd; none good. A town of narrow streets, with a park and promenade by the side of the canal. The church is constructed after the pattern of those of Carcassonne and Perpignan. On the surrounding plain an inferior wine is grown. The first-class vineyards, producing the generous white wines from 17° to 18°, are all on the neighbouring gravelly eminences.

8. m. S. by rail from Lunel is the more interesting town of AIGUES-MORTES, "stagnant waters," pop. 4300, 4 m. from the Mediterranean, and 4 ft. above it, and connected with it by a navigable canal. *Inn:* Saint Louis. It is of great historical interest, and is surrounded by the most perfect old embrasured wall in France, built in the form of a parallelogram, 596 yds. long by 149 yds. broad. It is 36 ft. high, and is flanked by 15 towers. On the western side rises the famous round tower of Constance, 96 ft. high and 72 in diameter, containing two vaulted superimposed circular chambers, used by Louis XIV. and Louis XV. as prisons for their Protestant subjects of both sexes, who here suffered such cruelties that the Dutch and Swiss Governments were roused to interfere in their behalf, and even Frederic the Great is said to have interceded for them, but in vain. From the platform at the top of this tower is the highly interesting view of the flat country at the mouth of the Rhône, whence the traveller may judge for himself whether the sea has, or has not, receded from the town since the time of Saint Louis—we think not. Both the tower of Constance and the walls are the work of Saint Louis, who had a predilection for Aigues-Mortes, as he considered it the most suitable place in his kingdom from which to embark for Palestine. On 25th August 1248, after having heard mass in the church Notre-Dame-des-Sablons (fronting his statue), he and his Queen Marguerite sailed from Aigues-Mortes on their first expedition to Palestine. On the 3d of July 1270 he again sailed from the same place; and on that same year, on the anniversary day of his first expedition, the 25th of August, he perished among the ruins of Carthage. 4 m. S. from Aigues-Mortes by omnibus, or steamer by the canal, is the bathing station of Port-Grau-du-Roi. *Inns:* Pommier; Dubois (see map, page 66).

49 m. N. from Lunel by rail is Vigan. (See page 105.)

96½ m. W. from Marseilles, 43 m. W. from Arles, 31 m. S.W. from Nîmes, and 15 m. S.W. from Lunel, is

MONTPELLIER, on the sides and summit of an eminence 145 ft. above the sea and 7 miles from it. Pop. 56,000. *Hotels:* H. Nevet, the best and most expensive, at the commencement of the Esplanade. On the same side, only a little farther up, is a block of handsome buildings containing the Public Library, closed on Sundays and Thursdays, and the Picture Gallery or Musée Fabre, open on Sundays and Mondays. Adjoining is the Lycée.

In the Place de la Comédie, near the Esplanade, is the H. du Midi, the next best hotel. In the Grande Rue, the H. Cheval Blanc, frequented by commercial men. Opposite the station is the H. de la Gare. In the fine broad street, the Rue Maguelone, leading from the station to the Place de la Comédie, is the H. Maguelone, second class. Their omnibuses await passengers.

Temple Protestant near station, in the Rue Maguelone. Telegraph Office in the Boulevard de la Comédie. Post in the Boulevard Jeu-de-Paume. From the Esplanade omnibus runs to Castelnau. From near the Place de la Comédie coach to Mauguio. From the Boulevard de Blanquerie, below the prison, coach to Claret and St. Hippolyte. (See map, p. 66.)

The most modern part of the town is the Rue Maguelone, leading from the station to the Esplanade, a delightful promenade bounded by the citadel. At the N.W. angle of the Esplanade a stair leads down to a line of boulevards, passing up by the "Hôpital Général" to the Botanic Gardens, the earliest institution of this kind in France, founded in the reign of Henri IV., and for some years under the direction of the famous botanist De Candolle. It contains an area of 9 acres, divided into three parts : at the N. end is a nursery ; at the S., in a hollow, surrounded by trees, the botanical part ; and between these two divisions the arboretum. Opposite the Botanic Gardens is the once famous École de médecine, said to have been founded by Arab physicians under the patronage of the Counts of Montpellier. It now occupies the old bishops' palace, built in the 14th cent., with additions in the 17th. At the entrance are bronze statues of Barthez, 1734-1806, and La Peyronie, 1678-1747. Within the entrance are busts of the most celebrated professors and divines connected with the college and the church of Montpellier. In the same building are also valuable anatomical and pathological collections, and a library with 55,000 vols. Adjoining is the Cathedral of St. Pierre, 14th and 15th cents., but the choir is recent, though in the same style. White marble statue of Mary and child by Canova.

Overlooking the Botanic Gardens is the beautiful promenade, the Place du Peyrou, on an eminence at the western side of the town. In cold weather invalids and nurses with their children frequent the lower terrace of this " Place," the promenade Basse du Midi. At the western end of the Peyrou is the Château d'Eau, a hexagonal Corinthian building, which receives and distributes through the town the water brought from the fontaine de St. Clement, 5½ m. from Montpellier. The aqueduct, which conveys the water across the valley from the opposite hill, consists of two tiers of arches 70 ft. high and 2896 ft. long. The gate at the end of the promenade was erected to commemorate the victories of Louis XIV. Adjoining is the Palais de Justice, with statues of Cambacérès and Cardinal Fleury. Eastwards, by crooked streets, are the Mairie and the markets.

A short way north from the Hôtel Nevet, by the Rues Ste. Foi and also on the Esplanade, is a handsome modern edifice, comprising the **Musée Fabre**, the Bibliothèque publique with 65,000 vols., and the "Collection de la Société archéologique." The Musée Fabre, open on Sundays and Mondays and feast days, contains, among many works of inferior merit, some good pictures by great artists, such as Berghem,

Fra Bartolommeo, P. C. Champaigne, Cuyp, L. David, G. Dow, Van
Dyck, Ghirlandajo, Girodet, Granet, Greuze, Metsu, Palma, P. Veronese,
Porbus, P. Potter, Poussin, Samuel Reynolds, Salvator Rosa, Rubens,
Ruysdael, Andrea del Sarto, D. Teniers, Terburg, Titian, and Zarg.
The library contains some curious MSS. connected with the Stuarts,
which belonged to Prince Charles Edward.

Montpellier produces a lovely coloured wine with good bouquet,
called St. Georges d'Orgues. The manufacture of verdigris, the preparation of preserved fruits, dye works, chemical works, and distil-
leries, are the principal industries.

From the railway station, opposite the Hôtel de Nevet, a line extends
through the lagoon Pérols, covering a surface of 3000 acres, and yielding annually 2000 tons of salt, to the port of Palavas, 5 m. south (pop.
1000), with a beautiful beach.. At the Palavas terminus is the Casino
hotel, and on the Canal the Hôtel des Bains and the Restaurant Parisien.
A cabine (bathing-house), including costume and linen, costs 1 fr.
Leave the train at the Plage station. 3 m. from Montpellier, in the
retired valley of the Mosson, is the mineral water establishment of
Foncaude. Water saline, unctuous, and sedative. Good for indigestion and nervous disorders. 12½ m. north from Montpellier is the Pic
du Loup, rising from the village St. Mathieu (pop. 500) to the height
of 680 ft., commanding an extensive view, and having on the top a
chapel visited by pilgrims.

From Montpellier a line extends 43½ m. W. to Faugères on the
line from Beziers to Capdenac by Rodez. (See map, page 27.)

109½ m. from Marseilles and 4½ from Cette is **Frontignan**, pop.
3000. Possessing 570 acres of vineyards producing rich amber-
coloured, luscious, and spirituous wines, made principally from the
clairette and picardan grapes. The neighbouring marshes yield
annually about 50,000 tons of salt.

114 m. from Marseilles is **Cette**, pop. 29,000. At this point the
Chemins de Fer de Paris à Lyon system joins the Chemins de Fer du
Midi, and consequently carriages are often changed here. For Cette
to Toulouse and Bordeaux, see Table "Bordeaux à Cette" in the
"Indicateur des Chemins de Fer du Midi." Cette is 271 m. east from
Pau, 266 from Bordeaux, and 84 from Perpignan. Omnibuses and
coaches await passengers. *Hotels:* Barrillon ; Grand Galion ; Bains ;
Souche. Cette makes a pleasant halting-place. The best walk is to
the top of Mt. Setius, 590 ft. Ascend by the Rue d'Esplanade, and
when at the highest part of the Public Gardens take the road to the
right. The view is magnificent. In front is the Mediterranean, and
behind Lake Thau with its villages. At the base of the mountain is
Cette, and beyond Frontignan. The Port of Cette is protected by a
breakwater 548 yds. long, which encloses a harbour of 210 acres, furnished with two jetties ; the western, constructed by Vauban, is 656
yds. long, and the eastern 548 yds. This busy port, besides having
an extensive carrying trade, has a large wine manufactory, where above
100,000 pipes of imitations of all the well-known wines are made
annually, by mixing different wines with each other.

From the first bridge over the canal (not including the railway bridge) a small steamer starts three times daily for Balaruc and Meze, on Lake Thau. Meze, like Cette, is entirely devoted to the wine trade. Balaruc has a bathing establishment, supplied by intensely saline springs, resembling strong sea-water, temperature 125° Fahr. A quart contains 106 grains of chloride of sodium, 13½ of the chloride of magnesia, and a fraction of the chloride of copper, 15 grains of the sulphate, and 13½ of the bicarbonate of lime. Pension, 8 to 9 fr., and the bath treatment 4½ fr. additional. The Canal du Midi enters Lake Thau at Les Onglous, 11 m. W. from Cette. (See map, page 27.)

503 **34**
MIRAMAS, pop. 900, south from the station at the head of the Étang Chamas. At the station there are a small inn and a large plantation of almond trees, which, when in flower, exhale a delightful perfume. Passengers to Avignon by Cavaillon and L'Isle change carriages here (p. 65). Also for Port Bouc, 16¼ m. south.

MIRAMAS TO PORT BOUC.

Miramas to Port Bouc by rail through a flat plain (see map, p. 66). The two most important towns passed on the way are : Istres, 6¼ m. from Miramas station and 10 N. from Port Bouc, pop. 4000, founded in the 8th cent. on Lake Olivier, and possessing still part of its ancient ramparts. The principal industry is the manufacture of salt and of the carbonate of soda. 13¼ m. from Miramas is **Fos** (Fossae Marianae), pop. 1100, on a hill crowned with the ruins of a castle, 14th cent. At the foot of the hill, by the side of the Arles canal, are large tanks for the manufacture of salt. From Fos, other 3 miles south by rail, or 16¼ miles altogether from the Miramas railway station, or 29 miles S. from Arles by the canal, is **Port Bouc**, pop. 1000. *Inns:* near the stations of the railway and the canal steamer, the Hôtel du Commerce ; near the jetty, the Hôtel du Nord. Port Bouc, on the Étang Caroute, near the entrance to the great lake, the Ltang de Berre, is an important fishing-station with a large and well-protected harbour. At the end of the jetty is a fixed light, seen within a radius of 10 m. At the other side of the entrance is Fort Bouc with a massive square tower in the centre and another lighthouse. About 7 miles west from Port Bouc by the coast road is the Port of St. Louis, page 72. (For Port Bouc to Martigues and Marseilles, see p. 118.)

Port Bouc to Arles, 29 m. S. by the canal steamboat ; time, 5 hrs ; fare, 3 frs. The canal is 62 ft. wide and 8 deep. The embankments are very solid, and along a great part of them extends the railway between Arles and Saint Louis. The only town the canal passes is Fos, about ½ m. E. The Miramas railway passes it on the other side. Passengers drop into the steamer from the farmhouses. The steamer moors at the S.W. corner of Arles. (See p. 72, and map p. 66.)

506½ **30½**
SAINT CHAMAS (Sanctus Amantius), pop. 3000, about ½ m.

from the station. It is situated on the N. end of the Étang de Berre, and on both sides of a short narrow ridge of soft sandstone pierced with excavations. The Government have one of their most important powder manufactories in this place. Hardly ½ m. E. from the Hôtel de Ville is the Flavian Bridge, built by the Romans, across the stream Touloubre, with at each end a kind of triumphal arch of 12 ft. span and about 22 ft. high. At each of the four corners is a grooved Corinthian pilaster surmounted by a frieze and a projecting dentilled cornice. On the top at each end stands a lion ; the two on the east arch are apparently ready to spring eastward, and the other two westward. The bridge is in a state of perfect repair, but the sculpture and inscription on the two arches over the entrances are slightly effaced. The road to it is by the Hôtel de Ville and the parish church with a rudely sculptured "Pieta" over the portal. The bridge is to the E. of St. Chamas, and is well seen from the railway, especially when crossing the viaduct of 49 interlaced arches, which carry the rail over the little valley of the Touloubre. 8½ m. E. from St. Chamas is Berre station. The town, pop. 2100, is directly south, on Lake Berre, a sheet of water 14 m. long and 38 in circumference.

519½ ROGNAC, pop. 900. Junction with rail to Aix, 16½ m. E., 17¼ passing under the Roquefavour aqueduct, 7½ m. E. The canal, which brings 200 cubic ft. of water per second from the Durance to Marseilles and the neighbouring plain, commences opposite Pertuis, directly north from Marseilles. It is 94 m. long, of which more than 15 are under ground ; it has a fall of 614 ft., traverses, by 45 tunnels, 3 chains of limestone hills, and crosses numerous valleys by aqueducts, of which the largest crosses the ravine of the river Arc at Roquefavour. This aqueduct is 270 ft. high on three tiers of arches, is 1312 ft. long, 44½ ft. wide at the base, and 14 ft. wide at the water-way. It consists of 51,000 cubic yards of masonry, and cost £151,394, while the cost of the whole canal from the Durance to the sea, near Cape Croisette, a little to the east of Marseilles, has been £2,090,000. A branch from the principal channel throws 198,000 gallons per minute into the city, while five other ramifications fertilise by irrigation the country around it. The canal water is purified in the basins of Réaltort. The large reservoir for Marseilles is behind the Palais de Longchamp. (See p. 114, and for the course of the canal, maps pp. 66 and 123.)

To visit the aqueduct, take the road to the left from the station, pass under the railway bridge, and then ascend partly by a steep path and partly by steps to the house of the concierge.

16½ m. E. from Rognac, or 33 m. N. from Marseilles by Rognac, but only 18 m. N. by Gardanne, is **Aix-en-Provence**, pop. 29,000. *Hotels :* Negre-Coste, the best, in the Grand Cours ; at the east end of the Cours, Mule-Noire, and near it at the Palais de Justice, the Hôtel du Palais ; at the station end of the Cours, the Louvre and the France ; at the baths, the Hôtel des Bains ; opposite the Hôtel de Ville, the Hôtel Aigle d'Or. Best cafés in the Cours René. Post and telegraph offices in the street behind the Cours, or behind the division opposite the Hôtel Negre-Coste. Aix, formerly the capital of Provence, was founded 120 B.C. by the Consul Sextius Calvinus around the thermal springs, which he himself had discovered. The temperature of the water is 95° F., and the ingredients, iron and iodine, the carbonates, sulphates, and chlorides of soda and magnesia, together with an organic bituminous matter strongly impregnated with glairine. The establishment is situated at the extremity of the Cours Sextius. Pension, 8½ frs. Each bath 1 fr. At the high end of the Cours René is a statue, by David, of René of Anjou, "le bon Roi," king of Naples, Sicily, and Jerusalem ; died in 1480 at the age of 72, and buried at Angers, where he was born. He was endowed with every virtue, was a poet, painter, and musician, and was skilled in medicine and astronomy. During his reign in Aix the people were prosperous, and art and science flourished. From the right of the statue streets lead up to the principal square with a monument to Lodovico XV., the Palais de Justice with statues of the jurists Portales and Siméon, and the church of the Madeleine, built for the perpetual adoration of the host. A little higher up are the Hôtel de Ville, built in 1640 ; the Halle-aux-Grains, reconstructed in 1760 and adorned with bold and spirited sculpture. Next the Hôtel de Ville is the great clock tower, bearing the date 1512. In the centre of the court of the Hôtel de Ville is a statue of Mirabeau, and on the staircase a white marble statue of Marshal Villars, by Coustou. In the Hôtel de Ville is also the public library with 100,000 vols. Among the MSS. is the prayer book of King René, with illustrations said to have been done by himself. No. 569 is a small 4to volume, with copies of letters written by Queen Mary Stuart. The first 57 pages relate to her early history. At page 645 commences a defence of her conduct, written by a warm partisan of the queen. The street, ascending through the gateway of the clock tower, leads to the university buildings, the palace of the archbishop, and the Cathedral of **Saint Sauveur**, built in the 11th cent., partly on the foundations of a temple to Apollo. The tower, 195 ft. high, was built in the 15th cent., and the chancel in 1285. The façade was commenced in 1476, and the beautiful sculpture on the great entrance door executed in 1503. It is generally covered by a plain outer door. In the interior to the right is the Baptistery, an octagonal chapel with six antique marble and two granite Corinthian columns about 30 ft. high, each shaft being of one stone. The ornamental sculpture on the panels and in the spandrels is by Puget. On the same side are two triptychs, one by Crayer, "Mary worshipped by Saints," and the other by some artist of the Jean Van Eyck school, representing in the centre Moses and the burning bush, with Mary up in a clump of trees. On one wing is King René on his knees, attended by the Magdalene, St. Maurice, and St. Anthony ; and on the other wing is the king's second wife, Jeanne de Laval, attended by her patron saints.   On the outside of the shutters are the angel Gabriel and Mary.

On each side of the chancel is an organ case, but only the one on the left hand has pipes.   Under each is a large tapestry dating from 1511, representing scenes in the life of J. C.   Both pieces are said to have belonged to St. Paul's of London.   Among the relics the church possesses are : the skull of St. Ursula, the arm of one of her 11,000 virgins presented by Nicolas V. in 1458, a rib of St. Sebastian presented by King René, and three thorns from the crown of our Lord.

The last street at the S. E. end of the Cours René leads directly to the church of St. Jean and the **Picture Gallery** adjoining ; free on Sundays and Thursdays from 12 to 4.   St. Jean was built in the 13th cent. by the Princes of the house of Aragon for the order of the Knights of St. John of Jerusalem.   The spire is 220 ft. high.   To the left of the altar is the tomb of Raymond and wife, Comte de Provence.

On the ground-floor of the picture gallery are sarcophagi, inscriptions, and statues ancient and modern.   Upstairs is a large collection of paintings, water-colours, and drawings ; but few have either labels or numbers.

The "Biscotins" seen in the shop windows are round sweet biscuits about the size and shape of walnuts.   The better kind, "Gallissons," are flat and diamond shaped.   The olive oil made in the farms around Aix is reputed to have a very fine fruity flavour.   The reason alleged is—the trees being small the berries are gathered, or rather plucked, by the hand before they are quite ripe.   Where the trees are large, as in the more favoured parts of the Riviera, the fruit must be allowed to ripen to allow of its being shaken down by long poles.   The trees are pruned in circles, leaving an empty space in the centre.

(For the following see maps, pages 66 and 123.)   Coach daily from the "Cours" to Rians, 20 m. N.E., passing Vauvenargues, 8 m. E.   The castle, 14th cent., and village of Vauvenargues are situated near the cascades of the Val Infernets, and within 3 hrs. of the culminating point, 3175 ft. above the sea, of the Sainte Victoire mountains.   **Rians**, pop. 2900, *Inn:* Hôtel Barème, is situated amidst olive trees and vineyards.   Coach daily from Rians to Meyrargues, on the railway 34½ m. N. from Marseilles, and 155½ S. from Grenoble, passing Jouques, 7½ m. N., with the ruins of its castle, both situated in the gorge of the Riaou, in which rise the copious springs of the Bouillidous, which irrigate the fields and set in motion numerous mills.   2 m. beyond Jouques is **Peyrolles** (pop. 1200.   *Inn :* Hôtel du Grand Logis), on the Durance, and at the foot of the Grand Sambiu, 2560 ft. above the sea.   In the chapel of the old fortress is a painting on wood attributed to King René.

Meyrargues (pop. 2000.   *Inn :* Reynaud) is situated with its castle in the valley of the Volubière. Coach at station awaits passengers from Rians.

Diligence also from the Cours to Pélissanne, 18 m. W., passing by La Barben, with one of the best castles in Provence, 14 m. W. Coach from Pelissanne to Salon, 4 m. W. (For Salon, see p. 66.) 5 m. N.E. from Pelissanne is Lambesc.

Diligences leave the Cours also for St. Cannat and Lambesc ; but the best way is to go on to the next station N. from Aix, La Calade, where a coach awaits passengers for St. Cannat, 5 m. N.W., and Lambesc, 3½ m. farther. In the village of St. Cannat is the chapel of N. D. de la Vie, visited by pilgrims. **Lambesc**, 14 m. from Aix, pop. 3000, is a pretty little town, agreeably situated at the foot of the hill Berthoire. The manufactures of olive oil and silk form the principal industries.

7 m. S. from Aix, and 11 m. N. from Marseilles, is **Gardanne**, pop. 3500, with extensive coalfields. Junction here with branch to Carnoules, 52 m. S.E., on the line between Marseilles and Cannes. (See under Carnoules, p. 142.)

From **Rognac** the train passes by the Étang de Berre, and halts at Vitrolles, on the east side of the rail, 2½ m. S. from Rognac. 3¼ m. S. from Vitrolles and 11¼ m. N. from Marseilles is Pas-des-Lanciers, junction with line to Martigues (see p. 66), 12¾ m. E.

Four and a half miles south from the Pas-des-Lanciers, and 7 miles north from Marseilles, is the station of **L'Estaque**, a village on the sea, full of large brick and tile works, extending a good way up the valley of the Séon. This is the birthplace of the painter, sculptor, architect, and engineer Pierre Puget, born 31st October 1622, died at Marseilles 2d December 1694, in the 51st year of the reign of Louis XIV., to the glory of which his genius had contributed. He was the youngest of three brothers, the children of Simon Puget, a poor stonemason, who died while Pierre was still a boy.

Marseilles (see p. 111). Cabs and the omnibuses from all the principal hotels await passengers in the large open court just outside the arrival side of the railway station. At the east end of the departure side of the railway station is the Station Hotel, very comfortable, but the prices are rather more than moderate.

LYONS TO NÎMES.

172 m. south by the west bank of the Rhône, passing Oullins, Givors-canal, Ampuis, Peyraud, Tournon, La Voulte, Le Pouzin, Le Teil, Laudun, and Rémoulins. Thence to Marseilles other 79 miles.

Maps, pages 26, 46, 56 and 66.

NIMES
MILES FROM
172

LYONS : start from the Perrache station. The train after passing Oullins and Irigny arrives at Vernaison, 9 m. from Lyons, pop. 1400, with manufactories of pocket-handkerchiefs, and a large castle converted into a school. 4 m. farther is **Givors-canal**, where the Nîmes line separates from the line to St. Etienne, 29 m. W. The canal of Givors, commenced in 1761, is 13 m. long, and is used chiefly by the coal barges. Near Tartaras it traverses a tunnel 118 yards long. The train now proceeds to Loire, 16½ m. S. from Lyons, pop. 1400, famous for chestnuts, and then 8 m. farther down the Rhône to **Ampuis** (opposite Vaugris), pop. 2000, H. du Nord, producing apricots, melons, and chestnuts, and possessing 94 acres of the Côte-Rotie vineyards, of which 46 acres belong to the first class, yielding one of the best wines of France, remarkable for its fine colour, flavour, and violet perfume. It is a little heady, and gains much by a voyage. 3 m. farther south by rail is Condrieu, with 87 acres of vineyards, producing luscious white wines, becoming amber-coloured. 31 m. S. from Lyons is Chavanay, pop. 1800, with old castle and suspension bridge. *Inns:* H. Commerce ; Soleil ; omnibus at station. 4 m. from Chavanay by coach is Pelussin, pop. 4000. Romanesque church with crypt and ruins of Virieux castle. 7 m. farther is Serrieres, pop. 1700. Railway viaduct of 66 arches.

39¼
PEYRAUD, pop. 400. Junction with line to Annonay, 9 m. 132¾ W., and to Grenoble, 60 m. E. by Rives and Voreppe. **Annonay**, pop. 16,500, built in the hollow and on the sides of the surrounding mountains, at the confluence of the Déôme and the Cance. *Inn :* H. Midi, in the principal square, occupying the centre of the low town. The ruins of the old castle are on a rock by the side of the Cance. The Hôtel de Ville is on a hill beyond. The spot from which the brothers Joseph and Etienne Montgolfier made the first air-balloon ascent, 3d June 1783, is indicated by a pyramid. They were also the founders of one of the celebrated paper mills of Annonay ; whose paper was long esteemed the best in France. 27 m. N.W. from Annonay by coach, traversing a beautiful mountain-road, is St. Etienne. From Annonay the road ascends 9¾ m. to Bourg-Argental, pop. 3600. *Inn :* France. Bourg, as the inhabitants call it, is a silk-rearing and manufacturing town, on the Déôme, in a hollow surrounded by mountains

G

covered with vines and mulberry trees. 2 m. farther the road passes
the castle of Argental, and shortly after reaches its culminating point
on a vast tableland to the south of Mont Pilat. The country around
is covered with a great forest of firs. The obelisks along the road are
to guide travellers when snow is on the ground. The road now crosses
the plateau called La République, bounded, by the Bois de Merlon,
and then descends to St. Etienne by Planfoy, 5 m. from St. Etienne,
and La Rivière 2 m. 17½ m. by rail from Annonay is Tournon.

56½ m. S. from Lyons, 115½ N. from Nîmes, and opposite Tain,
with which it is connected by two suspension bridges, is **Tournon**,
pop. 6100, on the Rhône. Hôtel de l'Assurance between the bridges,
and opposite the landing-place from the Lyons and Avignon steamers.
Fishers can easily reach from Tournon many of the tributaries of the
Rhône. Next the hotel is the castle of the Counts of Tournon, now
the Palais de Justice. Beyond it is the church of St. Julien, built in
1300. The interior is on lofty early pointed arches. Wine, silk, and
olives supply the principal industries. Coach daily to Le Cheilard,
5½ hrs., ascending all the way (see p. 83). Coaches also to St.
Félicien, 3 hrs. W. ; to St. Agrève, 9¼ hrs. W. ; and to St. Martin de
Valamas, 7½ hrs. W. 3 m. N. from Tournon is Vion, with a beautiful
church. (See map, p. 46.)

^{65¼}
⤳ SAINT PERAY, pop. 3000. *Inn :* H. du Nord. Omnibus ^{106¼}⤳
at station. Also omnibus for Valence. An uninteresting village about
ten minutes from the station, situated on the sunny side of the valley
of the Merdary. The vineyards here produce an excellent sparkling
wine, the taste of which is natural, not given to it by the addition of
prepared cordials, as is the case with the other champagnes.

69 m. from Lyons is Soyons, pop. 900, under an eminence crowned
by the Tour Maudite, an old fortress. 77 yards above the village is
a cave, La Grotte de Néron, in which prehistoric remains have been
found. 2½ m. farther is Charmes, pop. 1000, and other 3 m. Beauchastel, pop. 1000, 2 m. from St. Laurent du Pape. (Map, p. 46.)

⁷⁷
⤳ LA VOULTE, pop. 5000. *Inn :* H. du Musée. Temple Pro- ⁹⁵⤳
testant. Railway and steamboat stations. A dirty and badly-paved
town on the right bank and on the steep sides of a hill rising from the
Rhône. On the summit are the Grande Place, the parish church, and
the castle, commenced by Bernard Anduze in 1305, and finished by
Gilbert III. de Ventadour in 1582, who also built the chapel. The
castle is now inhabited by workmen, and the chapel is a magazine.
By the side of the castle is a large iron-foundry, employing 170 men.

The ores come from rich mines a little way up the valley, near the decayed mineral water establishment of Celles-les-Bains. *Inn:* H. Chalvet, 2 m. down the Rhône, but behind the hills. The water contains iron with a little free carbonic acid gas. Coach daily from La Voulte to Le Cheilard (or Cheylard), 30 m. N.W., 6 hrs., and to St. Pierreville, 24 m. W., 5 hrs. The road to the two places separates at St. Sauveur, 8½ m. E. from St. Pierreville, and 15 m. S.E. from Le Cheilard. (See map, p. 46.) St. Sauveur, pop. 2000. *Inns:* Poste; Voyageur. Is prettily situated on the Erieux, which descends from Le Cheilard, between high rocky banks cultivated to the summit by a series of laboriously walled terraces, on which are small fields of wheat intermingled with walnut, chestnut, apple, pear, and cherry trees, and in the more favoured spots vines and peach and mulberry trees. The road skirts the cliffs, and is itself terraced the greater part of the way. A few miles up the river, opposite the village Chalançon, *Inn:* H. Astier, is a very good specimen of an old donkey-backed bridge, Le Cheilard, 2130 ft. above the sea, pop. 3500. *Inn:* H. Courtial. This, the great diligence centre of Ardèche, is a dingy, dirty town, with narrow streets, beautifully situated on the Evreux, in a hollow between lofty terraced mountains. Coaches daily to Valence, La Voulte, and Tournon. Every other day to Annonay by the same road as the Tournon coach as far as a little beyond Mastre, 1280 ft. above the sea, whence it diverges northward. Coach daily also to Le Puy, 36 m. N.W., by St. Martin-de-Valamas, pop. 2200, at the confluence of the Eysse and the Erieux and Fay-le-Froid, 22 m. E. from Le Puy, near the river Lignon, pop. 900. (Map, page 46.)

ROAD TO THE SOURCE OF THE LOIRE.

Saint Sauveur to Le Beage by St. Pierreville, Marcols, Mezillac, and Lachamp-Raphaél (Gerbier-de-Joncs). The road from St. Sauveur to St. Pierreville ascends the Gluyère or Glaire in much the same way as the road to Le Cheilard ascends the Erieux. St. Pierreville, 1788 ft. above the sea, pop. 2100. *Inns:* Rochier; Commerce. Temple Protestant. On an eminence rising from the Gluyère. At St. Pierreville passengers for Marcols enter a smaller vehicle. The whole way the road follows the course of the Gluyère, between great granite cliffs. 2 m. before reaching Marcols is the clean little village of **Olbon**, on both sides of the Gluyère, with a nice inn, the H. des Voyageurs, and a Temple Protestant. A little farther by the side of the stream is a spring of mineral water containing iron and carbonic acid gas.

6 m. W. from St. Pierreville is **Marcols**, 3380 ft. above the sea, a small village with three silk mills, on an eminence rising from the Gluyère. *Inn:* H. de l'Union. This is the terminus of the stagecoaches, for the other places westwards vehicles must be hired. As conveyances cannot always be had at Marcols, the most prudent plan for those going on to Le Beage, and not disposed to walk the distance, is to spend the night at St. Pierreville, and to start early next morning in a vehicle hired from the "Bureau des Diligences," 15 frs. per day,

with one horse. Gig from Marcols to Lachamp-Raphaél, 11 frs. Le
Beage is 28¼ m. N.W. from St. Pierreville, passing through Marcols
6 m., Mezillac 11¾ m., and Lachamp-Raphaél 16 m.

The road from Marcols to Mezillac, 2¼ hrs., coils up the sides of
steep terraced mountains. Near the summit of one, in a very exposed
situation, is the small hamlet of Mezillac, consisting of low massive stone
cottages, and a modern church built in the style of the former one,
10th cent. Refreshments can be had at the Bureau de Tabac. A little
farther down is the inn. At Mezillac the road from Le Cheilard to
Aubenas intersects the road from Mezillac to Le Beage. Thus far the
prevailing rock has been granite, but about ½ m. from Mezillac the
road skirts the face of a mountain one mass of basaltic prisms.

4½ m. W. from Mezillac is the hamlet of Lachamp-Raphaél, 4364
ft. above the sea. Most of the better cottages take in travellers, where
generally abundance of good milk, butter, eggs, coffee, and potatoes
may be had, with a bed. There are no trees in this region. About 1
hour from Lachamp by a bad road is the cascade du Ray-Pic, which
plunges down into a dark abyss. Any lad can show the way.

THE GERBIER-DE-JONCS AND MONT MEZENC.

2 m. beyond Lachamp-Raphaél, just under the culminating point
of the road (4600 ft. above the sea), is a farmhouse called La Maison
Bourlatié, and near it a flattened peak. Just beyond this Maison
Bourlatié a road diverges to the right (eastward) from the main road,
which take for the Gerbier-de-Joncs, the top of which is distinctly
seen after having proceeded a short way, and is hardly an hour's easy
walking from Bourlatié. It is a most interesting and easy excursion.
The Gerbier-de-Joncs (*Gerbiarum jugum*) is an isolated pointed cone,
composed of masses and fragments of trachyte, rising 325 ft. above the
tableland, 5125 ft. above the sea, and commanding a wide and extensive view. At the base, south side, from under a block of trachyte
and some loose stones, wells gently forth the infant Loire, running
first into a little circular basin for the use of the adjoining farmhouse,
whence it runs down the bank in a tiny streamlet from 3 to 4 inches
wide, but soon becomes sufficiently powerful to turn the wheel of a
mill. The continuation of the road from the Gerbier goes to Les
Etables, 22 m. S.E. from Le Puy, at the foot of Mount Mezenc, 5755
ft. above the sea. Now go on to Le Beage, or return for the night to
Lachamp, 22½ m. N. from Aubenas by Antraigues.

Lachamp-Raphaél to Le Beage, 12½ m. W. Char-à-banc, 10
frs. The road, which has been ascending all the way from Valence and
La Voulte, continues to ascend till about 1¾ m. beyond Lachamp,
where it attains its culminating point, about 4600 ft. A little farther
the road to the Gerbier diverges to the right. Less than 2 m. from this
the road crosses the Loire, and soon after is joined by the road from
the village of St. Eulalie on the way to Montpezat.

Le Beage, pop. 850. *Inns:* La Maison Brun; H. des Voyageurs. A
dirty cattle and swine breeding village, 4122 ft. above the sea, beauti-

IRE

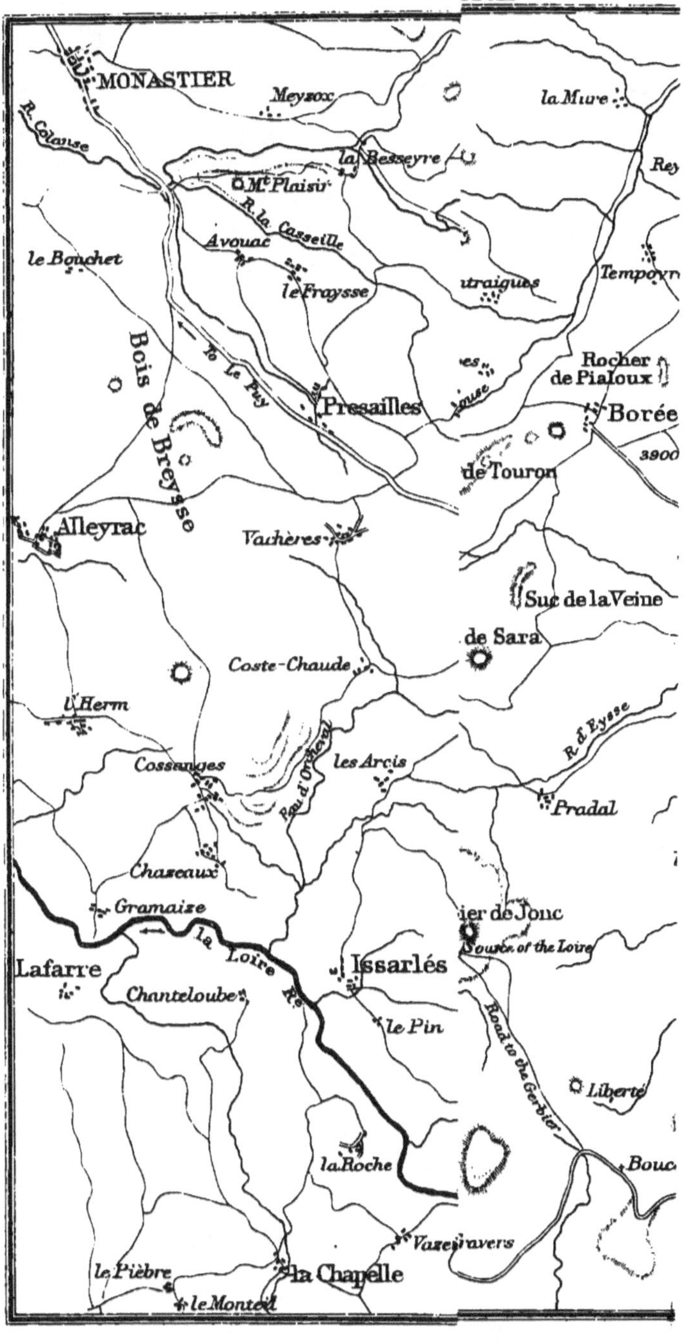
MONASTIER
Meyzoc
la Mure
R. Colanse
la Besseyre
Rey
Mt. Plaisir
R. la Casseille
Avouac
le Bouchet
le Fraysse
utraigues
Tempoyr
Rocher de Pialoux
To Le Puy
Bois de Breysse
Presailles
Borée
3900
de Touron
Alleyrac
Vachères
Suc de la Veine
de Sara
Coste-Chaude
l'Herm
R. d'Eysse
Cossanges
les Arcis
Rau d'Orcheral
Pradal
Chazeaux
Gramaize
ier de Jonc
Source of the Loire
la Loire Re
Issarlés
Lafarre
Chanteloube
le Pin
Road to the Gerbier
Liberté
la Roche
Bouc
Vazeilles
ravers
le Pièbre
la Chapelle
le Monteil

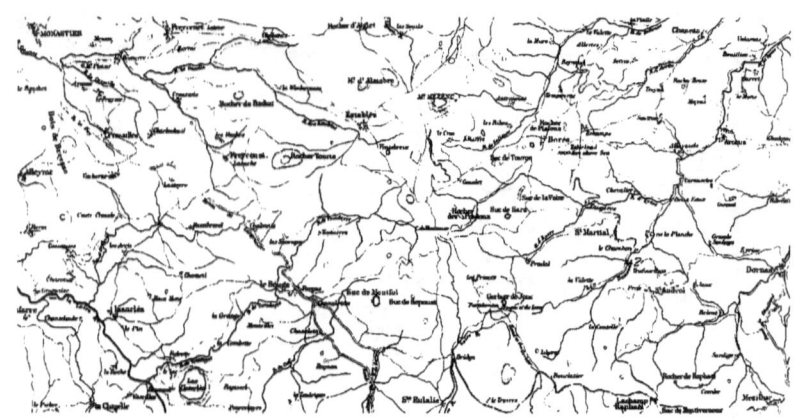

fully situated on an eminence rising from the Veyradère, which rushes past in a dark ravine below. Pasture being the principal crop cultivated, the mountain sides have no terraces. Four great fairs are held annually here. The winter is long and severe, but from June to October the weather is pleasant. The staple occupation of the females is lace-making on a pillow with bobbins. The design is on paper fixed to a short cylinder, and is further indicated by pins with coloured glass heads. The linen thread is given them by the merchants, who pay them at the rate of from 2d. to 4½d. the yard, according to the breadth of the lace, from 2 to 4 inches. A most industrious lacemaker can earn 1 fr. per day. 3¼ m. S.W. from Le Beage in an extinct crater is the lake Issarlès, occupying a surface of 222 acres.

From Le Beage the trachytic mountain of **Mezenc** (pronounce Mezing) is visited. But the best plan is to go on to Les Etables, 4410 ft. above the sea, 7½ m. N. from Le Beage by the wheel road, but only half that distance by the direct path. *Inns:* Testud; Chalamel, where pass the night. The hamlet is situated at the foot of Mont Mezenc, 5755 ft. above the sea, or 1345 ft. above Les Etables, and 866 ft. above the hamlet of Mezenc. The ascent takes about an hour.

LE BEAGE TO LE PUY.

Le Beage is 12 m. S.E. from Monastier, passing through Chabanis. On the opposite side of the river are seen Freycenet, 3905 ft. above the sea, and Crouziols, 4½ m. S. from Monastier. Char-à-banc between Le Beage and Monastier, 10 frs.

LE MONASTIER, pop. 4000, on an eminence rising from the Colanse. *Inns:* Commerce; Voyageurs. Coach daily to Le Puy, 11 m. N.W. 10¼ m. S. is Salettes, and 22 m. S. St. Paul de Tartas, 3393 ft. above the sea, at the foot of Mont Tartas, 4424 ft. St. Paul is near Pradelles, connected by diligence with Le Puy and Langogne. The parish church, St. Théofrède, of Le Monastier was, along with the abbey, founded in 680, and rebuilt in 961 by Ufald, 10th abbot of Monastier, and repaired and enlarged in 1493 by Estaing, the 45th abbot. The edifice exhibits throughout the Auvergne style of architecture. The portal consists of a semicircular arch with 6 mouldings resting on four short columns with sculptured capitals. Above the tympanum and also over the large rectangular window are rude mosaics. Under the eaves of the roof runs a string moulding of grotesque sculpture, representing men and animals. In the interior the capitals of the columns and the corbels on the vaulting shafts are similarly adorned. In the apse is the chapel of Saint Théofrède, with sculptured stone roof. He is the "protecteur du Monastier"—"le bon pasteur, qui s'expose a la mort pour son troupeau"—the "conservateur des fruits de la terre." (See his litany.)

11¼ m. N. from Le Monastier by diligence along a beautiful mountain-road is Le Puy. The bureau at Le Puy of both the diligence and the courier is at No. 1 Rue du Pont-St. Barthélémy near the large "Place" and the hotels. About half-way from Le Monastier is the village of Arsac, *Inn:* H. des Voyageurs, and about 1 m. more, on an eminence, the village and the still imposing remains of the fortress of Bouzols, 10th cent.   Shortly after having crossed the Loire at the town of Brives, the diligence enters Le Puy, 2 m. from Brives.

36 m. S.W. by rail from St. Etienne, 89½ m. from Lyons, and 33 m. S.E. from St. George d'Aurac junction, on the line between Clermont and Nîmes (see maps, pp. 26 and 46), is

Le Puy,

pop. 20,000, from 2000 to 2250 ft. above the sea, between the rivers Borne and Dolezon, affluents of the Loire, 2 m. from the town.   *Hotels :* Ambassadeurs ; Europe ; Nord.   To visit Le Puy, the best plan is to begin with the Cathedral.   From the high side of the Place de Breuil, at the N.W. corner, ascend by the streets St. Gilles, Chenebouterie, and Raphaël, to the Place des Tables, with a stone pinnacle fountain in the centre.   From this ascend by the R. des Tables to the flight of 40 steps, leading up to the tetrastyle portico in front of the church. Forty-one more steps lead up through this portico to the portal of the west façade of the church, built up in the 18th cent., and having against it an altar to Mary.   The oblong flat stone at the base of the table of the altar belonged to a dolmen which stood on this hill from the earliest times, and is called the "Pierre aux fièvres," from its once supposed power of curing of fever those who lay upon it.

From this altar a flight of 27 steps ascends to the left, to the cloisters, while the flight to the right of 32 steps ascends to one of the two south side entrances into the church.   The other south side entrance, called the Porte du Fort, 12th cent., presents an extraordinary composition of the florid Byzantine style.   On one side of it is the square belfry in 5 stages, commenced in the 11th cent., on the other is the bishop's palace, and in front a small terrace.   At the north side of the church is the Porte St. Jean, 12th cent., preceded by an arch of 28 ft. span.   The cloisters are in the form of an oblong square, with 9 arches on the long sides, and five on the short, supported on square piers with attached colonnettes.   The south side is the earliest, beginning of the 10th cent., and the western the most recent.   The church, built in 550, received a succession of alterations up to 1427, when it was injured by an earthquake.   In 1846 it was repaired and restored.   The interior consists of eight square compartments, each, excepting the 7th, covered with a dome resting on four massive piers. Above the 7th rises an octagonal lantern tower.   Under it is the high altar, with a replica of the miracle-working image,[1] brought from Cairo in 1251, and presented to the church of Le Puy by Saint Louis in 1254, but destroyed in the Revolution of 1793, when, according to the marble tablet on the pier of this compartment, 20 priests of the diocese were

---

[1] The original image was of cedar, with the face, both of it and of the child, painted black.   It was 2 ft. 3 in. high, and weighed 25 lbs.   The form was rudely carved, stiff and Egyptian like, and the members of both were swathed in two plies of linen.

executed at the same time by the same party. On the south wall a large picture represents a numerous concourse of church and civic dignitaries carrying in procession the original image to make it stay the plague, which raged in Le Puy in 1660. The picture opposite represents the Consuls of Le Puy, attired in red, thanking the image for its protection. In the sacristy is the Théodulfe Bible, 9th cent. Near the north portal is the baptistery of St. Jean, built in the 4th cent. on the foundations of a Roman edifice.

From Saint Jean commences the ascent of the Rocher Corneille, a mass of volcanic breccia, which forms the summit of Mount Podium. On the top is the image of Notre Dame de France, 433 ft. above the Hôtel de Ville, and 2478 ft. above the sea. It was unveiled on the 27th September 1860, was made from 213 cannons taken at Sebastopol, is 52½ ft. high, and weighs 2165 cwt. The foot is 6 ft. long, the hands 5 ft., and the hair 22 ft. The circumference of the head of the child, J. C., is 14 ft. In the interior of the image a spiral stair of 90 steps leads up to the shoulders, whence an iron ladder of 16 steps extends to the crown of her head. From little openings in this colossal figure are most enchanting views. From the orifice in her right side is seen (2½ m. N.W.) the village of Polignac, likewise on a hill 2645 ft. above the sea, clustering round its old castle. Immediately below is the Aiguilhe, and to the left, 1¼ m. S.E., Ours Mons.

On a projecting part of the rock is, in a kneeling posture, looking up to Notre Dame de France, the figure of Bishop Morlhon, b. 1799, d. 1861, one of the principal promoters of the statue. Bonnassieux is the sculptor of both of them.

Behind the Rocher Corneille rises the isolated volcanic rock called the Aiguilhe, 265 ft. high, 518 ft. in circumference at the base, 45 at the top, and ascended by 266 steps. Fee, 5 sous. On the summit is the chapel of St. Michael, commenced in 962 by Bishop Godescalk, and consecrated in 984. The present building dates principally from the end of the 11th and the beginning of the 12th cent. ; restored and repaired in 1850. Originally the interior of it as well as of the cathedral was covered with mural paintings. The views are superb.

Near the foot of the rock, and adjoining the Mairie of Aiguilhe, is an octagonal baptistery, 12th cent., called the Temple of Diana. Near the post office, in the Boulevard St. Louis, is the lower part of a tower which belonged to the town gate Pannessac. The church, at a little distance below, is St. Laurent, 14th cent. In the chapel to the left of the high altar is the grave and mausoleum of the chivalrous Duguesclin, who died on the 17th July 1380, while besieging the fortress of Châteauneuf-le-Randon, between Langogne and Mende.

In a large new building in the public garden off the Place de Breuil is the Musée, open on Sundays and feast days from 2 to 5. Everything is distinctly labelled. On the ground-floor in the hall to the left are architectural relics from Roman buildings in and about Le Puy. The best fragments belonged to the temple which stood on the site now occupied by the baptistery of Saint Jean. In the hall to the right is a miscellaneous collection of Egyptian, Celtic, and Roman antiquities, mixed up with a few articles belonging to the Middle Ages.

Upstairs is the Picture Gallery. In the centre room are portraits of the most celebrated natives of Le Puy, and a very good copy of part of the "Danse Macabre," dance of death, in the church of Chaise-Dieu. Among the portraits are Charles Crozatier, born 1795, died at Paris 1853, the munificent contributor to the museum of this his native town. In the right-hand hall the best paintings, chiefly belonging to the Flemish school, are in the low row, such as Begyer, d. 1664; Caravaggio; Coypel, d. 1707; Franck, d. 1616; Heem, d. 1694; Lippi, d. 1469; Maes, d. 1693; Mieris, 1747; Mierveld, 1641; Poussin, 1695; Rigaud, 1743; Terburg, 1681; Tyr, 1868; Weenix, 1719. In the adjoining small room is a complete collection of the minerals belonging to the Haute-Loire. In the left room among other pictures are: Annunciation, Tintoretto, 1594; Mdlle. de Valois, Mignard, 1695; Mary Stuart, F. Clouet, 1572; Henriette-Marie de France, wife of Charles I. of England, Van der Werf, 1722; Landscape, Hobbema, 1669; Concert, Teniers (vieux); Portrait of Girl, J. B. Santerre, 1717. In the next room are specimens of the lace, blond and guipure, worked by the females inhabiting the towns and villages among the mountains of Ardèche and the Haute-Loire, of which articles Le Puy is the great emporium. The specimens and sample books are in cases. In the centre case are specimens from Alençon, Binche, Brussels, Cevennes mountains, Malines, Russia, Valenciennes, and Venice; the Corsage with lace trimming of the gown Marie Louise wore on the day she was married to Napoleon I.; also some of her ribbons.

1¼ m. S.E. from Le Puy is **Ours Mons**, 2463 ft. above the sea, and 180 ft. above the plain. The prospect from the top is considered by Mr. Scrope most remarkable; "exhibiting in one view a vast theatre of volcanic formation, in great variety of aspect, containing igneous products of various natures, belonging to different epochs."

LE PUY TO LANGOGNE BY PRADELLES. (Map, p. 46.)

Le Puy, 2045 ft., to Langogne, 2940 ft. above the sea, 26 m. S. by coach, along an admirably-constructed road, over a high, cold, treeless tableland, whose culminating point, 3900 ft., is about a mile south from the hamlet of La Sauvetat, 6 m. N. from Pradelles. 8 m. from Le Puy is Montagnac, on the Cagne, 3123 ft. From this hamlet a road diverges 8 m. S.W. to Cayres, 3727 ft. above the sea, pop. 1450. *Inn:* Du-Lac-du-Bouchet. A lace and cheese-making village, about 1½ m. by a good road from the extinct crater of Le Bouchet, 231 ft. higher than Cayres, now a lake of 222 acres and 92 ft. deep. It is very similar to Lake Issarlès, near Beage (which see p. 85). After Montagnac the coach arrives at Costaros, 3510 ft., 12 m. S., where the horses are changed. Then Sauvetat, 16 m. from Le Puy, pop. 300, and afterwards Pradelles, 3771 ft., pop. 2000, with two small inns, 21 m. from Le Puy and 5 m. from Langogne. The coach stops at Langogne railway station, where the omnibus of the Cheval Blanc

awaits passengers.   Pradelles is 24½ m. S. from Le Monastier by St.
Paul-de-Tartas, and 2½ m. from Les Sallettes (see map, p. 46).

Pradelles to Mayres, 18 m. S.E., char-à-banc, 20 to 25 frs., by
a good but a high and exposed road, passing Peyrebelle (p. 95), La
Narce, 8¾ m., pop. 900, the Col Chavade, 4170 ft. above the sea, near
the source of the Ardèche, whence the road descends rapidly, passing
above the hamlet of Astet.   This is not a good entrance into Ardèche.

From Le Puy a coach starts daily from near the post office for St.
Bonnet, Usson, and Craponne, pop. 4000, directly N. from Le Puy,
and 12½ m. E. from Chaise-Dieu by stage-coach.

LE PUY TO LANGEAC BY ST. GEORGES. (Map, p. 46.)

For geological excursions the railway between Le Puy to Langeac
by St. Georges d'Aurac is very useful.   The culminating point of the
line, 3658 ft., is in the tunnel between Darsac and Fix-St. Geneys.
This railway crosses at right angles the Velay mountains, full of
extinct volcanoes, extending from Chaise-Dieu to Pradelles.

Le Puy to Langeac, 36½ m. W. by rail.   The first part of the
line traverses a most picturesque country among great basaltic cliffs.
1 m. from Le Puy the train passes the village of Espaly, and by the
face of basaltic columns rising from the Borne and its little affluent
the Riou-Pézeliou, in whose bed zircons and blue sapphires have been
found.   On the opposite side of the Borne is the great mass of basalt
called the Croix de la Paille, with a display of prisms in three tiers,
called les orgues d'Espaly.   The village, pop. 2300, is built at the foot
of a rock of volcanic breccia crowned by the scanty ruins of a castle
built in 1260 by Guillaume de la Roue, bishop of Puy.

8¾ m. from Puy is **Borne**, 2535 ft. above the sea, pop. 390.   A
ramble in the ravine of Borne forms a pleasant and easy excursion
from Le Puy.   5½ m. E. from this station, or 3½ m. W. from Le Puy,
is Polignac, passed by the train.   The village, pop. 2500, with church
of 11th cent., is at the foot of a rock of basaltic breccia crowned by the
imposing ruins of a fortress dating from the 11th cent.   A stair of 132
steps (ascent dangerous) leads up to the terrace of the Keep, 14th
cent., commanding an extensive view.

13 m. W. from Le Puy is **Darsac**, 2914 ft. above the sea.   A small
hamlet, with a restaurant, the **station for Chaise-Dieu**, 13¾ m. N.,
fare 2½ frs., and for Arlanc, 24¼ m. N., or 10½ m. beyond Chaise-Dieu.

The coach first passes through Allègre, pop. 1700, a dirty little
village, 5 m. N., on the side of Mont de Bar, 3583 ft. above the sea,
with the ruins of a castle built in the 14th cent.   Mont de Bar and
Mont du Bouchet are the best specimens of extinct volcanoes in the
Velay chain.   From this the diligence, after having skirted for 8 m.
the high cold region of the Velay mountains, arrives at **La Chaise-
Dieu**, 3576 ft. above the sea, pop. 2000.   *Inns:* Lion d'Or; Centre;
Nord.   A dirty, decaying village, in which its imposing church par-
ticipates.   Robert, a scion of the ducal house of Aurillac, and canon
of St. Julien in Brioude, obtained permission from the canons of N.

D. du Puy to build a small house and oratory in the wildest and most inaccessible part of the forests on their domains, where he and his companions might lead a more austere life than in their monastery at Brioude. This house, built in 1043, by degrees attained the goodly proportions of a convent, which the peasants called La Chaise-Dieu, or Casa-Dei. Clement VI., formerly Roger de Beaufort, abbot of Chaise-Dieu, born in the village, commenced, shortly after his elevation to the papal throne, to build at his own expense a church on the site formerly occupied by the oratory of St. Robert. The work was continued and finished by his nephew, Gregory XI., in 1420, by whom are the façade with the two short massive square towers, 128 ft. high, and the horse-shoe staircase of 41 steps. The tower, 30 ft. square and 110 high, attached to the S. point of the apse, was built by the abbot de Chanac to protect the church and convent, which he surrounded with a wall. The gateway, part of the wall, and part of the old convent, are just under the tower. Adjoining the remains of the abbey buildings are the cloisters, a parallelogram, 140 ft. by 77, of which only two sides remain. The long side has nine low, wide, massive, mullioned and traceried unglazed windows, and the short side four.

The interior of the church is 301 ft. long, surrounded by 22 tall plain slender octagonal piers, from which springs the groining, which spreads itself over the stone-vaulted roof. The nave is 44 ft. wide, and the aisle on each side 15, all the three roofs being of the same height. The church is lighted by long narrow pointed windows, one between each two columns, excepting at the apsidal termination, where a triangular projection affords space for three windows. The tracery has little depth, and is of the simplest design. The choir, 131 ft. long, is separated from the nave by an ugly rood-loft. It contains 144 carved cedar-wood stalls, and above them on both sides 17 pieces of Arras tapestry, 16th cent., from designs by Taddeo Gaddi. In the centre is the mausoleum of Clement VI. His white marble effigy, with the hands folded and the papal Triregnum on the head, reclines on an altar table of black marble.

On the N. side of the screen of the choir, just behind the pulpit, is the "Danse Macabre," or dance of death, a favourite subject with artists from the 12th to the 14th cent. The ironic grin and jocund gait of the skeleton death contrast vividly with the dismayed and demure expression of the great and mighty kings, priests, and warriors, young and old, gay and sedate, he marshals off, in the midst of their projects and plans, to the dark silent grave. Under it is the sadly mutilated mausoleum of Queen Edith of England, wife of the unfortunate Harold. Near it is the more perfect mausoleum of the last abbot of La Chaise-Dieu.

La Chaise-Dieu to Vichy by Arlanc and Ambert.

10½ m. N. by coach from La Chaise-Dieu, 24¼ m. N. from Darsac, and 11¼ m. S. from Ambert-du-Puy, by a beautiful road, is **Arlanc**, pop. 4500, *Inn :* H. des Princes, between the rivers Dore and Dolore,

AMBERT. FIX-ST. GENEYS. ST. GEORGES-D'AURAC. MONISTROL.

consisting of the Bourg with the parish church and the Ville, composed mostly of old houses. A great deal of lace and blond is made here. 11¼ m. N. is the manufacturing town of Ambert, pop. 8000, 43 m. N. by rail from Vichy; whence the ascent is made, 3 hrs., of the culminating point of the Forez mountains, the Pierre-sur-Haute, 3882 ft. above the sea. 15 m. from Ambert, and 11¾ m. S. from Thiers, is Olliergues, pop. 2000, on a hill rising from the Dore. It contains an old bridge, some 13th cent. houses, and the ruins of a castle which belonged to the family of the Tour d'Auvergne. 13 m. farther N., or 8¾ m. S. from Thiers, is Courpière, pop. 4000, on the Dore, with some old houses and the ruins of the castle of Courte-Serre. 61 m. N. from Darsac, or 36¾ m. N. from Ambert, is Thiers, south from Vichy. For Vichy see p. 358 ; Thiers, p. 367.

The next station west from Darsac by rail (see map, p. 46) is Fix-St. Geneys, 18 m. from Le Puy, 3274 ft. above the sea, pop. 900. *Inn :* H. des Voyageurs, situated on a tableland above the valley of the Sioule, covered on one side with firs. 2¼ m. farther is the station for the hamlet La Chaud, 2950 ft. above the sea, on the Sioule. 7½ m. farther is Rougeac, with a castle 1923 ft. above the sea.

The most westerly station on the line is St. Georges d'Aurac, 1872 ft. above the sea, 86¼ m. W. from St. Etienne, and 32 from Le Puy. 58½ m. N. by rail is Clermont, and 131 m. S. by rail is Nîmes (see map, p. 26). Near the station is the inn Lombardin. The village, pop. 500, is 2 m. S.E. Other 2 m. E. is the château Chavagnac, the birthplace of General Lafayette. 5½ m. W. is Voute-Chilhac, pop. 800, most picturesquely situated on a narrow peninsula formed by the Allier, opposite the mouth of the Avesne. The church was built in the 15th cent. by Jean de Bourbon, bishop of Le Puy. Passengers going north change carriages at the station of St. Georges d'Aurac. 4½ m. S.W. from St. Georges, 90½ W. from St. Etienne, and 36½ from Le Puy, is Langeac, 1690 ft., 63 m. S. from Clermont, and 127 m. N. from Nîmes. All the trains halt here. *Inns :* H. Lombardin ; Pascon. Their omnibuses await passengers. Langeac, on the Allier, is a pleasant town near the station, situated in a vast plain. The parish church dates from the 15th cent. To the N.E. of the town, in the valley of Morange, is a coal-basin of 1450 acres. (Map, page 46.)

15 m. S. from Langeac is Monistrol-d'Allier, 2000 ft. above the sea, pop. 1200. The station is on the E. side, and the town on the W. side of the river. Coach by a picturesque road to Le Puy, 17 m. N.E. by St. Privat, 2930 ft., pop. 1600, on the stream Rouchoux, which runs in a deep gully between high cliffs. A little way beyond the hamlet of Chiers the road attains its culminating point, 3739 ft. above the sea. 10 m. from Monistrol is Bains, 3235 ft., pop. 1300, with a very old church. 1¼ m. farther the road passes the picturesque rock of Cordes, 3012 ft., and then descends to Le Puy by La Roche, 2895 ft., and Mont Bonzon. Coach from Monistrol to Saugues, 6½ m. W., 3116 ft., pop. 4000, on the side of a hill, rising from the beautiful valley of the Margeride. In the neighbourhood is a monu-

ment called the tomb of the "English general." It consists of a
square vaulted roof of small stones resting on four round columns 13
ft. high and 6⅜ ft. apart. It has no inscription, and bears a resemblance to the mortuary chapel at Valence (see p. 44).

81   **91**
⌒ LE POUZIN, pop. 3000, *Inn:* H. Lion d'Or, on the Ouvèze, ⌒
which here enters the Rhône. The town has foundries and the remains
of its old castle. Junction with line to Privas, 13¼ m. W. **Privas,**
pop. 8000. *Inns:* Croix d'Or ; Louvre. On an eminence 1060 ft. above
the sea, at the foot of Mt. Toulon, 838 ft. higher, and at the confluence of the Chazalon, the Mezayon, and the Ouvèze. The town, looking
well from a distance, consists chiefly of narrow, crooked, steep streets,
and dingy houses. From the promenade called the Esplanade, planted
with plane trees, is an excellent view of the picturesque valley of the
Ouvèze, and of the volcanic chain of the Coiron, especially of Mount
Combier. 1¼ m. from Privas, on the plain of the Lai, is a house called
the Logis du Roi, in which Louis XIII. established his headquarters
in 1629, when, with Cardinal Richelieu, he besieged the Protestant
inhabitants in the town, commanded by the brave Montbrun.

From Privas, coach daily, 11 m. N. to Ollières, on the Eyrieux.
Inn: H. du Pont, comfortable. This coach meets at Ollières the
coaches to La Voulte and Valence on the Rhône, and the coaches to
Le Cheilard and to St. Pierreville. The latter is the coach to take
for the Source of the Loire and Mont Mezenc (see pp. 84, 85). Coach
also to Aubenas, 18 m. S.E. (See next page, and map p. 46.)

98   **74**
⌒ ROCHEMAURE, pop. 1300, Auberge Gabarre. Suspension ⌒
bridge across the Rhône. The modern part of the village is built
along the high road, but the old on the steep slopes of the basalt
rocks crowned by the ruins of the castle. There are many ways up
to the top ; the best and most frequented commences just opposite
the "auberge," traverses the centre of the curious old stony village,
passes on the right the chapel with the arms of Ventadour and Soubise
on the portal, then ascends by the battlemented wall to some miserable habitations, among what was the seigneurial manor, of which
large portions still remain. Next to it, on a needle-like peak of nearly
horizontal columns of basalt, rises the Keep, like a spear piercing the
sky. A narrow path leading so far up will be found round the N.W.
corner. The views are superb, of the valley of the Rhône on one side,
and on the other of the Coiron mountains. These ruins, which from
below look slim and airy, are the remains of a massive edifice constructed principally of basaltic prisms in the 12th cent. by the family
of Adhémar de Montheil, and reduced to its present condition by order
of Louis XIII.

A road up the gap on the N. side of the hill leads in a little more than an hour to Mount Chenavari, 1668 ft., distinctly seen from the top of the gap. On the summit is a tableland bordered with massive basaltic columns. At Rochemaure the olive trees begin to appear.

$\frac{95\frac{3}{4}}{}$ LE TEIL, pop. 3200, with some small inns. Omnibus awaits $\frac{76\frac{1}{4}}{}$ passengers for Montelimart, 3¼ m. E., on the other side of the Rhône (p. 48). Branch line to Alais, 62¼ m. S.W., on the line between Nimes and Clermont-Ferrand. From Vogué, on this branch, 17½ m. S.W. from Le Teil, and 44¾ m. N.E. from Alais, a smaller branch extends 12 m. N. to Nieigles-Prades. The Nieigles-Prades line forms a convenient entrance into Ardèche (see maps, pages 26, 46, and 56).

Vogué, Aubenas, Vals, Neyrac, Thueyts, Mayres.

5 m. W. from Teil, on the branch line to Alais, is Aubignas (Alba Augusta), pop. 530, once an important Roman station. 6¼ m. N. from Vogué is Aubenas, pop. 8000, *Inn:* H. Durand, on a hill covered with vines, olives, and mulberry trees, rising 328 ft. above the Ardèche, and commanding an extensive view of the valley of the river. On the highest part of the town are the church and the fine old castle, now containing the college, the hospital, and some other public institutions. Aubenas is the centre of an important trade in raw silk, butter, and cheese. At Vesseaux, a village to the north of Aubenas, excellent chestnuts are grown. (Maps, pages 56 and 46.)

3¼ m. N. from Aubenas is La Begude, the station for Vals. Omnibus awaits passengers. VALS, pop. 4000, on the Volane, famous for its **Mineral Waters.** *Hotels:* Des Bains, on an eminence above the bathing establishment and the gardens. In the same neighbourhood are the Hotels Parc ; Juliette ; Délicieuse ; Lyon ; Orient. All the important springs are also in this part. In the town are the Hotels Europe ; Durand ; Nord ; Poste. The Pension in the Hôtel des Bains is from 12 to 15 frs., in the others from 9 to 10 frs. Season from 1st May to October. Vals is prettily situated on the Volane, in a hollow among hills covered with vineyards and studded with mulberry and chestnut trees. The springs, gardens, baths, and best hotels are all at the eastern extremity. Near the H. du Parc is the intermittent fountain, and from it, across the bridge, are the springs Vivaraises, under a grotto ; and, adjoining them, the spring Juliette, while a little beyond is La Délicieuse. The springs Madeleine, St. Jean, Précieuse, and the others, belonging to the Société Générale, are all farther up the river, nearer the town, at the second bridge. None of them are so pungent nor so agreeable to the palate as the Juliette and the Délicieuse. The properties of all are much the same. They give tone to the stomach, assist the action of the liver and kidneys, and remove paralysis of the bladder. They are all cold, easily digested, and may be drunk at any time. They contain bicarbonate of soda, lime, and magnesia, lithia, iodine, iron, and some of them traces of the arseniate of soda, and owe their pungency to the free carbonic acid gas.

5 m. N. from Vals, or 9 m. from Aubenas and 16 m. from Privas, is **Antraigues**, pop. 2000, situated on the side of three basaltic rocks, at whose base flow three impetuous mountain torrents—the Bise, Mas, and Volane. From the heights behind the town there is a magnificent view. In the neighbourhood is the extinct crater, the **Coupe d'Aizac**, covered with a beautiful reddish lava. *Inns:* Brousse ; Glaise.

AUBENAS TO LANGOGNE BY MAYRES. (Maps, pp. 56 and 46.)

Coach daily from Aubenas to Mayres, 18 m. W. It passes through Pont-de-la-Baume, 945 ft., and by the eminence on which is **Neyrac-les-Bains**, the Nereisaqua of the Romans. *Inns:* H. des Bains ; H. Fournier. 2½ m. from Pont-de-la-Baume, 7 from Vals, and 9½ from Aubenas. It is situated within the crater of Saint Léger, containing 8 acidulous, alkaline, and chalybeate springs, temp. 81° Fahr. From several fissures issues carbonic acid gas ; from one place, the Trou de la Poule, in sufficient quantity to kill birds and dogs in 2 or 3 minutes. In the neighbourhood is the volcano of Soulhiol. 2 m. W., on the left bank of the Ardèche, at its confluence with the Médéric, is **Thueyts**, pop. 2600, *Inn:* H. Burine, situated on a bed of lava from the crater of Mont Gravenne, 2785 feet above the sea. Through this bed the Ardèche has, in cutting a passage for itself, laid bare a grand display of basaltic columns from 150 to 200 ft. high, extending nearly 2 m. down the valley. To the W. of the Bourg are a bridge with two stages of arches across the Médéric, called the Pont du Diable, and the falls of the Gueule d'Enfer, 330 ft., which, unless in rainy weather, have very little water. From this part commences the Pavé-des-Géants, a tableland composed of granite and basalt of an average height of 214 ft. from the base, lined with vertical prisms. To the right, at the extremity of this wall of rock, is the Echelle du Roi, a staircase of 192 steps of broken prisms, within a natural shaft or chimney, leading up to the top of the tableland, where there is a good view. The best is from Mont Gravenne. The ascent requires about 1 hour.

The diligence now ascends the Ardèche to Mayres. About half-way, near the hamlet of La Mothe, are the cliffs called the Rocher d'Abraham, 4358 ft. above the sea, of which the Bauzon is the continuation.

5½ m. from Thueyts is **Mayres**, pop. 2900. *Inns:* France ; Commerce. 1810 ft. above the sea, at the foot of the Croix de Bauzon, 5055 ft. above the sea, and on the Ardèche, which here flows in a narrow gorge between granite cliffs. The stage-coaches go no farther than Mayres. For Langogne, 22 m. N.W., it is necessary to hire a vehicle. From Mayres the road commences to ascend the Col, passing above the hamlet of Astet at the foot of the Rocher d'Astet, 4925 ft. above the sea.

7 m. from Mayres is the summit of the pass or Col de la Chavade, 4170 ft. above the sea, near the source of the Ardèche. 2½ m. farther is La Narce, pop. 900. A little beyond, or 26 m. from Aubenas and

14 from Langogne, is the roadside inn of Peyrebelle, 4195 ft. above the sea, where for 25 years the landlord and his wife robbed and murdered the travellers that came to their house. Nearly 4 m. N. from Peyrebelle is Coucouron, pop. 1400.

The road now attains the height of 4266 ft., where, on account of the snow and wind, it becomes very dangerous in winter.

35 m. from Aubenas and 5 from Langogne is Pradelles, 3771 ft., 16 m. from Le Puy by coach and 5 from Langogne (see p. 88, and maps, pages 26, 56 and 46).

Prades, Pont-de-la-Baume, Jaujac, Montpezat, St. Eulalie, and Source of the Loire.

For the main loopline, see map p. 56 ; for the rest, map p. 46.

11¾ m. N. from Vogué station and 5½ from Aubenas station is the terminus of this branch line, called Nieigles-Prades, as from it coaches take passengers to both of these towns. Nieigles, pop. 1600, is situated on an eminence rising from the N. side of the Ardèche. In the vicinity are coal-pits and rows of basalt columns supporting terraces covered with chestnut trees. On the south side of the Ardèche, and to the east of Jaujac, is Prades, pop. 1200, on the Salindre, in the centre of an important coal-basin.

Near the railway terminus is the village of Pont-de-la-Baume, pop. 900, *Inns :* H. du Louvre, etc., 955 ft. above the sea, at the confluence of the rivers Fontaulière and Alignon with the Ardèche. One of the best headquarters for visiting the basalt rocks in the neighbourhood, both from its own position and the facility afforded here for going elsewhere, as the coaches for Vals, Mayers, Burzet, Neyrac, Montpezat, and Jaujac pass through it.

3¾ m. from La Baume, or 7½ from Aubenas by coach, is Jaujac, the Jovis aqua of the Romans, pop. 2600. *Inn:* Union. On an eminence above the Alignon, of which nearly the whole of the right bank from Pont-de-la-Baume to Jaujac is lined with countless basaltic prisms. From the town cross the bridge, and at the mill descend to the path by the side of the river, where there is an admirable view of the columns, which, however, are not vertical. About ½ m. from the town is the Coupe de Jaujac, an extinct volcano, which has burst through the coal formation of this valley, bounded by mountains of granite and gneiss. It is ascended easily in 20 minutes. At the foot of the crater, just where the path leading to the top commences, is a gaseous chalybeate spring ; not unlike those of Vals.

14 m. N.W. from Aubenas, or about 8 from Pont-de-la-Baume by diligence, is **Montpezat.** The road from Aubenas ascends by the Ardèche, which it crosses ; La Baume at the foot of the hill, on which are the ruins of the castle of Ventadour, 14th cent. Farther on, within a mile of Montpezat, are seen the ruins of the castle of Pourcheyrolles, built in 1360 on a plateau of prisms 115 ft. high, over which flows the Pourseilles, an affluent of the Fontaulière or Fontollière. Near the

suspension bridge across the Fontaulière is Mt. Gravenne, the best specimen of an extinct volcano in the whole region. The toll-keeper from the bridge can point out the path leading to the top. The bridge is about 10 minutes' walk from Montpezat.

Montpezat-sous-Bauzon, pop. 2600, on an eminence 1877 ft. above the sea, rising from the Ardèche. *Inns:* Europe ; Poste. This is the terminus of the diligences. The river Fontaulière has its source in the crater of Mount La Vestide, the largest in the Vivarais. By the new road La Vestide is 6½ m. N.W. from Montpezat. Coach to the base of the peak and back, 10 frs. The peak is 325 ft. high from the base, but the crater is nearly 900 ft. deep. By the old road, ascending by the village of La Faud, La Vestide is only 4 m. distant.

MONTPEZAT TO LE PUY.

To go from Montpezat to Le Puy, 43 m. N.W., hire vehicle to Le Beage, 16 m. N.W., 20 to 25 frs., and from Le Beage to Le Monastier, 12 m., 10 frs. Diligence between Le Monastier and Le Puy. From Montpezat the road ascends by the hamlet of Le Pal, 3888 ft., opposite the extinct volcano, the Suc du Pal, 724 ft. higher, with 3 cones. North is Lake Ferrand, and still farther north, Lake Bauzon, 4832 ft. above the sea. After the hamlet of Le Pal the road passes the hamlet of Rioutort, crosses the river Padelle, and arrives at the village of Usclades, 9 m. N. from Montpezat, pop. 600, whence a winding road ascends to Le Beage, 6¼ m. N. (see p. 84).

From Montpezat a road extends 13 m. N. to the source of the Loire by Rioutort and Sainte Eulalie. Sainte Eulalie, pop. 650, *Inn:* Faure, in a little valley on the left bank of the Loire, about 2 m. S. from the road between Lachamp-Raphaél and Le Beage. The large peak seen in the distance is the Gerbier-de-Joncs, at the foot of which is the source of the Loire. To go to it, from the main road walk down to the one-arch bridge which crosses the still infant Loire, and walk up the path by the side of the stream (see p. 84, and maps pp. 46 and 85).

Ruoms, Largentière, Vallon, Pont d'Arc.

See map, page 56.

25½ m. S.W. from Teil, 8 m. S.W. from Vogué, and 36½ m. N.E. of Alais, is Ruoms. Station for Largentière, 9 m. N., 1¼ fr. For Joyeuse, 8 m. W., and for Vallon, 6¼ m. S. Largentière, pop. 3000. *Hotels:* Europe ; France. Coaches to Joyeuse, Les Vans, and St. Ambroix. St. Ambroix, pop. 5000, on the Cèze, H. Luxembourg, is a town with silk-mills and glass-works. Near Ambroix is Robiac, station for Besseges, with important coal-fields. Largentière, or properly L'Argentière, situated in the ravine of the Ligne, derives its name from the argentiferous mines in the neighbourhood. On the tableland behind the Palais-de-Justice is the picturesque village of Chassiers, pop. 1300. Joyeuse, pop. 2300. *Inns:* H. Nord ; Europe. Situated with its suburb, Rosières, on the Baume. The town has part

of its ancient ramparts, and the castle which belonged to the Sires de
Joyeuse. In the church the chapel to the right of the choir contains
an Annunciation, with the arms of the family of Joyeuse.

The town of Ruoms, pop. 1300, has an interesting church, and a
considerable part of its old walls, towers, and gates.

VALLON TO THE PONT D'ARC. (Map, p. 56.)

One hour from Ruoms station by omnibus is Vallon, pop. 2500.
Inns: *H. du Louvre; Luxembourg; Temple Protestant. From
Vallon the Pont d'Arc is 75 minutes distant by the stony road over
the hill, which, as far as the shoulder of the last ridge, is also the
road to the caves. A boat from Vallon to the Pont costs 10 frs. ; to
St. Martin it costs 35 frs., time 7 hrs. St. Martin is 3 m. from the
railway station of St. Just, on the railway on the west side of the
Rhône (see p. 98). The landlord of the Louvre can procure either a
guide for the Pont, 2 frs., or for the caves, 5 frs., or the boatman for
sailing down the Ardèche. The Pont d'Arc is a natural bridge across
the Ardèche, composed of a calcareous rock, pierced with a span of
180 ft., through which the river flows majestically. The soffit of the
arch is 100 ft. high, but the total height of the parapet is 230 ft., and
48 thick. There are several rocks similar to this in France, but this
one is unrivalled in size, and in the beauty and grandeur of the surrounding scenery. A lovely little plain, covered with vines, peach
and mulberry trees, is enclosed by the circle of vertical cliffs 500 ft.
high, which at one part extend over the river. In these cliffs are
great stalactite caves, approached by iron ladders from the top. One
of them is 490 ft. long and 100 ft. high. Vallon is famous for black
truffles, honey, and chestnuts. Pigs are used for finding the truffles.
They are better than dogs, because they are not so apt to be carried
off by other scents, as, for example, when a hare or a partridge suddenly appears upon the scene. (See under Carpentras, page 54.)

102¼ VIVIERS, pop. 3300. *Inn:* Louvre. The station and the 69¼
new town are along the road parallel to the Rhône: the old town
with the cathedral is on the hill behind. The streets are narrow,
crooked, and steep. Here, along the W. side of the Rhône, are lofty
limestone cliffs, the quarrying and preparing of which forms the principal industry of the place. Coach to Aps, 8 m. N.W. on the Teil and
Alais railway, passing St. Thomé, pop. 600, at the junction of the
Nègue with the Escoutay, which flows through a deep ravine. Omnibus to Châteauneuf, on the opposite or east side of the Rhône.

109¼ BOURG-ST. ANDEOL, pop. 4500. *Hotels:* Luxembourg; 62½
Europe ; their omnibuses await passengers. Omnibus also for Pierrelatte (page 50), on the opposite or E. side of the Rhône. Le Bourg
has handsome quays alongside the Rhône, a church founded in the

H

11th cent., and some houses of the 15th and 16th cents. About 350 yards from the town, at the foot of a rock, rises the spring Fontaine de Tournes, which, after turning various mills, flows into the Rhône. About 20 ft. above it is a much effaced sculpture in relief, representing the sacrifice of a bull to the god Mithras.

$\overset{115}{\sim}$ ST. JUST and St. Marcel station, from which both towns are $\overset{57}{\sim}$ less than a mile, but in different directions. 2½ m. from the village of St. Just is St. Martin, pop. 600, on the left or N. bank of the Ardèche. A ferry-boat crosses the river. On the other side, a little farther up, is Aiguèze, pop. 450, with ruins of castle, and farther down St. Julien, but not seen from St. Martin.

Boats are hired at St. Martin to visit the caves of St. Marcel, 4½ m. up the river, or 3¾ m. W. from the village of St. Marcel. The price depends upon the time the visitors make the boat wait. The cave consists of a tunnel, 4¼ m. long, which here and there widens out into spacious lofty caverns hung with stalactites. Some parts are very steep, slippery, and fatiguing. The visit requires from 6 to 7 hours, and certainly none but ardent lovers of walking in dark caverns should undertake the labour. The sail, however, is pleasant. The nearest hotels are at Pont-Saint Esprit and at Bourg-St. Andéol.

$\overset{119}{\sim}$ PONT-ST. ESPRIT, pop. 5000. H. de l'Europe. Coach to $\overset{53}{\sim}$ La Croisière, on the other or east side of the Rhône. (See for bridge and Croisière page 50.) Station of the steamboat between Lyons and Avignon. Pont-Saint Esprit, on the west side of the Rhône and on the western Rhône railway, makes a convenient and comfortable resting-place, with pleasant promenades by the side of the Rhône. Down from the bridge are the church of St. Pierre, now abandoned, and St. Saturnin, built in the 15th cent. Near it is the citadel, built between 1595 and 1620. Within, down a steep stair of 36 steps, are the remains of a chapel constructed in 1365, now a military storehouse. On the south side is a beautifully-sculptured portal, supported on each side by an elegant pinnacled buttress. The arch, 20 ft. span, is richly decorated. In the Hôtel Dieu (infirmary) are a few specimens of old (faïences) pottery. Carriage from the hotel to Valbonne (4½ m. S.W.) and back 15 frs. At Valbonne is a beautifully-situated Chartreuse convent with about 30 inmates. The drive is pleasant (see map, page 56).

Carriage also from the hotel to Saint Martin, on the Ardèche, 4½ m. N.W., there and back 12 frs. (For St. Martin see above.)

7½ m. south from Pont-St. Esprit is Bagnols-sur-Cèze, pop. 5000. H. du Louvre. Omnibus at station. A manufacturing town. Coach to Uzès, 17 m. W.

132½ LAUDUN, pop. 2200, about 2½ m. west from the station, and 39½ 10 m. from Orange, is built on a hill 350 ft. high. The vineyards in the neighbourhood produce a good white wine. Junction with branch to Alais, 35½ m. west, by Connaux, St. Pons, Cavillargues, Seyne, Celas, and Mejannes ; small and uninteresting towns (see map, p. 26).

137½ ROQUEMAURE, pop. 3100. *Inns:* H. du Nord ; H. du 34½ Midi. Omnibus at station. Situated on the small branch of the Rhône which encircles the island of Mémar, 1¼ m. long. The best part of this curious old town is in the neighbourhood of the Hôtel du Midi, where are the public promenade with large trees, the great embankment to protect the town from the invasions of the Rhône, and the ruins of the old castle, of which the most remarkable part is the square tower perched on the point of a great rock. Orchards, vineyards, and mulberry groves surround the village. Roquemaure, however, like all the other small towns on the Rhône, has a dingy and untidy appearance. Clement V., first Pope of Avignon, died here in 1314. 5 m. W. is Taval, pop. 2200, where a good wine is made.

144½ PONT-D'AVIGNON, station on the west side of the Rhône 27½ for Avignon (p. 63). Omnibuses from the hotels await passengers. The omnibus between Avignon and Villeneuve passes the station every hour. Tram every ¼ between the station and Avignon.

7 m. S. from the Pont-d'Avignon is Aramon, pop. 2800, on the Rhône, at a considerable distance from its station. 3¾ m. farther is Theziers, pop. 650, with the church of St. Amans, 11th cent., and the ruins of a castle. (Map, page 66.)

159½ REMOULINS, pop. 1400, with ruins of a castle. From 12¼ Remoulins branch to Uzès, 12¼ m. N.W. On this line, 3¼ m. from Remoulins and 9¼ from Uzès, is Pont-du-Gard station, on an eminence, whence walk down to the bridge. (For description and directions see pp. 64 and 104, and map page 66.)

UZÈS, pop. 5600, *Inn* Bechard : on an eminence surrounded by picturesque calcareous rocks. From the inn walk past the church St. Etienne, then turn to the left, and having gone down the avenue ascend the double stair leading up to the beautiful terrace, on which, to the left, stands the Cathedral, and to the right, projecting from the balustrade, the little house with about 9 yards of frontage, in which Racine resided with his uncle, a canon of the cathedral.   Below, in the deep narrow valley, is the stream Eure, which once supplied the Roman aqueduct at Nîmes.   At the S.W. corner of the church rises from a square basement a circular campanile, 12th cent., in six stages, of which five are composed of eight blind round arches, each pierced by twin open arches resting on an impost column.   On the top is a low tiled roof, partly hidden by an embrasure-like parapet.   On the north side of the church is the bishop's palace, now the Sous-Préfecture, and the seat of the tribunal.   Looking from the top of the stairs towards the town the most prominent objects are the large dungeon-tower of the castle, with turrets on three of the corners; the Tour Carrée de l'Horloge, surmounted by an iron grating and a bell ; and the Tour de Prison.   The octagonal tower, crowned with an image of the Virgin, rises from the École des Frères, and the low square tower from the church of St. Etienne.   At the other end of the promenade is the bronze statue by Duret of Admiral Comte de Brueys, né à Uzès le 11 Fevrier 1753.   Mort à Aboukir (battle of the Nile) le 2 Aout 1798. Now walk up the street to the Marché au Blé, with a pretty bronze fountain opposite the Mairie and Post Office.   Behind the Mairie is the entrance to the castle called Le Duché, which has for centuries belonged to the family of Crussol, Ducs d'Uzès.   Fee for a party 1 fr. On entering, to the right is the Tour de la Chapelle, 13th cent., restored ; to the left, the dungeon tower, 11th cent., ascended by 248 steps, commanding an extensive prospect ; and in front the façade, 16th cent., by P. Delorme.   The ground-floor of the "Tour de la Chapelle" contains the family vaults.   Over the tombs is a large crucifix made in England ; the figure is of bronze and the cross of copper.   Above is the chapel.   Of the house the best part is the stair, vaulted throughout and covered with sculptured stone panels.   The best wines in the department are grown in the neighbourhood of Uzès.   Besides the railway, Uzès is connected by a good diligence with Bagnols, 17 m. E. on the railway of the west side of the Rhône, 19 m. N. from the Pont d'Avignon, and 7½ m. S. from Pont-St. Esprit.

After Remoulins the train halts at the station **Sernhac-Lédenon. Lédenon**, pop. 700, is about 2 m. W. from the station, and **Sernhac**, pop. 1200, about the same distance E.   7 m. from Nîmes is the St. Gervasy-Bezouce station, and 2½ m. nearer, Marguerittes, pop. 2000, with a handsome modern church, and in the cemetery the ruins of the chapel of St. Gilles, 12th cent., seen from railway.

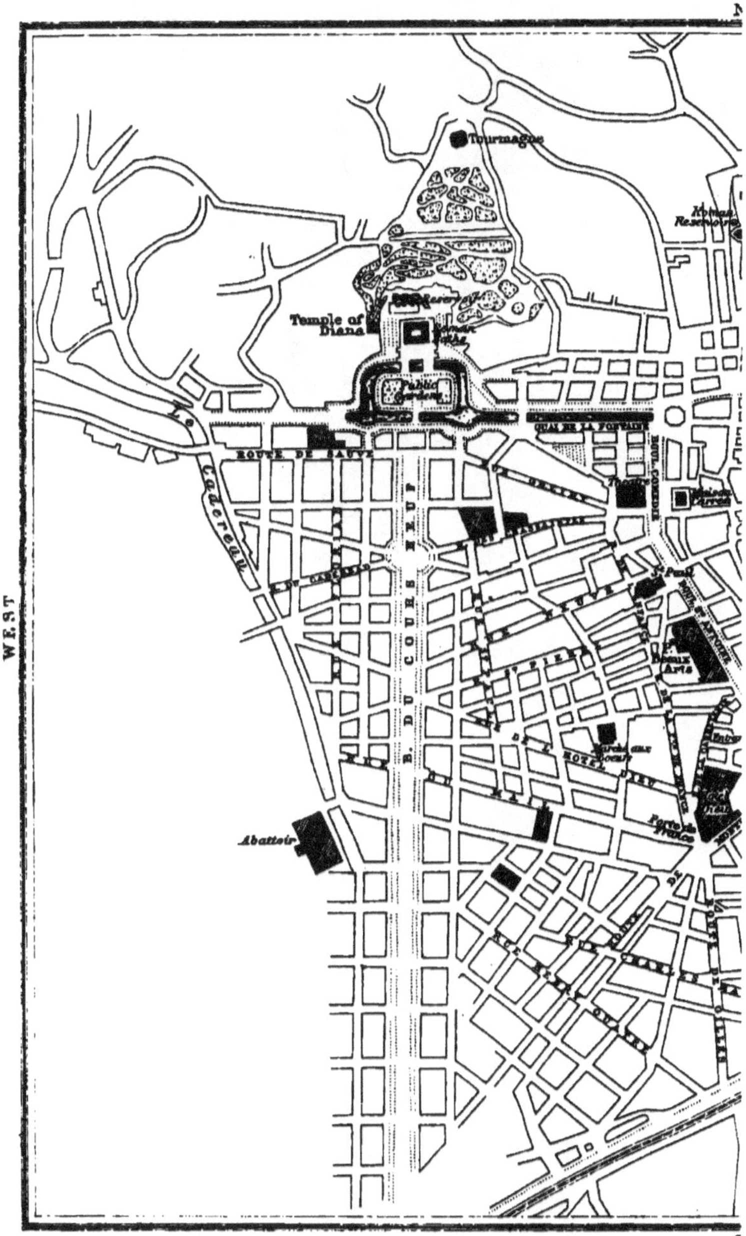

Tourmagne
Roman Reservoir
Temple of Diana
Roman Baths
Public Gardens
QUAI DE LA FONTAINE
ROUTE DE SAUVE
Le Cadereau
Theatre
Maison Carrée
St Paul
Beaux Arts
B. DU COURS NEUF
RUE NEUVE
Marché aux Boeufs
RUE DE L'HOTEL DIEU
Porte de France
Abattoir
WEST

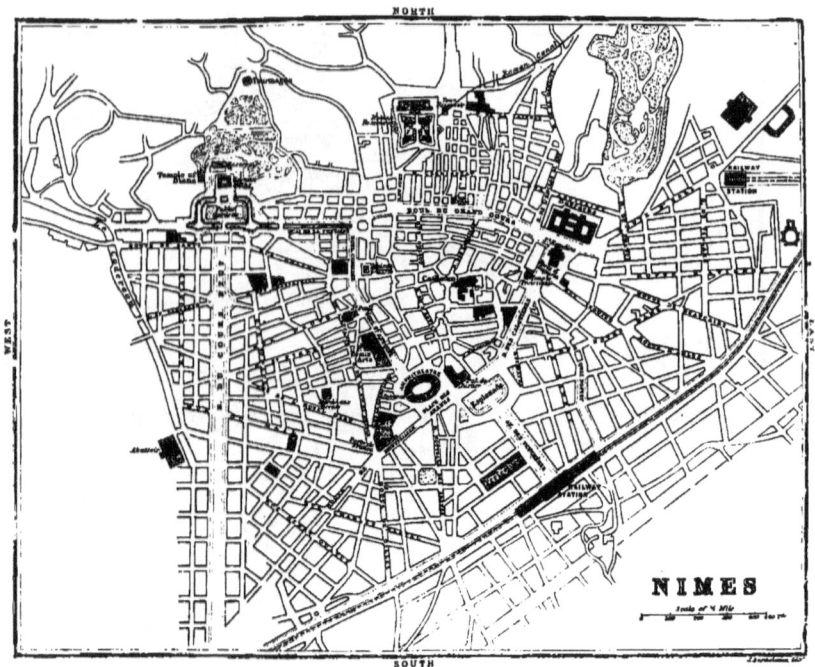

172 m. S.W. from Lyons, 27½ m. S.W. from Avignon, 31 m. N.E. from Montpellier by Gallargues, 17 m. W. from Tarascon, 80 m. N.W. from Marseilles, and 450 m. S.E. from Paris by Clermont-Ferrand, is

NÎMES,

population 64,000, on the Vistre, 150 feet above the sea. A flight of steps as at Tarascon leads from the town up to the station. At the foot of these steps is the Hôtel des Arts, pretty comfortable room 2 frs., dinner with wine 3 frs. The trams start from in front of the house. In the town are: On the Esplanade, the H. Luxembourg, the most expensive. By the side of it, fronting a garden, the H. du Midi or Durand, from 9 to 12 frs. Fronting the amphitheatre the Cheval Blanc, commercial, 8 to 10 frs. Opposite the Maison Carrée, the H. Manivet, 9 to 12 frs., the most conveniently situated for visiting the sights. Their omnibuses await passengers at the foot of the station stair. Post Office, No. 4 B. du Grand Cours, between St. Baudine and the Public Gardens. Telegraph Office in the Place de la Salamandre, a small "Place" off the B. des Calquières. Temple Protestant, the Porte d'Auguste, and the handsome new church of St. Baudine, with its two elegant spires, are at the north end of the B. des Calquières, beyond the Esplanade.

Sights.—The Amphitheatre, the Maison Carrée, and the Roman Baths. *Cab Stands* are found at the station, at the Amphitheatre, and at the Maison Carrée. Cab carrying 4, 2 frs. per hour.

A straight, wide, and handsome avenue extends from the station to the Esplanade ; having in the centre a large fountain with four marble colossal statues by Pradier round the base, representing the Rhône, the Gardon, and the fountain nymphs of Nemausa and Ura. On the top of the pedestal is a larger statue, also by Pradier, representing Nîmes, with its face towards the station. Behind it are the Palais de Justice and the Amphitheatre, and to the left the church of St. Perpetua.

The great sight in Nîmes is the Roman **Amphitheatre**, the most perfect extant. In form it is elliptical, of which the great axis measures 437 ft., and the lesser 433 ft., and the height 70 ft. Around the building are two tiers of arcades, each tier having 60 arches, and all the arches being separated from each other by a Roman Doric column. Above runs an attic, from which project the consoles on which the beams that sustained the awning rested. Within each arcade, on the ground-floor and on the upper story, runs a corridor round the building, the upper one being roofed with stone slabs 18 ft. long, reaching from side to side. There were four entrances, one facing each of the cardinal points of the compass. The interior contained 32 rows of seats in 4 zones, capable of accommodating from 18,000 to 20,000 spectators. The lowest zone corresponded to the dress circle, the others to the galleries. The present entrance is from the western side, fee 50 c., opposite No. 8 Place des Arènes. The stair that leads up to the top is under the fifth arch west. No description can express the sensation experienced from contemplating this vast Roman structure from the highest tier or from the edge of the outside wall. At the same time it must be remembered that there are no railings, and that an inadvertent step might have serious consequences. The date of the building is uncertain. Titus, Adrian, and Antoninus Pius have each been conjectured to have been the founder. The Visigoths converted it into a fortress, the Castrum Arenarum, occupied by the Saracens at the beginning of the 8th cent., till driven from France by the armies Charles of Martel ; died in 715.

On the N. side of the amphitheatre is the Boulevard St. Antoine, with, on the left hand or W. side, the Palais des Beaux Arts, including the Public Library, containing 60,000 vols. ; the Archæological Museum, containing many interesting articles, chiefly Roman, found in the neighbourhood ; and the Picture Gallery, containing, among other pictures, a Magdalene by Guido ; A Holy Family, a Head of John the Baptist, and a portrait of himself, by Titian ; A Head of a Girl and a Return from Hunting, by Rubens ; Portraits of Vanloo and of his mother, by himself; Cromwell regarding Charles I. laid out in his coffin, by Paul Delaroche, his chef d'œuvre ; "Nero and a Sorceress experimenting on a slave with the poison they were preparing for Britannicus," by Javier Sigalon ; An old woman, by Greuze ; also works by Gérard Dow, Claude Lorrain, Metzu, Ostade, Paul Potter, Ruysdael, Van den Welde, and Wouvermans.

At the N. end of this Boulevard is the church of St. Paul, with frescoes on gold and blue grounds by H. and P. Flandrin.

Beyond are the Theatre and the Bourse, and opposite them **La Maison Carrée,** a beautiful specimen of a Roman temple, probably part of the Forum, with which it was connected by colonnades extending east and west. It is 75 ft. long, 39 wide, and 39 high, and is supposed to have been erected in the time of Antoninus Pius. It stands on a platform, and is encompassed by a quadrilateral peristyle of 30 Roman-Corinthian columns surmounted by a plain architrave, scroll frieze, sculptured dentils, and a fluted cornice. All the columns are attached,

ROMAN BATHS. TOURMAGNE. FORT.

excepting the ten which support the pediment. In the area within the railing are mutilated statues and fragments of Roman columns.

Eastward, in the centre of the old town, is the Cathedral St. Castor, built in the 11th cent., but nearly rebuilt in subsequent times. The most venerable portion is the façade, constructed of large blocks of stone. A delicately-cut frieze, representing scenes from Genesis, extends under the roof. The eaves of the pediment are supported by brackets with acanthus leaves. The table of the third altar, right hand, in the interior, is sculptured in much the same style as the exterior frieze.

N.W. from the Maison Carrée is the Public Garden, adorned with vases and statues among shrubs and flowers, overshadowed by tall elm and plane trees. To the left are the remains of a temple or fane (called the temple of Diana), dedicated to the Nymphs, built B.C. 24, of huge carefully-hewn blocks of sandstone, and reduced to its present state in 1577. The little of the ornamental work that remains is very much mutilated. Opposite the temple, protected from the troublesome winds of Nîmes, are the **Roman Baths**, about 12 ft. below the level of the gardens, the vaulting being supported on small columns, over which rise open stone balustrades. Adjoining is the copious spring that supplies them, as placid but somewhat larger than the Fontaine of Vaucluse (p. 65).

From the fountain a road leads up the wooded slopes of Mont Cavalier to an octagonal structure called the **Tourmagne**, 90 ft. high, erected before the Roman invasion, and supposed to have been a tomb. It was originally filled with rubble, which was excavated in the 16th cent. in search of treasure. The winding staircase of 140 steps was added in 1843. The view from the top is extensive. Fee, 30 cents.

Eastward from the Tourmagne is the Fort, built by Louis XIV., now the town prison. On the western side of the fort are the remains of the reservoir, *castellum divisorium*, which received the water brought by the canal from the aqueduct of the Pont-du-Gard. This canal still brings water to the town reservoir, on the opposite or east side of the fort.

In the year of Rome 788 a strong wall was built round Nîmes, 7 ft. high, pierced with 10 gates ; of which there still remain two ; the Porte d'Auguste, originally fronting the road to Rome, now at the E. end of the Temple Protestant, and the Porte de France at the extremity of the Rue Carrèterie. (See plan.)

The ancient name of Nîmes is Nemausus, one of the cities of Gallia

Narbonensis, and the capital of the Volcæ Arecomici. As early as the reign of Augustus it was a "colonia," and possessed in the days of Strabo the "Jus Latii," and therefore was independent of the Roman governors. Its most notable product then was cheese, which was exported to Rome ; now it is raw silk, for which it is the principal emporium in the south of France. The wines of Nîmes are in repute in Paris, particularly the Costière and the St. Gilles, called also Vin de Remède. Both deteriorate after the sixth year in bottle. Nicot, who introduced tobacco into France, and Guizot, the minister of Louis Philippe, were born at Nîmes.

13½ miles from Nîmes is the **Pont-du-Gard**, built by the Romans in the reign of Augustus as part of the aqueduct, 25 m. long, which, from the neighbourhood of Uzès (page 99), brought the waters of the Eure and Airan to the reservoir beside the fort, of which only vestiges now remain. This "Pont," which spans the valley or banks of the river Gardon, consists of three rows of arches, whose total height above the bed of the river is 156 ft. The two lower stories are formed of hewn stones, placed together without the aid of any cement ; but the mason work underneath the channel of the third or top story is of rough stones cemented, by which all filtration was prevented. The first or lowest row consists of six arches, with a span of 60 ft. each, except the largest, which has 75 ft. The second row consists of eleven arches of the same dimensions as the first, and the third of 35 arches of 15 ft. span. A stair from the right bank of the river leads up to the watercourse above the topmost tier of arches. In the striking boldness of its design this bridge exhibits a decided improvement and superiority over all the other Roman aqueducts. The arches are wider, and the piers in proportion lighter, and had the same principle been extended so as to have formed it of one single row from top to bottom, it would have equalled in the skill and disposition of its materials the more judicious and more elegant structures of modern times (see Roquefavour, p. 77). Take ticket to Pont-du-Gard Station. But if with luggage, and on the way to Avignon, take ticket to Remoulins, where leave the luggage, and take another ticket to the Pont-du-Gard, which having visited, walk back to Remoulins station, where take ticket for Pont Avignon (see under Avignon, p. 64).

79 m. S.E. from Nîmes by rail is **Marseilles** (p. 111), passing Tarascon, 17 m. (p. 66), and Arles, 25 m. (p. 68).

NÎMES TO MILLAU BY VIGAN.

See Map, p. 26.

58 m. N. W. by rail from Nîmes is Vigan, whence coach 43 m. W.,
9 hrs., to Millau, on the line to Paris by Rodez. There are no towns
of importance on this line, though some parts, especially towards
Vigan, are very picturesque. 27 m. from Vigan, and 31 from Nîmes,
is Quissac, pop. 1800, junction with line to Lezan, 9 m. N., and
thence 4½ m. E. to Mas des Gard, on the Nîmes and Alais line. 9 m.
W. from Lezan is St. Hippolyte-Le-Fort, pop. 4500, on the sluggish
Vidourle. From this the line goes westward by La Cadière to Ganges,
9½ m. from Vigan, on the Hérault, 595 ft. above the sea, pop. 5000, H.
Croix Blanche, omnibus at station. The most pleasant town on the
line. 2½ m. farther is Jumène, 682 ft. above the sea, pop. 3000, with
coal and iron mines. 4 m. from Vigan, at Le Pont, 666 ft. above the
sea, the line crosses the Hérault, and entering the picturesque valley
of the Arre follows the course of that river to Vigan, pop. 6000. *Inns:*
Voyageurs; Cheval Blanc; both in the "Place," near the statue of
the Chevalier d'Assas, born at Vigan in 1733, and "Mort glorieuse-
ment à Clastercamp à 27 ans." Vigan on the Arre, an affluent of the
Hérault, is 860 ft. above the sea, in a hollow between steep mountains,
with terraces of vineyards, olive, mulberry, fig, and chestnut trees to
nearly their summits. The town consists of narrow, crooked, badly-
paved streets. The hospital was founded in 1190. In the promenade
near the post office are some old chestnut trees, disfigured with knots.
In the neighbourhood are several coal-pits, worked, however, with
difficulty, on account of the water they contain. Nearly a mile westward is the Fontaine Isis, the source of the water-supply of the town.
Beside it are the cold sulphureous springs of Cauvalat.

Coach daily to **Valleraugue**, *Inn:* Aresque, 14 m. N., in a very
picturesque region, on the Hérault, in a deep wooded valley between
the Aigoual mountains towards the N., and the Espéron mountains
towards the S. The principal source of the Hérault is a little higher,
towards the W., at Séreyrède. From Valleraugue the ascent is
made in about 2½ hours of Mt. Aulas, 4665 ft. above the sea, the culminating point of the Espéron, commanding a magnificent view.
The source of the Dourbie is just a little to the S. of Valleraugue, and
of the Tarn to the N., but on the other side of the Aigoual. Excellent fishing, botanising, and geologising in this neighbourhood.

Le Vigan to Millau, 43 m. W. by diligence, 9 hrs. The first
village the coach passes is Molières, on a hill above the road, with coal-
mines. From this the road ascends to the villages of Esparron, 5½
m., and Arre, 6¼ m., from Vigan. A little higher up the coach leaves
by a tunnel the valley of the Arre, and enters that of the Vis, with
the village Alzon, 12½ m. from Vigan, pop. 900. *Inn:* the Souterraine,
the best on the road. After a pretty steep ascent of 7 m. the coach
arrives at Sauclières, pop. 2200, *Inn:* H. du Nord, producing excel-

lent pork, cheese, and potatoes. The coach from this ascends the southern side of the Lenglas mountains, covered with vineyards, olive and mulberry trees, and farther up forests of chestnut trees. From the other side of the ridge it descends to the valley of the Dourbie, in which is St. Jean du Bruel, pop. 2000, *Inn:* Commerce, 23 m. from Vigan and 20 from Millau. The coach having traversed the valley of the Dourbie, full of chestnut trees, reaches Nant, pop. 2000, a poor village, on an eminence, 16 m. from Millau. Shortly afterwards the diligence crosses the monotonous tableland of **Larzac**, 2790 ft. above the sea, and arrives at the village of La Cavalerie, with some small dolmens. 7 m. W. is Millau, on the line to Paris by Rodez.

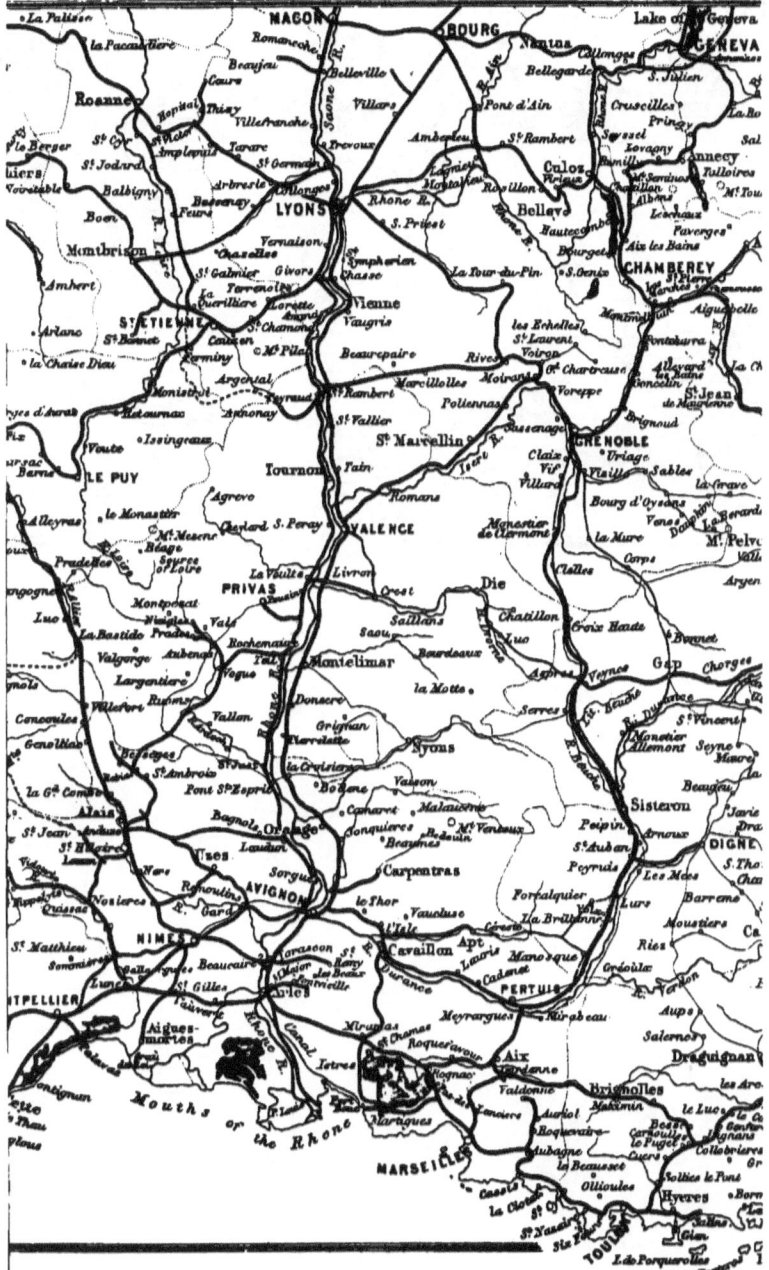

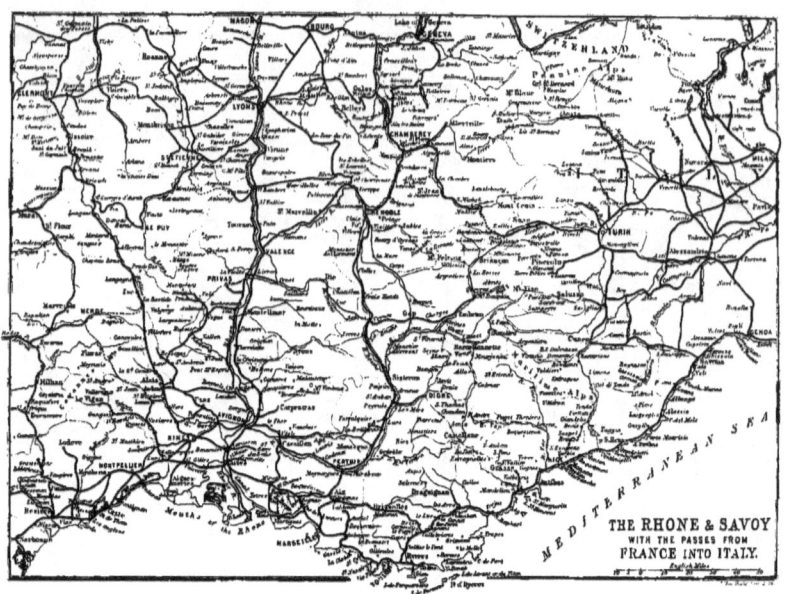

THE RHONE & SAVOY
WITH THE PASSES FROM
FRANCE INTO ITALY.

THE RIVIERA.

— ♦♦ —

HOTELS, PRODUCTIONS, AND CLIMATE.

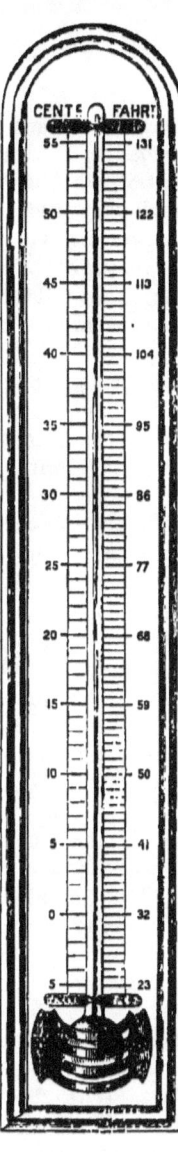

THE RIVIERA is a strip of land extending 323 miles along the coast of the Mediterranean at the foot of the Maritime Alps and their off-shoots. It is usually divided into two portions — the Riviera from Hyères to Genoa, 203 miles long; and the Riviera from Genoa to Leghorn, 112 miles long. The milder and more frequented of the two is the former—the Western Riviera—which has been subjected to most careful and minute meteorological observations, and the various stations classified according to their supposed degree of temperature. Yet in the whole 203 miles the difference may be said to be imperceptible. No one station in all its parts is alike, the parts of each station differing more from each other than the stations themselves. Yet each station has some peculiarity which suits some people more than others; this peculiarity being more often accidental and social—such as the people met with, the lodgings, the general surroundings, and many other little things which exercise a more powerful influence upon the health and well-being of the mind and body than the mere fractional difference of temperature. None of the protecting mountains of any of the stations are sufficiently high, precipitous, and united to ward off the cold winds when the higher mountains behind are covered with snow. All the ridges have deep indentations through which the cold air, as well as the streams, descends to the plain. Hence no station is exempt from cold winds, and all delicate persons must ever be on their guard against them—the more sunny and beautiful the day, especially in early spring, the greater is the danger. All the stations suffer also, more or less, from the famous Mistral, a north-west wind, which in winter on the Riviera feels like a north-west wind on a sunny summer day in Scotland. The mean winter temperature (November, December, and January) of Hyères, considered the coolest of the winter stations, is 47°·4 Fahr., and of San Remo, considered the mildest, 48°·89 Fahr. The coldest months are December and January. With February the temperature commences to rise progressively. Throughout the entire region bright and dusty weather is the rule, cloudy and wet weather the exception. "In December wild flowers are rare till after Christmas, when the long-bracted orchid, the purple anemone, and the violet make their appearance. These by the end of January have become abundant, and are quickly followed in February by crocuses, primroses, and pretty blue hepaticas. Meanwhile the star-anemones are springing up in the olive-woods, with periwinkles and rich red anemones. In March the hillsides are fragrant with thyme, lavender, and the Mediterranean heath, to which April adds cistuses, helianthemums, convolvuli, serapiases, and gladioli."—*H. S. Roberton.* There is a much less quantity of wild flowers now than formerly. The date-palm flourishes in the open air. Capital walking-sticks are made of the midrib of the leaf. Among the trees which fructify freely are the orange, lemon, and citron trees, the pepper tree (*Schinus molle*), the camphor tree (*Ligustrum ovalifolium*), the locust tree (*Ceratona siliqua*), the Tree Veronica, the magnolia, and different species of the Eucalyptus or gum tree and of the true Acacia. In marshy places the common bamboo (*Arundo donax*) attains a great height; while the *Sedum dasyphyllum*, the aloe, and the Opuntium or prickly-pear, clothe the dry rocky banks with verdure. The most important tree commercially is the olive, which occupies the lower part of the mountains and immense tracts in the valleys. The higher elevations are divided among the cork tree (*Quercus suber*), the Maritime, Aleppo, and umbrella pines, and the chestnut tree. The Japanese medlar (*Eriobotrya japonica*) is common in the orchards, flowers in December, and ripens its fruit in May. With the exception of the orange, lemon, and cherry, all the other orchard trees ripen their fruit too late for the winter resident.

On the Riviera generally, but especially in Hyères, St. Raphael, Grasse, and Menton, board and lodging in good hotels can be had for 8s. or 9s. per day, which includes coffee or tea in the morning, and a substantial meat breakfast and dinner, with country wine (vin ordinaire) to both. In some boarding-houses (Pensions) the price per day is as low as 6s. If two are together, especially two ladies or a gentleman and his wife, an excellent plan is to take a furnished room, which, with a south exposure and good furniture, ought to cost about £2 per month. They can easily prepare their own breakfast, and they can get their dinner sent to them. If the party be numerous, apartments should be taken, which vary from £2 to £30 per month. For the season, from October to May, furnished apartments are let at prices varying from £18 to £100. As a general rule it is best to alight at some hotel, and, while on the spot, to select either the pension or apartments, as no description can give an adequate idea of the state of the drains nor of the people of the house. A maid-servant costs nearly £1 per month, a cook about one-half more, but they are not easily managed. Fluids are sold by the litre, equal to nearly a quart of four (not six) to the gallon. Solids are sold by the kilogramme, or, as it is generally called, the kilo, equal to 2 lbs. 3¼ oz.

Bread is about the same price as in England. The best beef and mutton cost from 1s. 10d. to 2s. the kilo. A good chicken 2s. 6d. Eggs when at their dearest cost 1½d. each. Excellent milk costs 4d. the litre. The best butter 3s. 2d. to 3s. 6d. the kilo. Of French cheese there are a great many kinds, all very good. Among the best are the Roquefort and the fromage bleu, both resembling Stilton, and cost from 2s. 6d. to 3s. 6d. the kilo. Fish are dearer than in England. The best caught off the coast are : the Rouget or Red Mullet, the Dorade or Bream, the Loup or Bass, the Sardine, and the Anchovy. The Gray Mullet, the Gurnard (Grondin), the John Dory (Dorée Commune), the Whiting (Merlan), and the Conger are very fair. The sole, turbot, tunny, and mackerel are inferior to those caught in the ocean. The cuttle-fish is also eaten. Good vegetables can be had all through the winter, such as carrots, leeks, celery, cabbage, cauliflower, peas, lettuce, spinage, sorrel, and artichokes. The cardon (*Cynara cardunculus*) and salsifis (*Tragopogon porrifolius*) are often served up at dinner in the hotels. The cardon tastes like celery, but the salsifis has a bitter flavour. The potatoes are of good quality, but often spoilt in the cooking. In all the stations are English clergymen, physicians, apothecaries, bankers, bakers, and grocers.

Before commencing to treat in detail the different stations of the Riviera, "some of the general advantages of the invalid's life in this region must be noticed. The chief of these is the amount of sunshine which he enjoys for weeks and even months together, when the sun often rises in a cloudless sky, shines for several hours with a bright-ness and warmth surpassing that of the British summer, and then sinks without a cloud behind the secondary ranges of the Maritime Alps, displaying in his setting the beautiful and varied succession of tints which characterise that glorious phenomenon of the refraction of light, a southern sunset ; when he imparts to the rugged mountains a softness of outline and a brilliancy of colouring which defy description. In the early stages of phthisis, and especially when the patient is young and active-minded, struck down by overwork or sudden ex-posure, this cheering influence is most beneficial. It is of great im-portance that, while taking the needful care of himself, he should not degenerate at an early age into a hopeless valetudinarian, especially as an every-day increasing mass of evidence warrants us in believing that under the influence of medicine and climate a large number of these patients gradually recover their health and lead useful lives, and, with due care, lives of no inconsiderable duration. Patients should never neglect to consult a doctor on their first arrival, as his experience and advice with regard to lodgings, food, etc., are of great value, and may often prevent them from falling into bad hands, or settling in un-healthy localities." To these remarks of Dr. Williams may be added, that patients should bring with them a letter from their physician describing their case and the treatment he thinks should be adopted.

The best time for walking and driving is between 9 and 12, as then there is rarely either wind or dust. For invalids requiring quiet sunny walks there are no stations· on the whole coast so suitable as Hyères and Bordighera.

Sea-bathing on the Riviera may be continued with advantage by many during the greater part of the winter season. As the rise and fall of the tide are so trifling, the beach is always in a fit state for the bather. The water of the Mediterranean is more highly mineralised than that of the ocean. It contains about 41 per cent of common salt.

Doctors' Fees.—French doctors charge their countrymen generally 10 frs. for each visit. English doctors charge for each visit 5, 10, or 20 frs., according to what they suppose to be the means of their patients. An extra charge is made for night work.

Tourists may find it convenient to take with them a little brandy, tea, arrowroot, Liebig's extract, Gregory's mixture, opium pills, and a little of whatever medicine they are in the habit of using. The ordinary wine at the hotels is neither so good nor so safe as formerly, and should always be watered.

MARSEILLES.

MARSEILLES, pop. 319,000, 15 hrs. 25 min. from Paris, and 6 hrs. 37 min. from Lyons. From Cannes it is 4 hrs. 31 min., and from Nice 5 hrs. 27 min. 536½ m. S. from Paris, 190¼ m. S. from Lyons, 120½ m. W. from Cannes, and 140 m. W. from Nice. On the departure side of the railway station is the **Terminus Hotel** (dear). The hotel omnibuses await passengers. Call out loudly the name of the hotel desired, to which the driver of its omnibus will respond.

A plentiful supply of **Cabs** is both at the railway and the custom-house station of the Bassin de la Joliette. Each coachman is furnished with an official tariff, which, though constantly changing, may be stated to be—Between 6 A.M. and midnight, for a cab with one horse, the course, 1 fr. ; the hour, 2 frs. With 2 horses, the course, 1¼ fr. ; the hour, 2¼ frs. From midnight to 6 A.M. 75 c. extra. Portmanteaus not above 30 kilo., or 68¼ lbs., 25 c. each. The hotel omnibuses charge each passenger 1 fr.

Hotels.—In the Rue Cannebière, ascending from the Port, are very fine **Cafés**, and in the eastern continuation of it, the Rue Noailles, the best **Hotels**. The Hôtel du Louvre et de la Paix ; the Hôtel Noailles ; and the Hôtel Marseilles ; all near each other, and charging from 12 to 20 frs. per day.

Less luxurious and expensive are : the Petit Louvre, No. 16 R. Cannebière, over the office of Messageries Maritimes steamboats ; between the Port and the Bourse, the Hôtel de Genève, a comfortable house ; on the opposite side of the Rue Cannebière and near the opera house, the Hôtel Beauveau ; near it, in the R. Vacon, the *Hôtel des Colonies.

In and about the Cours Belsunce, where there are a large cab-stand and an important tramway terminus, are some good second-class hotels, of which the best is the Hôtel des Phocéens, 28 R. des Récolettes. Rooms, 2½ frs. ; Dinner, 3½ frs. with wine. Next it, at No. 26, is the Hôtel de l'Europe, a "maison meublée," in which good rooms, including service, cost 2 frs. Breakfast and dinner can be had in the neighbouring restaurants. Of them, one of the most comfortable is G. Restaurant des Gourmets, adjoining the hotel. Near it is the Restaurant Bouches du Rhône, a cheap house. The other second-class houses in the Cours Belsunce which can be recommended are—the Californie ; Deux Mondes ; Hôtel St. Marie ; Négociants ; Alger. The Hôtel du Cours is good also, but it is only a "maison meublée." The continuation of the Cours Belsunce is called the Cours St. Louis, where a flower-market is held. Just off this Cours, in the Rue d'Aubagne, is a cheap, good, and clean house, the hotel and restaurant St. Louis; rooms from 1½ to 3 frs. ; dinner, à la carte. At No. 8 Place de Rome is a good and cheap house, the Hôtel Forer, well situated, but it is one of those for which either a cab or the general omnibus must be taken at the station.

Steamboats.—The steamers of the Messageries Maritimes, of Morelli et C¹ᵉ, of Fraissinet et C¹ᵉ, of the P. and O. Navigation Co., etc., arrive and depart from the Dock or Bassin Joliette. The custom-house is at the north end of the dock, and just outside the dock-gates are porters and a large cab-stand. The custom-house contains one waiting-room for the first and second class, and another for the third. Passengers before they can have their baggage examined have to pay 6 sous at the end of the baggage-room for each box, for which they receive an acknowledgment. A tramway runs from No. 1 Quai Joliette to Longchamps, entering the Port and the Rue Cannebière by the R. de la République. There are no hotels near the steamboat station.

Small boats' station at the head of the Port. Boats to and from the Château d'If, 8 frs. from 3 to 3½ hrs. On feast days small steamers make the round of the islands, starting from nearly the same place, but do not land the passengers, fare ½ fr., time 1 hr. At this part of the quay the feluccas from Spain discharge their cargoes of oranges and other fruits. From the Hôtel de Ville (1 in plan) on the port, the Bateaux Mouches cross over to the Place aux Huiles opposite, 1 sou. At the mouth of the port, from between La Consigne and the Fort St. Jean, other Bateaux Mouches cross over to the Bassin Carénage, by the side of Fort St. Nicholas, and just below the interesting old church of St. Victor, 1 sou. From this a road leads up to Notre Dame.

The principal Temple Protestant is in the R. Vincent, No. 2. There is another in the R. Grignan, No. 15, near the General Post Office at No. 53. Poste-Restante, "guichet," on the ground-floor, opposite the entrance door. Telegraph office, No. 10 Rue Pavé d'Amour. Anglican chapel, No. 100 Rue Sylvabelle, south from the Rue Grignan and parallel to it. The public library is in the Boulevard du Musée, in the École des Beaux Arts. Open daily except Sunday.

Best money-changers by the west side of the Bourse, 10 in plan.

The Opera is near the Port; the other theatres are around the Rue Noailles.

Sights.—Palais Longchamp, an artistic edifice, containing the Picture Gallery and the Natural History Museum; free. Closed on Mondays and every day between 12 and 2 (see p. 114). Near the

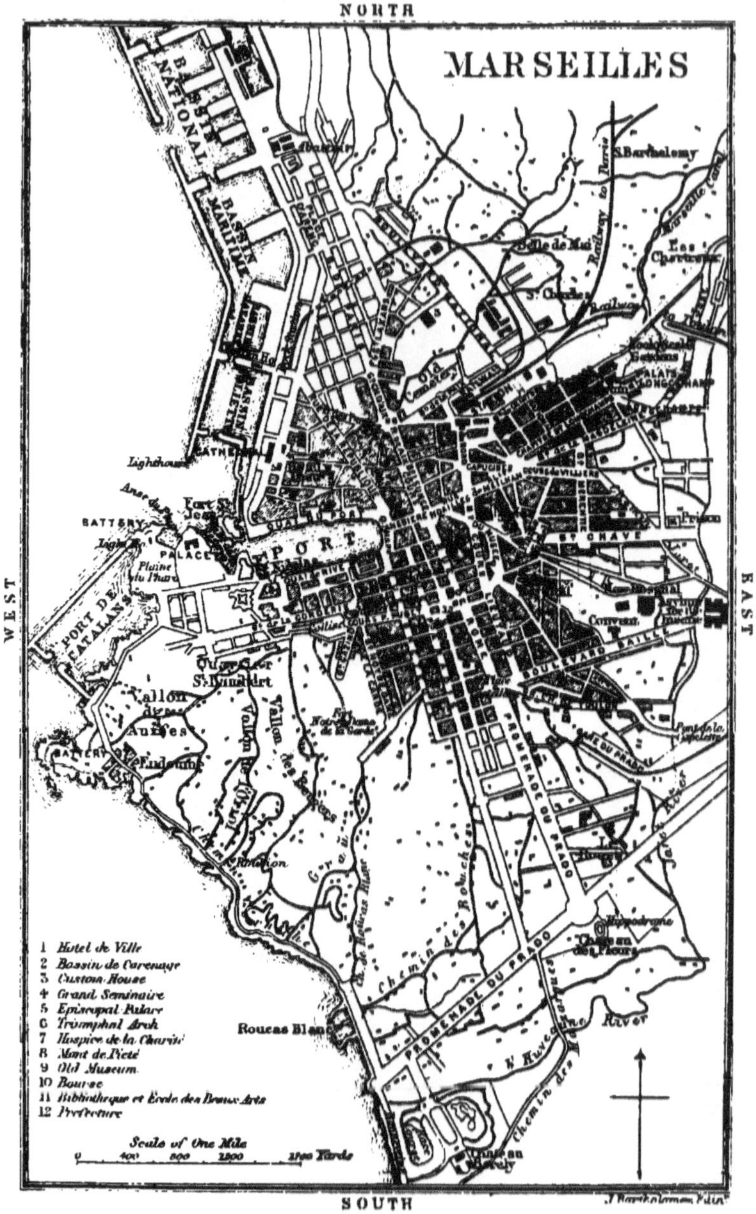

MARSEILLES

WEST

EAST

S. Bartholomy

BASSIN NATIONAL

BASSIN MARITIME

Lighthouse

Fort St Jean

BATTERY

PALACE

PORT

PORT DE CATALANS

BATTERY

St Dunstan

Vallon
des
Auffes

Endoume

ST CHAVE

Roucas Blanc

1   Hôtel de Ville
2   Bassin de Carenage
3   Custom House
4   Grand Séminaire
5   Episcopal Palace
6   Triumphal Arch
7   Hospice de la Charité
8   Mont de Piété
9   Old Museum
10   Bourse
11   Bibliothèque et Ecole des Beaux Arts
12   Préfecture

Scale of One Mile

0   400   800   1200   1700 Yards

J. Bartholomew, Edin

SIGHTS. TRAMS. CORNICHE. BOUILLABAISSE.

Palais is the Zoological Garden, free on Sundays. Notre Dame de la Garde (p. 116). The shops and cafés in the Rues Cannebière and Noailles. A drive on the Corniche road.

Of all the **Trams** the most important starts from the left of the statue in the Cours Belsunce, and runs by the Château des Fleurs and the Prado to its Bonneveine terminus, a little beyond the racecourse. Just behind the Bonneveine terminus is the **Château Borély**, containing the Musée d'Archéologie, including a collection of Phœnician relics found in the neighbourhood, which support the hypothesis of the Phœnician origin of Marseilles. Open on Sundays and Thursdays. On the ground-floor are Roman mosaics, busts, altars, tombstones, jewellery, mummies ; and in the end room is a stone with a Phœnician inscription, regulating the tariff of the prices to be paid to the priests for sacrifices in the temple of Baal. Upstairs are collections of antique glass, necklaces, fayence from Provence and Marseilles, bronzes, gold jewellery, lamps, vases, weapons, and an octagonal plan of Marseilles 18 ft. in diameter.

Return from the Bonneveine terminus by the tram for the Place de Rome, near 12 in plan. On its way it follows the Corniche road, considered the most beautiful drive about Marseilles, fare ½ fr. The gardens and pleasure-grounds in the whole of this neighbourhood are due to the irrigation afforded by the canal. Of the bathing establishments on the Corniche road the best is the Roucas Blanc ; and of the restaurants the best is the Hôtel Roubion, a first-class house, charging 15 frs. per day, and for vin ordinaire, lights, and service, 5 frs. additional. The house is situated on an eminence rising from the Corniche road, at the entrance into the Vallon de l'Oriol, commands a splendid sea view, has handsome dining-rooms, and is famed for its fish dinners and Bouillabaisse. Trams and omnibuses are constantly passing it. This establishment, as well as most of the other restaurants along the Corniche road, has tanks in the rocks on the beach, in which is kept a supply of live fish to make the Provence dish called Bouillabaisse, a kind of fish soup, which, like most national dishes—plumpudding, puchero, haggis, etc.—admits of considerable latitude in the preparation. The essentials are—whole rascasses and chapons (scorpion fishes), and rock lobsters stewed in a liquor mixed with a little of the best olive oil, and flavoured with tender savoury herbs. An extra good Bouillabaisse should include also crayfish, a few mussels, and some pieces of any first-class fish, such as the bass.

Those having little time to devote to Marseilles should, after taking

I

a short stroll about the Port and in the Rues Cannebière and Noailles, enter the Joliette tram on its way up to the Palais de Longchamp, fare 2 sous. The **Palais de Longchamp**, which cost £165,000, consists of two rectangular wings, united by a semicircular colonnade of Ionic volute-fluted columns. In the centre, under a richly-sculptured massive archway, an inscription records that the great undertaking of bringing the water of the Durance to Marseilles was begun on the 15th November 1839, and was accomplished on the 8th July 1847, in the reign of Louis Philippe I. Another records that the palace was commenced in the reign of Napoleon III., on the 7th April 1862, and finished on the 15th August 1869. From a group of colossal bulls under the colonnade gushes a copious stream of water, which in its descent makes a cascade of 90 ft. in three stages. The wing to the right, standing with the face to the palace, contains the Natural History Museum ; and the other, the picture and sculpture galleries.

All the pictures are labelled. On the first floor are some large pictures by French artists and a few statues. In the second small room left hand is a collection of sketches by famous painters. Among the best pictures in the large centre hall of the upper story are :—F. Bol, d. 1681, portrait of woman and of King of Poland ; Bourdon, d. 1671, portrait of P. de Champaigne ; Cesari, d. 1640, Noah inebriated ; Fontenay, d. 1715, Fruit ; Girodet, d. 1824, Fruit ; Gongo, d. 1764, Sacrifice to Venus and Jupiter ; Greuze, d. 1805, portrait ; Holbein, d. 1554, portrait ; Loo, d. 1745, portrait of lady ; Maratta, d. 1713, Cardinal Cibo ; Mignard, d. 1695, Ninon de Lenclos ; Nattier, d. 1766, Mme. de Pompadour as Aurora ; Peeters, d. 1652, marine scene ; Pellegrino, d. 1525, Holy Family ; Perugino, d. 1524, Holy Family ; F. Porbus, d. 1584, portrait ; Raphael, d. 1520, St. John ; Rembrandt, d. 1669, A Prophetess (sibyl) ; Reni, d. 1642, The Protectors of Milan ; Ribera, d. 1656, Juan de Porcida ; Rigaud, d. 1745, Duc de Villars ; Rubens, d. 1640, Wild-boar Hunt ; Salvator Rosa, d. 1675, Hermit ; Veronese, d. 1588, Venetian princess ; Zurbaran, d. 1662, St. Francis. In the room to the right is the "École Provençal," containing, among other paintings—Barry, The Bosphorus ; Duparc, d. 1778, The Milkmaid, and portraits of old man, woman, and girl knitting ; Papety, d. 1849, "La Vierge Consolatrice"; P. Puget, Madonna. In the left room are, among others, J. F. Millet, b. 1815, Woman feeding Child.

The most important parts of the Museum of Natural History are the conchological division and the collection of ammonites.

HÔTEL DE VILLE.   LA CONSIGNE.   CATHEDRAL.

From the Palace gardens is a good view of Marseilles. Behind the palace, on the top of the hill, is the great reservoir 242 ft. above the sea, supplied with water from the main channel by a branch canal. (See under Roquefavour, p. 77.) At this part of the hill is one of the entrances to the Zoological Gardens ; free on Sundays, when they are crowded with people. Near the entrance is the **Observatory,** one of the most important in France.

The port of Marseilles has in all an area of 422 acres, and is protected on the E. by Cape Croisette, and on the W. by Cape Couronne. Its approaches are lighted by 6 lighthouses, of which the most distant is on the Planier rock, 130 ft. above the sea, and 8 m. S.W. from Marseilles. The large steam vessels lie in the dock La Joliette, covering 55 acres, and finished in 1853 ; while the old-fashioned trading-vessels, with their lateen sails, crowd together in the harbour called emphatically the "Port," containing 75½ acres. From the end of the "Port" extends eastwards the handsome and greatly-frequented street La Cannebière, so called from the rope-walks, whose site it now occupies. At nearly the middle of the N. side of the "Port" is the **Hôtel de Ville** (1 in plan), built in the 17th cent., and adorned with sculpture by Puget, born at Marseilles ; while at the western extremity of the same side, next Fort St. Jean, is a low building called **La Consigne,** or Health Office. Over the chimney-piece in the council-room of the Consigne is a beautiful relief in white marble by Puget, representing the plague at Milan. To the right is a picture by Gerard, representing Bishop Belsunce administering the sacrament to the plague-stricken inhabitants of Marseilles in 1720. To the left, St. Roch before the Virgin, by David. Fronting the windows, "The frigate Justice returning from Constantinople with the plague on board," "l'an 4 de la République." Opposite the fireplace, "The cholera on board the Melpomene," by Horace Vernet. Next it, by Guerin, "The Chevalier Rose assisting to bury those who had died of the plague." Between them is a Crucifixion by Auber. Between the two windows is a portrait of Bishop Belsunce. (Fee, ½ fr.) Near the Consigne is the pier of the ferry-boats. Above the Hôtel de Ville is the town infirmary, and beyond it, on a terrace 30 ft. above the quay of Joliette, the **Cathedral,** a Byzantine basilica, 460 ft. from S. to N., and 165 ft. from E. to W. at the transept ; built of gray Florentine stone alternating with a whitish sandstone from the neighbourhood of Arles. The nave is 52 ft. wide, and the roof 82 ft. high. The great dome is 196 ft. high. Behind the cathedral are the Episcopal palace

(5 in plan), the Seminary (4), and the Hospice de la Charité (7). Eastwards, in the Place d'Aix, is the **Arc de Triomphe**, an imitation of
the arch of Titus at Rome, commenced on the 4th November 1825, to
commemorate the prowess of the Duc d'Angoulême in the Spanish
campaign of 1823. It is 58 ft. high and 58 ft. wide, has on the south
side statuary by Ramey emblematic of the battles of Fleurus and
Heliopolis, and on the north side similar statuary by David, representing the battles of Marengo and Austerlitz.   Over the arch is the inscription—"*A la République.*" From the arch a steep street, the R.
d'Aix, descends to the Cours Belsunce, with at the N. end a statue of
Bishop Belsunce, "pour perpetuer le souvenir de sa charité et de son
dévouement durant la peste ; qui desola Marseille " in 1720. By the
side of it are the terminus of the Bonneveine tram (p. 113) and the
Alcazar Lyrique, a kind of superior café chantant.

The continuation southwards of the Cours is the Rue de Rome, and
farther S. the spacious Promenade du Prado.   At the S. end of the
Cours are, to the right the R. Cannebière, and to the left the R.
Noailles, the two best streets in Marseilles.   At the W. or Port end of
the former is the **Bourse** (marked 10 in the plan), a parallelogramic
building, 154 feet broad by 223 long, erected between 1858 and 1860.
The principal hall, 60 feet by 94, is ornamented with mural paintings.
In the vestibule are allegorical statues of Marseilles and France, and a
bas-relief representing Marseilles receiving productions from all parts
of the world.   On the opposite side of the street, by the R. de Paradis,
are the Opera-house, the Palais de Justice, and the Préfecture (12 in
plan).   The Palais de Justice, built in 1862 in the Greek style, has on
the pediment and peristyle bas-reliefs by Guillaume, representing
Justice, Force, Prudence, etc.   The outer hall, the "Salle des Pas-
Perdus," is surrounded by 16 columns of red marble.   The Préfecture
is a splendid edifice in the Renaissance style, 300 ft. long by 260 ft.
wide, adorned with statues and bas-reliefs, and furnished with a grand
staircase, escalier d'honneur, communicating with handsome reception-
room ornamented with mural paintings.

From the Bourse a pleasant road leads up to the church of **Notre
Dame de la Garde**, one of the principal sights, and the most prominent
object in Marseilles.   From the Rue Paradis turn to the right by the
Cours Pierre-Puget, traverse the pretty promenade, the Jardin de Colline,
and then ascend the narrow road, the Montée des Oblats.   On descending
be careful to take the path to the left of the stone altar under a canopy
on 4 columns.   A small omnibus drives up the length of the Plateau

117

Notre Dame de la Garde.   Lycée.   Saint Victor.

de la Croix, whence a series of 178 steps has to be ascended to attain to the terrace on which the church stands, 535 ft. above the sea. The church is shut between 12 and 2, but the tower, ascended by 154 steps, can always be visited. Fee, ½ fr. It is 148 ft. high, crowned with a gilded image of Mary 30 ft. high, ascended by steps in the interior to the head. The view, which is just as good from the terrace, commands the whole of Marseilles. To the N.E. the culminating peak is Le Taoume, 2166 ft. ; to the S.E. is the Montagne de Carpiagne, 1873 ft.; and S. from it Mont Puget, 1798 ft. In front of Marseilles are the islands Ratonneau and Pomègue, connected by a breakwater. Between them and the mainland is the little island of If (p. 118). Off Cape Croisette are the islands of Maïre and Peirot. The road down the little ravine (the Valon de l'Oriol) leads to the Corniche.

NOTRE DAME DE LA GARDE.

Notre Dame, an edifice in the Roman-Byzantine style, consists of an upper and a lower church. The dome over the apse is 48 ft. high. The interior of the church is lined with Carrara marble, but the pilasters and columns are of marble from Africa and the Alps. Over the high altar in the low church is the miracle-working image of Notre Dame. It is about 6 ft. high, stands on a pedestal of olive wood, is hollow, and made of a kind of stucco (carton-pierre) silvered over, excepting the face and hands of both it and the child. It weighs 1 cwt. 1 qr. and 14 lbs. On the high altar in the high church is a replica, nearly all of silver. The walls are covered with expressions of gratitude to it, and with pictures illustrating the manner in which its miraculous interposition was displayed. .

From the streets Cannebière and Noailles other handsome streets ramify, such as the Rue de Rome and the Cours Liautaud. Just where the Cours Liautaud leaves the Rue Noailles is the **Lycée** or head grammar-school, and in the neighbourhood (marked 11) La Bibliothèque et l'École des Beaux Arts, forming together a palatial edifice off the Boulevard du Musée, 177 ft. long by 164 ft. wide. On the ground-floor are the class-rooms, and on the first story, the library, the collection of medals, and the reading-room, 131 ft. long by 19½ wide. Among the medals are 2600 belonging to Provence. The library contains 95,000 vols. and 1300 manuscripts.

At the mouth of the Port, on an eminence above Fort St. Nicolas and the Bassin de Carenage (graving dock), is the oldest church in Marseilles, **Saint Victor**, all that remains of one of the most famous monasteries in Christendom, founded in 420 by St. Cassien, ordained deacon of the church in Constantinople by Chrysostom. . The exterior of St. Victor resembles a badly-built small fort surrounded by 7 unequal and uncouth square towers, the two largest at the N. side having been added by Pope Urban V., a former abbot of the monastery. Over the entrance door under these towers is a rude representation of St. George and the dragon. The upper church dates only from the beginning of the 13th cent. Near the sacristy in the S. side a stair of 32 steps leads down to the original church, a large and spacious crypt. Of this crypt the most ancient part is the small chapel shut off from the rest, with several tombs hewn in the rock. Among those buried here were St. Victor, and, according to the tradition of the place, Lazarus also, who is said to have died at Marseilles. The ancient appearance of this chapel is marred by a modern altar with a stone reredos, sculptured, it is said, by Puget. The shaft of one of the columns has a sculptured rope coiled round it. Pieces of ornamental sculpture are seen at different parts of the crypt, and remnants of a fresco painting. This also is the sanctuary of a miraculous wooden image of Mary and Child, said to have been carved by Luke. It is of a dark colour, is $3\frac{1}{2}$ ft. high, and is called Notre Dame de Confession, whose intercession is sought by crowds of votaries from the 2d till the 9th of February. The best of the sarcophagi have been removed to the museum in the Château Borély (p. 113). At the foot of the eminence on which the church stands are Fort St. Nicolas and the Bassin de Carénage, whence a sou ferry steamboat crosses every four minutes to the other side. Among the modern churches perhaps the best is Saint Vincent de Paul, built in the style of the 13th cent.

Excursions.—The principal excursion from Marseilles is to the **Island of If,** with its old château built by Francis I., long used as a state prison. Boats for the excursion lie at the Cannebière end of the Port. They charge from 5 to 9 frs. ; but it is necessary to arrange the price before starting. The landing-place is at some low shelving rocks, whence a stair ascends to the terrace, on which are, to the right the entrance to the Château, and a little to the left a restaurant. A man conducts visitors over the castle, of which the most interesting parts are the cell of Monte Christo, and the place where he was thrown over into the sea.

Marseilles to Martigues, 24 m. N.W. by rail (see map on p. 66). At Martigues station omnibus for Port Bouc, $3\frac{1}{4}$ m. W. ; fare, $\frac{1}{2}$ fr. From Port Bouc rail to Miramas, or steamboat by the canal to Arles (see p. 76). After leaving Marseilles the first station of importance is L'Estaque (see p. 80), 7 m. W., with large brick and tile works, at the foot of a wooded hill. 4½ m. farther is Pas-des-Lanciers, with an inn close to the station. Here the Martigues branch separates from the main line, and the Martigues passengers change carriages. Here also an omnibus awaits passengers for Marignane, 3¾ m. W. on Lake Marignane, pop. 7000. Remains of castle which Mirabeau inhabited. Lake Marignane is separated from Lake Berre by a narrow strip of land. The train after passing Marignane station arrives at the station for Châteauneuf, a village S. towards the hills.

Les Martigues, pop. 10,000. At station, omnibus for the inn, Hôtel du Cours, and omnibus for Port Bouc. Martigues is situated on both sides of the outlet from Lake Berre, and on the islets within this outlet, all connected by bridges. The railway station, the hotel, and a large part of the town are on the E. or Jonquière side. On the first or smallest of the 3 islets are the Tribunal de la Pèche and the fish-market ; on the middle one is the Hôtel de Ville ; and on the third and largest are the hospital and the parish church with sculptured portals. On the N. side of the canal is the part of the town called Ferrières, containing the harbour and the reservoirs for the manufacture of salt. Fishing is the principal industry of the inhabitants.

There are in Marseilles numerous charitable institutions. The infirmary (Hôtel Dieu), founded in 1188 and rebuilt in 1593, can accommodate 750 patients. The workhouse (Hospice de la Charité) contains generally from 600 to 680 orphan children and aged men and women. Near the Prado is the Hôpital de la Concepcion, with 800 beds.

The leading industry is soap-making, which occupies sixty factories, with 1200 artisans, and produces annually 65,000 tons, valued at £2,000,000 sterling. With this manufacture are connected oil and chemical works ; in the former, which employ 2000 to 2500 workmen, 55,000 tons of different oils are produced yearly. The chemical works employ 2000 operatives in the manufacture of the salts of soda and concentrated acids, the value of whose annual production may be estimated at £320,000. Metallurgy is another great industry ; a large quantity of ore, imported from Elba, Spain, and Algeria, is smelted in the blast furnaces of St. Louis in the suburbs. The Mediterranean ironworks and yards, together with other private companies, have large workshops for the construction or repair of marine steam-engines, and for every branch of iron shipbuilding, employing several thousand workmen. Marseilles is a great centre for the extraction of silver from lead ore ; 16,000 tons of lead and 25 tons of fine silver are separated annually.

Commerce.—The chief imports in point of bulk are cereals from the Black Sea, Turkey, and Algeria ; but the one of greatest value, raw silk, £4,000,000 yearly, comes from Italy, Spain, the Levant, China, and Japan. Then follow metals, ores, timber, sugar, wool, cotton, and rice. The principal exports in respect of value are silk, woollen and cotton fabrics, refined sugars, wines and spirits ; those of greatest bulk are cereals in the form of flour, building materials, oil-cakes, manufactures in metal, oils, glass and crystal.

History.—The Greek colony of Massalia (in Latin, *Massilia*) was founded by the enterprising mariners of Phocæa in Asia Minor, about 600 B.C. After the ravages of successive streams of invaders it was repeopled in the 10th century under the protection of its viscounts. In 1112 the town bought up their rights, and was formed into a republic, governed by a podestat, appointed for life. In the remainder of the Middle Ages, however, this arrangement was modified, the higher town was governed by the bishop, and had its harbour at the creek of La Joliette. The southern suburb was governed by the abbot of St. Victor, and owned the Port des Catalans. The republic or lower town, situated between the two, retained the old harbour, and was the most powerful of the three divisions. The period of the Crusades brought great prosperity to Marseilles. King René made it his winter residence. Louis XIV. came in person to Marseilles to quell the disturbances under the Fronde. He took the town by storm, and had Fort St. Nicolas constructed. Marseilles repeatedly suffered from the plague, and an epidemic raged from May 1720 to May 1721 with a severity for which it is almost impossible to find a parallel ; Bishop Belsunce, Chevalier Rose, and others immortalised themselves by their courage and devotion.

During the Revolution of 1793 the people rose against the aristocracy, who up to that time had governed the commune. In the Terror they rebelled against the Convention, but were promptly subdued by General Carteux. The wars of the empire, by dealing a severe blow to their maritime commerce, excited the hatred of the inhabitants against Napoleon. Since 1815 the prosperity of the city has received a considerable impulse from the conquest of Algeria and the opening of the Suez Canal.

The Marseillaise.—The famous anthem called "The Marseillaise" was composed by Joseph Rouget de l'Isle, born at Lons-le-Saulnier on the 10th May 1760, and died (it is said in poverty) at Choisy-le-Roi, 6¼ m. S. from Paris by rail, on the 27th June 1836. On the 24th April 1792, the day before the departure of a detachment of volunteers, Dietrich, the Mayor of Strasburg, gave a banquet to their officers, and during dinner requested Rouget, then an officer in the engineers, to compose a war-song for them. Although it was late before Rouget retired to his room, he had both the music and the words ready before going to bed. In the morning he handed the paper to his host, saying : *" Tenez, voilà ce que vous m'avez demandé, mais j'ai peur que cela ne soit pas trop bon."* *" Que dites vous mon ami ? "* said Dietrich, after casting his eye over the MS. ; *" vous avez fait un chef-d'œuvre."* The mayor's wife having tried it on the piano, the orchestra of the theatre were engaged to perform it in the principal square of Strasburg, when such was the enthusiasm it created that the detachment marched off with nearly 1000 instead of 600 volunteers. For them Rouget called the air "Le Chant de guerre de l'armée du Rhin." In July of the same year a detachment of volunteers was sent to Paris from Marseilles by order of Barbaroux, and as they were in the habit of singing this song both on their march and in the capital it received the name of the "Hymne des Marseillais." Charles Barbaroux, born at Marseilles in 1767, died on the scaffold June 1794, was one of the deputies who contributed most to the fall of the monarchy. He belonged to the party called the Girondins.

MARSEILLES TO MENTON.

By Hyères, Cannes, Nice, and Monaco. 155 Miles.

See Maps, pages 113, 155, and 185.

MENTON
MILES TO
155

MARSEILLES. See under "Marseilles, Toulon, Nice et ⌣⌣
Menton" in the "Indicateur." The train, after leaving Marseilles
on its way to Toulon, traverses beautiful fertile valleys opening to
the sea, and bounded by mountains mostly with whitish calcareous
tops. Having crossed the stream Huveaune and traversed several
tunnels and the Durance and Marseilles canal, the slow trains halt
at the villages of St. Marcel, with the chapel of N. D. de Nazareth,
and St. Menet, and La Penne, all situated at the foot of Mont
Carpiagne.. During the season, from May to October, a coach at
the St. Menet station awaits passengers for the cold mineral baths of
Camoins, 2 m. distant, or 5 m. by omnibus from Marseilles. The
bathing establishment is about ¼ m. from the village, in an undulating hollow, among plane trees, olives, and vines. The water is
cold, and contains iron and iodine, with a great deal of sulphur. It
is very effective as a tonic, and in diseases of the liver. The establishment is quiet but comfortable. Pension 8 to 9 frs. per day.

10½ m. from Marseilles is **Aubagne**, pop. 8100. H. Notre Dame.
Omnibus daily to Marseilles, stopping at H. St. Louis. Every train
halts at Aubagne. Junction with loop-line to Valdonne, 10½ m. N.,
with coal-mines and potteries. Coach from Valdonne to Aix by
Fuveau, where take rail.

After Aubagne the train passes through the tunnel of Mussaguet,
and, if a slow train, halts at the next station, Cassis, a pleasant fishing village in an oasis at the head of a small bay, between Mont
Gardiole (to the west), culminating point 1800 ft., and Mont de
Canaille (to the east), culminating point 1365 ft. *Inn:* Hotel
and Pension Liautaud. An omnibus awaits passengers at the station,
30 cents. A very pretty path, passing by the Grotte de Regagne
and through a forest of pines on the sides of Mont Canaille, leads
to La Ciotat, 6½ m. east by this road, and 23 m. from Marseilles
by rail. The station for La Ciotat is 2½ m. from the town, but an
omnibus awaits passengers. *Inn:* H. de l'Univers, at the head of a
well-protected harbour, nearly encircled by two strong stone jetties.
At the western side of the little bay is a curious promontory, the Bec
de l'Aigle (well seen from the station), composed of three lofty rocks
in a row, perpendicular on the W. side. Beyond the point is the

For continuation westwards see map, page 66.

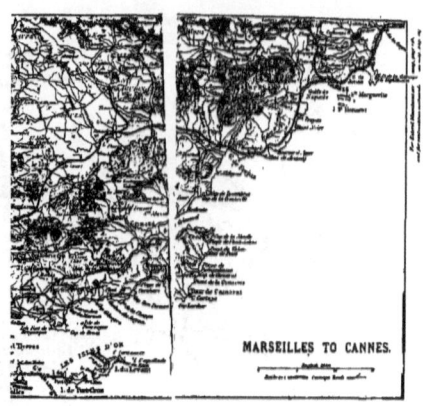

MARSEILLES TO CANNES.

small island Ile Vert. A little quarrying and coral fishing is carried on in La Ciotat; but the main business of the place is derived from the great shipbuilding yards of the Messageries Maritimes, which may be said to employ directly and indirectly the whole town.

4¼ m. beyond La Ciotat, or 27¼ from Marseilles, is the pretty village of St. Cyr, close to the station. 4¼ m. farther is the station for Bandol, a fishing village at the head of a shallow bay with small islands. The industries are cooperage and the culture of immortelles in fields on the plain and on terraces on the sides of the hills.

36 m. E. from Marseilles is the station Ollioules-St.-Nazaire, where omnibuses await passengers for St. Nazaire, pop. 2500, a port on the Mediterranean, and for Ollioules, pop. 3900, *Inn:* Trotobas; situated a short way inland on the Reppe, in a deep hollow surrounded by limestone cliffs, which, about 2 m. up the river, are so close to each other as to form a gloomy ravine, at one time the haunt of the brigand Gaspard de Besse. The great industry of Ollioules, Nazaire, and Bandol is the culture of immortelles, which, when made up into wreaths, are sent all over France. The largest and best cost 24 frs. the dozen. Yellow is the natural colour of the flower, but they are variously dyed or bleached. They are cultivated on terraces among olive trees. Oranges and lemons grow freely here. The coach for Beausset halts in the Place of Ollioules, and then runs up the right bank of the Reppe to Beausset, pop. 3000. *Inn:* France.

38½ m. E. from Marseilles, and 6 m. W. from Toulon, is **La Seyne** station. An omnibus awaits passengers for the town, pop. 11,000, H. de la Méditerranée, situated on the roads opposite Toulon, between which two ports there is constant communication by steamers. Near the hotel is the office of the omnibus for Tamaris, a village 1¼ m. S.E., at the foot of Fort Napoleon, and on the Rade (roads) du Lazaret. The omnibus returns by Brguier. The Toulon omnibus for Reynier passes through La Seyne, fro which Reynier is 3 m. W. On the hill above Reynier are the new fort and what remains of the ancient village of **Six Fours**, once a town of importance. The greater part of the crumbling walls has been cleared away, and in their stead a strong fort has been built, which occupies the entire summit of the hill. The old church still remains, of which the earliest part, 6th cent., is at the entrance extending east and west, and was originally the whole building. To the right hand are two stone altars (6th cent.), with windows behind them to give light to the officiating priest, who at that time said mass with his face to the audience. The nave, extend-

ing N. and S., was added in the 15th cent.   It contains a Madonna
by Puget, and some pictures on wood of the 15th cent.   Under the
church is a large cistern, formerly, according to the "Annales de Six
Fours," the chapel or house where Mary, sent by her brother Lazarus,
told the inhabitants about Jesus.   She was buried in the crypt of St.
Maximin (p. 143).

TOULON.

42 m. E. from Marseilles, 13 m. W. from Hyères, 22 m. S. from
Carnoulles, 59 m. S.W. from St. Raphael, 79 m. S.W. from Cannes,
98½ m. S.W. from Nice, and 113 m. S.W. from Menton, is **Toulon**,
pop. 71,000 (see maps, pp. 123 and 129).   *Hotels:* near the station,
the Grand Hotel, a large first-class house ; a little farther and near
the post, the theatre, and Temple Protestant, are the Victoria and
the Louvre ; in the Place Puget is the Nord, and at No. 15 an office
where carriages can be hired for Mont Faron and other excursions.
From this "Place" start the omnibuses for Hyères, 11 m. E. by the
road ; also omnibuses for Ollioules and Beausset.   The porpoises and
scallop shells on the fountain in the centre of the "Place" are by
Puget.   In the Place d'Armes is the H. Place d'Armes, fronting the
Arsenal and the Promenade, where the band plays on Sundays.

The omnibuses for Cap Brun, Ste. Marguerite, Le Pradet, La Valette,
La Garde, and La Crau, and the diligences for Pierrefeu, Collobrières,
Cuers, Solliès-Pont, Belgentier, Meounes, Neroules, and Brignoles, start
from the Place d'Italie at the east end of Toulon.   In this "Place"
are the inns H. Petit, St. Jean, and H. Croix-Blanche.   (For the above
places see maps, pp. 123 and 129.)   In the Place Puget are several
cheap restaurants.   The best restaurants are on the quay of the port.

The Quai du Port.—The bronze statue on this quay, representing Navigation, is by Daumas, by whom are also the colossal statues
in front of the theatre.   Near it are the berths of the steamers for
Saint Mandrier, 3½ m. S., and for the Iles d'Hyères.   More to the
right is the berth of the large steamers for La Seyne.   At the west
end is the hulk of the famous *Belle Poule*, covered with a roof of
sloping planks.   This was the vessel in which Napoleon's body was
brought from St. Helena and deposited in the Hôtel des Invalides on
the 15th December 1840.   The Chamber of Deputies granted £40,000
to defray the expenses of the expedition, and entrusted the command
to the Prince de Joinville, with whom were associated Bertrand,
Gourgaud, the younger Las Casas, and Marchand the Emperor's valet,
all the latest and most devoted of Napoleon's adherents.   On the

16th October the coffin was opened, when the body was found in an excellent state of preservation. On that same day the remains were embarked on board the *Belle Poule,* and on the 18th the ship set sail. On the 30th November it reached Cherbourg, where the body was transferred to the steamboat *Normandie,* which conveyed it up the Seine to Courbevoie, where it was placed on a most magnificent car.

Cab fares.—The course, 1¼ fr. ; the hour, 2 frs.

The strongly-fortified port of Toulon occupies a plain rising gradually from the sea to the lofty ridge of Mont Faron, which runs east and west, and sends out lower branches, enclosing the town and harbour on either side. On the summit, immediately behind the town, are Fort Croix and large barracks ; to the east is La Platrière, 1000 ft., and immediately behind it Mt. Coudon, 2305 ft. To the west is the Cap Gros, 1735 ft., and behind it Mt. Caoume, 3268 ft. On every commanding position is a fort ; while from the water's edge at the west end of the port rises Fort Malbousquet. Similarly situated on the eastern end is Fort Lamalgue, the last held by the English in 1793. The Petit Rade offers a spacious and most secure roadstead. From it are walled off, at the east end, the Port Marchand and the Vieille Darse, or town-docks, whence the steamers sail. Then follow the Government docks of Vauban, Castigneau, and Missiessy, all communicating with each other by swing bridges, and surrounded by well-built quays. The most conspicuous features of Toulon are the arsenals and the establishments connected with them, which are on a scale of almost unrivalled magnificence, occupying 717 acres, and employing above 10,000 men. Near the west end of the Port a large gateway with marble columns forms the entrance into the "Arsenal Maritime," covering 240 acres, and containing a general storehouse, 100 forge fires, two covered building-slips, a ropery 1050 feet long, and an armoury with at the entrance two caryatides and a colossal eagle by Puget. Adjoining is the Arsenal de Castigneau, constructed on piles along the bay towards La Seyne, with the bakery, ironworks, and ship-equipment departments.

Although Toulon, rather a dirty town, is crowded with marines and sailors, it maintains by the constant influx of the peasantry all the characteristics of a town of Provence. Theatres of every grade abound, from the Grand Opera House down to the poor little café chantant, where gaudily-dressed females electrify the audience with popular ballads. The most pleasant lounge in winter is on the Quai du Port, as the wharf fronting the town-dock is called. As long as the sun is above the horizon it shines there, consequently during the cold season it is crowded with all kinds of people, most of whom, unfortunately, are poisoning the air with execrable tobacco. On it are good cafés and restaurants, and booksellers' shops where plans of the town and neighbourhood are sold. This now gay sunny promenade was in November 1793 the scene of one of the most horrid butcheries of human life recorded in history, when the infuriated Republican soldiers, mad with vengeance, slaughtered above 6000 of their countrymen, not sparing even those of their own party, in their blind rage. Sir Sydney Smith, amidst the flames of burning ships and dockyards, and the shrieks and imploring cries of the terrified populace, succeeded in rescuing and embarking some 1500. Napoleon, then a lad of 23, by whose military genius the discomfiture of the English had been effected, exerted himself to the utmost, but in vain, to stay the carnage.

Among the houses which border the Quai du Port is the **Town Hall**, adorned with two admirable caryatides by Pierre Puget. In front is the statue representing Navigation, and at No. 64 of the street behind is the corner house Puget built for himself. It contains four stories of nearly square windows, those in the lowest and highest rows being the smallest. The small side has three windows in each row, and the large four, the windows of the first three rows over the doorway being in couples. On the angles are shallow grooved foliated pilasters, and under the eaves a projecting dentil cornice.

The most sheltered street in winter, and the coolest in summer, is the Rue Lafayette, a broad avenue lined with shops and shaded with immense lime trees. It commences at the east end of the Port and bends round to the Place Puget. About half of the street is occupied by a fruit, flower, and vegetable market. In the second story of the narrow five-storied house, at No. 89 (the Port end), is one of the cannon-balls fired by the English during the struggle of November 1793. (See above.) At the Port end of the street is the "Place," whence the omnibus starts for Mourillon; also the church of St. François de Paule. The interior contains pictures and statues of some merit. The reredos of the altar to the left represents one of the interviews between J. C. and Marguerite Alacoque, while that of the altar to the right represents Mary announcing herself to the girl swineherd at Lourdes to be the "conceived without sin."

The street ramifying from the west side of the Rue Lafayette, between houses Nos. 77 and 79, leads to the cathedral of **Sainte-Marie-Majeure**, commenced in the 11th cent., and finished in the 18th.

The exterior is unattractive.   The interior is better.   The organ-loft over the entrance is of carved oak.   The alabaster reredos of the altar in the chapel to the right of the high altar is by the sculptor Veyrier. The tabernacle and the two angels under it are by Puget, who is said to have executed also the alto-relievo on the side wall of the chapel representing the apostles looking into the empty tomb of Mary.   Over the arch of the chapel on the left of the high altar is a Madonna in wood by Canova.   Several very good pictures adorn the church.

All the steamers sail from the Quai du Port.   The best and largest are those which cross to La Seyne (p. 123).   The steamers for the Iles d'Hyères and for St. Mandrier sail also from this wharf.   The St. Mandrier steamer makes the trip six times daily, calling first at Balaguier, where the landing-place is between Fort Aiguillette to the north and Fort Balaguier to the south, the latter being easily recognised by its round tower.   The restaurant and houses are situated towards Fort Aiguillette.   On the other side of the point of Fort Balaguier is Le Tamarin, or Tamaris, consisting chiefly of pretty villas in luxuriant gardens full of palms and orange trees.   Behind Tamaris rises Fort Napoleon, commanding a splendid view.   An excellent carriage-road leads up to the top.   It commences near the neck of land of the peninsula of Cepet.   An omnibus runs between Le Tamaris, Balaguier, and La Seyne.   The steamer, after touching at Balaguier, crosses the roads or Rade du Lazaret and enters the small bay of St. Mandrier.   At the landing-place is a comfortable inn, charging 8 to 10 frs. per day.   Round the point, in a warm nook among the hills, is the hospital of St. Mandrier, with 1200 beds, one of the most important establishments of this kind in France.   It occupies three sides of a parallelogram, has a handsome chapel, and a great cistern vaulted with concentric circles.   Adjoining is a large and well-sheltered garden with orange trees.   Visitors are readily admitted.   In Toulon, near the Place d'Armes, is the Hôpital de la Marine, exclusively for the navy.   Although well ordered, it is hardly sufficiently ventilated.

One of the most interesting walks is to the top of Mont Faron, 1792 feet above the sea.   From the Porte Notre Dame, at the E. end of Toulon, take the broad road or street leading northwards by the bridge across the railway.   Then passing one of the artillery establishments, leave the town by the Port of Ste. Anne—the name is on the gateway.   From this the real road commences, excellent all the way, and in its gentle ascent and continuous windings ever unfolding the most lovely views of the town and the bay.   When not far from

the summit three roads meet. The road to the left goes to the barracks and to the top. The nearly level road to the right goes to Fort
Faron, and the steep road to the left to Fort de la Croix on a rock
above Fort Faron. Both are on the east or the La Valette side of
the mountain. The summit consists of a stony tableland, from
which rise knolls of various elevations. It can be done in a carriage.

Toulon Omnibuses.—Among the omnibus-drives from Toulon the best
are to Hyères (p. 133) by La Valette, and to the village of Dardenne,
on a stream in the picturesque valley between Mont Faron on the right
or S. side and the steep Tourris mountain, with bald calcareous summits, 1426 ft. high. As far as the omnibus goes the road is good.
The road eastwards through the valley leads to La Valette, and the
short road northward to the village of Le Revest, on the top of an
eminence commanding a good view of the ravine of the Dardenne.
The village of La Valette, pop. 1700, is 3¼ m. E. from Toulon and
7¾ W. from Hyères by the omnibus. The carving on the church door,
representing John writing the book of Revelation in the island of
Patmos, is said to have been done by Puget. From this village the
ascent is made of Mt. Coudon, 2305 ft., in about 2½ hours. "From
Mt. Coudon there are grand views in all directions. I have sought
for them a great deal, and seen a great many, but have never beheld
any scene so lovely as the graceful yet bold indentured coast of France
as exhibited from Coudon."—*George Sand.* A carriage-road leads up
to the very top, but unfortunately, when only a few feet from the
summit, farther progress is stopped by a fort, and the best of the
view lost. Commence the ascent from the narrow lane opposite the
Hôtel de Ville, and, once on the high road, never leave it. On the
way up many very beautiful land and sea views disclose themselves.

The next best omnibus-drives are to Cap Brun and Ste. Marguerite,
eastward on the coast, and to Le Pradet, a village N.E. from Ste.
Marguerite, on the road to Carqueyranne. Both omnibuses start from
the Place d'Italie. Although this road skirts the coast, very little of
it is seen on account of hills and garden-walls. Cap Brun and Ste.
Marguerite are both forts on cliffs projecting into the sea. To the
east of the Fort Ste. Marguerite is the village, consisting of a few
houses, with a small chapel among villas and cottages scattered over
the slope of an eminence rising from a tiny cove. Le Pradet is
a considerable village a little to the S. of La Garde. La Garde, on
its hill crowned with the ruins of a castle, forms a marked feature in
the landscape. At Cap Brun is the villa of Sir Charles Dilke.

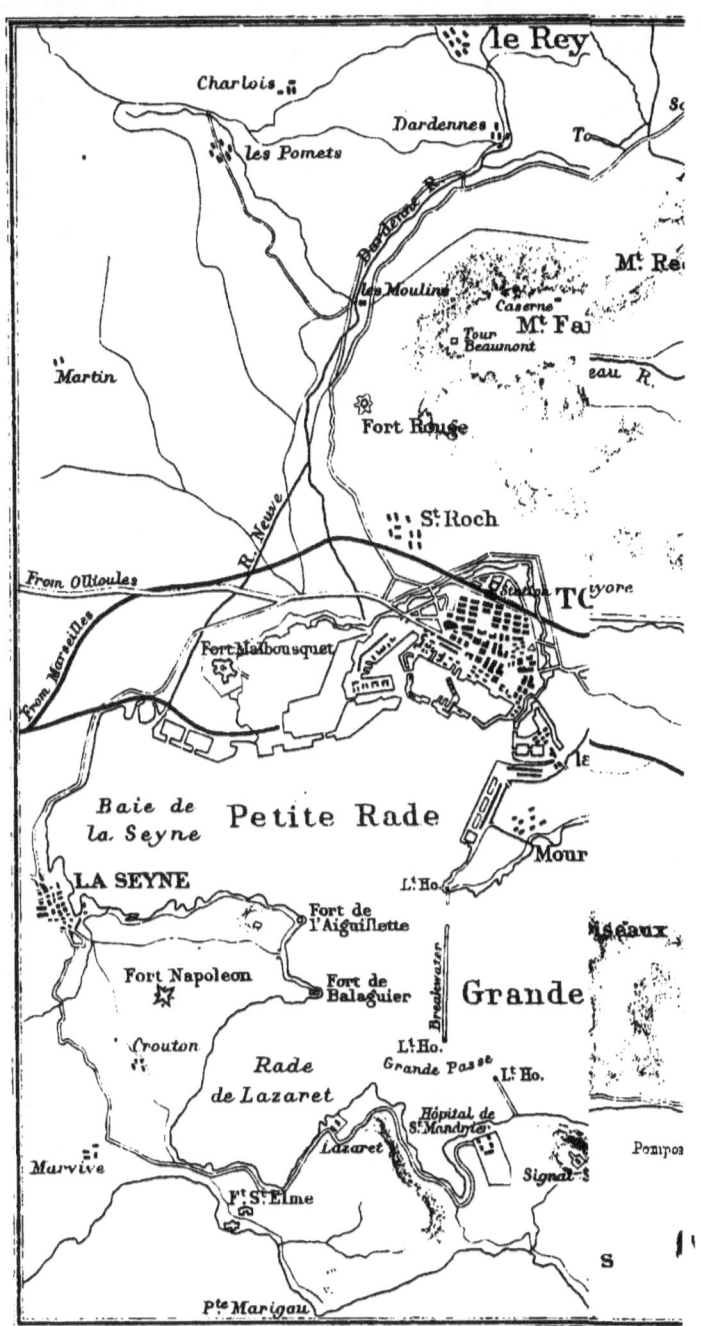

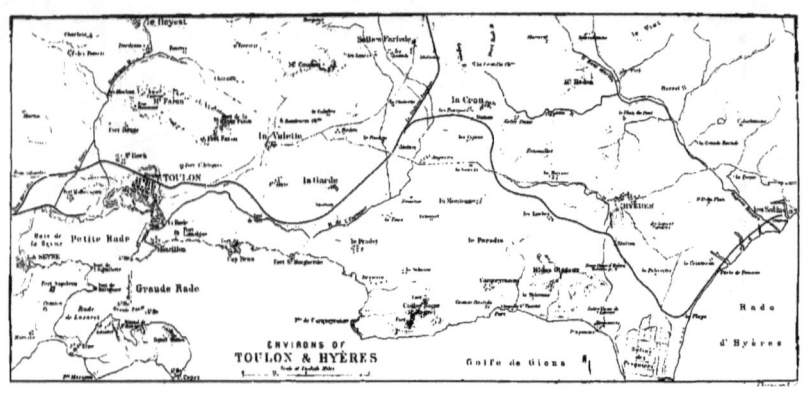

ENVIRONS OF
TOULON & HYÈRES

The omnibus to the sea-bathing suburb of Mourillon, 3½ m. E., behind Fort La Malgue or Malague, starts from the Port end of the Rue or Cours Lafayette.

Diligence Drives.—Toulon to Meounes, 19¼ m. N. by diligence from the Place d'Italie. Time, 3 hrs. ; fare, 2½ frs. (see map, p. 117).

The diligence, after passing through La Valette, Farlède 4¾ m., and Solliès-Ville, arrives at Solliès-Pont, 272 ft. above the sea and 10½ m. from Toulon, situated on the railway and on the Gapeau. The diligence halts near the inn H. du Commerce, where passengers from Hyères can await its arrival. The coach to Brignoles passes by the same way, but at an earlier hour. From Solliès-Pont commences the beautiful part of the route, up the fertile valley of the Gapeau between lofty and precipitous calcareous mountains. The slopes are covered with large olive trees, and the plain with fields and vineyards and numerous cherry trees. Nearly 2 m. farther up the valley, but on the other side of the Gapeau, is Solliès-Toucas (328 ft.), situated in a sheltered nook. 5 m. higher up, and 12½ m. from Toulon, is Belgentier (pronounced Belgensier), on both sides of the Gapeau. The horses are changed here. The inn (auberge), which is indifferent, is round the corner to the right. From Belgentier the olives cease to be continuous. The diligence, after passing the flour-mill Pachoquin, 558 ft., arrives at the best headquarters in the valley, Meounes, 919 ft., on the stream Naille, an affluent of the Gapeau, 3½ m. N. from Belgentier, 8¾ m. N. from Solliès-Pont, 6 m. E. from Signes, 4¾ m. S. from Roquebrussane, 12 m. S.E. from Le Camp, 5 m. S. from Garéoules, and 7½ m. S. from Forcalqueiret railway station, which is 7 m. E. by rail from Brignoles (see map, p. 123).

The inn of Meounes is behind the church. On a small peak overlooking the village is an image of Mary. Round three sides of the pedestal are the words "Mary conceived without sin, the tower of David, the refuge of sinners, pray for us." On the fourth side "June 1870." Eastward is a great circular mass of mountains, which rises abruptly on the eastern and southern rim, and sinks towards the western and northern. Going round from south to east the culminating points reach the elevations of 1794 ft., 1860 ft., 2073 ft., 2248 ft., 1934 ft., 2326 ft., and 2060 ft. Tablelands, more or less fertile, and peaks of various elevations, occupy the centre. The rocks are calcareous, and most of the paths which traverse this region are excessively stony.

Scarcely 3 m. from Meounes by a very pretty road is the Carthusian Monastery of Montrieux (pronounced Monrieux), on an eminence 945 ft. above the sea. To go to it descend the high road for about 1½ m. to a bridge and first road right, which take. A little way up, the road divides into two ; take the left one, which crosses the Gapeau. The building, which is prettily situated, is small, and contains only about from 30 to 35 inmates. It was founded in 1117, and had very large possessions, which, with the house, were taken from the monks at the fatal revolution of 1793. In 1845 the building was re-

K

purchased, along with 74 acres of land, and peopled with a detachment of friars from the head monastery of the order, the Chartreuse of Grenoble. The Carthusians and Trappists resemble each other in dress and in their rules, the chief difference being that the Trappists sleep in the same room, and dine together in the same room, while the Carthusians have each a separate suite of small rooms or cells, where the inmate sleeps and feeds by himself. Both affirm: "Nous ne permettons jamais aux femmes d'entrer dans notre enceinte; car nous savons que, ni le sage, ni le prophète, ni le juge, ni l'hôte de Dieu, ni ses enfans, ni même le premier modèle sorti de ses mains, n'ont pu échapper aux caresses ou aux tromperies des femmes." A nearer but very stony path, commencing opposite the church door of Meounes, leads also to the convent.

Through Meounes pass the Toulon courrier to Brignoles by Roquebrussane, the Toulon coach to Brignoles by Garéoules, and the Toulon coach to Garéoules. The drive between Meounes and Brignoles is monotonous, and the inns in the villages poor. Fare from Meounes to Brignoles 3 frs., distance 15 miles. (For Brignoles, see p. 142.)

Toulon to Collobrières.—From the Place d'Italie a coach starts daily to Collobrières, 25 m. N.E. by E., passing through La Valette 3¼ m., La Garde with its castle 5 m., and La Crau 7¼ m. *Inn:* H. de France. Beyond the inn are the post and telegraph offices, and a few yards farther, in the Rue de Gapeau, the halting and meeting place of this diligence with the coach that runs between Hyères and La Crau.

From La Crau the diligence proceeds to Pierrefeu, 18 m. from Toulon, where the horses are changed near the first terrace, a little higher than the inn. From Pierrefeu the diligence proceeds to Collobrières, up the thinly-peopled valley of the river. Fare, 2½ frs.; time, 4½ hrs. Excursionists from Hyères should await the diligence at La Crau, where it arrives about 4 P.M.; or take the rail to Cuers station, and then the courrier, which leaves Toulon every forenoon for Collobrières, passing through Pierrefeu (p. 142).

From Toulon to Pierrefeu the road traverses a fertile plain more or less undulating, covered with olive trees, vineyards, and wheat fields. The Gapeau, the river that supplies Hyères with water, is crossed a few yards beyond La Crau, and shortly afterwards the road to Pierrefeu takes a northerly direction up the valley of the Real-Martin, the principal affluent of the Gapeau. Pierrefeu, pop. 4000, is a dirty village on a hill, 482 ft. above the sea, with narrow, crooked, steep streets. From the terrace there is a pleasing view of the plain below. From Pierrefeu the coach ascends the valley of the Réal-Collobrier to Collobrières, pop. 3600, on an eminence rising from the stream. *Inn:* H. de Notre Dame, near the diligence office, good and clean. The office of the courrier is in the principal street, near the Post and the Hôtel de Ville with the promenade. From the top of the hill, where stands the old church, now abandoned, is an excellent view of the valley. The lower part is covered with fields and vineyards interspersed with fruit trees. On the side of the mountains facing the north are forests of

chestnut trees, some very old and of most fantastic forms, while on the
opposite side are forests of sombre cork oaks. Cork-cutting, wine-making,
and the exportation of chestnuts form the principal industries.   The
wine, when four years old, makes an agreeable vin ordinaire.   In the
tenth year it is at its best, when it becomes straw-coloured.

A winding coach-road across the Maure mountains extends northwards to Gonfaron, a station on the railway to Cannes.   Between this
road and Pignans station is the culminating point of the Maures, on
which is the chapel of N. D. des Anges, 2556 ft. above the sea.

The Islands of Hyères, or the Iles d'Or.

Steamer every other day from Toulon to Porquerolles ; time 2 hrs.,
fare 2 frs. ; thence to the Ile Port-Cros, time 1 hour.   Fare there and
back to Porquerolles, 2 frs.   Steamer also every other day from Les
Salins of Hyères to Porquerolles by the Iles du Levant and Port-Cros.

The finest of the views of Toulon and neighbourhood is from
the deck of the steamer while sailing through the roads.   To the
north rises the massive and precipitous Mont Faron with its forts and
barracks, and to the east is La Malgue with its forts and batteries.
To the west is La Seyne, by the north side of the hill on which is Fort
Napoleon, and southwards is the peninsula of Cepet with the large
Military Hospital of St. Mandrier.   The whole coast from Toulon to
Hyères is afterwards seen distinctly from the steamer.   Just before
arriving at Porquerolles the steamer sails closely along the southern
shore of the peninsula of Giens (see p. 140, and map, p. 123).

Porquerolles, pop. 500, is 5 miles long, and of an average breadth
of 2 miles.   The culminating point is 479 ft. above the sea.   The
northern coast is low, the land sloping upwards to the south, where
it terminates in vertical cliffs of schistose and quartzose rocks.   The
vegetation is nowhere luxuriant.   Pines, arbutus, and heaths cover the
mountains, while the more fertile plains and valleys have vineyards
and fields.   The climate is very dry, and the water-supply is obtained
from wells.   Mosquitoes can hardly be said to exist.   Many rare plants
are found in the woods, such as the Delphinium requienii, Galium minu-
tulum, Pelargonium capitatum, Latyrus tingitanus, Alkanna lutea,
Genista linifolia, Cistus Porquerollensis, and the Cistus olbiensis.

The Port of Porquerolles is situated in nearly the centre of the N.
side of the island, exactly opposite Hyères, and 9 m. from Les Salins.
The pier has not sufficient water to allow the steamer to moor
alongside.   In the "Place," quite close to the pier, are the church,
the museum of the island collected by the most worthy curate, and
the two inns, of which the H. du Progrès is the larger of the two.
Above the town, at an elevation of 215 ft., is the castle, with some small
buildings formerly used as an hospital, now a prison.

There are three main roads in the island—the road by the N. coast
westward is called the **Chemin du Langoustier**, the road by the N.
coast eastward the **Chemin des Mèdes**, and the road up the centre
of the island, from N. to S., the **Chemin au Phare**.   This last road

commences at the N.W. corner of the "Place" and terminates at the lighthouse on Cap d'Armes, the most southern point of the island, 210 ft. above the sea. The lighthouse, first-class, is ascended by 70 steps, is 46 ft. above the ground, and has a white light.

The first road right from the N.W. corner of the "Place" is the Chemin du Langoustier, which, on its way westward, traverses a comparatively open country. The building in ruins, seen on the top of the ridge to the left, 370 ft. high, is an old watch-tower, considered the most ancient structure on the island. Near the end of the road is a decayed soda manufactory. At the terminus on the peninsula is a Vigie, a watch-tower and signal-station combined, 108 ft. above the sea.

The road along the N.E. coast, the Chemin des Mèdes, traverses the most fertile part of the island. About half-way, near Point Lequin, it passes round the N. end of a ridge, extending N. and S., on whose summit, 479 ft. above the sea, is a semaphore or signal-station, commanding a perfect view of the whole island, while the view of the other islands, of the peninsula of Giens, of Hyères, and of the coast to beyond Cannes, is admirable. The way up is by the first branch road right at the commencement of the wood. The road at the commencement looks as if it led up the plain. The Chemin des Mèdes terminates at a farmhouse called Notre Dame, formerly a monastery, whence the continuation is by a path leading to a fort on Cap des Mèdes, to the N. of a hill 449 ft. high.

Port-Cros.—11½ m. E. from Porquerolles port is the island of Port-Cros, 12½ m. S. from Les Salins, on the western side of the island, at the head of a small landlocked bay. An inn is near the pier. The main road extends from the landing-place up the valley by the church and the proprietor's house to **Port Man** at the eastern end of the island. Port-Cros consists of a picturesque wooded ridge, whose culminating point is to the south, 669 ft. above the sea; it is 2½ m. from S.W. to N.E., and 1¼ m. from N. to S., and contains 1482 acres. The rocks in Porquerolles and Port-Cros are similar—mica, schist, and quartz. Round the coast are numerous little coves with tiny smooth beaches. Excellent sea fishing may be had at all times.

About a mile east from Port Man is the western extremity of the more sterile island of the **Levant**, 5 m. from E. to W., and 1½ from N. to S. The culminating point is in the centre of the island, the Pierres Blanches, on which there is a signal-tower, 423 ft. above the sea. Mica, amianthus, actinolite, and tourmaline abound.

Toulon to Hyères.

Toulon to Hyères.—Passengers at Toulon for Hyères, 11 m. E., can go either by the omnibus, which starts three times daily from the Place Puget, fare 1 fr., time nearly 2 hours, or by train. If by rail they should examine the Indicateur, and select a direct train, otherwise they may have to wait some time at La Pauline, where the branch line commences by La Crau to Hyères, 13 miles by rail from Toulon.

HYÈRES,

pop. 13,000, the most southerly of the stations on the Riviera, the nearest to England, and only 18¼ hours from Paris. It is not so gay as Cannes, Nice, Monte Carlo, and San Remo, nor perhaps even Menton ; but none of these places have such beautiful boulevards, nor such a variety of charming country walks and drives either by private or stage coaches. The hotel omnibuses await passengers at the station. The station is ¾ m. S. from Hyères, and ¾ m. N. from the Hermitage.

Hotels.—At the west of the town are the Hôtel des Palmiers, below the Place des Palmiers ; the *Iles d'Or, with garden off the main road ; the H. Continental, on an eminence above the Iles d'Or. These three are first-class houses, and charge per day from 15 to 20 frs., including bedroom, service, wine, candles, and three meals with coffee or tea in the morning. Next the Iles d'Or is the Hesperides, 8 to 12 frs. Off the main street are the Ambassadeurs and the Europe, both from 10 to 12 frs., frequented chiefly by those who come only for a few days. At the east end of Boulevard des Palmiers the H. du Parc, 12 to 15 frs. On opposite side, and well situated for the sun, is the second-class house, the H. Iles d'Hyères, 7 to 10 frs. Near it, but not well situated, is the Méditerranée, third-class. The principal hotel on the east side of Hyères is the H. Orient, 10 to 13 frs., a comfortable and old-established house, opposite the public gardens. Farther east, and off the high road to St. Tropez, is the Beau-Séjour, from 12 to 15 frs. Down by one of the roads to the sea is the H. des Étrangers, 10 to 13 frs., in a sunny situation. About 1½ m. S. from Hyères, near the Hermitage chapel, but in a sheltered nook overlooking one of the warmest and most favoured valleys of the Montagnes des Oiseaux, is the *Hôtel and Pension de l'Hermitage, 9 to 12 frs., retired and comfortable, and frequented chiefly by English. As it is near the sea, in a forest of pines and cork oaks, it combines the advantages of Arcachon with those of Hyères. All the above prices include tea or coffee in the morning, and meat breakfast and dinner, with wine to both. Abundance of furnished apartments and villas to let. In the Place des Palmiers are a French and an English bank. Both exchange money. In the same "Place" is the Temple Protestant, and a little beyond the English Pharmacy. The Episcopal chapel is in the Boulevard Victoria. The town hospital is at the west end of the town.

There are several clubs ; the best are the Siècle and the Progrès, which take in English newspapers. Here, as well as in the other stations on the Riviera, all the first-class clubs or "cercles" have large gambling-rooms, as productive of evil as Monte Carlo.

Cab fares.—Per hour, 2 frs. A coach per month with driver and 2 horses, 500 frs. With 1 horse, 300 frs.

Drives.—A 3 to 4 hours' drive in a coach with 1 horse costs 6 to 8 frs., with 2 horses 10 to 12 frs., but, as there is no recognised tariff, it is necessary in every case to settle the price beforehand. The drive to Carqueyranne by the coast and back by the road between the Paradis and Oiseaux mountains, with 1 horse, 8 frs. The same price to La Crau, round by the west side of Mt. Fenouillet, and back by the valley of the Gapeau. The great drive, forming a good day's excursion, is to the Chartreuse of Montrieux, 18 m. N., by La Crau, Solliès-Pont (a railway station), and Belgentier (pronounced Belgensier). (For description, see p. 129.) Coach with 2 horses, 25 frs. there and back. The other great drive (costing the same) is to the Fort of Brégançon, 16 miles east by the coast-road, passing by Les Vieux Salins, at the eastern extremity of which a road strikes off due north towards the St. Tropez road, passing Bastidon (7 m. from Hyères) amidst large olive trees. After Les Salins the road enters the part of the plain called La Plage Largentière, in which is situated the Château de Bormettes, built by Horace Vernet (7½ m. E. from Hyères). A little farther east, on the Plage de Pellegrin, are the châteaux of Léoubes (11 m.) and Brégançon; and, on the western point of Cap Bénat, Fort Brégançon, about 4 miles west of Bormes. (For Bormes, see p. 142.) Another pleasant drive is to Cuers, 14 m. N.W. by the Gapeau and Pierrefeu. The first road that ramifies to the right, from the Gapeau valley road, leads up into the Vallée de Borel, in the heart of the Maure mountains. This road passes by the large farm-house of Ste. Eulalie, in a plain full of large olive trees, some 6 feet in diameter. There are also some large pines. Besides these excursions there are a great many little drives which may be taken in the wooded sheltered valleys running up between the ridges of the Maure mountains, but for them a light vehicle should be selected, as some parts of the roads are not good.

Coaches.—From the Place de la Rade start daily coaches for Carqueyranne 6¼ m. W., for Les Vieux Salins 4 m. E., for La Crau 4½ m. N. (see p. 130), and for St. Tropez 32½ m. E., whence a steamer sails to St. Raphael. Near the "Place," opposite the Hotel and Restaurant du Var, start several times daily large omnibuses for Toulon by La Valette (see maps, pp. 123 and 129).

MASSILLON. ST. PAUL.

Hyères proper is a little dirty town of narrow streets, running up the south-east side of the castle hill ; like, however, all the other winter stations, the new quarter, with its handsome streets and villas, has far outgrown the original limits. A plain, 2 m. wide, is between the town and the sea. The beautifully-wooded Maure mountains surround it on the land side, mitigating the keenness of the north, north-east, and east winds, but affording indifferent protection from the mistral or north-west wind. The Toulon road, extending east and west, forms the principal thoroughfare. On it, and in its proximity, are the best shops and the best hotels. From it rise the steep streets of the old town, of which two of the gateways still exist. At the east end, fronting the Place de la Rade, is the Porte des Salins, and at the west end the Porte Fenouillet. Exactly half-way between these two stood the principal gateway, the Porte Portalet, from which the street R. Portalet leads directly up to the *Place Massillon, containing the fish-market, a bust of Massillon, and the Maison des Templiers, 12th cent., now the Hôtel de Ville. Standing with the face towards the Hôtel de Ville, we have to the left a dirty narrow street called the Rue Rubaton, in which is the house, No. 7, where Massillon, the greatest of the pulpit orators of France, was born on the 24th of June 1663. In the pulpit he appeared sedate, without gesture and parade. On one occasion, when he preached to the Court at Versailles, his sermon produced such a powerful effect on Louis XIV. that he exclaimed in the presence of the Court—"Father, I have heard several good orators and have been satisfied with them, but whenever I hear you I am dissatisfied with myself." The language of Massillon, though noble, was simple, and always natural and just, without labour and affectation. When he preached for the first time in the church of St. Eustache in Paris his famous sermon on Matthew vii. 14, and had arrived at the peroration, the entire congregation rose from their seats, transported and dismayed. This prosopopœia, which still astonishes in the perusal, has been chosen by Voltaire in the article "Eloquence" in the *Encyclopédie* as an example presenting "*la figure la plus hardie, et l'un des plus beaux traits d'éloquence qu'on puisse lire chez les anciens et les modernes.*" His father, who spelt his name Masseilhon, was a notary. The business was continued from father to son in the same house from 1647 to 1834.

Above the " Place " is the church of St. Paul, 12th cent., on a terrace commanding a view towards the sea. The figures by the side of the altar represent the apostles Peter and Paul. In the clumsy modern addition to the church is an ancient baptismal font.

HYÈRES. ST. LOUIS. COSTEBELLE.

At the low part of the town, in the Place Royale or de la République, is the church of St. Louis, built in the 12th cent. in the Byzantine style and restored in 1840. The floor is 11 steps below the entrance. The quadripartite vault is supported on lofty wide-spanned arches. The pulpit, of walnut, is beautifully carved. The 19 stalls display elegance and originality of design in the form and arrangement of the canopies. The confessionals are also tastefully carved, and are set into the wall. Behind the altar, to the right, is a large and remarkable picture representing the landing of St. Louis with his queen and their 3 children on the beach of Hyères (the Plage du Ceinturon) on the 12th of July 1254, when the royal family were the guests of Bertrand de Foz in the castle. The other picture, which is modern, represents St. Louis about to enter Notre Dame of Paris. The statue over the fountain in this square, the Place de la République, represents Charles of Anjou and Provence, 9th son of Louis VIII. of France, and brother of Louis IX. In 1245 Charles married the great heiress the Countess Beatrice, which event closed the independent political life of Provence by uniting it to the house of Anjou. In 1257, on the principle that might is right, he dispossessed Count Foz of the castle and territory of Hyères. At the western end of the town is the Place des Palmiers, with palms planted in 1836. Those which adorn the Boulevard des Palmiers were planted in 1864, and came from Spain. Napoleon I. lodged in the house No. 7 of the Place des Palmiers after the siege of Toulon. Around Hyères are numerous nursery-gardens, and on the plain, down by the Avenue de la Gare, is the "Jardin d'Acclimatation," where animals, birds, and plants are reared for the Jardin d'Acclimatation of Paris, of which it is a branch. These gardens form a most enjoyable and amusing retreat, are well sheltered, and plants, flowers, and milk are sold in them. Open to the public.

From the railway station to the sea extends a tract called the Costebelle, about 2½ m. from N.E. to S.W., on the wooded slopes of the Montagnes des Oiseaux. The winter. here is exceptionally mild, and some of the villas stand in little hollows clothed with pine and olive trees. Near the southern end of Costebelle, on Hermitage Hill, 320 ft. above the sea, is the chapel of Notre Dame d'Hyères, visited by pilgrims. From this hill are lovely views, not obstructed by trees. In the valley on the western side are old olive trees.

THE CHÂTEAU OF HYÈRES.

On the top of the hill on which the old town is built is the **Château of Hyères**, which should be visited as early as possible, for the sake

CHÂTEAU. MONT FENOUILLET.

of acquiring a topographical knowledge of the environs. Ascend by the Hôtel de Ville and the steep narrow streets beyond, keeping to the right, as the entrance into the castle-grounds is at the S.E. end of the wall. The castle, 657 ft. above the sea, is believed to have been founded in the 7th cent., although not mentioned till the 10th, when it is called *Castrum arœarum* or *arœis,* "air-castle." Considerable portions of the walls, and some of the towers and dungeons, still remain, the most perfect part being on the western side, above the Hôtel des Iles d'Or. The view from the ramparts is beautiful. Immediately beneath are the town and its dependencies, like a map in bold relief. Southwards, towards the sea, is the great plain, studded with farmhouses, cypresses, olive plantations, and vegetable gardens. Beyond is the roadstead, with generally one or more vessels of war moored off the village of Les Vieux Salins. Out at sea, to the east, are the islands of Levant, Port-Cros, and Bagaud, the smallest of the three. Farther west, towards the peninsula of Giens, is Porquerolles (p. 131), the largest of the islands. Giens is distinctly seen, with its two necks of land 3 m. long. On the land side from Giens the view is bounded to the west by the little hermitage hill bearing the chapel of N. D. d'Hyères, and the Oiseaux mountains, on whose sunny flanks is Costebelle. North from Oiseaux peak is Mt. Paradis, 982 ft., which looks as if the top had been shaved off. Northwards from Mt. Paradis, on the other side of the plain, are Mt. Coudon, 2305 ft. (see p. 125), and the eastern extremity of Mt. Faron, behind Toulon. Towards the east the view is bounded by the Maure mountains and the Pointe de la Galère, with Fort Brégançon. From this fort, northwards by the beach, are the châteaux of Brégançon and Léoubes. The highest peak of the Maures is 2556 ft. above the sea, crowned by the chapel of Notre Dame des Anges. (Refer to maps, pp. 123 and 129.)

Behind Hyères Castle is the highest of the ridges in the Maurette group, the culminating point being Mt. Fenouillet, 981 ft., at the western extremity. The path to it, which skirts the whole ridge, commences at the back of the castle, just under the peak of La Potence, 633 ft., on which is a fragment of a tower. A gibbet for the execution of malefactors stood there, hence the name. The small hill above the east end of Hyères, and standing between the old and new cemeteries, is a favourite walk, and commands a good view. Before descending from the castle observe the road to Mt. Fenouillet.

Excursion to Mont Fenouillet. — Behind the castle ramify three paths. The path to the right leads eastward along a lower ridge of the Maurettes by the Potence to Mt. Decugis, 585 ft.   The path to the left, called the "Chemin St. Bernard," leads down to the west end of Hyères, near the octroi office and the hospital.   The centre path leads to Mt. Fenouillet through plantations of olives, cork oaks, and firs, and some fine brushwood, of which the most beautiful in winter is the *Arbutus unedo*, or strawberry tree.   When less than half-way a road at Mt. Roustan, 608 ft., diverges N.E. by a ridge projecting into the valley of the Gapeau.   Just under the peak of Fenouillet is a small chapel visited by pilgrims.   From the summit, at the foot of the cross (3 Mai 1877), there is a superb and extensive view.   Numerous paths lead from it down to the road between Hyères and Toulon.

Excursion to the Montagnes des Oiseaux.—The best way is to take the path commencing in the first valley N. of the Costebelle road, ascending by the N. shoulder.   The whole way the path is good, only in some places it is nearly concealed by brushwood, especially by the *Quercus coccifera*.   The trees on the summit, 982 ft., obstruct the view, but on the way up charming landscapes now and then unfold themselves of Hyères on one side and of Carqueyranne on the other.

The Trou des Fées.—On the top of the hill (345 ft.), opposite the E. side of the Oiseaux peak, is a cave called the Trou des Fées.   The entrance is by a vertical cavity, resembling a well.   The interior, covered with stalactites, is about 96 ft. long by 40 wide.   To explore it lights are necessary.   The hole is not very easy to find, though a path leads directly to it.   It is situated under some fir trees.   The road down by the eastern valley of the Montagnes des Oiseaux to the Costebelle road passes near one of the principal springs which supply the town.   The other source is in the plain, on the road "du Père-Eternel," nearly 2 m. S.E. from the town.   It is pumped up by an engine of 26 horse-power.   This water filters to this place from the Gapeau, 1 m. E., through the gravelly soil of the plain.

To mention all the drives and walks would be both difficult and confusing.   As all the roads and paths are free, the tourist may ramble in whatever direction he pleases, either through the orchards or up the lonely but beautifully-wooded valleys and mountains.   The only sound heard is the occasional report of a gun, fired by the "chasseurs" at such game as blackbirds, thrushes, jays, bullfinches, and larks.   In the swamps about Giens are occasionally snipes and wild ducks.   The Maure mountains and their interminable valleys offer ample scope for the walking powers of the most indefatigable pedestrian.

The principal agricultural products of Hyères, as indeed of all the Riviera, are olives, wine, and cork.   The olive-berry harvest commences in December. The small berries make the best oil. The trunk has a curious propensity to separate and form new limbs, which by degrees become covered with bark. If the sap be still in a semi-dormant state, and the weather dry, the trunk and branches can bear a cold of 12° Fahr., while the orange and lemon are killed by a cold of 22°. The cold of 1820 killed the orange trees about Hyères, and nearly all the trunks and branches of the olive trees, but not the roots ; from each of which sprang, in the course of time, two or three saplings, now trees growing round one common centre. Next to the Aleppo, maritime and umbrella pines, the most numerous of the forest trees is the cork oak, or *Quercus suber*, generally accompanied with the diminutive member of the oak tribe, the *Quercus coccifera*. The bark forms an important article of commerce. When the stem of the young cork oak has become 4 inches in diameter, the bark is removed for the first time, but it is of no use. Ten or even fifteen years afterwards, when the bark is about an inch thick, the trunk is stripped again, by making two circular incisions 3 to 4 feet apart, and two vertical on opposite sides. This operation is repeated every tenth year in the month of June, when the sap is in full vigour. A cork tree does not produce fine-grained cork till it is fifty years old. Cork-cutting, which formed an important industry in the mountain villages, is gradually leaving them and settling in the towns on the railways, on account of the greater facility of transport. The curious caterpillar of the Moth, *Bombyx processionaria*, feeds on the leaves of the Aleppo and maritime pine trees. Their nests, made of a cobweb material, and shaped like a soda-water bottle, are firmly attached to the branches. On cutting them open the caterpillars are found coiled up in a ball, and do not endeavour to escape. They feed during the night. When they leave the nest they go in procession, following each other with great precision. On the summits of the Maures, and on all the mountains bordering the Riviera, grows the heath *Erica arborea*, from whose roots pipes are made. The digging up and the preparing of these roots for the Paris manufacturers form now an important industry in the mountain villages. In England they are called briar-root pipes, briar being a corruption of the French word *bruyère*, signifying heath.

The "specialité" of Hyères is the rearing of early vegetables, fruits, and flowers, for the northern markets, especially roses, strawberries, peaches, apricots, artichokes, and peas. The broad flat alluvial plain between the town and the sea is admirably suited for this purpose. The gardens are easily irrigated, and besides, within a few feet of the surface, there is always abundance of water.

"About Hyères are many rare butterflies. Among the best is the Nymphalis-Jasius, the only representative in Europe of the genus Charaxes. The first brood appears early in June, the second at the beginning of September. It is found all over the Riviera, but most abundantly at Hyères. The Vanessa Antiopa appears in July and September, many of the latter generation living through the winter. Thais Medesicaste, T. Hypsipyle, Anthocaris Eupheno (the Aurore de Provence), Polyommatus Ballus, and Rhodocera Cleopatra may be taken in April. A little later there is an abundance of the Podalirius (scarce Swallow Tail), the Machaon, the Thecla Betulæ, the Argynnis Pandora, the A. Niobe, the A. Dia, the A. Aglaia, the A. Valenzina, the Arge Psyche, the Satyrus Circe, the S. Briseis, the S. Hermione, the S. Fidia, the S. Phædra, the S. Cordula, the S. Actœa, the S. Semele, and the S. Bathseba, all common more or less throughout the summer." —*W. A. Powell of the English Pharmacy of Hyères.*

Climate. —Hyères is especially fitted for old people and young children, and all those whose weakened constitutions require to be strengthened by a winter abroad. Indeed, all of limited means coming to the Riviera should try this place first, as it is the nearest, the cheapest, and the most rural. For such as require gaiety, Hyères is not suited. "The chief attractions of Hyères are its climate and the beauty of its environs, which render it an agreeable place of winter abode, even for persons in health, who do not require the animated movement and recreative resources presented by large towns, and who are in tolerable walking condition ; the walks and rides, both on the plain and through the cork-tree woods, by which the hills are for the most part covered, presenting considerable variety, while from the more elevated positions charming prospects may be enjoyed."—*Dr. Edwin Lee.* The mean winter temperature is 47°·4 F., and the average annual rainfall is 26 inches. But on the Riviera, as in England, every winter varies in the rainfall and in the degree of cold ; and therefore the chances are that the traveller's experience will not agree with the carefully-compiled stereotyped meteorological tables. The climate of Hyères is less stimulating and exciting than at Cannes and Nice ; and, "generally, it may be said to be fitted for children or young persons of a lymphatic temperament, or of a scrofulous diathesis, either predisposed to consumption, or suffering from the first stage of that disease."

THE BRANCH-LINE BETWEEN HYÈRES AND LES SALINS.

The railway from La Pauline and Hyères to Les Salins extends 11 m. south-east. The beautiful mountain standing in full majesty before La Pauline station is Mont Coudon (see p. 128, and map p. 129).

8¾ m. S. from La Pauline, and 2½ m. S. from Hyères, is the station for La Plage, consisting of some pretty villas built between the beach and a wood of umbrella pines. From the pier the *Zephyr* sails every afternoon (excepting Sunday) to Porquerolles (p. 131). The beach adjoining the E. side is Le Ceinturon, where St. Louis landed in 1254. At La Plage station commences the larger of the two necks of land which connect the peninsula of Giens, 3¼ m. S., with the mainland. The large neck is traversed by a line of rails extending nearly to the Tour Fondue, whence a boat sails to Porquerolles, the town opposite (p. 131). The road along the neck, which at some parts is very hot and sandy, skirts large square basin-like marshes, where salt is made by the evaporation of the sea-water by the heat of the sun. At the south

end of the marshes is the little village of the saltmakers. The salt
is heaped up in pyramid-shaped piles, covered on the top with tiles,
and on the sides with boards, which gives them the appearance of
houses. Very fine views both of Giens and Hyères are obtained on
the way to the saltworks. The easiest way to approach the narrow
neck is by the Carqueyranne coach. It leads directly to the village of
Le Château, with a neat church and the ruins of a castle. Many rare
plants and immense quantities of uni- and bivalve shells are found at
Giens, especially on the smaller of the two necks.

From Le Château a road leads westward to the small fishing hamlet
of La Madrague, passing on the left a huge block of quartz with
layers of mica. From a little beyond La Madrague take the road
leading up to a house with a pepper-box turret, whence the continuation
leads up to the semaphore or signal-station, on the highest point of
the isthmus, 407 ft. above the sea. The hills are well wooded, and
the tiny valleys covered with orchards, vineyards, and fields. Many
pleasant rambles can be had on the isthmus.

After La Plage station the train, having passed the sea-bathing
station of Capé (Gapeau) and crossed the river Gapeau, arrives at

Les Salins, 18 m. from Toulon and 5 from Hyères by rail. The
omnibus from Hyères to Salins stops at the small "Place" opposite
the pier. Fare, ½ fr. It traverses a road bordered by mulberry trees,
between vineyards and olive groves. Les Salins is a poor hamlet
with a little harbour frequented by feluccas and the boats of the
training ships anchored in the bay. Behind the hamlet are immense
shallow reservoirs for the evaporation of sea-water principally in
July and August. These reservoirs or Salins occupy above 1000
acres, and produce annually 20,000 tons of the value of £10,000.
It is very coarse grained, but is much esteemed by the fish-curers.
60 workmen are employed permanently, but during the hot or busy
season 300 (see map, p. 129).

Coach to Carqueyranne, 6¼ m. W., by Costebelle and the coast.
After having rounded the base of Hermitage Hill the coach arrives
at the commencement of the small neck of land where passengers for
the peninsula of Giens alight. Scarcely 200 yards beyond this are
the almost buried ruins of the Roman naval station of Pomponiana,
some fine olive trees, and several villas. A road from this leads to
the Hermitage, passing an olive-oil mill. West from Pomponiana
by the high road is Carqueyranne, a small straggling village, from
which the little port is about ½ m. distant by nearly a straight road
southwards. The Toulon omnibus from the Place d'Italie halts at the
port, but passes through the village on its way to Toulon. The peak
to the west of Carqueyranne is Mt. Negre, 985 ft., and to the east
are the peaks Oiseaux, 982 ft., and Paradis, 980 ft. Mt. Paradis may
be conveniently ascended from Carqueyranne, commencing from the
valley between the two chains. In Carqueyranne are produced the
earliest strawberries, peas, potatoes, and artichokes for the Paris market.
It is 3½° warmer than Hyères.

BORMES. CARNOULES. GARDANNE.

Coach to Bormes, 14½ m. E. from Hyères. The coach, after passing the ramification southwards to Les Salins, halts a few minutes at La Londe, 7¾ m. E., a little village with an inn, situated on both sides of the St. Tropez road. Shortly afterwards the Bormes and Lavandou road separates from the St. Tropez road, and extends S. through a wood of fir and cork trees. Bormes is picturesquely situated among a group of hills to the east of that long ridge which terminates with Cape Benat and the Fort Brégançon. In the Place de la République or St. François is the inn, commanding a good view from the back windows. At the east end of the inn is the old churchyard, and a little beyond the new cemetery on the road to Collobrières, 14 m. N. On the other side of the " Place " is the parish church, from which a path leads up to the ruins of the castle, 12th cent., built by the Seigneurs of Bormes. Latterly it was occupied by monks. From the castle a path, passing six small chapels, ascends to the church of Notre Dame, commanding, especially from the portico, a pretty view of the plains, sea, and mountains, as far as Toulon. Bormes suffers from want of water. Less than an hour's easy walking from Bormes is Lavandou, a prosperous fishing village on the coast road from Brégançon to St. Tropez. Savoury "langousts" or rock-lobsters are caught in the bay (see map, p. 123).

⁴⁹⁻ᵕ LA PAULINE, a few houses with a new church, near the foot ¹⁰⁶⁻ᵕ of Mont Coudon. Junction with line to Hyères, 6½ m. E. Passengers who have missed the train for Hyères should await the omnibus at the little café below. From La Pauline the train arrives at Solliès-Pont, pop. 3000 ; Inns: Victoria ; Commerce ; on the Gapeau. Four hundred feet higher, on a steep hill, is the partially-walled and half-deserted Solliès-Ville, almost of the same colour as the cliffs it stands on. Then Cuers, on the side of the hill. Inn: Poste. From the station the courrier leaves for Collobrières (see p. 130).

⁶³½⁻ᵕ CARNOULES. Inn: H. de la Gare. Junction with line to ⁹¹½⁻ᵕ Gardanne, 52 m. N.W., on the line between Marseilles and Aix.

Gardanne to Carnoules.

Gardanne, pop. 3100. H. Truc, with large coalfields, 11 m. N. from Marseilles and 7 m. S. from Aix (see p. 77). On this line, 16 m. N.W. from Carnoules and 36 m. E. from Gardanne, is Brignoles, pop. 6000, on the Carami. Inns: Poste ; Cloche d'Argent ; Provence. This rather dirty town, situated in the midst of plantations of plum and mulberry trees, has long been famous for its dried plums. When ripe, they are first carefully peeled and the stone taken out, then dried and gently pressed. They are put up in small flat circular boxes. The church,

BARJOLS. ST. MAXIMIN.

13th cent., is in the highest part of the town. St. Louis of Anjou, Bishop of Toulouse, was born in the palace of the Counts of Provence, now the Sous Préfecture, situated a little higher up the street than the church. In the sacristy are preserved several of his sacerdotal vestments. Diligence daily to Barjols, 16½ m. N., pop. 3000 ; H. Pont d'Or ; situated at the confluence of the Fouvery and the Crevisses (p. 167). Diligence also to Toulon by Meounes (see p. 129).

On this branch line, 12 m. W. from Brignoles, is St. Maximin, 1043 ft. above the sea, pop. 3400. *Inns:* H. du Var ; France. The church of this ancient town was commenced by Charles II. of Sicily towards the end of the 13th cent. over the underground chapel of St. Maximin, 1st cent. It has no transept. The nave is 239½ ft. long and 91½ ft. high, and the aisles on each side 211 ft. long and 58 ft. high. The width of the church is 127½ feet. The exterior is ugly and unfinished. The interior of the roof rests on triple vaulting shafts rising from 10 piers on each side of the nave. Above the western entrance is a large and fine-toned organ, which was saved from destruction by the organist Fourcade playing upon it the Marseillaise. The case, the pulpit, and the lovely screen of the sanctuary are of walnut wood from the forest of Ste. Baume. Few parts of any church present such an admirable combination of beauty, elegance, and symmetry as this sanctuary, by a Flemish monk, Frère Louis, in 1692. Round the screen are 20 sculptured panels, each bearing within a wreath a representation in relief of one of the incidents in the life of some celebrated member of the order of St. Dominic. Under them are 92 stalls in 4 rows ; at one end is the rood-loft, and at the other the high altar against the apsidal wall. The entrance is by one door on each side, adorned with chaste sculpture and spiral colonnettes. To the left, or N. of the altar, is a relief by Puget (?) in marble, representing the Ascension of Mary Magdalene, and on the other side, in terra-cotta, Mary receiving the Communion from St. Maximin down in the crypt where she died. The reredos of the altar at the east end of the N. aisle consists of a painting on wood by an Italian artist in 1520. In the centre is a large Crucifixion, and on each side 8 paintings on panels representing the Passion. Below, on the table of the altar, is an Entombment. In the second chapel from this is another reredos in the same style, representing St. Laurent, St. Anthony, St. Sebastian, and St. Aquinius. Here, in a small window-like recess, is a very ancient iron Crucifixion. From the chapel behind the pulpit is the entrance into the cloister and convent, 13th and 14th

144

MARSEILLES
MILES FROM

MONT BRETAGNE. TRETS.

MENTON
MILES TO|

cents. The sculpture above the sound-board of the pulpit is of one piece, and represents the Ascension of Mary Magdalene. The undulating fluting on the panels and the sculpture on the railing are very graceful. Behind is the stair down to the crypt in which Mary Magdalene died after having swallowed a consecrated wafer given her by St. Maximin. Her body was afterwards put into the elaborately-carved alabaster sarcophagus on the left side of the altar. The marble sarcophagus next it contained some bones of the Innocents Mary is said to have brought with her from Palestine. Opposite Mary's is the marble sarcophagus of St. Maximin, 1st cent., and then follow the sarcophagi, also in sculptured marble, of St. Marcella (Mary's maid) and St. Sidonius, 2d cent. They are all empty, having been rifled at the Revolution of 1793. In the shrine on the altar is the skull of Mary Magdalene, and in a sort of bottle the greater part of one of her armbones. (See also under Six Fours, p. 123.) The cave of Ste. Baume, in which Mary Magdalene is said to have lived 34 years, is situated among the picturesque mountains, partly in the Var, and partly in the Bouches du Rhône, of which the culminating point is Mont Bretagne, 3498 ft. To go to it, coach to La Poussiere, 5½ m. S.W., then ascend to the cave by Nans, 5 hrs. distant. Frequented by pilgrims. From the chapel St. Pilon, 3285 ft. above the cave, glorious view. (See map, p. 123.) 12 m. W. from St. Maximin and 12 E. from Gardanne is Trets, pop. 2200 ; *Inn :* France ; a dirty town surrounded by its old walls garnished with square towers. In the neighbourhood are coal-pits, but they are small and unimportant.

75¼ — LE LUC station, 1½ m. from the town, pop. 3900. 79¾ *Inns :* Poste ; Rousse. Coach daily from the station by a beautiful road across the Maure mountains to St. Tropez, 26 m. S.E., by La Garde Fraisenet and Cogolin. Fare, 5 frs. Time, 4 to 5 hours. The coach, shortly after leaving the station, begins the ascent of the Maures, amidst vines, olives, chestnuts, and firs. On the top of the pass, 1495 ft. above the sea and 12 m. from Luc, is the village of La Garde Fraisenet, pop. 750, where the horses are changed. This was the site of the Grand-Fraxinet, one of the strongholds of the Saracens. 17 m. from Luc and 5 from La Garde is, on an eminence, Grimaud, pop. 1400, an interesting village with arcaded streets. In the principal square is a deep well hewn in the rock. The massive walls of the church are built of large blocks of granite. On the top of the hill is the castle built by Jean Cosse in the 15th cent., and occupied till the

145

middle of the 18th. 19 m. from Luc, 7 from St. Tropez, and 25½ E. from Hyères, is Cogolin, pop. 1000; *Inn*: Piffard; situated on an eminence. On the top of the hill the Saracens had a castle, from which they were driven (p. 187), and all the fortifications destroyed excepting one tower, now the town clock tower. By the roadside, about half-way between Cogolin and St. Tropez, is a very large fir tree. 32 m. N.E. from Hyères and 26 m. S.E. from Luc station is

St. Tropez, pop. 3300, *Inn*: Grand Hotel, a house with large rooms, at the head of the port on the quay, commanding an excellent view of the bay. The town, as usual, consists of dirty narrow streets. The church is in the style found in the valley of the Rhône and along the east coast of the Mediterranean. Nave surrounded by arches on high piers or tall slight columns, such as at Tournon and Hyères. Small chancel and no apsidal chapels, but generally an altar on the right and left of the high altar, one of the two usually being to "Maria sine labe concepta." Behind the church, on a hill, is the citadel; and at the foot of the hill, close to the sea, the cemetery. At the head of the harbour, opposite the Grand Hotel, is a statue of Pierre André de Suffren, one of the greatest admirals France ever had. He was born at St. Cannat, in Provence, 13th July 1726, and died at Paris 8th December 1788. The promenade has seven rows of large Oriental plane trees. The sea-urchins of St. Tropez are very good. The drive by diligence from Luc to St. Tropez is more beautiful than from Hyères to St. Tropez. Coach daily to Hyères, 32½ m. W.

84½ LES ARCS, pop. 1200, H. de France. Branch line 8 m. N. 70½ to **Draguignan** on the Nartubie, pop. 10,000. *Hotels*: *Bertin; Poste; France; Var. From the side of the H. Bertin diligences start for Salernes, pop. 2250, on the Bresque. *Inn*: H. Bernard; 13¼ m. N.W. from Draguignan (see map, p. 123). From Salernes the coach proceeds to Aups, pop. 2350, on the Grave, 1657 ft. above the sea, and 7½ m. N. from Salernes. *Inn*: Gontard, with good beer. From Aups diligence to Manosque by Riez (see p. 166). Also diligence to Brignoles by Barjols (see p. 143). From Draguignan diligence 3 times in the week to Fayence, pop. 1000, situated half-way to Grasse. Diligence also to Lorgues, pop. 3000; *Inn*: Bonne Foy; 6 m. W.

Draguignan is situated on the south side of the Malmont mountains, which attain an elevation of 1995 ft. In the old town is the clock-tower, 58 ft. high, commanding an extensive view of the plain and of the surrounding mountains. In the new town the streets are broad and intersected by avenues and a beautiful promenade containing

L

146

MARSEILLES
MILES FROM

FREJUS. COLOSSEUM.

MENTON
MILES TO

thirteen rows of lofty Oriental plane trees, about twenty in each row.
The Jardin des Plantes is small. In the Place aux Herbes is one of
the ancient gateways. Preserved fruits, oil, raw silk, and leather are
the principal products. ¾ m. from Draguignan, by the road to Comps,
is a large dolmen composed of one flat stone resting on four similar
stones. The top slab is 16 ft. long by 12½ wide and 1½ thick. The
others are each 7 ft. high, excepting one, which is broken. Indications
of markings may be traced. Growing around this interesting Celtic
monument are an oak, a splendid specimen of a "micocoulier" (*Celtis
australis*), and a juniper, 20 ft. high, of a very great age. The way to
it is from the H. Bertin, ascend the street, and take the first road left.
When within a few yards of the kilomètre stone, indicating 1 kil.
from Draguignan and 30 from Comps, take the private road to the
left, leading into an olive tree plantation (see map, p. 123).

98   57
⌣⌣ FREJUS, pop. 3400, H. Midi close to station. Situated on ⌣⌣
the Reyran at the S.W. extremity of the Estérel mountains, a picturesque
group 13 m. from N. to S. and 10 from E. to W., traversed by the
"Route de Paris en Italie," which, from Frejus to Cannes, 22½ m.
E., passes by their highest peak, Mont Vinaigre, 2020 ft. above the sea.
The peculiar charm of the Estérels is due to the warm reddish hue and
fantastic forms of the bare porphyry cliffs rising vertically from the
midst of the sombre green pines which clothe these mountains.

To the west of the station are the remains of the city walls, the
Porte de Gaules, and the Colosseum, or Arènes, of which the greatest
diameter was 224 ft., with accommodation for upwards of 9000 spectators. On the eastern side of the station are the Porte Dorée and
the terrace called the Butte St. Antoine. East of the Butte stood a
Roman lighthouse. At this part are remains of Roman towers and
walls. The masonry throughout is admirable, composed of stones of
the size of large bricks. The Porte Dorée has alternate layers of stone
and brick. Having visited the ruins by the side of the railway, pass
up by the church, and leave the town by a road having on the left
hand a large building—the seminary. Having walked a few paces,
there will be seen to the left rather an ugly square tower, which
marks the site of the theatre. The lofty ruins of arches in this
neighbourhood are the remains of the Roman aqueduct which brought
water to Frejus from the Siagnole, near Mons, 24 m. N.E., and contained 87 arches. To the right of the road is a terrace supported by
(once) powerful masonry. Below is the old Chapelle St. Roch. In the
higher part of the town is the parish church, which, with the adjoining

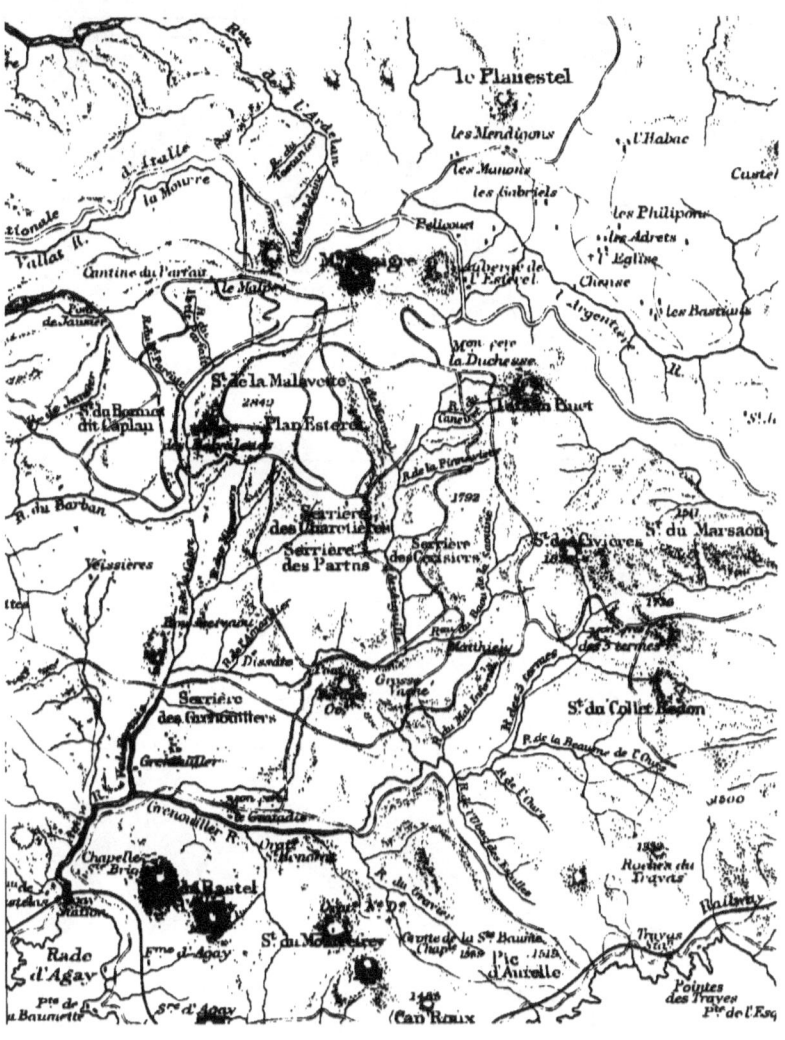

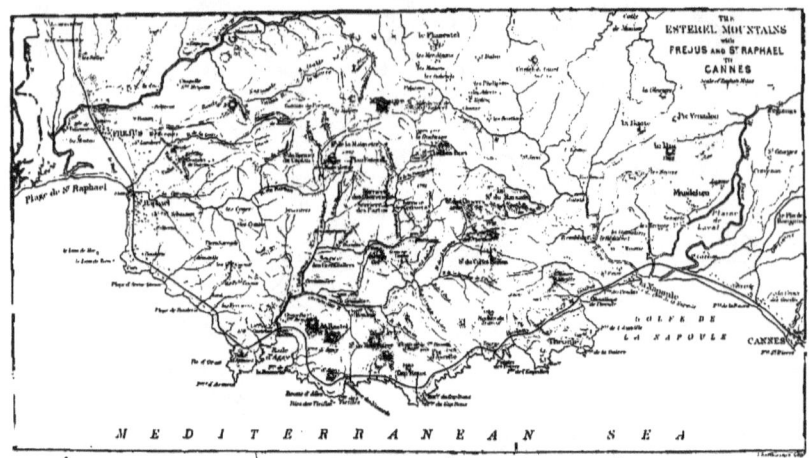

147

MARSEILLES
MILES FROM
SAINT RAPHAEL. AGAY.
MENTON
MILES TO

"'éveché," belongs to the 12th cent. To the left on entering is the
baptistery. In the Rue Éveché is a house with a sculptured doorway
and well-executed caryatides. From Frejus commence the pleasant views
and glimpses of the Mediterranean, which continue all the way to Genoa.
The Phœnician merchants of Massilia (Marseilles) founded the cities of
Forum Julii or Frejus, Antipolis or Antibes, Nicæa or Nice, and Agatha
or Agde. Agricola, the father-in-law of Tacitus, was born at Frejus.

100½
SAINT RAPHAEL, a rapidly-increasing place of 3000 inhabit- 54½
ants. In winter its guests come from the colder regions in quest of
warmth, and in summer from the hot interior in quest of the cooling
breezes and the still more refreshing sea-bathing. *Hotels:* close to
the station, the France, 8 to 9 frs. More expensive houses : G. H. de
St. Raphael, on an eminence, with garden ; near the beach, the *G. H.
des Bains, 9 to 13 frs. ; and Beau Rivage. Among the numerous
handsome villas is the cottage built by Alphonse Karr. : Temple Protestant, Anglican Chapel. Little steamer daily to St. Tropez ; whence
diligence to Hyères (p. 134). Omnibus runs between St. Raphael and
Valescure, 2 m. inland, with G. H. de Valescure. St. Raphael, only
43 minutes from Cannes, makes a salubrious and agreeable residence,
with pleasant walks, either by the beach or up the valley of the Garonne
into the Estérel mountains, where the rambles are endless. At the E.
end of St. Raphael is a very pleasant park, rising from the rocks on the
coast. A little farther towards Cannes is the Boulerie, with a large hotel.

Napoleon landed at St. Raphael on his return from Egypt in 1799,
and here he embarked when he sailed for Elba. Along this part of
the coast are fine specimens of the *Pinus pinea.*

105
AGAY, a small custom-house station, with a few houses at the 50
head of a small but deep bay, into which flows the stream Grenouiller.
On the top of the conical hill, on the S. W. side of the station, is the
Tour de Darmont, a signal-tower. The great excursion from Agay
is to La Sainte Baume, 4¼ m. distant, and a little to the N. of the
peak of Cape Roux, 1444 ft. above the sea. From the station take
the path eastward to the old château, which leave on the right hand,
and pass under the railway to an abandoned farmhouse. There a
good path begins and winds upwards to the summit of a small hill.
From there descend boldly into the valley in an eastwardly direction
towards the rugged red summit of Cape Roux till a stream is reached.
Leaving the stream, a pathway will be seen going upwards to Cape
Roux. Follow that till a high ridge is reached, close to the summit,

where is a splendid view to the east and west and north-west; then take to the left, and in a few hundred yards a platform, with a spout of running water and a couple of abandoned buildings, is reached. Distance about 3½ miles. About 260 ft. above this, in the face of the rock, is La Sainte Baume, the holy cave of St. Honorat, in which this saint is said to have lived a hermit's life for some years. The best way back to Agay is by the wide path seen from the hermitage leading westward to the river in the valley. On the way remark, on the left hand, a truncated stone pillar, a Roman milestone, with an inscription. Some archæologists base upon the existence of this stone their assertion that the Via Aurelia passed this way. At the bottom of the valley cross the Grenouiller, and join the road to Agay.

After Agay the railway sweeps round by the base of Cape Roux, where a magnificent panoramic view displays itself, just before arriving at **Le Trayas**, the next and last station before reaching Cannes, 11 m. E. from St. Raphael, 6¼ m. E. from Agay, and 8¾ m. W. from Cannes. From Trayas also a road leads to the chapel of Ste. Baume, which is considered nearer though not so good as the road from Agay. At Trayas the train passes from the department of Le Var to the department of the Alpes Maritimes, then traverses the Saoumes tunnel, 886 yards, and having passed the pretty villages of Theoule and La Napoule, enters the beautifully-situated town of Cannes.

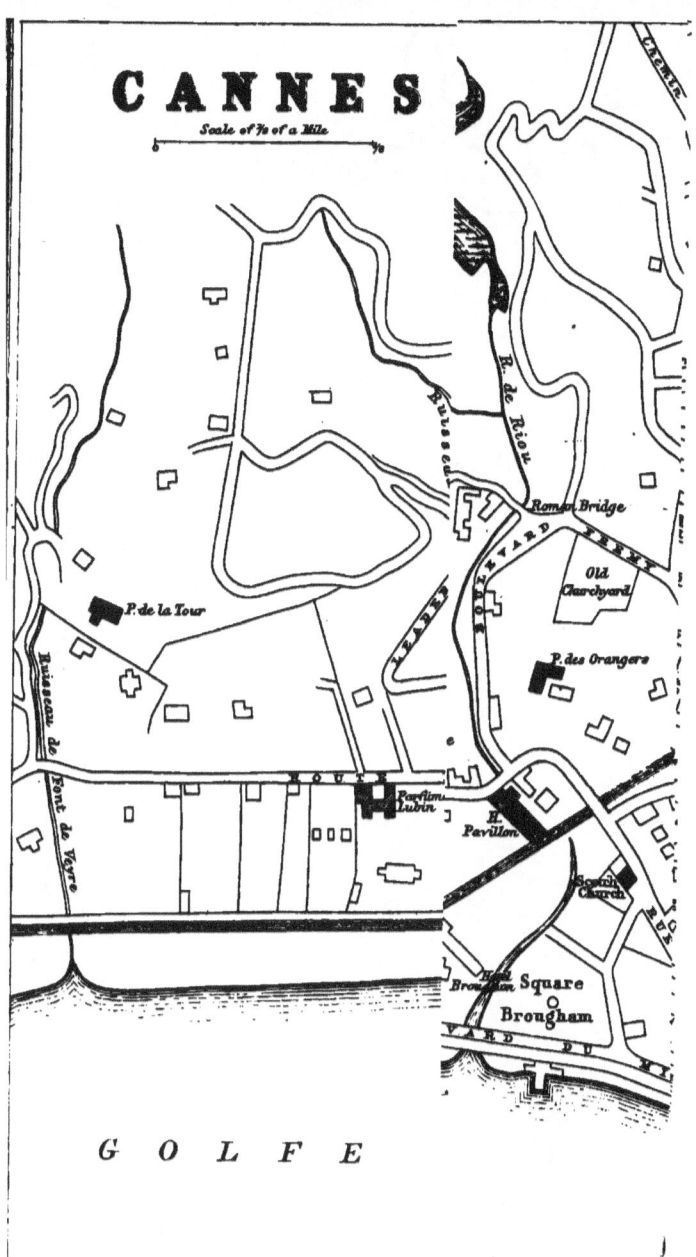

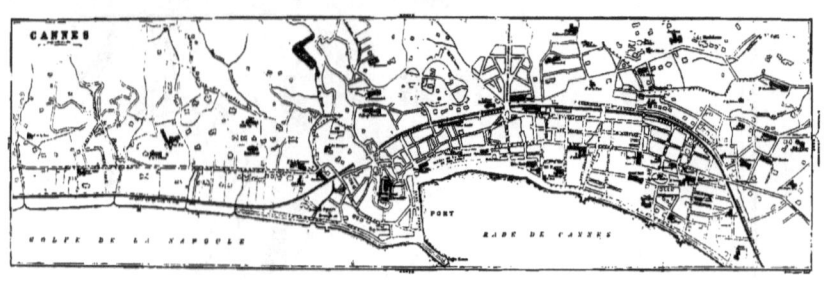

CANNES,

on the Gulf of Napoule, 120½ m. E. from Marseilles, 79 m. N.E. from Toulon, 78¼ m. N.E. from Hyères, and 19¼ m. S.W. from Nice. Fixed population, 19,400. **Hotels and Pensions.**—Although there are already very many hotels, their number continues to increase. Of villas there are about 450, which, with the exception of some 110 belonging to resident French and English proprietors, are let by the season, from the 1st of October to the last of May, at rents varying from £80 to £1200, including plate and linen. Many have coach-house, stables, and gardens attached. For information regarding them apply to Taylor and Riddett, agents, bankers, and money-changers, 43 Rue de Frejus. They have also a well-supplied reading-room, which they place at the disposal of the public without any charge. The first-class hotels charge from 10 to 25 frs. per day ; the second from 8 to 12, including everything. A fair gratuity for service during a prolonged stay is from 50 c. to 75 c. per day.

Those requiring to study economy will find the most reasonable hotels and pensions at the east end of the town. The Pension Mon Plaisir, 8 frs., in garden, Boulevard d'Alsace, near railway station. In the Boulevard Cannet, Pension d'Angleterre, 9 to 10 frs., in garden. Farther up the same Boulevard the Pension St. Nicolas, 8 frs. Near Trinity Church, the *Pension Victoria, 8 to 11 frs., with very large garden fronting the promenade.

Cab, with one horse and seated for two, from the station to the hotels, 1½ fr. ; each portmanteau, ½ fr.

The atmosphere on the hills, and at some little distance from the sea, is supposed to be in a less electrical condition, and not so liable to produce wakefulness, as in those places near the beach, and therefore many prefer the hotels and pensions situated inland. *Hotels :* fronting station, the Négociants ; the [1]*Univers, 7½ to 9 frs. In the Allées, on the beach, the Hôtel Splendide, 12 to 20 frs. At E. end of R. d'Antibes, the Pensions Luxembourg ; Wagram, 8 to 11 frs. ; and the H. Russie, 9 to 12 frs.

Hotels to the east of the Allées, fronting the beach, taking them in the order from west to east :—The National, 9 to 15 frs. ; Midi, 8 to 12 frs. ; *Beau-Rivage ; *Gray and Albion ; *Grand Hotel ; Plage ; the last four are first-class houses, charging from 10 to 20 frs. The

---

[1] The asterisk, here as elsewhere, prefixed to the name of a hotel indicates that it is one of the best of its class.

H. Suisse ; Augusta ; Anne Therese ; *Victoria, in large garden, 8 to 12 frs.   Behind the Grand Hotel is the Theatre.   Behind the H. Midi, in the R. Bossu, No. 8, the Post and Telegraph Offices.

On the north side of the railway, but a little higher, are the Louvre ; H. Central ; Alsace-Lorraine, all 10 to 20 frs.   St. Victor ; La Paix. A little way back are the Pension d'Angleterre ; H. de France ; H. Méditerranée, 9 to 13 frs.

Farther east, and approaching the region of Californie, are Hotels Windsor ; Mont-Fleuri ; *Beau-Séjour ; St. Charles ; Des Anges ; *Californie ; Des Pins, 10 to 25 frs.   On the hill overlooking the H. de Californie is the Villa Nevada, where the Duke of Albany died on Friday morning, 28th March 1884.

In the interior, on eminences on the west side of the Boulevard Cannet, are the *Prince of Wales ; *Provence ; Des *Anglais ; *Richemont ; all with gardens, and charging from 12 to 25 frs. per day.

At the foot of this hill, on the Boulevard Cannet, is the Pension Lerins, a plain but comfortable house, charging 7 to 8 frs.   A little higher up this Boulevard is the English church of St. Paul ; whence a road ascends to the Hôtel *Paradis, which, although a first-class house, on an eminence in a garden, charges only from 10 to 15 frs.   Next it is the Hôtel de Hollande, similarly situated.   Also well inland, on the Nouveau Chemin de Vallergues, is the H. *Beau-Lieu, 10 to 20 frs.

On the west side of Cannes, near the agency of Taylor and Riddett, is the *Hôtel des Princes, 10 to 20 frs.   On the hill above this part is the H. Continental, 10 to 20 frs.   Between the Scotch church and the beach, and fronting the public garden, is the H. *Square Brougham, 8 to 10 frs., well situated.   Beyond, between the railway and the beach, is the H. Pavillon, 12 to 25 frs.   A little beyond is Christ Church, and on an eminence opposite the H. *Terrasse, 12 to 16 frs., a large house with garden.   Farther west, and considerably inland, upon separate eminences, are two handsome hotels, the *Belle-Vue, behind the Rothschild villa ; and the *Beau-Site, 12 to 25 frs., behind Lord Brougham's villa.   Farther west, and on the same level, is the H. Estérel, same price.   On a hill, a little beyond the perfume distillery of M. Lubin, is the Pension de la Tour, well situated, and not expensive.   The western suburb of Cannes is called La Bocca, and sometimes La Verrerie, from the bottle-works there.   From this a road runs up the broad valley of the Siagne, where there are fields of the fragrant red Turkey rose, gathered in May for the perfumeries (see page 161).

Churches. — Christ Church, Rue de Frejus ; St. Paul's, Boulevard

CAB FARES.   STEAMERS.   LORD BROUGHAM.

du Cannet ; Trinity Church, a little to the east of the Cercle Nautique.
Scotch Church, Rue de Frejus. Near the Church of St. Paul is the
Invalid Ladies' Home. French Churches, on the Route de Grasse,
and in the Rue Notre Dame. German Church, Boulevard Cannet.

Bank and money-changer opposite post office. In the neighbourhood
the office of Cook & Son, where their railway and hotel tickets are sold.

Cab Fares.—One horse with 2 seats, the course 1½ fr. ; the hour, 2½ frs.
Two horses with 4 seats, the course 2 frs.; the hour, 3½ frs. Portmanteaus,
½ fr. each. *Steamers* from No. 20 Quai St. Pierre for Marseilles and Cette.
Twice daily for the islands of St. Marguerite and St. Honorat, 1 and 2
frs. there and back. On Thursdays and Saturdays trips to Theoule, 2 frs.

Cannes extends 4½ m. from east to west, partly on the Gulf of
Jouan, and partly on the Gulf of Napoule, covering likewise with its
houses and gardens Cape Croisette, which separates these two gulfs.
Landwards it extends nearly the same distance, where large hotels
crown the hills, and pretty villas with gardens occupy the valleys.
The principal square, called the Allées de la Liberté, is nearly in the
centre of the town, at the head of the Gulf of Napoule, and is about
700 yards long by 110 wide. It contains the Hôtel de Ville and the
H. Splendide. Between them is a marble statue, life-size, "A Lord
Brougham, né à Edinburgh, le 19 Septembre 1778. Décédé à Cannes
le 7 Mai 1868." He is in his official robes. In his left hand, resting
on the top of a palm, he holds a rose. The Hôtel de Ville contains
the Public Library and interesting collections illustrating the natural
history of the neighbourhood. The obliging director gives every assistance in naming the plants, insects, and minerals. At the head of the
Allées, and on the adjoining eminence, is the old or original town. On
this hill is the Church of Notre-Dame-d'Espérance, 17th cent., with a
reliquary of the 15th. In front is a rudely-constructed wall with
embrasures. Above it are St. Anne, 13th cent., the old chapel of the
castle, and the square tower commenced in 1080 by the Abbot Adalbert II., of the monastery of St. Honorat. From the top is an extensive view. Near the foot of the tower is a small observatory. On a
much higher hill behind is the new cemetery, where Lord Brougham
was buried on the 24th of May 1868. The monument consists of a
massive lofty cross on a double basement, bearing the following inscription :—"HENRICVS BROVGHAM. Natus MDCCLXXVIII.
Decessit MDCCCLXVIII." Near him lies James, fourth Duke of
Montrose, K.T., died December 1874.

The climate, though dry and sunny, is at times precarious. In nooks sheltered by hills from the wind the heat is often oppressive, but on leaving their protection a chilling current of air is experienced. The mean winter temperature is 47° Fahr. The average number of rainy days in the year is 52, and the annual rainfall 25 inches, the same as at Nice. " The electrical condition of the climate of Cannes, as well as its equable warmth and dryness, together with the stimulating properties of the atmosphere, indicate its fitness for scrofulous and lymphatic temperaments."—Madden's *Resorts.* "While Cannes, therefore, possesses a winter climate well suited for children, elderly people, and many classes of invalids, especially those who require a stimulating atmosphere, it is not so well adapted for the majority of those suffering from affections of the respiratory organs."—*Dr. Hassall.*

Drives.—In Cannes there are great facilities for driving in carriages, light open cabs, and omnibuses. The omnibuses start for their destinations either from the east corner of the Cours (Allées de la Liberté), or from the Rue d'Antibes, near the Cours. The largest livery stables are in the Rue d'Antibes. They charge for a carriage, with coachman and two horses, per month £30. The cabmen carry their tariffs with them, and are bound to show them when required. Copies of the " Tarif des Voitures " are kept for distribution in the Kiosque on the Cours. The recognised gratuity given to coachmen is at the rate of 3 frs. for a 25 frs. fare.

THE CORNICHE OF CANNES.

The best of the drives is to **Vallauris** by the low road to the Golfe de Jouan, 4 m. N. E., then up the valley to Vallauris, 2 m. N., and 250 ft. above the sea. From Vallauris return to Cannes, 5½ m. S. W. by the Corniche road and La Californie. Carriage and pair, 25 frs. Cab with one horse, 14 frs. ; with two, 18 frs. Omnibus to Vallauris, 1 fr. By taking the omnibus to Vallauris the remainder makes a delightful and easy walk along the Corniche road. Cross the Vallauris bridge a little below Massier's pottery, and ascend the broad road. About ½ m. from the bridge is the "Observatoire de la Corniche," where tea and coffee can be had, and whence there is a charming view east from Cannes to Bordighera. About half-way between this and the observatory at the Cannes or S. W. end of the road is the large hotel Cannes-Eden.

The Belvédère, at the Cannes end of the road, in La Californie, is 545 ft. above the sea, and can be approached by omnibus from the Cours, 1 fr. each. Behind it is the terminus of the branch of the canal which supplies the east part of Cannes. The terminus of the other branch, by which the west of Cannes is supplied, is just above the Belle-Vue hotel on the road up to the Croix des Gardes. The canal commences near the source of the Siagne, a few miles from St. Cesaire.

From the Belvédère an excellent carriage-road ascends to a still higher summit, 795 ft. above the sea, or 250 ft. above the Belvédère. The view is similar, including more of the interior. A short distance N.E. from this is another summit, 804 ft. above the sea, which from the top looks as if it were nearly over Antibes.

Many prefer to commence this drive by Californie, and to return from Vallauris by the Golfe de Jouan and the low road. Opposite the Golfe de Jouan station is C. Massier's pottery, and a few yards along the road towards Antibes is Napoleon's column (p. 169).

Vallauris, pop. 4000, is a poor village, with small cafés and restaurants. The omnibus stops in the "Place" opposite the church and the Hôtel de Ville, containing a large flat stone bearing an inscription, stating that "the Emperor Tiberius remade the road it refers to in the 32d year of his tribunician authority." Also a column, 4 ft. high and 14 inches in diameter, bearing an inscription to Constantine. Vallauris has long been famous for the manufacture of kitchen pottery, "Potteries Réfractaires," earthenware utensils, principally of the "marmite" or stewpan class, capable of bearing great heat without cracking. A dozen marmites, in assorted sizes, are sold for 2 frs. To this the Massiers and others have added the manufacture of artistic pottery, of which there is a good display, both in the showrooms in the village and in those down at the Golfe de Jouan. Several of the clay-beds may be seen by the side of the road leading up northwards from Vallauris; but the best and richest strata, all of the Pleiocene period, are in that valley near the spot where this road meets the road to Antibes. About 220 yards beyond this meeting-place a cut-up road ramifies, left, into the valley containing the clay-mines. The entrances into them are covered with roofing. Any one may descend into them. The colours of the clay are blue, red, black, and gray, all in various shades. The most valuable is the blue. Most of the common articles are made of a mixture of all the clays. Red clay from Estaque, near Marseilles, is also used in the making of artistic pottery.

Vallauris to Antibes.

The road leading northward from Vallauris and afterwards S.E. to Antibes traverses beautiful hills and valleys covered with Aleppo pines. Having passed the junction and the valley of the mines, we come to a firebrick and marmite manufactory, 410 ft. above the sea. The road behind, extending N.W., ascends to Castelaras. Afterwards a bridge is passed, and some arches of the aqueduct built by the Romans to convey water to Antibes. (For Antibes, see pp. 154 and 169.)

CANNET.

Two miles N. from Cannes, by the beautiful Boulevard Foncière, is
Cannet, 265 ft., pop. 2600. At the head of the Boulevard is the
H. *Bretagne, 10 to 20 frs. A little to the east of the church Ste.
Philomène is a smaller house, the H. and Pension Cannet, 8 to 10 frs.
Immediately opposite the church is the Villa Sardou, where in 1858
the accomplished tragedian Rachel died of consumption. At that time
none of those broad roads existed which now encircle the house. Above
the church is the "Place," commanding a very pretty view. Omnibus, 6 sous. Cab to Cannet, and return by the Grasse road, 7 or 9 frs.

Drive to La Croisette, the first cape east from Cannes, by the beautiful road 2 m. long, skirting the sea. Cab, 1 horse and 2 seats, 1½ fr.,
or 2½ frs. the hour. 2 horses with 4 seats, 2 frs. Tram, 6 sous.
Omnibus 6 times daily, fare 30 c. This is a most enjoyable walk or
drive by the beautiful esplanade fronting the sea. Near to La Croisette
is the entrance to the orange orchard "Des Hesperides," occupying 4
acres. The trees stand in rows 12 ft. apart, and were planted in 1852,
when they were from 5 to 8 years old. In gardens in the country the
oranges cost about a sou each, but in the Hesperides they are dearer.
The best are those the second year on the tree. Frosts retard the
sweetening process, and in some years damage the trees. In the village of La Croisette there is a place for pigeon-shooting, and also the
remains of fortifications begun by Richelieu, but never completed.

Cannes to the Cap d'Antibes, 7 m. E. Cab with 1 horse and 2 seats,
18 frs. With 2 horses and 4 seats, 22 frs. Private carriage, 30 frs.
Omnibus between Cannes and Antibes 3 times daily. In Cannes it starts
from the Allées de la Liberté, and in Antibes from the "Place," fare 1 fr.
Very near this "Place" are two comfortable inns, the H. Escouffier and
the H. des Aigles d'Or ; pension 7 to 8 frs. Their omnibuses await
passengers at the railway station. Antibes has a little harbour and pier,
and strong fortifications by Vauban, who also built the fortress Fort
Carré, near the northern side of the entrance. From the N. ramparts,
but more especially from the high walk above the pier on the roofs of
some small houses, are seen distinctly Nice, the fishing village Cros de
Cagne, and Cagne. Inland from Cagne are St. Jeannet, La Goude,
Vence, and St. Paul, and, farther west, Le Bar. In the background
are the Maritime Alps, generally tipped with snow in winter. In the
centre of the town are two ancient towers. One of them stands in
front of the church, and is used as the belfry ; the other forms part of
an adjoining building, the "Bureau du Recrutement."

The Cap d'Antibes affords a delightful little walking excursion.
To visit the "Cap" from Antibes, leave the town by the small gate, the

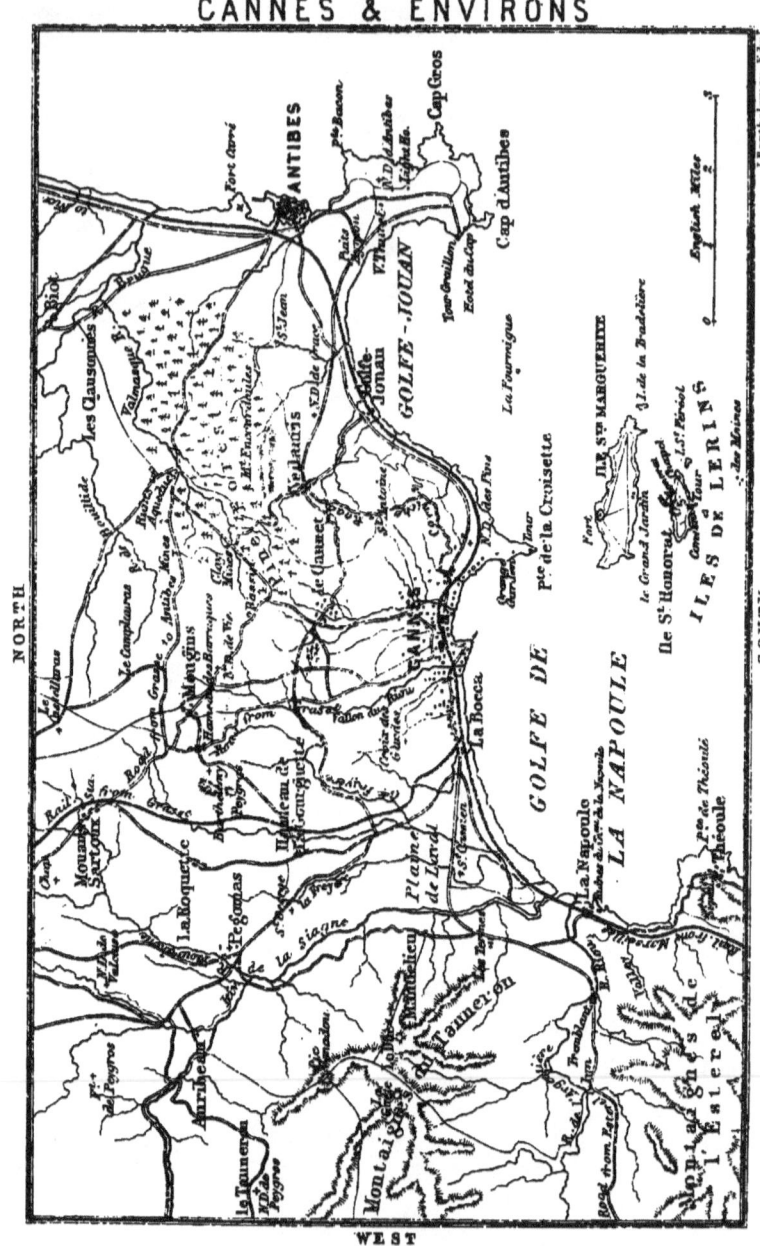

Porte Fausse, between the sea and the Porte de France, and then take the first road left by the side of the sea and the telegraph-posts. Ascend the hill, to the church, by the terraced steps of a "Via Crucis," bordered with the usual 14 chapels, each with a group representing some part of the passion of our Lord. At the top is N. D. d'Antibes, frequented by pilgrims. The north aisle, which is the oldest part of the building, is of the 9th cent. Behind it is the lighthouse built in 1836, on a hill 187 ft. above the sea. The building is 82 ft. higher, and ascended by 115 steps. On the top is a fixed white light, visible at a distance of 28 miles. Fee for one person, ½ fr. The view is splendid. Before descending, observe the road to the Villa Thuret and to the Hôtel du Cap, a first-class house, 10 to 14 frs. Omnibus at station. The villa and grounds of Thuret are now a Government school for the culture and study of semi-tropical trees and shrubs. It is said that the first gum trees introduced into France were planted in 1853, and those in this garden in 1859. (For Antibes, see also p. 169.) The great tower on a rock to the W., overlooking the sea, is a powder-magazine.

Drives to the west of the Hôtel de Ville.—*La Croix-des Gardes*, 2½ m. N.W., and 498 ft. above the sea. The nearest way ramifies from the Frejus road by the E. side of the Belle-Vue hotel. The cross rises from a column on a block of granite. The view is extensive. By the side of the road will be observed considerable plantations of the *Acacia farnesiana*, from whose flowers a pleasant perfume is distilled.

Cannes to Napoule, 6 m. W. Cab with 1 horse and 2 seats, 12 frs.; with 2 horses and 4 seats, 16 frs. 1 hour's rest allowed. By omnibus, 30 c., leaving Cannes at 1 for the Bocca. At the Bocca it corresponds with the omnibus to Napoule, 50 c.; which, as it does not return till 4.30, affords ample time to walk on to Theoule and back, 2 m. W. The Napoule road commences from the western, or what is also called the English, portion of Cannes. It passes the little Scotch church, behind which are the Square Brougham and the public gardens. Farther W. is Christ Church, one of the three Episcopal Chapels. A short distance beyond, on the right side of the road, is the villa Eléonore-Louise, where Lord Brougham died. The house is hidden among the trees, but the garden is easily recognised by 2 large cypress trees growing by the side of the rail. Three m. from Cannes, on an eminence covered with pines, oaks, and cypresses, on the S. side of the road, is the poor little chapel of St. Cassien, the patron saint of Cannes, whose day is held on the 23d of July, in much the same manner as the Pardons in Brittany, called here Roumeiragi. Napoule is a small hamlet by the side of an old castle on the beach, at the foot of wooded hills. From it a very pretty road by the coast, cut in the face of the cliffs, leads to the hamlet of **Theoule**, on a tiny plateau over the beach, at the foot of the Estérel mountains. The restaurant of Theoule is better than that at Napoule. Between these two hamlets, and spanned by the railway viaduct, a narrow precipitous valley penetrates into the mountains. From Theoule a road extends to Trayas.

Cannes to the Inn of Estérel, 12 m. S.W. and 830 ft. above the sea.

Estérel. Pégomas. Mougins. Castelaras.

Carriage there and back, 35 frs. Cab with one horse and two seats, 18 frs.; with two horses and four seats, 22 frs. After passing the Bocca and St. Cassien, the carriage crosses the Siagne, having on the right or north Mandelieu nestling in the sun, at the foot Mt. le Duc, 1265 ft., a little to the east of the flat peak La Gaëte, 1663 ft. Afterwards the Riou is crossed at the village of Le Tremblant, 167 ft. above the sea, whence the ascent is continued by an excellent road amidst picturesque scenery to the Inn and Gendarmerie of Estérel. The inn is situated to the N. of Mt. Vinaigre, having to the east the Plan Pinet, 876 ft. above the inn, and to the west Mt. Vinaigre, 1193 ft. above the inn. The path to the summit of Mt. Vinaigre commences near the inn. The culminating part, 1030 ft., of the carriage-road is about 1¼ m. west from the inn at a place where four roads meet, almost immediately below Mt. Vinaigre, which is ascended from this point also.

7 m. N. from Cannes by the Plaine de Laval and the wide valley of the Siagne, passing the Hôtel Garibondy, is the village of **Pégomas**, pop. 1350, on the Mourachone, a slow-running stream, in some parts hidden among bamboos. Beyond the mill of the village is a pretty but difficult walk up the ravine of the stream. Omnibus, 75 c. Cab, 12 or 16 frs.; 1 hour's rest.

About 3 m. N.W. is **Auribeau**, pop. 480, prettily situated on the Siagne. Cab, 18 or 22 frs., with 2 hours' rest.

4¾ m. N. from Cannes, on a hill 820 ft. above the sea, is **Mougins**, pop. 1680. The road ascends all the way, passing by the cemetery and traversing vineyards and large olive groves. The omnibus goes no farther than Les Baraques, about ¼ m. below the town. Fare, 75 c. Cab there and back, one horse, 12 frs.; two horses, 16 frs.; 1 hour's rest. Mougins still retains a few low portions of its walls and one gate, just behind the church. In the shop near the gate is the key of the church tower. The church dates from the 12th cent. From the tower, ascended by 75 steps, is a beautiful view. To the west is La Roquette, N.W. Mouans-Sartoux, and beyond Grasse. To the S.W. near the sea, and on the border of the Estérels, is the village of Mandelieu.

4 m. N. from Mougins, by the stony old road, or a little farther by the new road, is **Castelaras**, 1050 ft. above the sea. It is half a villa and half a farmhouse, commanding from the tower a splendid view of Grasse, Le Bar, the valley of the Loup, Tourettes, Vence, etc., to the north; Biot, Antibes, Nice, etc., to the east; Mouans, Auribeau, and the Estérel mountains to the west; and Cannes with its islands to the south. The easiest way to approach Castelaras on foot is to take the train to Mouans-Sartoux, pop. 1010, then ascend the hill by the steep road to the east of the station. When on the top the farmhouse and tower are distinctly seen. Carriage there and back, 35 frs. The column farther north marks the tomb of a gentleman who died at Grasse in 1883.

Sail by steamboat to the Iles de Lerins. Time, 1 hr. The steamer makes two trips, so that passengers may land by the first at Ste. Marguerite, and by the second be carried on to St. Honorat, where the steamer remains sufficient time to visit the castle.

THE MAN OF THE IRON MASK.

ILES DE LERINS.

The Island of Ste. Marguerite, 4½ m. in circumference and 1½ m. from the mainland, is covered entirely with a pine forest, except at Point Croisette, on which stands the fort founded by Richelieu, containing the apartments in which Marshal Bazaine was confined and the far more interesting vaulted cell in which the Man of the Iron Mask was closely guarded. The present entrance did not exist at that time, the only communication then being by the now walled-up door which led into the house of the governor, M. de St. Mars. From behind the prison a road, bordered by the *Eucalyptus globulus*, goes right through the pine plantation to the other side of the island.

The name of the Man of the Iron Mask was Hercules Anthony Matthioli, a Bolognese of ancient family, born on the 1st December 1640. On the 13th of January 1661 he married Camilla, daughter of Bernard Paleotti, by whom he had two sons, one of whom only had posterity, which has long since been extinct. Early in life Matthioli was public reader in the University of Bologna, which he soon quitted to enter the service of Charles III., Duke of Mantua, by whom he was finally made Secretary of State. The successor of Charles III., Ferdinand Charles IV., the last sovereign of Mantua, of the house of Gonzaga, created Matthioli supernumerary senator of Mantua, and gave him the title of Count. Towards the end of 1677 the Abbé d'Estrades, ambassador from France to the Republic of Venice, conceived the idea, which he was well aware would be highly acceptable to the insatiable ambition of his master, Louis XIV., of inducing the weak and unfortunate Duke Ferdinand Charles to allow of the introduction of a French garrison into Casale, a strongly-fortified town, in a great measure the key of Italy. The cession of the fortress of Pinerolo to the French by Victor Amadeus, Duke of Savoy, in 1632, had opened to them the entrance into Piedmont, while the possession of Casale would have opened to them the broad and fertile plains of Milan.

The great difficulty Estrades had to encounter at first in the prosecution of this intrigue was to find a medium of communication between himself and the Duke. This channel was at last found in the person of Matthioli, who enjoyed the Duke's confidence and favour, and was besides a complete master of Italian politics. Through him the schemes of Estrades progressed so well that he was invited to the French court, where he was received and rewarded by Louis XIV., who at the same time presented him with a valuable diamond ring. Shortly after Matthioli's return to Italy he allowed himself to be bought over by the Austrian party, which frustrated the French negotiations and so exasperated the vindictive Louis that he sent orders to the Abbé Estrades to have him kidnapped at all hazards. For this purpose Matthioli was induced to go to the frontier beyond Turin, where he was arrested as a traitor to France by the Abbé, accompanied by four soldiers, on 2d May 1679. Such a scandalous breach of international law required the adoption of extraordinary precautionary means of concealment. His name was changed to Lestang, he was compelled to wear a black velvet mask, and when he travelled armed attendants on horseback were ready to despatch him if he made any attempt to escape, or even to reveal himself.

By the direction of Estrades he was comfortably lodged and fed in prison, till orders came from Paris, stating—" It is not the intention of the king that the Sieur de Lestang should be well treated, nor receive anything beyond the absolute necessaries of life, nor anything to make his time pass agreeably." He was handed over to the charge of St. Mars, who took him to the castle of Pinerolo, whence in 1681 they removed to the castle of Exiles. From Exiles St. Mars removed his unfortunate and now crazy prisoner to the Island of Ste. Marguerite, where they arrived 30th April 1687, after a journey of twelve days.

Among the erroneous anecdotes told of Matthioli during his ten years' sojourn on the island are :—On one occasion he is alleged to have written his name and rank on a silver plate, which he threw out of the window. A fisherman picked it up and brought it to St. Mars, who, on finding the man could not read, let him go. On another occasion Matthioli is said to have covered one of his shirts with writing, which he likewise threw out of the window. It was found by a monk, who, when he delivered it to St. Mars, assured him that he had not read it. Two days afterwards the monk was found dead. The origin of these stories is to be found in a letter from St. Mars to the Minister, dated 4th June 1692, in which he informs him that he has been obliged to inflict corporeal punishment upon a Protestant clergyman named Salves, also in his keeping, because he would write things on his pewter vessels and linen, to make known that he was imprisoned unjustly on account of the purity of his faith.

In 1697 Matthioli with his keeper left for the Bastile, of which place St. Mars had been appointed governor. They arrived on 18th September 1698.

On the 19th November 1703, about 10 P.M., Matthioli died in the Bastile, after a few hours' illness, and was buried next day at 4 P.M. in the cemetery of St. Paul. — Extracted from the *History of the Bastile*, by R. A. Davenport.

The Island of St. Honorat contains 97 acres, or is ¼ the size of Ste. Marguerite, from which it is 750 yards distant. A pleasant road of 2½ m., shaded by umbrella pines, leads round the island. Straight from the landing-place is a convent of Cistercian monks, settled here only since 1859. The original monastery was founded by St. Honorat in 410. In 730 and 891 the Saracens invaded the island, pillaged the establishment, and massacred the monks. In the 10th century the again flourishing brotherhood received Cannes as a gift from Guillaume Gruetta, son of Redouard, Count of Antibes. In 1073 they built the tower on the island, and in 1080 the Abbé Adalbert II. commenced the castle of Cannes. In 1148 the monks strengthened and enlarged the fortifications of their tower. In 1788 the monastery was suppressed on account of the irregularities of the inmates. In 1791 the island and buildings were sold. In 1859 they were finally bought by the Bishop of Frejus, who handed them over to the present occupiers, a colony of Cistercian monks, 50 in number, of whom about two-thirds are lay brethren.

" What Iona was to the ecclesiastical history of northern England, what Fulda and Monte Cassino were to the ecclesiastical history of Germany and southern Italy, St. Honorat was to the church of southern Gaul. For nearly two centuries the civilisation of the great district between the Loire and the Mediterranean rested mainly on the Abbey of Lerins. Sheltered by its insular position from the ravages of the barbaric hordes who poured down the valleys of the Rhône and of the Garonne, it exercised over Provence and Aquitaine a supremacy such as Iona, till the Synod of Whitby, exercised over Northumbria. All the more illustrious sees of southern Gaul were filled by prelates who had been reared at Lerins. To Arles (p. 70) it gave in succession Hilary, Cæsarius, and Virgilius.

"The present cloister of the abbey is much later than the date of the massacre of the monks, which took place, according to tradition, on the little piece of green sward in the centre of the cloister.

" With the exception of the masonry of the side walls, there is nothing in the abbey church earlier than the close of the 11th cent."
—J. R. Green's *Stray Studies.*

The tower or rather castle, as it now stands, represents two tall rectangular elevations of unequal magnitude, crowned by projecting cornices. On the ground-floor, with entrance from the beach, is a large hall with groined roof, said by some to have been a chapel, and by others a bakery, but most likely a "parloir" or reception-room. In the wall, a little to the left or west, and about 30 ft. from the ground, is a cannon-ball fired by the English when they took possession of the islands in 1746. The interior of the castle is shown by the concierge of the convent. The first part entered is the oblong cloister, in three stories, of which two remain entire. The corridor of the first is supported on short columns standing round the edge of a cistern. From this corridor open the doors into the bedrooms and refectory. From the upper corridor is the entrance to the chapel, which opened into the library. Above the library was the infirmary, of which not a vestige remains. A good view is had from the top. Visitors are next taken to the convent. The church and buildings are modern, excepting one of the cloisters. It is therefore a pity to spend much time there, especially for those who have arrived by the last steamer, and have consequently little time to spare.

By the road round the island are the remains of chapels of the 7th cent., or even earlier. Going from west to east there is, against the wall of the convent, a little to the west of the castle, the Chapel of St. Porcaire (restored), where, it is said, the saint was buried. At the western extremity of the island, within an old fort, is the Chapel of St. Sauveur. To the west of the landing-place, near the large gateway, are little better than the foundations of the Chapel of St. Pierre. Farther east, beside the Orphanage, is St. Justine, now a stable. The Orphanage contains about 25 boys. They are taught different trades. The franc charged for showing the castle goes to their support. On the eastern point of the island, beside a fort, is the most interesting chapel of all, the Chapel of the *Trinity, 35 ft. long by about 25 wide, placed from east to west. The great corner-stones of this small temple, by their size and solidity, are the main supports of the building, illustrating thereby the reason why in Scripture so much importance and honour are attached to them in edifices. The roof of the nave is semicircular, strengthened by three arches, the centre one springing from two round columns. The roofs of the three apsidal chapels are semispherical.

Cannes to Grasse, 12½ m. N. by rail, pop. 12,100. *Hotels:* the G. H. International, 9 to 12 frs., a first-class house on the road to Le Bar. In the town, H. Muraour and the Poste, 8 to 10 frs. Their omnibuses await passengers. Those who wish to walk commence by the stair to the right of the station, and then the steep road on the other side of the highway. Grasse, a town of charming views, delicious water, and the best of air, makes an excellent and beneficial change from Cannes. The town, with its terraces and labyrinth of narrow, crooked, steep streets, is situated 1090 ft. above the sea, on the southern slope of Mt. Rocavignon, which rises almost perpendicularly 695 ft. above the town. To the N. E. of Rocavignon is the Marbrière, 2920 ft. above the sea. The short but stony road to the top of Rocavignon commences opposite the fountain used by the washerwomen. On the summit is a stony plateau, commanding extensive and exquisite views. A little way inland is a grassy plot, called the Plain of Napoleon, because here, on 2d March 1815, he breakfasted at the foot of the three tall cypresses, and then went on to St. Vallier. In the face of the large calcareous cliff a few yards beyond the trees is a cavern or "foux," whence, after heavy rains, a large body of water issues in the form of a roaring cascade. The path which leads down into the beautiful valley below commences about 500 yards farther inland. It joins that very pretty road among olive trees, seen from the plateau, which, after passing the large white house, a hospice for the aged, enters Grasse by the powder-house, formerly the chapel of St. Sauveur, a little circular building with flat shallow buttresses, built in the early part of the 10th cent. On entering Grasse by this way, and just at the commencement of the promenade called the Cours, is the hospital. The large door gives access to the chapel, in which are hung, at the west end, three pictures attributed to Rubens —the Crown of Thorns, the Elevation of the Cross, and the Crucifixion. The concierge uncovers them. Immediately below, and opposite the entrance into the public gardens, is the house of M. Malvillan, containing paintings by a native of Grasse, Jean Horace Fragonard, who died at Paris in 1806. The best of them are five pictures, which were painted for Madame Dubarry, representing frolicsome scenes, young people playing games. At the foot of the Rue des Dominicains, in a large house with bulging iron grating, are some decorative paintings attributed to Flemish artists. These pictures are shown by courtesy. In the centre of the old town is the parish church, built in the 11th cent., but altered and repaired in the 17th. It contains several pictures, but the only good one is an Ascension of Mary, by Subleyras, behind the high altar. From the terrace at the east end of the church is one of the many beautiful views. Adjoining is the Hôtel de Ville, and attached to it is a great square tower of the 11th cent.

A stair at the head of the main street leads down to the principal square and market-place, with a fountain at one end and one of the sides arcaded. The best promenades are the Cours, the terrace of the Palais de Justice above it, and the Jardin des Plantes below it.

PERFUMERY.

The standard industries of Grasse are the distilling of perfumes and the preserving of fruits. The flowers are cultivated on terraces resembling great nursery-beds. Of the perfumes, the most precious are the Otto of Roses and the Néroly. It requires 45 lbs. avoirdupois of rose leaves (petals) to make 1 gramme, or $15\frac{1}{2}$ grains troy of the Otto of Roses, which costs from $2\frac{1}{2}$ to 3 frs. the gramme ; and $2\frac{3}{4}$ lbs. troy of the petals of orange flowers to make 1 gramme of Néroly, which costs 8 to 10 sous the gramme. The best Néroly, the Néroly Bigarrade, is made from the flowers of the bitter orange tree. It is used principally in the manufacture of Eau de Cologne, of which it constitutes the base. In colour it resembles sherry, and the odour is that of Eau de Cologne. The water that comes off in distilling Néroly forms the orange-water of the cafés. The Otto of Roses of Grasse is superior to that of Turkey. Extracts for scenting pocket-handkerchiefs are made from freshly-gathered flowers laid between two sheets of glass, held by their frames 4 inches apart, and piled one above the other, without pressing the flowers. On each side of the glass is a layer of lard $\frac{1}{4}$ of an inch thick, which, in 12 to 24 hours, absorbs completely the odoriferous oil. When the flowers are abundant they are renewed every 12 hours, sometimes even every 6. The operation is repeated several times on the same lard with fresh flowers. Jonquilles are changed 30 times, the cassia and violet 60, the tuberose (a kind of hyacinth) and the jasmine, both 80 times. The lard is then melted in a large iron vessel, and mixed with spirits made from grain, which, combining with the volatile oil, rises to the top. The fluid is then filtered.

M

This is called the cold method. Orange and rose petals require the hot methods, either by the still or by the "bain-marie." The distilling of the fragrant oil from the petals requires the most vigilant attention, and the maintenance of the same degree of heat. Rose and orange pomade are made by the bain-marie method by submerging a large iron pot full of lard in boiling water. When the lard is melted the petals are added, and after having remained there for 12 or 24 hours the mass is filtered to remove the now inodorous petals. The operation is repeated from 30 to 60 times, according to the required strength of the perfume. The red Turkey rose is the only rose used.

At the very foot of the Rue des Cordeliers is the confectionery of *Negre. He has showrooms and priced catalogues of his preserved fruits, which are made up in the candied (cristallisé) state, in the glazed-sugar (glacé) state, whole and in syrup (compotes), or as jams and jellies (confitures). At No. 22 Rue des Cordeliers is the perfumery of Bruno-Court, where purchases of the best material may be made from a franc upwards. Below the church is the perfumery of Warwick and Co., and in the B. Fragonard that of Pilar Frères, both of whom supply Atkinson of London with the raw material.

Grasse to St. Cesaire.—9 m. W. by a beautiful road. Carriage there and back, 20 frs. Diligence, 1½ fr. Time, 2 hours. This little village, pop. 350, is situated on an eminence above the Siagne, 1560 feet above the sea, or 470 feet higher than Grasse. In front of a large elm in the "Place" is a plain but clean inn, the Hôtel de la Siagne (pension from 6 to 8 frs.), where those who desire to fish in the river or ramble in the environs can live comfortably. From the end of the street, right from the inn, is a terrace, left hand, whence there is a view of the valley of the Siagne, with the Cannes canal on its eastern side. The path to the cave "Grotto de la Foux" goes by the upper side of this canal, and requires 1½ hour's easy walking. The commencement of the Cannes Canal is about a half-hour's walk farther up. No guide is necessary, unless it be desired to inspect the cave with lights. Guide, 5 frs. Like the more famous caves of Cahors and of Vaucluse (p. 64), this cavern or "foux," at the base of a calcareous cliff, contains a great basin of limpid water, but no stalactites. The Cannes Canal is a narrow uncovered conduit 31 m. long, exposed to animal and vegetable impurities throughout nearly its entire course. Of greater interest is the commencement of the Roman aqueduct, which conveyed water from the Siagnole to Frejus (p. 146, and map, p. 117) by a channel covered with bricks, and stones of the size of bricks, through the Roquotaillado tunnel, 164 ft. long, 27 wide, and 82 high, in all probability originally a cave, but adapted by the Roman engineers to their requirements. It is most easily visited from Montauroux, on the hill opposite, 3 m. distant by a bridle-path, *Inn:* Bourgarenne, where pass the night. From this village the tunnel is about 9 m. distant by an excellent carriage-road. 1½ m. from Montauroux is the village Callian, *Inn:* Castel, 1200 ft., supplied with water by the Roman aqueduct.

Nearly 2 hours' walk from the Cannes Canal up the Siagne, and

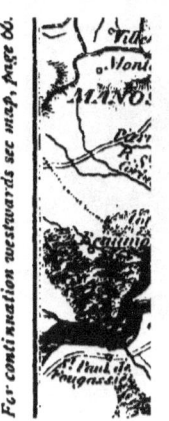

For continuation westwards see map, page 66.

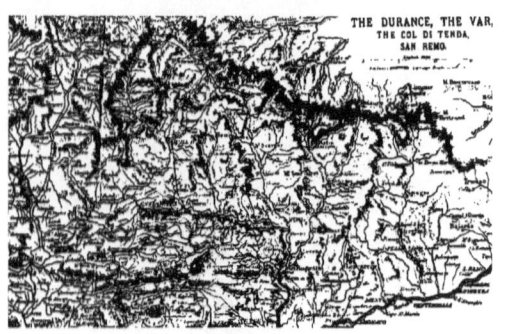

situated at a considerable elevation, is the stalactite cave of Mons. Those who have already seen such caves will find in this one nothing new nor striking. To visit it not only is a guide necessary, but the keeper of the cave at Mons must be advised beforehand, that he may be at the mouth of the cave with the key. It is much the better plan to return from the commencement of the Cannes Canal to St. Cesaire, and drive back to Grasse. The olives of St. Cesaire are considered among the best flavoured of the Riviera.

Grasse by Coach to Cagnes Station.

Grasse to the railway station of **Cagnes** by the **Pont du Loup** and **Vence,** 21 m. By omnibus, 3 frs. By private carriage, 30 frs. This drive is generally taken in two parts—Grasse to the Pont du Loup; then from the Pont du Loup to Vence or Cagnes.

Grasse to the Pont du Loup by Le Bar, 7½ m. N.E. Carriage with two horses there and back, 15 frs. Omnibus to Le Bar 3 times daily, 1 fr. Distance, 5½ m. N.E. ; whence it is a pleasant walk of 2 m. up the valley of the Loup to the inn and Pont du Loup, at the mouth of the Gorge du Loup. From the Pont 2½ hours of fatiguing walking up the ravine of the Loup brings the traveller to the falls of the Loup, which requires a good deal of rain to make them imposing. The whole way from Grasse to Vence is by a beautiful Corniche road, nearly on the same level (1090 ft.) throughout its entire course, disclosing at every turn exquisite views towards the sea. The Pont du Loup, with its little cluster of houses and orange-gardens, is at the top of a long narrow valley, just at the point where the Loup rushes forth from a rocky gorge. On the top of a plateau, about 500 ft. over the Pont du Loup, is the village of Gourdon. From the terrace adjoining the church of Le Bar there is an excellent view of Gourdon, the valley of the Loup, and of the carriage-road on both sides of it. Those who visit the Pont du Loup generally content themselves with a ramble in the gorge, and then, after having taken some refreshments, either return to Grasse or go on to the railway station of Vence-Cagnes (see p. 169), 13½ m. farther, or 21 m. from Grasse. The drive from Grasse to Vence-Cagnes station in a private carriage costs 30 frs. The very same road is traversed by the omnibus from Grasse to Vence, 15 m. eastward. Fare, 2 frs. Time, 4 hours. A seat should be taken in the "Imperial." Next day, at one, start from Vence to Cagnes railway station by another omnibus. Fare, 1 fr. Time, 1 hour. Distance, 6 m. The road from the Pont to Vence continues to follow the course of the Loup till within a few miles of the village of Tourette, pop. 980, at the foot of Le Puy de Tourette, 4158 ft. above the sea, where the omnibus halts.

Vence, 1100 ft. above the sea, pop. 2800. *Inn :* Lion d'Or, pension 9 frs. Picturesquely situated on a hill in the midst of mountains clothed with olive trees and studded with houses standing singly and in clusters. This, the ancient Vintium, has still large portions of its old walls and ramparts, with massive square towers (11th cent.) next the gates. At the northern entrance is the ancient palace of the Lords of Vence, with a beautiful tower, built in the 15th cent., in the style of the palaces of Florence, only without a court, for which there was no space. In front is a fine old ash tree, sadly mutilated.

The bishopric of Vence, founded in 374, was afterwards united to that of Frejus. In the centre of the town is the cathedral, 110 ft. long, 68 ft. wide, and about 70 high, inside measure. Two aisles with massive piers and semicircular arches (slightly stilted) are on each side of the nave. Above is a triforium 15 ft. wide. Roof waggon-vaulted. The choir, containing 50 stalls in dark carved oak, is in a gallery opposite the altar, in the position usually occupied by the organ. At the N.E. corner of the church is an ancient and beautiful baptismal font, of which, unfortunately, a large piece of the pedestal is sunk into the ground. The chancel was formerly a Roman temple. The column now in the square behind the church, and the other over a well at the west end, stood formerly at the entrance into the temple. On the table of the second altar right is part of a sculptured stone which formerly adorned this temple. In the next chapel is the tomb of St. Lambert, many years Bishop of Vence, with Latin inscription on table of altar. Under the chancel is the vault in which the bishops were buried, while the vault of the Lords of Vence was under the nave. The present "Place" behind the chancel was the public cemetery. Several stones with inscriptions are on the walls. One slab bears an eagle in relief, and under it is a still larger stone sculptured in a diaper pattern, with a stork and crowing cocks worked into the design. The style resembles that of the old carved door in the first chapel right of altar, all probably of the 14th or 15th cent.

To the N. of Vence is a row of four calcareous mountain cliffs, extending eastward to the Var, and each about 2000 ft. above the sea. The most prominent is the mighty cliff above Vence called the **Roche-Blanche**, commanding a superb view. On the summit are the remains of a walled village and castle, and less than half-way up the ruins of a castle of the Knight-Templars. The road up to the summit is by the first narrow path beyond the castle, ascending through beds of wild thyme and bushes of the prickly broom. The next hill is the Rocher-Noir, having on its eastern side, right above the bed of the Cagnes, a "foux," an immense cave called the Riou, containing a large basin of water, whence flows a copious stream. It is $3\frac{1}{2}$ m. from Vence. The next cliff rises over St. Jeannet, and bears its name. The most easterly is La Gaude, with vineyards producing one of the better wines of Provence, drank as vin ordinaire during the first year, when still sweet and unripe, but of good body and agreeable in the fifth and sixth years, when it costs $1\frac{1}{2}$ to 2 frs. the litre bottle. Vence is famous for double violets. They are cultivated in hollows between furrows, and are sold to the makers of perfumes at the rate of 3s. 8d. the pound. A woman will gather 4 kilogrammes (8 lbs. 13 oz.) in a day, for which she is paid at the rate of $2\frac{1}{2}$d. the kilo.

The road from Vence to the Cagnes railway station descends the whole way, passing at some distance the village of St. Paul, pop. 700, with part of its old walls, and below it the village of La Colle, pop. 1500. The coach drives through the low or modern town of Cagnes. *Inn:* Savournin, not comfortable during the mosquito season. The real town occupies, as usual, a hill, on the summit of which is a castle built by the Grimaldi, a polygonal tower bought by the present owner at an auction ; who has restored the painting by Carloni on the ceiling of the Salle Dorée, representing the Flight of Phaeton, and has also added a small picture gallery. A little way down from the castle are the ruins of the small abbey church of St. Veran, 6th cent. The chancel is still in good preservation. From Cagnes the views are not equal to those from Vence. (For the Vence-Cagnes station, see p. 169.)

ST. VALLIER.

Grasse to Digne, 63 m. north.—By the courrier 16 frs., changing coach at Castellane. Fare to St. Vallier, 2½ frs., Escragnolles 4 frs., Castellane 8½ frs., Barrème 11½ frs., and Digne 16 frs. By private coach from Grasse, with two horses, 100 frs. Dining first day at Escragnolles, and passing the night at Castellane. Next day breakfasting at Barrème, and then driving down to Digne (see map, p. 165).

The road between Grasse and Digne is broad, well constructed, and rises at an angle from 5 to 7 in the 100. From Grasse to St. Vallier (2350 ft. above the sea, or 1260 ft. above Grasse, and 6½ m. distant, population 536) the ascent is continuous, disclosing all the way grand views of Cannes, the sea, and the Estérel and the Tanneron mountains. The courrier and private carriages halt generally a few minutes in the "Place," near the column with a marble bust of Napoleon I., indicating the spot where he reposed "2 Mars 1815." The Hôtel du Nord is about 100 yards from this. The house is pretty comfortable, and charges per day from 8 to 9 frs. A carriage from this hotel, towards the Ponte-à-Dieu, as far as it can go, 3½ m., costs 5 frs. The remainder can be walked in about half an hour. A carriage from Grasse to St. Vallier, and towards the Pont-à-Dieu and back, 20 frs. The Pont-à-Dieu is a calcareous rock which spans the Siagne in the form of a bridge, like the "Pont" across the Ardèche.

From St. Vallier the road makes very circuitous windings on the steep sides of the mountains, ascending nearly all the way to Escragnolles, a hamlet, pop. 320, consisting of a few houses and a small roadside inn, with clean but hard beds, and plain and scanty fare, situated 3282 ft. above the sea, or 2192 ft. above and 18 m. north from Grasse. A little before arriving at Escragnolles is seen, in a deep valley, one of the principal sources of the river Siagne. The views from Escragnolles and Castellane exhibit lofty, wild, and partially-wooded mountains, with fields of wheat on laboriously-terraced ground.

19 m. N.W. from Escragnolles, or 37¼ from Grasse, is **Castellane**, 2370 ft. above the sea. Pop. 2000. *Inns:* Levant ; Commerce. A village of crooked streets on the Verdon, crossed by a bridge of one

arch. A narrow path leads to the top of the lofty cliff on which is the chapel of Notre Dame, rebuilt in 1703, commanding a most extensive prospect. Napoleon I. descended into Italy by the road on the left bank of the river. Those in private carriages generally spend the night here. A small coach runs between Castellane and Digne, which, although not very comfortable, is much better than the courrier in bad weather. 18 m. W. from Castellane by a mountain-road is Moustiers Sainte Marie (see p. 167). From Castellane the road by a series of zigzags reaches the top of the Col St. Pierre, 3600 ft., and then descends to **Taulanne**, 7 m. N.W. from Castellane. From Taulanne the road descends 5 m. S., chiefly through a picturesque ravine, to **Senez**, pop. 620, among wild barren mountains, at the foot of Mont La Combe, on the river Asse. The hamlet has a poor inn, and a cathedral built during 1130 to 1242.

44¼ m. N.W. from Grasse, and 18¾ m. S. from Digne, is **Barrème**, pop. 1100, on the confluence of the Clumane with the Asse. Breakfast is taken here, and the diligence changes horses. Cloth-mills and trade in dried fruits, especially prunes. In the neighbourhood is a saline spring. The road from Barrème to Digne descends by a ridge between the valleys of the Asse and the Clumane.

Digne, pop. 8000, 2000 ft. above the sea, 14 m. E. by loop-line from the station St. Auban on the main line. St. Auban is 80½ m. N. from Marseilles, 62¼ m. N. from Aix, and 20½ m. N. from Manosque. It is 109½ m. S. from Grenoble; 45½ m. S. from Aspres, the terminus of the road from Die; 41 m. S. from Veynes, whence commences the loop-line to Gap; and 31¾ m. S. from Serre, the terminus of the road from Nyons (see map of Rhône and Savoy). *Hotels:* Boyer; Remusat, both in the Boulevard Gassendi, near the statue of Pierre Gassendi (1592-1655), one of the most eminent philosophers of France. This, the ancient Dinia, the capital of the Avantici, is situated chiefly on hilly ground rising from the Bléonne and the Eaux-Chaudes. On the highest part is the cathedral, and on the plain up the river, near the seminary, the much more interesting church of Notre Dame, 12th cent., numbered among the historic monuments of France. 1¼ m. up the Eaux-Chaudes, at the foot of Mt. St. Pancras, are sulphurous springs, temp. 115° Fahr., efficacious in the cure of wounds and rheumatism. Bath, 2 frs. From Digne Napoleon issued his proclamation of March 1815. Digne makes a good resting-place and good headquarters. Both of the hotels are comfortable and moderate, 8 to 10 frs. per day, and both supply carriages at so much per day (see map, p. 165).

Among the many diligences that start from Digne, the most important is to **Riez**, 26 m. S.W., fare 4 frs., time 4½ hrs., a great diligence centre. Riez, pop. 3000, on the Colostre, at the foot of Mont St. Maxime. *Inn:* H. des Alpes, whence start coaches daily for Manosque, 22 m. W., by Allemagne, 5 m.; St. Martin, 8 m.; and to Gréoulx (see p. 167), 12½ m. S.W. from Riez, and 9¼ m. E. from Manosque, fare 4 frs. For Moustiers Sainte Marie (see p. 167), 9 m. E., by Roumoulles, fare 2 frs. For **Montmelian**, 18 m. S., by Quinson. Travellers on their way to Draguignan spend the night at Montmelian, H. Sicard, and proceed next morning to Aups, 9½ m. E., *Inn:* H. du Cours, and thence to Draguignan. From Montmelian a coach runs to Barjols, *Inn:* H. Pont d'Or, 9½ m. S., whence other coaches run to Brignoles (see p. 142). For **Valensole**, 7½ m. W., whence to Volx railway station, other 7 m. W. From Volx coach to **Digne**, 25 m. N., by Puymoisson, 3¾ m. N.; Le Begude, 8 m.; Estoublon, 11¾ m.; Mezèl on the Asse, *Inn:* H. du Cours, 15¾ m.; and Châteauredon, 7½ m. S. from Digne. All these roads traverse sometimes deep valleys and at other times extend across wide elevated tablelands. Down in the valleys are olive trees, in the higher regions quinces, plums, walnuts, and cherries (see map, p. 165).

Riez, the Colonia Julia-Augusta of the Romans, is still partly surrounded by its old fortifications, of which the highest of the towers has been converted into a belfry. Up the main street, through either of the gateways, are houses with sculptured doors and transomed windows which tell of better days. Near the two inns, but on the other side of the river, is La Rotonde, a temple, square externally, enclosing a peristyle of 8 monolith granite Corinthian columns, bearing an elongated octagonal dome. The diameter of the circle is about 23 ft. Near it are the remains of a colonnade consisting of 4 composite monolith granite columns. On the top of Mont St. Maxime is the chapel St. Maxime, 10th cent., restored and altered in 1857. It is 17 yds. long and 10 wide, outside measure. On each side of the chancel are three Corinthian columns similar to those in the round chapel. At the S. W. corner is a short square tower with a spire. From the brow of the eminence, where there is a statue of Mary, there is an excellent view of the dingy town and of the pleasing valley of the Colostre.

A very pleasant drive of 9½ m. E., fare 2 frs., is to the curious village of Moustiers Ste. Marie by the courrier, starting at 2 and returning at 4. *Inn:* H. du Mouton Couronné. The village consists of poor dingy houses, partly in a narrow gully and partly on the slopes, at the base of vertical calcareous sandstone cliffs, rising to the height of from 500 to 1000 ft. Between two opposite points of these precipices is a chain 745 ft. long, from which was suspended a gilt iron star which fell in 1878. Up the cliffs, by the stair of the "Via Crucis," is the chapel of Notre Dame, almost immediately below the chain. Several caves are in the neighbourhood. Lower down is the parish church of the 10th and 13th cents. From the S. side rises a square belfry in three diminishing stages. Between Moustiers and Riez is Roumoulles, with the ruins of a castle. 18 m. E. from Moustiers is Castellane, but no public coach runs between them.

12½ m. W. from Riez, and 9½ m. E. from Manosque, is **Gréoulx**, pop. 1400, a dirty village on a hill rising from the Verdon. On the top are the gaunt ruins of a castle built by the Knight-Templars. Less than ¼ m. from the village is the hotel and the bathing establishment. The rooms cost from 2 to 5 frs. Coffee in the morning, 60 cents.

Breakfast and dinner, 7 frs. Service, ½ fr. Or the lowest price per day, 10 frs., which is dear considering the quality of the house and furniture. Bath, 2 frs. Cure lasts 25 days. The establishment is 1150 ft. above the sea. The mineral water, of which there is a most abundant supply, is limpid and unctuous, and tastes like slightly salt new milk. Temp. 95° to 100° Fahr. The principal ingredient is the chloride of soda, and, in less quantities, the chloride of magnesia, the carbonate of lime, and the sulphate of lime and soda. The water is also rich in organic substances, such as baregine and glairine along with other sulphurous compounds, which develop themselves rapidly when the water is exposed to the action of the air. This organic matter is used in the mud-baths for the cure of sores and tumours. The baths are partially sunk into the floor, and are easily entered. The flow of water into and out of them is constant. Coaches daily from Gréoulx to Manosque, Mirabeau, and Riez (map, p. 165).

Manosque, pop. 6200, on the railway between Marseilles and Grenoble, 22 m. north from Pertuis, 41½ m. from Aix, 48½ m. from Gardanne, and 59½ m. from Marseilles. 4½ m. south from Volx, 20½ m. from St. Auban, 31 m. from Sisteron, 61½ m. from Veynes, 66 m. from Aspres, and 130½ m. from Grenoble (see map of Rhône and Savoy).

Hotels: Pascal; Eymon, commanding an extensive view of the surrounding mountains; near it the G. H. de Versailles; and the Poste. Manosque is situated on an eminence rising from the plain of the Durance, nearly surrounded by hills covered with vineyards and olive trees. Portions of the town walls and towers still remain, and the eastern and western gateways have been repaired and restored. Entering the town by the gate close to the hotels, we ascend the narrow and badly-paved principal street to the church of St. Sauveur, easily recognised by the square belfry attached to the S. E. end. Within the main entrance are two large caryatides. The windows of the façade are circular, the others small and round-headed with modern glass. On each side of the nave are semicircular arches of a great span; the chancel is extremely shallow, the roof 4 partite, and the floor considerably lower than the street. The narrow lane opposite the corner of the façade leads to the principal "Place," where there is a fountain, and whence there is a good view. Higher up the principal street is Notre Dame, in exactly the same style as St. Sauveur. The table or altar in the chapel to the left of the high altar is formed of a marble sarcophagus, 5th cent., with figures, in bold relief, of the apostles, and in the centre a crucifixion. Above is a black image of Mary and child, supposed to date from the 6th cent. In the Hôtel de Ville is a silver bust by Puget of Gérard Jung, the founder of the order of the Hospitallers, a religious community whose office was to relieve the stranger, the poor, and the sick. In the neighbourhood are deposits of gypsum and lignite. Coach daily to Riez, 5 hrs., 22 m. E.; to the baths of Gréoulx, in the same direction; to **Apt** (see index), 26 m. W., by Reillane 15½ m., and Céreste 20½ m. W. **Volx** station is the intended terminus of the rail from Apt.

124
-~ GOLF JOUAN or VALLAURIS. A few yards straight up **-~ 31**
from the station is a short column, which marks the spot where Napoleon bivouacked after his arrival from Elba on March 1, 1815. A very pleasant road, lined with villas, connects this small port with Cannes. Opposite station are pottery showrooms.

127   **28**
-~ ANTIBES, pop. 6000. *Hotels:* Escouffier, Aigles d'Or. A **-~**
fortified port founded by the Greeks, but, with the exception of two old towers, without any mark of antiquity. The streets are lined with tolerable houses. In the square the inhabitants have erected a monument to their valour. Those wishing a bird's-eye view of the town should ascend the tower beside the church. The bellman's house is close by. The wine of Antibes is of superior quality (see p. 154). From Antibes station omnibus to Biot, pop. 1400.

132   **23**
-~ VENCE-CAGNES. At this station coaches await passengers **-~**
for Cagnes, pop. 3000, about 1 mile distant. It is built on the slope of a hill, and contains the old mansion of the Grimaldi. Six miles northwards by the same road is **Vence,** pop. 3000, with an old cathedral and several interesting antiquities. It is famous for figs, and flowers for perfumery. One mile distant is St. Martin, with a splendid view from the terrace, and most picturesque environs. Between Vence-Cagnes and Nice runs a diligence (see p. 165).

136   **19**
-~ VAR. This station is on the left or Nice side of the river **-~**
Var, at the eastern end of the viaduct over the mouth of the river. ¾ m. N.W. from the station by the road to St. Martin are the Nice nurseries or pépinières, extensive, but not well kept. About 2 m. N.E. from the station, up on the hill, is the Caucade cemetery, in three stages. The first is used by the French, the next by the English, and the highest by the Russians. The last two contain many beautiful marble monuments.

At the mouth of the Var is the racecourse. The races take place in January.

NICE

is 140 m. N.E. from Marseilles, 95½ m. N.E. from Toulon, 95¼ m. N.E. from Hyères, 39 m. N.E. from St. Raphael, and 19¼ m. N.E. from Cannes. It is 9½ m. W. from Monaco, 15 m. S.W. from Menton, 23½ m. S.W. from Bordighera, and 30 m. S.W. from San Remo (see railway map, fly-leaf). Situated on the Bay des Anges and on the embouchure of the Paillon, mostly covered over, pop. 66,300.

Hotels and Pensions on the Promenade des Anglais, taking them in the order of east to west. The Hôtel des Anglais, with one side to the "Jardin Public." Next it is the Cercle (club) de la Méditerranée; and opposite it, projecting into the sea, a casino. On the other side of the cercle is the H. Luxembourg. Then follow the Pension Rivoir, 13 to 18 frs.; the H. Méditerranée, H. Westminster, and the H. West End, all first-class houses charging from 15 to 25 frs. per day.

The following are at the western end of the Promenade, and, as they have considerable gardens in front, the inmates do not hear the noise of the sea so much. The H. de l'Elysée, No. 59; the Pension *Anglaise, 8 to 11 frs., No. 77; the H. Continental, 10 to 15 frs. On the Boulevard du Midi, the eastern prolongation of the Promenade des Anglais, are the Beau Rivage; the H. des Princes, 12 to 15 frs.; and on the Quai des Pouchettes, the *H. et P. Suisse, 8½ to 12 frs.

Around the "Jardin Public" are the first-class houses, the Angleterre and the Bretagne. On the Quai Massena the H. de France; while in the Place Massena are the best cafés and restaurants, large cab-stands, and the terminus of the trams. Over the river near the Place Massena is the Casino Municipal, fronting the Quai St. Jean Baptiste, on which are the hotels Cosmopolitain; the Paix; and the Grand Hotel, fronting the garden in the Square Massena. These hotels are first-class, and charge from 10 to 20 frs. Higher up is a second-class house, frequented chiefly by French, the H. Ferrand, 8 to 10 frs.

On and near the Avenue de la Gare are some excellent hotels and pensions. Taking them in the order of the Place Massena towards the railway station we have, under the arches, the hotels Meublés, Deux Mondes, and opposite the Univers. Then follow the hotels Ambassadeurs with garden, Iles Britanniques, Prince of Wales, all the three from 10 to 20 frs. Opposite, at No. 42, is the H. and R. Duval, 9 to 12 frs. At the top of the R. de la Gare, the H. National, 9 to 12 frs., and the Hotel des Alpes.

In the streets at right angles to the R. de la Gare near the H. Iles Britanniques are the Russian, German, English, and Scotch churches, and some comfortable hotels and pensions, mostly with gardens. The best of the hotels are the *Paradis and the *Louvre, in the Boul. Longchamp, near the Scotch Church. At the western end of the Boul. Longchamp, the H. et P. des Palmiers, and the H. Splendide, all from 10 to 20 frs. Near the Splendide is the P. Java, 9 to 11 frs.

Behind the Scotch Church are the P. Internationale and the H. et

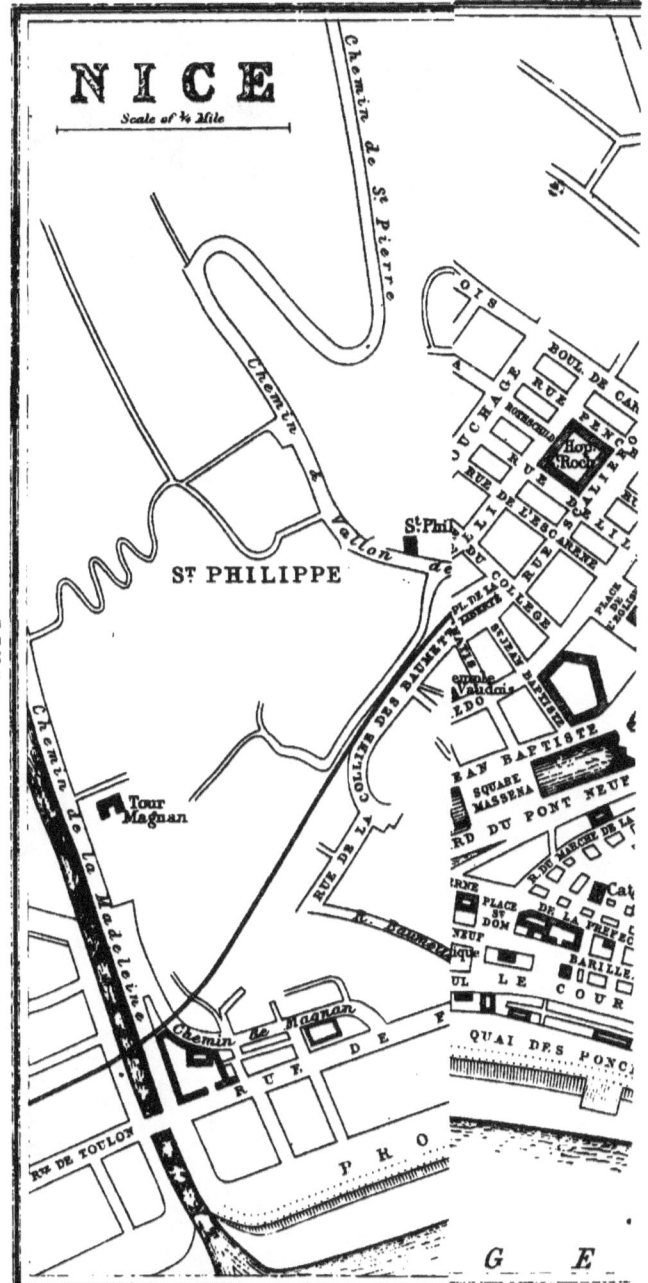

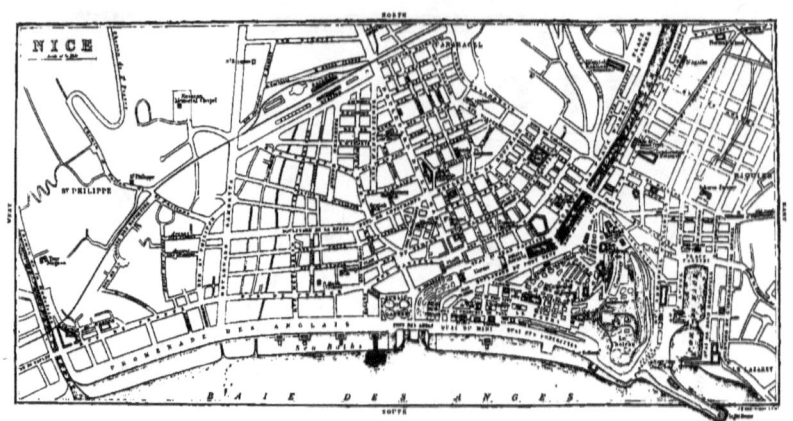

NICE. HOTELS AND PENSIONS.

P. de Genève. Next the Russian Church is the P. Helvétique. Near it the H. Royal; the H. et P. Mignon and the P. *Millet, entered from R. St. Etienne, 8 to 12 frs.

At W. end of the R. de la Paix the H. Raissan, 10 to 12 frs.; near it the Russie and the Beau Site, both quiet houses with gardens.

Opposite the station the H. et P. du Midi, 9 to 11 frs. Farther down the H. et P. Interlaken, 8 to 11 frs. with wine.

From the E. side of the Avenue de la Gare parallel streets extend to the Boulevard Carabacel. In the first of these, the Rue Carnieri, is the Theatre Français. In the Rue Pastorelli the Pension St. Etienne and the H. Négociants, 8 to 12 frs. In the broad B. Dubouchage are the first-class houses — the H. Littoral; *Empereurs; *Albion. Behind the Albion, in the Rue Alberti, the H. et P. d'Orient. The large building in the B. Dubouchage is the Bourse. Near it is the American Episcopal Church. In the Avenue Beaulieu are the H. Central and the G. H. *Rubion.

The hotels, pensions, and villas at the end of the B. Dubouchage, and about the B. Carabacel, are frequented by delicate people, who sun themselves in the gardens and boulevards of this quarter. At the Carabacel end of the B. Dubouchage are the first-class houses — the H. Hollande; H. *Windsor; and opposite, the H. *Julien. On an eminence in a garden off the B. Carabacel is the H. *Nice. Then follow, on the B. Carabacel, the H. Bristol, P. Londres, H. de Paris, and houses with furnished apartments. In this quarter is the Carabacel Episcopal Church, and near it the Hôtel Carabacel.

On the way up to Cimiès, the G. H. Windsor. On Cimiès Hill, near the Convent of St. Barthélemy, is the H. et P. *Barthélemy, on the road to the Val Obscur, and near many pleasant rambles. On the Cimiès Hill, on opposite sides of the Amphitheatre, are the H. et P. Cimiès, and the Pension Anglaise, in the three houses from 9 to 12 frs. They are about 2 m. from Nice, and 430 ft. above it. The tram from the Place Massena has its terminus near the P. Barthélemy. The H. Cimiès has its own omnibus. The town omnibus runs within a short distance of the P. Anglaise.

In the street behind the Promenade des Anglais, the R. de France, and its continuation the R. Massena, are hotels and pensions, with moderate prices. Commencing at west end and going eastward—at No. 100, in garden, the P. Torelli. On the hill behind the H. de Rome, 12 frs. At No. 121 is the H. de l'Elysée, with front to the Promenade des Anglais. At No. 46 the P. *Metropole, 8 to 10 frs.;

and opposite, the H. du Pavillon, with front to the Promenade des Anglais. At No. 34 the P. Lampiano, 9 to 11 frs. At No. 30 R. Massena the H. St. André, 8 frs. In the Place Massena the H. et R. Helder, 18 frs. For commercial gentlemen the best is the H. des Étrangers, R. Pont Neuf, 9 to 10 frs.

Those requiring to study economy will, by a little search through the private pensions, find very comfortable and moderately-priced lodgings. In the meantime they may alight at any of the following houses, where they can arrange at the prices given:—H. du Midi, opp. station, 8 to 11 frs., 3 meals, wine extra. At the head of the Avenue de la Gare the H. des Alpes and the H. National, 9 to 12 frs. At 17 B. Carabacel H. et P. de Londres, 8 to 10 frs. with wine. In the Rue de France the P. *Metropole, 8 to 10 frs. At the west end of the Promenade des Anglais the Pension Anglaise, 8 to 10 frs. In the Rue Massena the H. St. André, 8 frs., including everything. In the R. Gioffredo the H. and R. Montesquieu, 8 to 9 frs.

Cafés.—The best in the Place Massena. *Restaurants.*—The *London House, Pl. du Jardin Public. Restaurant *Française, 3 Av. de la Gare, and at No. 11 Rest. d'Europe. *Clubs or Cercles.*—The Cercle de la Méditerranée in the Prom. des Anglais. Cercle Massena, Quai St. Jean.

Banks.—The Banque de France, 6 Quai du Midi. The best for all kinds of banking business and money changing is the "Credit Lyonnais," 15 Avenue de la Gare. Other banks—the Banque de Nice, 6 P. Massena; Lacroix et Roissard, 2 P. Massena; Viterbo, 13 Avenue de la Gare.

House Agents.—John Arthur and Co., 1 Place Jardin Public; C. Jougla, 55 R. Gioffredo; Salvi and Co., 2 R. du Temple.

Post Office, 20 Rue St. François de Paul, behind the Quai du Midi. Most of the clocks have two minute-hands, one for railway or Paris time, the other for Nice time. The railway time is 20 minutes behind the Nice time. In the same street is the excellent public library, with 45,000 volumes. Open from 10 to 3 and 7 to 10 P.M. It contains a few antiquities, some Roman milestones, a collection of medals, and a bust of Caterina Segurana. The Museum of Natural History is in No. 6 Place Garibaldi. Observatory on the top of Mont Gros, 1201 ft. above the sea.

Booksellers.—Galignani, 15 Quai Massena, with well-supplied reading-room; Barbery, Place du Jardin Public; Visconti, 2 Rue du Cours. Cook's office adjoins Galignani's. Gaze's is at No. 13, and Caygill's No. 15 Avenue de la Gare.

Druggists.—Of these there are excellent English establishments in the principal streets.

Confectioneries and Perfumeries.—Of the confections the *specialité* of Nice is candied Parma violets, sold in little round boxes weighing 100 grammes, or 3½ oz., for 5 frs. the box. The most expensive of the glazed fruits are pine-apple, 10 frs. the kilogramme (2 lbs. 3¼ oz.), strawberries, 10 frs., and apricots, without the stones, 8 frs. All the others cost either 5 or 6 frs. the kilo. The best shops are—*Caëtan Féa, 4 Avenue de la Gare; Guitton and Rudel, 23 same street; and *Escoffier, in the Place Massena. Rimmel's garden and perfume distillery are near the slaughter-house, on the left bank of the Paillon.

Churches.—Temple Évangélique or Vaudois in the Rue Gioffredo; Russian Memorial Chapel, N.W. from the station; Russian Church, Rue Longchamp; German Church, Rue Adelaide; American Church, Rue Carabacel. Trinity Church, Rue de France; St. Michael's, Rue St. Michel; Carabacel Episcopal Church, at the east end of the Rue Notre Dame. Scotch Church, in the Rues St. Etienne and Adelaide.

Steamers to Marseilles, Genoa, Leghorn, and Corsica once weekly.

Coach hire.—A carriage with coachman and 2 horses, 750 frs. per month. Per day, 30 frs. There are many excellent livery stables, where carriages and riding horses can be had per day or per month.

Cabs.—Drivers have to produce their tariffs. Cab with 1 horse and seat for 2, the course 75 c.; seats for 4, 1 fr. The hour, seat for 2, 2½ frs.; seats for 4, 3 frs. Cabs with 2 horses, the course 1½ fr.; the hour, 3½ frs.

To or from the station. Cab with seat for 2, 1 fr.; with seats for 4, 1½ fr. Cab with 2 horses, 1 fr. 15 sous. Each article on top of cab 25 c., and 25 c. for each stoppage. It is better, if not sure of a hotel, to engage the cab by the hour.

All the *tram cars* start from the Place Massena.

Diligences.—From the office, No. 34 Boulevard du Pont Neuf, start daily:—Coach to St. Martin Lantosque, 3117 ft. above the sea, and 37 m. N. from Nice. Fare 6 frs., time 10 hrs. (see p. 180). Coach to Puget-Théniers, 1476 ft. above the sea, and 42 m. N.W. from Nice. Fare 2½ frs., time 9 hrs. (see p. 182). To St. Sauveur, 40½ m. N. (p. 182). Omnibus twice daily during the winter season to Monte Carlo, by the low Corniche road. From the office, Place St. François, start:—Coach to Cuneo, 80 m. N., by Tenda and the Col di Tenda tunnel. Fare 16 frs., time 18 hrs. Coach to Tenda alone, 2680 ft. above the sea, and 51 m. N. from Nice. Fare 9 frs., time 11 hrs. (see p. 182). From Hôtel Chapeau Rouge, Quai St. Jean Baptiste, coach to Levens, 1916 ft. above the sea, and 15 m. N. from Nice. Fare 3 frs., time 4 hrs. From the Cloche d'Or, Rue de l'Aqueduct, coach to Contes, fare 1½ fr., time 2 hrs., 10½ m. N. up the valley of the Paillon, passing the pretty village of Trinité-Victor, 5½ m. N., pop. 1300; Drap, on both sides of the Paillon; and then on a hill to the left, 2½ hrs. distant by a path, the ruins of the village Châteauneuf, abandoned on account of the want of water. Contes, pop. 1700, has good country inns, gardens full of orange trees, and vineyards producing good wine. Cab with 1 horse and 2 seats to Trinité-Victor and back, 5 frs.; ½ hour's rest allowed.

Climate.—If I should be asked to draw a comparison between Nice and Cannes with respect to climate, I should be inclined to call Nice a trifle colder in winter, especially if there be much snow on the mountains. M. Teysseire has preserved and published records of twenty years' meteorological observations taken at Nice with instruments placed outside his window, on a fourth floor facing the north-north-east. His mean results for the twenty years are as follow; to which, for the sake of comparison, I append the means of my six winter seasons at Cannes :—

MEAN TEMPERATURE.

	Nice.	Cannes.		Nice.	Cannes.		Nice.	Cannes.
November	53·8	52·6	January	47·1	48	March	51·8	51
December	48·5	46·3	February	46·2	48·8	April	58·1	55·5

The mistral is as well known at Nice as it is at Cannes. —*Health Resorts*, by M. Marcet, M.D.

Nice occupies a plain bounded by the limestone summits of the Maritime Alps, whence descend fertile wooded ridges composed of a reddish conglomerate and a gray-blue clay of the Pleiocene period. Between these ridges are deep vallons, gullies, or furrows, with precipitous sides, scooped out to a great depth by the intermittent action of torrents, the breadth and depth of the valleys depending on the volume of water in the stream and the degree of consistence of the conglomerate. The great vallons have tributary vallons. The pleasant Vallon de Magnan exemplifies both kinds. From the Pont de Magnan (near which a tram stops) the first tributary is nearly a mile up the stream, opening from the right or west side. This vallon is short, the walls nearly perpendicular, and in some parts scarcely 2 ft. apart. Higher up the Magnan, and opening from the left or east side, next a church, is the more beautiful and more extensive tributary vallon, the Madeleine, which high up becomes so narrow and so choked with troublesome brambles as to be almost impassable. The banks are covered with vegetation, and the more level parts with maritime pines and olive trees. At the entrance are beds of clay of immense thickness, of which fire-bricks are made. The Mantéga Vallon, entered from the Chemin de Mantéga (see plan), has great walls of clay and conglomerate. The softer conglomerate is quarried and broken up for its sandy dolomitic material, which, mixed with lime, makes excellent mortar.

The city of Nice consists of three distinct parts :—1st, the new or fashionable quarter, stretching westwards from the Paillon, containing avenues and gardens, and broad and well-paved streets bordered with large and elegant buildings, of which a large proportion are hotels and "pensions ;" 2d, the Old Town, a perfect labyrinth of narrow, dirty, steep streets, radiating from the Cathedral as a sort of centre, and running up the sides of the Château hill, which separates it from, 3d, the Port, with its seafaring population, and about 16 acres of harbour.

During the season, from November to April, Nice is a luxurious city, with the attractions and resources of the great northern capitals. In winter the population may be estimated at 90,000, whereas in summer it is only about 54,000, a diminution in numbers apparent only in the largest and most elegant part of the city. The non-fluc-tuating population inhabit the crowded tenements in the narrow streets huddled together between the Paillon and the Château hill.

The glory of Nice is the Promenade des Anglais, commenced by the English in 1822 to employ the poor during a season of scarcity. This beautiful terraced walk, 85 ft. broad, extends 2 m. along the beach of the Baie des Anges, from the Quai Lunel of the Port to the mouth of the Magnan, whence it will be continued other 3 m. west to the mouth of the river Var, near the Racecourse.

Over the Port rises the Castlehill, 315 ft., commanding from the platform, in every direction, the most charming views. To the E. are the peninsula of St. Jean and Cape Boron, and rising from it, Fort Montalban, Mt. Vinaigrier, and the Observatory residence and buildings. To the N. is Mt. Chauve ; to the E. the roofs of Nice ; and in the distance the Roche-Blanche (p. 164), the peninsula of Antibes, and the Estérels. This fortress, founded by the early Phœnician colonists, and destroyed and rebuilt at various periods afterwards, was finally razed to the ground in 1706, by order of Louis XIV., by Maréchal Berwick. Now it has become the great park of Nice. A round tower that still remains, over the Hôtel des Princes, called the Tour Bellanda, was probably added to the Castle by Emmanuel Philibert in 1560. On the W. side of the hill (see plan) is the cemetery in five stages. At the entrance is the monument to the "Victimes de l'Incendie du Theatre, 23d March 1881." Towards the E. end, at the wall, is the grave of

CATERINA SEGURANA. MEMORIAL CHAPEL.

Rosa Garibaldi, d. 19th March 1852. The tombstone was placed by her son, General Garibaldi. In the highest terrace is the grave containing Gambetta and his mother. In a terrace by itself in the eastern end is the Protestant cemetery.

Near the harbour, and above the Quai Lunel, is the statue of King Charles Felix. In the Rue du Murier, leading down from the Rue Segurane to the Port, is the mulberry tree where Caterina Segurana had her tent. On the 15th of August 1543 she, at the head of a devoted band, attacked the allied French and Turkish forces commanded by François de Bourbon and the Turk Barbarossa, struck down with her own hand the standard-bearer, and put the enemy to flight. Giuseppe Garibaldi was born, 19th July 1807, in a house which stood at the head of the Port before its enlargement. In a small street, ramifying from the Rue Segurane, is the church of St. Augustin, in which Luther preached in 1510. At the east end of the R. de la Préfecture, last street left, No. 15 R. Droite, is the Palais des Lascaris, with ceilings painted in fresco by Carlone. It is now the "École Professionnelle." This is also the street of the jewellers patronised by the peasantry. Paganini died (1840) in the house No. 14 R. de la Préfecture. The jambs and lintels of the doorway are slightly decorated. The Cathedral and the other churches in the old town are in the Italian style, ornamented with gilding and variously-coloured marbles. The new church, Notre Dame, in the Avenue de la Gare, is Gothic in style. The first non-Romanist church erected in Nice was the Episcopal chapel of the Trinity in 1822. As it became too small, the present church was built on the same site in 1856 at a cost of £6000. To the N.W. of the railway station, by the Chemin St. Etienne, in an orange grove, is the Russian Memorial Chapel, a series of ascending domes, built over the spot on which stood the villa in which the Prince Imperial of Russia died, April 24, 1865. The interior is covered with designs in gold leaf, varied here and there by a light-blue ground. Round the base runs a white marble panelling, enclosing frescoes of saints in niches.

The principal thoroughfares in Nice are the Place Massena and the handsome broad street the "Avenue de la Gare," extending in a straight line northward from the "Place" to the station. Next in importance are the Quais Massena and St. Jean Baptiste. In the above are all the best shops. The Rue Massena, and its continuation the Rue de France, behind the Promenade des Anglais, contain shops principally of the provision kind, British stores, grocers, wine merchants, confec-

tioners, and dressmakers.   At the east end of the Rue de France is
the Croix de Marbre, a marble crucifix under a canopy on four marble
columns, erected in 1568 to commemorate the visit of Charles V.,
Francis I., and Paul III. in 1538, and the partial reconciliation of the
two potentates through the intervention of the Pope.   The column
opposite commemorates the visits of Pio VII. in 1809 and in February
1814.   Near this is Trinity Church, and in the Rue Gioffredo the
Temple Évangélique, the second Protestant church built in Nice.

On the arched part of the Paillon, fronting the Quai St. Jean, is
the large and handsome Casino, and a little farther up the river the
pretty public garden called the Square Massena, with a statue in the
centre, in an animated posture, of André Massena, Prince of Essling
and Marshal of France, who was born on May 7, 1758, in a house now
demolished, which stood on the Quai St. Jean Baptiste.   In 1810
he was chosen by Napoleon to stop the advance of Wellington in
Portugal, and was commissioned "to drive the English and their
Sepoy general into the sea."   But the wary strategy and imperturb-
able firmness of the British general proved resistless, and Massena was
compelled to save his military fame by a masterly retreat.   On the
pedestal Clio is seen writing his name in the chronicles of his native
city.   This garden forms a pleasant lounge, but it is not so fashionable as the other farther down, at the mouth of the river, called the
"Jardin Public," planted with magnolias, acacias, Japan medlars, and
gum, cork, camphor, and pepper trees.   The band plays here in the
afternoon.   The most beautiful of the public gardens is on the Castlehill, intersected by footpaths and carriage-roads up to the summit.
On one side of the hill is the public cemetery.

All the side streets which ramify eastward from the Avenue de la
Gare lead to the Quartier Carabacel, one of the most sheltered parts of
Nice, and inhabited by the most delicate invalids.   Above it, about
2 m. distant, or 3 from the Place Massena, is Cimiès (430 ft. above
the sea), another favoured spot, frequented principally by nervous
invalids requiring a sedative climate.   On the top of this hill stood
the Roman city Cemenelium, of which all that remains are the ruins of
an amphitheatre 210 ft. long by 175 wide.   Just under the Boulevard
Prince de Galles are artistic ruins composed of ancient material gathered
in this neighbourhood.   They stand in the spacious grounds of the
superb villa Val Rose, which in shape resembles Noe's ark.   Entrance
from behind G. H. Windsor.   The first road right from the theatre leads
to a Franciscan convent built in 1543 on the site of a temple of Diana.

N

The altar-pieces of the two chapels to the right of the altar were painted by Ludovico Brea, a contemporary of Raphael, and the only artist of eminence Nice has produced. The cemetery contains some beautiful tombstones. In the centre of the "Place," on a spiral marble column, is a crucifix with a winged J. C. Above is a pelican feeding its young, a favourite Christian symbol of charity during the Middle Ages.

A path in the corner of the "Place" leads down to St. Pons (p. 179).

At No. 6 Place Garibaldi is the Museum of Natural History. The first hall contains a collection of the fungi growing in the department ; and separate, under a glass case, specimens of those allowed to be sold in the market for food.

The best of the drives from Nice is to Menton, 20 m. east, either by the high Corniche road along the flanks of the mountains, passing above Monaco, or by the beautiful new road which seldom rises much above the coast, and passes through La Condamine to Monte Carlo. An omnibus runs daily between the Boul. du Pont Neuf and Monte Carlo by this road (see p. 187).

Cab with 1 horse and 2 seats to Villefranche and back, 5 frs. ; ½ hour's rest allowed. With 2 horses and 4 seats, 7 frs. Above the Pont Neuf, near the Place St. François, omnibuses (without fixed time) start for Villefranche, ½ fr. ; St. Jean, 15 sous ; and Beaulieu, 15 sous. On feast-days a steamer generally sails to Monaco. In the village of St. Jean there is a very comfortable country inn, H. Victoria, where bouillabaisse can always be had. Pension, 8½ frs. And at Beaulieu, close to the station, is the *H. et P. des Anglais, pension 9½ to 12 frs. Those who go from Nice to St. Jean with luggage should leave in the omnibus, but for Beaulieu the rail should be taken. A carriage with 2 horses to St. Jean and Beaulieu and back, 25 frs. The tour round Mt. Boron, ascending by the new and descending by the old road, costs, in a coach with 2 horses, 15 frs. Time, 1½ hour.

Nice to the Val-Obscur, 4 m. N.—Take tram from the Place Massena to St. Maurice, 2 m. N. It stops in front of the gate of the Villa Chambrun, by the side of the Octroi. For the Vallon des Fleurs ascend by the road to the right. For the Val-Obscur ascend by the road to the left, passing the Chapelle du Ray. Carriages can drive the length of the water-conduit. From this part the bed of the stream may be followed, but as it is very stony it is better to keep on the path by the side of the conduit as long as possible. The Val-Obscur is a deep ravine, 440 yards long, between cliffs of an earthy conglomerate from 200 to 300 ft. high, and 7 ft. apart at their narrowest point. By continuing this path for a little distance past a house on the side of the hill, then crossing over by a path to the right, we reach the chapel of St. Sebastien, whence a road ascends to Mt. Chauve, passing by Le Ray, with an inn, 1446 ft. above the sea, or only 1324 ft. below the summit of Mt. Chauve.

The **Vallon des Fleurs** ou des Hepatiques is renowned for its olive trees and its wild flowers in early spring. The commencement of the valley is about 10 minutes' walk from the St. Maurice terminus of the tram. A path leads to the top of the valley. From the summit it leads round by the head of other two vallons to the Cimiès road, which it joins nearly opposite to the observatory, only a little higher up the valley of the Paillon. The whole forms a very agreeable walk. (For Cimiès, see p. 177.)

A much-frequented drive or walk is to the Grotte St. André, about 3¾ m. N. from Nice by the west bank of the Paillon and the Vallon St. André. A cab with 1 horse and 2 seats there and back, 5 frs.; with 2 horses and 4 seats, 7 frs.; ½ hour's stay allowed. Carriage, 15 frs. But if the return to Nice be made by Falicon, 25 frs. When about 1½ m. up the Paillon there is a large gate which gives access to the orchard of the Villa Clery, containing some orange trees above 100 years old, yet in the whole plantation there is not one well-developed specimen. The oranges are sold at from 4½ to 6 frs. the 100, and packed and despatched to order. Almost opposite, on the east side of the Paillon, are the more beautiful gardens and perfume distillery of Rimmel. On the top of the hill (430 ft.), above the Clery orchard, is seen the monastery of Cimiès, built in 1543 after the original house, which stood near the Croix de Marbre, had been destroyed by the Turks. The next large edifice passed on the west bank is the monastery of St. Pons, built in 775 by St. Syagrius, a contemporary of Charlemagne, on the spot where the Roman senator St. Pontius suffered martyrdom. The emperor is said to have spent some days here in 777 while on his way to Rome. In 890 it was destroyed by the Saracens, and in 999 rebuilt by Fredericus, Bishop of Nice. In 1388 the treaty was signed here by which Nice was annexed to the house of Savoy. A short distance beyond, at the part where the stream St. André unites with the Paillon, 3 m. from the Place Massena, is the asylum for the insane. First-class boarders pay 4 frs. per day, second 3 frs. A little higher up the stream are the village, pop. 660, and (on a hill) the château of St. André. The château is a plain house with a small chapel at the west end, fronted by a terrace built by the brothers Thaon of Lantosque in 1685. Part is occupied by a school and part is let. The chapel is now the parish church. At the east end is a small petrifying spring. From the château an avenue of ill-conditioned cypresses (the best have been cut down) leads to the Grotte St. André. Fee, ½ fr. each. It is a natural tunnel, 114 ft. long and 25 ft. high, through the limestone rock, under which flows the stream St. André, dammed up at the outer end to enable the man to take visitors through it in a boat. Near it are a restaurant and shop in which petrifactions are sold.

From the "Grotte" up to the 8th kilomètre stone the ravine becomes so narrow that there is barely room between the high cliffs for the road and the stream. It is so picturesque that those who have come to visit the cave should walk up this distance, 1 mile, before returning. Those in carriages generally pass up this way and return by Falicon, a village perched on the top of a steep hill above the river St. André.

To the Observatory, 1215 ft. above the sea, constructed in 1881 at the expense of M. Bischoffsheim. Take the Abbatoir tram the length of the Place Risso (see plan), where take the corner to the right and ascend by the Corniche road. If on foot, on arriving at a well beside a house, ascend the hill by the mule-path. The views are charming. The establishment possesses 1235 acres of land. On the highest part are the various buildings for astronomical purposes. A few yards below, on the west side of the mountain, is a handsome building 228 ft. long and 46 broad. In the centre is the library, and the wing at each end dwelling-houses.

Nice to Cuneo by St. Martin Lantosque.

(Map, page 165, and Map of Rhône and Savoy.)

Nice to Cuneo by St. Martin Lantosque.—Diligence from Nice to St. Martin, 37 m. N. From St. Martin to Entraque, on the north side of the Col di Finestra, 8 hrs. by mule, considered equal to 25 m. From Entraque to Cuneo by Valdieri and Dalmazzo, 24 m. N. by coach.

The diligence from Nice ascends by the west side of the river Paillon, and after passing the villages of St. André (p. 179) and Tourette, near the ruins of Châteauneuf, arrives at Levens, 1826 ft. above the sea, pop. 1560, *Inn:* H. des Étrangers, where the coach halts a short time. After Levens it crosses the Col du Dragon, and then descends into the prettiest part of the valley of the Vesubie, where it passes through the village of Duranus, 18 m. from Nice, pop. 1500. Then, after having traversed a tunnel 88 yds. long, crossed the Vesubie, and passed by the hamlet of Le Suque (Suchet), 25 m. from Nice, it reaches the village of Lantosque, 28½ m. from Nice, 1640

St. Martin Lantosque. Col di Finestra. Valdieri.

ft. above the sea, pop. 1910, *Inn:* H. des Alpes Maritimes. On a plateau 765 ft. above Lantosque, and 1¼ m. distant, is La Bollène, with a large hotel, charmingly situated amidst hills covered with chestnut trees. The coach next halts at Roquebillère, pop. 1800, on the Vesubie, 3½ m. from Lantosque, 32 from Nice, and 1968 ft. above the sea. It is the station for the village of Belvédère, pop. 1250, with a comfortable hotel on a plateau 755 ft. above Roquebillère. From Roquebillère the coach proceeds up the valley of the Vesubie by the villages of Berguerie, St. Bernard, and St. Sebastien, to St. Martin Lantosque, 37 m. from Nice, pop. 1956, and 3117 ft. above the sea. An ancient village at the junction of the Vesubie with the Salèses. In the "Place" where the diligence stops is a very good inn, the H. des Alpes. Down in the town is the Belle-Vue pension, 6 frs. Up by the side of the promenade are some good pensions. On the opposite hill, ½ hour walk from St. Martin, and 700 ft. higher, is the village of Venanson, pop. 250, commanding splendid views of the surrounding valleys. The lower parts of the mountains are covered with chestnut and cherry trees, and the higher with large firs. From St. Martin commences the bridle-path to Entraque, by the valley of the Vesubie and the Col di Finestra, 8269 ft. above the sea, called thus from a fancied resemblance of a cleft in the peak to a window. Mule and guide to Entraque, 22 frs.; time, 8 hrs. 1¼ m. up the Vesubie is the stone which marks the boundary between France and Italy, and 6¼ m. farther the inn and the chapel of the Madonna di Finestra, 6234 ft. above the sea. Many rare plants are found here, especially the remarkable *Saxifraga florulenta*, on the ridges of rock above the sanctuary. Half an hour beyond, a lake is passed among jagged peaks, and, in about another ½ hour more, the summit of the pass, 8269 ft., is attained, commanding an extensive view both towards Italy and France. At Entraque there is an inn, and a coach daily to Cuneo.

A mule-path from St. Martin extends to the Baths of Valdieri, about 20 m. distant, time 7 to 8 hrs., by the Salèses, which it follows all the way to the Col de Moulières, 6890 ft. A few miles farther northward it crosses also the Col di Fremamorta, a depression between two mountains, 8745 ft. and 8964 ft. respectively above the sea. It then descends by a long dreary road to the Val di Vallaso, where it turns eastwards to the river Valletta and the Baths of Valdieri. From the baths a carriage-road extends 24 m. N.E. to Cuneo, passing by the village of Valdieri on the Gesso, 2493 ft. above the sea, 10 m. N. from the baths, and 7½ m. S. from the next village, Roccavione, in the picturesque valley of the Vermanagna. The coach then passes through the Borgo San Dalmazzo, 5 m. from Cuneo, in a well-cultivated plain at the junction of the Vermanagna with the Gesso.

A more direct but not such a good path separates from the Fremamorta road at a small hamlet about 4 m. N. from St. Martin, whence it ascends northwards by the Col de Cerise, 8500 ft., and then follows the course of the Valletta to the baths. "The Baths of Valdieri make excellent headquarters for exploring this part of the Western

Alps.   In every village an inn of more or less humble pretensions is to be found ; and, though the first impressions may be very unfavourable, the writer [Ed.] has usually obtained food and a bed such as a mountaineer need not despise.   Apart also from the advantage of being accessible at seasons when travellers are shut out by climate from most other Alpine districts, this offers special attractions to the naturalist.   Within a narrow range may be found a considerable number of very rare plants, several of which are not known to exist elsewhere.   The geology is also interesting, and would probably repay further examination.   A crystalline axis is flanked on both sides by highly-inclined and much-altered sedimentary rocks, which probably include the entire series from the carboniferous to the cretaceous rocks, in some parts overlaid by nummulitic deposits."—*The Western Alps*, by John Ball.

Nice to Puget-Theniers, 42 m. N.W. by the Vallon du Var, which does not become picturesque till Chaudan, 22 m. N. from Nice, at the junction of the Tinée with the Var, where the horses are changed and where the coach from St. Sauveur (18¼ m. N. from Chaudan) meets the Puget coach.   Puget-Theniers (Castrum de Pogeto de Thenariis, pop. 1450, 1476 ft. above the sea, *Inn:* *Croix de Malte) is a dirty village on the confluence of the Roudoule with the Var at the foot of bare precipitous mountains.   Coach daily from the inn to Guillaumes, pop. 1300, on the Var, 22 m. N., *Inn:* Ginié.   The roads beyond are traversed by mules.   Coach also to Entrevaux, 3¾ m. W. from Puget.

The banks of the Tinée are more picturesque than those of the Var.   On the Tinée, 40½ m. N. from Nice, is **Saint Sauveur**, pop. 800, *Inn:* Vial, with Romanesque church containing a statue of St. Paul, dating from 1309.   Hot and cold sulphurous springs issue from a granite rock called the Guez.   From St. Sauveur a good road extends northwards by the Tinée to St. Etienne, where there is an inn. From St. Etienne, pop. 150, a good mule-path leads by the Col Valonet to Vinadio (see map, p. 165).

Nice to Turin by the Col di Tenda.

Nice to the village of Tenda, by coach, 51 m., 11 hours, 9 frs. ; Tenda to Cuneo, 29 m., 7 hours, 7 frs.; Cuneo to Turin, by rail, 3 hours (see maps, pp. 165 and 107).   This is rather a fatiguing journey. The most beautiful views are seen during the descent from Tenda to the Mediterranean.   **Nice.**—Start from the Place St. François.   The road ascends the E. bank of the Paillon by the villages of **Trinité-Victor**, pop. 1300, and **Drap**, pop. 800, with a sulphurous spring called Fau de Lagarde.   Beyond this it leaves the Paillon and crosses over to **Escarène** on the Braus, 12½ m. N.E. from Nice, pop. 1500. About 1½ m. farther is **Touet**, pop. 400, whence commences the tedious ascent of the Col di Braus, 3300 ft., between the Tête Lavine on the S. and Mt. Ventabren on the N.   The road now descends to **Sospel**, 1125 ft., pop. 3500, on the Bevera, an affluent of the Roja, 25½ m. N.E. from Nice.   H. Carenio ; coach daily to and from Menton, 14 m. S.   The road now ascends the Col di Brouis, 2871 ft., whence passengers in this direction have their last view of the Mediterranean. The descent is now made through bleak and barren mountains to Giandola, 39¼ m. N.E. from Nice, 1247 ft., at the base of lofty frowning rocks. *Inns :* Étrangers, Poste. Coach daily between this and Ventimiglia. To the E., on the Roja, are Breglio, pop. 2580, and the ruins of the castle of Trivella. The road now ascends a narrow defile of the Roja, which, suddenly widening, discloses Saorgio, pop. 1600, 400 ft. above the torrent, composed of parallel rows of dingy houses among almond and olive trees. On the top of the hill is the castle of Malemort, destroyed by the French in 1792. From this the valley contracts so much that the road has repeatedly to cross and re-cross the river on its way to Fontana on the Italian frontier, 43 m. from Nice, pop. 1230. Luggage and passports are examined here. Almost the only habitat of the curious plant *Ballota spinosa* is between Fontana and Breglio. The road from this to St. Dalmazzo, 5 m. N., passes through one of the most formidable defiles in the Alps, the Gorge de Berghe, between steep massive walls of igneous rock. "The bold forms of the cliffs, and the luxuriant vegetation which crowns every height and fills every hollow, make the scenery of this road worthy to compare with almost any other more famous Alpine pass."—*Ball.* At St. Dalmazzo is a hydropathic establishment, pension 8 frs. Coach daily between Ventimiglia and Tenda.

51 m. N.E. from Nice, 2 m. S. from the tunnel, and 12 m. S. from Limone, is the village of Tenda, pop. 1800 ; *Inn :* H. National ; 2680 ft. above the sea, and 1516 ft. below the tunnel ; situated on the Roja at the base of a rock, on which are the picturesque ruins of the castle of Beatrice di Tenda, executed on the 13th Sept. 1418 by her jealous and tyrannical husband, Duke Fil. Maria Visconti. Many rare plants are to be found on the rocks over the village. The village church (1476-1518) is a good specimen of Lombardian architecture. The tunnel, opened in 1882—4196 ft. above the sea at the Tenda end, and 4331 ft. at the Limone end—is 9844 ft. long and 23 ft. high. The Tenda end of the tunnel is at the hamlet called La Punta, and the Cuneo end at the hamlet La Panice. From La Panice the road descends rapidly by the Vermanagna to Limone, 3668 ft., 63 m. N.E. from Nice and 17 m. S. from Cuneo ; *Inn :* H. de la Poste ; pleasantly situated in the valley of the Vermanagna, from which an occasional glimpse may be had of Monte Viso, 12,670 ft. The road, after passing Robillante, Roccavione, and Borgo-San-Dalmazzo, pop. 4600, arrives at Cuneo, 80 m. N E. from Nice, 1500 ft. above the sea, pop. 1200 ; *Inns :* Barra di Ferro, Albergo di Superga ; situated at the confluence of the Stura with the Gesso. 55 m. N. by rail is Turin.

The easiest way to go to Turin from Nice is to take the rail to Savona, whence rail to Turin, 91 m. N W. by Carru, Bra, and Cavallermaggiore. On this rail, 4 m. W. from Savona, is the Santuario di Savona, a pilgrimage church with large hospice for poor devotees (p. 210). From Carru station, 50 m. N., a branch line extends 8 m. S.

to **Mondovi**, pop. 17,000, on the Ellero. *Inns:* Croce di Malta ; Tré Limoni d'Oro. From Mondovi is visited the Cave of Bossea, about 15 m. S., in the valley of the Corsaglia. Each seat in the conveyance, 8 frs. ; cave, 2½ frs. each, shown from June to October. 12 m. S.W. from Mondovi, and about the same S.E. by coach from Cuneo, is the **Certosa di Val Pésio**, formerly a monastery, founded in 1173, now a hydropathic establishment, open from 1st June to 30th September. Pension, 8 to 10 frs. It is well managed, and well situated for botanists, fishers, and sketchers.

At the station S. Giuseppe di Cairo, 13 m. W. from Savona, is the junction with line to Alessandria, 52 m. N., by Acqui, 31 m. N., traversing a picturesque country, between S. Giuseppe and Acqui, where it passes down the beautiful valley of the Bormida.

Acqui, pop. 8000, on the Bormida, and 21 m. S. by rail from Alessandria. *Hotels:* Italia ; Moro. The town is partly on and partly round the Castello. On the other side of the river is the bathing establishment, a large building with abundant accommodation. The pension price per day is from 9 to 12 frs., including the use of the water, which, besides being drank, is employed both in water and in mud baths. The waters are sulphurous and alkaline, temp. 120°, and were known to the Romans under the name of the Aquæ Statielæ, yet of their times nothing exists but the ruins of an aqueduct. The mud-baths of Acqui are remedies of considerable power. The patient remains immersed for about half an hour in the humus or mineralised mud of a temperature as hot as he can bear. Immediately after he receives a warm mineral water bath. "The therapeutic influence of this application is most evident in chronic articular enlargements, rheumatic arthritis, some indolent tumours, intractable cases of secondary syphilis, and rheumatism."—Dr. Madden's *Health Resorts.*

142½   **VILLEFRANCHE**, pop. 3500. Approached by omnibuses 12¼ from the Pont Vieux at Nice, also by rail. Station at the head of the bay. *Hotel :* Marine. Pleasant boating excursions may be taken here to the peninsulas of St. John and the Hospice. The climate of Villefranche resembles that of Cimiès and Carabacel. 2 m. E. from Nice, at the head of a deep narrow bay, 2 m. long, are the arsenal, fortress, and port of **Villefranche**, founded in the 13th cent. by Charles II., King of Naples. The bay is a favourite place of anchorage of the French squadron, as well as of other ships of war and yachts. Boat from the mole to the little pier on the peninsula of St. Jean, 1 fr. each person. From Villefranche commences the splendid Road to **Monaco**, 8 m. long and 18 ft. wide, exclusive of the space for foot-passengers. This most enjoyable carriage-drive skirts with the railway the base of the precipitous cliffs which rise from the sea. 1 m. from Villefranche by rail, or 1¾ by road, is

143½   **BEAULIEU**, famed for its large olive trees. A little above 11½

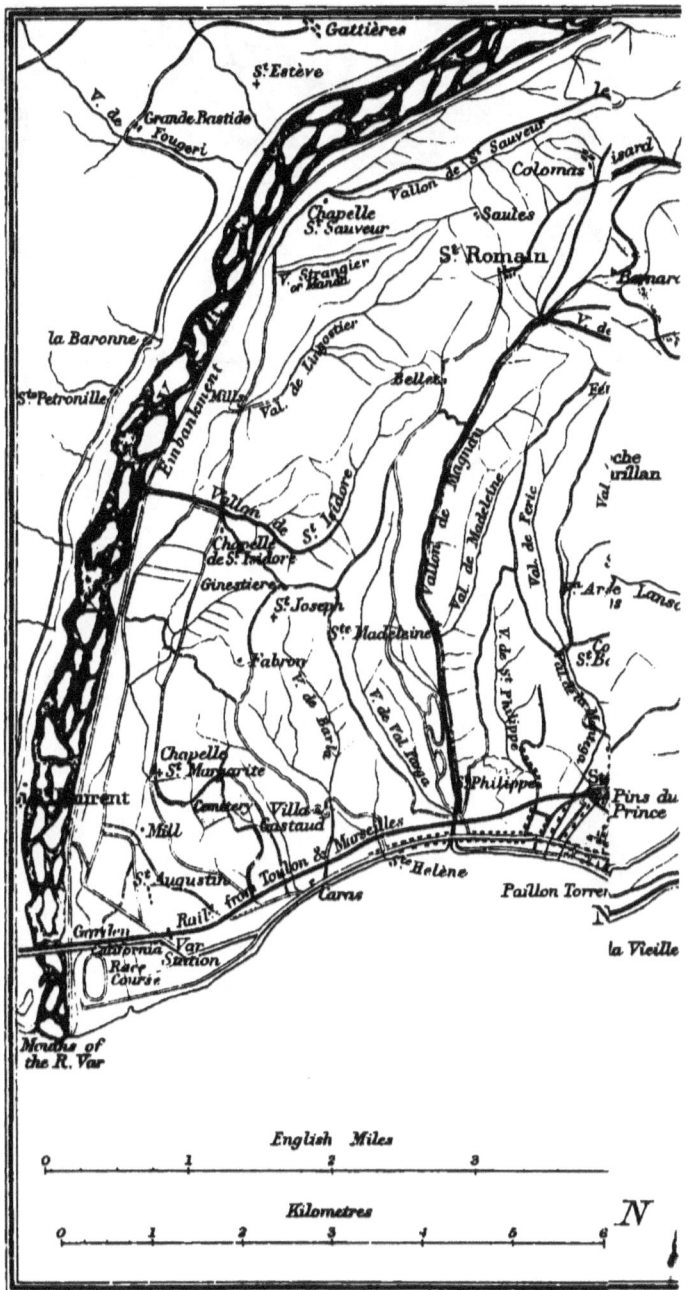

Gattières

St Estève

V. de Grande Bastide Fougeri

Vallon de St Sauveur

Colomas

izard

Chapelle St Sauveur

Saules

V. Strangier or Banel

St Romain

Benar

la Baronne

V.de

Ste Petronille

Mills

Val. de Lingostier

Belles

Éé

che urillan

Embancement

Val

Vallon de St Isidore

Vallon de Magnan

Val de Forte

Chapelle de St Isidore

Ginestière

V.de St Philippe

Arte

Lans

St Joseph

Ste Madeleine

St B

Fabron

V. de Barla

V. de Val

Chapelle St Margarite

Philippe

Pins du Prince

urent

Cemetery

Villas Gastaud

St

Mill

from Toulon & Marseilles

Ste Helène

Paillon Torre

St Augustin

Caràs

N

Rail

la Vieille

Garibu

Var Station

California

Race Course

Mouths of the R. Var

English Miles

0   1   2   3

Kilometres

0   1   2   3   4   5   6

N

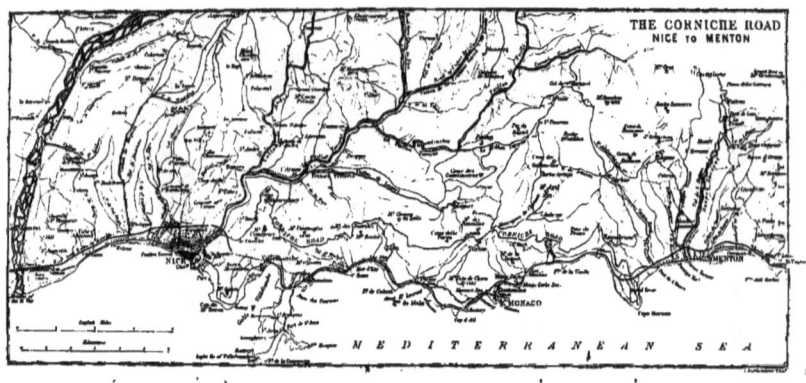

the station is one of the oldest trees, and near it the H. des Anglais among "countless terraces, where olives rise unchilled by autumn's blast or wintry skies." Down towards the village is another old olive tree, not far from a restaurant. Near the Church on the Monaco road is the Restaurant Beau-Rivage, where a Bouillabaisse lunch can be had. In the creek below are small boats for hire. Beaulieu is really a beautiful place. It is situated in one of the most sheltered nooks of the Riviera, at the foot of gigantic cliffs with patches of strata of reddish sandstone. The edges of this grand precipice are fringed with trees, which in the bright atmosphere look almost as if they were transparent; while below, groves of stately olive trees cover the base and struggle as far up as they can by the fissures in the rocks. Behind the olives, and intermixed with them, are orchards of orange and lemon trees, bending under the weight of their beautiful fruit. Trees and tall shrubs hang over the edges of the abrupt banks, which enclose the tiny creeks and bays bordered with diminutive sandy beaches, or with long ledges of marble rocks, dipping gradually down into the deep-blue water, carpeted in some places with the thin flat siliceous leaves of the Posidonia Caulini, a Naiad not an alga, which covers the shore of the Mediterranean, and of which great accumulations are seen thrown up at various parts. It makes a poor manure, but prevents in some degree evaporation.

A charming road, at some parts rather narrow for a carriage, leads from Beaulieu round by the edge of the bay and east side of the peninsula to the **Port of St. Jean.** The real carriage-road commences at the railway bridge, goes round by the west side of the peninsula, and descends to St. Jean, a little before reaching the chapel of St. Francis. The continuation past the chapel, of the road, extends to the lighthouse, passing the signal-tower to the right.

The port of St. Jean, *Inn:* H. Victoria, is used principally by the tunny fishing-boats from February to April. It makes a very pleasant residence for artists and naturalists. It is situated among creeks and bays, gardens, orchards, villas, and woods, in the most fertile part of the peninsula. Beyond, on the highest point of the peninsula of St. Hospice, is a round tower, the remains of the fortifications razed by the Duke of Berwick in 1706. The more ancient crumbling masonry around belonged to a stronghold of the Saracens, whence they were driven in the 10th cent. "A fir-clad mound amid the savage wild bears on its brow a village, walled and isled in lone seclusion round its ancient tower. It was a post of Saracens, whose

fate made them the masters for long years of lands remote and scattered o'er a hundred strands."—*Guido and Lita*, by the Marquis of
Lorne.   Below, towards the point, are a cemetery, a church, 11th
cent., visited by Victor Emmanuel in 1821, and a battery.

At the south extremity of the peninsula of St. Jean is the lighthouse (second-class), built in the 17th cent., but repaired, and the top
story added, in 1836.   It is 98 ft. high, or 196 ft. above the sea, and
is ascended by 120 steps.   The light is white and revolving, and is
seen at a distance of 20 m.   The Antibes light is fixed, and is of the
first-class.   By the east side of the lighthouse is the grave of Charles
Best, who died at Tenda, on the 30th day of July 1817, aged 38.   The
tomb is hewn in the rock and arched over.   His friends have laid him
in a grand place to await the call of the resurrection trumpet.   Large
euphorbias and myrtles cover this stony part of the peninsula.

EZE.

The most picturesque part of the Monaco road is between Beaulieu
and Eze, the next station, 2 m. distant by road, but only 1½ by rail.
The steep flanks of the mountains between Beaulieu and Cape Roux
are so exposed to the sun, and so protected from the cold, that this
region has been called the Petite Afrique.   Cape Roux itself, the abrupt
termination of a lofty ridge, looks as if it would topple over into the
sea, to which it is so close that both the rail and the road have to pass
through it by tunnels.   On the eastern side of this cape is the equally
picturesque and sheltered bay, the Mer d'Eze, backed by a phalanx of
lofty stalwart cliffs and mountains.   On the peak (1300 ft. high) of one of
this confused assemblage of lofty calcareous rocks is the nearly deserted
village of Eze, pop. 770, with the ruins of its castle founded by the
Saracens in 814, and its small church, recently restored, built on the
foundations of a temple of Isis, whence the name Eza or Eze is said to
be derived.   From the floor of rock of the castle, under the remains
of a vaulted roof, a charming marine landscape displays itself, while
inland is seen the Pass or highest part (1750 ft.) of the Corniche road,
which here crosses the ridge terminated by Mt. Roux.   At the Pass are
an inn and a few houses.   The road up to Eze commences near the
station.   In some parts it is steep, and much exposed to the sun, and
throughout very picturesque and stony, passing through plantations of
firs, olives, and carouba or locust trees.   The ascent requires, doing it
leisurely, 75 minutes.   From Eze a road ascends to the Corniche road,
and another descends to St. Laurent, on the road to Monaco.   A little
beyond Eze is the station for La Turbie.

100 min. from Cannes, 35 from Nice, and 44 from Menton, is

$\frac{149}{\sim\sim}$ MONACO station, situated in La Condamine. At the station $\frac{6}{\sim\sim}$ an omnibus awaits passengers for Monaco on the top of the S.W. promontory, 195 ft. above the sea. For Monte Carlo, on the top of the N.E. promontory, alight at the next station, 1¼ m. N.E.

Monaco proper, pop. 1200. Hôtel de la Paix, 7½ frs., splendid view from the square. Pharmacies under the direction of MM. Cruzel and Muratore. Till the arrival of F. Blanc in 1860, Monaco was a poor place, where the Prince and his subjects had to maintain themselves from the produce of a few small vineyards and orchards scattered over patches of scanty soil on the slopes of the mountains. But now that the gambling-tables have brought a flood of gold into the principality, wealth has taken the place of poverty, the palace has been furnished anew, the humble Grimaldi church, 13th cent., thrown down, and in its stead a majestic cathedral erected, the barns have been filled with plenty, costly roads have been cut through the cliffs, the formerly arid hills clothed with exuberant verdure, and beautiful villas have been built in the midst of enchanting gardens, in places where, only a few years ago, hardly enough of short wiry grass could grow to feed a goat. The gambling establishment of Monaco was opened in 1856 by a company with the sanction of Prince Charles III. The first house was in the Place du Château ; whence, after sundry changes, the company commenced to build a house in 1858 on Monte Carlo. Becoming short of funds, they sold their rights and property in 1860 to François Blanc.

The Grimaldi family have been in possession of this small territory since 968, when the Emperor Otto I. gave it to Grimaldi I., Lord of Antibes and father of Giballin Grimaldi, who drove the Saracens from the Grand-Fraxinet of St. Tropez (p. 145). The greatest length of the principality, from the cemetery wall at the western extremity to the brook St. Roman at the eastern, is (including curves) 3½ m., and the greatest breadth, from Point St. Martin northwards, 1 m. Population 10,000, distributed among four different centres—the city, or Monaco proper; the port, or La Condamine ; Monte Carlo ; and Les Moulins. They are all united excepting the city, which, like an eagle's nest, occupies its own isolated rock, and is the one clean old town on the whole coast of the Mediterranean, and, although about 200 ft. above the sea, is most easily accessible by well-planned and gently-sloping roads. At the landward or north end of the promontory is the palace, of which the rooms in the upper floor on the west side are shown to the public on certain days. The earliest parts, including the crenellated towers, date from the commencement of the 13th cent., but the rest is much more modern and of different dates. It is in the form of an oblong rectangle, the south small side being occupied by the entrance and the north by the chapel, sumptuously decorated with marble, gilding, and mosaics. Within the entrance is the Cour d'Honneur, decorated on the east side with friezes and designs in fresco by Caravaggio, retouched in 1865, representing the triumphal procession of Bacchus. On the opposite side a horse-shoe marble staircase, of 30 steps in each branch, leads up to an arcaded corridor. Under the 12 inner arches are frescoes by Carloni, representing the feats of Hercules. The rooms shown are to the left and right of the entrance passage, at the north end of the corridor. To left the first room is the usher's room. The second is in blue satin; hangings and furniture in style Louis XV.; some family portraits on the walls. 3. Reception-room in red; handsome chimney-piece of one stone. Bust and full-length portrait of Charles III., Prince of Monaco. Ceiling painted in fresco by Horace Ferrari. 4. Room with brown hangings and green furniture. On the walls are some indifferently executed pictures representing the exploits of the Grimaldis. 5. Bedroom with red furniture ; style Louis XIII.

Rooms on right hand of passage. 1. Sitting-room of the Duke of York, brother of George III. ; red furniture and hangings ; family portraits, some very good, and frescoes by Annibale Carracci. 2. The bedroom in which he died, 1760; the walls hung with rich embroidered scarlet satin; ceiling painted in fresco by Ann. Carracci. Table in mosaic. Elegant bedstead, shut off by a richly-gilt banister or low screen. 3. Sitting-room in pale yellow; style Louis XV. 4. Bedroom. Furniture and walls covered with white satin richly embroidered.

The door in the N.W. corner of the court gives access to a very pretty garden, 130 ft. above the sea, full of palms, orange trees, and flowers. Below, near the beach, is the kitchen garden.

At the southern part of the town is the cathedral, built with money bequeathed by Blanc. It is placed from north to south, is 75 yards long, and at the transepts 32 yards. In front, handsome terrace and good view. Northward, in the Rue de Lorraine, is the Church des Penitents Noirs, and a little way farther down the same street are the Église de la Visitation, founded in 1663, its schools, and the Hôtel Dieu. Down on the face of the southern cliffs is the domain of the washerwomen. They spread their clothes to dry on the hot rocks, or

LA CONDAMINE. ST. DEVOTA. MONTE CARLO.

over the prickly pear plants, here very abundant. At this end is also the Jardin St. Martin, a very pretty promenade, with charming views. 500 yards west from the foot of the Monaco rock, on the splendid road to Villefranche, is the cemetery, whose wall forms the western limit of the principality. Among the many tombs there is a beautiful marble monument to Pierre and Modestine Neri, brother and sister.

On the little plain between the promontories of Monaco and Monte Carlo is La Condamine, whose handsome houses extend, where practicable, a considerable way up the surrounding mountains. In the picturesque gully, entered from beneath the railway viaduct, is the parish church, on the spot where the body of Santa Devota, a Roman martyr, the patroness of Monaco, was washed ashore. In 1070 Hugues, Prince of Monaco, caused the nose and ears of Captain Antinopes to be cut off for having stolen the relics of St. Devota. La Condamine contains the harbour and the principal railway station, as well as the less expensive hotels, such as the G. H. des Bains between the sea and the gas-works, and the Bristol on the terrace. Within the town, the Condamine ; Étrangers ; Angleterre ; Beau-Séjour ; Beau Site ; France ; Marseille ; in all, board and lodging from 8 to 10 frs. At the station the H. Nice and Des Voyageurs. On the road up to Monte Carlo are the first-class hotels : Princes ; *Beau Rivage ; *Monte Carlo, occupying the house the late Madame Blanc built for herself. On Monte Carlo are the first-class houses : the Paris ; the *Grand Hotel ; *Des Anglais ; Russie ; Londres ; Colonies ; still higher up, the *Victoria in the principality, but on the confines of France ; in all, 15 to 20 frs. per day. Behind the Londres a narrow lane leads up to the Corniche road by the village of Le Carniet. Those hotels marked in this instance with an asterisk do not receive promiscuous company. Abundance of excellent restaurants, cafés, and furnished rooms. English chapel in France, above the Hôtel Victoria. Mean winter temperature, 49°·3. *Cabs.*—The course, within the principality, 1½ fr. ; the hour, 3 frs. To Menton and back, 15 frs. The omnibus that runs between Monte Carlo and Nice by the new road starts from the Casino (see page 178).

Monte Carlo is not an isolated rock like Monaco, but the abrupt termination of a ridge sloping upwards from Point Focinana to the Corniche road and the Château Mountains, both a considerable way beyond the territory of Monaco. On the face of Monte Carlo, or rather of Focinana Point, is the Casino, a large and showy building, erected in 1862 by F. Blanc (d. 1877), a native of Avignon, and formerly the

proprietor of the Cursaal of Homburg. To the right of the entrance
into the Casino are the cloak-rooms, the ladies' (dames) and gentlemen's
(hommes) lavatories, and the reading-room. Fronting the entrance is
the concert-room—a superb rectangular hall profusely decorated with
gilt ornaments intermingled with paintings in fresco representing the
Muses and mythological subjects. It is furnished with 600 cushioned
arm-chairs covered with scarlet velvet. The stage, or the part occupied
by the orchestra, is less ornamented, and the colours are more subdued.
Directly opposite is a sumptuous gallery for the use of the prince and
his suite, entered from the large door at the west side of the Casino.
The orchestra consists of nearly 80 first-class musicians, of whom about
three-fourths play on stringed instruments. To the left of the entrance
are the gambling-rooms and the office where visitors give their names
and addresses before entering. In the first three rooms are the
tables for roulette, which is played with one zero, and at which the
smallest sum admitted is 5 frs., and the largest 6000 frs. or £240. The
fourth room, ornamented with panel paintings by Clairin and Bou-
langer, representing young lady riders, croquet-players, fencers, fishers,
archers, mountaineers, shooters, and sailors, is devoted to trente-et-
quarante, at which the smallest sum admitted is 20 frs., and the
largest 12,000 frs. or £480. Only French coin and notes taken at
the tables.

Charming gardens and lawns with exquisite turf surround the
Casino, and under it, at the foot of the cliff, is a large pigeon-shooting
gallery. Entrance, 5 frs. Well-constructed carriage-drives and footpaths ramify in all directions, up the hill to the Corniche road, and
along the coast either to Menton or to Nice by the magnificent coast-
road to Villefranche (see p. 184). The whole hill itself, or rather
slope, is studded, even beyond the boundaries of Monaco, with
beautiful villas, partially hidden among orange, lemon, and olive
trees. On the eastern side of Monte Carlo is Les Moulins, now
quite a town, with shops, hotels, restaurants, and furnished lodgings. Up on the main road is the Hôtel de la Terrasse, 20 frs.,
dear. Down below on the coast-road, fronting the sea, is a small
house, the Hôtel du Parc.

At the Casino it is not necessary to gamble, while those inclined to that horrid vice will find more dangerous traps laid to
catch them in the clubs of the principal towns on the Riviera. In
Monte Carlo no one can gamble on credit. About a quarter of
an hour eastward from Moulins by the main road is the valley of

LEMONS.   TÊTE DE CHIEN.

St. Roman, with some very large olive and locust trees.   In the principality are also large groves of lemon trees.   They flower and bear fruit throughout the whole year.   The lemons, which ripen in spring, are called graneti, and those which ripen in summer verdami. They are the juiciest, and as they keep longest, are the most suitable for exportation.   The best paper for wrapping them in is that made from old tarry ropes.   The manure preferred for the lemon and olive trees is composed of the waste of horns, woollen rags, and refuse.

Excursions.—1640 feet above Monaco is La Turbie, ascended by a road containing 860 terraced steps, of which the best are 14 feet long by 9 feet wide, but a great many are smaller, and the most are in bad condition.   The ascent, walking leisurely, requires one hour.   It commences from the Rue de Turbie, the second street left from the railway station.   At Turbie, pop. 2400, there are three restaurants—the France, Paris, and Ancre ; the first is the most frequented.   Bedrooms, 2 frs.   Delicious lemonade, most grateful after a hot climb.   When up at La Turbie ascend by the tower of Augustus to the little knoll close by and take a seat under the rock at the top, whence " From ancient battlements the eye surveys a hundred lofty peaks and curving bays." But the one great view, which excels all the others, is from the

Tête de Chien.

The road to it ramifies from the Corniche road at the west end of La Turbie.   Carriages drive all the way.   As there is a Fort on the top, permission must be procured from the captain to approach the brow of the mighty projecting precipice, which by its position commands a splendid uninterrupted view east and west, but spoils that from the other places.   From the Tête de Chien eastward are seen every mountain, town, village, cape, creek, and bay the length of San Remo.   On the western side the view is much more extensive, reaching to St. Tropez and the Maure mountains.   The east side embraces Monaco, Monte Carlo, Les Moulins, Mt. de la Justice, Mt. Gros, Roquebrune, Cape St. Martin, Menton, Ventimiglia, Braja and Bordighera on the Cape San Ampeglio, which conceals San Remo, but not the entrance into the bay.   The western side embraces Eze, Cape Roux, Beaulieu, the whole of the peninsula of St. Jean, a piece of Villefranche, the greater part of Nice, Antibes, the lighthouse and peninsula, the Lerins islands, the Esterel mountains, and the Maures above Saint Tropez, which close the view.   A good opera-glass should be taken.   A stony road leads down the west side of the Tête, through a plantation of firs, to the Monaco road, which it joins near the battery (see map, p. 185).

LA TURBIE. ROQUEBRUNE.

La Turbie, the ancient Trophæa Augusti station, on the Via
Julia, is a poor village, composed of narrow streets, old houses, and
gateways close to the massive Roman fort, which, after having stood
nearly intact for 1700 years, was reduced to its present dilapidated
condition by a prince of Monaco in the reign of Louis XIV. The village
is supplied with excellent water from a spring to the N.W. of Mt.
Agel. To the west of Turbie, at the Colonna del Ré, a road descends
northwards to the sanctuary of Notre Dame de Laguet, at the foot of
Mt. Sembole, 13 m. from Nice, but scarcely 2 from La Turbie.

The conical hill, rising over La Turbie, is Mt. la Bataille, and the
long ridge farther east, leading up to Mt. Agel, 3771 ft., are the
Château mountains. The view from none of these mountains equals
that from the Tête de Chien ; moreover, the ascent is uninteresting, by
stony paths. Ascend by the first road east from Turbie, and when at
the Turbie reservoir turn to the left for the Montagne de la Bataille ;
but for the Château mountains take the path to the right. This path
leads round into a narrow ascending valley, at the top of which is the
summit of the Château mountains, and the commencement of the peak
of Mt. Agel, one half-hour higher. The mountain immediately over
Monte Carlo and Les Moulins is La Justice, 911 ft., used as a quarry.
On the top is a pillar of rough stones, rudely plastered together. By
the side of it are the remains of a similar column. At the chapel of
St Roch a road leads up to the Corniche road (see map, page 185).

150¾
~~ MONTE CARLO station. Alight here for the Casino, for 4¾
~~ the hotels on Monte Carlo, and for Les Moulins and its hotels.

152¾
~~ ROQUEBRUNE station, where the Corniche road from La 2¼
~~ Turbie joins the low road from Menton.

Roquebrune, pop. 1080, is 150 ft. above the station and the sea,
among great masses of brown conglomerate rocks. From the main
road a series of paved steps leads up to the village through a plantation
of lemon trees. The streets are steep and narrow, but the houses are
better and more comfortable than those of the villages similarly situated in the neighbourhood of Menton, Bordighera, and San Remo.
Near the terrace is a small restaurant. On the summit of the hill are
the ruins of the great castle built by the Lascaris of Ventimiglia, who,
in 1363, ceded it to Charles Grimaldi. On a lintel on the eastern
square tower is the almost defaced sculpture representing a bishop's
mitre, with the armorial bearings of the Grimaldis, and the date
August 17, 1528. This bishop is supposed to have been Augustine

Grimaldi, councillor to Francis I. of France, who repaired this castle in 1528.   A broken staircase leads up to the top.   "No warrior's tread is echoed by their halls, no warder's challenge on the silence falls.   Around, the thrifty peasants ply their toil, and pluck in orange groves the scented spoil from trees that have for purple mountains made a vestment bright, of green and gold inlaid."—*Guido and Lita*, by the Marquis of Lorne.

699 m. S.E. from Paris, 155 m. N.E. from Marseilles, 34½ m. N.E. from Cannes, and 15½ m. N.E. from Nice, is

MENTON,

population 11,100, 16 miles S.W. from San Remo.   *Hotels and Pensions.* —Commencing with those at the west end of the Promenade du Midi, near the Gorbio, and going eastward through the town to the Garavan. Those hotels with ² prefixed have a front to the sea and esplanade, and another to the Avenue Victor Emmanuel II.   The asterisk signifies recommended.   W signifies bottle of wine, and the price given that of the cheapest quality.   P signifies pension or boarding-house.   At the west end of the esplanade the ²H. du Pavillon ; the H. St. George, 9-12 frs., W 1½ fr., by the side of the Borrigo; ²*P. Condamine; *H. et P. Londres. These 4 houses charge from 9 to 12 frs., W from 1½ to 2 frs.   Near the Carrei and the Episcopal Church of St. John are the *H. Splendide, 9-12 frs., W 1½ fr.; the Parc, 8-10 frs., W 1½ fr.; and the ²*Russie, 9-12 frs., W 1½ fr.   Now cross the Carrei, on which is a very sheltered promenade up the eastern bank.   By the side of the Place (where the band plays), built over the mouth of the torrent, is the ²*H. de Paris, 10-14 frs., W 1½ fr.   Same side, ²H. et P. d'Angleterre, 9-12 frs. Opposite, the H. Camous, 9-12 frs.; and the Banque Bottini.   Situated in the busiest part of Menton are the *P. and H. Méditerranée, 9-12 frs., W 1½ fr.   Next it the house agencies of Amaranté et Cie and Tonin-Amaranté ; and a little farther, the Menton Bank of Biovès et Cie.   Opposite, the ²H. Westminster, ²H. Victoria, and ²*H. de Menton, all large good houses, charging 9-15 frs.   The H. Menton is patronised by Messrs. Cook.   Nearer the harbour, but with a front only to the sea, is the Midi, same price.   We now enter the eastern or most sheltered quarter, called the Garavan.   The hotels are large and first-class, and charge from 10 to 20 frs., and wine from 1½ to 2½ frs.   The most westerly is the H. Italie, and, about 100 feet up the bank behind, the principal house of the hotel.   A little farther east, on the same eminence, is the *Belle-Vue.   Near the Belle-Vue, and on

O

the same level, is the Villa Helvetia, a benevolent home for ladies not younger than 18 nor older than 40, who are received for 20s. a week, which includes everything "except laundress and fire in bedroom." For conditions of admission apply to Ransom, Bouverie, and Co., bankers, London ; Mrs. Seton Karr, 30 Lancaster Gate, Hyde Park ; or Miss Mackenzie, 16 Moray Place, Edinburgh. Below, on the terrace along the beach, is Christ Church, and adjoining is the Paix, a well-furnished house. Then follow the *H. des Anglais, the H. et P. Santa Maria, *Beau Rivage, Grand Hotel, Beau Site, Britannia. Queen Victoria spent the spring of 1882 in the Châlet des Rosiers, about 200 yards from the H. des Anglais.

Inland, on the east side of the Carrei, in a warm nook, under the shelter of a high hill, is a cluster of large and small hotels, just behind the busiest part of the town. Of these the most prominent are the first-class houses of the *H. des Iles Britanniques (expensive), *H. National, *Orient, *Louvre, and Princes. Rather lower down are the Ambassadeurs, Turin, Venise, Malte, Alpes, 9-15 frs., W 1-2 frs.; the last five being less costly. Up the west side of the Carrei is the P. des Orangers, pleasantly situated. On the road down from the station, on the right or west bank of the Carrei, is the H. de l'Europe, 9-14 frs., W 2 frs. Almost adjoining is a second-class house, the H. and P. des Deux-Mondes, 6-7 frs. The above prices include service, coffee in the morning, and meat breakfast and dinner, but never wine, excepting the G. H. de Menton, whose price includes wine but not coffee.

Menton has certainly some very sheltered nooks, but this only renders the more exposed parts the more dangerous. The distinguishing feature of the neighbourhood is the abundance of lemon trees in the small valleys watered by mountain streams. The annual yield of the trees amounts to 30 million lemons, of which the minimum price is from 12 to 15 frs. the thousand.

Bankers.—Bank of France, Maison Palmaro. In the Av. Victor Emmanuel are : Biovès et Cie, Credit Lyonnais, A. Bottini, and Credit de Nice. In 17 R. St. Michel, the Palmaro Bank and the English Consulate. *House Agents.*—G. Amaranté and T. Amaranté, 12 and 19 Av. V. Emmanuel ; Willoughby, R. St. Michel. English doctors, chemists, and grocers.

Protestant Churches.—Christ Church, adjoining the H. de la Paix ; St. John's, near the Pont Carrei ; Presbyterian, above H. Italie ; Vaudois, R. du Castellar ; German Church, R. Partouneaux.

Cabs.—One-horse cab—the course, 1 fr. 25 c.; the hour, 2¾ frs. Two-horse cab—the course, 1 fr. 75 c.; the hour, 3 frs. 75 c. A one-horse cab for the whole day costs 20 frs.; a two-horse cab, 25 frs. Donkey for the whole day, 5 frs.; gratuity, 1 fr. Boats, 2 frs. the hour.

MENTON. CAPE ST. MARTIN. GORBIO.

Menton is situated round a large bay, bounded on the west by Cape St. Martin, and on the east by Mortola Point. This bay is divided into two smaller bays by the hill, 130 ft. high, on which the old town is built. The platform of the parish church, St. Michel, is reached by 95 steps in 8 divisions. All the streets about it are narrow, dirty, steep, and even slippery. The new town stretches out a great way along the beach. The public promenade (about 40 ft. wide) bends round the west bay from the town to Cape St. Martin. A kind of gloom pervades Menton. The strip of ground on which it stands is narrow, and so are the streets. Immediately behind rise great mountains with dark gray limestone cliffs, intermingled with deep green olive trees and stiff straggling pines. The valleys are narrow and sombre. The roads up the mountains are steep, badly paved, and are generally traversed on unwilling donkeys.

The pleasantest walks and drives are those along the coast, extending from Cape St. Martin to the Italian frontier, to which there are two roads, an upper and a lower. The former, the main road, crosses the bridge of St. Louis, while the latter skirts the beach to the famous bone-caverns. The *débris* found in these caves, like the shell-banks in the north of Scotland, consisted of the waste accumulation from the food of the early inhabitants, together with the stone implements they had employed. Four of the caves are above the railway, a little beyond the viaduct under the Italian custom-house, and two are just below the line close to the beach.

Cape St. Martin, 2 m. W. Tram from Garavan to St. Martin, 50 c. The tram stops at the N.E. corner of the cape. On the road northward from the cape leading to Roquebrune is, right hand, a Roman sepulchre, consisting of a centre arch with a smaller arch on each side, all that remains of the Roman settlement Lumone, mentioned by Antoninus. From this a straight road leads directly S. through a grove of large olive trees to the signal-tower in the centre of the peninsula. Beside it are the ruins of a nunnery, which was connected with the monastery of St. Honorat (p. 158). Afterwards the road leading westward joins the carriage-way, which sweeps round the peninsula. A stony path on the W. side, parallel to the road, extends along the coast by the rocks and cliffs (see map, p. 185).

Gorbio, 2½ hrs. or 5 m. N. up the valley of the Gorbio, and 1427 ft. above the sea. Take the road E. from the Pont de l'Union, passing by the entrance into the Villa (Palais) Carnolès, and traversing groves of lemon and olive trees. When about 1 hr. from the village the road becomes steep, and pines take the place of lemon trees. Gorbio, pop. 500, occupies the summit of a hill rising from a valley formed by the stream Gorbio and by one of its affluents. The streets are narrow, steep, and roughly paved ; the houses poor but substantial ; and the little church, built in 1683, is dedicated "Soli Deo." At the upper end of the village is a beautiful tulip tree. The path northward from the tree leads to Mt. Gorbio, 2707 ft., and to Mt. Baudon, 7144 ft. The rough stony road leading to the right or eastward from the tree ascends, in less than 2 hrs., to St. Agnès. It is easily followed, and unfolds lovely views. St. Agnès, pop. 580, is situated 2180 ft. above the sea, or 330 ft. below the mountain peak, crowned with the ruins of the castle built in the 10th cent. by Haroun, a bold Saracen chief. A narrow path leads up to the top in 45 minutes, whence there is an extensive prospect.

From the village descend to Menton by the path on the W. side of the village, which, after innumerable windings, reaches the road by the side of the Gorbio. On the way down it is difficult, among the network of execrable paths, to follow the right one, which in descending is not of much consequence, but in ascending adds immensely to the fatigue. If the traveller should stray into the Vallon Castagnec or Primevères, the bed of the stream should be followed as much as possible. One excursion should be made of Gorbio and St. Agnès, commencing with Gorbio.

Convent and Chapel of the Annonciade, 722 ft. above the sea, on the ridge between the Carrei and the Borrigo. Walk up the right or west bank of the Carrei to beyond the railway bridge, the length of the Hôtel Beau-Séjour, whence the path commences. Opposite, on the other side of the river, is seen the Hôtel des Iles Britanniques. The object of this easy excursion is the charming view from the terrace in front of the convent. The walls of the church are covered with votive offerings.

Castellar, 1280 ft. above the sea, 4 m. north, pop. 770. The road commences from the narrow street, R. de la Caserne, a few yards W. from the Place du Marché. Having passed a church, it enters on the broad highway which skirts the flanks of the steep mountains, covered with lemon and olive trees, rising from the left or east side of the stream Menton. With a few interruptions the road is excellent all the way. Castellar, on the plateau of St. Sebastian, surrounded by olive trees, is a poor village, consisting of three narrow dirty parallel streets lined with ugly dingy houses, and terminating

BENNET'S GARDEN. LA MORTOLA. HANBURY GROUNDS.

at the N. end with the parish church, rebuilt in 1867. Near the church are the crumbling ruins of a castle of the Lascaris, descendants of the Byzantine Emperors. From the terrace, where there are some beautiful elm trees, is a charming view. Here also the village feast-day is held on the 20th of January. From Castellar 2 to 3 hrs. are required for the ascent of the Berceau, 3640 ft. above the sea, commanding a magnificent prospect. Guide advisable.

Pont St. Louis, Bennet's Garden, Hamlets of Grimaldi and Ciotti.—At the east end of the Garavan is the boundary between France and Italy, a narrow ravine with cliffs 215 ft. high, spanned by a bridge of one arch 72 ft. wide. From this, on the first projecting point, are an Italian custom-house station and the two entrances into the Bennet Garden. The lower entrance is just before reaching the top of the point, the other is by the path ascending from the point to Grimaldi. The upper entrance is by the side of the square tower converted into a villa. The garden on terraces is an oasis among cliffs, rocks, and stones, and is chiefly remarkable for the number of English garden flowers in full bloom in the middle of winter. The views from the walks are charming.

The continuation of the path, or rather stair, up the steep rocky hill leads to Grimaldi, a few straggling cottages among olive and lemon trees. After Grimaldi the path crosses the top of the ridge, and having passed up by the E. or left side of the Vallon St. Louis, ascends the hill, on the top of which is the hamlet of Ciotti (1090 ft.), consisting of some 20 houses compactly grouped together. N.E. from Ciotti is Mt. Belinda, 1837 ft.

La Mortola, about 2 m. E. from Garavan. The Menton and Ventimiglia omnibus passes through Mortola by the gate (200 ft. above the sea) of the Hanbury Grounds, consisting of 99 acres, sloping down to the beach by terraces. Large olive trees occupy the larger portion, while in the more sheltered nooks are palms, orange and lemon trees. On a level with the house, the Palazzo Orengo, 150 ft. below the entrance, is the Pergola, a charming walk covered with trelliswork supported by massive pillars, up which climb above 100 different species of creeping plants. Queen Victoria visited the grounds on the 25th March 1882. An excellent view of the house and grounds, as well as of Ventimiglia and Bordighera, is had from the stone seat a little below the Mortola cross, on the highest part of the road, a little to the W. of Mortola. For time and conditions of admission into the Hanbury Grounds apply to the Palmaro Bank, 17 R. St. Michel. The generous founder and father of the present owner died a few years ago. Just beyond is the Piano di Latte, one of the most favoured little valleys in the Riviera. Mortola is nearly an hour's drive from Bordighera. The most important drive towards the interior is to **Sospel,** 14 m. N., on the road between Nice and Cuneo by the Col di Tenda (see p. 182). Excellent carriage-road all the way, ascending by the western or railway station side of the Carrei. In the lower part of the valley are large plantations of lemon trees. To the left of the road near the octroi are Les Moulins olive-oil mills, with four stages of water-wheels. 4 m. farther up the valley of the Carrei, on a eminence considerably above the stream, are the church and straggling village of Monti. The bridle-road that descends here to the Carrei crosses over to Castellar, well seen on the opposite side. About a mile beyond Monti, opposite the part of the road where it makes a sudden bend to the left, is seen a small stone bridge on the other side of the Carrei. This bridge crosses the stream that forms the cascade called the Gourg-d'Ora.

About a hundred yards to the west of the bridge, on the face of an almost vertical rock, and at a considerable height, is a kind of window or cavity called the Hermit's Grotto. Over the entrance is an illegible inscription in red hieroglyphics. By the side is another inscription giving the name of a hermit who once lived in this cave :—

CHRISTO LA FECE. BERNARDO L'ABITO.
1528.
(Christ made it. Bernard inhabits it.)

The inside of the grotto is composed of two rooms ; the first, 6 yds. by 4½, is continued by steep staircases up into the mountain for about 27 yds. At this extremity a large cavity leads into a second room, 8 yds. long, with a floor sloping in the opposite direction to the opening. Into this cave the crusader Robert de Ferques is said to have retired from grief.

At the time when King Philip Augustus had summoned all his nobility to take part in the third crusade, a lord, named Robert de Ferques, hastened to join the banner of the Count of Boulogne, his sovereign. This Robert de Ferques had been recently married, and his young bride, Jehanne de Leulinghem, unable to bear the thought of separation, resolved to follow her lord and share his toils. She succeeded by concealing her sex under a man's dress, and set out with joy in the capacity of esquire. Unhappily, during the journey she fell from her horse, and was forced to stop at an inn. Robert de

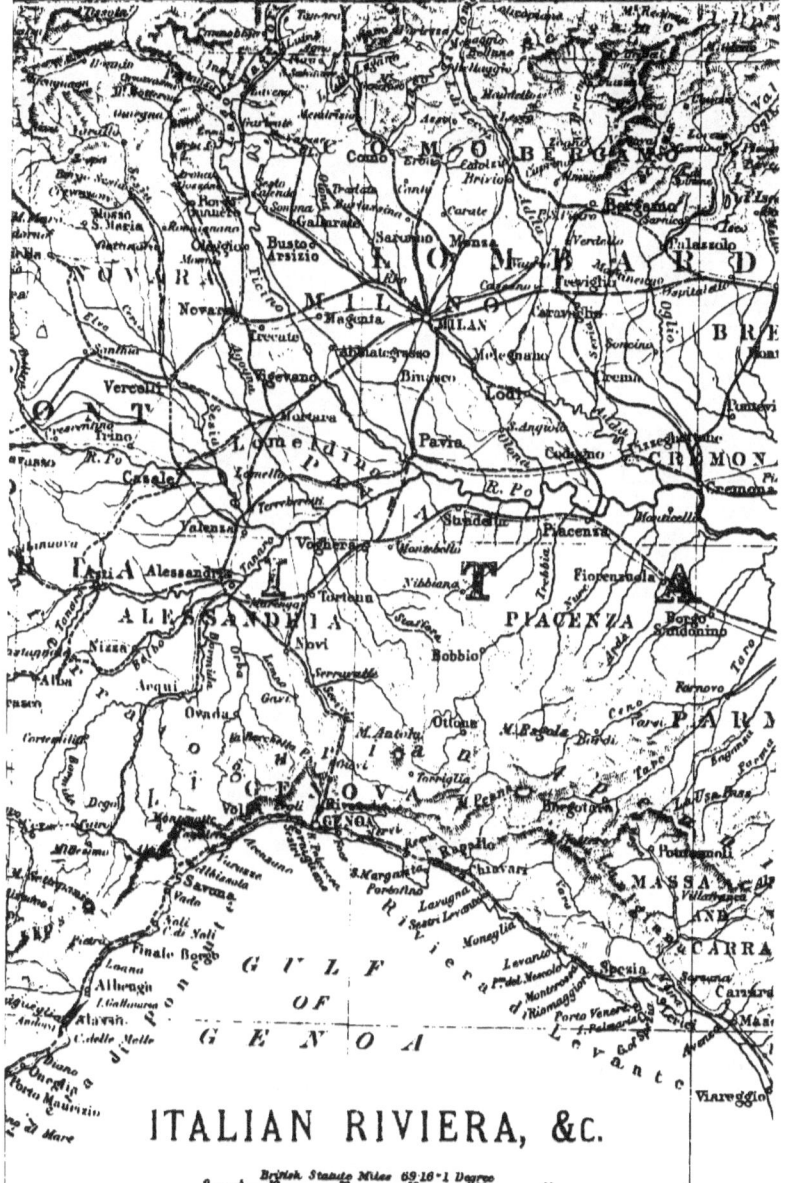

ITALIAN RIVIERA, &c.

ITALIAN RIVIERA, &C.

Ferques was obliged, with broken heart, to follow the army, and abandon his young wife to the care of a faithful servant. But in a few days the old esquire came with tears in his eyes to announce to his master the death of the courageous Jehanne. The poor knight was so overwhelmed with grief that, with the consent of the Count of Boulogne, he resolved to give up the world, and consecrate to God, in the most austere solitude, a life which he had already almost sacrificed to Him in war with the infidels. In 1528 he seems to have been succeeded by the anchoret Bernard.

The Sospel road now begins to ascend the Col de Guardia, pierced near the top by a tunnel 260 ft. long, and shortly after it reaches the walled town of Castellon or Castiglione, on an eminence 2926 ft. above the sea, commanding an extensive view, 8¼ m. from Menton, pop. 320. 5¾ m. farther is Sospel, pop. 3500 (p. 182).

Climate.—Menton being protected by an amphitheatre of high hills from the northerly blasts, the winters here are generally milder.

"A cool but sunny atmosphere, so dry that a fog is never seen at any period of the winter, whatever the weather, either on sea or on land, must be bracing, invigorating, stimulating. Such, indeed, are the leading characteristics of the climate of this region—the Undercliff of western Europe. Such a climate is perfection for all who want bracing, renovating—for the very young, the invalid middle-aged, and the very old, in whom vitality, defective or flagging, requires rousing and stimulating. The cool but pleasant temperature, the stimulating influence of the sunshine, the general absence of rain or of continued rain, the dryness of the air, render daily exercise out of doors both possible and agreeable. I selected Menton as my winter residence six years ago, because I was suffering from advanced pulmonary consumption, and after six winters passed at Menton I am now surrounded by a little tribe of cured or arrested consumption cases. This curative result has only been attained, in every instance, by rousing and improving the organic powers, and principally those of nutrition. If a consumption patient can be improved in health, and thus brought to eat and sleep well, thoroughly digesting and assimilating food, the battle is half won ; and helping the physician to attain this end is the principal benefit of the winter climate of the Riviera." — Bennet's *Winter Climates.*

"With all its vaunted security from biting winds, and its mountain shelter from the northern blasts, Menton lies most invitingly open to the south, south-east, and south-west, and winter winds from these directions can be chilly enough at times. What tells so keenly upon the weak and susceptible is the land breeze, which regularly at sundown steals from the mountains towards the sea. The mean temperature of November is 54°, December 40°, February 49°, March 53°. When the air is still, a summer heat often prevails during the day, though in the shade and within doors the mercury seldom rises above 60°."— *Wintering at Menton,* by A. M. Brown.

For the Excursions, see maps pp. 163 and 185.

THE ITALIAN RIVIERA,

OR

Menton to Genoa.

By VENTIMIGLIA, BORDIGHERA, SAN REMO, and SAVONA.

MENTON MILES FROM	Distance 100½ miles. See accompanying Map.	GENOA MILES TO

MENTON. The road from Menton to Genoa crosses the 100½ frontier at the bridge of St. Louis, spanning a ravine 215 ft. deep.

6½ m. E. from Menton by the carriage-road, passing the village of Mortola, and traversing the Piano di Latte, is

6¼ VENTIMIGLIA, pop. 8500, on a hill at the mouth of the 93¾ Roja. *Inns:* near station, the Hôtel Suisse ; in the low town, the Hôtel Tornaghi. All the trains halt here ¾ of an hour, and luggage entering France or Italy is examined. The new station is commodious. At one end of the luggage-room is a clock with Paris time, and at the other one with the time of Rome, 47 minutes in advance of Paris. The waiting-rooms, "Sale d'Aspetto," cloak-rooms, "Camerini di Toeletta," and the refreshment rooms are all at the French end, as well as the way out to the train. The town is well seen from the station. The church occupies a prominent position ; and close to it, in the Via Lascaris, are the post office, theatre, and the best café. The walk up this same Via to the town-gate shows the best part of the town, while the avenues in continuation beyond it lead up to the best sites for views. Not far from the station, on the right bank of the Nervia, on a large sandbank, are the remains of a theatre and of a cemetery, which probably mark the site of the ancient Albintemelium. What remains of the theatre is composed of large blocks of greenstone from the quarries of Mortola. The excavations have been carried on under the direction of the inspector of historic monuments in the province. Omnibus between Ventimiglia and Bordighera. Diligence once daily between Ventimiglia and Tenda, p. 183.

10 BORDIGHERA, pop. 2800. The old town, the Bordighera 90½ di sopra, is compactly built on the summit of the eminence rising from the cape S. Ampeglio, whose sides are covered with olives and palms. Down below, on almost a level with the sea, is the low or new town, where most of the invalids reside, though it is doubtful if the site is well chosen. *Hotels:* the best is the [1]*H. Angleterre, a first-class house in a garden, near the station. Similarly situated is the 'H.

Bordighera. Both charge from 10 to 20 frs. Behind the Angleterre is the Episcopal chapel. West from the Angleterre is [2]*Beau-Rivage, 6 to 10 frs. Immediately opposite station are [2]H. and P. Continental, 9 to 11 frs. ; the [2]H. and P. Sapia, 8 to 9 frs., and the Bordighera bank, where money can be changed. Eastward are the hotels [2]Victoria and [2]Windsor. Admirably situated on an eminence overlooking the Moreno palm-garden is the [1]*H. and P. Belvédère, 8 to 12 frs. Near it is the [2]*Pension Anglaise, 6 to 9 frs. At the commencement of the Vallecrosia valley is a Home with industrial school for orphans of poor Italian Protestants, founded by an English lady. Omnibus between Bordighera and San Remo, passing through Ospedaletti, a beautiful drive. Also omnibus every half-hour between Bordighera and Ventimiglia. It passes through the low town of Ventimiglia and stops at the commencement of the ascent to the high town.

The great feature of Bordighera are its plantations of palms, whose tufted tops wave above the more lowly lemon trees laden with pale yellow fruit, while the whole of the background is crowded with vigorous olive trees. Some of the palms are 800 years old. The lemon, after the olive, is the most profitable tree.

To the *Tower of Mostaccini*, 1½ hr. there and back, by the Strada Romana, till near Pozzoforte, where ascend by path right hand. This tower, of Roman origin, and still in excellent preservation, served as an "avisium" or watch-tower in the Middle Ages. From it is obtained a delightful view of part of the coast.

2½ m. west from Bordighera is the commencement of the valley of the Nervia, 16 m. long from north to south, with a varying breadth of 1½ to 2½ m. A good carriage-road extends all the way up to Pigna, 11 m. from Bordighera. On this road, 1½ m. up the Nervia, or nearly 4 m. from Bordighera, is Campo-Rosso, on the Nervia, at its junction with the Cantarena, pop. about 250. It possesses two churches, both 12th cent. St. Pierre has frescoes, 15th cent., on principal entrance and on the sacristy, also some pictures attributed to Brea of Nice. The confessionals are in the gallery. From Campo-Rosso a bridle-path leads up to the top of the hill, on which is the chapel of Santa Croce, commanding an extensive view. About 2 m. farther up the valley is Dolce-Acqua, on both sides of the Nervia, crossed here by a stone bridge with a span of 108 ft. Over the village, consisting of houses crowded together and piled above each other, rises the imposing feudal castle of the Dorias, reduced to its present dilapidated condition by the Genoese in 1672. 2¼ m. from Dolce-Acqua, or 8½ m. from Bordighera, is Isola Buona, pop. 1200, with paper and olive mills, heath pipe manufactories, and cold sulphurous springs. From Isola, a little way up the Merdanio or Merdunzo, is Apricale, pop. 1000. South from Apricale is Perinaldo, the birthplace, 8th June 1625, of Giovanni Domenico Cassini, the most famous of a family distinguished as astronomers, who succeeded one another as directors of the observatory at Paris for four generations.

A little more than 11 m. from Bordighera is Pigna, on the Nervia,

202

MENTON
MILES FROM

LA COLLA. OSPEDALETTI.

GENOA
MILES TO

at the foot of Mont Torragio, 3610 ft. above the sea, a village where the principal occupation is the cutting and sawing of the timber from the surrounding forests. The church, built in 1450, has on the rose window a representation of the descent of the Holy Ghost on the apostles. The frescoes on the choir are nearly of the same date as the church, and are attributed to Jean Ranavasio. In the wild and picturesque ravine of the Nervia, above Pigna, is a copious sulphurous spring, temp. 79° Fahr., utilised by a bathing establishment. Near Pigna, on a hill covered with chestnut trees, is the village of Castel-Vittorio or Franco. From Pigna a bridle-path leads, 4 m. N., to Les Beuze, the last village in the valley of the Nervia.

The most pleasant of the drives is to San Remo, 6¾ m. N.E., by Ospedaletti. About a mile from the E. side of Cape S. Ampeglio is the hamlet of Ruota, with a small chapel containing a group in alabaster representing the Annunciation. A short way farther a path descends from the road to a house on the beach in a luxuriant garden of palm and lemon trees. At the inner end of this orchard, near the railway, is an excellent sulphurous spring, temp. 70° F. After this the Corniche road bends round to Ospedaletti (see below). On the hills behind Ospedaletti, about 2 m. N., is La Colla, 1000 ft. above the sea. In the Town Hall is a valuable collection of 120 paintings, mostly by great Italian masters, such as Frà Bartolomeo, I. Bassano, F. Barocci, A. Carracci, Caravaggio, Cortona, C. Dolci, Domenichino, Sasso Ferrati, Reni, Salvator Rosa, Andrea del Sarto, and Spagnoletti. In another room is the library. The pictures and books were collected by the Abbé Paolo Rambaldi during his long stay at Florence, who at his death (1864) bequeathed them to this his native city. In the sacristy of the parish church is a beautifully-carved ivory crucifix, bequeathed, along with some other articles, by the Prelate Stefano Rossi, also a native of this quarter. A coach with 2 horses from Bordighera to La Colla and back costs 20 frs.

La Colla is the native town of the sea-captain Bresca, who, contrary to the orders of Pope Sixtus V., broke the silence by calling aloud to "wet the ropes" when the obelisk was being raised in front of St. Peter's. 2 m. E. from La Colla is San Remo, which is 3 m. from Ospedaletti.

The climate of Bordighera is similar to that of San Remo ; but as a residence it is more rural and has fewer resources. The mistral at Bordighera, instead of being a north-westerly wind, deviates by the configuration of the coast into a west wind.

Bordighera supplies Rome with palm-leaves for the Easter ceremonies, as also the Israelites in Germany and Holland for the feast of Tabernacles.

13½
—~ OSPEDALETTI, pop. 1000, a small village with nearly a mile ~87~ of frontage towards the sea, from which it is separated by the railway. In the village is the [2]H. and P. Ospedaletti, room 40 frs. the month.

Upon an eminence with garden is the [1]H. de la Reine, 12 to 20 frs. Adjoining is a handsome Casino, in which there is dancing even during the day. The gambling is private, and on a small scale.

16½
—— SAN REMO, 16¼ m. E. from Menton by the coach-road, pop. ——
in winter 18,000. As Italy is entered it will be observed that the women, the maidens and their mothers, are the hewers of wood and drawers of water, and that to their lot falls the menial work of the most laborious trades.

Hotels.—Those with the figure [1] are first-class houses, with [2] second-class. The asterisk signifies that they are especially good of their class. Commencing at the railway station and going eastward by the principal street, the Via Vittorio Emanuele, we have the [1]G. H. de la Paix, close to the station and fronting the public garden. Then follow the [2]H. and P. Nationale, 7 to 8 frs.; the [1]*H. San Remo ; the [2]P. Suisse ; the Rubino Bank ; the Squire-Pharmacy; the Asquasciate Bank; the Vicario Store; the [2]P. Molinari, and the [2]H. Bretagne, frequented principally by commercial travellers. Behind Squire's is the Episcopal Chapel, and a little farther west, left hand, the Post Office.

On the Corso Garibaldi, the eastern continuation of Via Vittorio Emanuele, are the [1]H. Nice and the [1]*H. Angleterre. Near the Angleterre are the Pensions [2]*Allemagne; [2]Rossi; and [2]Lindenhof ; and the Home for invalid ladies of limited means. Twenty-five shillings the week ; which, as at the similar institution at Menton, includes doctors' fees, comfortable living, wine or beer, and everything except washing and fire in bedroom. For particulars apply to Messrs. Barnetts & Co., bankers, 62 Lombard Street, London.

At the end of the corso are two large houses in gardens, with one front to the sea and the other to the road—the [1]H. Méditerranée and the [1]*H. Victoria. Near the harbour, behind the Via V. Emanuele, are the [2]*Beau-Séjour with garden, and the H. Bains.

At the west end of San Remo are some good houses, mostly on eminences in gardens. Taking them in the order from E. to W. we have the [2]P. Anglo-Americaine ; the Presbyterian Chapel ; the [2]P. Tatlock (German) ; [1]*Hôtel Royal ; [1]*Belle-Vue ; [1]Paradis ; [1]*Londres ; [1]Pavillon (moderate) ; [1]Anglais ; [1]Palmieri ; and the [1]*West-End, the most important hotel on this side of San Remo, and situated at the commencement of the pleasant walk by the Strada Berigo. In the first-class hotels the pension is from 9 to 18 frs., in the "pensions" from 7 to 11 frs.

Omnibuses run between the two ends of the town; also between San Remo and Bordighera ; San Remo and Taggia by Bussana ; San Remo and Dolce-Acqua ; and San Remo and Ceriana, 6½ m. N. (see map, p. 165).

Cab Fares.—The course, 1 horse, 1 fr. during the day, and 1½ fr. night. Per hour, 2 frs.; at night, 3 frs. The course, 2 horses, 1½ fr. during the day, and 2½ frs. at night. The hour, 3 frs.; at night, 4 frs.

Old San Remo is built on two hills, and the modern town at the foot of these hills, on the Nice and Genoa road, called at this part the Via Vittorio Emanuele, where are now all the best hotels, restaurants, booksellers, confectioners, and dealers in inlaid woods. "The mean temperature is 49°·1 Fahr. (Sigmund), nearly as high as Dr. Bennet's estimate of that of Menton; while it would appear, from a comparison of the thermometrical tables kept by Dr. Daubeny with those of Dr. Bennet for the same winter, that the range of temperature at Menton is nearly 3° more than at San Remo. The climate is warm and dry, but from the protecting ranges not rising precipitously as at Menton, the shelter from the northerly winds is less complete. At the same time the vast olive groves screen the locality from cold blasts and temper them into healthful breezes, imparting a pleasing freshness to the atmosphere, and removing sensations of lassitude often experienced in too well-protected spots. The size of the sheltered area gives patients a considerable choice of residences, which can be found either close to or at varying distances from the sea, according to the requirements of the case; while the numerous wooded valleys, abounding in exquisite wild flowers, provide plenty of donkey and foot excursions." —Williams' *Winter Stations.*

San Remo has many pleasant walks, in valleys full of lemon trees, as at Menton, or up mountains covered with olive trees, generally on terraces built up with low stone walls without plaster.

The best of the drives is to the Madonna della Guardia, on Cape San Martino, by the village of Poggio, and back by the coast-road. From the Hôtel Victoria the Corniche is continued till arriving at a part where the road divides into two; one descends, the other ascends; take the latter, which an inscription on a marble slab indicates to be the "Strada Consortile de San Remo à Ceriana." This road ascends through olive trees to Poggio. Just before entering Poggio, the carriage-road to the Madonna strikes off to the right by the east side of the promontory, while a stony bridle-path goes right over the centre. The town seen on the opposite side of the valley is Bussana. Poggio, one of the many wretchedly poor villages, has two churches. The road, which has ascended all the way from San Remo to Poggio, still continues to ascend by the Ceriana valley to Ceriana. *Inn:* H. Etoile d'Italie, 6½ m. from San Remo, commanding ever-extending views, which, together with the profusion of wild flowers, form the principal

attraction of the excursion. Cab with 1 horse to Ceriana and back, 14
frs. ; 2 horses, 20 frs., with ½ hr. rest. The Madonna road from Poggio
is nearly level. The chapel, with a few tall cypresses, stands at the
extremity of Cape San Martino. The prospect is extensive. To the
east are, on the coast, Arma, Riva, San Stefano, and in the distance
San Lorenzo. On the hills behind them are Bussana, Pompeiana, and
Linguegliectta. Behind is Poggio. To the west are San Remo, La Colla,
and Bordighera. Cab with 1 horse to the chapel and back, 7 frs. ; 2
horses, 10 frs., with ½ hr. rest (see maps, pp. 163 and 199).

A good carriage-road, commencing near Cape Nero, leads up to La
Colla, on one of the spurs of the Piano del Carparo, 1000 ft. above the
sea, and 2 m. from San Remo, by the bridle-path. Cab with 1 horse,
8 frs.; 2 horses, 12 frs., with ½ hr. repose. See page 199.

St. Romolo to Monte Bignone.

One of the most frequented excursions is to San Romolo, 1700 ft.
above the sea, and 4 m. northwards, either from the Place St. Etienne,
or the Place St. Sir. Donkey, there and back, 5 frs. San Romolo
consists of some villas, an old convent, and a chapel, built over the
cell which was inhabited by the hermit St. Romolo. It commands
splendid views, and from it the ascent is made of the Piano del Ré, a
ridge 3500 ft. above the sea, between Mounts Caggio or Cuggio and
Bignone. To reach the ridge, descend a short way the Romolo road,
then take the path to the left, and make for the corner next Monte
Bignone, whence the bridle-path ascends to the summit, 4235 ft.
above the sea, 5 hrs. from San Remo, or about half that time from San
Romolo. "In making the ascent of Monte Bignone, it is always safest
to be accompanied by a guide. For those who are strong the ascent
on foot is the pleasantest, but the road is quite practicable for sure-
footed donkeys, although in places it is somewhat trying for those
whose nerves are not strong. The whole route is exceedingly beautiful, glorious prospects meeting the eye at almost every turn ; the path
sometimes traverses forests of fir trees, with amongst them innumerable bushes of the bright-leaved holly, at others it runs along the
edges of steep ravines and precipices : many curious and rare wild
flowers attracting the eye on the way ; till at length, after an ascent
of about two hours from San Romolo and four from San Remo, the
broad sloping and grassy summit of the mountain is reached. Continue the ascent until its highest point, marked by a stone obelisk, is
gained, and from which one of the most magnificent prospects imagin-

able lies stretched out on all sides, embracing an area in some directions of more than a hundred and fifty miles, astonishing and enchanting the beholder.   To the south, the glorious expanse of the
Mediterranean, and in the far distance the island of Corsica, with the
snowy peaks of Monte Rotondo ; on the right Monte Caggio, and the
mountains forming the western half of the San Remo amphitheatre,
terminating at Capo Nero surmounted by Colla, and the valleys of
San Remo and Bordighera ; farther away, the mountains of the Men-
tonean amphitheatre, and along the coast successively the various
capes and promontories as far as Cap d'Antibes and even the Esterels ;
on the left the Ceriana and Taggia Valleys, with on the farther
side of the latter Castellaro and the Madonna di Lampeduza, and
Pompeiana and Riva on the seashore ; while far away to the east are
the mountains of the Eastern Riviera or of the Riviera di Levante,
with the Apennines in the distance ; lastly, to the north is a broad
and deep valley, having on the other side a range of mountains still
loftier than the one on which we are standing, and above these again,
the snow-capped Alps stretching away in the one direction towards
the Esterels, and in the other to Turin.   Looking now more closely
into the valley below, on a narrow ridge on the near side of the valley,
is seen the town of Perinaldo, and on a hill on the opposite side,
Apricale ; both of a singularly deep red hue, from the fact that the
tiled roofs only of the houses are seen from this great altitude.   There
is a pathway leading down to Bajardo, and thence to Pigna, where
accommodation at a small but clean inn may be had for the night ;
whence the return home can then be made by the Nervia valley and
Bordighera, altogether a most beautiful and varied excursion.   (For
the valley of the Nervia, see p. 201, and map, p. 165.)

" It is impossible to convey in words anything like a correct idea
of the splendour of the prospect on a clear day from Monte Bignone ;
it must be seen to be appreciated ; it has been described as one of the
finest in Europe.   The excursion is one which may be safely undertaken with ordinary precautions, and is within the compass of any
person of fair health and strength.   An additional charm consists in
the number of rare and beautiful wild flowers, which are different from
those found at a lower elevation.   Amongst the most noticeable of
these is the blue Hepatica, Anemone, Hepatica L., a pink variety of
which is sometimes met with, the pink cyclamen-like flower, Erythro-
nium Dens Canis L. with its trefoil-like and spotted leaves ; in shady
places the Primrose, Primula acaulis All. ; everywhere over the sum-

207

MENTON
MILES FROM
TAGGIA. PORTO MAURIZIO.
GENOA
MILES TO

mit of the mountain the Cowslip, Primula veris ; two species of Gen-
tian, Gentiana verna and G. acaulis L.; Ophrys fusca Link, also a
species of Asphodel, Asphodelus albus Willd.; Saxifraga cuneifolia ;
Sempervivum arachnoideum L.; and lastly, in shady dells, Daphne
laureola L. With two or three exceptions, these flowers were found
in blossom at the end of April, but they had been so for some weeks
previously. On my way up the San Romolo valley I noticed many
plants of Helleborus fœtidus L., as also for the first time in flower
the large and handsome pink Cistus, C. albidus L.; this is the species
so commonly found above the region of the olive trees."—*San Remo
and the Western Riviera*, by Dr. Hassall.

San Remo to **Taggia**, there and back, cab, 1 horse, 8 frs.; 2
horses, 12 frs., with ½ hr. rest ; by coach, 2 horses, for the day, 20
frs. Or from San Remo by rail to Arma, whence omnibus to Taggia,
10 sous. Donkey from **Taggia** to Lampedusa, 2 frs. The best place
for refreshments in Taggia is the Albergo d'Italia, formerly the palace
of the Marquis Spinola. The stream Taggia or Argentina is crossed
by a long curved bridge of unequal arches. From the east end of this
bridge a steep road leads up to the town of Castellar, whence a well-
kept path ascends to the chapel of the Madonna di Lampedusa. From
both places there are charming views. The Taggia road ascends the
valley the length of Triora, by the village of Badalucco.

21½   79
⁓ TAGGIA, pop. 5000, on the Giabonte, 3 m. from the sta- ⁓
tion. An omnibus awaits passengers (½ fr.) In Taggia it halts at the
Locanda d'Italia, at the termination of the Via Curlo ; whence commences the road to Castellar, situated upon a hill on the opposite side
of the river, and about ½ hour's walk from Taggia. Castellar is visited
on account of the gaudy sanctuary and the view from the hill. Taggia,
though a poor dirty town, with steep, narrow, and slippery streets, has
two very fair churches. At No. 1 Via Soleri—the principal street in
the town—is the habitation of Giovanni Ruffini (Dr. Antonio). To
reach it, on entering the town, after having passed through the archway, take the street to the left, the Via Ruffini, then, first left, the
Salita Eleonora. On the beach, near the Taggia station, is the little
port of Arma, with the ruins of a fort built in the 15th cent. 2 m.
farther east by rail is San Stefano, pop. 600, at the foot of Mont
Colma, with a climate like that of San Remo.

31   69½
⁓ PORTO MAURIZIO, pop. 8000. *Hotels:* France ; Commerce. ⁓
Porto Oneglia, pop. 8000, H. Victoria, on the opposite sides of a
small bay. The most important part of San Maurizio is the high town,

containing the principal church, of which the porch consists of a double
row of Corinthian columns flanked by two square towers. The interior
represents the Roman-Greek style met with in all the churches on this
coast, only here the details are more elaborate and more highly finished.
The roof, instead of being plain barrel-vaulted, is divided into arches,
domes, and semi-domes, resting on massive piers with attached Corinthian pillars. The soffits of the arches and domes are covered with
diaper mouldings, with rich friezes and dentils along the edges. The
form of the pulpit is graceful, and the staircase nearly hidden. Many
of the old houses have handsome cornices over their windows and doorways. A good and much-frequented road, or rather promenade, connects Porto Maurizio with Oneglia, about a mile distant, beautifully
situated at the mouth of the Impero. This is the birthplace of
Admiral Andrea Doria, 1466. After passing through a long tunnel we
reach the Port of Diano Marina. The broad valley inland up the
Piètro is covered with fine olive trees. Farther east is Cervo, on an
eminence overlooking the station and the sea. Then Laigueglia, with
gardens full of orange trees. From Laigueglia a fine smooth beach
extends all the way to

Alassio, pop. 5000, a new winter station, 44½ m. east from Menton,
and 56 m. west from Genoa, built along the beach, and nearly surrounded
by a high wall, with at both ends a suburb beyond the walls. *Hotels:*
H. et P. Suisse, opposite station, 6 to 9 frs. On the beach at the E.
end, the *G. H. Alassio, 8 to 9 frs. On the beach at the W. end, the
H. Méditerranée, 6 to 8 frs. Near the station, the Episcopal chapel.

Alassio and its neighbour Laigueglia are partially protected from
some of the cold winds by low but compact mountains belonging to
the chain of the Ligurian Alps. Pleasant walks and well-paved cause-
ways extend up the hills, while along the coast are pretty drives to
Loano and Ceriale, or up the valley westwards from Albenga. Around
both towns are many large carouba and orange trees. Palms are less
abundant. Between Alassio and the next station, Albenga, is the
small island of Gallinaria, with a castle on the summit of the hill.

Albenga is 4 m. N. from Alassio, on the Caprianna, and at a little
distance from the coast. *Hotels:* Hotel d'Albenga ; Italia ; Vittoria.
Their omnibuses await passengers. This, the ancient Albium In-
gaunum, the birthplace of the Emperor Proculus, is situated on low
ground, in a broad valley watered by the Caprianna. Around Albenga
are many deciduous trees, and here and there in the sheltered spots
orange and lemon trees trained as espaliers. A good carriage-road

extends up the valley of the Nerva and across the Col di S. Bernardo, then by the town of Garessio and the valley of the Tanaro to Ceva, 4 hours by rail from Turin.

After Albenga follow Loano, pop. 3800, pleasantly situated on the beach at the foot of a gentle sloping hill, and Pietraligure, on the Isola, pop. 1000, a sheltered town, with abundance of palms, orange, and lemon trees, principally at the eastern end, round the cape.

$\frac{59\frac{1}{2}}{}$ FINALMARINA, pop. 3500. *Hotel:* Garibaldi. The $\frac{41}{}$ church of St. John the Baptist, after the design of Bernini, is richly ornamented with marbles of various hues, mingled with rich gilding and bright frescoes, presenting a grand combination of gorgeous colour. In Final Borgo is the church S. Biaggio, resplendent also with colour, but more subdued. The pulpit and altar display most delicate workmanship. There is a great deal of fine scenery in the neighbourhood, and pleasant walks in the valleys, and up the heights to the numerous dismantled forts (15th cent.), and to the Castello Gavone, a picturesque ruin. Five miles N. from Finalmarina is Noli, pop. 1000, *Inn:* Albergo del Sole, at the commencement of the arcade, fronting the beach. This curious town, formerly a republic under the protection of Genoa, is still partially surrounded by walls garnished with rectangular towers. It is pierced from E. to W. by narrow parallel streets, the best being the Via Emanuele II., which commences at the beach on E. side by the clock-tower, near the inn, and traverses the town to the W. side by the new church. The continuation, outside the town, the Via Monasterio, leads up to the mountains covered with vines, olives, and maritime pines. On the top of the hill are the ruins of Noli castle, with walls garnished with circular towers. The old church, 11th cent., is near the station. Fishing is the chief industry. A beautiful road, 2 m. N. by the coast, leads to Spotorno.

$\frac{74}{}$ SAVONA, pop. 17,000. *Hotels:* Suisse, a large house in the $\frac{26\frac{1}{2}}{}$ Piazza di Teatro ; *Roma, under the Arcades ; and the Italia, opposite the Suisse. In the ancient seaport of Savona, Mago the Carthaginian deposited his spoils after the capture of Genoa. The greater part of the town is now modern, consisting of handsome gardens, boulevards, and well-paved broad streets lined with massive arcades, and substantial houses built in enormous square blocks of from four to five stories high. The rock, the Rupe di S. Giorgio, on which the acropolis formerly stood, is occupied by the castle, and pierced by an elliptical tunnel. At both ends are small harbours with shallow water. The

P

Cathedral, built in 1604, is, in the interior, entirely covered with orna-mental designs in different shades of brown and orange, relieved here and there by stripes of gilding. The two large frescoes in the choir, and the other at the western end, are by V. Garrazino. In the last chapel, N. side nearest the altar, is a triptych by Brea, 1495. Near the Cathedral, in the Sistina chapel, is the tomb of the parents of Pope Sixtus IV., the uncle of Julius II. In the church of San Domenico there is in the first chapel, left on entering, a "Nativity" by A. Semini. The figure of the Virgin appears rather large, but the contour and expression of the others are admirable. In another chapel on the same side of the church is an "Adoration of the Magi" by Albert Durer, in the form of a triptych. In a small church, called the Capella di Christo, over the altar within a niche, is a wooden figure of our Lord, said to be 800 years old. In the sacristy are two reliefs in black marble from 400 to 500 years old. The Emperor Pertinax, and the Popes Gregory VII., Sixtus IV., and Julius II., were born in or in the neighbourhood of Savona. 4 m. from Savona by coach and rail is the sanctuary of Nostra Signora di Misericordia. The church, built in the 16th cent., is covered with precious marbles, and ornamented with paintings by Castello, the intimate friend of Tasso. At Savona junction with line to Turin, 91 m. northwards (see p. 183).

$\frac{77}{\frown}$ ALBISSÓLA, pop. 2000, on the Sansobbia. This town is $\frac{23\frac{1}{2}}{\frown}$ about a mile from the Port or Marina. 4½ m. farther eastwards by rail is **Varazze**, pop. 10,000, a pleasant town at the head of a large bay. A little shipbuilding is carried on here. Beautiful palm, lemon, and orange groves. This is the birthplace of Jacopo di Voragine, the author of the *Golden Legend*, the reading of which was the principal means of transforming Ignacio Loyola from an intrepid soldier into a zealous missionary. Between Varazze, 64 m. N.E. from San Remo, and Arenzano, 6¼ m. N.E. from Varazze, is another favoured part of the Riviera, sheltered by a ridge of most picturesque hills, of which Monte Grosso (1319 ft.) is the culminating point. The road here passes through firs, umbrella pines, carouba trees, cypresses, evergreen oaks, arbutus trees, and some fine shrubs of *Phillyrea angustifolia*, with here and there just enough olive trees to afford evidence of the comparative mildness of the climate. About half-way between Varazze and Cogoleto is the village of Inoria.

$\frac{85}{\frown}$ COGOLETO, pop. 1000. From the station walk down to the $\frac{15\frac{1}{2}}{\frown}$ town; and on reaching the main street, the Via Cristoforo Colombo,

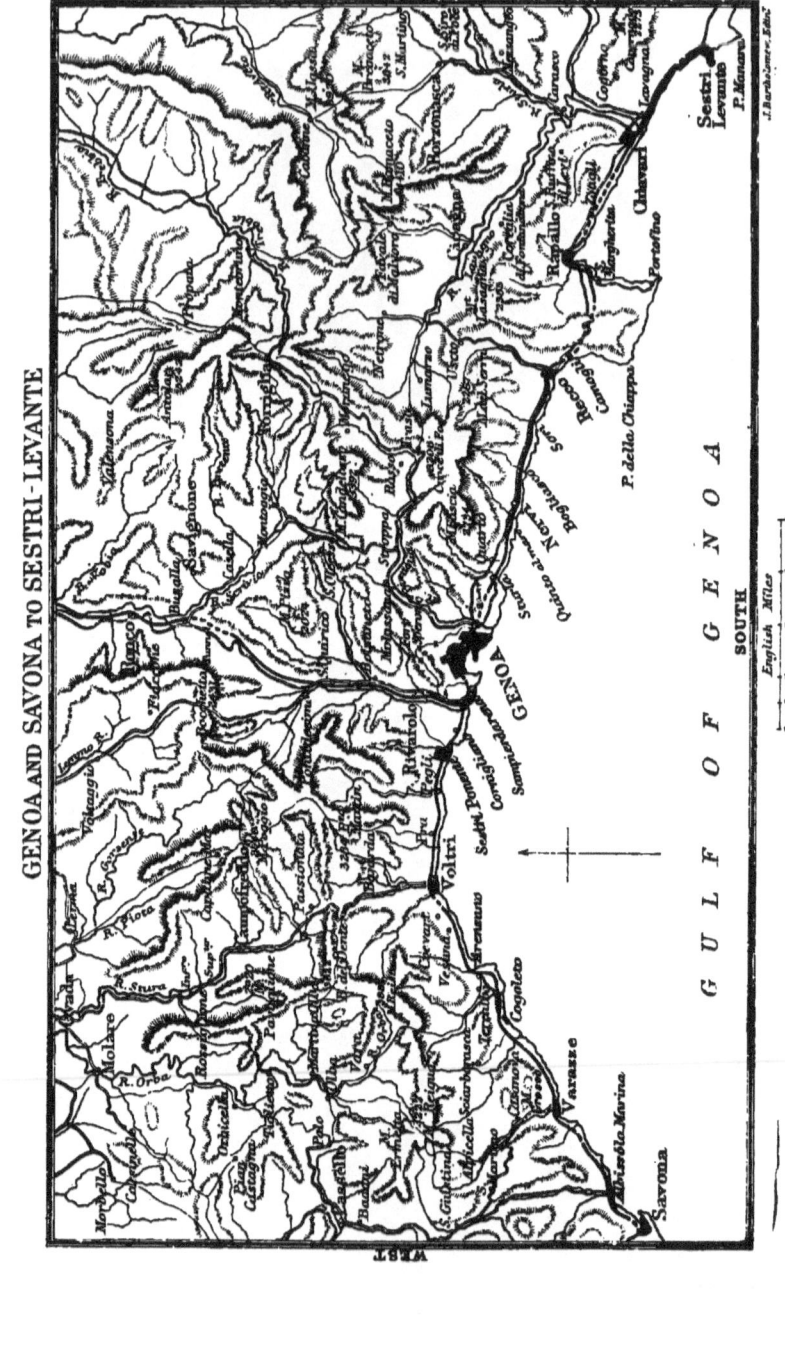

GENOA AND SAVONA TO SESTRI-LEVANTE

turn to the left. In the second division, right hand, at No. 22, is
the house of Columbus, with the following inscription :—

> *Hospes, siste gradum. Fuit hic lux prima Columbo;*
> *Orbe viro majori heu nimis arcta domus!*
> *Unus erat mundus. Duo sunt, ait iste. Fuere.*

It consists of three stories, with one side fronting the sea, and the
other the main street. The rooms are small, and with arched roofs.
That in which Columbus was born (1435) is on the first story.
Fronting the adjoining room is a large balcony overlooking the
Mediterranean, where it is possible the boy Columbus learned to con-
ceive the idea of a continent beyond the Atlantic by having been
accustomed to gaze on this sea at his feet, with the knowledge that
beyond it there lay the vast continent of Africa. Although his parents
were in humble circumstances, they were descended from a family belonging to the most illustrious nobility of Piacenza, who had lost their
estates during the wars of Lombardy. Boatbuilding and fishing are
the principal industries of Cogoleto. Map, p. 220.

$87\frac{1}{4}$ ARENZANO, pop. 5000. *H. Arenzano, 7 to 8 frs., near $13\frac{1}{4}$
station. One of the cleanest towns on the Riviera, pleasantly situated
in a picturesque country and commanding extensive views of the coast.
The road between Arenzano and Cogoleto passes by Monte Grosso.

$91\frac{1}{4}$ VOLTRI, and the next town, Pra, may be called one. Paper- $8\frac{3}{4}$
making and shipbuilding are the principal industries. Map, p. 220.

95 PEGLI, pop. 1000. *A winter station.* The largest hotel is $5\frac{1}{4}$
the *H. Pegli et de la Méditerranée, with one side to the sea and the
other to the public garden and English chapel. Pension in winter, $9\frac{1}{2}$
to 15 frs. On the beach the H. Gargini, second class. Pegli is a
quiet little village, prettily situated on the sea, and among hills. It
has constant communication by tram and rail with Genoa, and is
visited on account of the grounds around the Villa Pallavicini, ornamented with statues of Roman divinities, temples, triumphal arches,
huts, and an obelisk. But the remarkable object is the artificial cave,
covered with large stalactites, in the midst of a lake 5 feet deep, surrounded by evergreen shrubs and trees so arranged as to produce
wonderfully pretty vistas. At one part the edge of the lake seems to
join the sea, although many miles distant. All this has been created
on the formerly sterile side of a hill, where almost nothing would
grow from the want of water and of soil. Water was brought from a
great distance, and caused to tumble down the mountain in cascades

into the lake, which had to be lined with porcelain to retain it. The cave was then built of brick, and covered with consummate art with stalactites, as in nature. The visitor is rowed in a boat about this most curious piece of land and water. In other parts there are a multitude of surprises, in unexpected jets of water, and in beautiful peeps of scenery no larger than a picture. Attendant, 1 fr. ; for party, 2 frs.

1¾ m. E. from Pegli and 3¾ W. from Genoa is **Sestri-Ponente**, pop. 10,800. *Hotel:* *G. H. Sestri, 8 to 12 frs., with commodious bathing establishment at the foot of the garden. The beach, composed of small pebbles, has a rapid slope. Good sea water can be brought to bedroom every morning. The station is near the hotel, and the trams pass by the gate. The interior of the parish church is superbly gilt and covered with frescoes. Just under the wide spanned roof are painted statues of the patriarchs and prophets. Sestri makes a better winter station than the next town, **Cornigliano**, *H. Rachel, 9 to 12 frs., with sheltered garden, 2½ m. W. from Genoa. Both of these towns are considered from 4° to 5° colder than Menton. The tram passes the garden gate of both hotels. After Cornigliano the tram and train traverse the populous suburb of Sampierdarena and arrive at Genoa. The principal railway station is at the W. end of Genoa. The Piazza Annunziata is the terminus of the Pegli, Sestri, and Cornigliano trams.

100½
~~ GENOA, pop. 145,000. The hotels most conveniently situated for visitors are the G. H. de Gènes, 9 to 15 frs., in the Piazza de Ferrari, opposite the theatre and the post office ; the *G. H. Isotta, 10 to 15 frs., No. 7 Via di Roma, parallel to the glass arcade, and also near the post ; the *Londres, 9 to 10 frs., near the station ; the Victoria, in the Piazza Annunziata, and the H. Étrangers, No. 1 Via Nuovissima. The above are in a line with the palaces, and cost 8 to 10 frs. Down in the port in the Via Carlo Alberto, and most conveniently situated for those who have to embark, are—taking them in the order from W. to E.—the Croix de Malte, the H. de la Ville, the H. Smith, the *H. Trombetta, and the *France. They charge from 8 to 14 frs. By the side of the last two hotels is the Bourse, and in the neighbourhood of the Bourse are the best money-changers.

For **Genoa to Turin**, see p. 279.

Anglican church in the Via Goito, a small street leading northwards from the Acqua Sola Promenade. In the same neighbourhood is the broad street Via Assarotti, with at No. 37 the Valdensian and Presbyterian churches. Shops for filigree work in gold and silver in the Via degli Orefici by the side of the Bourse, and at the foot of the Sestiere della Maddalena, which descends from the Piazza delle Fontane Morose. At No. 17 of that Piazza is a good shop for coral ornaments.

Cafés.—*Café Roma, by the Teatro Carlo Felice ; *Stabilimento delle Nazioni, Via Roma ; *Concordia, Via Garibaldi. The principal sights are the church of the Annunziata, p. 212 ; the Cemetery approached by the Staglieno omnibus from the Piazza de Ferrari ; the Palaces between the railway station and the Piazza Nuova. The church of Santa Maria in Carignano, approached by the Carignano omnibus from the Piazza de Ferrari, passing through the Acqua Sola Gardens, 138 ft. above the sea (p. 218). North from the Acqua Sola is the Villa Negro, containing the Museum of Natural History. The best of the drives is along the Via di Circonvallazione.

Florio-Rubattino have steamers to Bastia (Corsica), Cagliari, Civita-Vecchia, Leghorn, and Porto Torres, in the north of Sicily. Peirano, Danovaro, and Co. have steamers to Ancona, Brindisi, Catania, Gallipoli, Leghorn, Messina, Naples, and Triest. For the English steamers between Liverpool, London, and the ports of the Mediterranean, apply to Lertora Fratelli, No. 2 Via S. Lorenzo.

1-horse cabs—the course, 1 fr. ; the hour, 1½ fr. ; every successive ½ hour, 80 c. 2-horse cabs—the course, 1½ fr. ; the hour, 2 frs. ; every successive ½ hour, 1 fr. Boats to and from the steamers, 1 fr. each. Rail from Genoa to Turin, 104 m. N.W. (p. 279).

Post Office in the Galleria Mazzini. Telegraph Office in the Palazzo Ducale. Best money-changers near and around the Bourse.

Genoa is singularly constructed around a small bay on shelving ground, rising rapidly from the water's edge to the height of from 500 to 600 feet. The old part of the town is a labyrinth of crooked streets from 6 to 12 feet wide, and frequently so steep that steps have to be cut in them. The most remarkable of the new streets is the Via di Circonvallazione, composed of a series of lofty terraced "corsos" skirting the face of the hills, commencing at the E. end from the Piazza Manin, 330 ft. above the sea, and extending westward in a zig-zag form to the railway station by the Albergo dei Poveri. They are reached from the upper ends of the Vias Palestro, Mameli, Caffaro, and Brignone di Ferrari, by ramps and long stairs. The palaces, another feature of Genoa, are large gaunt mansions, all similar in style —gates 40 feet high, with marble columns—courts paved with various coloured marbles—broad staircases, all of marble—rooms 30 feet high with arched ceilings, and adorned with gilded columns, large mirrors, crystal lustres, and mosaic floors ; the roofs panelled, and the panels divided by sculptured figures, and filled with finely executed paintings in oil. The best churches and palaces are in the streets extending in a continuous and slightly curved line from the railway station, at the west end, to the Piazza de Ferrari at the eastern end of Genoa.

The visiting of the palaces is rather fatiguing, as the best works of art are preserved in the upper stories, reached by splendid but lofty staircases. The best two are close to each other, the Palazzo Durazzo Pallavicini, No. 1 Via Balbi, and the Palazzo Rosso, No. 18 Via Garibaldi. They contain specimens of everything for which the palaces are remarkable. A fee of 1 fr. is sufficient to leave with the keeper of the gallery. Most of the palaces have each of the rooms provided with a list of the pictures and frescoes it contains printed on a card, which makes the visitor quite independent of the servants and guides.

As there are so many places to visit between the railway station and the cathedral, the best plan is to do that portion on foot, and after having visited the cathedral, to take a cab from the stand at the foot of the Via S. Lorenzo, and drive by the Via Vittorio Emanuele, round by the ramparts, and up the Via Rivoli to the church of Sta. Maria di Carignano.

The only palace west from the station is the Palazzo Doria, reconstructed by Montorsoli, 1525, and decorated and embellished by Perino del Vaga, a pupil of Raphael's, and a contributor to the paintings in the Vatican. Perino's best works here are Jupiter defeating the Giants, in the principal hall, and the Triumph of Scipio, at the entrance. In the centre of the garden is a fountain representing Andrea Doria as Neptune, with his Sea-horses, by P. Carlone. In the garden, on the other side of the railway, are a colossal statue of Hercules, erected by Doria, and a monument to the memory of his dog Rolando, given him by the Emperor Charles, who conferred upon him the title of "Il Principe." The tomb of Andrea Doria is in the church of San Matteo, and over the altar the sword presented to him by Paul III.

Adjoining the Doria palace is the Via Milano, a terraced promenade lining the western side of the harbour, as the less beautiful but more costly terrace by the Via Carlo Alberto lines the eastern front. Walking *eastward from the station* the first large building is the Royal Palace, No. 10 Via Balbi. This palace, formerly the property of the Durazzo family, was erected after the plans of P. F. Cantone and J. A. Falcone, while the staircases and terraces, which have been so greatly admired, were by the Chevalier Charles Fontane. The accommodation is extensive, but the rooms are small, excepting the principal

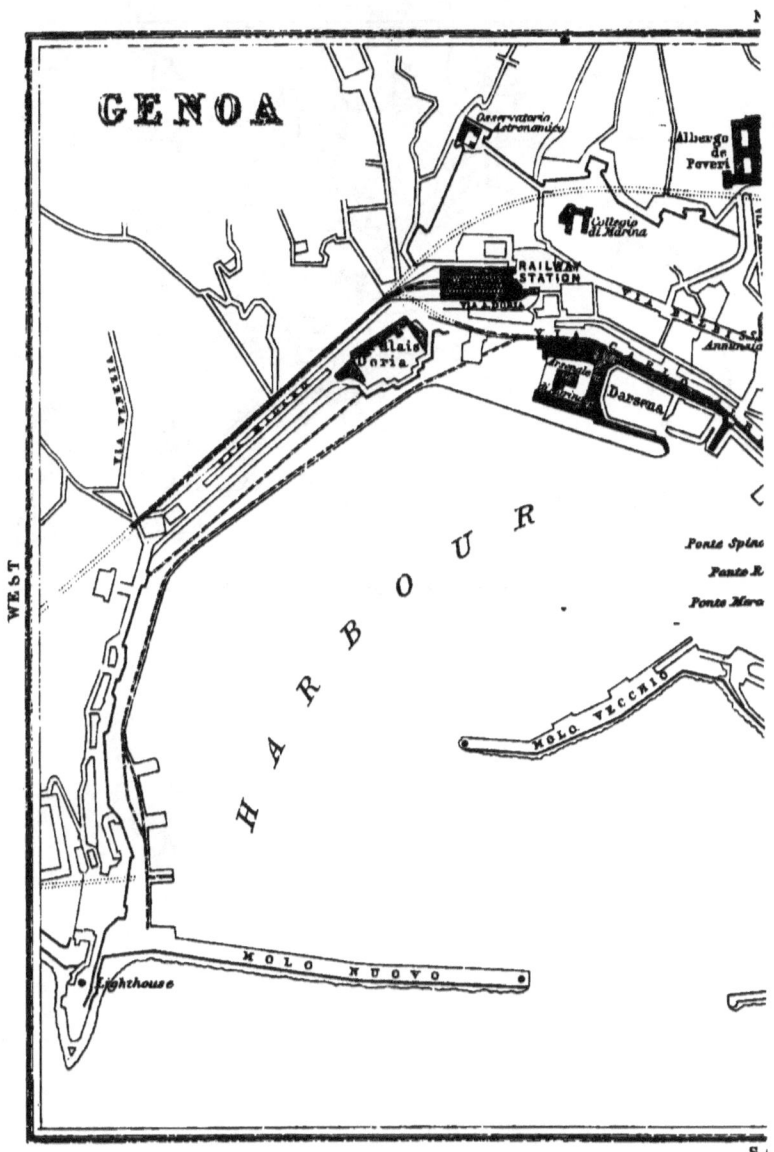

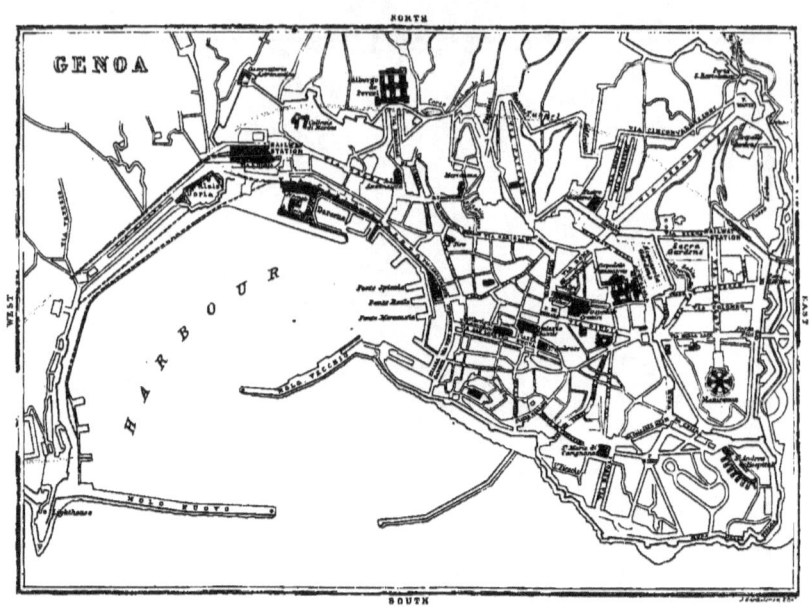

reception hall, the theatre, and the library.   The pictures are indifferent.

The Balbi Palace, No. 4 Via Balbi, built after the plans of B. Bianco, and improved by P. A. Corradi, contains a large collection of paintings—among others a Lucrecia, Cleopatra, and a St. Jerome, by Guido ; St. Jerome, a Virgin, and Jesus scourged, by Tizziano ; a St. George and St. Catherine ; and the Infant Jesus, by Coreggio.

No. 1 Via Balbi is the P. Durazzo Pallavicini, one of the most important to visit.   The architect was B. Bianco, but the vestibule and staircases (considered the finest in Genoa) are by A. Tagliafico. The paintings are almost entirely by Italian masters, such as Molinaretti, Guercino, Franceschini, Leida, Carracci, Lanfranco, Procaccini, Cappuccino, Langetti, Castelli, Ferrari, Vercelli, Reni, Merone, Cogorano, Zanotti, and Merighi.   In the first room there is a valuable triptych by A. Durer, and the gem of the collection, James I. of England and Family, by Van Dyck.   In the reception room are other three choice works by the same master.   The frescoes on the roofs are by Boni, Piola, Davolio, and Bazzani.   In each room there are cards with the names of the artists and subject.

From the Via Balbi we pass into the Piazza dell' Annunziata, with, on the left hand, the church of that name, the most sumptuous in Genoa, built in 1228 by the Monaci Umiliati, but altered and left in its present state by the Conventurati in 1587.   The façade, supported on six stately marble columns, is unfinished.   The interior is full of beauty, and resplendent with glowing colours harmoniously blended.   Over the entrance is Procaccino's masterpiece, the Last Supper.   The frescoes on the cupola are by A. Ansaldi, those on the choir by J. Benzo, and the remainder principally by the Carloni. Among the other beautiful things are the angels supporting an altar, the spiral pillars in the apse, and the elegant columns of the nave.   In front of this church trams start for Cornigliano, Sestri Ponente, and Pegli every 10 minutes.

We now pass along the Via Nuovissima, and at No. 6 descend to San Siro, which was the cathedral church of Genoa till 985.   The high altar is by Puget.   The fresco on the roof by G. B. Carlone.   The marble columns are all of one piece.   Near San Siro, in the confined little square No. 6 Piazza Pellicceria, is the Palazzo Spinola, with many beautiful paintings, such as the Martyrdom of St. Barthélemy and St. Laurent by Ribera, the Four Seasons by Bassano, Virgin and Child by Guercino, a Magdalene by Guido, St. Anne and the Virgin by L. Giordano, the Last Supper by G. C. Procaccini, S. Jerome by Spagnolletti, a Holy Family by Albani, the Four Evangelists by Van Dyck. In the fourth room is the gem of the collection, a Holy Family by Rubens. The frescoes are by Tavarone, G. Sebastiano, Ferrari, and Gallery.

In the Via Garibaldi, No. 18, is the **Palazzo Rosso** (Galleria Brignoli), with a small but valuable collection of pictures by Italian masters, distributed among the rooms denominated Spring, Summer, Autumn, and Winter. The frescoes on the roofs are by Toila, Ferrari, and Carloni. It contains also a good library.

No. 9 Via Garibaldi is the *Municipicio* or City Chambers, a splendid building, entirely of marble, and covered with frescoes representing incidents in the history of Genoa. All the rooms and galleries are open to the public excepting the council-chamber, the Sala Rossa, and the Sala Verde. In the first hall (the council-chamber) is a portrait of Columbus in mosaic, and on the roof a fresco representing him in the presence of Ferdinand and Isabella. In the second, among other paintings, is a triptych ascribed to A. Durer, and in the third (the Sala Verde) a beautiful bust of Columbus. The architect was Rocco Lugaro, the ornaments and figures over the windows are by G. T. Carlone, and the frescoes by Pavarone, Paganelli, Passano, and M. Canzio.

At No. 12 Via Nuova is the **P. Serra**, built, like most of the other palaces in this street, about the year 1552, by the celebrated architect Galeazzo Alessi. The size and distribution of the principal apartments are excellent, and many are beautifully ornamented in fresco by the brothers Semini, particularly the ceiling in the first antechamber, representing the funeral games instituted by Æneas in honour of Anchises. The dining-room was the work of the famous Genoese architect Tagliafico, and is greatly admired for its simplicity and good taste. But the greatest object of attraction in this palace is the grand salon, shining with gold. Along each side are columns of marble gilt, alternating with lofty mirrors reaching from the floor to the roof. The architraves and panels are curiously carved and gilt. The fresco on the roof is by Leon, and represents the triumph of Spinola over the Turks. The roof of the next room was painted by A. Semini.

The Palazzo Adorno, No. 8 Via Garibaldi, contains a good though smaller display of paintings and frescoes. The same may be said of No. 5 in this same street, the P. Spinola.

At No. 6 Via Garibaldi is the P. Doria, with a handsome portico and splendid halls containing a choice collection of paintings by P.

Veronese, Guercino, Murillo, Van Dyck, Domenichino, and Tintoretto. We now enter the Piazza de Ferrari, with the post office, the principal theatre, the H. Gènes, and the Accademia delle Belle Arti, where young men assemble at night to study drawing, painting, and sculpture. Important trams start from this Piazza. The Staglieno tram stops at the cemetery ; the Carignano tram at the church of Carignano.

The second street left from the P. de Ferrari leads to S. Matteo, built in 1278, but altered in 1530 by G. A. Montorsoli at the request of Andrea Doria, relating to whose family are the numerous inscriptions on the church. Over the altar is his sword. The "palaces" in front of the church belonged to the Doria family.

In the Piazza Nuova is S. Ambrogio, entirely covered with beautiful marbles and adorned in much the same style as the church of the Annunziata. Among other paintings it contains a large picture of the Assumption by G. Reni, third chapel right ; St. Ignatius healing one possessed of devils, by Rubens; and over the high altar, by the same master, the Circumcision. The frescoes in the cupolas are by Carloni and Galeotto. The large building to the right is the former Ducal Palace, now the government house. The grand reception room up stairs is ornamented with 54 columns of Brocatello marble, with bases of Siena marble. From the windows is seen the tower of the Embriarci, constructed by Guglielmo Embriarco, the inventor of the movable wooden towers used by Godfrey de Bouillon in his attacks upon Jerusalem.

On the other side of the Ducal Palace is the Cathedral, built in the 11th cent., but repeatedly restored. The exterior and interior are of black and white marble in alternate bands. The façade consists of three large portals resting on spiral, plain, and twisted columns. The arch of the centre porch has an immense span, bordered by bold fascicled work, while over the doorway is the Martyrdom of St. Laurence in relief. In the interior there is a strange mixture of styles. The nave is separated from the aisles by sombre coloured pillars supporting pointed arches, over which runs a series of round-headed arches. The roof of the choir has frescoes by Teverone. The marquetry of the stalls was executed in the 16th cent. The leading feature, however, in this church is *the chapel of St. John the Baptist*, in the centre of the left aisle. It was built in 1490, and ornamented with statues by G. Porta and M. Civitali, of which the best are those representing Zacharias in his official robes, Elizabeth, and Habakkuk. Under a canopy supported by four porphyry columns is the shrine by D. Terrano (1437), said to contain the ashes of John the Baptist, brought from Mirra in

1097. At the end of the right or south aisle is the chapel of Mary, with a Crucifixion by Van Dyck. In the sacristy is preserved a vase once famous under the name of the Sacro Catino (sacred vessel). It was found at Cæsarea, in Palestine, and tradition asserted that it had been presented by the Queen of Sheba to Solomon, and that out of it the Saviour had eaten the paschal lamb with his disciples. It was believed to be of emerald; and a law was passed in 1476, declaring that if any one applied a hard substance to the vase he should suffer death, because it was suspected that the material was only glass.

Below the cathedral at the foot of the Via S. Lorenzo is a cabstand, whence drive by the church of Carignano and the Acqua Sola Gardens to the Via di Circonvallazione, commanding a series of beautiful views of Genoa. From the P. de Ferrari an omnibus runs to Carignano, passing through the Acqua Sola Gardens, 30 c.

S. Maria in Carignano, built 1555-1603 after designs of Galeazzo Alessi, is 165 ft. square, and 174 ft. above the sea. The statues above the entrance, of Mary, Peter, and Paul, are by David. Of the four colossal statues below the dome, St. Sebastian and Bishop Sauli are by Puget; the other two are by Parodi and David. The best of the paintings (covered) are—St. Francis by Guercino, Mary with Sts. Francis and Charles by Procaccini, St. Peter by Piola, and a Descent from the Cross by Cambiaso. But better than all the pictures is the view from the highest gallery on the dome, 368 ft. above the sea, ascended by an excellent stair of 249 steps, fee 25 c. each. The omnibus in the square goes to the Acqua Sola Gardens. From the top of the little wooded hill at the N. W. extremity of the Splanata della Acqua Sola is another fine view.

About 2 m. from Genoa by the western side of the Bisagno is the Campo Santo, the Staglieno cemetery, approached by omnibus every ½ hour from the Piazza de Ferrari. The greater part of the road runs parallel to the Genoa aqueduct arches, which follow the sinuosities and inequalities of the mountain sides for nearly 15 miles.

The front portion of the cemetery is rectangular, 656 ft. wide and 820 ft. long, surrounded by a double arcade of marble arches with a span of 21 ft., and 18½ ft. high. Each arch can contain seven tiers of three coffins each, the end space of each narrow cell allowing just room enough to label the date of the death and the name of the occupant. The poorest people are buried in the ordinary way, in the ground surrounded by the arches. The richest have a whole arch to themselves, where all that money can command in talented sculpture is made to do service to the feelings of bereaved friends, by perpetuating the memory of those they have lost, in the choicest and most costly marbles. These lovely statues appeal more to the sympathy of the spectator than the medley contents of even a famous sculpture-gallery. Above this rise other two galleries, and behind the second on the hill side is another large piece of ground. On a level with the first upper gallery, and approached by 77 long white marble steps bounded by a massive parapet of dark greenstone from the quarries of Pegli, is the mortuary chapel, consisting of a great dome supported on 16 round columns, each of one block of black marble 32½ ft. high. In eight niches round the interior are colossal statues of Bible personages, beginning with Eve. The façade rests on six white marble columns 21 ft. high. The whole vast structure of galleries, stairs, walls, and floors is arched into cells and vaults for the dead. At the N.W. end of Genoa, above the Annunziata, is the workhouse, Albergo dei Poveri, 318 ft. above the sea, on the Via di Circonvallazione, founded in the 17th cent., and containing accommodation for 1300 poor. At the E. end of the city is a large establishment for the insane, called the Regio Manicomio.

The Riviera di Levante; or, Genoa to Pisa.

GENOA   Distance 102½ miles, time 4½ hours by "direct" train.   PISA
MILES FROM   See Maps, pages 199 and 211.   MILES TO

GENOA.—The best winter stations on the Italian Riviera are, $\frac{102½}{}$ with the exception of Bordighera and S. Remo, those situated between Nervi and Rapallo. The coast is exceedingly picturesque and sheltered from the N. winds by precipitous mountains, covered at the base with vineyards, orange and lemon trees, and on the higher zones with olive, peach, and fig trees. Lord Carnarvon has been the first to take advantage of the superior beauties of this part of the Riviera in the choice of a site for a villa on Cape Portofino. Map, p. 211.

$\frac{7½}{}$ NERVI, pop. 8000. *H. et P. Anglais, E. from the station, $\frac{95}{}$ with large garden, 8 to 15 frs. H. et P. Victoria, on the W. side of station, 9 to 12 frs. On the face of the mountain, about 100 ft. above the H. et P. Anglais, the *H. et P. Belle-Vue, 8 to 9 frs., including wine; admirably situated. In the Piazza, near the station, and at the terminus of the Genoa and Nervi trams, is the *P. Suisse, 6 to 8 frs. Opposite, the H. et P. Nervi, 9 to 12 frs. English doctors. Episcopalian service.

Nervi, with the neighbouring town of Bogliasco, forms one continuous narrow street 2 m. long, hemmed in between houses and

220

GENOA
MILES FROM

CHIÁVARI. SPEZIA.

PISA
MILES TO

walls. On the S. side is the sea, on the N. high hills covered with olive trees and studded with churches and cottages. Ten m. S.E. from Nervi is **Santa Margherita** Ligure, pop. 5000. *H. et P. Belle-Vue, 7 to 10 frs. A charmingly situated town at the head of a sheltered tiny bay. In the neighbourhood is the sumptuous villa Spinola, in the midst of beautiful gardens. The prettiest walk is by the road skirting the beach to the village and promontory of Portofino, 3 m. S. To the right or N. is the villa Castello di Pagi, and on the fourth hill from the end of the promontory the villa of Lord Carnarvon overlooking the little fishing village of Portofino, and commanding a glorious view.

$\frac{18\frac{1}{4}}{}$ RAPALLO, pop. 6000. H. et P. Europe, 8 to 10 frs. At the $\frac{84}{}$ head of a small bay. A good deal of lace and olive oil is made here. Among the many pretty walks is the one to S. Margherita, 2 m. N., by the low road skirting the beach. The high road is more beautiful, and a trifle longer.

$\frac{24\frac{1}{4}}{}$ CHIÁVARI, pop. 12,000, at the mouth of the Entella. *Inns:* $\frac{78\frac{1}{4}}{}$ Albergo della Fenicé ; Locanda Nazionale ; Caffé Ristorante Priario. One of the best towns on the coast, with well-paved and arcaded streets, substantial houses, and handsome churches containing a few valuable pictures. The most profusely ornamented is, close to the station, the church of the Virgin of Orta, whose "sacred" picture hangs over the high altar. Chiávari manufactures lace and chairs of light wood with twisted straw seats, plain and coloured, called Sedié di Chiávari. Many of the organ-grinders are said to hail from this town. 4½ m. from Chiávari, across the Lavagnaro, is Sestri Levante, pop. 8000. *Hotels :* Grand Hotel, with palm-garden ; Italia. Trains halt a few minutes at this pleasant place, the Segeste of the Romans. Sestri is situated on a bay terminating with a promontory, on which is a garden commanding a grand view. Shortly after passing Riomaggiore, 51½ miles from Genoa, the Gulf of Spezia comes into view, with the promontory of Porto Venere and the island of Palmaria on the right, and in front numerous capes, the chief of which is Cape Corvo. From Sestri to Spezia by carriage and pair, 45 frs.

$\frac{56\frac{1}{4}}{}$ SPEZIA, pop. 11,500, 1 m. from station. Spezia, although $\frac{46}{}$ near good scenery, has nothing attractive itself ; neither does it make a suitable winter residence. It has some excellent hotels bordering the spacious corso along the beach, the best being the "Croce di Malta," a large and handsome building, 10 to 15 frs. Then follow the H.

National ; the Italia ; and, below the arcade, the Brettagna, all first-class, but the Brettagna is the most moderate. Boats with one man, 1½ fr. per hour ; with two men, 2 frs. In 1861 Spezia was made a station of the Italian navy. As a harbour it is one of the finest and largest in the world. Napoleon I. intended to have made it the Mediterranean harbour of France. The Royal Dockyard, at the south-west side of the town, occupies 150 acres ; while the artillery maga-zines, in the bay of S. Vito, cover an area of 100 acres. On the W. side of the bay is the picturesque Porto Venere, the ancient Portus Veneris, 8 m. distant by land, 10 frs. per carriage 1½ hr., or boat 2½ hrs. The marble of Porto Venere is black, with gold-coloured veins.

"To the N.W. and W. of Spezia is a chain of mountains, of which Monte Bergamo, 2109 ft., is the most distant. It may be ascended from the Genoa road, which runs under its N.E. flank. Nearer to Spezia is Monte Parodi with a carriage-road to the top, whence there is a grand panoramic view of the surrounding country. Near this is the village of Biassa, whose inhabitants are supposed to be of Moorish origin. While the N.W. coast of the Gulf of Spezia is rugged and hilly, the northern and eastern portion for about three miles is com-paratively level, which renders it a good walking place for invalids. The valleys of the Migliarini, at the northern extremity of the eastern half of the Spezia valley, are also excellently adapted for invalids, especially at that time of the day when the sea-breeze is blowing freshly. A favourite excursion from Spezia by water is to Lerici and San Terenzo, about 6 m. S.E. The steamer sails at noon, and returns at 4. Lerici is in a most sheltered situation, and remains in sunshine an hour after the sun has set at Spezia. The house, a square old-fashioned Italian villa, which Shelley occupied in 1822, is on the shore close to the sea, near the village."—*The Riviera*, by Dr. Sparks. After Spezia, the train crosses the Magra, the ancient boundary be-tween Italy and Liguria, and arrives at

67¾
— SARZANA, pop. 11,200. *Hotels :* New York ; Londres. 34¾
— This ancient town, with the picturesque fortress of Sarzanella, formerly belonged to the Grand Duke of Tuscany, who, in the 15th century, ceded it to the Genoese in exchange for Leghorn, at that time a mere village. Sarzana was the birthplace of Tommaso Parentucelli, who, from a simple monk, was in 1447 elected pope under the title of Nicholas V., and who constituted his native place into a bishopric. He was a great patron of learning and founder of the Vatican library.

The Bonaparte family lived in this town till 1612, when they removed

222

GENOA
MILES FROM

AVENZA.—CARRARA.

PISA
MILES TO

to Corsica. The cathedral (14th cent.) is a plain cruciform edifice, partly of marble and partly of stone. Behind the cathedral, by the first street right, is the citadel, two minutes' distant; and about fifteen minutes' farther, the fortress built by Antelminelli, Lord of Lucca, a beautiful though low machicolated structure on the top of a hill overlooking the railway. Both citadel and castle are partly in ruins, and well seen from the station.

79
⏜ AVENZA. Station for Carrara, 3¼ miles N.E. by branch line. ⏜
Gigs also for Carrara await passengers at the station. Fare, 5 fr.

Carrara (pop. 14,000), situated on the Carrione, formed by the union of the Torano, Fantiscritti and Colonnata streams, descending valleys with valuable marble strata. *Hotels:* The Nazionale, close to the theatre; The Posta, adjoining the Post-office and close to the Accademia. Near the Nazionale is the Italian Protestant chapel. At the station great blocks of marble meet the eye. Passing them and crossing the bridge by Walton's marble works, walk up the Corso Vittorio Emanuele to the Piazza Alberica, with a statue of Maria Beatrice and a short arcade. Near the right side of this piazza are the two hotels. The road to the left leads up the Carrione to the valley of the stream Torano, and the village of the same name, ¾ of a mile from Carrara. The valley now becomes narrower, the road worse, and the heavily laden bullock-carts more numerous, carrying and dragging blocks of marble. To the left rises Mount Crestola, and immediately opposite Poggio Silvestro, Polvaccio di Betogli, and the Mossa del Zampone, from all of which the Romans procured statuary marble, and which still continue to yield some of the finest quality. All the quarries (cavé), of which there are 400, employing 6000 men, are a good way up the face of the mountains. The ascent to them is over steep slippery marble debris. The nearest and the easiest " cavé " to visit are on Mt. Crestola. The other quarries are in the valleys of the Colonnata and of its affluent the Fantiscritti. In the Fantiscritti mines Roman relics have been found. Any boy will do to show the way to the rivers Carrione and Torano, and when there it is impossible to go wrong; but to visit any particular mines a guide is necessary. Fee 4 fr. Besides the common road there is a railway for the conveyance of marble blocks from the valley of the Torano to the Marina or Port of Carrara. Many antique Roman statues are of marble from Carrara, anciently called Luni. The marble of which the Greek statues are made is from Paros, and from Mount Pentelicon, near Athens. Carrara is a healthy and busy town, not troubled in the least with mosquitoes in winter and spring. The great business of the town is the transporting and dressing of marble; and the principal establishments the studios of the artists, where statues, monuments, chimney-pieces, and ornaments are sculptured and exposed for sale. Admission readily granted.

The churches present nothing remarkable; the marble of the exterior walls of the cathedral has become brown, while that of the interior is nearly black. In the Accademia delle Belle Arti are some good copies of the works of great artists and a few Roman antiquities found chiefly in the mines of Fantiscritti.

78½

26½ MASSA is about a mile from the railway, by a good road, at the foot of Mt. Castagnola, which, with the still loftier peaks in the rear, Mts. Tambura and Rotondo, protect it from the northerly and easterly winds, so that it may be considered one of the winter stations on the Mediterranean. The climate is mild, as the vigorous orange trees in the gardens testify. In the neighbourhood are many pleasant walks, both on the plain and up the valleys. The Hotel Giappone in the Piazza Aranci, although a plain house, is clean, and is kept by kindly people. The town is quiet; there are a few workers and dealers in marble, but the principal occupation is agricultural. The ducal palace in the square was once the residence of Elisa Bacciocchi, Napoleon's sister. Valuable marble quarries. Pop. 5000.

84½ PIETRASANTA, pop. 1000. *Inn:* Europa. A poor town, 20½ with marble works near the station outside of the walls, where baths are chiefly made. On the first large house, right hand of square, a tablet informs us that in it Michael Angelo Buonarrotti, on the 27th April 1518, "strinse nuovi contratti per la facciata di S. Lorenzo in Firenze." S. Martino (13th cent.) has a fine wheel window, of the kind found in nearly all the churches in this neighbourhood. At the entrance opposite the Campanile (1380) is a font about the same period. In the interior of the church are handsome marble columns, confessionals, pulpit, and font. The domes and semidomes are painted in fresco. Next is the Uffizio Municipale, with, in front, a statue to Leopold II., 1848. Then follows St. Agostino (14th cent.), all within a few yards of each other. In the neighbourhood are quicksilver and argentiferous mines and the Quarceta marble quarries.

90¾ VIAREGGIO, pop. 20,000. *Hotels:* Russie; Pension Anglo- 14½ Americaine; Commercio. A favourite sea-bathing station of the inhabitants of Pisa and Florence. On the 22d of July 1882 the body of Shelley was found cast on this beach. A few miles eastward, towards Lucca, is Lake Massaciuccoli, and the Roman ruins called the Bagni di Nerone, about 6 m. W. from Lucca in a beautiful country.

105 PISA, pop. 26,300. *Hotels:* On right bank of the Arno, in the Lung 'Arno Regio, the *Grand Hotel; *Bretagna; *Nettuno; Londra. Close to station, right hand, the *Minerva et de la Ville; Washington;

left hand, Commerce. Behind the H. Bretagna is the Anglican church. On the left side of the Arno, opposite the Victoria, is the Post-office. Cab-stand at the station. *Fares.*—From the station to the cathedral, with from one to two passengers, 1 fr. ; from three to four, 1 fr. 15 sous. The hour, 2 fr. From the station go straight up the Via Vittorio Emanuele to the Arno, where cross the bridge and walk down the river to the fifth street right, the Via Santa Maria, crossed by an arch at the commencement. The Via Santa Maria leads directly to the Piazza del Duomo, containing, in a row, the Leaning Tower, the Cathedral, and the Baptistery, and immediately behind, the Campo Santo, with frescoes considerably effaced, yet valuable as specimens of the Tuscan school of the 14th and 15th centuries. Fee for the Campo Santo 25 cents each.

The *Cathedral*, commenced in 1063 by the Greek architect Buschetto, was completed in 1092. The exterior is adorned with a range of blind arches decorated with party-coloured marble. Four open arcades, similarly constructed, rise over the western entrance, with the beautiful bronze doors of John of Bologna, as well as over those at the southern entrance by Bonano. Both doors are covered with a profusion of figures in delicately wrought iron, representing saints, prophets, and various other objects, enclosed in an elegant border of birds, foliage, fruits, and flowers. The internal length of the church is 311½ ft., and of the transepts 252 ft. The roof of the nave is 109 ft. high. A double row of columns runs up the nave, and a single row along the transepts and choir. Sixty of them are of oriental granite, and the rest (14) of fine marble, and each of one piece. The arches resting on them are semicircular, and are mostly in alternate layers of white and black marble. The roof is covered with richly gilt panelling. The altars are by Michael Angelo, and are arranged in pairs, each couple opposite each other being alike, excepting the two at the opposite ends of the transepts, which, however, are similar in design. One represents the fall by woman, and the other the reconciliation by woman in the ascension of the Virgin. Over the high altar, on the semidome, is a colossal Mosaic by G. Gaddi, in 1325. Among the best of the paintings are four of saints by A. del Sarto, near the bishops' chairs. Here also are paintings of Moses and Aaron, St. Luke and St. John, by Beccafumi, and the Sacrifice of Abraham and the Entombment by Sodoma. Upon a pier of the right transept is a St. Agnes by A. del Sarto, and on the corresponding pier of the left transept a Madonna by Perino del Vaga. In the right

Pisa. Leaning Tower—Baptistery—Cemetery.

transept notice the altar of St. Blaise, the chapel and tomb of S. Ranieri, the great picture of the Virgin with Saints by del Vaga and Sogliani. In the left (north) transept is the chapel of the Holy Sacrament, with a beautiful silver ciborium. The windows are small, but have some fine stained glass of the 14th and 15th cents. Galileo, while a student at Pisa, discovered, by observing the oscillations of the lamp suspended in the nave, that the vibrations of a pendulum are synchronous, or recur at equal intervals whether great or small.

The *Campanile* or leaning tower is a cylindrical edifice built of square blocks of compact marble, and consisting of a well-designed solid basement, 159 ft. in circumference, with walls 13 ft. thick, above which rise six open arcaded galleries, supported by 200 granite and marble columns. Over the sixth arcade rises a round tower 27 ft. high. The entire height is 183 ft., the mean diameter of the main portion 52 ft., and the deflection from the perpendicular 11 ft. 2 inches, exclusive of the cornice, which projects 32 inches more. It was commenced in 1174, and finished 1350. The ascent is very easy, by a stair 3 ft. wide, formed in the wall ; but not fewer than three are allowed to visit the top at the same time. Fee for the party, 1 fr. The keeper lives in one of the small houses (No. 14) nearly opposite.

The Baptistery is a circular building, 361½ feet in circumference, surmounted by a dome 180 feet high, and constructed after the designs of Diotisalvi. It was commenced in 1153 and finished towards the end of the 14th cent. Above the third storey rises the dome, intersected by long lines of very prominent fretwork, meeting in a cornice near the top, and terminating in a small dome crowned with a statue of St. John the Baptist, the titular saint of all such edifices. In the interior eight large Sardinian granite columns and four marble piers support twelve arches, over which rises the tier of piers and arches which support the cupola, within conical, but externally hemispherical. In the centre stands an octagon marble font for the baptism of adults, with four circular compartments at opposite sides for the baptism of infants. The beautiful pulpit by Niccolo da Pisa (1260) is ornamented with bas-reliefs, and supported on seven columns. Behind the Baptistery is the *Campo Santo*, founded about the year 1189 by the Archbishop Ubaldo. It is a rectangle 424 feet long by 145 broad, and surrounded by a broad gallery with a plain wall to the exterior, and 62 mullioned arches with quatrefoil tracery towards the interior. The inner side of the wall is covered with paintings in fresco, begun about the year 1300, and continued till 1670. Immediately to the left on entering is the

Q

monument of the oculist Andrea Vacca by Thorwaldsen. To the right commence frescoes illustrating incidents in the life of St. Ranieri, the patron saint of Pisa, by Andrea da Firenzi, 1377. Those beyond the second door illustrate the temptations and miracles of hermits in the Theban wilderness, by the Lorenzetti. Between Nos. 39 and 40, Hell. Above 38, the Day of Judgment. Then, by Orcagna, the Power of Death,—filling those living in pleasure with horror, but those in sorrow with joy. Now follow (in the eastern side) the oldest of the three chapels, and frescoes illustrating the Crucifixion, Resurrection, and Ascension. On the north wall the most interesting frescoes are by Puccio Orvieto, 14th cent., illustrative of events in the Old Testament. On the west wall is hung part of the chain the Pisanos caused to be drawn across the mouth of the harbour, which, however, Conrad Doria broke through in 1290, burnt the fleet of Pisa, and carried off the chain to Genoa. A few years ago, according to the inscription, the Genoese returned it to Pisa. On the wall, under the chain, is the monument to Giov. Niccoli Pisano ; and, a little to the right, a Madonna by that famous sculptor. The empty space within the cloisters was once the common burying-ground of the city. It is filled, to the depth of ten feet, with earth brought from the Holy Land by the galleys of Pisa. Among the other churches may be mentioned Santa Maria della Spina, on the bank of the Arno (a low square church)—an excellent specimen of the Moorish-Gothic introduced into Italy in the 11th cent. The churches of St. Matteo, St. Pierino, St. Michele in Borgo, St. Andrea, and St. Francisco, contain a few curious and some good paintings, with other antiquities. The church of St. Stephano is reputed to contain the bones of St. Stephen. The palaces of the Cavaliers, Lanfreducci, Seta, and Casa Mecherini, are worthy of notice.

Near the Grand Hotel is the Sapienza or University, founded by the Emperor Henry VII. The quays and bridges of Pisa are extensive, and well-constructed. Four miles from Pisa are the baths of St. Julian, considered beneficial for diseases of the liver and gout (see next page).

Between Pisa and Leghorn there are trains nearly every hour, distance 11¼ miles. **Leghorn** (pop. 90,000). *Hotels :* In the Piazza del Cantiere, the Nord, fronting the harbour ; and close by, in the Via Vittorio Emanuéle, the Bretagne ; New York ; France ; and at No. 59 of the same street, Il Giappone. Anglican church in the Scala degli Hollandesi. Presbyterian church, No. 3 Via degli Elisi. Cabs per hour, 1½ fr. Boat from the hotel to the steamer, 2 fr. Leghorn has many handsome and well-paved streets ; among the best of them is the

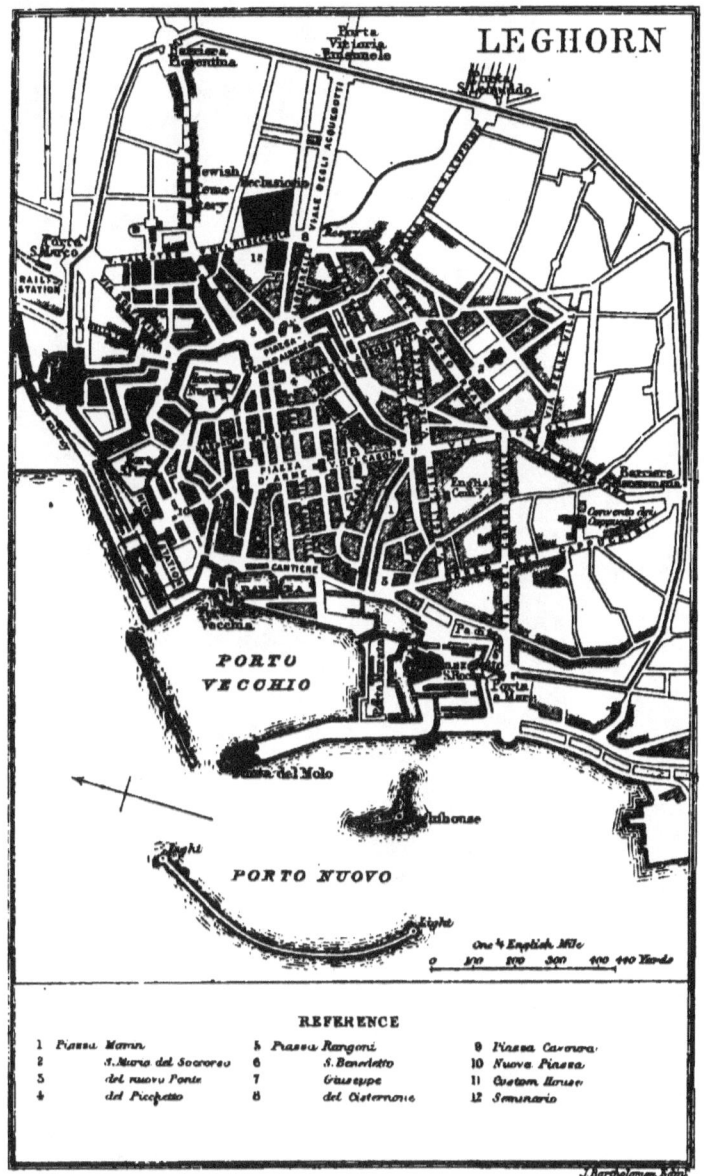

LEGHORN

REFERENCE

1 Piazza Mann
2 S. Maria del Soccorso
3 del nuovo Ponte
4 del Picchetto

5 Piazza Rangoni
6 S. Benedetto
7 Giuseppe
8 del Cisternone

9 Piazza Cavoura
10 Nuova Piazza
11 Custom House
12 Seminario

J. Bartholomew, Edin.

Via Vittorio Emanuele, which, commencing at the head of the harbour from the Piazza dei Cantieri, traverses the principal square, the Piazza d'Armi, with the cathedral, and extends to the Piazza Carlo Alberto. Its continuation, on the other side of the square, the Via Larderel, extends to a large building on the right hand crowned with a semi-dome. This is the grand reservoir, supplied with water from the mountains Colognone by an aqueduct 12 m long. Smollett died at Leghorn just after completing "Humphrey Clinker," and was buried in the English cemetery. Steam-boats every week for Bastia in Corsica, for Porto Torres in Sardinia, and for Marseilles and Genoa.

Pisa to Florence by Lucca and Pistoja.

Distance 62 miles east. See Map of Turin to Florence, page 199.

PISA   FLORENCE
MILES FROM   MILES TO

                                                62

PISA. The direct line to Florence is by Pontedera and Empoli. Distance, 49 miles. Time, 2 hours and 10 minutes. The first station by the Lucca route is *San Giuliano*, with its thermal springs, temp. 109° and 84° Fahr., rising from a calcareous rock at the foot of the wooded Monti Pisani. The waters "are used internally in chronic hepatic complaints, in gravel, and some renal affections; in dysentery, and dyspepsia attended with pain and vomiting."—Madden's *Health Resorts*. After Giuliano, we reach the Rigoli station, whence the line extends along the left side of the Serchio, enclosed within its bed by expensive embankments.

15 / LUCCA (pop. 22,000). Each portmanteau taken from the 47 / station to the cab, 6 sous; bag, 2 sous. Cabs await passengers, 1 fr.; portmanteau, 4 sous.

Sights.—A walk on the ramparts, 3 miles in circumference, and a visit to the Duomo and to the Picture-Gallery. To the south of Lucca, near the station, is an ancient aqueduct of 459 arches.

Hotels: Universo, between the Duomo and the Piazza Napoleone, a first class-hotel; Croce di Malta, near the Piazza Napoleone; and the Corona, near the Piazza also, but towards the church of St. Michele. Diligence to the Baths of Lucca start from a court opposite the H. Corona. Distance, 17 miles. Fare, 3 fr. Carriage, 15 fr. Money-changer in the Piazza dell' Erba, off the P. Napoleone. Lucca is one of the most ancient cities in Italy. Originally it belonged to the Etrurians, but was taken from them by the Ligurians, and colonised by the Romans about 170 years before the birth of our Lord. The most remarkable event that distinguished it in ancient times was the interview which took place here between Cæsar, Pompey, and Crassus, and which attracted to the town half the senate and nobility of Rome. After the fall of the Roman empire, Lucca was governed by princes of its own, from one of whose race, Azon II., of the house of Este, the royal families of Brunswick and England are descended. The town is in the form of the letter O, surrounded by ramparts which afford a most agreeable drive. At the railway end is the Piazza Napoleone, and near it all the principal sights. One entire side of the Piazza is occupied by the Palazzo Ducale, now the Palazzo Provinciale, a vast and substantial edifice, built in 1578, enclosing two large courts, and containing the prefecture, the post-office, the picture-gallery, and the government offices. The Picture-Gallery, open every day (except Mondays), between 10 and 2, although small, contains some precious works, in handsome halls. In the first room is a Madonna della Misericordia, and in the second, the Creator with Mary Magdalene and St. Catherine, both by Fra. Bartolommeo, in 1515 and 1509. Also pictures by Reni, Zucchero, and Tiziano. In the Sala da Ballo, painted in fresco by Luigi Adamolli Milanese in 1819, are a Madonna by Perugini ; a full length portrait of Napoleon's sister Elisa ; and two ancient pictures on wood—a Nativity, and a Christ with Saints. The remainder of the pictures are in the rooms which were occupied by Maria Aloysia Borbonia (Marie Louise), whose monument by Bartolini (1843) stands in the centre of the square. Leaving the Piazza Napoleone, by the street at the end of the small avenue, we come to another open space containing San Giovanni and the Duomo, and between the two churches a house called the "Administrazione del opera della chiesa ;" where, among other things, are preserved *La Croce dei Pisani*, an elaborately wrought gilt silver cross, by B. Baroni in 1350, and the gold lamp, weighing 24 lbs., which formerly hung in front of the Tempietto in the Duomo. They are shown at any time, but a fr. is expected. The Cathedral or Duomo of St. Martino was commenced by Anselmo Badagio, who, three years afterwards, as Pope Alexander II., blessed the enterprise of the Norman invader of England. The façade, with its three tiers of columned galleries, was built in 1204, the choir in 1308, and the triforium in 1400. The sculptures of the portico are subjects from the life of St. Martin. Over the door on the left is a Descent from the Cross, by Nicolo di Pisa, 1233.

LUCCA. CATHEDRAL—THE TEMPIETTO—S. GIOVANNL

Loftiness and simplicity, verging on plainness, characterise the interior of this church, as well as those of all the others in Lucca, with the exception of San Romano, which is profusely decorated. The windows are small and filled with modern glass, excepting the three at the eastern end, which are by P. Ugolino. All the pictures are covered, excepting on Sundays and feast-days, but the custodian can always be found in the sacristy, who shows the church for a franc. Commencing at the first altar, right hand from main entrance, Nativity, by Passignano ; second, Adoration of the Magi, P. Zucchero ; third, Last Supper, Tintoretto ; fourth, Crucifixion, Passignano ; fifth, Resurrection. In south transept, west side, is the monument to Pietro da Noceto, one of the many admirable works by Matteo Civitali, to whose genius the church owes its best sculpture, which he contributed during a period of nearly thirty years from 1472. The angels on the altar in the Chapel del Sagramento, opposite the monument, as well as the whole of the chaste white marble altar in the Chapel of St. Regulus, adjoining the sacramental chapel, are by him. On the left side of the high altar is the altar to "Christo Liberatori," by G. Bologna, and adjoining, La Cappella del Santuario, where again we find the beautiful handiwork of Civitali displayed on the altar and reliquaries on both sides. The Madonna which forms the reredos of the altar is by Fra Bartolommeo. This picture and the Madonna by Ghirlandaio (1400), in the sacristy, are the two gems in the church. Just outside the Cappella del Santuario is a recumbent figure of *Ilaria del Carretto* by Jacopo della Quercia (1444), unfortunately slightly mutilated, yet a beautiful imitation of the repose of nature transferred to statuary. In the north aisle is the Tempietto, a small octagonal chapel standing apart, in which is preserved the cedar wood crucifix, 8th or 9th cent., said to have been carved by Nicodemus with the assistance of an angel. The fresco on the left side of the main entrance into the Duomo represents him cutting it out. This cross is exhibited three times a year. The embroidery on the red curtain is an exact copy. The figure of S. Sebastian on the Tempietto, as well as the elegant pulpit opposite, are by Civitali. Opposite the cathedral is San Giovanni, founded in the 12th cent. The baldness of its great walls is partly relieved by the coloured panelled ceiling. Leaving the Piazza Napoleone by the western corner of the Palazzo Provinziale, we soon reach the Piazza and Church of San Michele, founded in the 8th cent., with a lofty façade composed of tiers of variously shaped columns. Continuing in the same direction towards the ramparts, we reach S. Frediano, of the

7th cent., with a large Mosaic (12th cent.) over the main entrance. Just within it, on each side, are frescoes by Ghirlandaio. To the right is an ancient circular font about 9 feet in diameter, beautifully carved in relief by Magister Robertus in 1151. The font at present used is against the wall, and is by N. Civitali, the nephew of Matteo. The second chapel on the right contains the tomb of St. Zeta, the patroness of Lucca, in a sarcophagus on the altar. Third chapel beyond this (east side) is a coronation of the Virgin by Francia, and on the opposite wall of the same chapel a curious old carving in relief, representing the assumption of the Virgin. On the opposite side of the church is a chapel covered with ancient frescoes by Aspertino, one of which represents the transporting to the church of the cross made by Nicodemus after it had been found in the sea. By the side of it is St. Augustine being baptised by St. Ambrosius at Milan ; and above them, in the semicircle, an entombment. Opposite is S. Frediano (who was an Irishman) staying by prayer an encroachment of the sea, and an Adoration of the Magi. Above is St. Ambrosius instructing his disciples. On the ceiling, God surrounded by Angels, Saints, and Prophets. 3½ m. from Lucca is the Villa di Marlia, in the midst of beautiful grounds.

The Baths of Lucca.

17 miles from Lucca. See Map, page 199.

The road ascends by the left bank of the river Serchio, through pleasing scenery, passing the town of Muriano, situated on the right side of the river. About 13 miles from Lucca is the curious bridge of the Maddalena, consisting of four arches, the arch next the village of Borgo being disproportionately large, and with a gradient from the bank to the centre of 60°. It is only 4 feet wide, and, although built in 1322, is the only bridge across the Serchio that withstood uninjured the great flood of 1836, when the Serchio attained in three hours a height till then unknown, and swept away with irresistible fury all the other bridges, and broke up the mounds, dikes, and embankments. The two villages (pop. 9500) which go under the name of the Baths of Lucca are *Il Serraglio* on the left bank, and *Corsena* on the right bank of the Lima, near its junction with the Serchio. On the hill behind Corsena are the springs and bathing establishments. By the side of the Lima is the Bagno Cardinali, close to the Casino ; and about 100 feet above the Cardinali is the Bagno Bernabó. A short way westward, overlooking the valley of the Lima, is the Bagno Doccebasse, and immediately below it the Bagno dello Spedale-Demidoff, for the exclusive use of the poor. On the top of the hill, among some houses, is the Bagno Caldo, and a little to the east, standing by itself, the Bagno San Giovanni. *Hotels:* the best are Pagnini's Hotel and Pension, next the Casino ; and the America, nearer the bridge. On the opposite side of the river, in Il Serraglio, are the New York, and the Corona, plainer houses. A mile up the river by the right bank, along a beautiful road, the Strada Elisa, is another village, which is also included in the Baths of Lucca, the Bagno alla Villa, the most beautifully situated of the three. *Hotels :* At the entrance of the village, the H. and P. Queen Victoria. At the foot of the hill on which the bathing establishment is situated, the H. and P. du Pavillon and the Anglican chapel. Near them the H. and P. du Parc. The pension price in all, both here and at Corsena, is from 7 to 11 frs. *Cabs :* First hour, 2 fr. ; afterwards 1½ fr. Numerous furnished houses to let. From 400 to 1000 fr. for six months.

The bathing establishments are fitted up with every modern appliance. The baths are rather small. Chemically the different springs are very similar, but in temperature they vary ; the coolest is the Doccebasse, 85° Fahr., and the hottest the Bagno Caldo, 133° Fahr. The principal ingredients are sulphates and carbonates of lime, chlorides of soda and magnesia, and carbonate of iron. The total amount of saline matter being 15 grs. to the pint. On a tablet at the entrance to the baths of La Villa is inscribed a list of the diseases cured by the water ; but their principal action is on the digestive organs, and through them sympathetically on the whole animal economy. Besides, a great deal of the beneficial effect said to be produced by the water ought with more reason to be ascribed to the delightful mountain air, and the charming walks, drives, and rides, which entice visitors to spend the greater part of the day in healthy rambles. The surrounding country is beautiful—steep mountains covered with vines, chestnuts and oaks rise on each side of the river ; while well-made paths and roads wend their way up through these vineyards and forests to multitudes of points of various heights, commanding charming views. Season, May to October.

$\frac{40\frac{1}{2}}{\cdot}$ PISTOJA (pop. 13,600). *Hotels* : Globe et Londres ; Inghil- $\frac{21\frac{1}{2}}{\cdot}$ terra, both in the Piazza Cino. Cabs from the station to the hotels, 1 fr. ; portmanteau, 20 c. Next the H. Inghilterra is the church of S. Giovanni, erected at the end of the 12th cent., in alternate layers of black and white marble. The sculptured pulpit, resting on lions, is supposed to be by Fra Guglielmo of Pisa, 1270. The centre of interest is in the Piazza Duomo, easily found from different parts of the town by means of the lofty Campanile, the "Torre del Podesta," which rises above all the other buildings. By the side of it is the Duomo, a plain edifice, built in 1240. Over the central door is a Madonna, with angels, by A. della Robbia, and over the side-door frescoes by Balducci and Giovanni Christiani, 1369. To the right, on entering, is the monument to the jurist Cino (1336). In the upper tier he is represented addressing an assembly, accompanied by six other doctors, while below he is represented in his class-room lecturing to nine students. The altar of the chapel, to the right of the high altar, is of solid silver. It is generally covered, but by applying at the sacristy a man will uncover it for 2 fr. It remained unfinished for more than 150 years (1314-1466), and is said to be the finest piece of silversmith's work of that time in Italy, and that 416 lbs. of silver were employed in its execution. Below the chancel is a crypt. Fronting the Duomo is the *Baptistery*, begun 1339 (by C. di Nese), an elegant octagonal structure, also in alternate layers of black and white marble, each corner terminating in a pinnacle. The font is quadrangular, of pan-elled marbles, and constructed in the 13th cent. Outside, near the door, is a beautiful stone pulpit. Adjoining is the Palazzo del Podestá (now the seat of the Tribunale Civile), constructed in 1367, and restored in 1864. The vaults and soffits of the massive arches are covered with the armorial bearings of the former mayors of the town ; while, to the left of the entrance, are still the stone-seats and tables where they sat in judgment. Opposite is the Palazzo Municipale (14th cent.), and a little way down the street, the Ospedale del Ceppo (13th cent.), with a coloured terra-cotta frieze. Near the two hotels is the church of *S. Maria dell' Umilta*, built in 1509 by Ventura Vitoni. In the vesti-bule are large frescoes by Vasari. Near it is *S. Andrea* (12th cent.), with quaint reliefs over the entrance door, and in the interior a pre-cious marble pulpit, sculptured by Giovanni da Pisa, 1298-1301. The beadle, for a trifle, illuminates this piece of elaborate sculpture, when it is seen to still greater advantage. Between the two last churches is *S. Filippo da Neri*, with such a quantity of frescoes, representing angels and saints in glory, that even the visitor on entering feels himself among clouds also. In the Piazza Prato is S. Francesco, with some good frescoes and altar pieces. In the centre of the nave is the tomb of an Englishman, Thomas de Weston, Doctor Legum, 1408. The word pistol is said to be derived from the name of this town, as they have been manufactured here from a very early date. Catiline lost his life in a battle fought near Pistoia, B.C. 62, and the precise spot where he is said to have fallen is marked by a tower.

Passengers from Pisa to Florence have generally to change carriages at Pistoja.

11¼ m. from Florence and 50¼ m. from Pisa is Prato, pop. 13,100. *Hotels :* Giardinetto, Contrucci, surrounded by ancient walls, and de-fended by a castle built by the Ghibelines. The interior and exterior of the Cathedral are faced with white and green marble in bands. The nave has columns of serpentine. The elevated choir has good frescoes by Filippo Lippi, and in a chapel are others by Agnolo Gaddi (1365).

FLORENCE.   HOTELS AND PENSIONS.

61½ m. from Pisa by Lucca, or 49 m. by Empoli, is Florence, 357 m. from Turin, 82 m. from Bologna, 134 m. from Piacenza, 196 m. from Rome, and 60¼ m. from Leghorn.

FLORENCE, on the Arno, pop. 169,000. *Hotels and Apartments:* On the right or north side of the Arno, the Grand Hôtel Royal de la Paix ; de la Ville ; Grand Hôtel d'Italie ; Washington ; Grand Hôtel Nueva York ; Gran Bretagna ; del Arno ; and just behind the Paix, the Russie.   All these hotels have a south exposure, and are greatly run after in winter.   Charge from 10 to 16 frs. per day, according to the room.   The following charge from 9 to 13 frs., and are situated in the new streets a little way back from the Arno, and near the Cascine or Park of Florence (north-west side of plan) :—Hôtel and Pension Corona d'Italia, Via Montebello ; Hôtel and Pension Iles Britanniques in No. 42 ; and Hôtel and Pension Venise in No. 33 Via della Scala.   In the Iles Britanniques are also furnished apartments at from 250 frs. to 400 frs. per month.   Hôtel and Pension Couronne d'Angleterre, Via Solferino ; Hôtel and Pension Anglo-Americain, Via Garibaldi ; and the Universo in the Corso Vitt. Emmanuele. In the busy parts of the town, and charging rather less than the above, the Hôtel Milan No. 12 Via Cerretani ; Hôtel and Pension Angleterre, Via Panzani ; and at No. 21 of same street, Hôtel Bonciani, with front also to the Piazza S. Maria Novella.   Near the bridge La Santa Trinitá, and in the Via Tornabuoni are the Europe and Nord.   In the Via Porta Rossa the Hôtel Porta Rossa ; in the Via della Spada the Ville de Paris ; in the Via Condotta, La Luna ; in the Piazza S. Maria Novella (near the station) Hôtel Roma ; Minerva ; Bonciani, with furnished apartments ; and by the side of the station, La Posta and Rebecchino.   In the Piazza Maria Novella there are omnibuses for Sesto Fiorentino and a large cab-stand.   Conveniently situated for visiting the sights, and not expensive (from 7 to 9 frs. per day), are the H. d'Espagne above the Restaurant Etruria and the Etoile d'Italie in the V. Calzaioli.   Pension Suisse, Via Tornabuoni ; Le Phœnix, Via dei Martelli ; Lion Blanc (in which also single rooms are let), Via Vigna Nuova ; Cavour, Via del Proconsolo ; Commerce, Piazza di S. Maria Novella ; Hôtel and Pension Rudolfo, Via della Scala.   Furnished apartments all over the town. Just outside the Porta Romana, in the Viale Petrarcha, furnished apartments cost from 250 to 400 frs. the month.   The most expensive as well as the most fashionable are those situated on the right bank of the Arno ; but in the streets a little way back from the Arno apartments can be had for less.   It is of very great importance in winter to have bedrooms with a south exposure. Those with a north exposure feel cold even on a sunny day. People who take furnished rooms can dine at very moderate rates in restaurants, such as the Toscana or the Etruria, both in the Via Calzaioli. Best money-changers and restaurants in the Via Calzaioli, between the Piazza della Signoria and del Duomo. Fioravanti and Co., 5 Via Cerretani, change circular notes as well.

Protestant Churches.—American Church, 17 Via dei Serragli ; American Episcopal, 11 Piazza del Carmine ; English Episcopal, 5 Via del Maglio ; Scotch Church, 11 Lungarno Guicciardini.

Cab Tariff.—The course, 1 fr. ; night (between 7 P.M. to 6 A.M.), 1 fr. 30 c. Time, first half-hour, 1 f. 30 c. ; every successive half-hour, 70 c. Large trunks, 50 c. ; portmanteau, 25 c. Omnibuses run between the Piazza della Signoria and the old city gates. Fare, 10 c. ; Sundays, 15 c.

Best maps of Italy and of the environs of Florence at the office of the Topografico Militare, No. 8 Via Sapienza, near the Annunziata. Best plans of the town published by Pineider, in the Piazza della Signoria, and Bettini, No. 12 Via Tornabuoni. They also publish excellent little guides to Florence, with complete catalogues of all the pictures and statues in the various museums and churches. Pineider's is published in English likewise, and costs only a franc. They have a similar one for Rome. For the investigation and study of art in Florence, see the works, *Walks in Florence* by Susan and Joanna Horner, 2 vols., Isbister and Co., London, and volume 3 of *Hare's Cities of Italy.*

It is fatiguing, and unwise in those who are not students, to wander into every part of Florence to gaze upon every picture and every figure by a great master. The best are all in a few places, which, fortunately, are near each other. For oil-paintings the combined galleries of the Uffizi and Pitti are sufficient. In them the most important room is the Tribuna (p. 238), containing the concentrated excellence of both galleries in painting and antique sculpture. Besides what are in the Tribuna, Raphael has eleven pictures in the Pitti, of which the most famous is No. 266 in the Stanza dell' Educazione di Giove (see p. 244). Michael Angelo's finest sculpture is in the new sacristy of San Lorenzo (see p. 265), but the best collection of his works is in the *National Museum* (see p. 261). His David is in the *Accademia delle Belle Arti* (see p. 272). In the National Museum is the best collection of sculpture by great *Italian artists,* such as Michael Angelo, G. Bologna, Luca and Andrea della Robbia, Ghiberti, Brunelleschi, Donatello, Pisano, Ben-

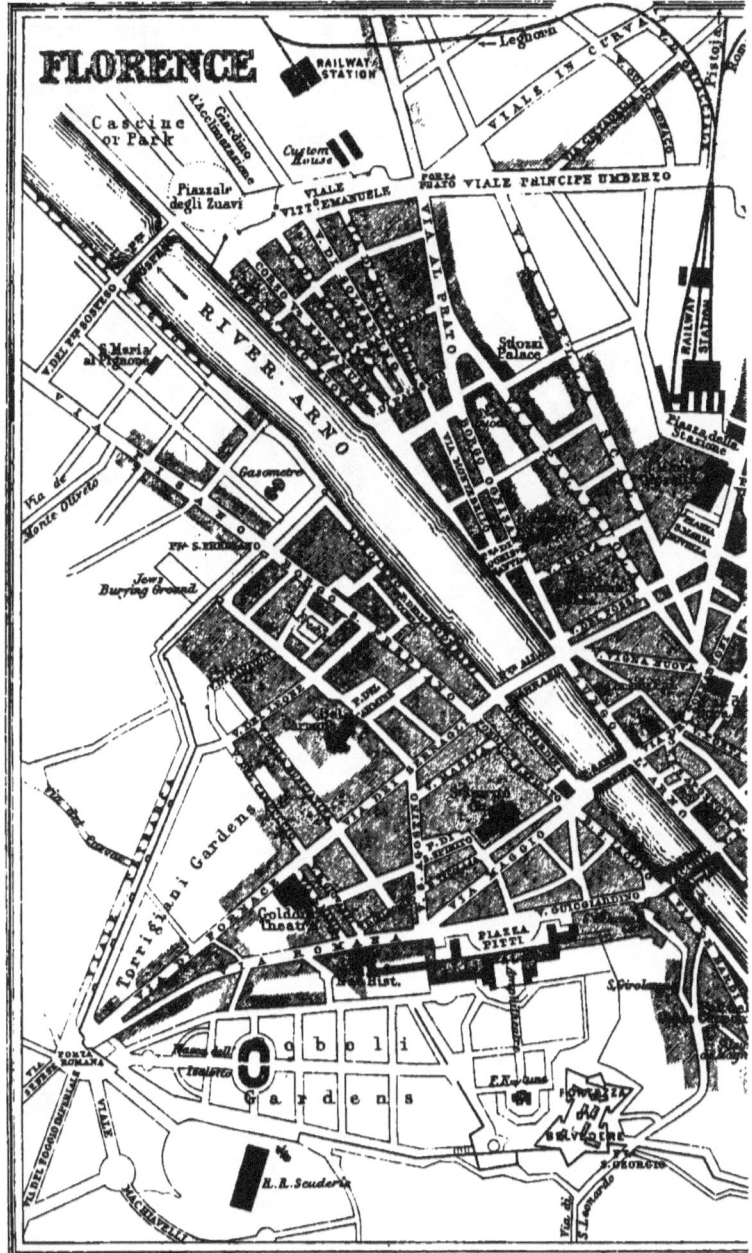

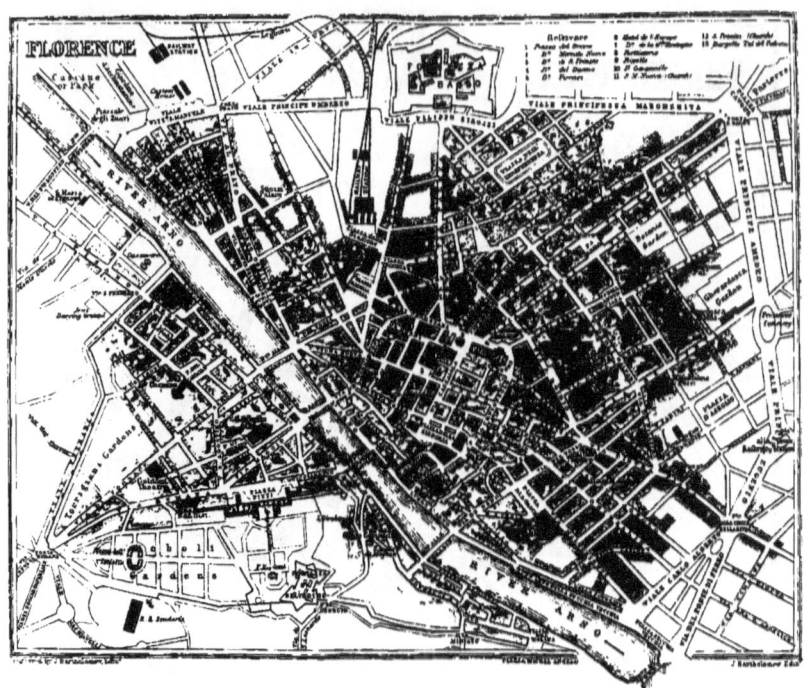

235

venuto Cellini, Rossi, Mino da Fiesole, and Verrochino, chiefly in the
first and sixth rooms of the first floor, and in the sixth room of the
second floor. Of the churches, the most important are the Duomo or
Cathedral, the Baptistery and Campanile, Santa Croce, San Lorenzo
(but particularly the Sagrestia Nuova and the Cappella dei Principi, attached to St. Lorenzo), S. Maria Novella, and the Annunziata. They
are open from early in the morning till mid-day, and again from three
till six. The best specimens of fresco painting are in the churches and
their cloisters. Remarkable ancient frescoes in the Brancacci chapel
of Del Carmine (page 252). Best painting by Cimabue, a Madonna,
executed in 1240, in the Rucellai chapel of S. Maria Novella (page 268).
Best frescoes by D. Ghirlandaio on the chancel or recess occupied by
the high altar in S. Maria Novella (page 268). Best frescoes of A. del
Sarto in the narthex of the Annunziata (page 269). Best frescoes of
Giotto in the first and second chapels of S. Croce (page 260). Of the
palaces the best are the Palazzo Vecchio (page 274), Palazzo Strozzi
(page 275), and the Palazzo Corsini (page 275). The best view of
Florence is from the top of the dome ; the ascent is very easy. The
pleasantest drive, with views, is to the Piazza Michel Angiolo, by the
Porta Romana and the Boulevards Machiavelli, Galileo, and Michel
Angiolo (page 249), studded with handsome villas.

At Florence the Arno is crossed by six bridges. One of these, the
Ponte Vecchio, differs from all the rest in having shops on each side.
By referring to the plan it will be observed that the road to the Pitti
Palace with the Boboli gardens, commences at the south end of this
bridge ; while, at the northern end, commences the Via Por S. Maria,
leading to the Piazza della Signoria. From the north-west corner
of the Piazza della Signoria a fine broad street, the Via Calzaioli,
leads to the *Piazza del Duomo;* from the eastern corner the street
called the Borgo de' Greci leads into the Piazza Santa Croce. It
is of great importance to understand the relative position of these
three squares. The chief feature of the Piazza della Signoria is the
Palazzo Vecchio, a fine specimen of the Florentine castles of the Middle
Ages (page 274). On either side of the main entrance are the terminal
statues of Baucis and Philemon, by Bandinelli, and in front the
colossal group of Hercules and Cacus, also by him. Opposite is the
spacious Gothic arcade called the Loggia dell' Orcagna, from the name
of the architect, or dei Lanzi, from the name of the watchman who formerly guarded the building. It was usual in the early period of the
Republic to provide a space near the government-house where the people

could meet and take part in public affairs ; and for this purpose this open gallery was built opposite the Palazzo Vecchio about the year 1376. Five steps, running along the front, lead up to the platform, covered by a vaulted roof, supported on four arches, resting on three columns terminating in beautiful capitals of the Corinthian order. Two shaggy lions, in Cipollino marble, ornament the entrance. The lion on the left is by F. Vacca, 17th cent. ; the other, on the right, as well as the six statues of Sabine priestesses, along the inner wall, beautiful in attitude and drapery, are antiques, and were brought from the Villa Medici in Rome in 1788. In front, under each arch, stand three separate groups, by celebrated masters of the 16th cent. To the right is the Rape of the Sabines, by G. Bologna, in 1583. Originally this group was intended to represent Youth, Manhood, and Old Age. To the left the statue in bronze of Perseus, with the head of the sorceress Medusa, by B. Cellini. The posture is fine, and full of power and animation, but the head and body of the Medusa are represented streaming with blood with a revolting exaggeration. Also left, Judith and Holofernes in bronze, by Donatello. Behind Perseus is the Rape of Polixena, a marble group, by Pio Fedi, in 1864. In the centre is an antique group supposed to represent Ajax dragging the body of Patrocles—restored by S. Ricci. Next it is the marble group, by G. Bologna, representing Hercules slaying the Centaur. In this Piazza is also the Fountain of Neptune, by Ammanati (pupil of Bandinelli), 1571. It is crowded with nymphs and satyrs, presided over by a statue of Neptune (19½ feet high) in a car drawn by four horses. Adjoining is a superb equestrian statue of Cosmo, by Bologna. The horse is admirable. To the left of the statue is the Palazzo Uguccione (considered to have been designed by Raphael), built in 1551. Adjoining the Loggia dei Lanzi are the extensive buildings " degli Uffizi," the great storehouse of art treasures. On both sides of the Piazza, along the basement floor, extends a wide and lofty colonnade, by Vasari (1560-74), ornamented with 24 statues of the most eminent Italians. On the same side as the Loggia is the Post-Office (Reale Poste). On the opposite side, at the second door from the end, is the entrance to the Galleria degli Uffizi, and six doors farther down, the entrance to the *Biblioteca Nazionale*, with about 250,000 vols. and 14,000 MSS. Open from 9 to 4. Any book may be had for consultation in the reading-room by writing the name on a slip of paper. The National Library was formed in 1864 by the union of the Palatine Library collected by the Medici with the Magliabecchian Library collected by Antonio Magliabechi in 1700. The arch at the S. end of the colonnade leads to the river Arno and the Ponte Vecchio.

GALLERIA DEGLI UFFIZI

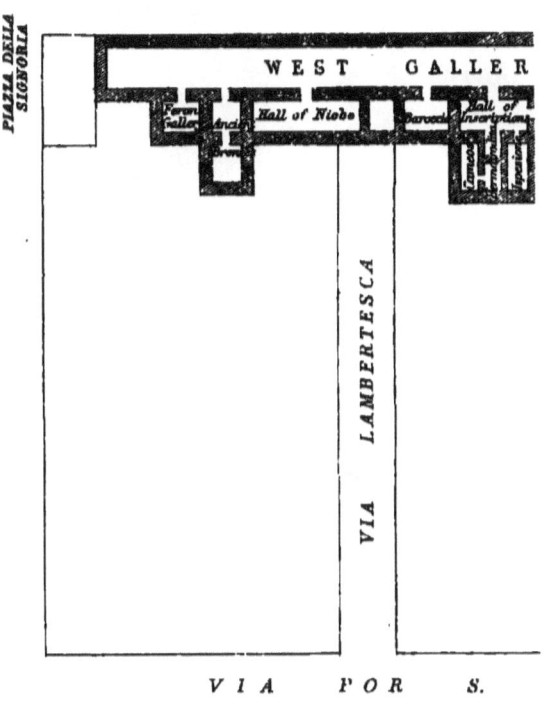

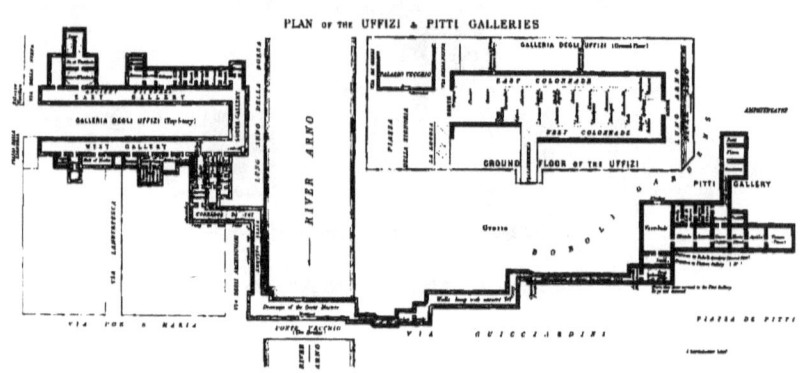

PLAN of the UFFIZI & PITTI GALLERIES

Galleria degli Uffizi.

Open daily from 10 to 3. Fee, 1 fr. each. Sundays, free. W.C.'s near the portrait rooms; key with the keepers in the corner of the southern gallery. In the top storey of the Uffizi buildings is the famous collection of paintings, statues, and antiquities, united with a similar collection in the Pitti Palace, by long galleries which cross the Arno by the Ponte Vecchio, and extend along the street Via Guicciardini, by the tops of the houses. The payment of a franc admits to both collections, and the visitor may commence at either end; either from the second door left hand, under the Uffizi colonnade, or from the door at the N. E. corner of the Pitti Palace, next to the iron gate opening into the Boboli gardens. But the easiest plan is to commence with the Uffizi, and to descend towards the Pitti gallery by the stair at the top of the western gallery. The only part of the way in which it is possible to go wrong, is where (after having passed through the gallery of birds, fishes, and plants, admirably drawn in 1695 by Bart. Legozzi, and a small room with a few beautiful miniature paintings representing scenes in the life of our Lord,) we come to a common stone staircase, which, to enter the Pitti galleries, *ascend*, but to go out, descend. Downstairs, outside, are the Piazza Pitti and the entrance to the Boboli gardens.

Entering the Uffizi by the second doorway under the colonnade, those who wish to save themselves the fatigue of the 126 steps up to the galleries may, for a franc, be carried up in a lift. In the first vestibule are Roman statues and bas-reliefs representing festivals and sacrifices, and busts of Lorenzo the Magnificent, Cosmo I., Francis I., and of others of the Medici. Second vestibule, more Roman statuary, and an inimitable Greek figure of a wild boar; the whole expressing admirably the growling ire kindling in an irritated animal. Two exquisite wolf-dogs, bold, spirited, and true to nature. The horse, said to have belonged to the Niobes group, does not bear close examination.

We now enter the eastern corridor, 178 yards long, with the ceiling painted in arabesques by Poccetti. Ranged on both sides are valuable specimens of ancient statuary, and of Roman busts of emperors and members of the imperial family, Augusti et Augustæ. On the walls is hung a valuable and interesting series of pictures, beginning with the stiff gilded Byzantine style of the infancy of the art, as No. 1, a Madonna by Andrea Rico di Candia (1102), and advancing gradually by No. 2, St. Cecilia, by Cimabue, 130 years later. A marked improvement in colour and grouping is seen in No. 6, Christ in Gethsemane, by Giotto, pupil of Cimabue. No. 17 is a beautiful triptych by Fra. Angelico ; No. 24 a Madonna by Credi ; No. 29 a Battlepiece by P. Uccello ; and No. 61 a Crucifixion by Lippi.

From the two long sides of the gallery large doors open into halls where the pictures are arranged in schools; the first of these being, as is shown on the plan, the Scuola Toscana, contained in three rooms, and consisting of 165 paintings, by M. Albertinelli, A. and C. Allori, B. Angelico, M. A. Anselmi. B. Bandinelli, Fra. Bartolommeo, G. Biliverti, S. Botticelli, A. Bronzino. F. Cambi, J. Casentino, Cigoli, P. di Cosimo, L. di Credi, F. Curradi. C. Dolci. Empoli. P. Francesca, M. A. Franciabigio. A. L. Gentil, D. and R. Ghirlandaio, F. Giorgio, G. S. Giovanni, B. Gozzoli, F. Granacci. Ignoto (unknown). Fra F. Lippi. O. Marinari, Masaccio, T. Manzuoli, G. da Milano, F. Morandini. G. Pagani, M. Pasti, S. Pieri, A. Pollaiolo, Pontormo. G. Ramacciotti, Razzi, Il Rosso, G. F. Rustici. V. Salimbeni, C. Salviati, A. del Sarto, L. Signorelli. Fr. Ubertini. R. Vanni, O. Vannini, G. Vasari, Dom. Veneziano, A. Verrocchio, Leonardo da Vinci, Volterrano. F. Zucchero. The earliest painters are in the inner room. Among the most remarkable of them are, B. Angelico, 1294. A. Botticelli, 1286, a large picture, and 1289 and 1299. Fra. F. Lippi, 1307. D. Ghirlandaio, 1295 and 1297. G. da Milano, 1293, in ten compartments. A. Pollaiolo, 1301 and 1306 ; D. Veneziano, 1305.

In the middle hall—Albertinelli, 1259. Fra. Bartolommeo, 1265 ; Bronzini, 1271. Cigoli, 1276 his best work. F. Lippi, 1257 and 1268 ; Razzi, 1279, formerly a banner carried in processions. Leonardo da Vinci, 1252, an unfinished picture.

First hall—Albertinelli, 1259 ; Allori, 1165 ; Biliverti, 1261, one of his best works ; Bronzino, 1271 ; Cigoli, 1276 ; Credi, 1168 ; Leonardo da Vinci, 1157 and 1159 remarkably fine.

Next to the rooms occupied by the Scuola Toscana is the Tribuna, a plain 8-sided hall, 30 ft. in diameter, designed by B. Buondelmonti, and painted and decorated by Poccetti. In this room are preserved five of the most famous antique statues in the world, and forty-two of the choicest pictures in the collection by Alfani, F. Barocci, Fra. Bartolommeo, A. and L. Caracci, Correggio, Domenichino, A. Durer, Guercino, L. Kranach, F. Francia, Lanfranco, B. Luini, Mantegna, Michael Angelo, L. d'Olanda, P. Perugino, Raphael, G. Reni, Giulio Romano, Rubens, A. del Sarto, Schidone, Spagnoletti, Tiziano, Van Dyck, P. Veronese, and D. Volterra. Facing the door is the Venus de Medici, 4 ft. 11 inches high, supposed to be by Cleomenes, son of Apollodorus, which, along with the statue of the Apollino, were brought from the Villa Hadrian, in Tivoli, during the reign of Cosmo III. The group of the Wrestlers, exquisitely finished, wants animation. The Dancing Fawn, attributed to Praxiteles, is one of the most exquisite works of art that remains of the ancients. The head and arms were restored by Michael Angelo. In the *Knife-Grinder*, the bony square form, the squalid countenance, and the short neglected hair, express admirably the character of a slave, still more plainly written on his coarse hard hands and wrinkled brow.. Among the paintings, six are by Raphael—all gems. 1120 Portrait of a Lady, painted when he was 20 ; 1123 the Fornarina, every hue as perfect as if transferred to the canvas by the sun—the expression is pert ; 1125, the Madonna del Pozzo (Well), attributed also to Franciabigio, beautifully finished ; 1127 St. John in the Desert, colouring tawny, but admirable light and shade ; 1129 the Madonna del Cardellino (nightingale), one of Raphael's best works, painted when he was 22 ; 1131 Portrait of Julius II., considered one of the finest portraits in the world. In the Hall of Saturn, in the Pitti Gallery, and in the National Gallery of London, are likewise portraits by Raphael of this impetuous and warlike pope. 1139 Holy Family by Michael Angelo. This picture, one of the few by him in oil, exhibits powerful drawing with dexterous execution. 1112 the Madonna between St. Francis and St. John, called also the Madonna delle Arpie, by Andrea del Sarto—rich but subdued colouring, very pleasing to the eye. 1117 the famous recumbent Venus, by Tiziano. 1118 the Rest in Egypt, by Correggio—wonderful colouring.

Six rooms follow in succession from the south side of the Tribuna, and contain respectively the Italian, Dutch, Flemish-German, and French schools, and the collection of gems. The Italian, or more properly the Lombardo-Venetian Schools contains 115 paintings by Albano, D. Ambrogi. Baroccio, J. Bassano, G. Bonatti. Cagnacci, Canaletto, A. Caracci, G. da Carpi, G. Carpioni, B. Castiglione, M. Cerquozzi, C. Cignani, Correggio. Domenichino, B. and D. Dossi. C. Ferri, D. Feti, L. Fontana. Garofalo, L. Giordano, Giorgione, F. Granacci, J. Guercino. J. Ligozzi, B. Luini. A. Magnasco, A. Mantegna, L. Massari, L. Mazzolini, Fr. Minzocchi, Moretto da Brescia. Palma (both), G. P. Pannini, Parmigianino, P. Piola, C. Procaccino, S. Pulzone. G. Reni, P. Reschi, S. Rosa. E. Savonazzi, J. Scarsellino, B. Schidone, F. Solimena. A. Tiarini, Tinelli, Tintoretto, Tiziano, A. Turchi. G. Vanvitelli, P. Veronese, A. Vicentino. B. Zelotti. S. Zugo. Of those, the most noteworthy are Guido Reni, 998 Madonna; Parmigi-

THE DUTCH, FLEMISH, AND FRENCH SCHOOLS—ROOM OF GEMS.

nnino, 1006 Madonna, and 1010 Holy Family; Coreggio, 1016 Child's Head; A. Mantegna, 1025 Virgin, with Child in her lap; Caravaggio, 1031 Medusa.

The Dutch School contains 135 paintings, of which the best are by Berkeyden, Borch, G. Dow, Galle, Hemskerch, Metsu, Mieris, Netscher, O. Paulyn, Poelemburg; Rembrandt, 922 an Interior, with Holy Family. R. Ruysch, Ruysdael, Schalken, Stingelandt, Van Aelst, Van der Heyden, Van der Werf, Van Kessel.

The Flemish and German Schools, in two rooms, consist of 157 paintings, of which the best are by Cranach 822, Catherine Bore, wife of Luther; 838 Luther; 845 John and Frederick, Electors of Saxony; 847 Luther and Melancthon. C. Gellé or Claude Lorraine, 848 Landscape, considered the gem of this department. G. Dow, 786 Schoolmaster. A. Durer, 766 His father; 777 St. James; 851 Madonna. Holbein, 765 Richard Southwell. 784 Zwinglius, and 799 Sir Thomas More. Quintin Matsys, 779 St. Jerome. Rubens, 812 Venus and Adonis, but his best pictures are in the Sala della Niobe. Susterman, 699 and 709 Portraits. Teniers, 742 a Chemist, and 826 a Landscape. Van Dyck, 783 a Madonna.

The French School is represented by 47 paintings, of which the most noteworthy are by Fabres, 679 the poet Alfieri, and 689 the Countess of Albany, wife of, firstly, Prince Charles, the young Pretender, and afterwards of Alfieri. Gagneraux, 690 A Lion-hunt. Mignard, 670 Madame de Grignan and her Mother, and 688, Madame de Sévigné. N. Poussin, 680 Theseus before his Mother. Rigaud, 684 Portrait of Bossuet.

The Room of Gems has six upright glass cases, in which are exposed to view statuettes, vases, cups, caskets, and a variety of ornaments made of lapis lazuli, rock crystal, jasper, agate, aqua marina, turquoise, and gold. In the second glass case is the most valuable article, a casket of rock crystal, with twenty-four events from the life of Christ engraved upon it by Valerio Belli, by order of Clement VII., who presented it to Catherine of Medicis as a wedding present. The Room of Gems opens into the south or connecting corridor, painted in fresco by Ulivelli, Chiavistelli, and Tonelli. The most remarkable sculptures here are 129 reliefs on a sarcophagus, representing the Fall of Phaeton into the Eridanus (the river Po), with the Transformation of his Sisters into Poplar Trees; and the races in the Circus Maximus of Rome; 137 Round altar with reliefs representing the Sacrifice of Iphigenia; 145 Youth extracting a Thorn, a replica of the more famous statue in the Vatican; 145 Venus Anadyomene; 146 Nymph. (The key of the W.Cs. is kept in the little office in the corner of this corridor).

FLORENCE. THE VENETIAN SCHOOL—PORTRAITS OF ARTISTS.

West Corridor and rooms. Rows of Roman statues stand on both sides, and the walls are covered with Italian paintings of a much later date than those in the eastern corridor. The first two rooms contain the Venetian School, represented by 82 paintings, and the next four contain portraits of artists, nearly all by themselves. The room behind the Venetian school contains a collection of 80,000 medals and coins. The 82 pictures which illustrate the *Venetian School* are by twenty-five great masters, T. Bassano, G. Bellini, P. Bordone, C. Caliari, D. Campagnole, Giorgione, L. Lotto, A. Maganza, Moretto, Morone, G. Muziano, Padovanino, Palma (both), Pini, Porta, Savoldo, A. Schiavone, Tinelli, Tintoretto, Tiziano, P. Veneziano, C. Veronese, P. Veronese, A. Vicentino. At the head of all stands the immortal Tiziano. His finest portraits are those of the Duchess (599) and of the Duke of Urbino (605), Francesco della Rovere I. ; of "Flora," called his Mistress (626) ; of Giovanni, father of Cosimo I. (614) ; and of Sansovino (596). Also by Tiziano, 633, Holy Family ; 609 Battle between the Venetians and Austrians ; 648 Catherine Cornaro, Queen of Cyprus ; and 618 Sketch of Virgin and Child for his celebrated picture in Sta. Maria at Venice. P. Veronese, 589 Martyrdom of St. Justina ; 596 Esther before Ahasuerus, and 636 The Crucifixion. Tintoretto, 617 The Marriage in Cana. In the next two rooms are Portraits of Artists of all nations, from the 15th cent. to the present time. In a niche is the statue (338) of Card. Leopoldo de' Medici, and in the middle of the hall the celebrated Medici Vase (339), with the sacrifice of Iphigenia in relief, by a Greek sculptor. Cardinal Leopold, brother of the Grand Duke Ferdinand, founded this collection in the 17th cent., and left it with 200 portraits ; now it has about 500. Among the most remarkable are—288 Raphael, by himself, in 1506, when 23 ; 225 Van Dyck ; 228 Rubens ; 232 Holbein ; 292 Leonardo da Vinci ; 384 Tiziano ; 378 Tintoretto ; 874, 384, and 459 Annibale Caracci ; 368 Antonio Caracci ; 403 Guido Reni ; 546 Sir Joshua Reynolds ; 465 Thomas Murray. The door adjoining the hall of portraits of painters opens into the long series of corridors and stairs leading to the Pitti Gallery. See page 243. Sala delle Iscrizione.—The walls are covered with Greek and Roman inscriptions, arranged in 12 divisions according to the subject. In this room are also some very interesting ancient sculptures. Among others (315) the Torso of a Faun. *Cabinet of the Hermaphrodite.*—The most important piece of sculpture here is 306 Hermaphrodite reclining on a lion's skin, a valuable Greek work ; 318 Bust of Alexander the Great in suffering. *Cabinet of Cameos.*—A very

R

THE HALL OF NIOBE—THE HALL OF BRONZES.

precious collection of ancient and modern cameos, statuettes, and enamels, including those presented by Sir William Currie in 1863. *Sala del Baroccio.*—Against the walls are beautiful tables in pietra-dura or Florentine mosaic, and one in the centre of the room by Jacopo Antella, in 1615, from designs of Ligozzi. This hall contains 172 pictures, chiefly by Italian artists. The great picture in size and merit is 169, by Baroccio, The Madonna del Popolo or " The Virgin interceding with her Son ; " 163 is Susterman's portrait of Galileo ; 191, by Sasso-ferrato, a Madonna ; 207, one of Carlo Dolce's best works, " St. Galla Placida." *Sala della Niobe.*—The hall of Niobe was built in 1774, by the Grand Duke Pietro Leopoldo, for the famous statues supposed to have been by Scopas or Praxiteles, and found near the Porta S. Paolo at Rome in 1583, representing Niobe and her children struck by thunderbolts from Apollo. They constitute one of the finest and most powerful groups in the world, but stationed as they are round the cold, flat, white wall of an oblong saloon, each on his separate pedestal, the illusion of design and composition is not only destroyed but individual criticism invited, a test all of them cannot bear. It is believed that originally they formed a group on the pediment of a temple. Niobe is rather large, nearly nine heads high, but the child she protects is without a fault in form. This group is of one piece of marble. All the others are in single figures. But the soul and source of all that is interesting in these statues is the wonderful figure of the wounded and dying youth, represented lying on his back, his legs just crossing each other, the left hand reclining on his breast, and his right arm slightly raised. As a statue, it commands the highest admiration, and as a chaste and powerful picture of death, the keenest sympathy. Behind the statue of Niobe is a very large picture by Rubens—Henri IV. at the battle of Ivry—a performance of wonderful spirit, but un-finished ; and opposite it, 147 The entry of Henri IV. into Paris ; 144 Van Dyck, a portrait ; 152 Honthorst, Fortune-teller.

Sala dei Bronzi.—In two rooms ; among these ancient bronzes the most remarkable are the bronze heads of Sophocles and Homer, and the Torso 428 found near Leghorn—a torso is the trunk of a statue that has lost the arms and legs ; 426 The head of a horse ; 424 The figure of a youth, 5 feet in height, called the Idolino, found at Pesaro in 1530. The pedestal is attributed to Ghiberti. A tablet containing a list of the Roman Decurions, dated A.D. 223. *Galleria Feroni.*—In this room are arranged the pictures bequeathed by the Marchese Leopoldo Feroni, of which the best are, an Angel with a Lily, by C.

Dolce; A Butcher's Shop, by Teniers the younger ; and a Holy Family, by R. Schidone. Outside, in the corridor, is 131, Portrait of Pasquali Paoli, the Corsican patriot, by Richard Cosway ; and 110 and 113, Landscapes, by Agostina Tassi, the master of Claude Lorraine.

THE CONNECTING GALLERIES.

Between the Uffizi and Pitti Galleries is a series of passages and stairs finished in 1564, and opened on the occasion of the marriage of Francesco de' Medici with Joanna of Austria, of whom the statue of "Abundance" in the Boboli gardens is supposed to be a likeness. The walls of the stairs and corridors on the Uffizi side of the Arno are covered with a rich and valuable collection of engravings, constituting a complete history of the art from the 15th cent. to the present time. The corridor on the Ponte Vecchio crossing the Arno is occupied with a glorious collection of drawings by the great masters. The first part of the corridor on the south side of the Arno contains numerous portraits of the Medicean family, and then follows (on the long passage behind the Via Guicciardini) a vast collection of tapestry, executed in the 16th and 17th cent. in Paris and Florence. The best are those representing the festivities at the marriages of Henry II. with Catherine de' Medici, and of Henry IV. with Maria de' Medici, executed in 1560 after designs by Orlay. From the tapestry gallery a short stair ascends to a room hung with pictures painted in chiaroscuro, or in one colour, by several of the old painters. From this another short stair leads to the long narrow gallery on the wall of the Boboli gardens. This gallery is hung with water-colour drawings, by Bartolommeo Ligozzi, in 1695, representing with wonderful truthfulness, figures of birds, fishes, and plants. To these illustrations of natural history succeeds a series of miniature paintings of scenes in the life of our Lord. Now we come to the common stone stair leading upwards to the Pitti Gallery, and downwards to the door fronting the Piazza Pitti, and next the gate leading into the Boboli gardens. At the top of the stair is a large vestibule, with a window looking into the gardens. The names of the Sale and Stanze (Halls and Rooms) are on the catalogues. Each room is provided with two of these catalogues, one in Italian and another in French. The halls are painted in fresco, and adorned with statuary and rich tables of Florentine mosaic.

THE PITTI GALLERY.

The vestibule opens into the *Sala dell' Illiado*, painted by Sabatelli in 1837, and having in the centre a statue of "Charity," by Bartolini.

Nos. 191 and 225 are Assumptions, by Andrea del Sarto, and 184 is his Portrait, painted by himself. No. 185, a Concert, is a remarkable picture, and one of the few existing by Giorgione. Tiziano is represented by some of his best portraits:—No. 200, Philip II. of Spain; 201, Cardinal Ippolito de' Medici; 215, Portrait; and 228, the Head of Jesus. 208, the Madonna del Trono, by Fra. Bartolommeo. 219, P. Perugino, Adoration of the Child Jesus. 188, S. Rosa, his own Portrait; and 218, Warrior. 190, Sustermans, a Prince of Denmark. 224, Rod. Ghirlandaio, Portrait of a Lady. 230, Parmigianino, the Madonna col lungo Collo. 235, Rubens, Holy Family. 236, Bassano, House of Martha.

Sala di Saturno.—The frescoes on the ceiling are by Pietro da Cortona. The gems of this room may be considered :—151, Portrait of Pope Julius II. ; and 165, the Madonna del Baldacchino, by Raphael. The others by Raphael are the Portraits of (158) Card. Bibbiena ; and of (171) Inghirami and (174) the Vision of Ezekiel. 150, Charles I. of England and Henrietta Maria, by Van Dyck. 164, a Deposition, by Perugino.

Sala di Giove.—Ceiling painted by P. da Cortona. In the centre of the room statue of "Victory," by Consani, and at the sides five Tables in Florentine mosaic. The most remarkable picture in this, the Saloon of Jupiter, is 113, the Three Parcæ, or Fates, by Michael Angelo. Then follow Nos. 118, Andrea del Sarto and Wife ; and 124, an Annunciation, by A. del Sarto. No. 133 is a Battle-piece, by Salvator Rosa. In the lower corner, right hand, is his own Portrait, with the initials S. A. R. O. No. 140, an exquisitely finished Portrait of G. Benci, by Leonardo da Vinci. 139, Holy Family, by Rubens.

Sala di Marte.—Frescoes and decorations by Cortona. Raphael, Rubens, Van Dyck, and A. del Sarto, have in this room some beautiful paintings. The gem is (79) the Madonna della Sedia (chair), by Raphael. 94 is a Holy Family, also by him—called the "Impannata" or cloth window. No. 81, Holy Family ; and 87 and 88, Story of Joseph, by A. del Sarto. 82, Card. Bentivoglio, by Van Dyck. No. 86, Peace and War, by Rubens. 96, Judith, by O. Allori.

Sala di Prometeo.—The Mosaic Table in this room, by Giorgi, occupied him fourteen years. 338, Madonna, by Fra. Filippo Lippi.

Sala di Apollo.—Raphael has three portraits in this room :—59 and 61, M. and A. Doni ; and 63, Leo X. Tiziano has some fine works :— No. 67, a Magdalene, shows his power in colour ; and 54, Aretino, the poet, is one of his best portraits. 40, Madonna, by Murillo. 58, by

FLORENCE. PITTI GALLERY—ROOMS OF FLORA, ULLISSE, GIOVE.

A. del Sarto, Descent from the Cross, one of his best works. 64, the same subject admirably treated by Fra. Bartolommeo.

Sala di Venere (Venus).—Painted by Cortona. Nos. 4 and 15 are two most charming Sea-pieces, by Salvator Rosa. No. 18, La Bella Donna, by Tiziano. No. 27, Jesus appearing to Peter, by L. Cardi (Il Cigoli).

Galleria Poccetti. — Painted by Poccetti. Bust of Napoleon by Canova. Small corridor, or Corridor of the Columns, with two columns in oriental alabaster, and the walls hung with Florentine mosaics, and admirably executed miniatures in water-colours and oil, collected by Card. Leopold. No. 4, In glass cases are displayed valuable articles in ivory, amber, rock-crystal, and precious stones.

Stanza della Giustizia.—Painted by Fedi. The beautiful ebony cabinet was used by Card. Leopold. The most interesting picture in this room is 408, Portrait of Oliver Cromwell, painted from life by Sir Peter Lely, by request of Ferdinand II. of Tuscany.

Stanza di Flora.—In the centre is the famous Venus by Canova, called also the Venus Italica from its having been intended to replace the Venus de' Medici, when that still more famous statue was carried off to Paris, where it remained fifteen years. No. 415, Ferdinand II., by Sustermans. 416 and 421, Landscapes, by Poussin. 423, Adoration of the Shepherds, by Tiziano.

Stanza dei Putti.—Painted by Morini. No. 470 is a large picture by Sal. Rosa, called the Philosopher's Forest—Diogenes throwing away his drinking-cup. No. 465, Landscape, by Ruysdael.

Stanza d' Ullisse.—Painted by Martellini. No. 324 is a fine portrait by Rubens of the favourite of James I., George Villiers, Duke of Buckingham, assassinated by Felton in 1628. No. 289, Madonna, by Ligozzi. 297, Paul III., by Bordone. 306 and 312, Landscapes, by Sal. Rosa.

Stanza del Bagno.—This, the bath-room, is tastefully fitted up with a mosaic pavement. Four handsome columns in verd antique, and four marble statues, by Insom and Bongiovanni.

Stanza dell' educazione di Giove.—Painted by Catani. 266, the Madonna del Granduca, by Raphael, is one of the finest pictures in the Pitti Gallery. 245 is attributed to Raphael. 243, Philip IV. of Spain by Velasquez. 248, a "Descent" by Tintoretto. 256, Holy Family by Fra. Bartolommeo.

Stanza della Stufa.—The frescoes on the walls, representing the Four Ages of Man, are by Cortona, from sketches by the nephew of Michael

Angelo. The frescoes on the ceiling, representing the Virtues, are by Rosselli, in 1622. Among the treasures of this room are four antique statues in niches, a column of green porphyry, bearing a porcelain vase with a likeness of Napoleon I., and two justly celebrated bronze statues of Cain and Abel, modelled by Dupré of Siena, and cast by Papi in 1849.

THE BOBOLI GARDENS.

Now either return to the Uffizi by the very long galleries or descend to the foot of the stairs, and when outside, turn to the left and pass through the gate leading into the Boboli Gardens, open on Thursdays and feast-days. Permission to enter on other days is easily obtained at the office of the Minestero della Casa, under the south corner of the corridor. The gardens are laid out in a stiff style. Clumps of oleanders and oleasters among ilexes, laurels, pines, yews, and cypresses, encircled by tall myrtle hedges, make the grounds in many parts more like a labyrinth than a garden. Near the entrance is an artificial grotto, with, in front, a group by V. Rossi, and a Venus by G. Bologna ; and in the four corners unfinished statues by Michael Angelo, intended for the monument of Julius II. at Rome, and presented to Cosmo I. by L. Buonarotti. Opposite the palace is the Amphitheatre ; within the centre a granite obelisk and a large granite basin from Egypt, but brought to Florence from Rome. Beyond the palace, near the Porta Romana, is the Piazzale del Lago, with groups in marble by G. Bologna. In the flower-garden "del Cavaliere," are two more fountains, with monkeys in bronze, by the same artist, and a small villa, from the top of which there is a fine view (entrance 25c.) On the highest part of the gardens, facing the palace, is a colossal statue of Dovizia (Abundance), commenced by Bologna, and finished by his pupil Dacca.

THE PITTI PALACE was begun by Luca Pitti, a Florentine merchant, in 1436, from designs by Brunelleschi. In 1549 the still unfinished building was purchased by the Medici, who advanced it considerably, but not till quite recently was this vast pile finished. The façade is 659 feet in length, 148 feet in height, and the total surface occupied by the building 35,231 yards. Bart. Ammanati added the wings, and enclosed the beautiful court opposite the middle entrance with Doric, Ionic, and Corinthian columns, and placed at the extremity the pretty grotto covered in with Roman mosaic, supported on 16 columns, and ornamented with statues in marble and 'porphyry, and small trees and satyrs in bronze. To the right of the court is the Royal

FLORENCE. TRIBUNA GALILEO—MUSEUM OF NATURAL HISTORY.

Chapel. Above the altar is an ivory crucifix by G. Bologna. At the end of the portico, to the left, a door opens into the court, in which is the entrance into the room containing the splendid *Collection of Plate* by Benvenuto Cellini and Maso Finiguerra, and ivories by Bologna and Donatello. Zumbo, the famous artist in wax, has likewise some of his works here. The state apartments are sumptuously furnished.

Nearly opposite the Pitti palace, at No. 16 Via Guicciardini, is the house in which Machiavelli lived and died in 1527. A little farther up the Via Romana, in the house No. 19, is the

MUSEO DI STORIA NATURALE,

in the second floor, and the Museo Galileo in the first floor. Both open on Thursdays and Saturdays, from 10 to nearly 3. In the vestibule is an old terrestrial globe, black with age, 3 feet in diameter, probably by Ignazio Dante, a famous astronomer, brought to Florence by Cosmo I. He died in 1586. Upstairs is the Museo, or Tribuna di Galileo.* Explanatory catalogues in Italian and French are on the table. The statue of him is by A. Costoli. In the niche to the right are his telescopes, of which the lower one was constructed by himself, and by which he discovered the satellites of Jupiter. In the niche on the left are his compasses and magnet. The other philosophical instruments belonged to the Accademia del Cimento, instituted in 1657 and dissolved in 1667. It held its meetings in the palace of Prince Leopold de' Medici. All around are beautiful frescoes, illustrating scenes in the life of Galileo. Among the relics is the forefinger of Galileo, taken from the body when it was removed to its present resting-place in the church of Santa Croce. In the second storey is the excellent and comprehensive Museum of Natural History. The collections are admirably arranged, and in good condition. The botanical department contains the herbariums of Andrea Cesalpino, which he is supposed to have collected about the year 1563 ; of P. A. Micheli, collected about the year 1725 ; of Central Italy, by Parlatore, commenced in 1842 ; of Labillardière, who accompanied La Perouse in his expedition to New Holland ; of R. Desfontaines, the master of De Candolle ; and of the Englishman, P. B. Webb, who bequeathed his herbarium to this

---

* The word tribune is used in Florence to designate any large niche. But the real meaning of the word " Tribuna " is the semicircular cavity at the extremity of a Roman basilica, where the judges sat. In the early ages of the church some of these buildings were given to the Christians for public worship, who still retained their secular names, and worshipped in them without consecration.

museum. But the most wonderful objects in the museum are the
anatomical preparations in wax, chiefly by Clemente Sasini and his
assistants, under the direction of Tommaso Bonicoli, 1775 to 1791.
Like the great works of the great painters, they are executed with the
most minute care and truthfulness to nature, whether it be the magni-
fied anatomy of the cuttle-fish or of the silkworm, or the life-like
representation of the most delicate organs of the human body. They
are contained in twelve rooms, entered from the shell department, by
the door lettered "Ittiologia," opening into the Zootomia.

The House of Galileo,

at the head of the Via Romana, is the Porta Romana, the city gate by
which, in 1536, Charles V. and Pope Leo X. entered Florence. An
omnibus runs between it and the Piazza del Duomo. At the outer side
there is a cab stand, which is likewise the starting-place of the omnibus
for the Certosa (see page 250). Immediately outside the Porta commence three broad roads—the lowest is called the Via Senese and leads to
the Certosa ; the centre one, bordered with tall cypresses, is the Via del
Poggio Imperiale ; while to the left is the Viale Machiavelli, the first of
a series of magnificent boulevards (viali) leading to that noble terrace
the Piazza Michelangiolo. Let us first ascend the Via del Poggio to
the Royal Villa, formerly the property of the Medicis, now the Insti-
tuto della Annunziata, a boarding-school for girls. From it ascend by
the Via del Pian di Giullari, and when at the top of it take the road
to the right leading directly to the village of Arcetri, containing the
house in which Galileo spent the last years of his life, and in which
when blind, and 74 years of age, he was visited by Milton. Galileo
was born in 1564, at Pisa, and died in 1642. The house, a plain building, is indicated by a bust and tablet on the wall towards the street.
The steep little road to the left leads up to the farmhouse in which is
the Tower (Torre del Gallo) from which Galileo made his astronomical
observations. It contains several relics of the great astronomer—a
telescope, table, and chairs, a bust of him taken after death (il piu
antico che si conosca), a pen-and-ink sketch of him on marble by Sal-
vatelli, a smaller portrait of him by P. Leoni, 1624. From the farm-

house a steep narrow road leads down to the Boulevards between the Piazza Michelangiolo and the Porta Romana.

THE PIAZZALE MICHELANGIOLO.

There is no place about Florence which affords such an agreeable walk or drive as to the Piazzale Michelangiolo and the church of S. Miniato. They are situated on a hill on the left bank of the Arno, two bridges higher up the river than the Uffizi, and are distinctly seen from the Lung' Arno. The nearest way to approach them on foot is, having crossed the Ponte alle Grazie (the first bridge above the Ponte Vecchio), walk up the left bank of the Arno, passing the Piazza containing the fine marble monument to Prince Nicholas Demidoff, by L. Bartolini, in 1835, and continue the walk up the river till arrival at a square tower in the Piazza della Molina, whence commence the ascent by the stairs and road the Viale dei Colli. Or approach it from the Porta Romana by the fine avenues the Viali Machiavelli and Galileo, bordered by trees and handsome villas, disclosing as they wind round the steep sides of the hills a succession of ever-varying views. The Piazzale Michelangiolo is a splendid terrace, 165 feet above the Arno, commanding a grand prospect, and adorned with five statues in bronze, copies by C. Papi of Michael Angelo's famous works. To the right is the Viale Michelangiolo, the carriage road leading down to the Barriera San Niccolo, opposite the suspension-bridge (Ponte Sospenso). Above the Piazzale, by the convent church of San Salvatore del Monte (built in 1504 by Cronaca), is the Basilica of San Miniato, one of the earliest (1013) as well as one of the most perfect structures in the Byzantine style. Internally it is 165 feet long by 70 wide, and is divided longitudinally into aisles by pillars of classical design. The façade is faulty. The tower was erected in 1519. The floor of the nave is considerably under the level of the chancel, which terminates in a semi-dome, covered with mosaics executed in 1247, and of the same kind as those of St. Mark's at Venice. Behind the altar are five small windows of thin slabs of Pavonazzo marble. Between the stairs leading up to the chancel is the chapel constructed in 1448 by Michelozzi. Here lie the remains of Gualberto, the founder of the church and of the order of Vallombrosa. In the centre of the north aisle is the chapel of Cardinal Ximenes (died 1459). The monument is by B. Rossellino, and the beautiful terra-cottas on the ceiling by Luca della Robbia. On the south side is the Sacristy (built in 1387), exquisitely painted in fresco by Spinello Aretino, representing scenes in the life of St. Benedict. In

the centre of the nave is a curious piece of Byzantine pavement, executed in 1207. Below the chancel is the crypt, supported on 38 marble
columns, several being prolongations of those above. Under the altar
is the tomb of San Miniato. From the terraces of the adjoining cemetery there are splendid views of Florence and of the valley of the Arno.

THE CERTOSA.

From outside the Porta Romano a small diligence starts every hour,
at the hour, passing by the Carthusian Monastery of the Certosa, 3½
miles distant ; fare, ½ fr. Passengers alight at the great wall enclosing
the grounds at the commencement of the small by-road to the right,
leading up to the top of the circular hill on which the convent is picturesquely situated. It was erected by Niccolo Acciaiola in the 14th
cent., and is now the property of the State, who retain in it some twenty-
three friars of the order to take charge of the church, chapels, and
buildings. At the entrance-gate is the pharmacy, where the liqueurs
made in the convent can be bought and tasted. Their Chartreuse
cordial is not equal to that made in France, but the Alkermis is of good
quality. Fee to see the convent, ½ fr. At the top of the stair leading
up to the church is a fresco by Empoli. The church, paved with
marble in the cinque-cento style, has some good stalls (1590), and over
the marble altar a fresco by Poccetti. Right hand, chapel with frescoes
by Masari on the walls, and on roof by Poccetti and his school. From
S. aisle pass to chapel of S. Maria, in the shape of a Greek cross. Here
is a curious Trinity of the Giotti school. Descend to the Cappella di
Tobia, with the mausoleum of the founder, by Orcagna (1360), and
three monumental slabs over the tombs of his father, sister, and son.
Next, a narrow cloister with eight small windows, with vignette paintings
by Udine, 1560 ; Cappella del Capitolo, having for the reredos a Crucifixion by Albertinelli, and in the centre of floor the mausoleum of
Buonafede by Stogallo, 1545 ; then the Camere di Pio Sesto, his sitting-
room, and bedroom. He was a prisoner here nine months. Beautiful views
are obtained from various parts. In passing through the villages women
may be seen plaiting straw—a standard occupation in Tuscany.

Views.—From the Porta Romana commences also the road to the
Bello Sguardo and to Monte Oliveto (about a mile distant), both commanding splendid views of the city, of the valley of the Arno, and of
the surrounding mountains. Immediately outside the Porta turn to
the right, and walk by the side of the city wall by the Via Petrarcha
till the second road on the left, the Via de Casone, by which continue

to ascend till a road is reached on the left lettered, Via di Bello Sguardo. By it ascend to the next on the left, the Via dell' Ombrellino, where at the house No. 1 ring the bell. The view is from the pavilion of this house ; fee, ½ fr. To go from this to Monte Oliveto descend to the Via di Bello Sguardo, and from a house with a high railing turn to the right by the "Via di Monte Oliveto Per S. Vito," and descend to a large gateway and house on the left hand. At this house ask for the key of the Monte Oliveto, then walk forward past the old convent, now a military hospital, to the top of the knoll crowned with cypresses, and behold the view. Now descend by the Via di Monte Oliveto, which, at the foot of the hill, enters the Via Pisana opposite house No. 82, near the Porta S. Frediano, whence an omnibus runs to the Piazza della Signoria. If preferred, the tour may be commenced at this end, taking the omnibus from the Piazza to the Porta.

SANTO SPIRITO AND SANTA MARIA DEL CARMINE.—By referring to the plan it will be observed that a very short way north from the Pitti Palace are two churches, the Santa Maria del Carmine, containing the famous frescoes of Masaccio (b. 1402, d. 1429), and of Filippino Lippi (b. 1457, d. 1504), and the church of Santo Spirito, in which Luther preached as an Augustinian friar when on his way to Rome. The present church of the S. Spirito was commenced in 1446 by F. Brunelleschi, destroyed by fire in 1470, and rebuilt in 1488 according to Brunelleschi's design. The belfry, which is of admirable proportions, was erected by B. d'Agnolo. The church is 315 ft. long, and 191 at the transept, and is placed from south to north. The arches of the aisles rest on 47 pilasters and 35 columns, each of one piece of pietra-serena, brought from the quarries of Fiesole. Around the church are 38 semicircular chapels, ornamented with pictures by Alessandro Allori, Fra. Bartolommeo, Sandro Botticelli, Franciabigio, Raff. del Garbio, Rodolfo Ghirlandaio, Giotto, Filippino Lippi, Ant. Pollaiolo, and Cosimo Rosselli. Among the best of these are, in the choir, 12th chapel from entrance to church, a Madonna by Lippi. In left transept, 19th and 20th chapels, Martyrs, and The Adulteress, by Allori. 22d chapel, an Annunciation, by Botticelli. Among the sculptures the most remarkable work is in the 2d chapel, right hand on entering, a Pieta, by Baccio Bigio, a copy of the group by Michael Angelo in St. Peter's, Rome. The proportions of the dead body of our Lord are admirable, and the ribs, loins, and pectoral muscles skilfully marked. Before the choir is a screen erected in 1599, composed of bronze and rich marbles, and although rather out of place, full of beautiful details.

SANTA MARIA DEL CARMINE—BRANCACCI CHAPEL.

The high altar, under a ciborium or canopy supported on four columns of rare porphyry, is decorated with statuettes and candelabra by Giovanni Caccini. A door in the west aisle opens into the sacristy, the joint work of San Gallo and Pollaiolo, by whom it was finished in 1490. In the sacristy a door to the right opens into the cloisters, by A. Parigi, adorned with frescoes by Perugino, Ulivelli, and Cascetti.

The church **Del Carmine** was erected in 1475, destroyed by fire in 1771, and rebuilt in 1788 by Ruggieri and Mannaconi. Among the parts which escaped destruction in 1771 was the Brancacci chapel, at the end of the western or right transept, covered with valuable frescoes, in 12 compartments, by Masaccio, Lippi, and Masolino da Panicale. The four principal subjects are (left wall) "Christ directing St. Peter to take a coin from a fish's mouth to pay the tribute," by Masaccio, whose portrait is given in the last apostle to the right ; "the Restoration to Life of the Emperor's Nephew," painted by Filippino Lippi and Masaccio. On the right wall are—"St. Peter raising Tabitha," by Masolino ; "the Crucifixion of St. Peter ; " and "St. Paul before the Proconsul," by Filippino Lippi. These frescoes are said to have been studied by Perugino, Raffaelo, Leonardo da Vinci, and Michael Angelo. Of the eight small subjects, "The Expulsion of Adam and Eve," and "St. Peter and St. John Healing the Sick by means of their Shadows," on the left wall ; "St. Peter Baptising," and "St. Peter Distributing Alms," on the right wall, are all by Masaccio. "The Visit of St. Paul to St. Peter in Prison," on the left wall, and "the Deliverance of St. Peter from Prison," on the right wall, are by Lippi. "Adam and Eve under the Tree of Knowledge," and "St. Peter Healing the Cripple," are ascribed by some to Masolino, by others to Masaccio. In the opposite arm of the transept is the Corsini chapel, with large marble alti-rilievi by Foggini, and frescoes on the ceiling by Luca Giordano. In a chapel in the sacristy are some frescoes discovered in 1858, attributed to Spinello Aretino, but also, and with more probability, to Agnolo Gaddi, representing scenes in the life of St. Cecilia. The old church contained frescoes by Giotto, some fragments of which, removed the year before the fire, are now in the Royal Institution, Liverpool.

THE Duomo, or Cathedral Church of Santa Maria del Fiore was commenced by Arnolfo di Cambio, and the foundation-stone laid on

the 8th of September 1298, under the auspices of the first papal legate
ever sent to Florence, Cardinal Pietro Valeriani. Arnolfo died in 1310.
In 1330 Giotto was appointed master-builder, who, assisted by Andrea
Pisano, continued the work according to Arnolfo's design. Giotto died
in 1337. To Giotto succeeded Francisco Talenti, Taddeo Gaddi, and
Andrea Orcagna. In 1421 Filippo Brunelleschi commenced the dome,
and completed it in all its essential parts before his death, which took
place in 1446. In 1469 Andrea Verrochio added to the dome the
copper ball and cross. The dome, built without timber centrings,
consists of two vast vaults, an interior and an exterior, both supported
by strong ribs at the right angles, and surrounded at the base by a
strong iron chain. From the floor to the top of the dome the height
is 300 feet, the lantern 52 more, and to the top of the cross other 35.
The total height therefore is, from the floor to the top of the cross, 387
feet. The circumference of the dome is 466 feet. Three galleries are
carried round the drum. The first is reached by 153 steps; the next
by 62 steps more; and the third, which runs round the top of the
drum and the base of the dome, by other 65 steps. The appearance of
the church from the first and third galleries is most striking. Outside
the third gallery commences the cornice gallery of the dome. From
this part 180 steps (between the two vaults) lead to the top of the cupola.
From the top of the cupola to the ball the ascent is made up through
the lantern by 32 vertical bronze steps, and 13 steps in marble, and
23 in wood. The number of steps, therefore, from the floor into the
ball is 528; the only difficult part being the vertical bronze bear-like
ladder in the lantern, which is not worth ascending, as little can be
seen (and that little with difficulty) from an aperture in the ball. But
the view from the gallery at the top of the dome is truly magnificent.
Florence and neighbourhood lie stretched out below like on a map, and
as the clearness of the Italian air admits of the smallest objects being
seen distinctly, the traveller should visit this gallery as early as possible, to gain, by the assistance of the plan (page 234), a practical
acquaintance with the topography of the city. To the N.E., by the
Piazza Cavour and the stream Mugnone, is Fiesole, 3 miles distant, on
an eminence (see page 276). To the west of the town, on the Arno, is
the Cascine or Park, and the small hill with the clump of trees, on the
other side of the river, is the Monte Oliveto (page 250). To the S.E., on
the other side of the Arno, are the Piazzale Michelangiolo and San
Miniato (page 249), while a good piece beyond is the Torre del Gallo
(page 248). West from the Piazzale are the Boboli Gardens and

the Pitti Palace. Fee to ascend tower, 1 fr. Attendant to be found in south sacristy.

The length of the cathedral is 556 feet, and of the transept 342 feet. The breadth, including the aisles, is 132½ feet, and the superficial area 84,802 feet, or about 6000 feet less than the area occupied by Cologne cathedral. In 1860 Victor Emmanuel laid the foundation-stone of the gorgeous new façade, coated, like the whole exterior of the church, with polished white marble, and dark magnesian serpentine disposed in chastely ornamented panelling, an arrangement often met with in the churches of Italy.

In the interior, four arches of enormous span run down each side of the nave to the choir, which expands with unrivalled majesty under the magnificent dome. Walk in and behold its beautiful proportions. Do not struggle to perceive by means of the dim light the few relatively unimportant statues and pictures, or the intricate designs on the marble pavement by Agnolo, San Gallo, and Michael Angelo, but go at once and stand below the second greatest dome in the world, shaped like the narrow end of an egg, or more correctly, in the form of an elongated octagonal elipsoid, resting on six massive piers ornamented with statues of eight of the apostles, by Bandini, Donatello, Bandinelli, and Sansovini. The octagonal balustrade is by Baccio d'Agnolo, and the reliefs on the panels by Bandinelli. The fresco on the roof represents the Judgment Day. The upper portion is by G. Vasari, in 1572, and the rest by Federigo Zucchero, known in England by his portraits of Queen Elizabeth. The drum of the dome is lighted by seven circular windows, which, as well as the three over the main entrance, and the twenty-seven long windows in the choir, were the work of Domenico Livi da Gambassi, Bernardo de' Vetri, and others, from 1434 to 1460. Behind the altar is the last work of Michael Angelo (when eighty-one years of age), an *unfinished Pieta*, a heroic group, large but not colossal, composed of four figures, those of our Saviour, the Virgin Mary, Joseph, and an Angel. The interest of the piece lies in the melancholy but placid countenance of the Redeemer, and the inclination of the head lacerated by the crown of thorns. The Mask, Michael Angelo's first work, is in the sixth room of the National Museum, along with some other works of the great sculptor. His greatest productions are in the Sagrestia Nuova, see page 166. The reliefs in terra-cotta, over the elegant bronze gates of the sacristies, are considered amongst the best works of Lucca della Robbia. On the pier at the N.E. end of the nave is the statue of St. James, by Sansovino ; and just behind it, on the wall, is a painting by Domenico di Michelino, in 1465, representing Dante (holding in his hands a copy of his poems), with a view of Florence in the background, the only monument the Republic raised to him they had so unjustly banished.   In the north transept, covered by the wooden floor, just under the iron bar, is the gnomen and meridian line, formed by P. Toscanelli in 1408, and repaired by A. Ximines in 1756.   The line drawn on the true pavement, under the present boarded floor, runs in a direction nearly at right angles to the nave (the nave being nearly east and west).   It is only about 30 feet long, and receives the image of the sun, at and near the solstice, in June and July; at other seasons the image is lost on the sides of the cupola. The short diameter of the image in July is about 36 inches.   The height of the aperture, through which the ray enters by a window of the cupolina, is 277 feet 4 inches, 9.68 lines French measure ; so that, as the inscription states, it is the greatest gnomen existing.

Among the most interesting monuments in the church are : at the main entrance, an equestrian portrait, by Uccello, of Sir John Hawkwood, a captain in the army of the Florentine Republic, who died at Florence in 1394. The mosaic, representing the coronation of the Virgin, is by Gaddo Gaddi.   At the west end of the south aisle is the marble monument and portrait of Filippo Brunelleschi, by his pupil, And. Cavalcanti.   The third monument from the door is to Giotto, by Majano.   The beautiful water-stoup in front is by Giotto.   Opposite the southern entrance, in front of the Casa dei Canonici, are the statues, in a sitting posture, of Arnolfo di Cambio and Brunelleschi, by Luigi Pampaloni, in 1830.   To the right of Arnolfo's statue, at house No. 29, is a stone in the wall, bearing the words "Sasso di Dante," because on it the poet used to sit watching the progress of the cathedral from its commencement till 1301, when he was compelled to leave the city.

At the southern entrance is the **Campanile del Duomo**, designed and commenced by Giotto in 1334, and finished by Taddeo Gaddi. This dove-coloured marble gem of architecture, of admirable proportions and beautiful workmanship, towers 276 feet up into the air, by four storeys of elegant windows, and terminates in a grand square cornice projecting from the summit, from which, according to Giotto's plan, a spire of $94\frac{1}{2}$ feet was to have risen.   The niches are peopled with statues of apostles, saints, and philosophers, and the panels with Scripture subjects in bold relief, by Donatello, Giovanni Bartolo, Andrea Pisano, Niccolo Aretino, Lucca della Robbia, Giottino and N. di Bartolo.   Ascent by 414 steps.   Fee, $\frac{1}{2}$ franc each visitor.

Adjoining the cathedral is the church of San Giovanui, the baptistery of the city, founded in 6th cent., and repaired and restored in 1293 by Arnolfo di Cambio. It is an octagonal building, 94 ft. in diameter, covered by a cupola and lantern built in 1550. Three cele-brated bronze gates, of admirable workmanship, give access to it. The gate on the S. side (fronting the Via Calzaioli) was modelled by And. Pisano, and, after twenty-two years of incessant labour, cast and gilt in 1330. The architrave, ornamented with foliage, was added by Lor. Ghiberti in 1446, and the group at the top, representing the Beheading of John, by V. Danti, in 1571—a work full of expression. The N. gate is by Lorenzo Ghiberti, commenced by him when twenty-one, and finished (modelled and cast) when forty-one, in the year 1424. It is in twenty compartments, representing scenes from the life of Christ. The three statues above, and the ornaments, are by Rustici, 1511, a fellow-pupil of Michael Angelo, and friend of L. da Vinci. At the eastern end, facing the cathedral, is the bronze gate which Michael Angelo said was worthy to form the entrance into Paradise. This marvel of art was commenced by Lorenzo Ghiberti in 1425, cast in 1439, and finished, with the exception of the lower reliefs, in 1456, when Ghiberti died, and left the remainder to be completed by his pupils, among whom were the brothers Pollaioli. It is in ten compartments, representing as many scenes from the Old Testament. In grouping, drawing, grace, and beauty, the figures are truly admirable. The perspective is well sustained ; the distant objects being done in low, the nearer objects in middle, and those close upon the eye in high relief. Over the gate is the Baptism of Christ, by Sansovino, who, when he died, in 1529, had finished only the modelling ; but Danti, in 1560, produced it in marble. The Angels, executed nearly a century afterwards, are by Spinazzi, also from Sansovino's model.

The interior of the Baptistery rests on syenite columns and marble pilasters with gilded capitals. Above them is a triforium, with frescoes of saints on a gold ground painted on the panels. The roof and the soffit of the arch over the altar are covered with mosaics representing the Judgment Day, by Tafi, Torrita, and G. Gaddie, 13th cent. To the right of the altar is the monumental tomb of Pope John XXIII. (d. 1419), by Donatello and Michelozzi. To the left is the font, placed here in 1658, and attributed to G. Pisano. The silver altar of the Bap-tistery is kept in the "Uffizio del Comitate per la facciata del Duomo" (behind the east end of the cathedral), where it can be seen any day from 9 to 12, for 10 sous. It was constructed, during a long series of years from 1316, by the most eminent artists of the time, and represents in bold relief the story of John the Baptist. It weighs 335 lbs., is 12 ft. long by nearly 4 ft. high. The silver statue of St. John, made in 1452, weighs 14½ lbs., and cross 140 lbs.

Opposite the Baptistery, at the corner of the Via Calzaioli, is the very beautiful little arcade or loggia of the Bigallo, attributed to Orcagna, enclosed with iron gates by F. Petrucci. The oratory contains an image of the Virgin by A. Arnoldo, 1359 ; and a predella, with paintings, by Ghirlandaio.

OR SAN MICHELE.

Nearly in the centre of the Via Calzaioli, between the Piazzas del Duomo and della Signoria, is the Or San Michele, built at first of undressed stone, by Arnolfo di Cambio in 1282, for a granary or horreum. Having been destroyed by fire in 1304, it was rebuilt in 1337 under the direction of Taddeo Gaddi, the chief architect of the commonwealth. To Gaddi succeeded And. Orcagna, who received orders to transform the lower part (the loggia) into a church. In 1569 the upper storey was converted into government offices. Round the building, in deep niches, are statues in simple attitudes and of noble dignified forms, the result of a decree that each trade should bear the expense of furnishing one statue, which should be the protector and supporter of its own profession. St. Luke, by John of Bologna (good specimen of his style), was executed at the expense of the lawyers. Our Lord and St. Thomas, by Verrochio, for the mercantile tribunal. John the Baptist, by L. Ghiberti, for the guild of foreign wool-merchants. St. Peter, by Donatello, for the butchers. John the Evangelist, by Montelupo, under a graceful canopy of Robbia-ware, for the silk manufacturers. St. George, by Donatello, his noblest work, for the armourers. St. James, by N. Banco, for the tanners and furriers. St. Mark, by Donatello, for the flax-dealers. West front, St. Eloy, by Banco, for the blacksmiths and farriers. St. Stephen, by L. Ghiberti, for the wool-merchants. St. Matthew, by L. Ghiberti and Michelozzo, for the stockbrokers and money-changers. Statues of four canonised sculptors, by Banco, for the builders and carpenters. St. Philip, by Banco, for the hosiers. And inside the church, to the left of the altar of St. Anne, a Madonna, by Simone da Fiesola, for the physicians and apothecaries. These statues are considered the finest works of the ancient Florentine school. Over the niches are the arms of the respective trades, under graceful canopies.

s

SANTA CROCE—MICHAEL ANGELO—DANTE.

In the interior the most remarkable object is the canopied high altar, by Orcagna, otherwise called Cionis, with Ugolino's sacred picture of the Madonna. Inscribed on the altar is " Andreas Cionis pictor Florentinus hujus oratorii archimagister extitit, 1359." It is ornamented with Scripture histories in relief on marble, the different pieces being fixed together by pins of bronze run in with lead. The small but beautiful stained glass windows do not admit sufficient light into the church. Behind San Michele, in the Mercato Nuovo, is an admirable copy, by Pietro Tacca, of the celebrated Boar, adapted no less admirably to a Fountain.

SANTA CROCE.

South-east from the fountain, in the Piazza della Signoria, by the narrow street the Borgo dei Greci, is the Piazza Santa Croce, with, in the centre, the fine marble statue of Dante, 16½ feet high, by Enrico Pazzi. It and the new façade of the church were inaugurated in 1865, on the 600th anniversary of the birthday of the poet. The church of Santa Croce was commenced by Arnolfo di Cambio in 1297, to whom succeeded Giotto in 1344. The façade, although only recently finished, is according to the old design of S. Pollaiolo (d. 1509), and owes its erection in a very great measure to the liberality of an English gentleman, the late Francis Sloane, who died at Florence in 1871. The interior is divided into a nave and two aisles by seven acute Gothic arches. The pilasters, supporting columns as well as the roof, are of rude work, while the side chapels are not inclosed, but spread out on the walls of the aisles, an arrangement which greatly favours the display of the magnificent monuments erected in this church. The entire length from west to east is 385 feet, and from north to south at the transepts 128 feet.

Over the principal entrance, in the interior, is the statue of St. Louis, Bishop of Toulouse (d. 1297), the last work executed by Donatello. In the right or south aisle, commencing from the main entrance, after 1st altar, lies the monument and resting-place of Michael Angelo, who died at Rome in 1563, in his 89th year. The monument was designed by G. Vasari, and executed by three pupils of Michael Angelo. The bust, considered an excellent likeness, is by B. Lorenzione, one of the three. Next follows the great marble monument by S. Ricci, in 1828, to the memory of Dante, who died when in exile at Ravenna in 1321, in the 56th year of his age ; and 3d, a monument to the poet Vit. Alfieri (d. 1803), by Canova, in 1809, and one of his best works. Opposite this monument is an elaborately wrought pulpit, by B. da Majano, in 1470. 4th.

FLORENCE. MACCHIAVELLI—KETTERICK—COUNTESS OF ALBANY.

Monument and resting-place of Macchiavelli (d. 1527), by Spinazzi, in 1778. The originator of this monument was Lord Cowper, who, in 1707, raised a subscription for the medallion. Then follow a fresco of St. John and St. Francis, by A. Castagno, and an Annunciation in stone by Donatello ; and opposite it, on the floor, is the tombstone of John Ketterick, Bishop of Exeter, who died at Florence in 1419, when on a mission from Henry V. of England to the Pope. Then follow the monument to L. Bruni (d. 1444), by B. Rossellini. The Virgin, above, is by A. Verrochio, the master of Leonardo da Vinci. The tomb of P. A. Micheli, and the mausoleum of Leop. Nobili, by Leop. Veneziani. Turning to the right by the monument to Neri Corsini (died in London, 1859), and a slab on the ground, with an inscription by Boccaccio, in honour of the poet Berberino (14th cent.), we enter the Chapel of the Castellani, with frescoes by Starnini (the ablest pupil of Giotto), and reredos by Vasari. Over the altar is a crucifix, by Giotto ; at each side sarcophagi of the Castellani ; and statues of St. Bernard and St. Francis, by L. della Robbia. To the left is the monument to the Countess of Albany, widow of the young Pretender, died at Florence January 29, 1824 ; age, 72 years, 4 months, and 9 days. After the chapel of the Countess of Albany follows the Baroncelli or Guigni chapel, with reredos painting by Giotto, frescoes by T. Gaddi, and a Pietà by Bandinelli.

A handsome door by the side of the Baroncelli chapel opens into the cloisters. In the cloister, the first door left hand opens into the sacristy, built by the Peruzzi family in the 14th cent. Separated from the sacristy by an iron railing is the Rinuccini chapel, with frescoes and altars by Giovanni da Milano (1379), a favourite pupil of T. Gaddi. The reredos painting is by T. Gaddi, 1375. At the extremity of the cloister is the Cappella del Noviziato. At the entrance is a shrine by Mino da Fiesole, and opposite it, and also over the altar, admirable specimens of L. Robbia's terra-cotta work. The large relief is considered one of Robbia's master-pieces. The small door to the right of the altar leads to the room where the remains of Galileo were kept many years after his death (in 1642). There are also two mausoleums—one to a young American girl, Fauveau ; and another attributed to Donatello, both executed with much expression.

Returning to the church, we have, in the first chapel (right) frescoes of the Giotto school, and an Assumption by Allori. Second chapel, frescoes by Gio. da Giovanni. In the third, the Bonaparte chapel, is, to the left, the monument by Pampaloni, 1839, to the memory of the wife of Joseph Bonaparte ; and, to the left, another to the memory of their daughter, Julie Clary Bonaparte (d. 1845). The fourth, or the first to the right of the high altar, is the Peruzzi chapel, with reredos

GIOTTO'S FRESCOES—GALILEO—BARTOLINI'S LAST WORK.

by A. del Sarto. On the walls Giotto's best frescoes, representing the stories of St. John the Apostle and of John the Baptist. Fifth, the Bardi chapel. The painting on the altar, representing S. Francesco, is by Cimabue. The frescoes are by Giotto, and represent the life and death of San Francesco.

Chapels of the Choir.—Over the high altar, painting by Andrea Or-cagna. The walls and ceiling are covered with frescoes by Agnolo Gaddi, representing the legend of the finding of the cross, and the life of St. Francis. The five following chapels are not of much importance, excepting the third, in the north transept, painted in fresco by Luigi Sabatelli. The sixth is the Niccolini chapel, with frescoes on the roof, painted in the 17th cent. by Baldassarre Franceschini, surnamed *il Vol-terrano.* This chapel contains five mediocre statues by Francavilla, and two large paintings on wood by Alessandro Allori, and is also richly decorated with beautiful marbles. In the adjoining chapel, belonging to the Bardi family, is a crucifix by Donatello, one of his earliest and best works, yet not equal to that of his rival Brunelleschi in S. Maria Novella (page 267). After the Bardi chapel follow the Zamoyska mausoleum, with a painted reredos by Ligozzi, and the monument to the composer Luigi Cherubini (d. 1842), by Fantac-chiotti. Having arrived at the fine monument to Luigi, at the east corner of the north aisle, to avoid confusion it is better to return to the main entrance, and walk up the north aisle, commencing with the monument and resting-place of

GALILEO GALILEI,

who died in the village of Arcetri (p. 248), in 1642. Over the ceno-taph is his bust, and a representation of his first telescope. Then follows the monument to Pompeio Josephi, a jurist ; 3d, to G. Lani (1770), by Spinazzi,—on the column before this monument is a Pietà by A. Bronzino ; 4th, to Angelus Tavantus, sarcophagus below flat pyra-mid ; 5th, to Vitt. Fossombroni, by L. Bartolini, 1846 ; 6th, to Karolus Marzupinus, the learned secretary of the Florentine Republic, by D. Settignano, 1450 ; 7th, to Antoni Cocchio, 1773 ; and 8th, to *Raffœllo Morghen,* the illustrious Neapolitan engraver, a beautiful monument, by Fantacchiotti. Fronting it, on the column, is the monument to L. B. Alberti, the last work of Bartolini.

To the south of the façade a large doorway gives access to the clois-ters, around a spacious open court. At the far end, within this enclo-sure, is the chapel of the Pazzi, one of Brunelleschi's best works. To the right of the entrance into the cloisters is a building containing the refectory, with a Last Supper, by Giotto, and above it a Crucifixion and Tree of Jesse. In the smaller refectory, adorned with a fine fresco of Gio. di Giovanni, the Inquisition held its tribunals from 1284-1782. The doorkeeper at the gates has the keys of the Pazzi chapel and of the refectory. In the centre of the enclosure is a statue by Bandinelli which originally stood on the high altar of the Duomo.

THE NATIONAL MUSEUM OR BARGELLO.

At the southern end of the Via del Proconsolo, and between the Piazzas Sta. Croce and Signoria, is the National Museum, in the Palazzo del Podestà, built in the 13th cent. by Lapo Tedesco and two Dominican friars, Fra. Sisto and Fra. Ristoro. It bore various names, according to the functions of the different dignities who occupied it. When, in the 17th cent., it was converted into a prison and became the seat of the head of the police, it was called the Bargello. In 1864 it was chosen for the National Museum. Open from 10 till 3.30, 1 fr. Free on feast-days. The walls of the court are ornamented with the escutcheons of 204 Podestas (chief magistrates). The rooms on the ground floor are filled chiefly with armour, among which are a bronze cannon cast in 1636, and Donatello's seated lion, the Marzocco, or the Arms of Florence, a seated lion supporting a shield with its left paw. Ascend to the first floor by the *outside* staircase in the court. It was built by Agnolo Gaddi. At the top, in the vestibule, are two bells, one cast in 1228 by Bart. Pisano, and the other by Cenni in 1670.

First saloon.—All labelled. Principal objects—By *Michael Angelo*, Wounded Apollo, Bacchus and Satyr, Dying Adonis, and an unfinished group of Victory. Donatello, David with the head of Goliath. G. da Bologna. Virtue conquering Vice. A beautiful series of reliefs, illustrating Music and its effects, chiefly by L. Robbia and Donatello. *Second room.*—Furniture and glass ware. Wax group by Zumbo. *Third hall*, the audience chamber of the Podestà.—Majolica, porcelain, and enamelled ware. *Fourth hall*, originally a chapel, but afterwards the room in which prisoners under sentence of death were confined. The frescoes are chiefly by Giotto, 1301. Among the portraits on the fresco of the east wall, representing heaven, are those of Dante, and of his master Brunetto Latini. The St. Jerome and the Madonna are thought to be by Ghirlandaio. In the adjoining Sacristy are two frescoes, one of which is thought to be by Cimabue and the other by Gaddi. Those who wish to see them must request the door to be opened. *Fifth*

SCULPTURE—MICHAEL ANGELO—BOLOGNA—CELLINI.

saloon.—Two triptychs by Orcagna. Works in ivory and rock crystal by Cellini, Bologna, and N. Pisano. Wood carving by Gibbons. (In this saloon is the stair up to the second floor.) *Saloons 6 and 7.*— Sculptures by the best Italian artists of the 15th cent., all labelled. Among them may be noted, in the sixth saloon, Donatello's David, in the centre. In the seventh, in the centre, a Child by Donatello. The famous *Mercury*, by Bologna. David, by Verrochio. On the wall, a bronze table by Pollaiolo, representing the Crucifixion, and two bas-reliefs, the one on the right by Ghiberti, and the other on the left by Brunelleschi, prepared for the competition for the doors of the Baptistery of Florence, won by Ghiberti. Next, a fine ornament by Donatello. At the beginning of the third wall is a large bas-relief by V. Dante, representing the Brazen Serpent in the Desert ; and below it, another representing a Battle, by Bertoldo. These are followed by a cabinet full of sketches by the best artists of the 15th and 16th cents. After these, the famous bust of Cosmo of Medicis in Armour, by Benvenuto Cellini, and his model in bronze of the Perseus, under the loggia. Ascend now to the second floor by the stair in the fifth room. 1st room.—Portraits in fresco by A. Castagno (1450), transferred to canvas a few years ago : viz. Uberti, Acciaoli, Dante, Petrarch, and Boccaccio. Stained glass by Marcilla, 1470-1537. 2d room on the right.—Fine display of glazed terra-cotta work by Luca and Andrea Robbia. Stained glass window by Giovanni da Udini. 3d room (tower).—Tapestry 17th cent. 4th room (on the left of the entrance).—French tapestry and collection of coins. In the next two rooms, 5 and 6, are the **Masterpieces of Mediæval Sculpture**, which formerly stood in the galleries of the Uffizi. Room 5, in centre, John the Baptist, by Donatello. On the wall, in relief, by B. da Rovezzano, 1507, the Translation of St. Gualberto, on white marble, mutilated. Room 6, in the centre, St. John by Benedetto da Maiano. Young Bacchus, by Sansovino. Apollo, by Michael Angelo. On end wall, the Death of St. Peter, by L. Robbia. By Michael Angelo, the Virgin, Jesus, and St. John (unfinished) ; the famous Mask of a Satyr (executed in his 15th year) ; Martyrdom of St. Andrew (unfinished) ; and Bust of Brutus. Window wall, bust of Battista Sforza, and a Holy Family, by Mino da Fiesole. Entrance wall, Leda, by Michael Angelo. By Mina da Fiesole, a Madonna and a bust of Piero dei Medici. Left wall, by Rossellino, a Madonna and a St. John. Faith, by Civitale, 1484, one of his best works. Five children supporting festoons, by Quercia, 1150, one of his best ; and a Madonna, by Verrochio.

FLORENCE.   LA BADIA—HOUSE OF MICHAEL ANGELO.

At the end of the Via Proconsolo, and opposite the National Museum, is La Badia, founded by Willa, in 978, for the Black Benedictines ; rebuilt in 1284 by Arnolfo di Lapo ; and again, in part, in 1625 by Segaloni. The church, in the form of a Greek cross, has some good monuments and pictures. The Campanile was built about 1330. The handsome door is by Benedetto da Rovezzano, 1495. The second monument to the right of the entrance is to Gianozzo Pandolfini, by Ferrucci in 1457. On the adjoining altar are beautiful reliefs by Maiano, 1442 to 1497. In the north transept is the mausoleum of the Gonfalonier Bernardo Giugni, d. (1466), by Mino da Fiesole. In the south transept is the mausoleum of Count Ugo of Tuscany (d. 1000). Above is an Assumption, by G. Vasari, and in the Cappella de' Bianchi, a Madonna appearing to St. Bernard, by F. Lippi.

A little way east from the National Museum, at No. 64 Via Ghibellina, is the house of Michael Angelo Buonarrotti, a plain building, containing a collection of paintings, sculptures, and sundry objects connected with Michael Angelo, bequeathed to the care of the State by the last member of the family, Cosmo Buonarrotti, in 1858. The gallery is open to the public on Mondays and Thursdays, from 9 to 3. Catalogue in Italian or French, ½ fr. The collection is contained in seven rooms, some very small. In the centre of the first room is a small bust of Michael Angelo, and Nos. 1, 2, and 3 portraits of him at different ages. No. 14, Battle of Hercules, and No. 17, Madonna, both in relief, by Michael Angelo. Nos. 11, 13, 15, and 16 are glazed terra-cotta figures by the Robbias, displaying admirably the fine delicate surface of the enamel peculiar to their productions. Amongst those who have distinguished themselves in the manufactory of earthenware is Luca della Robbia, a Florentine goldsmith and statuary, born in 1388. He made heads and human figures in relief, and architectural ornaments of glazed earthenware, terra-cotta invetriata. The colours are white, blue, green, brown, and yellow. The art of making these glazed earthen figures invented by Luca was taught by him to his brothers Ottaviano and Agostino, and was afterwards practised by his nephew Andrea. The rooms to the left contain, drawings and plans of Michael Angelo, many being the original sketches of his greatest works. First room right, the principal room of all, contains the statue of Michael Angelo in a sitting posture, by Novelli ; and around the room sixteen pictures illustrating scenes in his life. The lower six are in grisaille. The ceiling is painted in fresco. The next or fourth room contains the family history, illustrated by twenty-one fresco paintings. In the small cabinet off this room are, among other things, a two-edged sword with the

Buonarrotti arms. In the fifth room, No. 74, Michael Angelo, a Madonna in relief, on marble. 77, a cast in bronze of 74, by Jean Bologna, by whom is also 81, a bust of Michael Angelo. Sixth room (the Library), large frescoes, representing the eminent men of Italy. In the seventh chamber, and in the small room off, are Etruscan antiquities.

San Giovannino, 264. San Lorenzo, 264. The Mortuary Chapel. The Sagrestia Nuova, 265. Biblioteca Laurentiana. Etruscan and Egyptian Museum, 267. Santa Maria Novella, 267. Spezeria, 268. See Plan, near station.

NORTH from the baptistery, at the end of the Via de Martelli, and next the Palazzo Riccardi (see page 275), is the Church of San Giovannino, rebuilt in the 16th cent., with frescoes representing scenes in the life of Christ, by Passignano, Barbieri, Bronzino, Tito, Corradi, and Ligozzi. A few yards west from San Giovannino is SAN LORENZO, considered in the earlier periods of the Republic the metropolitan church of Florence. Its existence is traced as far back as the year 393, when it was consecrated by St. Ambrose. In 1059 it was rebuilt and consecrated by Pope Nicholas II. Having been destroyed by fire in 1417, during a festival given by the Guelphs of Arezzo and the Guelphs of Florence, it was again rebuilt by Brunelleschi and Michael Angelo, and finished by Antonio Manetti in 1461. It is constructed in the form of a T, 400 feet long from east to west, and 170 from north to south. The aisles are lofty, and separated from the nave by 14 Corinthian columns. The two pulpits are adorned with subjects from Scripture, in relief, by Donatello and his pupil Bertoldo. The cupola is painted by Meucci. At the north transept is a monument in white marble by Thorwaldsen to Pietro Benvenuto, the painter of the cupola of the mortuary chapel. In the south transept is a monument to the memory of a daughter of General Moltke. A slab at the foot of the high altar bears the title and age of Cosmo I., but his remains repose in a black and white marble tomb in the subterranean church. Those pressed for time should, on arriving at the main or eastern entrance of St. Lorenzo, turn down to the left by that narrow busy street the Via del Canto de' Nelli, to the large folding-doors under the west end or apse of San Lorenzo, which gives access to the burial chapel, "Dei Principi," of the Medici family, and to the still more famous chapel called the Sagrestia Nuova. Both open on Sundays from 10, on Mondays from 12, and every other day from 9 to 3. Having entered the crypt, ascend the stair to the left, which leads into the mortuary chapel.

FLORENCE.   UNDERGROUND CHAPEL—·MORTUARY CHAPEL.

Guides offer their assistance, but they are of no use, as the sacristan
alone can unlock the doors. The Mortuary Chapel is octagonal, and
covered with polished marbles and other shining stones, glowing with
brilliant harmony of colour, yet chaste and simple. The splendid hues
are continued on the ceiling under the dome by the masterly frescoes
of P. Benvenuti, painted in 1835. In each of six of the sides is a
monument to a member of the Medicean family, from Cosmo I. to
Cosmo III. (d. 1723), whose son, G. Gastone (d. 1736), has his memorial
slab behind the altar in the crypt or lower church downstairs, where
repose the remains of Donatello near those of his patron Cosmo I., as well
as those of 35 other members of this once powerful family, which gave
three popes to the Church of Rome, two queens to France, and reigned
250 years over the sixteen cities of Tuscany, whose escutcheons in beautiful mosaic are set in panels round the mortuary chapel, below the granite
mausoleums of these princes. The Cappella dei Principi was designed
by G. de Medici, and built by M. Nigetti in 1604, for Ferdinand I., Duke
of Tuscany, to receive the "great stone" which Joseph of Arimathea
rolled " to the door of the sepulchre " of our Lord ; and which had been
promised him by the Emir Focardino, governor of Jerusalem. The
Emir not having fulfilled his promise, Ferdinand adopted the intention of his predecessor, Cosmo I., and had it converted into
the burial chapel of the Medicean family. From this chapel a
short narrow passage leads to the **Sagrestia Nuova**, or the
Cappella dei Depositi, containing the monuments and mortal remains
of Giuliano, Duke of Nemours, and brother of Pope Leo X. ; and of their
nephew Lorenzo, Duke of Urbino, and father of Catherine of Medicis ;
these two monuments, with the statue of Moses at Rome, are the greatest
works of Michael Angelo. The plan of the edifice was conceived by
Pope Leo, but the design and execution were entrusted in 1521 to
Michael Angelo. The interior is disappointing. A formal square
chapel, with walls partly encrusted with whitish marble, supported by
two tiers of Corinthian pilasters of that cold grey stone called pietra dura,
and pierced with doors and windows arranged in the same tame, flat style.
To the right on entering is the grand monument of Giuliano. He is
represented in a sitting posture, with his left hand gloved and raised.
The bent forefinger touches the upper lip, which seems to yield to the
pressure. The helmet throws a deep shade on the countenance. The
two statues reclining on the urn represent Day and Night. Day is
little more than blocked, yet most magnificent. To have done more
would have weakened the striking effect of the whole, which is

heightened by what is left to the imagination. Night is finely imagined. The attitude is beautiful, mournful, and full of the most touching expression—the drooping head and the supporting hand are unrivalled in the arts. Opposite is the monument of the nephew. The attitude of Lorenzo is marked by such a cast of deep melancholy brooding as to have acquired for it the title of "il pensiero." Beneath are the personifications of Evening and Dawn. Twilight is represented by a superb manly figure, reclining and looking down ; the breadth of chest and the fine balance of the sunk shoulder are masterly, while the right limb, which is finished, is incomparable. The Aurora is a female figure of exquisite proportions. In its serene countenance a spring of thought, an awakening principle, seems to breathe life into the face of stone, as if preparing it to open its eyes with the rising day. In front of the altar is a striking but unfinished Madonna, by Michael Angelo. On the right is a statue of San Cosmo, by Montorsoli, a pupil of Michael Angelo's, and on the left Santo Damiano, by Montelupo.

A door in the middle of the south aisle of the church of S. Lorenzo leads into the cloister, whence ascend the staircase, by Vasari, to the Bibliotheca Mediceo-Laurentiana. The books are kept in desks. Open from 9 to 3. Closed on feast-days. Fee, 1 fr. This library was founded by Cosmo in 1444. Amongst the remarkable manuscripts there is one of Virgil of the 4th cent. in Roman capitals, not very different in form from the letters on ancient Roman marbles ; it is on vellum, of the size of a small quarto, with notes ; the notes written in the 5th cent. by the Consul Turcius Rufus Apronianus, as his signature attests. This is one of the most ancient legible manuscript books in Europe of which the period is authentic. The manuscript of Virgil, in the Vatican library, with paintings, was said to be of the 4th cent., of the time of Constantine. The manuscripts of the middle ages, instead of being in Roman capitals, are written in letters resembling in some degree the small Roman printed letter now in use ; and, at a still later period, they are in a running hand. This library also possesses the celebrated manuscript of the Pandects, supposed to be of the time of Justinian, in the 6th cent., written in capital letters, which vary a little from the capitals on ancient Roman marbles ; it is on vellum, of the size of a large folio book ; it was brought from Pisa, and Cosmo I. caused an edition to be printed from it by Lelio Torelli. A Tacitus, of the 11th cent. is in a running letter. The library contains 8000 volumes of manuscripts. Many of them are chained to the desks.

Between S. Lorenzo and San Maria Novella in the Via Faenza, No.

FLORENCE. ETRUSCAN MUSEUM—S. MARIA NOVELLA.

144, is the Etruscan and Egyptian Museum. Open from 9 to 4. Fee, 1 fr. Free on Sundays.

First Room, The vases stand round the room in glass cases. The earliest are in the first case to the right. Next, case 11, is the entrance to an Etruscan tomb, which in its main features resembles that in which our Lord lay. From the frescoes, which are copies of the original on the tomb near Orvieto, it will be observed that the Etruscans seem to have treated death as a feast, to which the spirits were invited by the gods. *Second Room*, In the centre is the vase of Peleus, or vase of François, by whom it was discovered in 1845 near Chiusi. It is supposed to have been modelled by Ergatimos, and painted by Clitias. *Third Room*, Minor objects. *First Octagon Room*, Beautiful gold ornaments, beads, and glass bowls. Etruscan coins. From this room a corridor extends to a similar room, in which is a beautiful bronze statue of Pallas Athene with the ægis, and some fine Etruscan mirrors. *Fourth Room*, In the centre stands the Chimæra, one of the celebrated statues of antiquity. *Fifth Room right*, Armour. *Sixth Room*, Etruscan sculpture. Both of the gems of the collection are in this room— *The Orator*, a bronze statue above life size, discovered near Lake Thrasymene ; and an *Etruscan Sarcophagus*, which lay nearly 2000 years buried in the earth, and is supposed to have been made˙about 300 years B.C. From this we enter, by a passage covered with inscriptions, into the Egyptian Museum. *First Room*, In the centre, a Scythian war-chariot (the only specimen known), and by the side of it the remains of the Egyptian soldier who probably captured the chariot in battle. *Second Room*, The most interesting object here is the fresco of the *Last Supper, by Raphael*, in 1505, when only twenty-two. On the border of St. Thomas's dress are the date and name. In the last great hall are sarcophagi, reliefs, statues, obelisks, idols, mummies, portraits, and tabernacles.

Close to the railway station, and a short way west from the cathedral and S. Lorenzo, is the church of Santa Maria Novella, facing the piazza of the same name, adorned with two large obelisks of Serravezza Mischio marble, crowned with Florentine lilies in bronze, by G. Bologna, 1608.

This church, standing south and north, was commenced in 1221 and finished in 1371. The façade was designed by L. Alberti, and erected at the expense of G. Rucellai, whose name is inscribed on the frieze, " Joannes Orcellarius, 1470." Affixed to it are gnomonic instruments, made by Ignazio Dante in 1573. In the interior, the fresco over the principal door is after the Lippi school. The crucifix is by a pupil of Giotto, Puccio Capanna. On the wall to the right of the door is a remarkable fresco, a Trinity, by Masaccio ; opposite is a fresco attributed to Gaddi. But the most interesting objects are all at the northern or apsidial end of the church. At the extremity of the east or right transept, up some steps, is the Rucellai Chapel. On the reredos of the altar is the Madonna painted by Cimabue, considered his masterpiece. The walls of the chancel, or recess occupied by the high altar, are covered with exquisite paintings in fresco by D. Ghirlandaio, nearly all representing scenes from Scripture. The stalls are by B. d'Agnola, and the windows by G. Fiorentino. In the chapel on the left, or west from this, the Cappella Gondi, is the famous wooden *Crucifix by Brunelleschi.* A curtain is before it. At the end of the W. transept, up some steps, is the Strozzi chapel, with frescoes by A. Orcagna and his brother Nardo, representing the Day of Judgment, Heaven, and Hell. The open door at the foot of the steps leads into the sacristy, where, immediately on one side of the door, is a beautiful terra-cotta basin, by L. Robbia ; and, on the other side, one of marble by G. Fortini. A large door in the west, or left aisle, opens into the cloister called the Chiostro Verde, because the frescoes on the walls, by Paolo Uccello, 1390-1470, and Dello Delli, 1401, are painted in green. Here the keeper, for a few sous, opens the door leading into the Cappella degli Spagnuoli, designated thus from having been used by the attendants of Eleonora de Toledo, wife of Cosmo I. The ceiling and the left wall are covered with admirably conceived and executed frescoes by Taddeo Gaddi, while those on the right wall are by Simone Memmi. Adjoining is the Chiostro Grande, ornamented with 52 frescoes, by Cigoli, Allori, Tito, Poccetti, and other artists of the 15th and 16th cent., illustrative of the history of the Dominicans, with views of Florence in the background. At No. 16 Via della Scala is the entrance to the *Spezeria,* or pharmacy of the convent, long noted for its perfumes, as well as for a red liquor called Alkermes, a specialty of Florence, resembling in taste the liqueur made at the Chartreuse, near Grenoble, only sweeter. It is also made and sold at the Certosa (see page 250). The chapel contains some beautiful frescoes, illustrative of the last hours of our Saviour, by Spinello Aretino.

The Santissima Annunziata, 268. San Marco, 270. Picture-Gallery of San Marco, 270. Academy of Fine Arts, 271. Galleria dei Lavori in Pietre Dure, 273. North-east side of Plan.

FROM the N.E. end of the Cathedral the street, the Via dei Servi, leads straight to the Piazza and Church of the *Santissima Annunziata* the only church in Florence open the whole day. All the others close at 12; but most of them re-open about 2 or 3 P.M. On the right side of the Piazza is the Spedale degli Innocenti, a foundling hospital designed by Brunelleschi, and ornamented in 1470, by Andrea della Robbia, with pretty terra-cotta figures over the columns of the arcade. In the centre of the square is an equestrian statue of the Grand Duke Ferdinand I., by Bologna, in 1608, and two bronze fountains by Pietro Tacca. The **Church of the Annunziata** was built in 1250 by the Order of the Servi di Maria. At the entrance is a narthex or vestibule decorated with admirable frescoes, protected by glass. To the right, on entering, an Assumption by Il Rosso, 1515; then follow a Visitation, by J. Pontormo, 1516, pupil of A. del Sarto; a Marriage of the Virgin, by Franciabigio, 1513; a Birth of the Virgin, by Andrea del Sarto, as also the next picture, an Adoration of the Magi, both among his greatest works; a Nativity by A. Baldovinetti. The next five are by A. del Sarto; Children being Healed by touching the Dress of the Servite Filippo Benizzi; a Dead Child recalled to life by touching the Bier of Filippo; the Cure of a Woman possessed of a Demon; Men destroyed by Lightning who had insulted Filippo. He parts his Cloak with a Beggar. By Rosselli: Filippo assumes the habit of the Order. In the narthex is also the tomb of Andrea del Sarto (died 1606), with bust by Caccini.

The design of the interior of the church is by Ant. da S. Gallo. Gherardo Silvani added the marble decorations. The pictures between the windows are almost all by C. Ulivelli. On each side of the aisle are five chapels, and at the termination of the aisle are two short transepts and a circular tribuna designed by Alberti, covered with a cupola painted by B. Franceschini and Ulivelli. In the right transept is the tomb of Bandinelli, with a Pieta by himself. Immediately behind the high altar, adorned with a ciborium or canopy by B. Agnolo (1543), is the Cappella del Soccorso, with the tomb of Gian Bologna (d. 1608), who constructed this chapel for himself, and ornamented it with some of his best works. Under the organ in the second chapel is an Assumption by Perugino. In the third chapel is a Crucifixion by Stradano, his best work. In the fourth, a copy of Michael Angelo's "Judgment Day," by Allori. Next it, and to the left of the main entrance, is the chapel and shrine of the *Annunziata*, built in 1445, by Michelozzi, and lighted by forty-one silver lamps and one gold lamp glittering among costly polished stones. Over the altar is an Annunciation in fresco by Pietro Cavallini (d. 1364), said to have been done by angels. This picture is shown only once a year; but a duplicate of it, also by Cavallini, is in San Marco, on the wall to the right on entering. Over the altar is an "Ecce Homo," by An. del Sarto, in silver. Adjoining is the cloister built by S. Pollaiolo. Over the door opening into the church is a "Holy Family," by A. del Sarto, a production in the highest style of excellence, called the Madonna del Saco, as Joseph is seen in the background seated on a sack. The other fresco paintings in the cloister are by Poccetti, A. Mascagni, M. Rosselli, and V. Salimbeni (1542-1650), all displaying rich colouring without gaudiness. In this cloister is also the chapel of *St. Luke*, with the fresco of "St. Luke painting the Virgin," over the altar, is by Vasari, while those on the walls are by Bronzino, Pontormo, and Santi di Tito.

By referring to the plan, it will be observed that near to the Annunziata are the Academy of Fine Arts and the Church of S. Marco (standing from S.W. to N.E.) We shall commence with *San Marco*, erected in 1290, and enlarged in 1427 by Michelozzi. Interior.—Over central door a "Crucifixion" by Giotto. First altar right, Thomas Aquinas before the Cross by S. di Tito, and an Annunciation by P. Cavallini (covered). Second altar, Madonna and Saints, Fra. Bartolommeo. Third, Madonna. Here a small door opens into the sacristy built by Michelozzi, with statue of Christ by Novelli, and of S. Antonino by Montorsoli. To the left of the high altar is the Chapel of the Sacrament, with paintings by Tito, Empoli, Poccetti, and Passignano. In the left transept is the chapel of S. Antonino, with frescoes by Passignano in his best style, and a painting by Bronzino. Between the second and third altars on this the left side of the church, are the graves of the scholar Pico della Mirandola, d. 1494; the poet Girolano Benivieni, d. 1542 ; and of Poliziano, d. 1494, tutor to the sons of Lorenzo the Magnificent. To the right of the main entrance is the Convent, now the *Picture-Gallery*, of St. Mark. Open from 10 to 3. Fee, 1 fr. Sundays free. During the 15th and 16th cent. this convent had for its superiors the good Bishop Antonino (d. 1459), Fra. Angelico Fiesole (d. 1455), Fra. Girolamo Savonarola, the great preacher and martyr (1498), and Fra. Bartolommeo della Porta (d. 1517), the best collection of whose works is in this convent. Among the very fine frescoes are— On the door of the church, left hand wall, "St. Peter, martyr, with his hand on his mouth," B. Angelico. On the end or S.E. wall, "Crucifixion," with St. Dominic, B. Angelico. The door in the wall opposite the church opens into the refectory, with a fresco representing Angels bringing food to St. Dominic, by Sogliani (d. 1544), pupil of L. Credi. Above is a "Crucifixion" by Fra. Bartolommeo. The door in

THE FRENCH
WALDENSIAN VALLEYS.

English Miles

Railways   Carriage Roads

eastwards see map, page 304.

the south corner of the east wall opens into the chapter-house, with a
large fresco of the Crucifixion by B. Angelico.   A very famous work.
The crucifix on the left is by B. Montelupo, and the other by his son.
The door in the middle of the east wall gives access to the picture-gallery in the upper storey.   At the foot of this stair is a grand picture, a
Last Supper (Cenacolo) by Ghirlandaio, who has dressed the company
in the costume of the brotherhood.   From this ascend to the first floor
to what were the cells or rooms of the monks, ranged on each side of a
narrow passage ornamented with paintings in fresco.   At the head of
the stair is a very beautiful Annunciation by Fra. Angelico, and also by
him, on the opposite wall, a St. Dominic embracing the Cross.   Opposite
the Crucifixion is the best of the corridors.   The cells of the right corridor are ornamented with frescoes, principally by Fra. Benedetto, and
those of the left principally by his more famous brother, Fra. Angelico.
Next the staircase we have the library.   Second room, banners used for
Dante's festival in 1865.   Next, two frescoes by Benedetto.   In the
last two rooms, one a little higher than the other, Cosmo de' Medici
(Pater Patriæ) used frequently to reside.   His portrait is by Pontormo,
"The Jesus of Nazareth" is by Fra. Bartolommeo, and the beautiful
fresco by Angelico.   In the cell opposite is a Crucifixion by Angelico.
In the third room, painted on wood by Angelico, are an "Adoration"
and an "Annunciation."   In the fourth, also by him, other two famous
pictures on wood, the *Madonna della Stella* and the *Coronation of Mary*.
Turning to the right we find all the cells (as far as that of Savonarola),
with paintings by Fra. Benedetto or some pupil of Angelico.   In the
middle of this corridor is the beautiful Madonna enthroned, an admirable work of B. Angelico.   At the end, in a kind of chapel, are two
Madonnas on the wall by Fra. Bartolomeo : a Virgin in *terra invetriata*,
by L. della Robbia ; the bust of Savonarola, full of expression, modelled
by Bastianini ; and a sketch of the bust of Benivieni by Bastianini.   In
the two little cells at the side, in which dwelt Savonarola, are preserved
some manuscripts, a crucifix, and other objects which belonged to
him ; as also his portrait painted by Fra. Bartolommeo, and a view of
the Piazza della Signoria, with the burning of Savonarola and his companions.   Proceeding along the corridor, in which there are no cells on
the right for some distance, we come to more frescoes by Benedetto, the
best being a "Coronation" in the third cell.

At the south-west corner of the Piazza San Marco, at No. 34 Via
Ricasoli, is the entrance to the **Academy of Fine Arts.**   Open from 9
till 3.   Fee, 1 fr.   Sundays, free.   The principal door is by Paoletti.

ACADEMY OF THE FINE ARTS.

In the vestibule are reliefs and busts of contemporary artists by L. della Robbia. In the cloister are bas-reliefs by the brother and nephew of Robbia, and Bologna's models for his statues of Virtue and Vice, and of the Rape of the Sabines. A corridor, containing statues in stucco, to the right of the main entrance, leads to the library. Midway, left hand, a door opens into the principal gallery, the hall of the large pictures, with 124 paintings, by the following artists : M. Albertinelli, A. Allori, B. Angelico, Spinello Aretino, Fra. Bartolommeo, Biliverti, F. Boschi, Botticelli, Brina, Bronzino, Buffalmaccio, Calabrese, A. Castagno, Cigoli, Cimabue, Credi, Curradi, C. Dolci, I. Empoli, Gen. da Fabriano, A. and T. Gaddi, R. del Garbo, Ghirlandaio, Giotto, Ligozzi, Fra. F. Lippi, Aur. Lomi, Masaccio, Giov. da Milano, Monaco, S. P. Nelli, L. di Niccolo, D. Passignani, Perugino, F. Pesellino, Fra. P. da Pistoia, Poccetti, Fr. Poppi, C. Rosselli, A. Sacchi, A. del Sarto, L. Signorelli, G. A. Sogliani, A. Squazelli, Santi di Tito, Vasari, Veracini, Verrochio, Vignali. In No. 43, the Baptism of Christ, by Verrochio, the angel to the right of the spectator was painted by Leonardo da Vinci when he was twenty-three years old. No. 115, by Cigoli, St. Francis. It is said that in order to obtain the unearthly expression of the face the painter kept a poor pilgrim for many hours without food, until he fainted from hunger. This room is followed by a chamber communicating with the Tribune, built in 1875, for the celebrated statue of *David*, sculptured by Michael Angelo when 28 years of age. It was brought here in 1873 from the Piazza della Signoria, where it had stood 369 years. From the library a door opens into the Hall of Ancient Pictures, containing sixty paintings. The artists of a large number are unknown. The others are by B. Angelico, S. Aretino, M. Arezzo, A. Baldovinetti, B. Berlinghieri, Neri di Bicci, Sim. da Bologna, S. Botticelli, P. di Buonaguida, A. Ceraiolo, D. Ghirlandaio, Bicci di Lorenzo, G. Pacchiarotto, and Signorelli. In the hall of the small pictures there are seventy-one paintings, by artists already named, the most important being Fra. and B. Angelico, who, with Sandro Botticelli, Francesco Granacci, Luca Signorelli, and Lorenzo di Credi, are better represented here than anywhere else. The most remarkable are 41, "The Day of Judgment," by Fra. Angelico. 13, A "Nativity," by L. di Credi ; and 18, Portraits of two Vallombrosian friars, by Raphael or Perugino. Beyond this is a collection of original designs in a room called the Sala dei Cartoni. 2 and 5 are by Raphael. 6, Correggio. 3 and 12, Ben. Poccetti. 1, 4, 9, 10, 11, 18, and 22, Fra. Bartolommeo. 19, Bronzino. 7, 8, and 20, F. Barroccio. 24, Credi, and 23, Carlo Cignani.

FLORENCE. MOSAICS—GALLERIA DEI LAVORI IN PIETRE DURE.

From the vestibule a staircase leads up to the Galleria dei Quadri Moderni, a collection of 160 modern paintings, distributed in six rooms. The custodian of the academy keeps the keys of the Cloister dello Scalzo, No. 69 Via Cavour, adorned with fourteen frescoes by A. del Sarto, and two by his friend Franciabigio, in chiaroscuro, during 1517 to 1526, illustrative of the life of John the Baptist. They are not in a good state of preservation.

Adjoining the Accademia delle belle Arti, at No. 82 Via degli Alfani, is the entrance into the Galleria dei Lavori in Pietre Dure, open from 10 to 3 daily. Entrance free. Rooms 1, 2, and 3 contain, in glass cases, specimens of all the minerals and rocks used in Florence in the manufacture of mosaics. They are numbered, and accompanied with explanatory catalogues. They consist chiefly of varieties of marble and alabaster, agates of different shades, chalcedony, jasper, lapis lazuli, and red porphyry. The large room contains the finished mosaics, all for sale, at prices from £80 upwards. Mosaics are made and sold in numerous establishments throughout the city, but the best and most artistic are sold here.

THE PALACES OF FLORENCE.

The palaces of Florence are great square edifices of a grand and gloomy aspect, built of dark blue stones (pietra forte) measuring from 3 to 4 feet. The bases, to the height of from 20 to 30 feet, consist of coarsely chiselled rubble work, which lessens the baldness, and contributes character and effect to the from 200 to 300 feet of plain wall. At intervals are strong bronze banner-rings and torch-sockets, while at each corner is a curiously-shaped lamp of wrought-iron. Near the main entrance there is generally a niche, with an opening called a "cantina," just large enough to allow a quart bottle to pass through, whence various articles of food are transmitted into the house. Those that sell by retail the oil and wine from their estates have painted over this niche "Vino é Olio." The empty bottle, with the money, having been passed through, it reappears shortly after full. The windows of the first range are generally 10 feet from the ground, and are grated and barred like those of a prison. Under the eaves runs a deep cornice with bold projecting soffits. The roofs of the palaces, as well as those of the smallest houses, are of a low pitch, and covered with tiles of two different forms—a flat tile with ledges on the side, and a tile nearly semi-cylindrical and tapering upwards, which thus covers the interstice between the ledges of the flat tiles. The entrance to the palaces is by a high arched massive gateway, giving access to a court surrounded by

T

an arcade or loggia, whence massive stone staircases lead up to the highest storeys. The lofty ceilings of the principal rooms are decorated, and the beams though displayed, are carved, painted, and gilded, and contribute to the grandeur of the whole. The floors are of thin bricks, either laid flat or edgeways in the herring-bone or *spina di pesce* fashion. As in Genoa, several of the palaces contain collections of works of art open to the public on certain days. Of these the best are—first, the Palazzo Vecchio, in the Piazza della Signoria, erected in 1218 by Arnolfo di Lapo. It is surmounted by a noble antique tower 305 feet high, commanding an excellent view of Florence. The entrance is through a superb but gloomy court, surrounded by an arcade on massive columns, by Michelozzi, substituted for those of Arnoldo in 1434. They are 8 feet in circumference, and of admirable proportions. In the centre is a neat little fountain by Andrea Verocchio, intended originally for the Villa Careggi. Having traversed this court, ascend first stair left hand, and keep turning to the left the length of the first storey, where take first door right, which opens into the great hall or council chamber, 170 feet long by 77 broad, built in 1495, but altered by Vasari in 1540, who also added the frescoes on the walls and oil-painting on the ceiling illustrative of events in the history of Florence. Now ascend to the second storey, where enter the ante-room to the left, the Sala de' Gigli, with a grand but injured fresco by Ghirlandaio in 1482. The lintel of the door in this room opening into the next, the Sala d'Udienza, is by Benedetto da Majano. On one of the leaves of the door is a linear drawing of Dante, and on the other one of Petrarch. The Sala d'Udienza is painted in fresco by Salviati, illustrative of Roman history. It communicates with the Cappella S. Bernardo, beautifully painted in imitation of mosaic by R. Ghirlandaio. Near the chapel of St. Bernard (sometimes approached by the four rooms of Eleanora de Toledo, painted by Stradan of Bruges, and at other times by a narrow passage), is a small chapel beautifully painted by Bronzino, and an adjoining chamber painted by Poccetti.

North from the palace, by the Via dei Magazzini, is the Via S. Martino, in which is a house with a marble slab over the door, bearing the following inscription : "In questa casa degli Alighieri nacque il Divino Poeta."—*Dante.* He was married to Gemma in S. Martino, a humble little church close by, in the Via dei Magazzini. The Beatrice of Dante (like Petrarch's Laura) lived in the Palazzo Salviati, in the Via del Proconsolo. She married Giovanni delle Bande Nere, and became the mother of Cosmo I.

FLORENCE. PALAZZO STROZZI—CORSINI—RICCARDI.

In the Via Tornabuoni is the Palazzo Strozzi, open on Wednesdays from 11 to 1. It was built in 1489 from designs by Majano. The iron-work, rings, and lanterns are by Grosso di Ferrara, 1510. The picture-gallery on the first floor is contained in four large rooms elegantly and comfortably furnished. In each room there is a list of the paintings on a card. The two most remarkable are—Portrait of one of the ladies Strozzi by Leonardo da Vinci; and another of one of the children, "La Puttina," by Tiziano. Between the Strozzi Palace and the Arno is the Piazza S. Trinità. In it, opposite the Hotel du Nord, is a column of Oriental granite from the baths of Antoninus, presented to Cosmo I. by Pius IV. A short way down the Arno (see plan), at No. 10 Lungarno Corsini, is the Palazzo Corsini, built (1618-56) by G. Silvani, staircase by Ferri. The collection of paintings, contained in twelve rooms, may be visited on Tuesdays, Thursdays, and Saturdays from 10 till 2. Entrance by No. 7 Via Parione.

Next to the church S. Giovannino (see p. 264), at No. 1 Via Cavour, is the Prefettura della Provincia di Firenze, formerly the Palazzo Ric-cardi, 300 feet long by 90 in height. This, the cradle of the Medicean family, was erected in 1431, after the design of Michelozzi, by Cosmo Pater Patriae, and continued to be the residence of the Medici till 1540, when it was abandoned for the Palazzo Vecchio. The first row of large windows was opened by Michael Angelo; for originally the base, rising to 30 feet, presented one unbroken space, varied only by the projection of the vast and rudely chiselled stones of which it is composed. In the court below the corridor are statues and busts, and the sarcophagi which were formerly outside the baptistery, and a curtain beautifully sculp-tured in stone over one of the arches. Upstairs are the Biblioteca Ric-. cardi, a picture-gallery, and a small chapel covered with most charming frescoes by Benozzo Gozzoli 1400-1478, painted by lamplight, as the chapel at that time had no window. Palace open from 12.30 till 2.

Down the Arno, beyond the Ponte alla Carraia (see plan), is the Church of Ognissanti. In the chapel next the door of the sacristy repose the remains of Amerigo Vespucci, who gave his name to America. In the centre of the nave are frescoes by Ghirlandaio and Botticelli. The frescoes in the cloisters illustrating the life of St. Francis are by Giovanni and Ligozzi. The Last Supper, in the refectory, is by Ghir-landaio. A little way up the street called the Borgo Ognissanti is the Hospital S. Giovanni di Dio, founded by Amerigo Vespucci; while the house in which he lived and died stood on the site of the present No. 21 Borgo Ognissanti.

PARK OF FLORENCE—VILLA CAREGGI—PALAZZO TORRIGIANI.

At the west end of the town, near the Porta Prato, is the Cascine or Park of Florence, on the right or north bank of the Arno, much frequented in the afternoon. An omnibus runs every 10 minutes between the Porta Prato and the Piazza della Signoria. Opposite the Cascine is the hill Monte Oliveto, page 251. Nearly two miles north from the railway station by the Romito road is the Villa Careggi, built by Michelozzi for Cosmo Pater Patriae, in which he died on August 1, 1464, as also Lorenzo the Magnificent, on the 8th of April 1492. At the Ponte alle Grazie, the first bridge above the Ponte Vecchio, is the Palazzo Torrigiani, built by Baccio d'Agnolo, containing a valuable collection of paintings, accompanied with catalogues. Open daily excepting Saturdays and Sundays.

FIESOLE.

At the east side of the town, by the Via Alfieri or Pinti, is the Protestant cemetery, between the Boulevards Eugenio and Amedeo, the latter leading northwards to the Piazza Cavour with the Porta S. Gallo. From this Porta commences the road to the Etrurian city of Fæsula, the modern *Fiesole*, 3 miles from Florence, and about 600 feet above it, on the summit of a ridge composed of a dark-coloured sandstone. Rail to Fiesole. Carriage there and back, 8 to 10 fr. From the Porta S. Gallo it is an easy walk of about 2½ miles. See the excellent map of the environs (Dintorni) of Florence, published by the "Istituto Topografico Militare," 1 fr. Beyond the Porta S. Gallo take the road leading up the left or east bank of the Mugnone for about 1 mile, as far as the Villa Palmieri, where, in 1348, Boccaccio wrote his Decameron. From this the road ascends between walls about 1 mile more to the Church and Convent of S. Domenico, in which Beato Angelico was one of the monks. The church contains an Annunciation by Empoli ; a Baptism of Christ by Credi ; a St. Francis by Cigoli ; and in the choir a Virgin with Saints by B. Angelico. Near S. Domenico is the Villa Landore, which was occupied for many years by Walter Savage Landor. The road striking off to the left or towards the Mugnone, leads to the venerable abbey of La Badia di Fiesole, rebuilt in 1462 by Brunelleschi. The road from St. Domenico to Fiesole is rather steep, and passes, at about two-thirds of the way, the beautiful old mansion with terraced gardens called the Villa Mozzi or Spence, once a favourite residence of Lorenzo il Magnifico, and the place in which the Pazzi conspiracy was formed in 1478. A short way beyond, the road enters the Piazza of *Fiesole* (pop. 11,500. *Inns:* Locanda

Firenze ; Trattoria l'Aurora), famous for views and stone-quarries. One side of the Piazza is occupied by the Cathedral, dedicated to St. Romulus, commenced in 1028, and in form resembling S. Miniato. To the right of the high altar is the mausoleum of Bishop Salutati, and a marble tabernacle by Mino da Fiesole in 1465. The frescoes on the ceiling of the chancel are by Ferrucci ; and the statue of St. Romulus in a sitting posture by Luca della Robbia or his nephew. In a garden behind the church are the remains of a Roman theatre. The road passing this garden leads to the ruins of the ancient walls, formed of huge uncemented blocks, not parallel, but of different sizes, and some of them indented into each other. Fronting the Cathedral is the commencement of a little stony road leading up to the terrace of a Franciscan convent, commanding a glorious view, and to the church of S. Alessandro, with columns of Cipollino marble.

S. SALVI. VENCIGLIATO. SETTIGNANO.—1¼ mile east from the Porta S. Croce, by the road following the railway, is S. Salvi, containing a Last Supper, by A. del Sarto, in the refectory. From S. Salvi northwards to the Via Settignano, which follow for 1½ mile eastwards, then take the road to the left going northwards, and crossing the Mensola above its union with the Frassinaia, is the Castle of Vencigliato, founded in the 10th cent., 5 miles north-east from the Porta S. Croce, and situated on the summit of a hill commanding a splendid view. In 1860 it was restored at the expense of an Englishman, Temple Leader. 1¼ mile east from the part of Settignano road, whence the Vencigliato road ramifies, is Settignano, the birthplace of Michael Angelo.

Straw-plaiting gives employment to numerous females around Florence. The wheat used is sown in March, and is cut before the grain is ripe. The straw is then divided into pieces from 6 to 8 inches long, and exposed for sale in the markets in small bunches. In this state it is bought by the plaiters, who in their turn expose for sale yards of plaited straw to the hatters.

The vin ordinaire given at the restaurants of Florence is principally the Vino Monteferrata, which, when two or three years old, resembles an inferior dry claret. In Savoy and Tuscany large flat cakes are made of ground chestnuts. They are sold hot, have a sweetish taste, and are very nourishing to those who can digest them.

Excursion to Vallombrosa, Camaldoli, and Alvernia to the east of Florence. (See Map on page 199.)

To Vallombrosa. Take rail to Pontassieve, 13 miles east from Florence, pop. 11,000. *Inn:* Italia ; where hire coach for Pelago, 6

VALLOMBROSA—CAMALDOLI—SACRO EREMO.

miles east. Fare, 6 fr. Pelago (pop. 2000). *Inn:* Buon Cuore ; whence mule, 5 fr., guide, 2 fr., to Vallombrosa, 8 miles south. Or coach as far as Tosi, about 5½ miles from Pelago, and the rest by mule or on foot. At Pontassieve a carriage for two at 12 fr. per day, or for four at 20 fr. per day, may be hired for visiting the three sanctuaries. Having visited Vallombrosa, return to Pelago, and proceed to Bibbiena, 15 miles east, by the Consuma, Borgo alla Collina, and Poppi, 4 miles from Bibbiena. From Bibbiena mules or horses must be hired for Alvernia, 2 hours distant. From Alvernia a fatiguing path leads to Camaldoli, in about 6 hours. The better plan is to go to Camaldoli from Bibbiena, distant 4 miles northwards from Bibbiena.

A little beyond Pelago the road to Vallombrosa begins to ascend the Apennines, disclosing in the ascent many charming views of hills crowned with villas, and mountains covered with evergreen oaks, intermingled with bare perpendicular cliffs, and roaring torrents tumbling from the crags. *Vallombrosa* is situated 2980 feet above the sea, on the side of Mt. Protomagno, which rises 2340 feet higher. Although the scenery does not agree altogether with Milton's description in *Paradise Lost*, book iv. lines 131-159, it possesses that charming loveliness which inspired the divine poet with the ideas conveyed in these lines. The steep acclivity is clothed with a "woody theatre" of stateliest chestnuts, oaks, firs, and beeches, which in ranks ascend, waving one above the other, shade above shade ; or hang from the very brows of precipices, whose verdant sides are with thicket overgrown, grotesque, and wild. "Higher than their tops" an occasional glade breaks the uniformity of the sylvan scene, while on the summit expands a wide grassy down with enamelled colours mixed, from which there is a "prospect large" over foliaged hills, and the wild, bleak, sterile mountains of Camaldoli and Alvernia. The church and convent were erected in 1637. The latter is now occupied partly by a forestry school and partly by an inn. Nearly 300 feet higher, by a winding path, is Il Paradisino, a little hermitage romantically situated on a projecting rock commanding a grand view. The scagliola decorations in the chapel were by an Englishman, Father Hugford, who excelled in various branches of natural philosophy, and in the art of imitating marble by that composition called scagliola. He died in the last century. The ascent to the summit of the Protomagno occupies 1 hour ; guide 2 fr. The road to Camaldoli winds round the mountain that shelters Vallombrosa on the north side, and then descends into the Val d'Arno Inferiore. On a knoll, encircled with trees in the middle of the plain, is the noble now ruined castle of Romena, and behind it the villages of Poppi and Bibbiena.

The abbey of *Camaldoli*, founded by S. Romualdo, a Calabrian anchorite, in 1046, is situated on the torrent Giogana, in a valley surrounded by high mountains. About 2 miles above the monastery, on a hill to the north, by a zig-zag path through the forest, is Il Sacro Eremo, the hermitage of the convent. The church is neat, and possesses an Annunciation in relief by Robbia. From the culminating point of the ridge, the Prato al Soglio, is one of the finest views in this part of Italy.

About 1¼ miles from Camaldoli, on Mons Alvernus, a lofty rock towering above the neighbouring eminences, and split into numberless pinnacles of fantastic forms, full of grottoes and galleries hollowed out by nature, is situated the convent of *Alvernia*, founded by St. Francis in 1213, and inhabited by about 110 monks. From the church a covered gallery leads to the cave with the chapel of the Stemmate, in which St. Francis is said to have received, imprinted on his body, marks similar to those pro-duced on Jesus Christ by the crucifixion. From Camaldoli and from Alvernia return to Bibbiena, where the diligence may be taken to Arezzo, pop. 12,000, whence rail either to Rome, 141 miles south, or to Florence, 54 miles north-west. The drive from Pontassieve to Florence, by the Arno, is very beautiful.

Florence is 291 m. S.E. from Turin by Pistoja, Bologna, Modena, Parma, Piacenza, and Alessandria. Time by quick trains, 13 hrs. 1st class, 52 frs. 95 c. ; 2d class, 37 frs. 5 c. See Black's *South France*, East half, page 233.

Florence is 196½ m. N. from Rome by Arezzo, Terontola, Chiusi, Orvieto, and Orte. 8 hrs. by quick train. 1st class, 34 frs. 30 c. ; 2d class, 23 frs. 55 c. Florence is 60¼ m. E. from Leghorn by Empoli, Pontedera, and Pisa. 2 hrs. 20 min. by quick train. 1st class, 10 frs. 45 c.; 2d class, 7 frs. 15 c. See the "Indicatore Ufficiale." To the price given in the Indicatore the amount of the tax has to be added.

Genoa to Turin by Alessandria and Asti.

Distance, 103½ m. N.W.   Time by quick trains, 4¼ hrs.   Map, page 199.

Genoa.—The train after traversing the first tunnel emerges at the busy populous suburb of Sampierdarena, 1¼ m. W. from Genoa and 2½ m. E. from Sestri-Ponente. The rail now turns northward and ascends the valley of the impetuous torrent of the Polcevēra, travers-ing six tunnels. Having passed Rivarolo, Bolzaneto, and Pontedecimo, the train arrives at Busalla, 14¼ m. N. from Genoa and 89¼ m. S. from Turin. Busalla is situated on the culminating part of the line (1192 ft.), on the crest which divides the basin of the Adriatic from the Gulf of Genoa. Here also the gradients of the line are highest, being about 1 in 28½ or 35 in 1000. The longest tunnel on the line, the Galleria dei Giovi, 3390 yards, is just before arriving at Busalla. It perforates calcareous schists, and is ventilated by 14 shafts. The scenery, which has been hitherto very picturesque, becomes tame after traversing the last tunnel at Arquata, 26 m. N. from Genoa, in the narrow valley of the Scrivia. 33½ m. N. from Genoa, and 70 m. S. from Turin, is Novi, H. La Sirena, a town of 11,000 inhabitants, situated among hills ; where, in August 15, 1799, a great battle took place between the French under Joubert and the Austrians and Russians under Suwarrow, when the former were defeated and their general killed. Novi is 60 m. S.W. from Milan by Tortana, Voghera, and Pavia.

47¼ m. N. from Genoa and 56¼ m. S.E. from Turin is **Alessandria**, pop. 30,000, 234¼ m. N.W. from Florence by Piacenza, Parma, Modena, Bologna, and Pistoja. See Black's *South France*, East half. See map, page 199.

At the Alessandria station hot coffee and chocolate are always ready. *Hotels:* L'Universo; Italia; Europa. Alessandria received its name in compliment to Pope Alexander III. The citadel, capable of holding 50,000 men, was built in 1728. The cathedral has a façade in the modern taste, with granite columns; in the interior is a colossal statue of St. Joseph by Parodi. The other churches are the Madonna di Loreto and S. Lorenzo. The Ghilino palace, now belonging to the crown, was designed by the elder Alfieri. Two great fairs are held annually at Alessandria—one in April, the other in October. In the neighbourhood is the village of Marengo, near which took place (June 1800) the battle between the French and the Austrians that was first lost by Bonaparte and afterwards won by Desaix and Kellermann. From Alessandria the train ascends the valley of the Tanaro, passing the minor stations of Solero, Felizzano, Cerro, and Annone; then at 34¾ m. E. from Turin, and 68¾ m. N.W. from Genoa, arrives at

Asti (the *Hasta Pompeia*, or Pompey's Market, of the Latins), a place of 18,000 inhabitants. H. Leone d'Oro. Celebrated for its sparkling wines, both red and white. The cathedral is a large and fine Gothic structure (1348). The adjacent church of S. Giovanni is built upon a basilica, of which the existing part is borne by monolithic columns with capitals bearing Christian symbols, 6th cent. Near Porta Alessandria is the small Baptistery of San Pietro, 11th cent., resting on short columns with square capitals. Alfieri, the poet, was born here, in a palace built by his uncle, who was a count and an architect. He died in 1803. The tertiary strata of the neighbourhood are very rich in fossils. Loop-line from Asti to Milan in 3½ hrs.

From Asti the train descends by Villafranca, where there is a viaduct over the Standvasso, about 100 ft. above the stream. Farther W., at Trofarello, is the junction with the loop-lines to Savona, 82½ m. S. (page 183), and to Cuneo, 46½ m. S.W. (page 183).

Five miles S. from Turin is Moncalieri. On the hill-side, overlooking the town, is the large royal palace in which Victor Emmanuel I. died in 1823.

For **Turin**, see Black's *South France*, East half. Loop-line to Pinerolo, 23½ m. S.W., and to Torre-Pellice, 10½ m. farther west, in the Waldensian valleys. See Black's *South France*, East half.

Paris to Turin and the Italian Riviera.

By FONTAINEBLEAU, JOIGNY, DIJON, MACON, BOURG, AMBÉRIEUX,
CULOZ, AIX-LES-BAINS, CHAMBERY, MODANE, and MONT CENIS.
The continuation of this line southwards from Turin extends to
Genoa by Alessandria (page 279).

Part First.—PARIS to MODANE, 431 miles. Time by the Rapide, 13 hrs. 36 min.
Part Second.—MODANE to TURIN, 58½ miles. Time by Express, 3 hrs. 27 min.

Time-tables.—In England, see under "London to Turin" in the Continental
Time-tables of the London, Chatham, and Dover Railway, which Company give
through tickets. In Paris, start from the station of the Chemins de Fer de Paris
à Lyon. At the bookstall buy one of their Time-tables, 40 c. The best resting-
places are Dijon, Macon, and Chambery. For the whole route consult the Sketch
Map on the fly-leaf. For the northern part, between Paris and Macon, see map,
page 1 ; and from Macon to Turin, map, page 26.

PARIS
MILES FROM | **PART I.—PARIS TO MODANE.** | MODANE
MILES TO
431

PARIS. In front of the departure side of the Chemins de Fer ⌇⌇
de Lyon Station is the Grand Hôtel de l'Univers, and under it a Café
Restaurant. A little farther off is Hôtel Jules César. Good restaurant
also in the station. For the first 274 m. between Paris and Macon,
see pages 1 to 26. At Morel junction the Vichy line separates from
this one. At Montereau, 49½ m. from Paris (p. 10), the Express halts
4 min. ; but not the Rapide. At La Roche (p. 14) both the Rapide and
the Express halt 5 min. At Tonnerre (p. 17) they halt again 5 min.
At Les Laumes (p. 19) the Express halts 5 min. At Dijon (p. 20) both
halt 6 min. At Macon (p. 26) they halt 5 min. At Macon the Turin
line separates from the Marseilles line, and goes 23 m. E. to Bourg,
297 m. from Paris. At Bourg, in the church of Brou, are sumptuous
mausoleums. From Bourg a loop-line traverses a picturesque country
by Nantua to Geneva, 97 m. W. (See map, p. 27 ; and for description,
Black's *France*, North half. 5½ m. S.E. from Bourg the line crosses
the Ain at the village of Pont-Ain, and afterwards arrives at Ambérieu, 316¼ m. S.E. from Paris, and 114¾ m. N.W. from Modane. At
Ambérieu the Rapide halts 10 min., and the Express 15 min. Ambérieu,
pop. 4000, is a pleasant town on the Albarine at the base of the Jura
mountains, and connected by rail with Lyon, 32¼ m. west. From
Ambérieu another loop-line extends 11 m. S. through a mountainous
country to Montallieu, pop. 2000, with important quarries, on the
Fouron near its junction with the Rhône. Between Ambérieu and
Culoz the rail passes through the last ramifications of the Jura

mountains. In approaching Culoz it winds round the S. base of Mt. Colombier, 4733 ft., ascended in 4 hrs. either from Culoz or Artemart. The view is admirable—on one side the Savoy Alps, with the lakes of Bourget, Annecy, and Geneva ; while on the side of France it extends to Lyons and the mountains of Ardèche.

8 m. S. from Ambérieu and 3 m. N. from Montallieu is Lagnieu, pop. 3500, station for La Balme, pop. 1000, 3 m. S.W., on south side of Rhône. There is a cave here with great galleries and stalactites, and a lake 130 yards long, 8 yards wide, and 13 ft. deep. It is easily approached from Aix-les-Bains by the Lyons steamboats. Alight at the Salette station, 20 min. walk from the entrance into the grotto.

From Ambérieu the train ascends the valley of the Albarine, which, after St. Rambert-de-Joux, 7 m. S.E. from Ambérieu, becomes wild and imposing. At Tenay, *Inn :* Pittion, 4¼ m. farther, the train quits the Albarine and traverses a sequestered valley to

Virieu le Grand, 340 m. S.E. from Paris, pop. 1100. Junction with loop-line to Belley, 9½ m. S., pop. 5000 ; *Inns :* Rey ; Camus, with important quarries of lithographic stones. 442½ m. from Paris and 19¼ m. N. from Aix-les-Bains is Artemart, with the falls of Cerveyrieu.

347½ m. S.E. from Paris, 14½ m. N. from Aix-les-Bains, and 83½ m. N. from Modane, is Culoz, on the Rhône, about ¾ m. E. from the station, 771 ft. above the sea, pop. 1200. Near the station are the inns *H. Folliet ; H. Mémon. A great deal of carriage-changing takes place here. 41 m. N.E. is Geneva ; see Black's *North France*, and map p. 26. 4½ m. S. from Culoz and 10 m. N. from Aix-les-Bains is Châtillon, 700 ft. above the sea, on the N.E. extremity of Lake Bourget, 2 hrs. distant by row-boat from Aix. In the castle, 13th cent., commanding a charming view of the lake, Pope Celestin was born.

Lake Bourget is 700 ft. above the sea, 10 m. long, from 2 to 3 m. wide, and from 200 to 300 ft. deep. The W. side is bounded by the steep ridge of Mont Chat. Opposite to Aix is a depression, the Col du Mont Chat, 2070 ft., and immediately to the S. a bold craggy peak, La Dent du Chat, 5302 ft., ascended from the little village of Bordeaux in about 4 hrs., after a very fatiguing climb. One of the best points for a view over the lake and the surrounding country is the Revard, 5112 ft., one of the summits of the ridge Mont d'Azy, which bounds the E. side of the plain of Aix (see page 285). It is ascended from the village of Mouxy in about 4 hrs.

The best of the fish caught in the lake is the ombre-chevalier. The lavaret is peculiar to it. There are also trout, perch, pike, shad, carp, gudgeon, tench, and barbel.

362 AIX-LES-BAINS, 850 ft. above the sea, 1½ m. from Lake **69**
Bourget, pop. 6000. The Casino is a handsome building, with park of
its own extending to the railway station. First-class hotels—their
pension is from 12 to 20 frs., but it is necessary to arrange the price
at the commencement. On each side of the Casino are the *H. Aix,
with garden, and the Univers. Opposite are the H. de la Galerie and
the Nord. Then follow the *Hotels:* *Europe; *Venat, with large
garden; and opposite, at the end of R. du Casino, the H. Genève.
Second-class houses: in the parallel street, the R. Genève, behind the
R. du Casino, are the H. Durand; *Gaillard; in the Place Centrale
the H. Poste. Opposite the H. Poste is the office whence the omnibuses start for the lake and the Lyons steamboats, and for Marlioz.
Up by the side of the Bath-house is the H. de l'Établissement. In
front, the H. de l'Arc Romain. To the left, in the Rue des Écoles, is
a small clean family house, the H. Germain. A little beyond is the
H. Châteaux-Durrieux. Below the last, the H. Folliet and Italie.
The pension price in the above second-class houses varies from 7 to 11
frs. On road to station, the H. des Bergues.

On an eminence overlooking the park is the *Splendide Hôtel, a
really splendid first-class house. Below it is the H. Beau-Site, also a
new but a smaller first-class house.

The Port is nearly 2 m. from Aix by the R. de Genève, and then
to the left. At the pier is the inn Beau-Rivage, "Poissons frais."

Abundance of furnished lodgings. English chapel, Rue du Temple,
behind the H. Venat. Presbyterian chapel in the park.

Cabs or Fiacres.—One-horse cab—3 frs. for the first hour; every
succeeding hour, 2 frs.; per day, 20 frs. Two-horse cab—for first hour,
4 frs.; every succeeding hour, 3½ frs.; per day, 20 frs. Riding horses
—two hours, 4 frs. Donkeys—one hour, 1 fr.; half-day, 4 frs.

The bathing establishment is a very large edifice, especially fitted
up for the external application of the water, very little being drunk.
Mineral water flows from the fountain in front of the building. Behind
the establishment are the caverns whence the springs issue. To visit,
½ fr. There are three different springs, their temperatures being 112°,
114°, and 115° Fahrenheit, and their contents carbonates of lime,
magnesia, and iron, sulphate of soda, and some phosphates. Ordinary
bath with linen, 1½ fr. Opposite the establishment is a Roman arch,
3d cent., with the inscription "Lucius Pompeius, Campanus, Vius
fecit." Behind the arch is the château of the Marquis of Aix, now occupied by the Hôtel de Ville and the post and telegraph offices. A hand-

some stone stair of fifty-eight steps, under a quadripartite roof on round columns, leads up to the various offices. At the top is the museum. On the ground-floor, just beyond the foot of the stair, a door opens into what is called the Temple of Diana, a large rectangular hall of coarse masonry, recently restored. Adjoining are the Hôtel de l'Arc Romain, 9-12 frs., the parish church, and the park. The waters used for drinking are the cold sulphur springs, situated a little way out of town.

The most powerful and peculiar is the spring at Challes, 900 ft. above the sea, and 45 min. distant by omnibus from Chambery. *Hotels:* Château de Challes ; Terrason ; Perret. It, like the others, is used for indigestion and liver complaints, but especially for laryngeal affections.

Nearly a mile from Aix by the Chambery road is the Marlioz mineral water establishment, with hotel, furnished apartments, and villas, all within a large park. The water is cold, sulphurous, and alkaline, with bromine and iodine, and costs 10 c. the glass. About 20 min. walk from the town by the Geneva road, near the village of St. Simon, is the Raphy spring, frequently taken at meal-time and prescribed in certain gastric diseases, dyspepsia, and nervous disorders of the stomach.

Excursions from Aix-les-Bains.—The steamer on certain days makes the tour of the lake, stopping at the principal places, of which the chief is the Abbey of Hautecombe ; fare there and back, with small boat and two men, 9 frs. To Bordeaux and back, 5 frs. ; Bonport, 4 frs. ; Châtillon, 14 frs. Arrange price beforehand. No boat permitted to carry more than six passengers. An hour on shore allowed. Drive round the lake—one horse, 11 frs. ; two horses, 15 frs.

The Abbey of Hautecombe was founded in the 12th cent., but rebuilt in 1745. The church, containing 300 statues and many frescoes, is 215 ft. long, the transept 85 ft., and the height of the roof 34 ft. The interior, as well as most of the mausoleums, is of a soft white fine-grained magnesian limestone, from the quarries of Seyssel, near Culoz. The best of the statues are those of Charles Felix, King of Sardinia (died 1821), and of Marie Christine, his spouse (died 1849), on the right and left hands of the nave at the entrance. They are of Carrara marble. In the chapel of Notre Dame de Compassion, in the right-hand transept, is another beautiful group in Carrara marble ; in the left transept is a wood figure of St. Joseph, well executed.

About half a mile from the convent by a road following the shore of the lake is an intermittent fountain, very irregular in its action. To reach it continue the road till arriving at a clump of chestnut and horse-chestnut trees, some having stone seats round the trunks. The fountain is in the corner under the fourth tree. Near Hautecombe are the village and castle of Bordeaux, founded in the 9th cent., over which rises the Dent du Mont Chat (see p. 282).

Other Excursions. — To the S.W. the Colline de Tresserve, 1109 ft., good views, chestnut trees, and the castle of Bonport. To the S.E. the Roche du Roi, with quarries, which were worked by the Romans. The Rocher de St. Victor, by the chestnut forest of Mouxy ; there and back, 5 hours. The mountains of the Grand-Revard and the Cluse, 5154 ft., by mule-path ; there and back, 6 hours. To the N. the cascade of Gresy, 45 minutes, 3 m. Gresy, with its keep, 12th cent. 5 m., the defile of the Combes and the Prime rocks. To the N.N.W. the Montagne de Gigot, 2680 and 2762 ft.

Aix to the Grotto of Banges, *by Gresy and Cusy.* —Seat in car there and back, 5 frs. About 3 m. from Aix is Gresy, with its pretty waterfall. Beyond the village the road ascends by the stream Sierroz to an undulating plain, on which is Cusy, 3½ hours from Aix. To the N., on a rock rising from the Chéran, are the extensive ruins of a castle. On the opposite bank are seen the hamlet of Aiguebellette and the castle of St. Jacques, and, rising abruptly from the valley, three singular obelisks of rock. 2 hours from Cusy the Chéran is crossed by the Pont de Banges, and not far from this bridge, where the road is hemmed in between the rocks and the stream, is the entrance to the Grotte de Banges, containing a lake, 216 ft. below the level of the entrance, approached by a gallery 270 yards long, hung with stalactites.

This road may be continued to Le Châtelard, 1¾ hour from the bridge, 2500 ft. above the sea ; *Inns :* Des Beauges ; De la Poste ; pop. 950. This is the capital of the " Pays des Beauges," occupying a plateau 13 m. long and 8 m. wide, traversed from S.E. to N.W. by the Chéran, and surrounded by steep rocks. Cheese-making, the rearing of cattle, and the manufacture of articles in wood form the industries of the inhabitants, of whom there are 10,000. Châtelard, in its social and geographical position, resembles Le Beage (p. 84).

The road from Aix to Chambery is through the broad valley which separates the mountains of the Grande Chartreuse from those of the Beauges. Belonging to the former are Mont Grelle, 4649 ft., to the S.W., and Mont Granier, 6348 ft., due S. ; while to the N.E. is the Dent de Nivolet, 4597 ft., an advanced bastion of the Beauges.

At Aix-les-Bains, junction with branch to Annecy, 26 m. N., whence a diligence starts daily for Geneva, 27½ m. farther N. by Brogny, Cruseilles, and St. Julien (see map, p. 27).

Aix-les-Bains to Geneva by Annecy and Annemasse, by rail.

21½ m. by rail N. from Aix-les-Bains, and 3½ m. from Annecy, is **Lovagny**, the station to alight at to visit the " Galeries des Gorges " of the torrent Fier, about 10 minutes distant. From the station take the road to the left, cross a bridge, and walk on to the châlet, where refreshments are sold, and tickets, 1 fr. each, to visit the gorge, which is of the same nature, though much superior, to the galleries of Pfäffers. The gallery, or rather balcony, is 1162 ft. long, and on an average 72 ft. above the torrent. It rests on iron brackets driven into the face of vertical cliffs 310 ft. high, and on an average 8 ft. apart.

3½ m. farther by rail is

Annecy, pop. 11,000. *Hotels:* Angleterre, opposite the post office ; Verdun, at the head of the town, near the public gardens and the lake, and not far from the steamboat-pier ; Aigle ; Savoie.

The steamboat sails from the side of the public gardens opposite the Convent of St. Joseph. It makes the tour of the lake three times daily. Diligence daily to Bonneville, 23 m. N., passing the villages of Plot and La Roche ; also to Albertville, 28 m. N., on the road to Italy by the Little St. Bernard (see page 320).

This ancient town, with narrow arcaded streets, is situated on the north-west end of Lake Annecy. The two most prominent buildings in Annecy, as seen from the lake, are the Barracks, and the Castle of Tresun, in which St. François de Sales, the founder of the Order of the Visitation, was born August 21, 1567. Opposite the steamboat-pier is another prominent edifice, the Church and Convent of St. Joseph, both modern, but containing, in the garden behind, the first chapel erected by St. Francis, dating from 1610. The house Madame Chantale, his friend, inhabited adjoins this chapel.

The mortal remains of St. Francis are in a shrine above the high altar in the Church of the Visitation, at the western side of the Rue Royale. The house in which he resided is in No. 18 Rue St. Claire, entrance at the left-hand corner within the court. The house in which Madame de Warrens first received Rousseau stood in the parallel street, behind the Rue de l'Évêché, on the site of that house next the Episcopal palace, with railings in front. The best promenade is the garden around the Hôtel de Ville at the head of the lake. It contains a statue by Marochetti of the great French chemist, Claude Louis Berthollet, born at Talloires in 1748.

The Lake of Annecy is 9 m. long, 2 broad, and 1455 ft. above the sea-level. It is surrounded by vine-clad and wooded mountains, of which the highest is La Tournette, on the eastern shore, 6260 ft. above the lake. To ascend it land at the village of Talloires, where there are a comfortable inn, the Hôtel de l'Abbaye, and guides.

Near the shore of the lake, on the side of a hill about 2 m. east from Annecy, is the house in which Eugene Sué spent the last years of his life. It is one-storied, with garret-windows, and behind a small square tower. On the morning of August 1, 1857, he took his last walk on the hill, returning from which fatigued he went to bed, and died two days afterwards. The remains of Rousseau's house are seen a little farther south, above the village of Veyrier.

South from Veyrier, also on the lake, is the village of Menthon, the birthplace of St. Bernard, the founder, in the 10th cent., of the hospices of the Great and the Little St. Bernard. He is buried on the right-hand side of the choir in the cathedral of Lausanne. At the south extremity of the lake is the village of Doussard, at the entrance into the dark gorge of the Combe Noire. Here a coach awaits passengers for Faverges and Albertville, 18 miles south from Doussard. In this neighbourhood the best mountain to ascend for the view is Semnoz, 4148 ft. above the lake. The ascent is made from the straggling village of Leschaux, 1590 ft. above the lake, 10 m. S. from Annecy, and 14 m. N.E. from Aix-les-Bains. Donkeys can be hired at the village. The ascent takes about 2 hrs. On the top is a comfortable inn. Duingt, at the S.W. end, is the most picturesquely situated village on the lake. (See map of Mt. Cenis, p. 291.)

3 m. N. from Annecy and 24 m. S. from Geneva is the village of Brogny, where, in 1342, Jean Allarmet the swineherd was born, who became successively Bishop of Geneva, Viviers, and Ostia, Archbishop of Arles, and then a Cardinal. From Brogny the road passes the Pont de la Caille, 18 m. from Geneva, a small village near the suspension bridge, 212 yds. long, across Les Usses, and 665 ft. above the bed of the torrent. Higher up, in a ravine, are the baths of Caille.

16½ m. from Geneva is Cruseilles, pop. 2000, and 2576 ft. above the sea. The road from Cruseilles passes over the top of Mont Zion, 2586 ft., and then descends to Chable. 10 m. farther is St. Julien, 1535 ft., pop. 2500. French custom-house station, 6½ m. from Geneva.

370¾ CHAMBERY, pop. 20,000, and 815 ft. above the sea. Pass- 60¼ engers arriving late should spend the night at Chambery, and next morning proceed to Turin. *Hotels.*—Princes, in the Rue de Boigne, near the fountain. France, on the Quai Nezin. In the Rue d'Italie, the Poste and Europe, near the theatre. In the Rue de la Banque is the Banque ; and opposite it is the Temple Protestant.

Chambery is situated in a plain surrounded by high mountains. The first object that strikes the stranger on arriving from the station is the monumental fountain to General Boigne in the Boulevard du Theatre, opposite the termination of the principal street, the Rue de Boigne. It consists of four bronze elephants supporting a column crowned with a statue of the General. At the other extremity of the Rue de Boigne is the Château, formerly the residence of the Dukes of Savoy, built in 1230. The entrance is either by the stair in front or by the road round from behind, which leads also to the Botanic Gardens. Within the precincts of the château is the Préfecture, having attached to it one of the old massive round towers, ascended by a most handsome staircase of 160 low broad steps to within a short distance of the top, attained by 36 more steps in two short flights.   In the stair is the entrance to the Museum, chiefly archæological.   The Natural History Museum is in the Botanic Garden.   The view from the top of the tower is very pleasing, and overlooks the whole of the town.   Fee, ½ fr.   Opposite the tower is the Chapel of the Dukes of Savoy, 14th cent.   Fee, ¼ fr.   The three tall windows are filled with beautiful old glass.   The roof is covered with stone groining, with cleverly-executed arabesque painting between the nervures.   The roof of the cathedral is similarly painted, but on a blue ground.   It is situated near the Rue de Boigne, and was built in the 14th, 15th, and 16th cents.

The Rue de Bourgogne, the second street to the right up the Rue de Boigne, leads past the Hôtel de Ville and the post office to the Palais de Justice, with the Jardin Public behind.   In front of the Palais is a bronze statue of the jurist, Antoine Favre, who died 1624. On a hill on the other or eastern side of the railway are the Convent de la Visitation and the **Church of Lemenc**.   The upper church of Lemenc is of the 13th or 14th cent., but the under church or crypt is of the 7th cent.   In the centre of the crypt is a curious baptistery, six feet in diameter, under a peristyle.   Beside it is an Entombment.   In the upper Church are the mausoleum of General Boigne and the relics of Saint Concors, an Irish archbishop from Armagh, who died here 600 years ago.   His relics are said to have the power of working miracles on children.   In the adjoining cemetery, close to a small chapel, is the grave of Madame de Warrens.

Excursions.—The house which Jean Jacques Rousseau inhabited is on the height called the Charmettes, 395 ft. above and 2 m. from Chambery by a pleasant road shaded with walnut and plane trees. It is a mere cottage.   The room to the right on entering was the dining-room.   It contains in a drawer his watch, opposite the window his bookcase, and hanging on the walls, facing each other, the portraits of himself and of Madame de Warrens.   The next room was their sitting-room ; here are his card-table and mirror.   The room above was madame's bedroom, and the one over the dining-room Rousseau's. From the garden the view extends to the Dent de Nivolet, 4597 ft., ascended from Chambery in between 5 and 6 hrs. ; guide advisable. View not equal to that from the Dent du Chat (p. 282).   The pretty walk to the Bout du Monde, at the foot of the Dent de Nivolet, by the bank of the Laisse and the gorge of the Doria may be made in little more than an hour.   Omnibus in 45 min. to the cold sulphurous iodo-bromuride springs of Challes (p. 284).

289

376
55
LES MARCHES, a straggling village at the foot of a hill crowned by the chapel and image of Notre Dame de Myans. To the S.W., 4 hrs. there and back, are the Abimes de Myans, lakes between conical hillocks, formed by a partial landslip of Mt. Granier.

378
53
MONTMÉLIAN, pop. 1200. *Inn:* Voyageurs. Junction with line to Grenoble, for which change carriages (p. 338).

385½
45¾
ST. PIERRE D'ALBIGNY, 971 ft. (map, p. 291), pop. 3300, 1½ m. from its station. *Inns:* At station : H. des Voyageurs. In town: Croix-Blanche ; Soleil. Junction with line to Albertville, 14 m. N. E., whence diligences to Annecy, 28 m. N., passing close by Ugine, 1755 ft., and through Faverges ; *Inn:* Poste. Diligence also to Moutiers and Bourg St. Maurice on the road to the Little St. Bernard, one of the easiest of the Alpine passes (see p. 321). From St. Pierre take the N. window of the carriage to have a proper view of the immense cones and pinnacles of calcareous rocks, which tower in many places almost vertically above each other. These lofty walls afford protection from the chilling blasts to the pretty villages, vineyards, orchards, and maize fields ; which places only at a little distance from these mountains do not enjoy. Vineyards cease a little above St. Michel, 2400 ft., but patches with vines may be seen within 3 m. of La Praz. Up to La Praz the mountains are cultivated more or less in terraces. Higher up the valley of the Arc they are too steep and arid.

392
39
AIGUEBELLE, pop. 1100. H. de la Poste. Village close to station. Arch to Charles Felix. The valley now begins to widen.

409
22
LA CHAMBRE, pop. 800, on the confluence of the Bugion and the Arc. Afterwards, to the right, is the valley of the Glandon.

414½
16½
SAINT-JEAN DE MAURIENNE, pop. 3200. *Inns:* Europe ; Cheval Blanc ; Voyageurs. The cathedral, founded in the 15th cent., contains the mausoleum of Count Humbert, and some beautifully carved stalls. The arcades of the cloister are of alabaster, and were constructed in 1452. In the neighbourhood are the argentiferous mines of Rocheray and the saline thermal springs of Echaillon.

421
10
ST. MICHEL, pop. 3000. A village on the Arc, 2323 ft. above the sea-level, in a hollow at the foot of high mountains. *Inn:* Poste, near the post office. From St. Michel the Alpine region commences. The next station is La Praz, 6 m. from St. Michel, 3140 ft. above the sea.

U

431 MODANE STATION, 3445 ft. above the sea, and 727 m. from London, is really part of the village of Fourneaux. Modane is a little farther up, and the train passes through it on the way to the tunnel. Large refreshment-room at station. Opposite station—*Inn:* Hôtel International, where comfortable lodgings can be had, as well as carriages to visit the neighbourhood. The river Arc runs by the back of the house. There are also several restaurants. Luggage from France and Italy is examined here. In Italy every pound of registered luggage is charged. The scenery on both the French and Italian sides is beautiful, and the traveller ought to endeavour to pass through it during the day. The passage through the tunnel is done in 30 minutes. The air is at no part disagreeable. The entrance is 492 ft. above the station, and is reached by a winding railroad of $3\frac{7}{10}$ m., with a gradient of $2\frac{1}{2}$ per cent. The highest part of the tunnel is 4380 ft. above the sea, and 5250 ft. below the summit of the ridge perforated.

From Modane the ascent is made of Mont Thabor, 7100 ft. higher than Modane, in $7\frac{1}{2}$ hrs., by the Col de la Saume. Descent in 6 hrs., or a little over 5, by Bardonnecchia.

Modane to Susa by Mont Cenis.

From Modane a carriage-road leads over the **Pass of Mont Cenis** to Susa, 40 m. distant by Villarodin, pop. 220. On the right bank of the Arc up the valley is Avrieux, where Charles the Bold was poisoned by his doctor. Near this are passed the forts Esseillon or Bramans, connected with the road by a steep winding path. $8\frac{3}{4}$ m. from Modane is Le Verney, where the road crosses the Arc; $10\frac{3}{4}$ m. Solliers; to the left, the valley of the Laisse or Doron; $16\frac{3}{4}$, Termignon, pop. 1080, and 4251 ft. above the sea, at the confluence of the Laisse with the Arc, church with frescoes and a curious belfry; 18 m. Lans-le-Bourg, pop. 1500, consisting principally of inns, situated on the Arc, 4560 ft. above the sea, at the base of Mont Cenis. After crossing the Arc the ascent of the Pass is commenced. From Lans-le-Bourg to Susa are twenty-three houses of refuge. At the culminating point, 6882 ft. above the sea, is the inn Ramasse. The road now descends. 13 m. from Susa and 27 from Modane is Les Tavernettes, on a terrace 200 ft. above the lake, which is $1\frac{1}{4}$ m. long and 6234 ft. high, and contains good trout. This is one of the best headquarters in the Alps for a naturalist. 10 m. from Susa and $29\frac{1}{2}$ m. from Modane is the Hospice of Mont Cenis, on the great plateau. 2 m. farther is the hamlet of La Grande Croix, 6069 ft., on the edge of the plateau, and whence the descent becomes more rapid. $4\frac{1}{2}$ m. from Susa is the post-house of Molaret, and about 3 m. more, or $1\frac{1}{4}$ from Susa, the hamlet of Giaglione, with splendid views and rich vegetation (Susa, see page 291).

ard

La Chapelle

Bozel

Aig de la Vanoise

La Chambre

Pralognan

du Freue

Mont Denis

St Jean de
Maurienne

Lans le bourg

Varon des Encombres

Termignon

Solli

Montriond

R. Arc

S. Michel

le Vern

La

Entreit

M. Levirent

Freney

Bram

Rodin Mt CENIS

S. André

Modane

Valloires

Fourneau

Mt Ambin

Aig d'Arves

Col de Frenis

Chau

la Grave

Mt Tabor

Evilles

English Miles

Bardoneche

Salbertrand

10   15   20   25

Vum

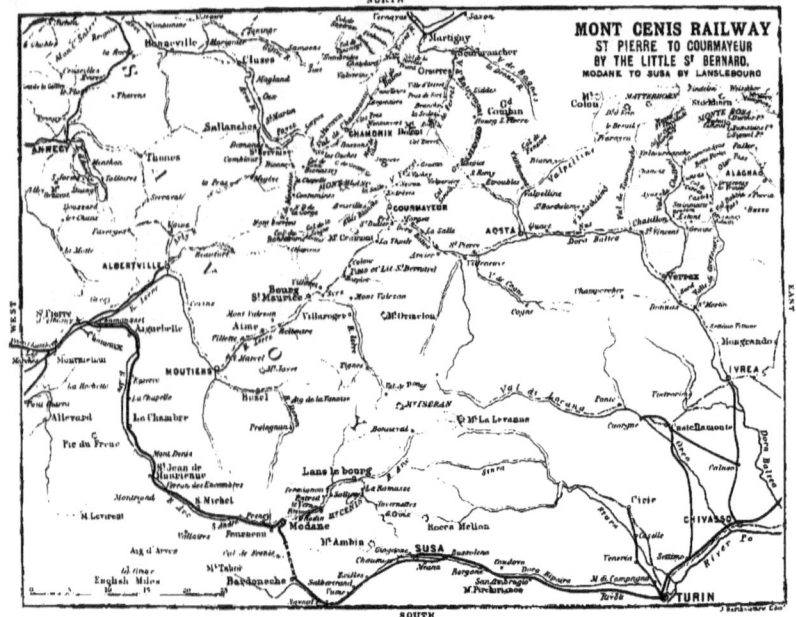

PART II.—MODANE TO TURIN.

See Map of Mont Cenis Railway.

MODANE. At Modane passengers enter the carriages of the 58½ Alta Italia Railway Company. The Italian time is 47 minutes in advance of the Paris time. The best time-table for Italy is the "Indicatore Ufficiale delle Strade Ferrate," 1 fr. ; also a smaller edition, 20 c., sold at all the railway stations. Waiting-room is Sala d'Aspetto. W.-C's., Cessi, or Latrine, or Retirate. For ladies, Cessi per le donne. Smoking carriages, Pei fumatori. Non-smoking carriages, È vietato il fumare. Way out, Uscita. Way in, Entrata. Station, Stazione or Fermata.

5 BARDONNECCHIA, 4127 ft., pop. 1600. At the station 53½ the Albergo della Stazione, and in the town the Hôtel de France. Situated near the Italian end of the tunnel, but in a more fertile country than that above Modane.

12 OULX, pop. 2000, and 3514 ft. high. *Inn:* Dell' Alpi Cozzié, 46½ at the station. At this pretty little village the road from Briançon, 17 m. S.W., by Mont Genèvre, joins the rail. The mountains, which extend from Monte Viso to Mont Cenis, were called the Alpes Cottiæ, from King Cottius, who, according to Pliny, reigned over this region some years before the beginning of the Christian era (Pliny, *Hist. Nat.*, lib. iii. cap. 20). Cottius erected the arch of Susa, and also constructed the road from that town over the Cottian Alps, by Oulx to Ebrodunum, now Embrun, on the Durance (see page 343).

21½ CHIOMONTE, 2526 ft. Beyond are some charming views. 36¾

25½ MEANA, 1 m. from Susa, and 325 ft. above it. The train, 33 having traversed beautiful chestnut woods, crosses the Dora and arrives at Bussoleno, 30½ m. from Modane, whence a loop-line of 5 m. extends to Susa, 1625 ft., pop. 5000. *Hotels:* France; Soleil. This, the ancient Segusium, the chief city of the Segusiani, who inhabited what is now called Savoy, is situated on the Dora, 1625 ft. above the sea. On the W. side of the town is the Roman Triumphal Arch erected about 8 B.C. in honour of Augustus. It is adorned with Corinthian columns and sculptured friezes on the entablature, but all are in a decayed condition. The cathedral, San Giusto, dates from the 11th cent.

12 m. from Bussoleno and 16 from Turin is San Ambrogio station, at the foot of Monte Pirchiriano, 3150 ft. above the sea and 1500 above the plain. On the summit is the convent of S. Michele della Chiusa, founded by Ugone Marino in 966, and finished in 1000. It was partially repaired by Carlo Alberto and Vittorio Emanuele II. The government intend to establish a meteorological station here. A good mule-path leads to the top in about an hour, passing the village of S. Pietro, with a good inn, 2617 ft. above the sea.

TURIN,

pop. 264,000, on the Po and the Dora Riparia, 785 ft. above the sea, and 490 m. S.E. from Paris. The city derives its name from the tribe Taurini, who were first the opponents and then the allies of the Romans. When Hannibal descended from the Alps he destroyed the city, that he might have nothing to dread from its hostility. Having risen speedily from its ruins, it received within its walls the army of reserve of Julius Cæsar when he marched against the Gauls. Under the Lombards it was made the capital of a duchy, and became the favourite residence of Queen Theodolinda, who, in 602, built the church of S. Giovanni Battista, now the cathedral of Turin, reconstructed in 1498. Francis I. so damaged Turin in 1536 that its entire reconstruction became necessary. The streets are wide, clean, and well paved, and pass through spacious squares ornamented with statues and bordered by handsome arcades. The most aristocratic part of Turin is the western end of the Corso Vittorio Emanuele II. and the streets ramifying southwards from this.

Hotels.—The *Europa, 19 Piazza Castello. In the same square, and less expensive, is the H. di Londra. This piazza is in the neighbourhood of the principal sights, and is the terminus of the most important trams. The other first-class houses are : the *Torino, opposite the arrival side of the station. The *Liguria, 14 Piazza Bodoni, with one end to the Via Carlo Alberto. Their new house is at 9 Via Madama Cristina, near the English chapel and the Vaudois church. The Liguria is patronised by Messrs. Cook. The H. Feder, 8 Via S. Francesco di Paolo. At 31 and 29 Via Roma, the Angleterre ; and the Trombetta. The Albergo Centrale, Via delle Finanze ; Bonne Femme (Buona Fama), Via Barbaroux. Less expensive : H. *Suisse ; H. Bologna, both opposite arrival side of station ; *France et Concorde, Via dell' Accademia Albertina, with one side to the Via di Po ; Albergo del Campo di Marte, 40 Via della Providencia ; the Dogana Vecchia, 4 Via Corte d'Appello ; Albergo del Gran Mogol, 41 Via Lagrange.

Cabs. — One horse, from 6 A.M. till midnight, the course, 1 fr. First half-hour, 1 fr. First hour, 1½ fr. Each successive half-hour, 75 c. The course from midnight to 6 A.M., 1¼ fr. From the central station to any part of the town, 1¼ fr. Trunks, 20 c. each. Cabs with 2 horses, ½ fr. additional. Porters, for carrying each portmanteau from the station to a cab, 2 sous. Each small article, either to cab or to the railway carriage, 1 sou.

Horse-trams traverse Turin in every direction ; while the steam-

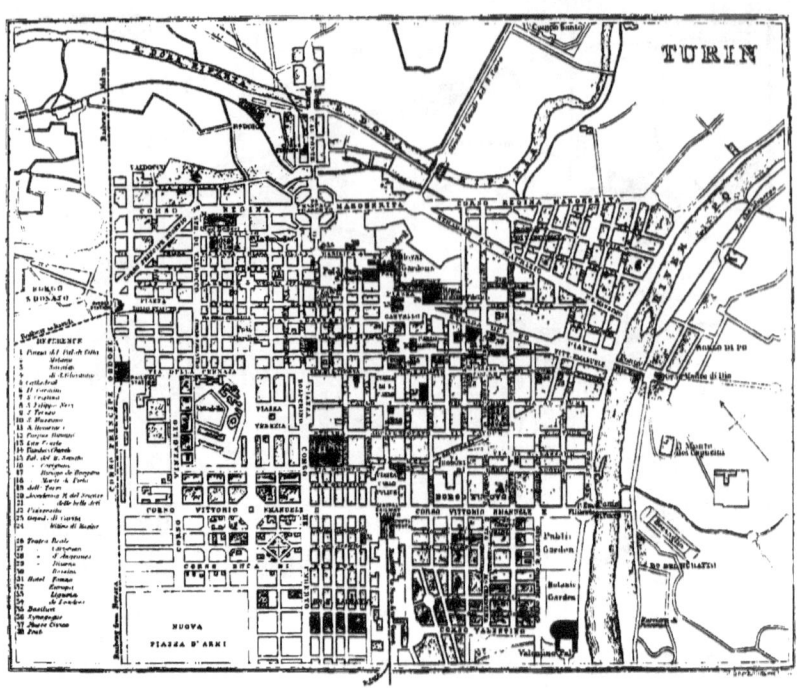

trams run from the city to the towns and villages not only within but beyond the suburbs. The fare of the horse-trams is universally 2 sous; that of the steam-trams from 12 sous to 3 frs. 18 sous. In the horse-trams no more than four may occupy one seat.

Stations.—The most important is the **Central Station**, a well-situated and well-arranged and spacious edifice. On a tablet on the departure side is an inscription to the honour of George and Robert Stephenson. Parallel to the station is the wide and handsome Corso Vittorio Emanuele, which traverses the city from east to west, having at the eastern end the Po and the Giardino Pubblico, and at the western the model prison, the Carcere giudiziario, the artillery barracks, and the cattle-market. In front of the station is a bronze statue of Massimo d'Azeglio, a poet and painter, who died in 1866, one of those who helped to throw off the yoke of Rome. Behind the statue is the garden or Piazza Carlo Felice, and the straight street, the Via Roma, extending to the Piazza Castello, by the Piazza S. Carlo, with, in the centre, a bronze equestrian statue, modelled by Marochetti in 1838, of Emanuele Filiberto, Duke of Savoy, and son of Carlo III. il Buono. He died in 1580. The attitude is rather theatrical. The station for Rivoli, at the west end of the Piazza dello Statuto, communicates with the P. Castello by the Via Garibaldi. The Cirié Lanzo station is on the Dora, N. side of plan, at the Ponte-Mosca. Opposite the Rivoli station, in the Piazza dello Statuto, is a monument to the engineers of Mt. Cenis tunnel, in the shape of a pyramid, 60 ft. high, composed of huge blocks of unhewn granite, up which scramble discomfited, colossal, naked Titans in white marble. On the pinnacle stands the Genius of Science, of a slighter make, and on a tablet the names of the engineers, Sommeiller, Gratoni, and Grandi.

Post and telegraph offices are in the Piazza Carlo Alberto, by the side of the Palazzo Carignano (p. 297). Stamps are sold at all the tobacco shops. This piazza is close to the P. Castello, and connected with the Via di Po by a lofty arcade, covered with glass, and bordered on both sides with well-stocked shops.

Booksellers.—For maps of Italy, Carlo Crespi, 2 Via Lagrange. For guide-books, Loescher and Brero, both in the Via di Po.

Money-changers in the central railway station and in the principal streets. In the main streets are also elegant **Cafés**, where the charge in all of them for a good cup of coffee with a piece of ice is 6 sous. The same price for an excellent ice cream heaped up in a glass.

Theatres.—See list on plan. A short way east from the central station, in the Corso Vittorio Emanuele, is the Vaudois church, built in 1853. Adjoining are the Vaudois schools, and behind, at 15 Via Pio Quinto, the Anglican chapel. Near the chapel is the synagogue, a handsome edifice with square towers crowned with balloon-like cupolas.

Sights.—The museums and picture gallery (Pinacoteca) in the "Accademia delle Scienze," with one side to the Piazza Carignano and another to the Via dell' Accademia delle Scienze. Nearly opposite is the Palazzo Carignano, containing the zoological and mineralogical collections. The white marble statue in front represents the philosopher, Vincenzo Gioberti, born 5th April 1801 in the house opposite, 5 Via Lagrange, where a white marble tablet states: "Il Conte Camillo di Cavour naque in questa casa, addi 10 Agosto 1810. E vi mori il 6 Giugno 1861. The armoury, enter by door headed "Reale Armeria Antica," under corridor, 13 Piazza Castello; adjoining is the Royal Palace. On the other side of the palace is the cathedral, San Giovanni. A walk down the Via di Po. Several drives in the horse-trams. All the above places are near each other, around the Piazza Castello. The only one that is at a little distance is the Museo Civico, up the side street, V. Rossini, from the Via di Po. The Superga, by steam tram from the Piazza Castello.

The Museum of Antiquities and the Picture Gallery.

The Palazzo dell' Accademia delle Scienze, designed by Guarini, was built in 1678 as a college for the sons of noblemen. It is a vast earthy-coloured brick edifice, of which the ornaments, mouldings, and cornices are also of dingy brick. On the ground-floor are the more massive, and in the first story the smaller antiquities. In the second story is the picture gallery, containing about 800 paintings in fifteen rooms. Open daily from 9 to 4, 1 fr. On Sundays and feast-days free, when it is open from 12 to 4. The large antiquities are contained in two halls. Hall 1. Left. In the centre, against the wall, under an inscription in honour of the Egyptologist Champollion, is the gem of the collection, a black basalt statue of Sesostris, Rameses II., 1388 B.C. On his right, in rose-coloured granite, is the colossal statue of Amenophis II., 1565 B.C., and on his left a small black basalt statue of Amenophis II., the god Ptah. Opposite are three figures in a sitting posture, representing the Egyptian Trinity, Osiris, Horus, and Isis. At the head of this hall is the colossal red sandstone statue of Seti II., in whose reign the exodus of the Israelites took place. From this a room ramifies at right angles, containing Greek and Roman statues, busts, friezes, vases, etc.

Parallel to Hall 1 is Hall 2. At the head of this hall, in a sitting posture, is the black basalt statue of Thothmes III., 1591 B.C., who was one of the most powerful of the Pharaohs.

Upstairs, first floor, are the smaller antiquities, contained in three large halls and several rooms. Near the centre of the first hall, left, is the oldest of all the articles in the museum, the pedestal of a table covered with hieroglyphics, supposed to have been made about 2654 B.C. A little farther down, in the centre of the hall, under a glass case, No. 13, is the Tabula Isiaca, a bronze tablet, 4 ft. long by 2 ft. 2 in. wide, inlaid with hieroglyphics in silver, made at Rome in the reign of Hadrian. Exactly opposite this tablet commences the passage that leads to the smaller rooms. In the first room, left, in the corner, is a colossal bust of Juno, hollowed, that the priest might the more easily work the oracle. In the first room, right, is a mosaic pavement, found at Stampacci in Sardinia. The rooms contain besides Phœnician terracotta figures, Etruscan vases, statuettes, urns, reliefs, ancient iron ornaments, lamps, etc.

The Centre Hall contains idols, jewellery, amulets, sarcophagi, mummies, Egyptian heads with the hair on, and bricks made by the Israelites.

In the Third Hall are the Papyri, of which the most important are : No. 4, near centre, against left wall, in second row, The Book of the Dead, 35 ft. long and 8 in. wide, illustrated with plain vignettes. Opposite, in centre of hall, is 126, fragments of the famous annals of Manetho, which contained a list of more than 300 kings of Egypt down to the 19th dynasty.

In the second story is the Picture Gallery. All the paintings are labelled. In Room 1 are portraits of princes of the house of Savoy, and battles in which they were engaged. Room 2. In this room are excellent specimens of the Turin painter, Gaudenzio Ferrari, No. 49, St. Peter and Donor ; 52, Madonna and St. Elizabeth ; 53, God ; 54, Descent from Cross ; 57, Joachim driven from the Temple. Rooms 3 and 4. Italian pictures, Massimo d'Azeglio, another Turin painter, 90, a Landscape. Room 5. Italian paintings of the 14th, 15th, and 16th cents.: Clovio, 127 bis, an Entombment, painted on silk ; Bronzino, 127 and 128, Portraits of Eleonora da Toledo and her husband, Cosimo I. de Medici. Room 6. J. da Ponte (Il Bassano), 148, Portrait ; P. Caliari (Paolo Veronese), 157, Queen of Sheba presenting

gifts to Solomon; A. Carracci, 158, St. Peter; Caravaggio, 161, Musician;
J. Robusti (Il Tintoretto), 162, The Trinity. **Room 7.** Guido Reni,
163, S. Giovanni; Spagnoletto, 174, St. Jerome. **Room 8.** Enamels
and paintings on porcelain by Constantin of Geneva. **Room 9.** A small
room entirely filled with fruit and flower pieces by Dutch artists.
Between rooms 9 and 10 is a dark lobby, hung also with pictures.
Room 10. Continuation of the Italian school, 16th, 17th, and 18th
cents.: B. Strozzi, 232, Portrait of Prelate; 251, Homer singing his
own Songs; Paolo Veronese, 234, Mary Magdalene at our Lord's Feet;
Guido Reni, 235, Apollo; 236, Cupids; G. Dughet (Poussin),
237, 238, Tivoli Waterfalls; G. F. Barbieri (Il Guercino), 239, 262,
*S. Francesca Romana, and in next room, Return of Prodigal Son.
Room 11. A. Canale (Il Canaletto), 257 bis, Ducal Palace, Venice;
F. Albani, 260, 264, 271, and 274, The Four Elements; S. Ricci,
272, Hagar sent away; 275, Solomon burns the Idols; C. Dolce, 276,
Head of Madonna; B. Bellotto, 283, 288, Royal Palace, Turin;
Old Bridge across the Po. **Room 12.** Flemish and German school:
Aeken (Bosch), 309, an Adoration; G. Van Eyck, 313, St. Francis;
Rogier Van des Weyden, 312, *Madonna; F. Franck, 335, Room
with Ladies and Gentlemen; Van Dyck, 338, 351, The three
Children of Charles I. of England; *The Princess Clara Eugenia of
Spain; Rubens, 340, Sketch of his apotheosis of Henri IV. in the
Uffici of Florence. **Room 13.** Containing the gems of the collection:
A. Mantegna, 355, Virgin, Child, and Saints; L. Credi, 356, *Virgin
and Child; G. F. Barbieri (Guercino), 357, *Virgin and Child;
Hans Memling, 358, *The Seven Sorrows of the Woman Mary; Saen-
redam, 361, *Interior of a Protestant Church, the figures by A. Ostade;
Van Dyck, 363, *Large equestrian portrait of the Principe Tommaso
di Savoia; his finest work is **384, Holy Family; D. Teniers, 364,
Tavern; G. Ferrari, 371, Jesus giving up the Ghost; Raphael, 373,
*La Madonna della Tenda; Donatello, 375, Virgin and child in
relief on marble; Sodoma, 376, *Death of Lucretia; P. Potter, 377,
*Cattle grazing in a meadow; H. Holbein, 386, Portrait of Erasmus.
Room 14. Dutch and German school: Picture by Jordaens; Sallaert,
398, Procession in Brussels; Floris, 410, Adoration; P. P. Rubens,
416, Resurrection of Lazarus; C. Vos, 417, Portraits of Snyders and
his wife; Teniers (the younger), 423, Card Players; Schalcken, 458,
Old Woman. **Room 15.** French school: C. Gélée (Claude Lorrain),
478, 483, Landscapes; I. Courtois (Bourguignon), 481, Cavalry Charge.
Catalogues sold of the contents of the museums and picture gallery.

Museum of Zoology and Mineralogy.

Opposite the Palazzo dell' Accademia, but a little to the left, is the Palazzo Carignano, also by Guarini, and also of earthy-coloured brick ; but the decorations are superior, more varied, and more pleasing than those of the Palazzo dell' Accademia.   In large gilt letters, on the façade fronting the Piazza Carignano and the statue of Gioberti, are the words, "Qui nacque Vittorio Emanuele II."   Within is a high and spacious court, surrounded by lofty halls, and at the east end, fronting the Piazza Carlo Alberto, with the beautiful bronze monument to him by Marochetti, cast in London, is the more pretentious stone façade, built in 1871, but not in harmony with the rest of the building.   (See also p. 293.)   In this palace, magnificently housed, are the zoological and mineralogical collections.   Open daily, 1 fr.   Sundays and feast-days free.

Royal Armoury.

No. 13 Palazzo Castello, open on feast-days from 11 to 3 free.   On other days procure admission from the secretary.   This collection is of great interest only to the inhabitants of northern Italy, as it is filled chiefly with relics of their kings, dukes, and wars.   In the first room is "Favorito," the favourite horse of the magnanimous Ré, Carlo Alberto. Above it, near the roof, are numerous tattered flags taken in battle. In the large hall are two rows of armed knights and foot-soldiers.   At the head of this hall, in a glass case, numbered 301, is an embossed oval shield, inlaid with gilding, and surrounded by a fringe of massive gold thread.   On five medallions are represented, in *alto-relievo*, scenes from the war of Marius against Jugurtha.   It belongs to the school of Giulio Romano, was executed probably in the latter half of the 16th cent., and was presented to the university of Turin by the Princess Vittoria di Sassonia Hilburghausen.   Among the relics are the sword worn by Napoleon at the battle of Marengo, the saddle of Charles V., and some beautifully inlaid body-armour of the Dukes of Savoy.   The large door at the end of this hall opens into the "Medagliere del Ré," containing 30,000 Greek, Roman and ancient coins and medals, including a complete series of those struck in the State of Sardinia ; and also 5000 medallions, seals and stamps.   In this same part is the Biblioteca del Ré, with 40,000 vols., 1800 MSS., numerous autographs, engravings and drawings by the great masters.   To visit these special permission must be obtained.   From the windows of the armoury is a view of the palace-gardens. At the N.E. angle of the Piazza Castello is the Teatro Regio, considered the finest work of Benedetto Alfieri. It is seated for 2500, and is open only during carnival and on extraordinary occasions. In the absence of the royal family the palace may be visited. It is a plain brick building, commenced in 1646, with the front to the Piazza Castello, plastered to imitate stone. Having passed the main entrance, turn to the left. At the end of this corridor is seen, through a glass door, the equestrian statue of Vittorio Amadeo I. (died 1675) in a niche at the foot of the grand staircase. The rider is in bronze, the horse in marble. Ascend the marble steps, then, to the right, two flights of narrow steps lead to the hall of the palace, where the servants will be found who show the palace. Fee, 1 fr.; party, 2 frs. After the guard-room succeeds a series of rooms with much gilding, inlaid floors, and rich furniture. The pictures are all modern, and of no great merit. The room called Maria Theresa's contains some fine china vases.

The Cathedral.

Adjoining the western end of the palace is the Cathedral San Giovanni Battista. To the left of the altar is the pew of the royal family. Behind the altar, and approached by two staircases of 37 steps each, is the Cappella del Sudario (open till 9 A.M.), a circular chapel, separated from the church by a glass screen. It was built by Guarini in 1694, and is encrusted with the dark grayish-blue marble from Fabrosa, near Mondoví, which brings out in striking relief the pure white of the statues and the rich gilding of the ornaments, cornices, capitals, and eight-limbed stars which spangle the interior. Double monolith columns of the same dark marble, with bronze pedestals and capitals, support six arches ornamented with diaper-work on the soffits. Above them rise six smaller arches containing the windows, while the dome or cupola is composed of an intricate series of interlacing zigzag arched ribs rising from the second tier, and intermingled with loop-holes, which throw light in such a manner upon the star at the summit as to give it the appearance of being suspended. The beautiful altar, lighted with gold and silver lamps, has two faces, so that two masses are said before it at the same time. The shrine on this altar is said to contain the shroud (Sudario) in which Joseph of Arimathea wrapped the body of our Lord when he laid Him in the tomb. Round the chapel are the beautiful white marble monuments of three kings of the house of Savoy—Em. Filiberto (ob. 1580), by Marchesi; Carlo Émanuele II. (ob. 1675), by Fraccaroli; and Amedeo VIII., first Duke of Savoy (ob.

1451), by Cacciatori. One prince, the Principe Tommaso (ob. 1656), by Gaggini. In a sitting posture is the lovely statue of Queen Maria Adelaide, consort of Vit. Em. II. (ob. 1855), by Revelli. The door behind the altar communicates with the upper corridors of the palace. Outside the palace gates is **San Lorenzo**, designed by Guarini, and finished in 1687. The interior is gorgeous, but it is chiefly distinguished for the boldness of its arches.

The Castello.

The large brick building in the centre of the Piazza Castello was erected in the 13th century, and called the Castello till 1718, when it became the favourite residence of the widow of Carlo Emanuele II., Madama M. G. Battista, who built the stone façade, and in honour of whom it has ever since been called the Palazzo Madama. Before the seat of government was removed to Florence the senators assembled in the great hall of this palace. One of the towers is used as an observatory, and another part of the palace by the "Accademia reale di Medicina," who here hold their meetings, and have also a museum of craniology.

Museo Civico.

Via Gaudenzio Ferrari, No. 1, near the Via di Po. Open from 12 to 3, 1 fr. Sundays and feast-days free. First room, autographs and MSS. of celebrated Piedmontese. 2. Water-colours, representing landscapes and historical scenes in Piedmont. Under glass frame is a solid oblong chased silver vase, 3 ft. and some inches in its greater diameter, and 2 ft. 8 inches in its smaller. At each of the two long ends is a lion's head with a ring in his mouth. Near this vase, and also under a glass frame, and also in solid silver, are two candelabra, a vase, and two flower-holders adorned with figures in relief. The first was presented in 1871 by the English Government, and the other by that of the United States to the Count Frederic Sclopis, President of the Geneva arbitration in the Alabama question, and given to this institution by his widow. None of them display much art; as for the English vase, it needs only a lid to turn it into a respectable soup-tureen.

The rooms from 4 to 11 contain modern oil-paintings, some very good, and all labelled. Down the centre are white marble statues; among the best are Eve and the Serpent by Fantacchiotti, and the Crucifixion of Eulalia by E. Franceschi. Second story.—Room 12, Embroidery; 13, Miniatures and illustrated MSS.; 14, Iron work; 15, Carving in wood and ivory—notice 947, Judgment of Solomon; 16, Glass and

300

Turin. Via di Po. University. Madre di Dio.

majolica ; 17, Italian porcelain ; 18, Busts ; 19, Small oil-paintings and uniform of Azeglio ; *20, Italian painted glass from 1300 ; 21, Egyptian pottery ; 22, Pottery and stone age.

The Via di Po.

The finest of the streets is the Via di Po, which extends from the Piazza Castello to the great rectangular square, the Piazza Vittorio Emanuele, on the bank of the Po ; and as both of these spacious squares, as well as this magnificent street, are lined throughout with wide and lofty arcades, they form together an excellent and interesting walk in all weathers. The Via di Po is 768 yards long and 19½ wide, and the pavement within the arcade 6½ yards wide. Good shops are ranged on both sides of the street under the arcades. In the Via di Po is also the University, built in 1713 by Vittorio Amedeo II., but founded in 1404 by the Prince Lodovico di Acaia. It is attended by 2500 students, and directed by 70 professors. The Library, open every day from 9 to 4, contains 200,000 volumes and 3000 MSS. In the court are Roman bas-reliefs, inscriptions, and statues, ancient and modern. Between the Via di Po and the Piazza Carlo Emanuele ramifies the Via dell' Accademia Albertina, containing at No. 6 the Accademia Albertina delle Belle Arti. Open daily. Apply to the custodi.

The **Piazza Vittorio Emanuele** is 394 yards long and 121½ wide. In front, on the other side of the Po, is a conspicuous church, the Gran Madre di Dio, built in 1818, in the style of the Pantheon at Rome, by Bansignori, to commemorate the return of Vittorio Emanuele I. to Turin after the fall of Napoleon. A little to the right on a hill (Il Monte) is a Capuchin convent, built towards the end of the 16th cent. The road up is very easy, and the view from the terrace admirable. Immediately above the Madre di Dio church is the palace, La Vigna della Regina, built by Prince Maurice of Savoy, which after his time was inhabited by one of the queens of Sardinia, from whom it acquired its present name, "The Queen's Vineyard." It is now a government school for the education of children of military men. Up the river, beyond the suspension bridge, is the Castello del Valentino, distinguished from a distance by its four pavilions with high-pitched roofs. It was built by the widow of Victor Amadeus I., daughter of Henri IV. of France, and is now used as a government school of civil engineering. It contains a good collection of minerals, the larger part of which, obtained from Sardinian provinces, are topographically arranged. The **Botanical Garden** belonging to the university is also here.

Monuments.

In the Piazza Carlo Emanuele II., a short way S. from Piazza Castello, is the monument to Camillo Cavour, by Dupré of Florence, for which he received £1200, contributed by the inhabitants of every part of Italy in 1872. The statues are in white marble, the tablets and friezes in bronze, and the pedestal in granite. The monument is tame and mystic. Cavour, in an upright position, holds in his hand a scroll bearing the words, "libera chiesa in libero stato." (See p. 294.) The climate of Turin is more suitable for bronze than for marble statues. To the west is the Piazza S. Carlo, with a bronze monument to Emanuele Filiberto (see p. 293). Farther west, in the Piazza Solferino, is the remarkable, almost painful, bronze group representing Ferdinando di Savoia (brother of V. Emanuele II.) at the battle of Novara in 1848. When about to lead the charge on the Bicocca his horse fell, mortally wounded. The poor animal, on bended knees, with gaping mouth and outstretched neck, seems about to breathe its last in an agony of suffering.

A short way west from the Piazza Castello by the Via Palazzo di Citta is the Piazza del Palazzo di Citta, having on one side the Palazzo di Citta, or the Municipality buildings, designed by Lanfrachi, and erected in 1659. At the entrance to the Palazzo are the marble statues of the celebrated Prince Eugene and the Duke of Genoa, brother of King Victor Emanuel, and under the portico statues of Prince Thomas di Carignano and Victor Emanuel. In the centre of the square is a bronze group representing Count Verde (Amadeus VI.) over a fallen Saracen. Close to this square is the church of Corpus Domini, with the interior encrusted with beautiful marble, and ornamented with frescoes and gilding. From this the Via Milano leads towards the Piazza Em. Filiberto, passing by on the left S. Domenico, and on the right the Basilica. In S. Domenico, in the first chapel to the right of the altar, is a picture of the Virgin by Guercino.

Near the Piazza Em. Filiberto, by the Via Giulio, is the church La Consolata, with an ugly square brick tower. It consists of three churches built at different periods. On the principal altar is a miracle-working image of the Virgin ; while a great part of the adjoining walls is hung with pictures illustrating the cures and deliverances effected by it. Two lovely kneeling figures, in the most precious Carrara marble, looking towards the altar, represent respectively Maria Theresa, queen of Carlo Alberto, and Maria Adelaide, queen of Vit. Emanuele, dressed in the same way as they used to be when they attended worship every Sunday in this chapel. They both died in 1855. In the square outside, on a granite column, is a statue of the Virgin, erected in fulfilment of a vow when the cholera raged in 1835.

In the Piazza Savoia, near the Piazza dello Statuto, is an obelisk 72 ft. high, erected in 1854 to commemorate the abolition of the ecclesiastical courts. On the four sides are the names of the towns which contributed to the monument.

Less than a mile from the Ponte delle Benne is the cemetery or Campo Santo of Turin. (See N.E. corner of plan.) It is badly kept and not worth visiting. The inner or new part is a little better.

A little to the W. of the P. Solferino, and parallel to it, is the citadel and the barracks of the Cernaia. In front of the entrance is the monument to Pietro Mico, who, to save the citadel from the enemy, sprang a mine at the cost of his own life.

La Superga.

Leave by the steam tram starting from the Piazza Castello ; the time-table is in the waiting-room, where the tickets are also sold half an hour before starting. As the train can take only a limited number, the tickets are generally all taken in the first 10 minutes. The tram runs down the Via Po, crosses the Ponte Vit. Emanuele I., passes by the western end of the church, the "Great Mother of God," and descends by the left side of the Po to the Cassale station, whence the ascent commences by the rope and locomotive railway constructed by Agudio, and opened in 1884. The ascent takes 20 minutes, the length is 3500 yards, the average inclination 13%, and the greatest 20%. At the Superga station are waiting-rooms, and a few feet below them a commodious restaurant. On arriving at the station ascend by the road, right hand, for the Superga. The walk down the mountain is very pleasant, and it is probable that the pedestrian will fall in with some tram when on the main road to Turin.

The Superga is situated 4½ m. N.E. from Turin, on a mountain 1420 ft. above the Po, or 2146 ft. above the sea, and cost £100,000. It was commenced by Vittorio Amedeo II. in 1717, and finished in 1731, to fulfil a vow made by him on 7th September 1706, for the victory over the French at the battle of Turin, when the house of Savoy regained the duchy. The architect was Filippo Juvara.

Enter by door at the north side of the building, where the men will be found who conduct visitors over the church. Gratuity optional. The first hall shown contains small and indifferent portraits of all the popes. Then down 27 large marble steps to the crypt. At the foot is a white marble group, St. Michael overcoming Satan. None of the monuments are worthy the name of royal mausoleums. The best are : in centre, Carlo Alberto, 1779-1849 ; at right hand end, Carlo Emanuele III., 1701-1773 ; towards left, Duke Ferdinando de Genova, a colossal white marble statue ; at left end, Vittorio Amedeo II., the founder, 1666-1732. In an adjoining vault children under seven are buried.

From this ascend by 357 steps from floor of church to the gallery outside the lantern. A door about 80 steps up opens into the gallery round the interior of the octagonal dome, whence the church is well seen. The top of the lantern is 229½ ft. above the pavement of the church.

The chief object for visiting the Superga is the splendid view from the outside gallery of the lantern. In one direction is the plain of Piedmont with the Po wandering across it ; everywhere else the horizon is bounded by a vast chain of snowy Alps, with Monte Rosa on one side and Mont Blanc on the other.

Among the delicacies of Turin are the lamprede, thin eels from 5 to 8 inches long, caught in the Po. They are killed by being plunged into milk. The white truffles are also celebrated, and when cooked "à la Piedmontese" or "à la fonduta," and taken with a bottle of Asti wine, make most enjoyable dishes. The vermouth of Turin is an agreeable aperitive, and is taken before sitting down to table. The best wines of Piedmont are the Caluzo, a white wine ; the Barolo, a dryish red wine with a taste of the soil ; the Barbera, a strong red wine ; and the Nebrolo. The Gressini are double baked bread in strips 18 inches long and a quarter of an inch thick. In the Italian houses a handful of them is put down to each cover at the dinner-table. They are made at very many places besides Turin ; even at Cannes on the Riviera. A great deal of maccheroni (macaroni) is consumed in Italy. In Turin are important silk mills.

Turin to Cuneo, 54¾ m. S., by Cavallermaggiore (see p. 153). **Turin to Genoa,** 103¼ m. S.E., by Asti, Alessandria, and Novi (see p. 279). **Turin to Savona,** 91¼ m. S.E., by Carmagnola, Bra, Carru, and Ceva (see p. 183, and map p. 27). **Turin to Florence,** 291 m. S.E., by Asti, Alessandria, Piacenza, Parma, Modena, Bologna, and Pistoja (see p. 309, and map p. 199).

THE VALLEES VAUDOISES, OR THE VALLEYS OF THE WALDENSES.

(See accompanying Map.)

The Waldensian valleys are very beautiful, are drained by splendid trout-streams, and possess a rich variety of rare plants.

The chief town, Torre-Pèllice (formerly called Torre-Luserna) is 34½ miles S.W. from Turin by rail, passing by Pinerolo, 23½ m. S.W. from Turin, and 10¾ m. N.E. from Torre-Pèllice. From ¦Pinerolo a steam tram runs 12 m. N.W. up the valley of the Chisone to Perosa, the second Waldensian town in importance. Time, 1 hr. 30 min. The tram station is near the railway station.

Pinerolo is connected with Saluzzo by steam tram, 2 hrs. 20 min. S., 2 frs. 15 c. and 1 fr. 55 c., passing Osasco and Cavour. This tram station is at some distance from the Pinerolo railway station.

The Italian steam trams run on single lines laid on one side only of the highroads. Some towns they traverse, while others they merely skirt. They afford excellent opportunities for seeing the country, but run neither so quickly nor so smoothly as the railway trains.

Rail between Cuneo and Mondoví, 11½ m. E. and 58 m. S. by rail from Turin. Mondoví, pop. 17,000, on the Ellero ; *Inn :* Tré Limoni d'Oro. On one side of the Ellero is the railway station, and on the other are the inn and town, built on the lower slopes of a wooded hill rising from the river. The Via San Agostino contains the best shops. On the top of the hill is another town nearly as large as Mondoví (see p. 184).

The country of the Italian Waldenses consists of parts of the valleys of Pèllice, San Martino, and Perosa or Chisone, is about 20 m. long from W. to E. by 13 broad, is divided into 15 parishes, exclusive of the isolated parish of Turin, and contains a population of about 25,000. They have besides a thriving colony in Uruguay. Till Cavour in 1848 procured for Italy civil and religious liberty, the Waldenses were confined by law to their valleys ; now, however, they have spread themselves over the best parts of Italy, while many emigrate every year to the United States and to Uruguay. Of late mills and manu-factories have been established on their rivers, which has caused a large influx of Piedmontese workmen, so that many Waldensian towns and villages which up to 1848 were inhabited almost exclusively by Protestants have now a larger population of Romanists.

These valleys are very fertile, bearing luxuriant crops of maize, wheat, barley, potatoes, French beans, etc., intersected by long rows

See map, page 291.

For continuation of the French Waldensian Valleys see map, page 375.

English Miles

0 1 2 3 4 5   10

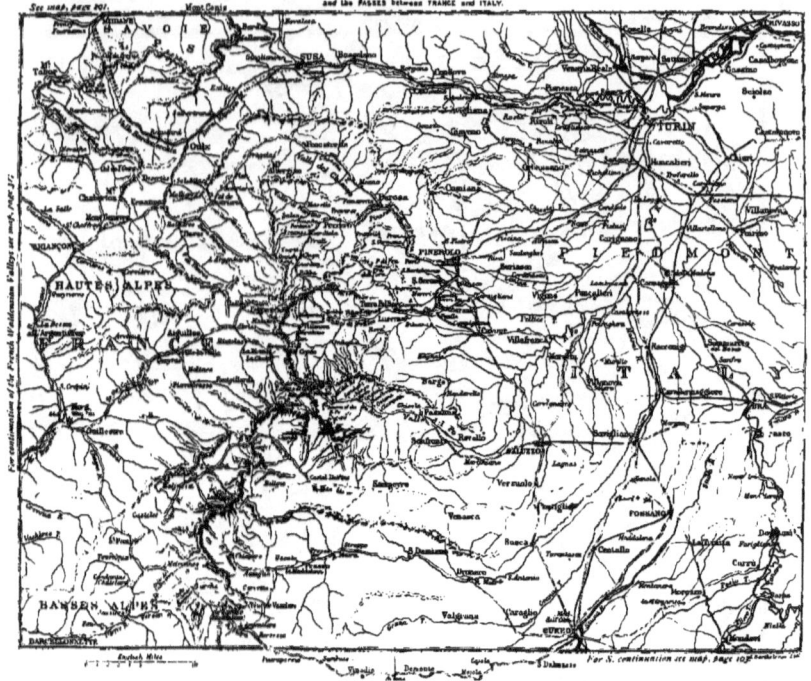

of vines on high trelliswork, and studded with mulberry, apricot, peach, apple, pear, and cherry trees, while at the base of the densely-wooded mountains which enclose them are walnut and chestnut trees. The only high mountain in the territory is Monte Meidassa, 10,185 ft., between the valleys of the Pèllice and the Po, which river has its source 6625 ft. above the sea among the snowy summits of Monte Viso, 12,607 ft., a short way south from Monte Meidassa by either the Col dell' Agnello or the Col Traversette, 9680 ft.

The Vaudois inhabited originally not only the valleys on the E. side of the Alps but also those of Louise, Embrun, and Barcelonnette on the French side (pp. 344, 345), and, as there was constant communication between them, French became the common language, as it is still in a great measure. They consider themselves a part of the Apostolic Church, which by its isolated position in the then almost inaccessible ravines had escaped the early innovations introduced by the church of Rome; albeit not altogether, for they admitted confession by contrite prayer to God and the mention aloud of their sins to a priest, the power of priests to bind and to loose, that sins were of two classes, mortal and venial, and the efficacy of fasts and penance. At the Reformation all these were swept away, and the doctrines and church polity of Calvin adopted. The independent church of the Waldenses, or valley-people, existed about a century before the arrival of Pierre Valdo from Lyons in 1180. Their name is supposed to be derived from "valle densa," contracted into Vallenses, Valdenses, and finally Vaudois. The first serious persecution of the Italian Vaudois was begun at the instigation of Yolande, sister of Louis XI. and wife of Amadée IX., Duke of Savoy. By her representation Innocent VIII. in 1487 fulminated against the Waldenses a bull of extermination. Whoever killed any of these heretics were to be absolved from promises they had made, property wrongly obtained by them was to be rendered legal, and they were to have a complete remission of all their sins. Persecution among the French Vaudois commenced in the 13th cent.

Torre-Pèllice, pop. 5200, *Inn:* H. de l'Ours, good and comfortable, is situated on the Pèllice and its affluent the Angrogna, 34¼ m. S.W. by rail from Turin, 10¾ m. from Pinerolo, and 1¼ m. from the station of Luserna-San Giovanni, pop. of both places together, 4200. Luserna is a considerable town to the N. of the station. *Inn:* Albergo del Belvédère. Opposite is San Giovanni, a large unfinished-looking village, with barracks, a "Tempio Evangelico," and several elementary Protestant schools.

Torre-Pèllice is a thriving town in the midst of a fertile valley enclosed within most picturesque mountains. At the west end are the Waldensian church, the manse, the college, and the higher school for girls. At the other end of the town are the inn, the post and telegraph office, the Romanist church and schools, and up by the Angrogna the Baptist chapel and manse. On the rivers are cotton and flour mills, and dye and calico-printing works. These establishments have attracted many Piedmontese to the town, which, from this and other causes, have made the Romanist population more numerous than the Protestant.

The wine made in the valley of Pèllice is principally red, and is drunk in the second year. A beautiful walk extends up the valley of the Angrogna to Perosa, about 6 hrs. N. by the defile of Pra de Tor, 4360 ft., and the village of Pramollo with Waldensian chapel and schools. Pop. of the district of Pramollo, 1350.

Torre-Pèllice to Mont Dauphin by Bobbio, Mirabouc, Les Granges des Pras, the Col de la Croix, La Monta, and Abriés, 47 m. W., 16 to 17 hrs. walking. Up to Bobbio, 2838 ft., 7½ m. and 2½ hrs. walking, pop. 1520, Tempio Evangelico, *Inns:* Camoscio, etc., there is nothing particular. Afterwards the valley gradually contracts till it becomes a mere gorge, having at the entrance the ruins of Fort Mirabouc. At Mirabouc, 4718 ft., the valley turns southward to the inn and custom-house station, 5683 ft., about 3½ hrs. from Bobbio, where provisions and accommodation may be had for the night. From this commences the ascent of the Col, 7576 ft., 17 m. from Torre-Pèllice and 30 from Mont Dauphin, commanding a splendid view of Monte Viso. The top (with an Hospice) is nearly level, and the descent by the French side easy. At La Chalp the track joins the char-à-banc road leading to Mont Dauphin by La Monta, Ristolas, Abriés, and Guillestre. (For Mont Dauphin and Guillestre, see p. 344, and map p. 304.)

PINEROLO.

23½ m. S.W. from Turin by rail and 10¾ m. N.E. from Torre-Pèllice is Pinerolo, 1237 ft., pop. 19,000. *Inns:* *Couronne d'Or ; Campana ; Cannon d'Oro. A handsome but rather a straggling town, with a large Piazza d'Armi, a good promenade, several hospitals, and representatives of the chief Italian banks. It contains besides a public library, various colleges and schools, including one for cavalry and another for music. The Waldenses have a chapel near the public garden, and a school for girls and another for boys. In the Via Sommeiller is a large seminary. The Cathedral is a handsome building, served by a large staff of dignitaries. In the Piazzetta Santa Croce is the Italian Alpine Club. *Cabs*—the course, 1 fr.; the hour, 1 fr. 75 c.; each successive half-hour, 1 fr.

Near the centre of the town is the terminus of the steam tram to Saluzzo, 2¼ hrs. Near the railway station is the terminus of the steam tram to Perosa, 12 m. N.W. from Pinerolo. **Perosa**, 2015 ft., pop. 2400, *Inn:* H. National, agreeably situated on the Chisone near its junction with the Germanasca. On the other side of the Chisone is Pomaretto, pop. 760, with a Waldensian chapel and school.

Perosa to Mont Dauphin. —There is a post-road up the Germanasca and down the Guil, an affluent of the Durance, to Mont Dauphin, passing by Perrero and Abriés. Abriés is 24 m. S.W. from Perosa and on the S. side of the Col d'Abriés, and 21 m. N.E. from Mont Dauphin. (For Mont Dauphin, see p. 344.) About 7 m. W. from Perosa is Perrero, 931 ft., pop. 560, on the Germanasca at its junction with the Germanasca di Massello. From this the road, still ascending the Germanasca, turns southward, and passing by the hamlets of Pomeifre, Fontana, Gardiola, and Bonous on the Germanasca at its junction with the Rodoretto, arrives at Prali on the Germanasca, 4502 ft., pop. of district 1370, about 4½ hrs. walk from Perosa. The road from Prali passes Cugno, Ghigo, Orgiere, and Pomé to Giordano, whence it becomes a mule-path, which at the hamlet of Ribba separates from the path to the Pass Giuliano, 8358 ft. to the S.E., and continues in a S.W. direction by the Germanasca to the Col d'Abriés, 8677 ft., frequented even in winter. The summit is 3 hrs. from Prali, and the descent to the village of Abriés by the hamlet of Roux, 2½ hrs. (For Abriés and Mont Dauphin, see p. 344, and map. p. 304.)

Perosa to Cesanne, 28½ m. N.W. by the river Chisone, Fenestrelle, Pragelas, and Sestrières. 9 m. above Perosa is **Fenestrelle**, pop. 1120, *Inns:* Croce Bianca; Scudo di Francia, one of the strongest Italian fortresses on the frontier. 7 m. from Fenestrelle is Pragelas, where the valley becomes more Alpine in character. Other 4½ m. is Sestrières, "whence the road mounts in zigzags to the Col de Sestrières, a nearly level plain 2 m. long, commanding a good view of Mont Albergian. The descent is by long windings to the level of the Dora, which is crossed to reach Cesanne, 8 m. from Sestrières" (Ball's *Alps*, p. 36). (For Cesanne to Briançon by Mont Genèvre, see under Briançon, p. 333, and map p. 304.)

SALUZZO.

Saluzzo is 42¼ m. S. by rail from Turin, and 4 hrs. by steam tram from the same city. Saluzzo is 2¼ hrs. N. from Cuneo by steam tram, passing Cavour, pop. of district 7220. Coach daily to Paesana on the Po, 14 m. W., fare 1½ fr.; also to Sampeyre, Albergo della Posta, 6 hrs. S.W., on the Vraita; and to Barge, 1½ fr., *Inn:* Lion d'Or.

The termini of the Cuneo and Saluzzo, the Pinerolo and Saluzzo, and the Turin and Saluzzo steam trams are just within the town. The tram to Pinerolo leaves Saluzzo near the railway station, passing by the marble statue to the poet Silvio Pellico, born at Saluzzo in 1788, d. 1854. Saluzzo, pop. 18,000, *Inns:* Corona Grossa; Gallo, is a town of considerable size, possessing great facilities for visiting various places in the neighbourhood, either by tram, rail, or coach.

Saluzzo to Mont Dauphin, 65½ m. W. by Paesana, Crissolo, Col de la Traversette, Abriés, and Queyras. Take the coach which starts in the evening for Paesana on the Po, 1778 ft., with two fair inns, passing Martiniana and Sanfront. Above Paesana the valley becomes very picturesque and the view of Monte Viso gradually more and more imposing. After having passed Ostana, 4266 ft., the road reaches the sanctuary of San Chiaffredo, and a little farther on is Crissolo, 8 m. from Paesana, 4374 ft. Next is the Borgo, 4954 ft., the highest village in the valley of the Po, consisting of three hamlets, the lowest having a small inn. On the opposite side of the valley and about 1 m. farther up is the cave, Balma Rio Martino, 5020 ft., in strata of dolomite. The valley shortly after becomes wild and Alpine, yet enclosing two small oases—the Pian Fiorenza, 6034 ft., and the Pian del Ré, 6625 ft., containing in summer a rich variety of rare Alpine plants. A little to the S.W. of the Pian del Ré is the source of the Po. The road to the Col de la Traversette leads N.W. from the Pian del Ré through a hollow covered with snow the greater part of the year, whence the real ascent commences. About 300 ft. below the crest and 9564 ft. above the sea is the tunnel, generally closed with snow, pierced in 1480 by Ludovico II The summit of the pass is 9680 ft. and about 4 hrs. ascending from Crissolo. The descent into the valley of the Guil is by the Buco di Viso. On the French side, 1897 ft. below the summit, is La Bergerie du Grand Vallon. (See Mont Dauphin to Saluzzo, p. 344, and map p. 304; also Ball's *Alps*, p. 22.)

CUNEO.

54½ m. S. from Turin by rail, and 2½ hrs. S. from Saluzzo by rail, is **Cuneo,** 1500 ft., pop. 1200, *Inns:* H. Barra di Ferro; Albergo di Superga. Steam tram to Borgo-San-Dalmazzo, pop. 4600, 45 min. S.W.; also to Dronero on the Maira, 1¼ hr. W. (See also pp. 182 and 279.)

Cuneo to Barcelonnette, 61¼ m. W., by Borgo-San-Dalmazzo, Demonte, Vinadio, Bersezio, the Col de Largentière and l'Arche, the frontier village of France, with two inns. (See under Barcelonnette : Cuneo to Nice by the Col di Tenda, see p. 182.)

Turin to Florence.

291 miles southwards by Alessandria, Piacenza, Parma, Modena, and Bologna.
Time by quick trains, 13 hours.   For London to Florence, and through tickets,
see the Continental Time-tables of the London, Chatham, and Dover Railway, 3d.

TURIN	FLORENCE
MILES FROM	MILES TO

291
TURIN. (For Asti, and the route as far as Alessandria, see ⏜
p. 280, and map p. 199.)

81   210
⏜ VOGHERA, pop. 10,000, on the Staffora.   Hotel: H. Italia. ⏜
Branch to Pavia, 17 m. N., and Milan.   Between Voghera and the
next station, Casteggio, is on the right Montebello, where the battle
took place, 9th June 1800, which preceded that of Marengo by five days.

117   174
⏜ PIACENZA, pop. 36,000, on the Po.   Hotels: S. Marco; ⏜
Italia ; Croce Bianca.   Cabs—the course, 1 horse, 70 c. ; 2 horses, 1 fr.
For the first hour, 1 horse, 1 fr. 50 c. ; 2 horses, 1 fr. 80 c.

In the middle of the town is the square called the Piazza de' Cavalli,
from the two bronze equestrian statues of Duke Alexander Farnese and
his son Duke Ranuccio.   On one side is the church of S. Francesco, and
on the other the Palazzo del Governo, and opposite it the picturesque
Palazzo del Comune, begun in 1281.   The pórtico underneath is used
as a market.   The upper part of the building is of red brick with
handsome windows.   The principal street, the Strada Diritta, leads to
the **Cathedral** (1122-1233), containing some admirable paintings.   In
the interior the arches are round, but the ribs of the roof meet at an
angle.   At the 3d altar is a picture, by A. Sirani, of the Ten Thousand
Martyrs ; at the 4th a painting of the Death of a Saint.   In the right
transept is an altar-piece, Three Saints, by Calisto di Lodi, and on the
ceiling frescoes by Agostino and Lodovico Carracci, in Correggio's style.
The Coronation of the Virgin is by Procaccini.   The **Cupola** is divided
into eight compartments ; six of them were painted by Guercino, with
figures of prophets and sybils ; the other two figures were by Morazzone.
Below are four allegorical paintings by Franceschini.   The roof of
the crypt under the church rests on 100 columns.   S. Antonino (the
former cathedral) was commenced in the 10th cent., and restored in
1562.   The curious vestibule and the massive columns bearing the
tower are relics of the earlier edifice.   At the W. end of the town is
Sa. Maria di Campagna, famous for paintings by Pordenone.   On

310

TURIN
MILES FROM

PARMA—MUSEUM.

FLORENCE
MILES TO

the left of the chief entrance is a fresco by him of St. Augustine and five Angels ; in the 1st chapel left are two large frescoes, the Nativity of the Virgin and the Adoration of the Magi. Crossing the transept we have on the left the "Marriage of St. Catharine," the faces being portraits of the Pordenone family, and a fine fresco also by him, representing the dispute of St. Catharine. By him are likewise the frescoes in the eight compartments of the cupola ; those in the pendentives are by B. Gatti. The most highly decorated church is *S. Sisto* (built in the 16th cent.), with an Ionic atrium. Raphael's Madonna, now at Dresden, was taken from S. Sisto.

The *Palazzo Farnese* is a great, unfinished, building, begun in 1558 by Margaret of Austria, now used as barracks. The Mandelli palace, now the Prefettura, has a handsome façade. 24 miles to the south of Piacenza is the site of *Velleia*, a town which was overwhelmed by a landslip in the 3d cent. Many interesting objects have been obtained there ; which have been deposited in the museum of Parma. In the vicinity are emanations from the ground of carburetted hydrogen gas, which takes fire on the application of a flame.

153 ⟶ PARMA, pop. 46,000, on the Parma. *Hotels:* Albergo Centrale ; ⟵ 138 Croce Bianca : Leone d'Oro. Parma, although founded by the Boii, and conquered by the Romans 183 B.C., is a neat clean town of modern appearance, surrounded by bastioned walls. The most important of the edifices is the Palazzo Ducale, forming, with the *Palazzo Farnese*, a large unsymmetrical assemblage of buildings in the Piazza del Corte behind the Piazza Grande. In the Ducal Palace is a collection of paintings belonging to the French school. In the Farnese are the Museum of Antiquities, the Picture-Gallery, the Library, and the Farnese Theatre, now in a ruinous condition. It was built in 1620, in the time of Duke Ranuccio, and for many years was the scene of splendid spectacles and grand public entertainments.

The *Museum of Antiquities* embraces a small collection, in four rooms, of Roman altars, bronzes, busts, and mosaics, principally from Velleia and Rome. Among the most remarkable, are "The Theft of the Tripoid," in 1st room. In the 2d room, a statuette of Hercules intoxicated, and the "Tabula alimentaria," a rescript of the Emperor Trajan, relating to the support of certain poor children. In 4th room, a bust of Maria Louisa, the first Napoleon's second wife, by Canova. Higher up on the same staircase is the *Library*, with 150,000 volumes, and some thousands of MSS., in several large galleries and halls, at the end of one of which is Correggio's fresco of the Coronation of the Virgin.

The *Pinacoteca* is on the same floor of the palace as the library, and is open daily during the same hours. The collection is not large, but is remarkable for the number and value of Correggio's pictures. In selecting the best pictures, we shall arrange the names of the painters alphabetically to facilitate reference.

Annibal Caracci.—Pietá. *Lodovico Caracci.*—Funeral of the Virgin ; the Apostles at the tomb of the Virgin (two large pictures). *Cima da Conegliano.*—Two very good pictures. (Correggio.)—1. The Madonna della Scala, a fresco. 2. The Flight into Egypt, known as the Madonna della Scodella, from the dish in the Virgin's hand. 3. The *Madonna with St. Jerome*, sometimes called Il Giorno, from its bright daylight effect and in contrast with La Notte at Dresden—this is Correggio's best picture here, perhaps it is the best picture he ever painted on canvas, and it is universally considered one of the marvels of art. The letters A. A. (Antonio Allegri) are worked into the silk that covers the walls of the cabinet. 4. The Martyrdom of St. Placidus and St. Flavia (such subjects are not agreeable, however skilfully treated). 5. The Entombment. 6. Christ carrying his Cross (some critics think this to be a work of Anselmi, others that it is an early production of Correggio). 7. A Portrait attributed to him. (On the walls of some of the rooms are the drawings that were made for Toschi the engraver from Correggio's frescoes at Parma.) *Albert Durer.*—Man with a Skull. *Francesco Francia.*—Descent from the Cross ; the Virgin enthroned with Saints ; the Virgin with the Infant and St. John (most charming). *Garofalo.*—Virgin and Child in the clouds, with a landscape below. *Giovanni di San Giovanni.*—A Singing party. *Murillo.*— St. Jerome. *Parmegianino.*—The Marriage of St. Catharine (an exquisite picture) ; Marriage of the Virgin ; Portrait of a Man with a music book (marked "incerto" on the frame). *Fra Paola da Pistoia.*—Adoration of Magi. *Pordenone.*—Portrait of a Man with an open book. *Raffaello* (?).— Christ in the clouds with the Virgin and St. John, and Saints below (it is by no means certain that this is a work of Raffaello). *Giuseppe Rosa.*— Landscape with Cattle. *Lionello Spada.*—Fortune-telling, three figures ; Marriage of St. Catharine. *Spagnoletto.* — Twelve pictures of Saints. *B. Schidone.*—The Entombment ; the Maries at the Sepulchre ; Virgin, Child, and St. John. *Vandyck.*—Virgin and Child ; Portrait of an Old Lady. *Velasquez.*—Portrait of a Man in a black dress (there are other portraits ascribed to him). *L. da Vinci.*—Sketch of a Female Head. *Zuccarelli.*—River Scene.

The *Ducal Garden*, open daily to the public, is on the other side of the river, and may be reached from the palace by a bridge called the Ponte Verde. It is a large piece of ground, laid out in a formal style; but when its chestnuts, limes, and acacias, are in leaf, it affords a pleasant promenade. Within the grounds is a palace called Palazzo di Giardino. The *Botanic Gardens* are at the other side of the town, near the citadel. The broad road near it, called the Stradone, is planted with trees, and is a favourite place of resort for the town's-people, both in carriages and on foot.

By a narrow street leading east from the Ducal Palace is the Cathedral, a good specimen of Italian Gothic, built in the 13th and 14th cents. The portals are adorned with lions, by B. da Bisoni, 1281. In the interior, along the top of clustered articulated columns, runs an elegant triforium, and over it extends a lofty elliptical roof, painted by G. Mazzola. The choir is above the level of the nave. Within the great door, left side, is a portrait of Correggio, and on the other, one of Parmegianíno. *The cupola* was painted by *Correggio* (1526-30), with frescoes representing the *Assumption of the Virgin*, but they are in a ruined state. Those on the vault of the right transept were by a son of Correggio, while those on the left transept were by Orazio Samma-chini. In the Capella dei Canonici, on the right side of the church, at the foot of the choir-steps, is an altar-piece by B. Gatti ; and near it a poor bust of Petrarch, with an inscription recording that he was arch-deacon here. Beneath the choir is a spacious crypt, supported by thirty-four marble columns. On the walls of the sacristy are frescoes of the 14th century, and intarsias by L. Biancho.

The *Baptistery* is a lofty octagonal building (1196-1281), with four deeply-recessed doorways, enriched with bas-reliefs. The four tiers of open galleries with columns, and a fifth tier of engaged arches, the pinnacled canopies at the top, and the ring of fantastic carvings below, combine to render this one of the most remarkable buildings of its class in Italy. In the interior there are two tiers of galleries, some rude sculpture, and a profusion of fresco painting—old, but not of much value. At the middle is a great font, hewn out of one piece of marble, and having in the centre a place where the priest could stand, pro-tected from the water, whilst he immersed the child. The font at which the Parmesans are now baptised is at one side, ornamented with carv-ings, and supported by a marble lion. S. Giovanni Evangelista (1510), a church standing near the cathedral, and much visited on account of the *frescoes painted by Correggio* (1520-25) *in the cupola ;* they represent the Vision of St. John, and, though blackened and badly lighted, they are fortunately in a better condition than those in the cathedral. The figures are on a large scale, and include the Evangelists and the Fathers of the Church, who look with astonishment at the glory above. Cor-reggio also painted in grey the decorations of the vault of the sanctuary ; and over the door of the sacristy in the left transept a fresco of St. John.

In the 1st chapel to the right of the principal entrance is a good painting of the Modenese school, and the monument of Sanvitale-Montenuovo; in the 2d an Adoration of the Shepherds, by Giacomo Francia (the painter's portrait is seen in the old man to the left); in the 6th chapel is a copy of Correggio's "Night," now at Dresden. On the arches of the 1st and 2d chapels on the left of the entrance are much-damaged *frescoes by Parmegianino* (four subjects); and in the 6th chapel is a picture, by Anselmi, of Christ with his Cross. The white marble holy-water fonts deserve notice. In the adjoining *convent* (now used as barracks) is a damaged fresco of two children by Correggio.

Near the Piazza Grande is the church of the *Madonna della Steccata,* from designs by F. Zaccagni in 1521. The best frescoes are by Parmeggianino, Moses breaking the Tables of Stone, Adam and Eve, and the Virtues, on the archway of the choir. On the vault over the high altar a Coronation of the Virgin, by Anselmi. Gatti painted the cupola. The wooden pulpit combines elegance with simplicity. A good Madonna in corner chapel left of main entrance. Near the Piazza di Corte is the church of S. Lodovico, and adjoining it the suppressed Convent of S. Paolo, now a school. In this small building are the best preserved works of Correggio, painted for the abbess of the convent on the walls and ceiling of this her reception-room. The subject is Children, or Amoretti, represented as being seen through the openings of a bower or piece of trellis-work. Their varied attitudes are most charmingly portrayed. Diana herself, whose Triumph is thus depicted, is painted over the fireplace. Below the principal subjects are smaller figures in grey. The frescoes in the next room are by Araldi. The custodian is generally to be found in the picture-gallery.

The famous Parmesan cheese is made chiefly in dairies around Milan, Lodi, and Pavia, and is called Formaggio di grana, because commonly used in a granular form with soup. 17½ miles S.E. from Parma is Reggio Emilia (pop. 24,000). *Hotels :* Posta ; Cavaletto. *Cabs*—80 c. the course ; 1½ fr. the hour. *Sights*—Cathedral ; house of Lodovico Ariosto, born here 1474. His *Orlando Furioso* went through sixteen editions in the 16th cent. 9 m. N.E. is Correggio, the birthplace of the great painter Antonio Allegri, called Correggio. To the Castle of Canossa and back, 14 frs.

185½
——— MODENA, pop. 31,000. *Hotels :* Reale ; San Marco ; Italia. ———
                                                                   105½
Their omnibuses await the trains. *Cabs*—one horse, 80 c. the course, 1 fr. 50 c. the hour; 2 horses, 1 fr. the course, 1 fr. 70 c. the hour.

Modena (*Mutina*, Lat.), the capital of the former duchy of Modena, is a clean and well-built town surrounded by ramparts, some of which serve the inhabitants as promenades. The country around is flat and fertile. A canal connects the town with the Panaro, a tributary of the Po, by which means water communication with the Adriatic is obtained.

The Cathedral, begun in 1099, is in the centre of the city. Its exterior is irregular, and encumbered with houses. The principal façade is small but pleasing, with a large rose window and three doorways. On the side next the Piazza Grande is a handsome porch, with columns resting on rudely-carved lions of red marble. The interior, though low, and destitute of paintings of merit, is interesting, especially for the sub-choral chapel, with a roof supported by many marble columns. At the entrance of this chapel is a group of lions, and in one corner life-size figures in coloured terra-cotta, by Begarelli, representing the Nativity. In the church notice the holy-water fonts, which look as if they were the hollowed capitals of ancient columns, and the stone pulpit with bas-reliefs. On the right side of the choir are some curious old bas-reliefs, including one of the Last Supper ; and on the left side of the choir is the mausoleum of the last Duke of the house of Este in the male line, died 1803. The *Campanile*, one of the finest in Italy, 315 feet high, was erected in the 13th and 14th cents. It received the name of Ghirlandina from its vane being ornamented with a bronze garland. At the head of the Corso Vittorio Emanuele is the Ducal Palace, an immense pile, containing the Picture-Gallery, occupying several halls in the upper stories, with an entrance on the north side. It is open daily from 9 to 4. The collection comprises between 500 and 600 pictures, amongst which, though there are no *chefs d'œuvre*, are many good ones. The gallery once ranked high amongst Italian galleries, but towards the end of the last century 180 pictures were sold, including five Correggios, to the King of Poland (they are now at Dresden) ; and the Duke when expelled in 1860 took away with him a few more of the best. In two of the rooms are glazed cases full of drawings and sketches by the old masters. Amongst them is a drawing in sepia for Tintoretto's masterpiece, the Miracle of St. Mark at Venice. In a room kept locked, but which the custode will open on application, are some interesting cabinets (one designed, it is said, by B. Cellini, another of amber, a third of tortoise-shell) ; also bronzes, carving in wood and ivory, majolica, enamels, etc. Amongst other curiosities is a " Presepio," with numerous figures in coral, the metal work being of silver.

The *Library*, on the same staircase as the Pinacoteca, contains

315

TURIN
MILES FROM
MODENA.—BOLOGNA.
FLORENCE
MILES TO

about 100,000 printed books (including 2500 quattrocentisti) and 3000 MSS. placed in several halls, one of which is very large. Also a few Roman and Etruscan antiquities, and the series of coins and medals struck at Modena. In the suppressed convent of S. Agostino, near the gate of that name, is the Museo Lapidario. Among the articles is a block of stone obtained from the ancient Via Mutina, at a depth of 18 feet below the surface. On the other side is a collection of mediæval tombs. In the church of St. Agostino is a terra-cotta group, by Begarelli, of the Entombment. M. Angelo spoke very highly of this artist's works.

The *Ducal Garden* is a prettily laid out piece of ground, which is open to the public daily from the early morning to the evening.

208½
— BOLOGNA, pop. 91,000. *Hotels:* Brun ; Italia ; Bologna ; 82¾
Aquila Nera ; del Pellegrino ; Tre Re ; Venezia ; Commercio. *Restaurants:* Stelloni ; Felsineo. Omnibuses from the hotels meet the trains. *Cabs*—one horse, the course, 75 c. ; by the hour, 1 fr. 50 c. To or from the railway station, without luggage, 1 fr.

Bologna is a walled city, with twelve gates, situate on a fertile plain near the foot of the Apennine range. The Bolognese school of painting is called the Scuola Caraccesca, from its founders, Lodovico Carracci (b. 1555, d. 1619), and his two cousins Annibale (b. 1560, d. 1609) and Agostino, a man of erudition, who furnished the general plan of the pictures. Their most distinguished pupils were Guido Reni (b. 1575, d. 1642), Domenichino (b. 1581, d. 1641), Lanfranco (b. 1581, d. 1647), G. Barbiere, called Il Guercino, from his squinting (b. 1590, d. 1666), Michel-Angiolo da Caravaggio (b. 1569, d. 1609), and Carlo Cignani (b. 1628, d. 1719) ; beautiful specimens of whose works are to be seen in the various churches, but especially in the picture-gallery of the "*Accademia delle Belle Arti,*" situated at the north-east end of the town, near the Porta S. Donato (see plan). It occupies eight rooms of the first floor, contains 360 paintings, all bearing the names of the artists, and is open from 9 to 3. Free on Sundays. The gem is St. Cecilia, by Raphael.

The other best works are :—12. *Guercino.*—St. William ; 13. St. Bruno ; 15. St. John the Baptist ; 18. St. John the Evangelist. 26. *Bugiardini.*—Marriage of St. Catharine. 34. *Agostino Caracci.*—Last Communion of St. Jerome, one of his finest paintings ; 35. Assumption. 36. *Annibale Caracci.*—Virgin and Child, with Angels and Saints ; 37. Virgin enthroned, with Saints. 39, 40. *Lodovico Caracci.*—Assumption :

42. Saints (Bargellini portraits) adoring the Virgin and Child ; 43. Transfiguration ; 44. Calling of St. Matthew ; 46. St. John the Baptist ; 47 to 53. Pictures by the same artist. 70. *M. Desubleo.*—Christ appearing as a Pilgrim to St. Augustine. 75. *Lavinia Fontana.* —St. Francis de Paul. 78. *Fr. Francia.*—Virgin and Saints (1490), extremely fine ; 79. Annunciation ; 80. Virgin and Saints ; 81. Virgin and Saints. There are several other unnumbered pictures by this master on frames. 84. *Giacomo Francia.*—Virgin and Saints ; 85. Virgin and Saints. 89, 90. *Innocenzio da Imola* (an imitator of Raffaello). — Virgin and Saints. 122. *Nicolo da Cremona.*—Descent from the Cross. 134. *Guido.*—Madonna with the Protectors of Bologna; 135. Massacre of the Innocents; 136. Crucifixion ; 137. Samson with the Ass's Jawbone ; 138. The Virgin of the Rosary (this is on silk, and was carried in processions) ; 139. Bishop Corsini ; 143. Portrait of a Carthusian. 152. *Raphael.*—ST. CECILIA, with other Saints, listening to the Music of the Angels (the instruments of secular music lie broken on the ground). This celebrated composition, painted in 1515, is well known from copies and engravings. 175. *Elisabetta Sirani.*—St. Anthony of Padua ; 176. Madonna. 181. *L. Spada.*—Melchisedec blessing Abraham. 183. *Tiarini.*—St. Catharine of Alexandria. 197. *Perugino.*—Virgin and Saints. 204. *Timoteo delle Vite.*—Magdalene. 206. *Domenichino.*—Martyrdom of St. Agnes ; 207. Madonna of the Rosary ; 208. Martyrdom of St. Peter of Verona (the same subject as that treated by Titian in a picture lately burnt at Venice). 212. *Unknown.*—Sleeping Child. 291. *Desubleo.*—St. John the Baptist. 292. *Innocenzio da Imola.*—Virgin and Saints. 294. *Bugiardini.*—Madonna. 360. *Aluno (Nicolo da Foligno).*—Virgin and Saints (given to the Gallery by Pius IX.)

In the same building is a collection of old arms and armour (*Oploteca*), and on the ground-floor a few good modern pictures. A collection of original drawings is preserved in the library.

Nearly opposite the Accademia is the University, with about 430 students, directed by 59 professors, of whom, among the most famous, have been Galvani, the first that observed the phenomena of Galvanism, Laura Bassi, a lady professor (d. 1778), and Giuseppe Mezzofanti (d. 1849), who spoke fluently upwards of forty-two languages. From the tower is a good view of the town. Attached to the University is a Museum of Antiquities and a Library. The Geological Museum is in a separate building. From the University, walking towards the leaning towers, we pass, in the Strada Donato or Luigi Zamboni (see plan), the oratory of St. Cecilia, the church of S. Giacomo, and (14) the Palazzo Maloezzi-Medici ; and shortly after, stand below two of the peculiar kind of watch-towers used in Italy during the middle ages.

S. Giacomo Maggiore was built in 1267, but subsequently restored. In the 6th chapel right is a fine work by Bart. Passarotti, the Virgin

BOLOGNA

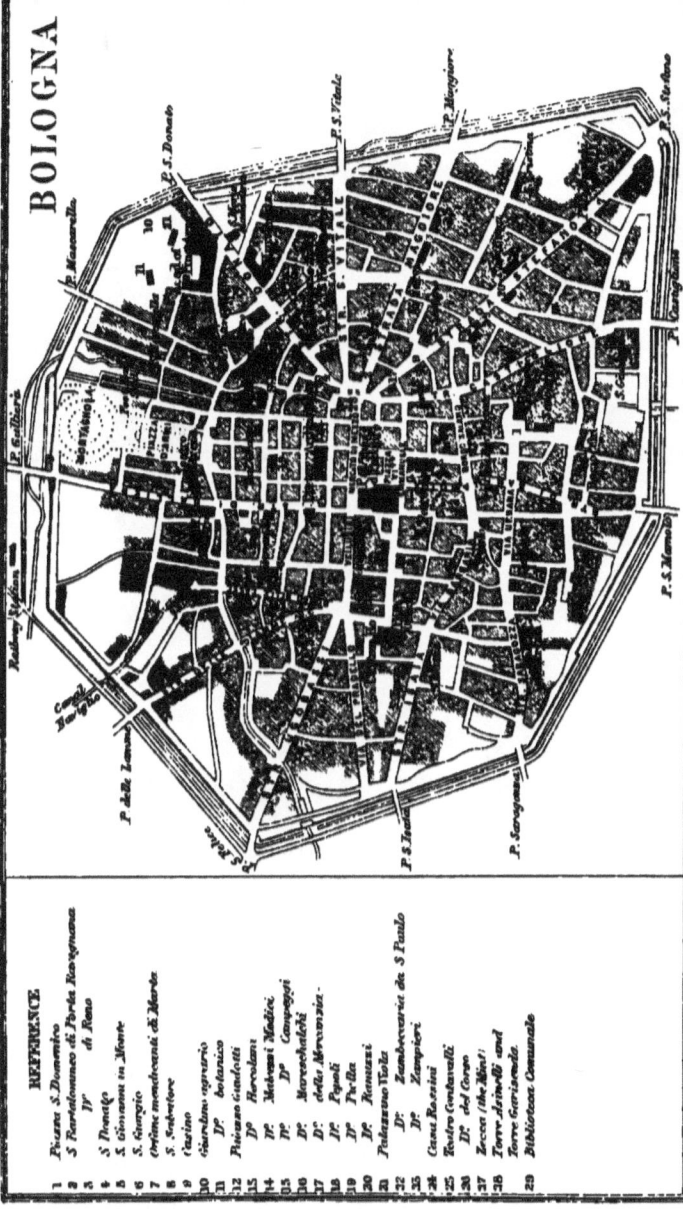

REFERENCE

1 Piazza S. Domenico
2 S Bartolomeo di Porta Ravegnana
3 D⁰   di Reno
4 S Petronio
5 S. Giovanni in Monte
6 S. Giorgio
7 Ordine mendicanti di Marte
8 S. Salvatore
9 Casino
10 Giardino agrario
11 D⁰   botanico
12 Palazzo Giustelli
13 D⁰   Marcolani
14 P⁰   Malvezzi Medici
15 P⁰   D⁰ Campeggi
16 D⁰   Marescalchi
17 D⁰   della Mercanzia
18 P⁰   Pepoli
19 P⁰   Pirilla
20 P⁰   Ranuzzi
21 Palazzo Viola
22 D⁰   Zambeccari de S Paolo
23 P⁰   Zampieri
24 Casa Rossini
25 Rostro Gentanelli
26 D⁰ del Corso
27 Zecca (the Mint)
28 Torre Asinelli and
29 Torre Garisenda
   Biblioteca Comunale

on a Throne, with Saints ; in the 7th, Prospero Fontana's St. Alexis ; in the 8th, Innocenzo da Imola's Marriage of St. Catharine ; in the 11th, three pictures by Lor Sabbatini ; in the 12th, two frescoes by Pellegrino Tibaldi, the Baptism in the same chapel is by P. Fontana. At the end of the church, to the left of the altar, is the Bentivoglio chapel, with Francesco Francia's best work, a "Madonna," the lunette above by Giacomo Francia. The 5th, 7th, and 10th chapels, on the left side of the church, contain good pictures, and in the 9th is Samacchini's Presentation in the Temple, which was engraved by Agostino Caracci.

In St. Cecilia are frescoes representing the legend of St. Cecilia and St. Valerian, by F. and G. Francia, Costa and Amico Aspertini. During the French occupation they were considerably damaged. At the commencement of the Strada Donato are the **Two Towers** (28 in plan), seen from a great distance. The taller, the *Torre degli Asinelli*, commenced in 1109, is 272 feet high, with an inclination of 3½ feet, and ascended by a rickety dirty staircase of 447 steps to the summit, whence there is the best view of the town. The Torre Garisenda, commenced in 1110, is 139 feet high, with an inclination of 8½ feet. From the towers, the Mercato di Mezzo leads W. to the *Piazza Vittorio Emanuele*, with, on the S. side, the church of S. Petronio ; on the N., the Palazzo del' Podesta ; on the E., the Pal. dei Banchi ; and on the W., the Pal. Pubblico,` an immense edifice, commenced in 1290, consisting of various buildings thrown together. In front is the Fountain, by Laureti, adorned with a statue of Neptune, by Bologna.

S. Petronio, commenced in 1390, but still unfinished, is of brick, and in the pointed arched Gothic style. The doorways of the façade are remarkable works ; the middle one was by Jacopo della Quercia (1425). In the interior, notice on the right side the stained glass of the 4th chapel ; Sansovino's statue of St. Anthony of Padua, and Treviso's grisaille pictures relating to that saint in the 9th chapel ; the windows are said to be from M. Angelo's designs ; in the 11th chapel, a bas-relief, an Assumption, by Tribolo, with Angels at the sides, attributed to Properzia de' Rossi, a Bolognese lady (d. 1535), who was at once painter, sculptor, engraver, and musician. The campanile is over this chapel. The large fresco of the choir is by Franceschini. On the floor of the left aisle is the meridian line traced by Cassini in 1652. In the 1st chapel, on this side, is some modern Milanese glass ; in the 7th, a Madonna, by L. Costa ; and in the 10th, Sa. Barba, by Tiarini. At the southern end of the church is (29 in plan) the Biblioteca Comunale, in the building called the Archigin·nasio Antico, originally the University, before it was removed to its present edifice. Besides the Library, open daily from 10 to 4, it contains a valuable Museum of Antiquities. Between S. Petronio and S. Stefano are (17) the *Pal. della Mercanzia*, the Chamber of Commerce, erected in 1294 ; (18) the Pal. Pepoli, 1344 ; [and (9) the Casino. Santo Stefano is a combination of ancient churches, chapels, and courts, on the site of a temple dedicated to Isis. Enter first the Church of the Crucifix, so named from the old painting at the great altar. In the 1st chapel on the right is a picture by Muratori ; in the 2d on the left St. Elisabetta, by Gessi. Then pass through a small chapel into the circular chapel styled San Sepolchro, which contains the tomb of St. Petronius, with curious carvings, and a miraculous well, considered to have healing virtues. This building is thought to have been formerly the baptistery of the next chapel (originally, perhaps, the principal chapel), dedicated to St. Peter and St. Paul. From a small court, called the Atrium of Pilate, from its alleged resemblance to that at Jerusalem, we gain access to the chapel of the Trinity, which contains four marble columns said to have belonged to the temple of Isis, and some pictures by Tiarini and others. There are ancient mural paintings in the sanctuary dedicated to Our Lady of Consolation ; and in the subterranean chapel of the Confession, a broken column is shown which is said to afford the measure of the Saviour's height. After visiting a cloister, where the columns show much variety of form, we have made the complete tour of this singular labyrinth of buildings, which are of great interest to the ecclesiologist. Behind Santo Stefano in the Strada Maggiore are (beginning at the leaning-towers' end, see plan), 2, S. Bartolommeo ; 23, the Pal. Zampieri ; 24 is the house of the celebrated composer Rossini, built by him in 1825. On the opposite side is the church Ai Servi, and No. 13 the Pal. Hercolani, once famous for its collection of pictures. *San Bartolommeo*, built in 1653, has some fine marbles and rather a gaudy dome. In 4th chapel right an "Annunciation," by Albano. The paintings behind the high altar are by Franceschini. In the left transept, an oval picture of the Madonna, by Guido. The Latin inscription on the wall relates how it was returned from London in 1859. *Palazzo Zampieri* (admission, ½ fr.), although deprived of most of the pictures, still retains the admirable frescoes by Agos. Annibale, and Lod. Caracci and Guercino. The church of *Ai Servi*, built 1393, has a fine interior, with thin columns. In the 2d chapel left is a "Touch-me-not," by Albano ; and in the 4th, a St. Andrew, also by him. In the 6th chapel an "Annunciation" by Inno da

Imola. South from the principal square is (No. 1 in plan) the church of S. Domenico, attached to a convent where St. Dominic lived and died. The church dates from the 12th cent., but restored in the 18th. Interior—2d chapel right, Miracle of Ferrerio, by D. Creti. Right of south transept—the splendidly decorated chapel of *St. Dominic*, with his sarcophagus ornamented with bas-reliefs, by Nic. di Pisa. The garlands and statuettes were by Nic. di Barri (Arca), 1469. The kneeling angel on the right, and St. Petronius, over the sarcophagus, were by Michael Angelo in his youth. The base of the tomb, with its bas-reliefs illustrating the life of the Saint, was not added until 1532, a work of Alfonso Lombardi. On the beautiful ceiling of the chapel is a fresco by Guercino, "The Transformation" of St. Dominic. The painting of the Saint burning Heretical Books (on the left wall) is by L. Spada ; that of the Saint recalling a Child to Life is by Tiarini. In a chapel on the right side of the high altar is the Marriage of Saint Catharine, by Filippino Lippi. The Adoration of the Magi at the high altar is by Bart. Cesi. In the left transept should be noticed the tomb of a Pepoli (1348), and on the wall a portrait of St. Thomas Aquinas, considered here an accurate likeness, though painted 100 years after the death of the saint. Opposite St. Dominic's chapel, and in the north transept, is the chapel of the Rosary, containing in the centre, under a slab, the grave of Guido Reni (b. 1575 ; d. 1642). Near him lie the remains of his favourite lady pupil, Elizabeth Sirani, who, with her master and the Caracci, executed the small paintings which adorn the frame of the reredos of the altar in this chapel.

Directly north from the Palazzo Pubblico is S. Pietro, rebuilt in 1605, containing, on the arch above the high altar, an Annunciation, the last painting by Lodovico Caracci, who died a few days after finishing it. Near S. Pietro is a small church Madonna di Galleria, with, in 1st chapel left, St. Philip Neri, by Guercino, and in the next, a fine Albani. N.E. from S. Pietro is S. Martino, 1217, restored. In the 1st chapel right, Giorlanno da Carpi's Adoration of the Magi ; and in the 5th chapel on the left side is an Assumption, attributed to Perugino ; in the next, a St. Jerome, by L. Caracci ; and in the chapel next the entrance, Madonna and Saints, by F. Francia. Old monuments in the cloisters. East from the leaning-towers is S. Vitale, consecrated in the fifth cent., and lately restored. At the 2d altar, right, is a Flight into Egypt, by Tiarini ; in a large chapel on the left, Angels, with a beautiful landscape, by F. Francia ; and at the first altar in the body of the chapel on the left, an Adoration of the Infant in Perugino's manner.

ENVIRONS OF BOLOGNA.

Beyond the Porta Maniola are the convent and church of the **Annunziata.** In the 2d, 3d, and 4th chapels of the church are three pictures by L. Costa, and in the Chapel of the Sacrament a Madonna by Lippo Dalmasio. In the choir is a very fine work by Fr. Francia (1500), and in the sacristy an Entombment by Giacomo Francia.

Beyond the Porta di Saragossa is the much-visited church of the **Madonna di S. Luca,** on the top of a hill commanding a beautiful view. It is approached by a portico of 640 arches, which begins just beyond the gate, and extends to the church, a distance of nearly 3 m. This portico was begun in 1672, but many years elapsed before it was finished. The church derives its name from possessing a picture reputed to have been painted by St. Luke. The best pictures have been removed from the church. Outside the same gate is the **Certosa,** formerly a Carthusian convent, now a cemetery. The church contains some pictures, and the chains of some Algerine slaves with the amount of ransom attached to each.

269¾ m. from Turin and 21¼ from Florence is Pistoja (see p. 231), and 291 m. from Turin is Florence (see p. 233).

St. Pierre to Courmayeur by the Little St. Bernard.

ST. PIERRE
MILES FROM

(74 m. N.E. See Map, page 290.)

COURMAYEUR
MILES TO

74
ST. PIERRE D'ALBIGNY (see p. 289), 15 m. S.E. from ᴗᴗ Chambery, and 45½ m. N.W. from Modane.

14
ᴗᴗ ALBERTVILLE, pop. 5000 on the Arly, and 1180 ft. above ᴗᴗ the sea. *Inns:* Million ; Balances. A diligence runs between Albertville and Annecy, 22 m. N.

22
ᴗᴗ LA ROCHE CEVINS, pop. 1000. *Inns:* Croix Blanche ; ᴗᴗ Lion d'Or. Hidden and sheltered behind a great rock which closes the valley. 2 m. beyond is the defile Pas de Briançon.

31
ᴗᴗ MOUTIERS, pop. 2100, and 600 ft. above the sea-level, ᴗᴗ on the confluence of the Doron with the Isère. *Inns:* Couronne ; Courriers. One mile from the town is the Roc du Diable, rising to the height of 8200 ft. At the base are the salt springs, utilised both

by salt-works and a bathing establishment.   From Moutiers the road
extends up a narrow and picturesque defile, following the course of the
Isère, past St. Marcel, pop. 500, then ascends to the summit of a rock
called the Detroit du Ciel, 945 ft. above the bed of the river, where
the valley is only 145 ft. wide; and after this enters a rich plain
with the village of Centron.   On the opposite side of the river is Mont
Jovet, 8375 ft., commanding a splendid view.   Then, after passing
the village of Villette, pop. 500, we reach

41
AIME, pop. 1100, and 2385 ft. above the sea-level. *Inn* : **33**
Petit St. Bernard.   This, the "Forum Claudii et Axuma," possesses
remains of extensive Roman fortifications, and a very ancient church
called St. Martin, built of stones from Roman buildings.   4 m.
beyond is Bellentre, pop. 1100, on the Isère, where the culture of the
vine ceases.   The Pass of the Little St. Bernard comes into view.

50
BOURG ST. MAURICE, pop. 2600, and 2780 ft. above the **24**
sea. *Inns:* Voyageurs; Royal. A village consisting of one long street,
near the confluence of the Isère with the Versoyen and Nantet.

52
SEEZ, the ancient Sextum, a pretty village between six **22**
mountains, pop. 2600, and 2985 ft. above the sea-level.   From Seez the
road passes the village of Villard-Dessus, and then crosses the Recluse
by a lofty bridge near an escarpment of gypsum, called the Roche
Blanche, supposed to be the place noticed by Polybius, where Hannibal
posted himself to protect his cavalry and beasts of burden.   3 m.
beyond is St. Germain ; the last inhabited village during the winter.
From St. Germain the ascent is easy to the

58½
HOSPICE, 7077 ft., founded by St. Bernard of Menthon, on **15½**
a grassy plain 3 m. long, and about a mile from the summit (7193
ft.), indicated by the Colonne de Joux, Jovis, or Jupiter, 23 ft. high,
of Cipolino marble.   From the Hospice, Mont Belvidere, 10,093 ft.,
may be ascended.   About 300 paces from the column is the Cirque
d'Annibal, consisting of a circle of large stones lying on the ground,
where Hannibal is said to have held a council of war, 218 B.C. A
few miles below are Cantine des Eaux Rousses, with a small inn, and
Thuile, a hamlet, 4685 ft. above the sea-level, 9 m. from Courmayeur.

70
PRÉ ST. DIDIER, pop. 1300, on the Doire. *Inns:* Poste ; **4**
Pavillon.   Junction with road to Aosta, 23 m. E. (See map, p. 290.)

Y

74
~~ COURMAYEUR, 4211 ft., the highest considerable village in
the valley of Aosta. *Inns:* Royal; Angelo; Mont Blanc; Union.
A public coach leaves daily for Aosta by St. Didier. Fare, 7 frs. ;
time, 5 hrs. Courmayeur is frequented by Piedmontese in considerable numbers every summer, both on account of the mineral springs
in its neighbourhood and for the sake of the exquisite freshness of its
climate. The waters, which rise from alluvium, are saline and pur-
gative. Those of La Saxe are sulphureous. All who have visited
Courmayeur, under favourable circumstances, agree in considering its
position one of the finest in the Alps. Six different routes diverge
from Courmayeur—the road to Aosta ; that of the Little St. Bernard ;
the Allée Blanche ; the Col du Géant ; the Col Ferret ; and the Col
de Serène, leading to the Great St. Bernard.

Paris to Modane by Lyons, Voiron, and Grenoble.

From Paris to Modane by this route the distance is 476 m., and Modane to
Turin 59 m. farther. This is the route to take for the Baths of Allevard, the
Monastery of the Grande Chartreuse, and for Grenoble, which is one of the
nearest railway stations to Mont Pelvoux and the other lofty mountains in the
Dauphiny. The best resting-places are Dijon, Lyon, and Grenoble.

PARIS
MILES FROM
    (Map, page 304.)
    MODANE
    MILES TO

476
PARIS. Start from the station of the Chemins de Fer de Paris ~~
à Lyon, where buy one of their Time-tables, 40 c. From Paris to Lyons
follow pp. 1 to 29, and examine the maps referred to.

318
~~ LYONS. Perrache station. (See p. 29.)
    158
    ~~

325½
~~ ST. PRIEST, pop. 2800. In the old castle here Charles VII.
confined his son Louis XI., then the Dauphin.
    150½
    •~

344
~~ BOURGOIN, pop. 5200. *Inns:* Europe ; Parc. Situated ~~
among 16,000 acres of bog, producing large quantities of peat. 10 m.
farther is La Tour-du-Pin, pop. 3200. *Inn:* Poste. On the Bourbre.
    132

358
~~ ST. ANDRE-LE-GAZ. A coach at this station awaits pass- ~~
engers for Chambery, 32 m. E., passing by Les Echelles, whence the
Chartreuse may be visited.
    118

363
~~ VIRIEU, pop. 2000. With a large old 14th and 16th cent. ~~
castle, in good preservation, containing tapestry and portraits, 16th
cent.
    113

368
~~ CHABONS, pop. 2000. 5 m. distant is Lac Paladru, 3 m. ~~ **108**
long and 160 ft. deep, surrounded by wooded slopes studded with
villages. At the N. end of the lake is Paladru, pop. 1000.

371
~~ RIVES, pop. 2900. *Inn:* Poste. Situated about 1 m. from the ~~ **105**
station, on the Fure. It has some of the largest paper-mills in France,
as well as some considerable forges. A great proportion of the inhabitants employ themselves in the weaving of silk and linen by handlooms. The parish church was built in the 14th cent. Here are the
ruins of the castle of Châteaubourg, destroyed by Richelieu in 1626.
Branch line from Rives to St. Rambert, 35 m. W., on the Lyons and
Marseilles line (see page 43).

378
~~ VOIRON, 939 ft., pop. 12,000. *Hotels:* Louvre; Cours; Poste. ~~ **98**
Coaches and gigs await passengers for the **Grande Chartreuse**, 15
m. distant by the village of St. Laurent-du-Pont, which is 9 m. from
Voiron and 6 from the Grande Chartreuse. Fare, 5 frs. Voiron is
a busy town on the river Morge, with important silk, linen, and
cloth manufactories. Here the monks of the Grande Chartreuse
have large premises for the sale of their famous cordials, which they
distil, not in the monastery itself, but in a large building a little
beyond St. Laurent. The road from Voiron to the Grande Chartreuse
joins the road from Voreppe just before reaching the village of St.
Laurent-du-Pont, distant from both stations 9 m., 1344 ft., pop. 2000.
Inns : Princes; Nord. After leaving St. Laurent we pass on our right
the distillery of the monks, and then ascend by a narrow gorge, among
fine woods and perpendicular cliffs, to the convent, consisting of an
immense square building, garnished with pavilions, situated on a
narrow plateau 3200 ft. above the sea-level, at the base of the Grand
Som, which towers 3460 ft. higher, easily ascended from this place
in about 3 hrs. This monastery, the head establishment of the
Carthusian friars, was founded by St. Bruno, the originator of the
order, in 1084. At first it consisted only of a small chapel, with six
poor cells, the habitations of St. Bruno and his followers, built in what
was then an almost inaccessible spot among rocks and forests.

The Grande Chartreuse now contains from 70 to 75 monks, each
provided with a suite of three small upper and two lower chambers,
and a small garden. They pray 3 hrs. every day, the rest of their
time being occupied in cultivating their gardens and working at any
of the handicrafts they understand, and in the preparation of their
simple vegetable fare. On Thursdays they take together a 3 hrs.

PARIS   MOIRANS.   VOREPPE.   GRENOBLE.   MODANE
MILES FROM   MILES TO

walk in the surrounding woods, during which time they may converse ;
and on feast-days they all dine together, when also they may converse.
Animal food and linen clothing are prohibited. At 7 A.M. they attend
mass, excepting on Sundays, when the hour is 8 A.M. Vespers are
said at 4 P.M., and matins at a quarter to 12 midnight. Visitors who
wish to see the monks should endeavour to be at the chapel-door at any
of these hours. For gentlemen guests there is ample accommodation
in the convent, clean beds, three large dining-rooms, good wholesome
food and excellent water. The men-servants, of whom there are 59,
inhabit the top story ; the wives, however, of these servants, not being
allowed to enter the convent, dwell in a house a few yards distant kept
by nuns. It is in this house also that ladies who accompany gentlemen must lodge, as no female is allowed to enter the monastery.

Their principal revenue is derived from the sale of the liqueurs they
distil at St. Laurent, and which are sold both wholesale and retail
at Voiron, at the following prices :—Liqueur verte, 8 frs. the litre
bottle ; liqueur jaune, 6 frs. ; liqueur blanche, 4 frs.

From the monastery the ascent is made of the Grand Som, 6660 ft.,
in about 3 hrs. It is necessary to make a considerable detour before
commencing the ascent. The first point reached is the Chapelle St.
Bruno, erected on the supposed site of the Hermitage. The view from
the top, though limited, is very beautiful. Coach to Grenoble, 17½
m. S., 5 frs. Guests in the monastery should pay 6 to 7 frs. per day.

381½ MOIRANS, pop. 1000. *Inn:* H. de Paris. Junction with 94½
branch line to Valence, 50 m. S.W., passing, at about half-way, St.
Marcellin, pop. 4000. *Inns:* Poste ; Courriers. From St. Marcellin
a coach runs daily to the picturesque village of Pont-en-Royan, on the
Saône, 11 m. S., whence another coach runs to Die by the Grands
Goulets and Chapelle. (For Die, see p. 47.)

385 VOREPPE, pop. 3000. *Inn:* Paris. Passengers for the 91
Grande Chartreuse may alight here also, from which it is 15 m. distant.

394 GRENOBLE, pop. 46,000, and 702 ft. above the sea, beauti- 82
fully situated on the Isère, by far the greater part being on the left
bank, while on the other there is a mere strip hemmed in between the
river and the steep declivities of the Bastile. *Hotels:* in the Place
Grenette, the *Monnet ; Europe ; the two principal hotels. Fronting
the promenade, in the Rue Montorge, is the Trois Dauphins, frequented
by commercial travellers. Napoleon I. on his way from Elba lodged
in this house from the 7th to the 9th March 1815. He slept in room

No. 9.   Among the cheaper second-class houses are the H. des Alpes ;
Marseille ; *Bayard ; all near each other and to the Place Grenette.
Of the small houses at the station, the best is the H. Savoie.   Temple
Protestant at the W. end of the Rue Lesdiguières.   Pleasant excursions for a very small sum may be taken to all the important places in
the neighbourhood by means of the rail and the diligences and omnibuses which start from the Place Grenette.   On the road to the railway
station is a large and handsome hospital, founded in the 11th cent. by
St. Hugues.   A little way down, on the other side of the river, is the
Esplanade, a very large oblong square, 430 yards by 120, surrounded
by trees, much frequented on feast-days.   The band plays in the Jardin
de Ville, off the Place Grenette.

From the Place de la Halle coaches start for Sassenage, Nogarey,
Seyssenet, and Seyssins ; from the P. Notre Dame for Domene and
Gières ; from the P. Grenette for La Chartreuse, time 4 to 5 hrs., fare 5
frs. ; also to Briançon by Bourg d'Oisans, 6 frs., 7 hrs.

The most important place to visit in the neighbourhood is the
summit of the **Bastile**, 915 ft. above the river.   To reach it cross the
river by the bridge highest up, then ascend by the first road to the
left in the village of La Tronche, beyond the gate.   After numerous
windings by a bullock-cart-road through vineyards, on the side of
the mountain exposed to the S., a square house is attained on the
plateau behind the fort.   The view is magnificent, but it is still better
from the peak immediately above, where there is one of the quarries of
argillaceous siliceous limestone, extensively used for making cement.
Ascend either by the continuation of the same bullock-road or by the
steep footpath.   The isolated mountain, so prominent from the village
of La Tronche, is Mt. Eynard, 4846 ft.   Although Grenoble is of great
antiquity, all that remains of its early history are some fragments of
the walls built by Diocletian.   The most interesting of the buildings
is the Palais des Dauphins, now the Palais de Justice.   In the square
in front is a bronze statue of Bayard, one of the most illustrious heroes
of a chivalrous age, esteemed by his contemporaries the model of
soldiers and of men of honour.   Born in 1476 at the neighbouring castle
of Pontcharrá, he died at Rebecq on the 30th April 1524 from wounds
received at the battle of Romagnane, and was buried in the church of
the Minimes, 1¼ m. from Grenoble, whence in 1823 his ashes were
removed to the church of St. André and deposited in the tomb in the
N. transept.   **St. André**, founded in the 13th cent., was the private
chapel of the Dauphins.   From the intersection of the transepts rises

a fine tower, terminating with a steeple 188 ft. high. Adjoining is the Hôtel de Ville, fronting the promenade. The tower of the 12th cent. attached to the Hôtel de Ville stands on foundations laid by Diocletian.

E. by the Rues du Palais and Brocherie is Notre Dame, from the 10th to the 15th cent. Next the altar is a beautifully-wrought stone tabernacle, and behind it, in the aisle, the chapel of St. Hugues, 13th cent. At the S. end of the town are the best streets and houses, the Place de la Constitution, and the Botanic Gardens. The Préfecture occupies the entire S. side of the "Place." Behind are the Botanic Gardens and the Natural History Museum. Opposite the Prefecture, in a handsome building, are the class-rooms of law, science, and literature. On the E. side are the Artillery School and a large handsome edifice containing the public library and the picture gallery. It is 279 ft. long and 156 ft. wide, and cost £67,585. The Library, open every day except Monday, contains 150,000 vols. and nearly 2000 manuscripts. There is a comfortable reading-room open to all. The great hall, 204 ft. long and 44 ft. wide, is lined with shelves of books in three stages, and lighted by handsome cupolas. Round the sides, under glass, are displayed richly-illuminated manuscripts, while down the centre are other glass cases containing medals and antiquities, many belonging to prehistoric times. Among the MSS. is a Bible (imperfect) translated into French by Raoul de Sestre in 1377 by order of Charles V.; also a New Testament, 12th cent., and another in Vaudois, 13th cent.

The Picture Gallery, open also every day excepting Monday, contains 550 paintings in four spacious halls, of which the centre one is the largest and contains likewise the best pictures. The principal artists are :—Albani, Alfani, Allori, Battoni, Bellini, Blanc-Fontaine, Bloemaert, Bloemen, Bol, Bonifazio, Bouchet, Breughel, Bronzino, Canaletto, Ph. Champaigne, Cock, Coypel, Crayer, Dagnan, Desportes, C. Dolce, Gustave Doré (landscape), Dubuisson, Faure, Feti, Flink, Foschi, Fouquières, Fragonard, Franquelin, Tadeo Gaddi, Gautier, Claude Gellée, Gerard, Giordano, Glauber, Guardi, E. Hebert, Heusch, Holbeina, Jordaens, Jouvenet, G. Lacroix, Lafosse, Lanfranc, Lepic, Licinio, Maltais Le, G. Manni, Massé, Meulen, P. Mignard, Millet, Monnayer, Montessuy, Moor, J. Ouvrié, Pannini, Parrocel, Perugino, Piombo, Procaccini, Rigaud, Rivera, Romano, Roos, Rubens, Ruisdael, Rysbraek, Salvator Rosa, Sassoferrato, Sneyders, Sueur, D. Teniers, Terburg, Thielen, Thulden, Tintoretto, Uden, Valentin, Van den

Veldt, Van Loo, P. Vannucci, Verelst, P. Veronese, Vos. Off the last room of the picture gallery is a chamber containing the busts and portraits of the most famous Dauphinois. Round the room are the Dauphins, Dukes Guigues I. to VI., Jean I. and II., Humbert I. and II.—Bayard, 1476-1524 ; Lesdiguières, 1543-1626 ; Vauconson, 1709-1782; Condillac, 1715-1780; Champollion, 1791-1831, etc. Upstairs is a collection of valuable antique furniture, porcelain, carved ivory, and other ornaments ; also one of those models of the Bastile which were distributed among the eighty-three departments of France after the fall of that stronghold of despotism on the 14th of July 1790. On one side of the picture gallery is the Rue Lesdiguières leading to the Temple Protestant. On the way is passed the entrance to the Botanic Gardens, with the Museum of Mineralogy and Natural History. The great interest of the museum consists in the well-arranged collection of specimens illustrating the organic and inorganic products of this part of the Alps. The birds and ores are well represented. Near the gate leading out to La Tronche is the church of St. Laurent, 11th cent. The crypt, 6th cent., is supported on twenty-four slender marble columns from 4 to 5 ft. high.

Twelve million pairs of gloves are manufactured annually at Grenoble, representing a value of £1,600,000. The material is given out to the workmen, both men and women, upwards of 25,000, who make it into gloves in their own houses. Certain improvements introduced by Xavier Jouvin in 1840 gave a great impulse to the glove trade and manufacture of Grenoble, but for some years both have been seriously on the decline. Excellent liqueurs, principally of cherries, are made in the department. The wines are indifferent, chiefly because the vines are not well selected.

Courrier every night at 9 to La Motte, 15 m. N., for 2 frs. Returns next day at 8. Coach daily to Barcelonnette, time 11 hrs. (see p. 341), passing Monètier, Allemont, the ancient Roman station of Mutatio on the Roman road and the Durance. 7½ m. N.E. are the ruins of N. D. de Chardavan, in a narrow valley. 1¼ m. N.E. is St. Geniès, with a saline sulphurous spring, and strata of anhydrite gypsum, black marble, anthracite, and lead ore.

3¾ m. N. from Grenoble by the Pont du Drac is Sassenage. Omnibuses start from the Place Grenette, fare 40 c. The Sassenage et Noyarez omnibuses leave their passengers at the entrance into the town near the H. Faure, but the Sassenage-Fontaine omnibuses go up to the "Place" and stop before the inn *H. du Commerce. To the left of the inn is the house of the guide for Les Cuves, whose services are necessary to be able to cross the Furon and the torrent from the Cuves.

This is a most enjoyable little trip from Grenoble, and Sassenage itself makes a very pleasant residence in May. An immense number of small vehicles are constantly running to the Pont du Drac ; whence it is a very pleasant walk of a little more than 2½ m. to Sassenage. The suspension bridge over the Drac was one of the first of this kind constructed in France, but instead of being hung on chains it is supported by long narrow plates held together by strong pivots. The gigantic and lofty cliffs about Sassenage are composed of limestone strata of great thickness, much valued for building purposes. The path to the Cuves commences at the left side (approaching) of the H. du Commerce, and, having passed through a doorway, enters a kind of park and ascends by the right side of the Furon. About 1½ m. up is a great cavern, so sharply cut that it looks as if it had been made artificially, out of which rushes a copious stream of pure water. After crossing the torrent, an ascent is made of a little more than 150 ft. to an enormous vault, within which are two caves, called Les Cuves, out of each of which rushes a great volume of water, which united passes under the cavern below called the Four des Fées. After this two or three beautiful cascades, quite near, are visited, and the Furon is crossed and the return made by the left side of this most picturesque river. From the Cuves side is seen part of the ruins of the old castle of the Berangers, to which a series of steps leads up, commencing near the mills, left bank. Their modern castle, built in the 17th cent., stands within a large park adjoining the village. The large halls are furnished with antique furniture and hung with paintings, a large proportion being family and historical portraits. The bedrooms of the marquis and marchioness are hung with old tapestry. The so-called Sassenage cheese is made in the mountains around Villard and Lans, some miles to the south of Grenoble. The general quality is not so good as formerly, as more of the cream now is used for making butter.

Grenoble to Briançon by Bourg d'Oisans and the Col de Lautaret (see map p. 304). Distance, 69 m. E. Diligence daily. When there is much snow, the Col is passed on sledges. Time, 15 to 18 hrs., according to the state of the road. Fare, 16 and 14 frs. As the diligence from Briançon to Grenoble stops several hours at Bourg d'Oisans, it is a good plan to alight there for the night. This magnificent mountain-road, commenced by Napoleon I. in 1804, opened in 1842, and finished in 1868, makes a charming walking excursion ; while from almost every village grand mountain tours may be made. Bourg d'Oisans, with a comfortable inn, the H. de France, makes capital quarters. There are besides very fair inns at Le Freney, H. d'Europe ; La Grave, H. Juge ; Le Dauphin, Inn Dode ; Le Monètier, H. Alliey, and even in the Hospice itself on the top of the Pass, where beds and food may be had at most reasonable charges.

5 m. from Grenoble by a straight road bordered with elms, between the river Drac and the railway, is the village of Claix. *Inn:* H. de France, with a bridge across the Drac, having a span of 85 ft. and 53 ft. above the river, built in 1611 by Lesdiguières. 5½ m.

farther S. by a road between poplars is Vizille, pop. 3900. *Inns:* Imbert ; Lion d'Or, near each other ; their omnibuses await passengers at the station. A manufacturing town on the Romanche, in a valley between high mountains. 15 m. from Grenoble is Séchilienne, pop. 1300. *Inn:* Petit Versailles, where the horses are changed. A village of one street, magnificently situated, 1182 ft. above the sea, in the valley of the Romanche, surrounded by steep mountains towering above each other. To the S. is Mont Taillefer, 9390 ft., ascended from Séchilienne in about 6 hrs. In 1½ hr. the hamlet of La Morte is reached, whence the ascent lies through pastures and pine woods to some steep rocks. The track then, leaving on the right a small tarn, keeps along the base of the rocks to an abandoned mine, where it runs along the ridge called the Arete de Brouffier, overlooking the valley of the Combe de Valloire on the right and the Combe de Gavet on the left. The ridge leads to a small plateau, usually covered with snow ; whence a second ridge leads up to the highest peak.

From Séchilienne the diligence passes through the hamlet of Riouperoux, in a narrow defile, among broken masses of rocks brought down by the terrible flood of the 14th September 1219, which desolated the plain from Oisans to Grenoble. 22 m. from Grenoble is the hamlet of Livet at the foot of the Grand Galbert, on the Romanche near its junction with the Olle. Up the Olle are the foundries of Allemont and the argentiferous lead mines of Chalanche. Here is also the Pointe de l'Infernet, 8184 ft., at the entrance to the defile leading up to the Bella Donna.

29 m. from Grenoble is Le Bourg d'Oisans, 2190 ft., pop. 3100. *Inns:* France ; Milan ; Poste. As the diligence from Briançon remains at the Bourg some hours, it is a good plan to break the journey here and start next morning. The village is situated near the Romanche, surrounded either by the vertical cliffs of mountains, upwards of 1000 ft. high, or by their steep but carefully-cultivated slopes studded with houses and hamlets. An easy excursion of 4 hrs. may be made to Lac Blanc, 6170 ft. above Le Bourg, one of the highest lakes for its dimensions in the Alps. It is nearly ½ m. long and 110 yds. wide, and commands an extensive view. From the Bourg a tract mounts nearly due N. in 3 hrs. by the villages of La Garde and Huez to the plateau of Brandes with ruins attributed to the Romans, abandoned mines and valuable deposits of anthracite worked in several places. 1 hr. farther is Lake Blanc.

Many interesting mountain excursions may be taken from this town, of which the most important is to the Ecrin Group, by Vosc, 7½ m., St. Christophe 13 m., and La Berarde other 10½ m. Entire distance to La Berarde from Oisans, 23½ m. A few miles above Oisans we leave the narrow gorge of the Romanche and follow the course of the Venéon to the hamlet of Pont Ecofier, commanding a magnificent view of the whole valley of Oisans, confined in its mural precipices, terminated by the distant peaks of the Bella Donna. In the extreme distance a glacier summit rises in glorious perspective precisely in the

330

Road to the Ecrins. St. Christophe. La Berarde.

prolongation of the valley; while midway stands Venosc, pop. 900; *Inn:* Paquet, on an elevated slope, clothed with exquisite verdure and noble walnut woods, on the right bank of the Venéon. Exactly opposite Venosc are the green pastures leading to the Col de la Muselle, 8300 ft. As the tributary valleys do not join the principal valley at common level, but are considerably higher, a waterfall, often of great beauty, almost invariably accompanies the meeting of the streams. In ascending the valley of St. Christophe the gorge soon becomes narrower, the rounded forms characterising the intruded lias are quickly left, and, the torrent having been passed on a substantial bridge, a very short distance brings us to a scene of sublime desolation. A mountain on the right hand has at some remote time crumbled into fragments and literally filled the valley from side to side with a colossal heap of ruins. Through and amongst these winds a narrow path practicable for mules, whilst the river dashes from rock to rock with excessive commotion, sometimes passing under the fragments which it was unable to displace. One huge slab of granite, wide enough for three carriages to pass abreast, forms a natural and ponderous bridge, harmonising with the desolation of the scene. On the right stands the romantic village of Enchastraye, a hamlet consisting of a few houses perched on a projecting rock in a tributary valley above one of the beautiful cascades. Not much farther on, the road leaves the stream and leads up the face of a rough hill to St. Christophe, pop. 600, which gives its name to the valley. Just before reaching the hamlet a bridge crosses a very wild and narrow cleft, through which foams a wild glacier stream called the Torrent du Diable. 2 hrs. farther up the valley is the village of Les Etages, commanding one of the finest Alpine views which the admirers of Swiss scenery can desire, terminated by the Montagne d'Arsine, standing immediately above the hamlet of La Berarde. It presents a series of rocky pinnacles in manifold rows, between which the snow can scarcely adhere; and as seen from Les Etages, especially by the morning light, is comparable to the Aiguilles of Mont Blanc, while the valley which stretches beyond it to the foot of Mont Pelvoux may almost rival the scenery of the Allée Blanche. La Berarde, which is placed in the midst of this savage landscape, consists of a few poor houses, with a small chapel distinguished from the rest by a belfry. Cultivation ceases just at the village; a few stunted pines are found still higher up, but there is no wood worth mentioning in the valley above Venosc. This excessive sterility peculiarly characterises the valleys of Dauphiné. The village of La Berarde is at a height of only 5710 ft., that of St. Christophe is 4825, and of Venosc 3365, but the character of the scenery is, like that of Switzerland, at a greater elevation. The unbroken rocky surfaces deceive the eye to such an extent that it is difficult to realise the enormous scale of these mountains. To ascertain their height we must attempt to mount them, and even then the eye has some difficulty to submit to the testimony of the limbs. The ascent of the Pointe des Ecrins is made from La Berarde, but it is extremely dangerous. Mont

LE FRENEY. LA GRAVE. COL DE LAUTARET.

Pelvoux is not accessible from La Berarde, but is ascended from Val Louise (see p. 333, and map p. 304).

Continuation of Road from Grenoble to Briançon.

After Le Bourg d'Oisans the road ascends by the side of the Romanche flowing several hundred feet below in a deep narrow ravine, by the side of La Combe de Malaval. 8 m. from Le Bourg and 37¼ from Grenoble is **Le Freney**, 3085 ft., pop. 900 ; *Inn :* H. Europe, with mines up in the mountains but of difficult access. It is in these mines that the crystals and the species of quartz containing gold are found, for which the Dauphiné is so celebrated among mineralogists.

2 m. farther, among masses of rocks, is the hamlet of Le Dauphin, with a small inn. From this place, until the summit of the Col de Lautaret is passed, every gap in the mountains shows a glittering glacier or a soaring peak. About 3½ m. farther up, near the hamlet of Les Freaux, a tributary of the Romanche pours its torrent over a precipice of granite, forming a beautiful cascade. 45 m. from Grenoble and 24 m. from Briançon is

La Grave, 5000 ft. ; *Inn :* H. Juge ; pop. 1500. Built on a slope rising from the road, with, behind, almost inaccessible cliffs containing copper mines, and opposite, on the other side of the river, the great glacier which streams from the summit of the Meije, 13,080 ft. To the E. of the Meije is the Bec de l'Homme, 11,372 ft., with a smaller glacier. The ridge called La Meije runs from E.S.E. to W.N.W., and is crowned by numerous aiguilles of tolerably equal elevation. The two highest are towards the eastern and western ends of the ridge, and are rather more than a mile apart. Any attempts to ascend the highest or western aiguille must be made from the northern side. The view of this mountain from the village of La Grave can hardly be praised too highly ; it is one of the very finest road views in the Alps, and one cannot speak in exaggerated terms of its jagged ridges, torrential glaciers, and tremendous precipices. The perpendicular cliff, extending from the Glacier des Etançons to the summit of the Meije, is about 3200 ft. From La Grave the road leads through a bleak region and several tunnels to Villard d'Arene, 4½ m. from La Grave and 32 from Briançon, a miserable hamlet, considerably under the high road, at the foot of the Bec de l'Homme.

51¾ m. E. from Grenoble and 17¼ m. W. from Briançon is the **Hospice of the Col de Lautaret**, a very fair inn on the summit of Pass, 6791 ft., where refreshments are taken and the horses changed. The two diligences pass it daily. An iron plate on the house indicates that it is 11 kilomètres (6⅘ m.) from La Grave and 13 kilomètres (8 m.) from Le Monètier. The pass commands a grand view down the gorge of Malaval and towards the lofty towering Meije or Aiguille du Midi, 13,081 ft. above the sea. From one side of the pass the Romanche descends to Grenoble, and from the other the Guisanne to Briançon. From the Hospice the road traverses several galleries, and passes by a mine of anthracite coal not far from the village of Lauzet.

The discovery of this mine has been a great boon to the inhabitants of this region, where wood is so scarce and where the winter is so long and inclement. 2½ m. from Lauzet and considerably below the road is the hamlet of Le Casset, at the foot of Mt. Vallon, 10,136 ft., at the entrance to the ravine of the Torrent Tabue, descending from the great glaciers which spread themselves over the eastern slopes of Mont Pelvoux. When the snow is melted the effect of the sun upon them is splendid. 60 m. from Grenoble and 9 from Briançon is

Le Monètier de Briançon, 4898 ft. above the sea, surrounded with barley-fields, pop. 2600, on the Guisanne, near the foot of St. Marguerite, 8328 ft., which, like Mont Vallon, belongs to the Pelvoux group. Horses changed here. *Inn:* Alliey; mineral bath establishment, with hot sulphurous springs. Mines of anthracite. The road then passes the villages of Les Guibertes, 4689 ft.; La Salle, with cloth and night-cap manufactories; and St. Chaffrey, 3¼ m. from Briançon and 4299 ft. above the sea. 69 m. E. from Grenoble is

Briançon, 4335 ft., pop. 6000. *Inn:* H. de la Paix. Temple Protestant. The Brigantium of the Romans, and now a fortified town of the first class, with eight strong fortresses, which guard this important entrance into France from Italy. The town stands on the steep sides of an eminence rising vertically from the Durance, here a roaring mountain torrent hemmed in between the cliffs of the Mont Infernet, with strong forts on all the salient points up to the very summit, 7810 ft. above the sea. At this part the Durance is spanned by a bridge of one arch, 120 ft. wide and 108 ft. above the river, erected in 1734, in the reign of Louis XV. On the right side of the river, above the town, is the Fort du Château, and opposite, on the left side of the river, are the Trois Têtes, the largest of the forts. The views from them are very extensive, especially from the fort Pointe du Jour. Carriage up to it, 30 frs. Permission to visit the forts must be procured from the commandant. The large building down the Durance seen from the bridge, in the suburb called St. Catherine, is a manufactory where the waste of silk on cocoons is carded and prepared for spinning. About 800 people are employed. The women earn 14d. per day, working from 5 in the morning to 6 P.M., 1½ hr. allowed for meals. The longitudinal streets of Briançon are narrow and steep, little better than staircases, down the centre of each of which runs a stream of water in a marble gutter, with such an impulse that all manner of garbage thrown into it quickly disappears. At the foot of Briançon is the fertile valley formed by the union of the Guisanne with the Durance, surrounded by carefully-cultivated mountains studded with villages. All the Briançon coaches start from the Place du Temple, in front of the church. "The neighbourhood of Briançon abounds in rare plants. Amongst them may be mentioned Astragalus austriacus and A. vesicarius, Oxytropus Halleri, Prunus brigantiaca, Telephium Imperati, Brassica repanda, Berardia subacaulis, Rhaponticum heleniifolium, Crepis pygmæa, Androsace septentrionalis, and Bulbocodium vernum." — Ball's *Western Alps*.

The great excursion from Briançon is the ascent of the Pelvoux group, whose highest peak is 12,975 ft. It can only be effected, however, in favourable weather and with experienced guides. A wheel-road extends by the village of La Bessée to Val Louise, 3780 ft., whence a path ascends by the hamlets of Claux and Aléfroide. The **Ville de Val Louise** lies near the union of the Valley des Entraigues with the principal branch of the Val Louise, called the Aléfroide, stretching up to the foot of the monarch of the group, the **Grand Pelvoux** itself, which, although at no great distance, cannot be seen from the village on account of the hill which rises immediately behind. (See p. 345, and map p. 304.)

Briançon to Oulx, 17 m. N.E. by diligence, 4 hrs., 7 frs., by a beautiful road winding up fir-clad mountains disclosing charming views of the valley of the Durance and of the Mont Pelvoux group. On the summit of the Pass or of Mont Genèvre, the Mons Jovis of the Romans, is the village of Genèvre (pop. 400), with the French custom-house, 6476 ft. above the sea or 2141 ft. above Briançon, and 7 m. from it and 10 m. from Oulx. An iron plate indicates that it is 11 kilomètres from Briançon, 61 from Embrun, 10 from Cesanne, and 40 or almost 25 m. from Susa (p. 291). A few yards beyond is an obelisk which marks the boundary between France and Italy, and which commemorates in French, Latin, and Italian the opening of this road in 1807 under Napoleon I., and its restoration or rather repair in 1835. 5 m. farther is **Cesanne**, at the confluence of the Dora with the Ripa, 4420 ft., or nearly at the same height as Briançon. Italian custom-house. *Inn:* Croix Blanche, where the horses are changed. A post-road leads from Cesanne to Perosa, 28 m. E. (p. 307). 5 m. from Cesanne is Oulx, 3514 ft., with a good inn, the Dell' Alpi Cozzié, close to the station. The diligence halts at and starts from the station. (See also p. 291. From Oulx rail to Turin, p. 291.) The road between Briançon and Oulx forms a pleasant and easy walking excursion, which can be considerably shortened on the French side by following the footpath.

Grenoble to Gap by diligence, 62 m. S. The Grenoble diligence goes only the length of Corps, where the Gap passengers enter the diligence for Gap.

Grenoble to Corps.

By diligence, 39½ m. S., 9 hrs., 9 frs., by a very beautiful road. From Grenoble the road extends nearly in a straight line between the railway and the Drac to Claix, 5 m. S. (pp. 328 and 345), and thence in another straight line between poplars to Vizille, 5½ m. farther. Coach from Vizille to La Motte les Bains. From Vizille the diligence takes nine horses, and having crossed the Romanche, ascends by the flanks of Mont Conex in 2 hrs. to the village of La Frey or Laffrey, 2000 ft. above, and 4¼ m. from Vizille, and 15 from Grenoble, in a cold situation on the top of this pass, about 3000 ft. above the sea; the horses are changed, and time given to take a cup of coffee. On this plateau, immediately beyond the village, is Lake Laffrey, 8050 ft. above the sea, 2 m. long and 875 yards wide. At its S. end is the village of the Petit-Chat, whence commences the Lake Pierre-Châtel. To the right or west of the road is Mt. Peychagnard, with rich anthracite coalmines, some of the beds being from 10 to 15 yards thick. The diligence next passes through Pierre-Châtel, 20 m. from Grenoble, a considerable village, with to the E. Mont Tabor, 7829 ft.

23¾ m. S. from Grenoble and 38¼ m. N. from Gap is La Mure, 2860 ft., pop. 3800, the largest town on the road, with the ancient castle of Beaumont, nail manufactories, and the anthracite mines of Availlans, 3½ m. distant. Horses changed. Between La Mure and La Salle, the next village, is perhaps the grandest scenery, the road running along the edges of high cliffs or in the profound depths of the ravine of the Bonne, which it crosses by the Pont-Haut. The hamlet of La Salle is exactly half-way between Grenoble and Gap, 31 m. from each, and 8½ m. from Corps. The road, after passing the village of Quet and the gorge of La Salette, arrives at

Corps, 39½ m. from Grenoble, on a plateau 814 ft. above the confluence of the Drac with the Souloise, or 3156 ft. above the sea. Pop. 1500. *Inns:* *Poste ; Palais ; next each other. Mules for La Salette with man, 4½ frs. Vehicles, 5 frs. the seat, or 15 frs. the whole. La Salette is 5½ m. from Corps, and 2750 ft. above it, by a wheel-road. The ascent by mule takes 2½ hrs. It is better to descend on foot. The excursion to La Salette is very picturesque, and, like all the journeys among the mountains of the department of Isère, of great interest to the botanist and geologist. The inhabitants of these mountains wander in winter to distant parts selling their plants, bulbs, and seeds. From the aromatic varieties most justly famous liqueurs are distilled at the Chartreuse, La Salette, Grenoble, and elsewhere. The rocks produce nearly every kind of metal, one of the best cements, and many beautiful crystals and marbles, of which the black variety of Beaumont is the most celebrated.

LA SALETTE.

This place, formerly a dreary and desolate mountain plateau, is now visited by thousands of pilgrims, especially on the great feast-day of Notre Dame de la Salette, sanctioned by Pio IX. himself. The church, a handsome and substantial edifice, built in 1860, of unpolished marble, is 146 ft. long and 49 ft. wide, and 60 ft. high, inside measure. Eighteen columns surround the nave and choir, while attached pillars support the walls, all covered with votive offerings. The pulpit was a gift from Belgian votaries. The façade, with three doorways, has on each corner a handsome square tower. The expenses, which were very great in a region of such difficult access, and where winter lasts six months, were defrayed by spontaneous contributions. Opposite the façade are well-executed colossal figures in bronze, the gift of a Spaniard, representing the events of the story. On the south side of the choir

Church of Notre Dame de la Salette.

a door opens into the large and spacious building occupied by the nuns, and on the north side another door opens into a similar building occupied by the monks. The hotel accommodation in each is exactly the same. The pension price, including wine and everything else, is 5½ frs. per day. Visitors can have a good meat breakfast for 1½ fr., dinner 2½ frs., supper 2 frs., a bowl of café au lait ½ fr., a cup of café noir 25 c. Both the monks and the nuns are very obliging. Books approved of by the bishop of Grenoble are sold in the "magasin" of the establishment, giving the history of the apparition, from which the following is extracted :—" On the 19th of September 1846, at 2.30 P. M., was seen by a girl and a boy in the place where the statue now is, a figure seated on a stone shedding tears so copiously that they caused a dried-up spring, about 2 ft. in diameter and 2½ ft. deep, a little to her left, to flow forth freely. Since then it has been fed by a pipe, and has been called the miraculous fountain. The girl's name was Françoise-Melanie Calvat Mathieu, 15 years old, and the boy's Pierre-Maximin Giraud, 11 years old, both employed as cowherds, and both so ignorant that they could neither read nor write. They understood only the patois, and had such frail memories that the girl had as yet been hardly able to remember a few lines of the catechism, while it had taken the boy three years to learn the Pater Noster and the Avé Maria. The statues of the children in the path between the railings indicate the place where they were standing when they first saw the figure. When the apparition became aware of their presence it arose, and calling them to her, said in French, shedding tears abundantly all the time, 'If my people will not submit, I shall be obliged to let loose the arm of my son ; it is so heavy and weighty that I cannot retain it any longer. You may pray and do what you like, you will never be able to recompense the labour I have taken for you. I have given you six days for work, and have reserved for myself the seventh, but they will not grant me it ; it is that that makes the arm of my son so heavy. Those who drive carts cannot swear without using (inserting) the name of my son. These are the two things which make the arm of my son so burdensome.' She continued a little longer in French till, observing the children did not understand her, she added in patois a long harangue in the same strain, a diatribe on the blasphemy of the age and the desecration of the Sabbath—' only some old women go to mass.' After her speech, and having twice charged the children to make known her discourse, 'a tout mon peuple,' she glided up the path between the railings, followed by the children, to the eminence where the colossal statue stands with the statues of the children before it, and, having ascended 5 ft., she disappeared, looking to the S. E." That this being was really Mary was acknowledged by Pio IX., who sanctioned the institution of a feast-day in her honour, and several plenary indulgences for pilgrimages and other acts of devotion, to Notre Dame de la Salette. On the 6th August 1867 the worship (culte) of her was publicly established in Rome. The first stone of the church, up on the mountain near the site where Mary appeared to the children,

336

PARIS
MILES FROM
GIÈRES. DOMENE. GONCELIN.
MODANE
MILES TO

was laid by Bruillard, bishop of Grenoble, on 25th May 1852, assisted by
Chatrousse, bishop of Valence, in the presence of 15,000 pilgrims. In
the churches all over France and in many of those in Belgium are
pictures representing N. D. de la Salette addressing the children. In
the litany addressed to Mary of Salette she is appealed to as "the
tower of David," "the gate of heaven," "the morning star," "the
refuge of sinners," "the queen conceived without sin," "the healer
of diseases," "thou by whose supplications the arm of the irritated
Lord against us is held back," "thou who hast said, If my people
will not submit I shall be forced to let go the arm of my son," "thou
who continually beseechest thy divine son to have mercy upon us,
pray for us."

The lad, Pierre Maximin, after serving his time in the army, kept
a shop at Corps, upon which was written, "Objets de Piété vendus par
Maximin Giraud." He died about the year 1880. Melanie, the girl,
was sent to a nunnery at Naples. A priest is said to have affirmed
that the pretended Mary was an eccentric lady called Mlle. Lamerlière,
born near Saint-Marcellin, Isère.

From Corps either return to Grenoble or take the diligence to
Gap, 22½ m. S. (See p. 333, and map p. 304.)

398 GIÈRES. At this station omnibuses await passengers for **78**
the baths of Uriage, 4 m. N., and 1358 ft. *Hotels:* Grand Hôtel ;
Cercle ; Ancien Hôtel ; Des Bains ; Du Rocher. The bathing establishment is comfortable and commodious, and is pleasantly situated in
a narrow wooded valley, about 400 ft. higher than Grenoble. The
water contains common salt, sulphates of magnesia and soda, and carbonate of lime, and rises in a deep valley at the junction of granite
and lias, which is, however, concealed for some way by an immense
mass of detritus, through which the spring forces itself. It is conveyed 700 yards in a subterraneous conduit to the establishment,
whence it issues with a temp. of 71° Fahr.

401 DOMENE, pop. 2000. *Inn:* Hôtel du Commerce. From **75**
this village is generally made the laborious ascent of the Pic de Belle-
donne, 9780 ft. above the sea-level. Guides necessary. The first
night is generally spent at the village of Revel. Two days required.

412 GONCELIN, pop. 1600. Station for Allevard-les Bains, **64**
6¼ m. distant by an excellent road through a beautiful country, in
comfortable omnibuses awaiting passengers at the station, fare 2 frs.
Here also a coach awaits passengers for Tourettes, pop. 400, in the
opposite direction, upon the right bank of the Isére.

Allevard on the Breda, 1837 ft. above the sea, pop. 4000. The three principal hotels are within the park, and the prices are from 8½ frs. to 12½ frs. per day, including everything. The Hôtel des Bains, with the casino, theatre, and mineral water establishment. At the other end of the park are the Louvre and the H. Parc. In the Place contiguous to the Temple Protestant is the H. du Rhône, 8½ to 10½ frs. In a garden of its own, Le Châlet. Near the diligence office, the France. The H. Very. Nearly a mile from Allevard at the junction of the lias with the primitive talc-slate rise the springs, temp. 61° Fahr., with a great deal of free sulphuric acid gas, especially efficacious in diseases of the throat and the respiratory organs, for the cure of which the establishment is especially adapted, the apparatus for inhalation and gargling being both complete and varied.

Allevard possesses also important ironworks, where the rich carbonate of iron ores from the neighbouring mountains are smelted.

Among the easiest of the many delightful walks around Allevard is the road that leads up the gorge of the Breda to what is called the "Fin du Monde," 1 m. distant, where masses of rock render it impracticable to proceed farther. To reach it, walk up the left bank to a bridge at the upper ironworks. Do not cross it, but continue on the left bank and ascend the road to the right. Finger-posts indicate the rest of the way. At one part of the road travellers are requested to pay a toll of 10 sous.

The ascent of the Brame Farine, 3983 ft., takes 1¾ hr. It is an elevated point on the ridge between the valleys of the Breda and the Isère. 25 min. from Allevard is the Tour de Treuil, 10th cent., the remains of a castle belonging to the family of Crouy Chanel. From this a path ascends through a ravine planted with walnut trees to the hamlet of Crozet. Descend by sledge, 2 frs.

There are a great many other excursions into the valleys and up the mountains, either by carriage or on horseback, for which there is a tariff by the authorities of the place.

The most remarkable of these excursions, and at the same time the most difficult, is 9 m. up the valley of the Breda by the hamlet of La Ferrière, to the Sept Laux or Lakes, 7144 ft. above the sea-level, and the Glacier of Gleyzin, 9480 ft. above the sea-level. Time required to go, 14 hrs. constant walking, but to the lakes only, about half that time. This series of lakes, above 30 in all, lies in a wild gloomy ravine, shut in on all sides by low bare peaks. They are fed by springs, and are not accumulations of stagnant water derived from the melting snow. The banks are surrounded with fragments of rock, covered with snow nearly the whole year, while the highest of the lakes, Lake Blanc, is almost always frozen over. Some of them contain trout, and a sluggish frog inhabits the marshy margins.

$\frac{418}{\sim\sim}$ PONTCHARRÁ station. An omnibus awaits passengers for $\frac{58}{\sim\sim}$ the village of Pontcharrá, pop. 2800, *Inn :* Domenjon, 1¼ m. distant. From Pontcharrá the coach proceeds 5 m. E. to the village of La

338

PARIS
MILES FROM

GARDANNE. PERTUIS.

MODANE
MILES TO

Rochette, in a beautiful valley. Near Pontcharrá, and seen distinctly from the station, is the castle in which Bayard was born.

426 LES MARCHES, a straggling village overlooked by a hill, on 50 which stands the church of Notre Dame de Myans, with a colossal statue of the Virgin. Beyond are some small lakes and mounds formed by landslips from Mt. Granier, 6520 ft. 2½ m. from Les Marches is Montmélian, where passengers by this route for Modane and Turin *change carriages* and join the direct line. For the rest of the journey to Modane (53 miles), see from Montmélian, p. 289.

Marseilles to Grenoble,

190 m. N., by GARDANNE, AIX, PERTUIS, ST. AUBAN, VEYNES, and CLELLES. Fare—first class, 36 frs. 70 c.; second, 27 frs. 55 c. Grenoble is 394 m. S.E. from Paris by Lyons (see p. 324).

MARSEILLES
MILES FROM

GRENOBLE
MILES TO

190
MARSEILLES. There are two ways from Marseilles to Aix, either by Rognac 33 m., or by Gardanne 16¾ m. The Rognac route must be chosen by those who desire to visit the aqueduct of Roque-favour (see p. 77).

11 GARDANNE, pop. 3500, on the stream Jaret. Both here 179 and at Septêmes are important coal-fields. Southwards, towards the Bouches du Rhône, are seen the chimneys of numerous tile, brick, and pottery works. From Gardanne a branch line extends to Carnoules, 52 m. S.E., on the line between Marseilles and Cannes (p. 142), on which the only towns of interest are Brignoles and St. Maximin.

18½ AIX-EN-PROVENCE (see p. 78). At Aix change carriages 171½ for Rognac. 5 m. N. from Aix is La Calade station, where a coach awaits passengers for St. Cannat, 5 m. N.W. (p. 80); and Lambesc, 3½ m. farther (p. 80). 5 m. S.W. from Lambesc is Pelissanne. 16 m. N. from Aix, or 34½ m. N. from Marseilles, is Meyrargues (see p. 79).

38 PERTUIS, pop. 5800. *Hotels :* Reynaud ; Thomas ; both 152 near each other. Their omnibuses await passengers at the station. Situated 2 m. from the Durance, at the junction of the branch line from Avignon, 48 m. W., passing Cavaillon, the station for Apt, and L'Isle, the station for Vaucluse (see pp. 64 and 66). The Marseilles canal from the Durance commences near Pertuis (p. 77). In the centre of Pertuis is the Tour d'Aigues, which was part of the old fortifications. From Pertuis the country becomes picturesque. 10 m. N. is the station of Mirabeau, pop. 800, with the castle in which Mirabeau spent his boyhood, and in which his father was born.

60 m. N. from Marseilles, and 130 m. S. from Grenoble, is Manosque, pop. 6200 (see pp. 166 and 168). 4½ m. N. from Manosque is Volx village and station, with beds of lignite. 69½ m. N. from Marseilles is La Brillanne, pop. 400, on the Oraison. 3½ m. N. from Brillanne is the station and village of Lurs, pop. 1000, on a hill overlooking the Durance. It contains the convent of Alaun, visited by pilgrims, and a Roman road called the Chemin-Seinet.

77¼ / PEYRUIS, pop. 1000; *Inn:* Latil; curiously situated on 112¼ / the Durance, at the base of cliffs of conglomerate more than 1000 ft. high, which by the action of water have been cut up into tall pinnacles.

80¼ / ST. AUBAN, pop. 250, junction with line to Digne. (For 109½ / Digne, see p. 166, and maps pp. 162 and 304.)

Digne to Barcelonnette by La Javie, Seyne, Le Lauzet, and Thuiles, 53 m. E., by coach; time, 11 hrs.; fare, 10 frs. 9 m. from Digne is La Javie, famous for plums; pop. 500; H. de France, at the junction of the Bléonne with the Arigeol. 2 m. beyond is Beaujeu, pop. 400, on the Combefère, whence a narrow valley leads to the Col de Labouret, 3990 ft. Thence descend to Le Vernet, pop. 300, on the Besse, with beds of gypsum, 19 m. from Digne and 33 from Barcelonnette. Near Le Vernet is commenced the ascent of the Col de Maure, 4708 ft.; from which descend to Seyne-les-Alpes, pop. 2800, on the flanks of a mountain, and half-way between Digne and Barcelonnette. It contains a church of the 11th and 12th cents. 18 m. from Barcelonnette, and 5 from Le Lauzet, is St. Vincent, pop. 600, situated on a grassy eminence overlooking the Ubaye. From Le Lauzet to Barcelonnette, see Gap to Barcelonnette, p. 341.

Digne to Barcelonnette by Draix, St. Thomas, Colmars, and Allos, 55 m. N.E. 10½ m. from Digne and 4 from La Javie is Draix, pop. 200, on a confluent of the Bléonne. 21¼ m. beyond is Colmars, pop. 1100, at the foot of Mts. Meunier and Draye, on the Sence at its junction with the Verdon. Excellent cheese, called Thorame. Cloth and saw mills. 5 m. beyond is Allos, pop. 1400, with a small inn, 18 m. from Barcelonnette. A short way from Allos by the hamlet Champ Richard, in one of the wildest and most sequestered valleys of the Alps, is Lake Allos, 7346 ft. above the sea, 4 m. in circumference, 140 ft. deep, containing capital trout, and surrounded by cliffs in some places 590 ft. high, over which tower bleak mountains, of which the most lofty is Mt. Pela, 8600 ft. The lake discharges its surplus water through a subterranean canal 1640 ft. long, whence it issues under the name of the torrent Chadoulin. From the village of Allos proceed to Barcelonnette by La Foux, pop. 150, with an interesting church, and Mourjouan, both on the Verdon, a tributary of the Ubaye. (For Barcelonnette, see p. 341. For Cannes and Grasse to Digne, see p. 165.)

91 / SISTERON, pop. 5000. Good resting-place. *Hotels:* Vassail; 99 / Negre; their omnibuses await passengers at station. Picturesquely

340

MARSEILLES
MILES FROM

SERRES. VEYNES. GAP.

GRENOBLE
MILES TO

situated, 1575 ft. above the sea, on both sides of the Durance at its confluence with the Buech. At the railway end of the town are the church of Notre Dame, 11th cent., and three towers, part of the fortifications built by the Counts of Provence. Notre Dame has been very much altered externally by restoration and repairs. The effect of the graceful octagonal tower has been destroyed by the square tower adjoining. In the interior the arches are early pointed, inclining to the stilted form. The three apsidal terminations are semicircular. The small window at the end of each is closed. The end of the town farthest from the railway is picturesque. From the gateway rise perpendicular cliffs of blue limestone, on the top of which is a fortress of the third class. Immediately opposite, on the other side of the Durance, are similar strata heaved up and twisted into an enormous pyramid. A little beyond the gateway, a good road leads up by the cemetery to a place where there is a good view of the valleys of the Durance and the Buech. 7 m. N. from Sisteron is **Mison** station, 2002 ft. above the sea, on the border of the Hautes-Alpes. 5 m. farther, Laragne station, 1883 ft. 3¼ m. N. from Laragne is Eyguians-Orpier station, 1979 ft.

112½ **SERRES**, pop. 1200; *Inns:* *Alpes; Voyageurs; Commerce; 77½ consisting of dirty, steep, narrow streets, on the sloping side of a calcareous cliff rising from between the Buech and the Blême. Diligence to Nyons, 41 m. E., p. 51. 8 m. N. from Serres is Chabestan, 2411 ft.

121½ **VEYNES**, 2614 ft. above the sea, pop. 1800. *Inns:* At station, 68½ H. and Rest. de la Gare; in town, H. Dousselin.

Junction with rail to **Mont Dauphin-Guillestre, 51 m. N.E.** This branch line extends to the passes leading to the roads which traverse the valleys of the Waldenses.

On this branch line, 16¾ m. E. from Veynes and 34¼ m. S.W. from Mont Dauphin, is **Gap**, on the Luye, 2895 ft. above the sea, pop. 9300. *Inns:* Poste; Nord; Provence; France. This, the ancient Civitas Vappium, has a large Champ de Mars, extensive barracks, long avenues of walnut trees, and a handsome modern cathedral, built on the site of one of the 11th cent. In the Préfecture is the mausoleum of the Connetable Lesdiguières, originally one of the leaders of the Protestants. In the hamlet of Tareau, close to Gap, Guillaume Farel, a celebrated French reformer, was born in 1489. He died on the 13th Sept. 1565. The most remarkable features of his character were dauntlessness and untiring energy and zeal. He possessed a sonorous and tuneful voice, fluency of language, and passionate earnestness; yet, although seldom failing to arrest the attention of large audiences, he often, by imprudent torrents of denunciation, aroused against his doctrines unnecessary opposition.

Gap to Barcelonnette, coach daily : distance, 42 m. ; fare, 8 frs. ; time, 8 to 9 hrs. The road follows the Luye to its confluence with the Durance, 5 m. S. from Gap. From this point it ascends by the N. side

of the Durance, passing the pretty village of Remollons, 10 m. from
Gap. 3½ m. farther is the roadside station of Espinasse, where the
horses are changed. 300 yds. above the confluence of the Ubaye with
the Durance the road crosses the Durance by the bridge of Saulze, and
ascends by the right side of the Ubaye to the village of Ubaye, 23 m.
from Gap, producing large quantities of walnuts, of which oil is made.
The apples of this neighbourhood were once famous. From almost
every part of the road between Espinasse and Ubaye are seen the picturesque fort and extensive forest of St. Vincent. 28½ m. from Gap is
Le Lauzet, pop. 1000, *Inn:* France, surrounded by great mountains,
with narrow gorges and lofty waterfalls. In the neighbourhood is a
lake abounding with trout. 3 m. higher up is the hamlet of Martinet,
at the entrance to the beautiful valley of the Laverq, extending to the
S. side of Mt. Siolane, on whose slopes the spire of the church of
Meolans occupies a prominent position. From Martinet the road
crosses to the right side of the Ubaye, whence, passing by Les Thuiles.
4½ m. from Barcelonnette, and St. Pons, 1½ m., arrives at Barcelonnette.
St. Pons contains the ruins of a castle, a church said to be of the 7th
cent., and a Via Crucis up a steep hill. The most curious part of the
church is the S. portal, under a soffit, having pillars on each side.
Above the pillars are small quaint figures of the apostles, and over the
door one of J. C. On the tympanum is a fresco representing the presentation of the kings to the child Jesus. On N. side of chancel is a
square tower with short spire, which seems to have served as a pattern
to all the church towers in the department of the Alps, the characteristics being that the height of the tower is proportionally great to the
height of the spire.

Barcelonnette, 3718 ft. above the sea, pop. 2100, *Hotels:* Nord ;
France ; on the Ubaye, in the midst of meadows, surrounded by mountains clothed with walnut, larch, and fir trees. The present village
was built in 1230 on ground given by Reymond Beranger, in honour
of whose ancestors, the Counts of Barcelona in Spain, the newly-erected
town received its name. The parish church, begun in 1230, was, on
account of a conflagration, nearly rebuilt in the 16th and 17th cents.
The tour de l'horloge at the corner of the "Place" is all that remains
of the church of N. D. de Confort, built in 1290 and destroyed in 1789.

From Barcelonnette, besides the coaches daily to Gap and Digne,
there is also one to the village of St. Paul, 4730 ft. above the sea, and
13½ m. N.E. from Barcelonnette, fare, 2½ frs. ; time, 3 hrs., by the
Maddalena road, the length of 2 m. above La Condamine, where it
diverges 6½ m. N. up the narrow and picturesque gorge of the
Ubaye. The wheel-road continues 10 m. beyond St. Paul to Maurin,
6565 ft. above the sea. From this a bridle-road enters Italy by the
Col Longet, 8767 ft., and the hamlets of Chenal (Italian custom-house
with a fair inn) and Château Dauphin and the river Vraita.

Barcelonnette to Cuneo by the Col della Maddalena, Vinadio,
Demonte, and Dalmazzo, 62 m. E., 12 hours' walk to Vinadio ; whence
there is a diligence to Cuneo. Wheel-road all the way (see map, p. 304).

Guide not necessary. 3¼ m. from Barcelonnette is the hamlet of Faucon.
3¾ m. more, Jausiers, pop. 1000, on the confluence of the Ubaye with
the Sanières and the Verdon. Church of the 14th cent. The road,
to avoid the narrow passage called the Pas de Grégoire, ascends to a
considerable elevation, and then descends to the village of Condamine-
Châtelard, 7 m. from Barcelonnette, under the fortress of Tournoux,
with remarkable excavations and stairs. 2 m. beyond La Condamine the road divides into two. One goes northward up the valley
of the Ubaye to St. Paul (see p. 341), the other goes to the Pass of La
Maddalena. 7 m. beyond Châtelard, or 14¼ m. from Barcelonnette,
is Larche, pop. 800, *Inns:* Alpes; Italie; 5570 ft., the last French
village. 5 m. beyond, or 19 m. from Barcelonnette, is the culminating
point of the Pass of the Maddalena or Argentière, 6548 ft. above the
sea, between Mt. Mourre and the Punta della Signora, 7190 ft. The
mule-path on the S. E. side now descends 850 ft. by the Lago della
Maddalena, the source of the Stura, to the hamlets of Maddalena and
Argentiera, 5596 ft., with an inn and Italian custom-house. A little
distance farther, or about 7 m. from the Col and 24 from Barcelonnette, is Bersezio, with an inn situated amidst much fine wild scenery.
14 m. from Bersezio is Vinadio, with an inn. The Baths are up a steep
glen, which ramifies southward from the Stura at the hamlet of Plancies,
about 4 m. beyond the village of Vinadio. 8 m. from Vinadio is Demonte,
near the junction of the Staura with the stream di Valcorera, descending from the pass of the Colle del Mulo, 8422 ft., leading over to the
picturesque valley of the Grana, about 25 m. W. from Cuneo. 12 m.
from Demonte, 5 from Cuneo, and 57 from Barcelonnette is S. Dalmazzo,
whence steam tram to Cuneo. (For Cuneo, see pp. 182 and 279.)

Gap to Grenoble by Laye, Corps, and La Mure, 62 m. Diligence to Vizille, the remaining 8 m. by rail.

From Gap the diligence road extends 62 m. northwards to Grenoble,
by **Laye**, 6½ m. N., where the Col de Bavard, 4088 ft., is traversed.
On the summit is a house of refuge. 4½ m. beyond Laye is Les Bar-
raques, *Inn:* H. Gentillon, near which is, at the mouth of the valley
of the Drac, St. Bonnet, 3350 ft., pop. 2200, the birthplace of Lesdiguières, in a most fertile district. 23 m. from Gap is Corps (see p. 333).

23¾ m. from Grenoble and 38¼ from Gap is **La Mure**, pop. 3800,
and 2860 ft. above the sea-level. *Inns:* Pelloux; Commerce. A
coach runs between La Mure and Grenoble by La Motte. Situated on
the Jonche. There is a large trade carried on here in cattle and grain.
3½ m. distant are the anthracite mines of Availlans. 20½ m. from
Grenoble is Pierre-Châtel, pop. 1200, to the E. of Mont Tabor, 7829
ft. 10 m. W. by a branch road is Motte-les-Bains. 10 m. from
Grenoble is Laffrey (see p. 333).

26¾ m. from Veynes junction is **Chorges**, pop. 1900. *Inn:* H. de
la Poste. This, the ancient capital of the Caturiges, occupies a
marshy unhealthy situation. The parish church was originally a
temple to Diana. In the "Place" is a marble pedestal with the
name of Nero. In and around the town are fragments of Roman

buildings. The chapel of Notre-Dame-de-Bon-Rencontre, in the valley of Chorges, is visited by pilgrims.

34¼ m. from Veynes is **Savines**, pop. 1300. *Inn :* H. de la Poste, on the Réallon. This is the place to alight to visit the forest and valley of the Boscodon, with splendid gorges. The road extends all the way to the valley of the Ubaye, which it enters near Martinet and Meolan. 6¼ m. beyond Savines is

Embrun, 3014 ft. above the sea, pop. 4000. *Inns :* Thouard ; Poste ; 8¾ m. S.E. from Réallon and 12½ from Pruntères. This, the Ebrodunum of the Romans and one of their important military stations, is situated on an eminence in the midst of mountains on the Durance, and the S. side of Mont St. Guillaume, 5550 ft. above the town. In a conspicuous situation stands the church of Notre Dame, said to have been founded in the time of Charlemagne. The walls, pierced with small round-headed deep-set windows with sculptured arches resting on colonnettes, are supported by flat buttresses rising to the eaves. The façade or west end consists of a flat gable with a 4-storied spired tower rising from the N. side. Above the portal is a rose window with valuable old painted glass. The N. portal is within a portico on four columns. The two outer rest on lions ; the two inner, each a cluster of four slender columns, rest on the shoulders of men in a sitting posture. The apse with its two apsidal chapels and part of the adjoining wall are probably the only parts of the church which date from the time of Charlemagne. The interior is about 60 yds. long and 25 wide. On each side of the nave are four wide spanned early pointed arches resting on massive rectangular piers. Above each arch is a small round-headed deeply-recessed window within a corniced arch resting on colonnettes. Below in the aisles are their exact counterparts, only about double the size. The roof of the nave is quadripartite, and that of the aisle semicircular. The high altar and angels are of white marble. The organ and most of the ornaments date from the time of Louis XI., who frequently visited this church to pray to Notre Dame d'Embrun, that white marble image of the Virgin and Child over the altar fronting the northern entrance. On the inside of the northern door-way (left hand) are two horseshoes, not exactly of the same size. It is said that Lesdiguières, the Protestant leader, attempting to ride into the church to the altar of the image of Notre Dame, the horse reared, and the shoes of its hind hoofs sticking to the pavement, the animal could proceed no farther.

Behind the cathedral is the archbishop's palace, now a barrack. In the centre rises a lofty square machicolated tower called the Tour Brune. 3 m. S. the road passes the village of Les Crottes.

After Embrun the rail passes Châteauroux, 3¾ m. N.E. from Embrun, with a bridge over the ravine of the Rabious, and St. Clement, 3¾ m. farther, near the Plan-de-Phazy, a poor village with a bathing establishment supplied by four hot mineral springs.

51 m. N.E. from Veynes is **Mont Dauphin**, an isolated rock of coarse reddish conglomerate rising from the junction of the Guil with

the Durance to the height of 3445 ft. above the sea, or 496 ft. above the road, the railway, and the rivers. A carriage-road leads up to the summit, where to the right are large barracks with the stables on the top story. To the left is the promenade, consisting of a group of stunted elms and horse-chestnuts, and immediately above is the village, which, like the other parts of the fort, has an untidy appearance. From the ramparts are magnificent views of valleys and mountains, including Mont Pelvoux. In the village is the inn Univers, and down at the foot of the rock is the inn St. Guillaume.

2 m. from Mont Dauphin, up the Rioubel, an affluent of the Guil, is the village of **Guillestre**, 3116 ft., pop. 1000, with an inn and church of the 16th cent. The road now ascends the valley of the Guil, passing through La Gorge de Chapelue, bounded by precipices from 700 to 800 ft. high. At the hamlet of Veyr, 9 m. from Mont Dauphin, is a cascade. 3 m. farther up the Guil, at the upper end of the defile, are the fort and village of **Queyras**, 17 m. S. from Briançon and 14 m. N.E. from Mont Dauphin, with an inn. "In the valleys around Queyras Protestants are numerous, especially in the **Val d'Arvieux**, reached by a road branching off on the left about 1½ m. below Château Queyras ; as well as in the Commune of Molines, and its hamlets, St.Veran, Pierre Grosse, and Fontgillarde. They have churches at Arvieux, St. Veran, and Fousillarde, in all of which service is performed once in three weeks by a pastor who resides alternately for a week in each parish" (see p. 304, and *Murray*, p. 216). A little higher up the left or S. bank of the Guil is the Ville-la-Vieille, with a church, 10th cent., and an inn. 18 m. from Mont Dauphin is Aiguilles, pop. 700, with an inn, on the right bank of the Guil. 21 m. from Mont Dauphin, and 5½ hrs. walk from the foot of Monte Viso, is **Abriés**, with an inn and Romanesque church, the highest village in the valley of the Guil. Although Abriés is a convenient halting-place, it is a most unattractive spot as headquarters. 4 m. S.E. from Abriés on the Guil is La Monta, with custom-house, where France is left.

For Perosa to Mont Dauphin, see p. 307 ; Torre-Pèllice to Mont Dauphin, p. 306 ; Saluzzo to Mont Dauphin, p. 308, and map p. 304.

Mont Dauphin to Saluzzo and Mont Viso, 65 m. E. From Mont Dauphin a good road extends 21 m. E. to Abriés, the highest village in the valley of the Guil, 5 hrs. walk from the foot of Monte Viso. From Abriés a mule-path leads over the Col de la Traversette, 9680 ft., on the S. flank of Monte Meidassa, 10,185 ft., to Crissolo, 7½ m. E. from the Col. 8 m. beyond by post-road is the village of Paesana, the chief town in the valley, and 1778 ft. above the sea. 5 m. farther E., on the road to Saluzzo, is Sanfront, whence a road strikes off, about 17 m. S., to Sampeyre, 3205 ft., the principal village in the valley of the Vraita. Saluzzo is 14 m. E. by coach from Paesana and 25 m. N.E. from Sampeyre (see p. 307, and map p. 304).

45¼ m. N.E. from Gap, and 9½ m. N.E. from Mont Dauphin, is La Bessée, 3420 ft. above the sea, pop. 1000. *Inn:* H. de la Poste. Here passengers alight for Mont Pelvoux, and proceed to the village of

Val Louise, about 6½ m. W. by the Col de la Batie, 3445 ft. (see
p. 333). 10½ m. N. from La Bessée is Briançon (see p. 333). "Nearly
opposite La Bessée to the N.W. opens out the Val Louise, which terminates in the glaciers and peaks of the **Mont Pelvoux**, whose top, rising
12,973 ft. above the sea-level, is visible from the road in clear weather.
The Val Louise branches into two; that on the right leads to Mt.
Pelvoux. Its summit, or Pic des Arcines, is a mass of ice. By the
other branch there is a difficult pass, called Col de Celar, into the
Val Godemar. Within the Val Louise was a cavern called Baume des
Vaudois, from a number of these people having concealed themselves
within it in 1488, carrying with them their children and as much food
as they could collect, relying on its inaccessible position and the snows
around for their defence. When the officer despatched by Charles VIII.
arrived with his soldiers in the valley, none of its inhabitants could be
found; but at length tracing out their hiding-place, he commanded
a quantity of wood to be set fire to at the mouth of the cave to burn
or smoke them out. Some were slain in attempting to escape, others
threw themselves headlong on the rocks below, others were smothered;
there were afterwards found within the caverns 400 infants stifled in
the arms of their dead mothers. It is believed that 3000 [French
Vaudois] perished on that occasion in this valley. The cavern has
fallen, and is nearly buried in the *débris*. The present inhabitants are
all Roman Catholics, and a miserable goitred race."—*Murray*, p. 218.

126
~~ ASPRES, pop. 2000, 2493 ft. above the sea. *Inn:* Ferdinand. **64** ~~
Junction with road to Livron, 68 m. W., on E. side of Rhône (see p.
46). The road after leaving Aspres crosses the Col de Cabres, and
then proceeds westwards by the valley of the Drôme (see p. 47).

154½
~~ CLELLES, 2400 ft., pop. 1000. *Inn:* Lion d'Or. Station **35½**
to alight at to make the ascent of Mont Aiguille, a limestone rock
6880 ft. high, near Chichiliane, about 7 m. distant towards Die.

163
~~ MONESTIER DE CLERMONT, pop. 1000. *Inns:* Europe; **27** ~~
France. Cold acidulous spring for diseases of the kidneys and stomach.

177
~~ VIF, pop. 3000. At the foot of a calcareous ridge, which **13** ~~
connects Mt. Moucherotte, 7454 ft., with Mt. Moucherolle, 7509 ft.

181
~~ VIZILLE, pop. 4000. *Inns:* Terrat; Europe; Parc. Vizille, **9** ~~
the Vigillia of the Romans, is an ill-built manufacturing town on the
right bank of the Romanche, with a castle built by Lesdiguières, now
restored and used as a manufactory (see p. 333).

185
~~ PONT DE CLAIX, pop. 2500, at the foot of mountains from **5** ~~
5000 to 6000 ft. high (see p. 328).

190
~~ GRENOBLE. (See p. 324.)

Paris to Lyons by St. Etienne.

PARIS. For time-tables, see under Paris, Roanne à Lyon par 〜〜
Saint Etienne. For the first 200 miles, between Paris and the important junction of St. Germain-des-Fossés, see pp. 351 to 358.

220 ST. GERMAIN-DES-FOSSES. All the trains halt here.   **129**
〜〜   〜〜

231   **118**
〜〜 LA PALISSE, pop. 3000, on the Bèbre. The ruined castle 〜〜
on the eminence overlooking the town was built in the 14th century.

235½   **113½**
〜〜 ARFEUILLES, pop. 3400, on the Barbenant. Fine water- 〜〜
fall, and castle of Montmorillon, 15th cent.

262   **87**
〜〜 ROANNE, pop. 20,000. *Hotels:* Centre ; Commerce ; *Nord. 〜〜
A busy, well-built, manufacturing town, on the Loire and the canal of
Digoin, possessing many interesting Roman remains. Among the
buildings the most noteworthy are—the church of St. Etienne, built in
the 15th cent. ; the ruins of the ancient feudal castle, and the college
built by the Jesuit Cotton, the confessor of Henri IV. The cotton-
mills employ 1200 workmen, and the annual value of the produce is
£1,120,000. After Roanne, the line to St. Etienne and Le Puy passes
through a picturesque country among the Cevennes and their offshoots.

282   **67**
〜〜 FEURS, pop. 4000, on the Loire. *Inn:* Poste. This, the 〜〜
ancient Forum Segusinorum, contains several antiquities, and a church
partly of the 12th century. In the neighbourhood is a chalybeate
spring, called La Fontaine des Quatre. Many Roman remains.

297½   **51½**
〜〜 SAINT GALMIER, pop. 3100, on the Coise. *Hotel:* Poste. 〜〜
Springs of mineral water of great repute, called by the Romans Aquae
Segestae. It is exported, and not utilised on the spot (see p. 348).

312   **37**
〜〜 SAINT ETIENNE, 1770 ft. above the sea, pop. 127,000. 〜〜
Hotels: Nord ; France ; both first-class. The Poste ; Europe ; Des Arts ;
Paris, are less expensive, and frequented by commercial travellers.
From the Europe the diligences start for Annonay. In the Rue de la
Paix is the Temple Protestant. East from the temple, in the Rue des
Jardins, is the Palais de Justice, a large handsome building.

This great manufacturing town, cold and muddy in winter, and
dusty in summer, was founded by the Romans B.C. 56, and from a very
early period became famous for forges and the manufacture of cables,
ribbons, firearms, and "faïence" or crockery. It is situated in the
long narrow valley of the Furens, amidst productive coal-beds. One
long street, bearing the names of the Rues de Roanne, Paris, Foy, St.
Louis, and Annonay, extends from west to east, dividing the city into
two nearly equal parts. Off this street are the principal squares or
"Places." In nearly the centre of this street, where it is intersected
by the Rue des Jardins and the Rue Royale, leading northwards to the
railway station, is the Hotel de Ville, with, at the west end, the Post

and Telegraph Offices.   On the south side of the part of the street
called the Rue St. Louis are : the Theatre, and on the hill behind, the
Ecole de Dessin, reached by 53 steps, passing an artificial grotto.
Above the Ecole, in the Rue St. Barbe, reside some of the many
weavers of ribbons, who exhibit their looms with pleasure to visitors.
On the summit of this hill is a Capuchin convent and church, surmounted with a gilded image of the Virgin.   The road from this convent, down the hill, passes the church of St. Etienne, built in the 12th
cent., containing some beautiful glass, and a relief representing the
martyrdom of St. Etienne.

A little to the east, and also on the side of the hill, is the **PALAIS
DES ARTS**, open from 10 to 12 and from 2 to 4.   It contains The
Picture Gallery, The Museum of Natural History, and complete collections of specimens of the manufactures of St. Etienne.   On the ground-
floor are the fire arms, labelled and ranged in rows.   Under glass-cases
are the separate pieces, from the smallest screw to the barrel ; including locks, triggers, cartridges, percussion-caps, shot, and balls.   The
centre room upstairs contains the Picture Gallery, nearly all modern.
The most striking is, " Nero beholding the effect of poison on slaves."
On one side of the Picture Gallery is the Natural History Museum,
and on the other, collections of ancient tapestry, enamels, cabinets,
and furniture.   In a separate saloon is the faïence, consisting chiefly
of plates.   In the second storey is the **MUSEE DE FABRIQUE**.
In the centre of the room are models of the ribbon-looms, and round
the walls, under glass, specimens of the ribbons, which, from their
small size and arrangement, do not show to advantage.   Even the
portraits, although most remarkable specimens of silk-weaving, are
apt to be passed by, as simply very good engravings.   Among
them is a group in a sitting posture representing the Queen, Prince
Albert, and the Prince of Wales, woven by Carquillat, who has several
other works of art in this room.   In the lower cases, in pattern books,
are specimens of all the varied fabrics from the looms of St. Etienne.
The annual value of the silk manufactures is estimated at £3,300,000,
employing 40,000 workmen and 280,000 spindles (broches), of which
165,000 work organzines and trames, and 114,000 work the silk intended for crapes and gauze ribbons.   The number of looms has been
estimated in all at 65,000 for weaving silks, and 80,000 for ribbons.
The coalfields occupy nearly 85 square miles, employ 5000 miners, and
produce on an average annually £1,600,000 worth of coal.   At the
west end of the long street, opposite the gas-works, are the Manufacture d'Armes of the Government, and adjoining their coal-pits (puits).
This large establishment is under the superintendence of artillery
officers of high rank, and employs about 2800 men.   There are, besides,
several private gun manufactories throughout the town, which turn
out annually as many as 300,000 stand of arms, including pistols and
revolvers.   The Promenade of St. Etienne is the Cours Fauriel.   It
adjoins the Jardin des Plantes, and is north from the Place du Palais
des Arts, by the straight street, the Rue de la Badouillière.

Excursions.—Nearly 2 m. S. is Valbenoite, pop. 7000, with large hardware manufactories, and the great reservoir of the city called the Gouffre d'Enfer. 2¼ m. farther by the same road is the village of Rochetaillée. This is also the road to take to ascend Mont Pilat. A carriage-road reaches the length of Bessat, 10 m. from St. Etienne. Thence a path leads to the farm of the Perdrix, 7 m. farther, where pass the night. Mont Pilat has two peaks—the Trois Dents, 4480 ft., and the Crête de la Perdrix, 4705 ft.

14½ m. by rail from St. Etienne is the St. Galmier station, 1260 ft. above the sea (see p. 346). An omnibus awaits passengers for the town, 1½ m. distant, on a hill 200 ft. above the station. It is a poor place with poor inns, the Commerce and Voyageurs. At the foot of the hill are the mineral springs and the establishments for bottling the water. The springs are at a considerable distance below the surface, reached by deep shafts, like the "Source Remy," cased with masonry, and furnished with spiral staircases.

From Roannes (p. 246), on the St. Galmier branch line, an omnibus starts for St. Alban, 6¼ m. distant, with a hotel and bathing establishment possessing cold acidulous chalybeate springs.

Nearer St. Germains, at the station of St. Martin d'Estreaux, a coach awaits passengers for Sail-les-Bains, 3¼ m. from the station. The bath-house has a hotel of its own. The establishment is supplied by six springs containing bicarbonate of soda, sulphur, and iron.

St. Germains is the station for Vichy (p. 358).

Paris to Lyons by Tarare.

PARIS
MILES FROM   Distance, 318 miles.   Time, 17¼ hours.   LYONS
                                                                     MILES TO

PARIS. This route is the same as the preceding as far as $\frac{318}{\sim}$ Roanne. For time-tables, see under "Paris, Tarare, et Lyon." The route becomes picturesque after Roanne.

$\frac{262}{\sim}$ ROANNE. (See p. 346.) 5 m. S. E. is L'Hôpital, and 19 m. $\frac{56}{\sim}$ more the manufacturing town of Amplepuis, pop. 7000, at the foot of a hill 1525 ft. above the sea-level, producing considerable quantities of muslin, calico, cotton, and linen cloth. 3 m. from Amplepuis commences the tunnel, 3200 yards, which pierces the ridge that separates the basin of the Loire from the Rhône. The temperature of the Rhône basin in winter is rawer and colder than that of the Loire.

$\frac{288}{\sim}$ TARARE, pop. 15,000. *Hotel:* Europe ; an uninteresting $\frac{30}{\sim}$ and unattractive manufacturing town on the Turdine, surrounded by steep mountains, among which is Mont Chevrier, one of the highest summits of the Beaujolais range. At the low end of the town is the railway station, and at the high end the viaduct of 21 arches across the valley of the Turdine. The arch which crosses the road has a span of 95 ft., the others average 35 ft. About 60,000 men in the town and environs are employed in the manufacture of velvet, embroidery, trimming, and especially in the particular kind of muslin called "tarlatan," a thin gauze-like fabric, for which it is celebrated.

318
_·~ LYONS (see p. 29).

Lyons to Clermont-Ferrand,

121 m. W. by GIVORS-CANAL, ST. ETIENNE, MONTBRISON, and THIERS.

At Givors-Canal passengers for stations on the west side of the Rhône change carriages. From Givors-Canal to St. Etienne the train passes towns with coal-mines and large smelting works and foundries. At St. Etienne (p. 346) a long halt is generally made. A little way up from the station will be found the steam tram, which, after traversing the best part of the town, returns to this terminus. 56½ m. W. from Lyons and 64½ m. E. from Clermont is **Montbrison** on the Vizezy, pop. 6700. _Inn:_ H. Lion d'Or. An uninteresting town, whose public buildings occupy religious edifices, secularised after the revolution of 1793. Of these the most prominent is the Palais de Justice, in the convent and church of the nuns of "Sainte Marie."

Behind the inn is the parish church of N. D. d'Esperance, founded in 1223, but recently repaired. The west portal (restored), with its heavy square tower and buttresses, was built in 1443 by order of Charles I. de Bourbon. The most interesting part is the five-sided apse, with in each side one long lancet window, and above it two small windows separated by an impost colonnette. To each corner is attached diagonally a long, narrow, slightly receding buttress. The church is 206 ft. long, and 62 ft. high from the pavement to the roof. At the E. end of the N. aisle is the mausoleum to Count "Fores and Niver, Guigo IV.," who founded the church in MCCXXIII. Opposite is the monument to the jurist Vernato, d. MCCCLVIII.

Fronting the E. end of the church is the Salle des Etats (house of Parliament) du Forez, built about the year 1300 by Jean I., Comte de Forez, and recently restored by the Duc de Persigny from plans by Violet-le-Duc. The name was afterwards changed into the Salle de la Diana (decana), from having been converted into the chapter-house of the church. It now contains the library of the Diana society, who also hold their meetings here. It is 64 ft. long, 26¼ ft. wide, and 26¼ ft. high. The roof is entirely covered with small painted representations of the escutcheons of the Counts of Forez, and of every family that has possessed land in the territory. The large end windows are modern additions. The chimney-piece, though modern, occupies the place of the original one.

Less than ⅓ m. from the inn, by the Clermont road, is a cold mineral spring, containing bicarbonates of lime, magnesia, and soda, with free carbonic acid gas. It makes a refreshing drink, as well as a tonic and diuretic. A little farther, about a mile from the town, is the old untidy village of Moingt, with church 12th cent., and in front of it a ruined gateway and round tower 13th cent. Montbrison is 49¼ m. W. from Lyons by the Dombes railway. The Lyons terminus of the Dombes railway is the station of St. Paul (p. 30).

Between Montbrison and Thiers there is nothing remarkable till just after St. Remay, the station before Thiers, when the train passes by the gorge of the Durolle at an immense depth below. At this part the train traverses eight tunnels, and crosses the valley of the Durolle by a viaduct of seven arches. 24¼ m. E. from Clermont, 40½ m. W. from Montbrison, 60 m. W. from St. Etienne, and 96¾ m. W. from Lyons is

Thiers, pop. 16,500, at first a small hamlet beside a fortress (Tigernum castrum) and a chapel dedicated to St. Symphorien (see p. 367).

Thiers is 72¼ m. N. from Darsac by coach, passing Olliergues, Vertolaye, Ambert, Marsac, Arlanc, and Chaise-Dieu (see p. 89).

Thiers makes a pleasant railway excursion either from Vichy or Clermont-Ferrand.

1¼ m. W. from Thiers and 23 m. E. from Clermont-Ferrand is

Courty. Junction with line to St. Germain des Fossés, 27½ m. W., passing Vichy, 21½ m. N.

13 m. W. from Courty and 10 m. E. from Clermont is Vertaizon, pop. 2200, situated 1¼ m. S. from the station. Junction with branch line to Billom, 5½ m. S., pop. 4300. *Inns:* Voyageurs ; Commerce. A prettily situated town among hills crowned with ruins of castles from 12th to 16th cents. Church St. Cerneuf, 11th to 13th cents.

The train from Vertaizon takes 30 minutes to reach Clermont-Ferrand (see p. 369).

Paris to Marseilles by Clermont and Nîmes.

This Route conducts to the volcanic region of Central France; to the famous Spas of Vichy, Royat, Mont-Dore, Bourboule, and St. Nectaire; and to the best towns for studying the architecture of Auvergne. (See Maps, pp. 1 and 27.)

PARIS   MARSEILLES
MILES FROM   MILES TO

PARIS. Start from the station of the Chemins de Fer de $\underline{\underline{530}}$ Paris à Lyon, and request a ticket for Nîmes by Clermont-Ferrand. The first stations passed are Brunoy (p. 2), Melun (p. 2), and Fontaine-bleau (p. 3). At Moret, 42 m. S.E. from Paris, the rail to Marseilles by Nevers and Nîmes separates from the rail to Marseilles by Dijon and Lyon. (For Moret, see p. 10.)

$\underline{\underline{73}}$ MONTARGIS, pop. 10,000, on the Loing and the canal Briare. $\underline{\underline{457}}$ *Inns:* Poste; France. The principal street leads directly from the station to the Hôtel de la Poste at the opposite end of the town. The streets about the old castle are narrow and dirty, and some of them steep. This castle, rebuilt by Charles V., called formerly the "berceau des enfants de France," became private property in 1809. A house has been built within the circle of the crumbling walls, of which a 14th cent. gateway still stands.

The parish church is of different epochs—the nave and the aisles belong to the 12th cent., and the chancel, which is four steps higher, to the 16th. It is supported on ten tall slender columns, from which the groining of the roof ramifies in all directions.

The town fairs are held in the promenade, called the Patis. In the adjoining forest, covering 21,030 acres, is the Dolmen of Paucourt. Montargis is a great railway junction on one of the main lines between Paris and the south of France.

10 m. S. by rail from Montargis is Nogent-sur-Vernisson, station for Châtillon-sur-Loing. Time, 75 minutes; fare, 1 fr. Admiral Coligny was born in 1516 in the old castle of this place, situated in the midst of the hereditary domain of the family.

$\underline{\underline{96}}$ GIEN, pop. 7600. *Inns:* Poste; Paris. An old town on the $\underline{\underline{434}}$ Loire, and an important railway junction. On the hill rising from the town is the church of St. Pierre, flanked by a square tower, 15th cent., commanding an admirable view. Adjoining is the château, a hand-some edifice built in 1494 by Anne de Beaujeu, daughter of Louis XI. It is now occupied by the Préfecture. Below, in the town, is the church of St. Louis, 17th cent. 38 m. N.W. by branch line is Orleans (see pp. 148 and 151 in Black's *Normandy*).

102½ BRIARE, pop. 5200. *Inn:* H. de la Poste. A pleasant town 427½
on the Loire, where large quantities of buttons are manufactured.
3 m. farther S. by rail is Châtillon-sur-Loire, pop. 3300. *Inn:* H.
des Trois Rois ; omnibus awaits passengers.

121 COSNE, pop. 7000. *Inns:* Grand Cerf ; Belle Étoile. This 409
little town, with ironworks of considerable importance, and still re-
taining parts of its old fortifications and castle, is situated on the Loire
at its junction with the Nohain. The best of the churches is St.
Aignan, of which the portal and apse are of the 11th cent. ; the rest
is modern. 6½ m. farther S. by rail is Sancerre on the Loire, pop.
3700. *Inn:* Pointe du Jour. With castle, 13th cent., on a hill 987 ft.
above the sea. In the neighbourhood are important quarries.

138 POUILLY-SUR-LOIRE, pop. 3500. *Inn:* Écu. The sur- 392
rounding vineyards produce a famous white wine, with a peculiar
flavour. It is drinkable in the second year, and deteriorates after
the 15th.

141 LA CHARITÉ, built on a hill sloping down from the rail- 389
way to the Loire, crossed by both a stone and suspension bridge.
Inns: Poste et G. Monarque ; Dauphin ; omnibuses await passengers.
It has still part of its fortifications and towers of the 14th cent. Of
the church St. Croix, consecrated in 1107 by Pope Pascal II., there
remain a vast narthex, the choir, and a high and profusely ornamented tower. This church belonged to a Benedictine convent, whose
deeds of charity gave to the town its name. The convent is now
occupied by the order of the Visitandines (Visitation). In the treasury
are the chasuble and mitre of St. François de Sales.

150 POUGUES LES EAUX, pop. 1400. *Hotels:* Near the 380
station, the H. du Châlet. At the entrance into the avenue, the H. de
l'Etablissement, and opposite the "Etablissement," the Hôtel Thermal.
Pougues, being a quiet place, can be recommended only to those in
search of repose, whose stomach or other internal organs have become
weak or deranged. The establishment, which has every kind of
apparatus for administering the water, is situated in a park extending
to the Loire, where fair rod-fishing may be had. The water, principally
used internally, is cold, has a pungent taste, and contains a large
amount of carbonic acid gas, both free and in combination with lime,
soda, potash, magnesia, and iron, and is serviceable in the cure of
dyspepsia, enlargement of the liver, gall-stones, and diseases of the
kidneys. Douche baths of carbonic acid gas are employed.

353

PARIS
MILES FROM

FOURCHAMBAULT. NEVERS.

MARSEILLES
MILES TO

$\overset{154}{\underset{\sim}{\quad}}$ FOURCHAMBAULT, pop. 6500. *Inns:* H. Bourges at $\overset{376}{\underset{\sim}{\quad}}$ station; in town, H. Berry. A town on the Loire full of large iron-works, employing above 5000 workmen. The Colonne de Juillet and the Pont du Carrousel were cast here. Omnibus at station.

$\overset{158}{\underset{\sim}{\quad}}$ NEVERS, pop. 20,400. *Hotels:* at the station, H. de la Paix; $\overset{372}{\underset{\sim}{\quad}}$ H. du Chemin de Fer. In the town the France, Europe, and Nièvre. A short distance N.W. from the station, or from the N.W. corner of the Park, is the nunnery of St. Giddard, containing the tomb of Bernadette Soubirous, to which establishment she was entrusted after her reported interviews with the "immaculately conceived one," and where she died, after a lingering illness, caused, it is said, by the knowledge that the present pope had not the same implicit faith in her story as his predecessor Pio IX. entertained (see under Lourdes, in Black's *South France*, West Half), In the garden of the convent, in a small chapel, is her grave, covered by a marble slab bearing the following inscription:—"Ici repose, dans la paix du Seigneur, Bernadette Soubirous, honorée à Lourdes en 1858 de plusieurs appari-tions de la Très Sainte Vierge. En religion Sœur Marie Bernard, décédée à Nevers, à la Maison-Mère des Sœurs de la Charité, le 16 Avril 1879 dans le 35e année de son age et la 12me de sa profession religieuse. C'est ici le lieu. Psalm 131, v. 15."

Julius Cæsar kept his military stores in Nevers; but after his defeat at Gergovia (p. 372) the inhabitants plundered his camp and massacred the soldiers. Of the old fortifications there remain the tower of the Loire, of which the lower part is of the 11th cent.; the tower of St. Eloi, 16th cent.; the tower Goguin, 12th cent.; and the Porte du Croux, a square tower of the 12th cent., but rebuilt in 1393, now containing an antiquarian museum. At the entrance into the town by the Paris road is a triumphal arch, erected in 1746 to com-memorate the victory of Fontenoy, 12th May 1745, when the French defeated the Anglo-German and Dutch forces under the Duke of Cumberland. Nevers stands on the slope of a hill rising from the Loire in the midst of a flat country abounding with iron, giving employment to important ironworks. In the most elevated part is the Grande Place, with the **Palais de Justice,** formerly the Palais Ducal, a stately edifice built in 1475 by Jean de Clamecy, Comte de Nevers, but altered and enlarged during the 16th cent. by his successors, belonging to the families of Clèves and Gonzaga. It is in the form of a parallelogram, flanked with four towers, each containing a staircase. In the centre turret is the "Escalier d'honneur," ornamented with sculpture representing scenes connected with the history of the house of Clèves. The market-place occupies the site of the old Palais de Justice, built in 1400 by Philippe de Bourgogne. Opposite the Palais de Justice is a fountain by Lequesne. In the Hôtel de Ville are the Library, the Picture Gallery, and an interesting collection of faïence, which has been manufactured at Nevers for eight centuries. Faïence is the French term for all descriptions of glazed earthenware, and corresponds nearly to the English word "crockery." The manufacture of majolica or enamelled pottery was introduced into France by Catherine de Médicis and her kinsman Louis Gonzaga, who, by marriage with Henrietta of Clèves in 1565, became Duke of Nevers. There are still important pottery works in the town.

Opposite the Palais de Justice is the Cathedral of St. Cyr, reconstructed in the 13th cent., with parts belonging to other epochs. The nave was rebuilt in 1188, the N. portal in 1240, the choir in the 14th cent., and the S. portal, which is flamboyant in style, adorned with complicated mouldings, in the 15th cent. In the interior we find a western and eastern apse; the former, 16th cent., covers a crypt of the 11th cent. Statuettes like Caryatides sustain the columns of the triforium. On the floor of the western end is the meridian traced by the astronomer Cassini while engaged in the triangulation of France.

The church of St. Etienne, 1097, is in the Romanesque style. St. Père was built in 1512, St. Genest, now in ruins, in the 12th cent., and the chapel of the Visitandines in 1639.

32½ m. E. by rail is Cercy la Tour, where a coach awaits passengers for the comfortable bathing establishment of St. Honoré. The water is hot, and in chemical composition resembles very much the springs in the Pyrenees. Hotel at the establishment. (See map, p. 1.)

Junction with branch to La Roche, 108 m. N. on the direct line between Paris and Turin (see p. 14). On this branch line, 8¾ m. N. from Nevers, is Guerigny, pop. 3050, on the Nièvre, with the important ironworks called the Forges de la Chaussade, employing upwards of 1300 men. 24¼ m. farther by the same line is Varzy, pop. 2890; *Inn:* H. de la Poste; with a very beautiful church, St. Père, 13th and 14th cents., surmounted by two square towers. In the interior are an elegant triforium and a beautiful Flemish painting (1535) of the Martyrdom of St. Eugenie. 44 m. S. from La Roche and 64 m. N. from Nevers is Clamecy, pop. 5400 (p. 15); *Inns:* Boule d'Or; Univers; *Poste; on the junction of the Yonne with the Beuvron. On the bridge across the Yonne is a bronze bust by David of Jean Rouvet, the inventor of those large rafts by which the wood from the forests is floated down to Paris and other parts. In the church of St. Martin, 12th to 15th cent., are a statue of Ste. Geneviève by Simart, a handsome organ-case of the 16th cent., and a beautiful reredos on the high altar. Under the markets are the vaults of the old castle of the Dukes of Nevers. The Palais de Justice, the gendarmerie, and the prison occupy one large building.

22 m. N. from Clamecy is Cravant (p. 14), an important railway junction. Junction also at Nevers with line to Chagny, 178 m. E. (see p. 24). Branch to Le Creusot and Autun (see p. 24).

$\frac{154}{\sim}$ SAINCAIZE, 600 ft. above sea ; junction with line to Bourges, 38 m. W. (See Black's *South France*, West Half.)

$\frac{195}{\sim}$ MOULINS, pop. 22,000. *Hotels:* At the station, H. du $\frac{335}{\sim}$ Chemin de Fer ; in the town, Dauphin, Paris, France, Allier. Omnibuses at the station. A cheerful town with extensive boulevards and pleasant walks along the banks of the Allier, crossed by a bridge built in 1763, of 13 arches, and 328 yards long. In the centre of the town is the Cathedral of Notre Dame, in the transition florid style of the 15th cent. The façade, over which rise two handsome spires, is of white sandstone, with colonnettes of dark Volvic lava. The tops of the buttresses are adorned with statues. The choir, which is seven steps higher than the nave, is lighted by windows containing valuable 16th cent. glass, and covered with a curious roof. In the chapel to the right of the altar is a small mausoleum with a recumbent figure illustrating the condition of even the fairest forms after death. Under the altar, in a little crypt, is an Entombment. In the first chapel, N. side of the choir, is an "Adoration of the Virgin" of considerable merit. Opposite the main entrance is a large square tower called "La tour mal coiffée," 15th cent., now a prison, which, with the handsome portico of the Gendarmerie, formed part of the famous castle of the Dukes of Bourbon. The most interesting old houses are within and around the Place de l'Allier. In that square is also the church of St. Nicolas, built in the style of the 13th cent. In the chapel of the Lycée, No. 15 Rue de Paris, a little beyond the Palais de Justice, is the marble mausoleum, by Coustou, Anguier, Renaudan and Poipant, of Henri II., Duc de Montmorenci, godson of Henri IV., and one of the bravest marshals of France. He had the misfortune to draw upon himself the enmity of Cardinal Richelieu and the displeasure of Louis XIII., which led to his execution in the Capitole of Toulouse on the 30th October 1632, where the knife is still preserved. His widow, Maria Orsini, caused his body to be brought to this chapel, then belonging to the convent of the nuns "de la Visitation." The statues, all of the finest Carrara marble, represent the duke in a half-recumbent posture and the duchess seated near him. Fee, ½ fr. In the Hôtel de Ville is the public library, with 25,000 vols. and a manuscript Bible of the 12th cent. called the Souvigny Bible. The town clock, with its moving statues, is mounted on a square tower, 15th cent., 40 ft. high.

Lord Clarendon, while on his way from Montpellier to Rouen, stayed some time at Moulins, where he wrote a part of his *History of the Rebellion*, which he finished while resident in Rouen, where he died on the 9th of December 1674, after having appealed twice in vain to Charles II. to be allowed to return to England. James Fitz-James, Duke of Berwick, a marshal and peer of France, natural son of James Duke of York, afterwards James II., by Arabella Churchill, sister of the great Duke of Marlborough, was born at Moulins on the 21st of August 1670, and died 12th June 1734. Montesquieu said of him: "In the works of Plutarch I have seen at a distance what great men were; in Marshal Berwick I have seen what they are." By the side of the Paris road, under a tree at the northern entrance into Moulins, the forlorn Maria, with her lute and her dog Sylvie, used to sit. Thwarted in love by the intrigues of the parish curate, she became the prey to a deep-seated melancholy. (See Sterne's *Sentimental Journey*, "Maria.")

9 m. W. from Moulins by rail is **Souvigny**, pop. 4000. *Hotel:* Croix d'Or. At the end of the village farthest from the station is a beautiful basilica, commenced in the 10th cent. and rebuilt and restored at various periods. It is 275 ft. long, 125 broad, and 56 high. In the Chapelle Vieille, to the right of the high altar, is the mausoleum of Louis II., Duc de Bourbon, and Anne his wife. On the other side is that of Duc Charles I. and Anne de Bourgogne his wife. Both chapels are enclosed in a stone screen with delicate flamboyant tracery. To the left of the principal entrance is an ancient column with the signs of the Zodiac sculptured on it. N. from the church, on the opposite side of the street, is the old castle of the Bourbons, occupied by people of humble rank. From the Souvigny station an omnibus runs 10 m. N. to Bourbon l'Archambault, passing at about half-way St. Menoux (Hôtel de l'Écu). It stops in front of the church just sufficient time to allow the traveller to cast a rapid glance over this

pleasing specimen of Aquitaine and Auvergne architecture of the 11th cent. (See map, p. 1.)

Bourbon-l'Archambault, pop. 4500. *Hotels:* Close to the bathing establishment, the Hôtel Montespan, on the site of the house which used to be occupied by Madame de Montespan and Louis XIV. About 100 yds. distant the Hôtel de France. On a hill at the northern side of this ancient town are the ruins of the once strong feudal castle of Bourbon, commenced by Louis I. in 1321, and finished in the 15th cent. by Duc Pierre II. Four massive towers, built of stone, with projecting points, still remain of the twenty-four which it had originally. On a hill at the opposite side of the town is the parish church, commenced in the 12th cent., resembling the church of St. Menoux. In the centre of the town is the copious spring of mineral water which, besides supplying the bathing establishment, is largely used for drinking and domestic purposes. It is clear, inodorous, unctuous, easily digested, slightly saline and aperient, and 128° Fahr. One-sixth of its volume is free carbonic acid gas, besides the same acid in combination with lime, magnesia, and soda; and some salts of bromine, iodine, and iron. It is eminently diaphoretic, diuretic, and tonic, and excellent for rheumatism, rheumatic gout, and scrofula. Between the bathing establishment and the church is the cold water spring called the "Source de Jonas," containing bicarbonates of lime and magnesia, chlorides of soda and magnesia, silicates of lime, alumina, and soda, the carbonate of iron and the oxide of manganese. The water is tonic and slightly laxative. 9½ m. S. from Bourbon is **St. Pardoux**, in a wooded and hilly country, forming one of the best drives from Bourbon. There is here a spring of remarkably sparkling water, ⅘ths of its volume being free carbonic acid gas. It contains the bicarbonates of lime, magnesia, and soda, silicates of lime and alumina, and the oxide of iron. It is delightful to the taste, very pungent, and, owing to the presence of so much carbonic acid gas, slightly heady. It is an excellent tonic, highly diuretic, and stimulates the secretion of bile. It is sold in litre bottles at Bourbon at 3d. per bottle. Madame Montespan, when in the height of her power, used regularly to visit Bourbon to recruit her health, and here she died, in solitude, on the 25th of May 1707, cast off and deserted by Louis XIV. 33 m. W. from Souvigny by rail is Commentry (see map, p. 1).

From Moulins branch line extends 73 m. E. to Montchanin, passing, at 17½ m. E. from Moulins, Dompierre; at 23 m. E., Gilly, station for Bourbon-Lancy; 29½ m. E., Saint Agnan; 35 m. E., Digoin; and 41½ m. E., Paray-le-Monial (see p. 27, and map, p. 1).

Dompierre-sur-Bebre, pop. 2230. *Inns:* Commerce; Lion d'Or. Coal and iron found in this neighbourhood. The country is undulating and well cultivated. Near the next station, Diou on the Loire, is the Cistercian abbey of Sept-Fonds, founded in 1132, rebuilt in the 17th cent., and now an agricultural school.

358

PARIS
MILES FROM
GILLY. ST. GERMAIN-DES-FOSSÉS.
MARSEILLES
MILES TO

Gilly, station for **Bourbon-Lancy**, pop. 3300, 8¾ m. N. by the Loire. Coach awaits passengers at station, fare 1½ fr. *Inn:* H. Trois Barbeaux, where carriages for drives can be had. The village, situated on an eminence, is full of old houses, of which the best are near the clock-tower, 15th cent. In the valley at the foot of the eminence is the suburb of St. Leger, with an excellent small **Bathing Establishment**, supplied by five alkaline springs, temp. 132° Fahrenheit, which flow into large basins in the court fronting the baths. The water contains free carbonic acid gas and 19 grains of the chloride of sodium to the pint. In lesser quantities the chlorides of calcium and magnesium, the sulphate of soda, the carbonates of lime and magnesia, and the oxide of iron. In Vichy the drinking of the water is the most important, but here it is the external application by baths and other means. They are very serviceable in the cure of nervous and cutaneous diseases, in neuralgia of the face, and in every form of rheumatism. The baths are of marble and easily entered, and furnished with ingenious contrivances to facilitate the application of the water to any particular part. Near the Casino, and standing by itself, is a swimming bath, 62 ft. long by 29½ wide and 5 deep, filled with the mineral water cooled down to 90° Fahr. The surplus water is still carried off by the underground channels constructed by the Romans. At intervals along their course perpendicular shafts are sunk down to the bed of the outlet.

On a height near the bathing establishment is a hospital built by M. and Mme. Aligre, and given by them to the town. A monument to their memory is in the Place of St. Leger, and a replica of the statue of Madame in silver is in the hospital. *Inns:* Opposite the establishment, the *Grand Hotel, 12 frs., and the G. H. des Termes, pension 8½ frs. A little farther, the G. H. des Bains, 7½ frs. ; for a lady, 6 frs. Opposite, the H. Allier. The charge for the baths and Casino is very reasonable. For particulars write to M. Le Regisseur des Bains de Bourbon-Lancy. The surrounding country is of considerable interest, the Loire is within an easy walk, while several important cities are within a few hours by rail.

A little beyond Gilly is Saint Agnan on the Loire. *Inn:* H. de Marion. A small town in the midst of iron and coal mines. 6 m. farther is Digoin, pop. 3300. *Inns:* H. des Diligences, in the town ; at the station, the H. de la Gare. Church of the 11th cent. Suspension bridge across the Loire.

220 ST. GERMAIN-DES-FOSSÉS, 845 ft. above the sea. Large 310 refreshment rooms. Always a great deal of traffic at this station. Change carriages for Vichy. Behind the station, on a little eminence, is the inn G. H. du Parc (bed 2 frs.), with garden. At the warehouse end of the station is the inn H. de la Gare. In the village, the Paix. 7 m. S. from St. Germain and 227 m. S. from Paris is

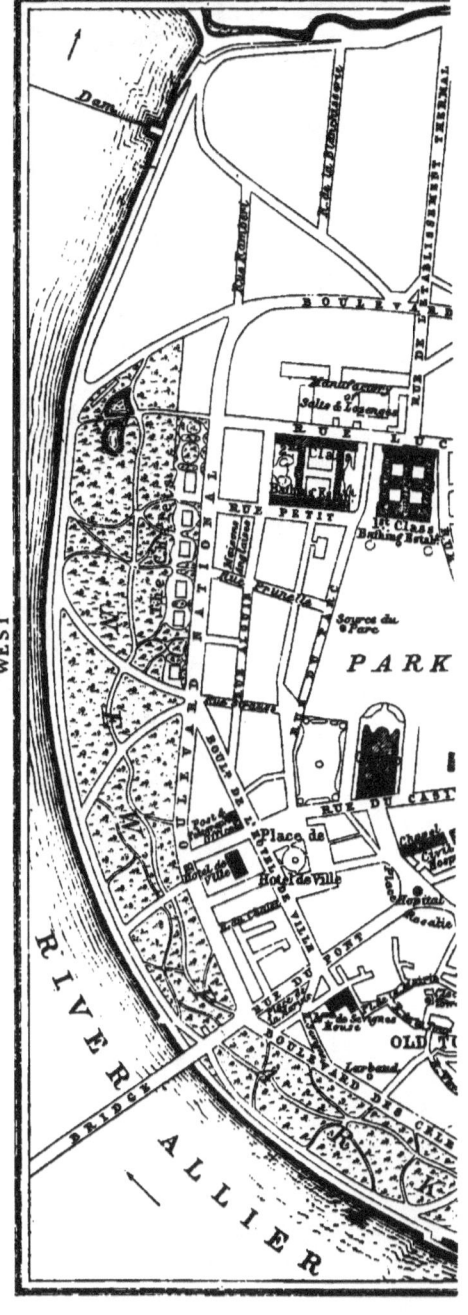

VICHY

on the Allier, pop. 7000, 8 hrs. by express from Paris. *Hotels :* The largest and best are around the Parc. Of them the most elegantly furnished are:—The Nouvel Hôtel, pension 25 frs. ; the H. Parc, 12 to 20 frs.; Ambassadeurs, 12 to 20 frs. ; Mombrun, 12 to 20 frs. ; and the Grand Hôtel, 12 to 16 frs., all first-class.

The following, also round the Parc, are equally comfortable, but the furniture is not so costly. The H. des Thermes, 10 to 12 frs., adjoining the Villa Strauss, in which Napoleon III. resided ; Cherbourg, 9¼ to 15½ frs. ; the Princes, 9¼ to 15½ frs. ; the G. H. de la Paix, 12¾ to 15¾ frs. ; the G. H. Velay et des Anglais, 9½ to 13½ frs. ; Royal Hotel, Amirauté, 7½ to 10½ frs. ; and H. de la Restauration. Almost adjoining the Ambassadeurs, the H. Molière, 8½ to 12½ frs., a smaller house. In all the above hotels, excepting in the first three, servants are taken at the rate of 6 frs. per day. The above prices include everything except the charge of 1 fr. for candles at the end of the stay.

Adjoining the north corner of the Etablissement, near the Grande Grille, is the G. H. des Bains, 9 to 14 frs. Opposite the Etablissement, the H. Britannique, 7½ to 10 frs.; the Richelieu, 8½ to 10½ frs. ; and behind it the H. Grande Grille, 8½ to 11½ frs., a more handsome house.

In the Rue Petit, near the Châlets in the Boulevard National, *H. d'Amerique, 9 to 10 frs., a clean quiet house, generally full.

In the Place de l'Hôtel de Ville at the south end of the Parc are the H. d'Espagne, 6½ to 10 frs., a small house served principally by the family ; and the Deux-Mondes, 8½ to 10½ frs., fronting likewise the Place Rosalie. The fraction in the prices is for service.

In the Place Rosalie are the Source de l'Hôpital and the Banque de Vichy, where circular notes are cashed and money changed.

In the Rue de Nîmes, a busy street, separated from the Parc by a row of houses, is the H. de Nice, 8½ to 10 frs.; one side faces the church. On the other side of the church is the *H. Notre Dame, 9½ to 10½ frs. Then follow the G. H. du Centre, 7 to 10 frs. ; H. Fénélon ; H. du Regence, 8 to 9½ frs. ; Orleans and Milan same price.

In the Rue de Paris, the street between the town and the railway station, are the G. H. du Louvre et de Reims, 7 to 10 frs., open all the year ; Univers, 8 to 10 frs. ; *Rome, 7½ to 9½ frs.; the Suisse ; H. Dubessay ; *Couronne, 8½ to 9½ frs. ; Beaujolais ; Brest, 7 to 8½ frs. ; Cote d'Or, 7 to 7½ frs. ; Globe, 7 frs., open all the year—all between the railway station and the Etablissement.

At the end of the Rue de Paris, in the Rue de Ballore, the G. Hôtel Maussant, 8 to 10 frs. In the Avenue Victoria, behind the military hospital, and in front of the petrifying spring, is the H. de Provence, 6 to 9 frs. In front of hospital, Hôtel Lucas.

In the Rue de Nîmes, between the Parc and the Parc des Celestins, are the G. H. Palais, 7½ to 10 frs. ; Genève ; Milan ; Bordeaux. Near the entrance into the Parc des Celestins, the H. Venise, 8 to 9 frs. and the H. Palais-Royal.

There are a great many maisons meublées, in which furnished rooms are let at prices varying from 4 to 8 frs., and ½ fr. for service. Lodgers can always have a breakfast prepared for them of coffee, bread, and eggs, without any extra charge, but the dinner is more troublesome. Among the maisons meublées are the Villa Sévigné (in which Madame resided) in the Boulevard National, near the Source Larbaud.

Travellers wishing to inspect the hotels and maisons meublées before deciding which to take should alight at one of the hotels in the Rue de Paris, as they are nearest the station, and sufficiently comfortable without being expensive.

Close to the principal establishment, in the Rue Lucas, is one of the best apothecary shops, the Pharmacie Durin, where information regarding the different doctors can be had.

Vichy, during the season, from 15th May till the end of September, forms a most enjoyable residence. It is full of comfortable hotels presided over by civil landlords, charging various prices from 6½ to 25 frs. per day, which includes wine, service, and everything else. The best situations are the Parc and in the contiguous streets. Tastefully-planned grounds, called the Neuf Parc, extend between the town and the Allier, crossed here by a handsome bridge, on the site where Cæsar built his wooden bridge. On an eminence at the southern end of Vichy are the old town and the old parish church of St. Blaise, 13th and 14th cents. In works undertaken for the railway numerous coins have been dug up bearing the effigy of the Gallic chief Vercingetorix, as well as many Roman objects belonging to all the epochs of the empire. In 1402 Louis II., Duke of Bourbon, surrounded Vichy with a moat and fortified walls, within which he erected his castle ; but of it all that remains is the great clock-tower or belfry.

At the head of the Rue de Paris, on the north end of the Parc, is the **Mineral Water Establishment**, composed of two large buildings —1st, The "Grand Etablissement," containing only first-class baths ; a parallelogram 167 ft. long by 250 broad, provided with 100 cabinets with baths, and traversed by a gallery from N. to S., having on the western side the gentlemen's baths, and on the eastern side the ladies'. At the extremity of this passage is an inhaling-room. Each bath costs 2½ frs., including service and linen. An hour and a quarter is allowed, including dressing. Below the baths are large reservoirs. In front of the entrance to the central gallery, near the spring Chomel, is the *office* for the taking down of the bathers' names and for the sale of the bath tickets.

2d, Separated by a narrow street is a similar edifice in which second and third class baths are given, costing respectively 1½ frs. and 60 c. each. The difference in the price of the baths arises from the quality of the accommodation and the amount of linen and towels supplied. The baths themselves are the same, and are filled too from the same springs. The two buildings contain together 350 baths and 150 shower-baths, and during the season as many as 4000 baths can be given in a single day. They commence at 3.30 A.M. and continue till 5 P.M., but at one part of the season till even later. But it must always be remembered that the external application of the water is not nearly so important as the internal. Patients may visit Vichy at any time; but the season suited to follow with success the course of treatment is from the 15th May till the beginning of October. The month of May is sometimes rainy. August and September are generally the driest months, and the most equable. The Vichy treatment lasts from 3 to 4 weeks. The waters are taken in the morning and during the day, and baths daily or every second day. For elderly people with sanguine and irritable temperaments and delicate constitutions the duration of the bath should not be more than 20 or even 15 minutes.

At the south or opposite end of the Parc is the Casino, a handsome comfortably-furnished edifice. The ballroom is 60 ft. long by 38 wide and 45 high, and lighted by five large bay windows looking into the park. The decorations are of the period of Louis XIV., with elegantly-painted walls and ceiling. A gallery, running across the building in a lateral direction, separates the ballroom from the theatre, which occupies the centre of the Casino and contains seats for 800 persons. The remainder of the building is occupied by the reading, billiard, and gambling rooms, and a saloon for ladies. One entrance ticket, 2 frs.; a month, 25 frs. There is music every morning, a concert in the afternoon, and theatricals in the evening. A great quantity of journals and reviews are at the disposal of members; also books, pianos, and music. A professor of billiards is attached to the Casino.

The Vichy Springs.—The Vichy waters are stimulating, but not tonic. They are gaseous and alkaline, their principal constituents being carbonic acid and the bicarbonate of soda. They differ materially from each other only in temperature. They are easily digested and readily eliminated into the system, where they restore the vitality of the organs below the diaphragm. None of the springs possess any special specific property, the best for the patient being that which agrees best with him. Nevertheless, experience has detected certain peculiarities which may assist him to discover the most suitable spring. The maximum quantity which can be taken daily with advantage is from 24 to 28 oz. The usual dose is four glasses of 5 or 6 oz., taken at different times throughout the day, and not necessarily from the same spring. The water may with advantage be mixed with the wine taken at dinner. Carafes are filled at the springs without any charge. In the shops are sold graduated glasses of 150 to 180 grammes, divided into three equal parts. 30 grammes equal 1 oz.

The Springs and their peculiarities.—Under the vestibule of the principal establishment are three important springs—the Grande Grille, the Puits-Chomel, and the Mesdames (see plan).

The Grande-Grille, 110° Fahr., is slightly aperient, and is employed with success by persons suffering from indigestion, obstructions of the viscera, congestion of the liver, spleen, biliary calculi, and gravel.

The **Puits-Chomel**, 113° Fahr. The water of this spring possesses marked anodyne properties, which render it very valuable whenever the weakened state of the constitution or its irritability requires to be moderately excited. Of all the Vichy waters it contains the least carbonic acid without being more difficult of digestion, and as, on the other hand, it is the most mineralised, it can in many cases profitably replace the other springs.

Mesdames, 61° Fahr., highly chalybeate, is beneficial in cases of chlorosis, amenorrhœa, and in debility following loss of blood. In cases where the constitution has been weakened without any evident derangement it stimulates the energy of the digestive functions so as to enable the patient to recover his usual strength.

The only other spring in the establishment is the Puits-Carré, 113° Fahr., which rises in the centre of the building, and is used for supplying the baths.

About 100 yards E. from the principal establishment, in a building opposite the military hospital, is the **Source Prunelle**, a cold spring, recommended for diseases of the liver, gravel, and calculi. A little farther E. is the **Source Lucas**, 84° Fahr., principally employed in baths for diseases of the skin. As a drink it is beneficial where the organs are more disturbed than diseased. In the park, opposite the Hôtel de la Paix, is the **Source du Parc**, 71° Fahr., recommended for sluggish action of the digestive organs, atonic derangement of the intestines, and affections of the bronchial tube caused by chronic irritation or catarrh. At the N. end of the Casino, in front of the town hospital, is the **Source de l'Hôpital** or Rosalie, 89° Fahr., resembling very much the Grande Grille, but less exciting. It is recommended to those affected with diseases of the digestive organs, dyspepsia, gastritis, obstinate diarrhœa, and dysentery ; and is particularly useful to literary men whose digestive functions are deranged from mental labour. It renders important service in ovarian tumours and other diseases of females.

A short way up the river by the Boulevard des Celestins are the five important springs, the **Sources des Celestins**, 54° and 58° Fahr., of which the nearest is under a handsome artificial grotto. They are largely exported, and have the same action, the only question being their respective degree of efficacy. Those who chiefly frequent these springs are invalids suffering from gout, gravel, and affections of the urinary organs, whose stomachs are sufficiently sound to be able to digest the water easily. Otherwise it is best to commence with either the "Hôpital" or the "Grande Grille" spring. In all cases the water of the Springs Celestins should be drunk moderately and with caution. Just beyond the Celestins, at the end of the Boulevard and near the Parc des Celestins, are the Lardy springs and establishment. The water, 77° Fahr., which rises from a depth of 620 ft., has a stimulating action on the mucous membrane of the stomach, is easily eliminated, and is generally drunk after meals by the Vichy invalids. "Stomach disorder, attended with heartburn and acidity, is in many cases capable of being cured or materially relieved by the use of one or other of the Vichy waters. When complicated with pain (gastralgia) and diminished power of the stomach, the Hôpital spring in some cases, the Lardy and Mesdames in others, would be most likely to have a beneficial effect: in other cases, where a more energetic action is required, the Grande Grille would be preferable."—*Dr. E. Lee.*

3 m. S. from Vichy, on the W. bank of the Allier, is the **Source Hauterive,** 57° Fahr., used principally for exportation. In therapeutical qualities it resembles the Celestins.

The principal use of the Vichy waters is in the treatment of gout, and in chronic diseases of the stomach and abdominal viscera, such as dyspepsia, chronic hepatic disease, biliary calculi, fatty degeneration or cirrhosis, and in hæmorrhoidal affections, which are so often connected with congestion of the liver. They are equally serviceable in enlargements of the spleen and in many cases of hypochondriasis. Moreover, this spa is specially adapted for the cure of some of the chronic diseases of women connected with disordered menstruation, and for the anomalous "critical complaints" which often set in at the period of life when this function ceases. "The complaint for which nine-tenths of the English visitors drink these springs is gout ; but it should be distinctly understood that Vichy water is not a specific for gout ; it can only act on the gouty diathesis by improving the tone of the digestive organs, augmenting the secretions, and correcting the abnormally acid condition of the blood."—*Madden's Health Resorts.* "The Vichy waters do not cure gout. They have, however, a very beneficial effect when administered with caution in cases of either hereditary or acquired gout, whether articular or internal, acute or chronic. The proper time to use the waters is in the interval of attacks, and as far as possible from the last attack. If too near the last attack, a repetition is to be feared, and there is almost as much danger in provoking nature as in resisting its action in a crisis."—*Dr. Daumas.* "We may then sum up the effects of a Vichy course, when judiciously prescribed, as restorative to the digestive and assimilative functions, and invigorative to the general health. The tone of the stomach is soon improved, digestion becomes easier and more rapid, pain and weight after food disappearing. The bile flows more freely. The bowels become regular. Diarrhœa, if previously present, ceases. The consequence of these changes is better assimilation, and therefore flesh is often gained. With the improvement in nutrition the colour returns to the cheeks and energy to the mind."—*Dr. P. James.*

CHEMICAL ANALYSIS of the Principal Springs.

Acids and Bases contained in each litre.	Grande Grille.	Chomel.	Mesdammes	Lucas.	Park.	Hopital.	Célestins.	Hauterive.
			NAMES OF THE SPRINGS.					
Carbonic Acid . .	4·418	4·429	5·029	5·348	5·071	4·719	4·705	5·640
Sulphuric ,,	·164	·164	·141	·164	·177	·164	·164	·164
Phosphoric ,, .	·070	·038	traces	·038	·076	·025	·050	·625
Arsenic ,, .	·001	·001	·002	·001	·001	·001	·001	·001
Hydrochloric Acid .	·332	·334	·222	·324	·344	·324	·234	·334
Silica	·070	·070	·032	·050	·055	·050	·060	·071
Protoxide of Iron	·002	·002	·012	·002	·002	·002	·002	·008
Lime . . .	·169	·169	·235	·212	·239	·222	·180	·168
Strontia . .	·002	·002	·002	·008	·003	·008	·003	·002
Magnesia . . .	·097	·108	·134	·088	·068	·064	·105	·160
Potash . . .	·182	·192	·098	·146	·151	·228	·163	·098
Soda	2·488	2·536	1·957	2·501	2·500	2·500	2·560	2·368
TOTALS . .	7·997	8·043	7·866	8·877	8·687	8·302	8·327	9·039
Saline ingredients in each litre.								
Free Carbonic Acid .	·908	·768	1·908	1·751	1·555	1·067	1·049	2·183
Bicarb. of Soda .	4·883	5·091	4·016	5·004	4·857	5·029	5·103	4·087
,, Potash .	·352	·371	·185	·282	·292	·440	·315	·189
,, Magnesia .	·303	·338	·429	·275	·213	·200	·328	·501
,, Strontia .	·303	·003	·003	·005	·005	·005	·005	·003
,, Lime .	·434	·427	·604	·545	·614	·570	·462	·432
,, Protox. of Iron	·004	·004	·026	·004	·004	·004	·004	·017
Sulphate of Soda .	·291	·291	·250	·291	·314	·291	·291	·291
Phosphate . .	·130	·070	traces	·070	·140	·046	·091	·046
Arseniate . .	·002	·002	·003	·002	·002	·002	·002	·002
Chloride of Sodium .	·534	·534	·355	·518	·550	·518	·534	·534
Silica . . .	·070	·070	·032	·050	·055	·050	·060	·071
TOTALS . .	7·914	7·959	7·811	8·797	8·601	8·222	8·244	8·956

The Larbaud spring, which is not given in this analysis, differs only slightly from the Célestins.

In a garden of a house in the Boulevard Victoria is a petrifying spring, containing a large quantity of the carbonate of lime.

Excursions.

CAB FARES.—The course within the town from 6 A.M. to 12 P.M. with 1 horse, 1½ fr. ; 2 horses, 2½ frs. By time, carriage and 1 horse, first hour, 3 frs., and 2 frs. each successive hour. Half the day, 9 frs. ; the day, 18 frs. Carriage with 2 horses, first hour, 4 frs., the following hours, 3 frs. each. The half-day, 12 frs. 50 c. ; the day, 25 frs.

Art. 17.—The price for the first hour, in or outside Vichy, is always fully charged although the coachman has not been employed the entire hour. All the other hours are divided and paid by quarters.

Art. 18.—The day is fixed at 12 hrs., which comprises 2 hrs. for rest ; the half-day at 6 hrs., and 1 hr. for rest.

For drives with a fixed destination the price should be settled beforehand. The following are the usual prices. To the Casino des Justices (about 2 m. beyond Cusset), there and back, 1 horse, 7 frs. ; 2 horses, 10 frs. The same prices are charged, there and back, from Vichy to Charmeil, Côte St. Amand, Hauterive, Les Malavaux, and Montagne-Verte. To the Ardoisière, there and back, 1 horse, 8 frs. ; 2 horses, 12 frs. To Chateldon and back, 1 horse, 15 frs. ; 2 horses, 20 frs. To Busset and back by the Ardoisière, 1 horse, 16 frs. ; 2 horses, 20 frs. To Maulmont and back, 1 horse, 15 frs. ; 2 horses, 20 frs. To Randan by Bois-Randenez, return by Maulmont, 1 horse, 18 frs. ; 2 horses, 24 frs.

Cusset, pop. 6200, on the Sichon, 2 m. E. from Vichy. *Inn:* H. du Centre, in the Place de la Halle, near the church. Omnibus, 20 c. At the entrance into the town is the **Etablissement Thermal Ste. Marie**, a neat building of red and black brick, with a large entrance flanked with turrets. Opposite are the "Sources Ste. Marie" and Elizabeth, both cold. The baths cost 1½ fr. From 9 in the morning till 2 in the afternoon only 1 fr. is charged. The waters are of the same class as those of Vichy, but have a little more soda and iron.

From Cusset a pleasant road leads to Les Malavaux, 2½ m. S.E. Take the road to Les Guitons the length of the bridge, which do not cross, but walk up by the course of the stream Joland. The hill to the right is called the "Côte des Justices," because on it criminals suffered the extreme penalty of the law. Shortly afterwards the valley narrows into a miniature gorge between basaltic rocks, and situated in the prettiest part, 1¼ m. from the bridge, is an inn with refreshment rooms. Pension per day, 10 frs. Beyond the inn the valley gradually widens and flattens. From the inn are visited the Puits du Diable ; and on the Malavaux the Fontaine des Sarrasins and the scanty ruins of a castle said to have been built by the Knight Templars ; admission, 1 fr. each.

2½ m. N. from Vichy by the Rue de Ballore is the Montagne-Verte, 1288 ft. above the sea, with a restaurant on the top, whence there is a good view of the surrounding country. This road makes the nicest walk in the neighbourhood of Vichy. At about a mile it passes by the cemetery.

Vichy to Busset by Cusset and the Ardoisière, 10 m. S. Return by St. Yorre, where the rail may be taken.

The road passes by Cusset and then extends southwards by the side of the Sichon. The first village passed on the Sichon is Grivats, famous for the manufacture of the Toiles de Vichy, called also Grivats, a variegated cotton stuff used for gowns and petticoats. The best quality, made only at Grivats, costs 1½ fr. the mètre (1¼ yard) ; the inferior qualities, made chiefly at Roanne, cost from 75 c. to 1 fr. the mètre. At Grivats they are all made by handlooms in the houses of the weavers. Among the best shops in Vichy for this article is that of Delorme-Desfougères, Rue de l'Hôpital.

From Grivats the road, after passing through a fertile country, reaches the **Ardoisière**, situated at the foot of Mont Peyroux, 7½ m. S. from Vichy. Inn with refreshment rooms. Here there is an abandoned slate quarry, charge to visit 1 fr., but it is not worth entering. The favourite excursions here are to the falls of the Sichon or the Cascade du Gourre-Saillant, fee 1 fr., which, unless after heavy rains, are very small; and to the ruins of the Château des Templiers on the top of Mont Peyroux, whence there is a beautiful and extensive view.

The road now leaves the banks of the Sichon and extends due S. towards Busset, 2½ m. from the Ardoisière, or 10 m. from Vichy by this road. Busset is a poor village at the foot of a hill, on which is the Château Bourbon-Busset, built in 1319, but restored since. Admission readily granted. Splendid view from the Tour de Riom. W. from Busset, on the E. side of the Allier, is St. Yorre (see below), where the rail may be taken to Vichy, 5 m. N.

Nearly 8 m. S.E. from the Ardoisière by the valley of the Suhan and the village of Arronnes is Ferrières, with, in the neighbourhood, the ruins of the old feudal castle of Mont Gilbert, the Roc St. Vincent, the Pierre-Encise, the Grotte des Fées, and the Puy-Montoncel. Time required from Vichy and back, 8 hrs.

Vichy to Randan.—Coach daily from the Place de la Marine at 11.20 A.M.; arrives at Randan at 1 P.M.; leaves Randan at 3.20, and is back to Vichy by 5. Fare there and back, 2½ frs. The castle of Randan is open on Thursdays and feast-days. The return journey, 4 m., by Maulmont costs 3½ frs.

The coach, having crossed the bridge of the Allier, passes on the left hand a small house with the sign SOURCE INTERMITTENTE. In the garden is the very interesting intermittent spring of Vesse, which acts every 6 or 7½ hours, when it rises from a depth of 375 ft. to the height of 16 ft. above the surface. During the irruption, which lasts 30 minutes, the water has a milky hue, from the quantity of air it contains. Admission, 25 c.

From this spring the road follows at a little distance the course of the stream Sermon, passing the villages of Les Séchauds and the Bois Randenez, and then enters the forest of Boucharde, at the southern extremity of which is situated Randan, with its large modern mansion belonging to the Orleans family. It contains a picture gallery with several drawings by the gifted Marie d'Orleans, the rooms of Madame Adelaide and of her brother Louis Philippe, a beautiful little chapel, and a large kitchen (see p. 368). From Randan the road leads due E. through the woods to the hunting-seat of Maulmont, constructed by Madame Adelaide in the Gothic style, on the site of an old commandery of the Knight Templars. From this the Allier is crossed by the suspension bridge of Ris, whence the return journey may be made by rail or by the high road along the E. side of the river.

Vichy to Thiers by rail, 22 m. S., changing at Courty. 5 m. S. from Vichy are the village of St. Yorre and the Larbaud mineral

St. Yorre. Ris. Chateldon. Thiers.

water establishment, with an intermittent spring in the grounds. The water, which is bottled here, rises from a depth of 340 ft.

The next station S. from St. Yorre is the station Ris-Chateldon, 5 m. from St. Yorre and 10 from Vichy. About 200 yards N. from the station the road that crosses the rail leads directly to the suspension bridge, or the Pont de Ris, over the Allier, about 1 m. W. The broad road opposite the station leads to Ris (pronounce the *s*) about 1 m. E. It is a large village, with dunghills, geese, and ducks in the principal street. The church, 12th and 13th cents., has narrow aisles and nave and semicircular apse.

For **Chateldon**, 3¼ m. S.E. from station, take the road that follows the rail southward to second road left. This village, more interesting than Ris, is situated in the little valley of the stream Vauziron, surrounded by hills covered with vineyards. In the "Place" is the principal inn, the H. Camin, pension 6 to 7 frs., whence the coach starts for the station, but not for every train. The house with the mineral water springs is up at the other end of the village, by the side of the Vauziron.

Maringues is 11¼ m. W. from the station by the Pont de Ris. Puy de Guillaume, 3¼ m. S. from the station.

23½ m. S. from Vichy by rail is the picturesquely-situated town of **Thiers**, pop. 16,230. *Inns:* *Paris ; Aigle d'Or ; Univers ; all near each other, and on almost the same level as the station. Also approached by rail from Clermont, passing through a mountainous country.

Thiers, with its old houses, and steep, tortuous, dirty streets, is built on the side of Mt. Besset, which rises to the height of 1716 ft. above the sea, but only 405 ft. above the old prison near the "Place." At the foot of this mountain flows the impetuous Durolle, which turns the wheels of the paper-mills and forges in the low town. From the different terraces are splendid views of the curiously-shaped surrounding mountains and of the plains of the Limagne. The manufacture of cutlery (coutellerie) is the standard occupation of the inhabitants. The steel is made in the forges ; all the rest is done in the houses of the workmen, each individual of the family taking the part in the manufacture corresponding to his or her ability. At the foot of Mt. Besset, near the Durolle, is the church of St. Moutiers, of the 11th cent., excepting the square apse, which is of the 7th. From the chancel a very pretty road leads up the valley of the Durolle to the Margeride. The church in the high part of the town to the left is St. Jean, 14th cent., with a cemetery. Considerably higher than St. Jean is St. Genest, built in about 1020. It has been recently restored. Over the second altar, left or north of the high altar, is a fresco, 16th cent., representing Mary among angels entering heaven. The painted glass is modern. 3 m. S.E. from Thiers is the village of Escoutoux, where a pleasant sparkling wine is made called Champagne de la Dore. Excellent butter and cheese are made at Thiers. The richest are flat and thin, but the most pungent is a cheese not unlike the Stilton in shape and colour. The best of the thin moist cheeses are those of

368

PARIS
MILES FROM
GANNAT. AIGUEPERSE.
MARSEILLES
MILES TO

Mont d'Or, near Lyons, not the Mt. Dore of Clermont. From Thiers
the country becomes most picturesque all the way to St. Etienne, the
line winding its way around the steep sides of lofty mountains with
roaring torrents in the deep ravines below. After leaving Thiers it
follows the course of the Durolle to its source. 3¼ m. from Thiers by
rail is the station for St. Remy, pop. 5000 (see below).

Vichy to the Château d'Effiat, 18 m. S.W. by the villages of Vesse
(or Vaisse) and Serbannes, and the forest of Montpensier.

The Château d'Effiat (15th cent.) belonged in the 16th cent. to
Antoine Coiffier Ruse, a marshal of France, whose eldest son was the
unfortunate Cinq-Mars. It was afterwards purchased by the famous
Scotch financier Law of Lauriston, who had to give it up to his
creditors. The castle was dismantled by order of the State, but is
now partially restored. 3¾ m. W., on the line between Gannat and
Clermont, is **Aigueperse**, pop. 2600. *Inn:* St. Louis. A coach runs
between Aigueperse and Randan, 8 m. E. (see below). Between
Vichy and the railway station of St. Remy is the modernised Château
of Charmeil on the Allier, 3¾ m. N. from Vichy. It forms a pleasant
afternoon drive.

2 m. N. from St. Germain-des-Fosses railway station are the
ruins of the Château de Billy (14th cent.), formerly one of the
strongest and most imposing in the Bourbonnais. In the village are
some old houses.

17 m. N.E. by rail from Vichy, on the Lyons line, is La Palisse
on the Bèbre, pop. 2830; *Inn:* H. de l'Écu; with a castle (14th
cent.) on an eminence overlooking the town (see p. 346).

224 SAINT-REMI-EN-ROLLAT, 867 ft. above the sea.

235½ GANNAT, pop. 6000. *Inns:* Nord; Poste. A town of **294½**
crooked streets, on the Andelot, at the confines of the plain of La
Limagne. The church of St. Croix (choir 11th cent., nave reconstructed in the 14th cent.), is a good specimen of the architecture of
Auvergne. Some of the windows are by J. du Paroy. In the "Place"
are two houses, one belonging to the Dukes of Bourbon, the other to
the Fontanges family, both 15th cent. Gannat is famous for beer.
Junction at Gannat with the railway system of the Chemins de Fer
d'Orleans, leading to Orleans and Tours, and the Feudal Castles on
the Loire. See Black's *Normandy, Brittany, and Touraine.*

242 AIGUEPERSE, pop. 2600. *Hotels:* St. Louis; Lion d'Or. **288**
The finest building is the Sainte Chapelle, built in 1475. The Hôtel
de Ville is in a convent of the Ursulines, built in 1650. A coach from
this station goes to Randan in the Limagne, 8 m. E., pop. 2000, with
a beautiful castle of bright and dark coloured bricks, reconstructed in

1822 by Mme. Ad. d'Orleans. 2½ m. distant, on the border of the
forest of Randan, is another castle constructed by Mme. in the style
of the Middle Ages. See under excursions from Vichy.

253
RIOM, 1105 ft. above the sea, pop. 11,000. *Inns:* H. Paris; 277
Poste; Puy-de-Dome. Diligences to Volvic, 3¼ m. S.W.; to Châtelguyon, 5 m. N.; and to Châteauneuf, 20 m. N.W. The most interesting church in Riom is St. Amable, 12th cent., with a large nave
supported on 14 piers, each pier having three engaged columns. On
the tower and south transept is the same kind of rude mosaic which
ornaments the church of Issoire. Near St. Amable is the Tour de
l'Horloge, 16th cent., and close to it a few 15th and 16th cent. houses.
Down this same street, the Rue de l'Horloge, is the church of Notre
Dame, 15th cent. Attached to the west end of the Palais de Justice
is the Ste. Chapelle, 14th cent., consisting of a choir, with a pinnacle
at each corner of the west end. In the building called the "Hôtel
Chabrol" is the museum and picture gallery.

20 m. N.W. from Riom, by diligence starting at 6 A.M., are the
mineral baths of **Châteauneuf,** pop. 1000. *Hotels:* Viple; Denys;
Mossier. Water saline. Temperature of the fourteen springs from 60°
to 102° Fahr. Recommended for obstruction of the liver, neuralgia,
nervous affections of the heart, cutaneous diseases, glandular swellings.
Bath, 1 fr.

5 m. N. from Riom by omnibus are the hot mineral springs of
Châtelguyon, most picturesquely situated among mountains. *Hotels:*
Bains; Thermes; Barthélemy; Marret; Lacroix. Bathing establish-
ment with every accessory. Recommended for dyspepsia, constipation
of the bowels, gall-stones, chronic bronchitis, syphilis. Water saline.
Temp. 100° Fahr.

3½ m. S.W. from Riom by diligence is Volvic, pop. 4000, built
on lava. Visit the church, the Musée in the Mairie, and the workshops where the lava brought from the quarries of the Puy de la Nugère
is hewn (see p. 377).

260½
CLERMONT - FERRAND, 1335 ft. above the sea, pop. 269½
43,000, on an eminence crowned by the cathedral, of which the
principal façade, the west entrance, is towards the Place de Jaude,
while the chancel or eastern end is towards the railway station.
Hotels: in the Place de Jaude are the *Univers; *Poste, for com-
mercials; Europe. Just off the Place de Jaude are the Paix; France.
All the above are large houses. Near the Académie and the Botanic
Gardens, the H. des Facultés, a small but good house. Among the
hotels in front of the station the best is the H. des Voyageurs.

Coaches from the Place de Jaude for Saint Mart, Royat, St. Amand, and Champeix. During summer, coach to nearly the top of the Puy-de-Dome (see page 372). In the "Place" are a large cabstand and offices where carriages may be hired for excursions.

The general post office is in the Place St. Herem, down from the N. side of the cathedral, just under the Promenade de la Poterne, whence there is a charming view of the Puy-de-Dome mountains. In the Place St. Herem is a bronze statue of Blaise Pascal, 1623-1662, in a sitting posture. A little beyond the foot of the stairs to the right of the statue is the Temple Protestant, service 1 P.M. The first narrow street beyond the post office leads down to the Fontaine Petrifiante.

Large quantities of fruit are preserved in Clermont, both in the moist and crystalline (glacé) state.

The most prominent edifice in Clermont is the Cathedral, founded in the 9th and rebuilt in the 14th cent. The material is basalt and Volvic lava, which admits of a very sharp edge. The narrow round belfry on the N. side is 165 ft. high. Round the nave and choir are twenty-eight, or, including those of the transepts, thirty-six fascicled piers, which rise nearly to the roof. Between are pointed arches, and immediately above, the triforium, having over each arch a treble window resting on four fascicled and three impost colonnettes. As the choir contracts towards the apsidal termination the piers become less massive and the arches $\frac{1}{3}$ narrower. The stained glass of the clerestory windows of the nave dates from the 15th cent.; but only a few are complete, having been injured by a hailstorm in 1835. The best glass is in the apse and in the N. transept, dating from the 13th cent. The glass in the rose of the S. transept, which is also beautiful, is modern. The clock, with its three men to strike the hours and quarters, dates from the 16th cent. Ten chapels radiate from the choir. In the first on the N. side is a miracle-working image of Mary and Child.

The house in which Blaise Pascal was born in 1623 is No. 2 Passage Vernines, a small kind of court near the right or S. angle of the principal entrance into the cathedral. It is more easily found by going to the front, No. 2 Place de la Cathedral, on the third story of which is a bust of Pascal. This part of the building is modern. Through the shop in a little room up a few steps is the exact spot where he was born.

The Rue des Notaires leads down from the cathedral to the Place de la Poterne, where there is a good view of the surrounding mountains.

NOTRE DAME DU PORT. BOTANIC GARDENS.

The large block of buildings passed on the right includes the Palais de Justice, the Hôtel de Ville, and the prison. The second street beyond these buildings, the Rue du Port, leads down to Notre Dame du Port, built in 578, destroyed by the Normans in 853 and restored in 866, according to the inscriptions on the tablet in the N. transept. The exterior is decorated with blind arches, mouldings, and dental friezes, while the apse and its radiating chapels have besides patterns in mosaic. From the intersection of the transept rises an octagonal tower.

In the interior the roof is waggon-vaulted with no groining. Round the nave are fourteen piers with attached columns, having on their capitals sculptured figures of men, animals, and plants. The chancel is surrounded by columns of the same kind, on which rest arches more or less stilted according to the width of the space. The triforium is massive and on short columns. All the glass is modern, excepting in the window behind the high altar and in each of the windows in the S. and N. ends of the chancel, which date from the beginning of the 13th cent.

Below the chancel is the crypt, supported on twelve massive columns. Over the altar is a miracle-working image, about 6 inches high, of Mary and child Jesus, found at the bottom of the well, 18 ft. deep, in 578, when the foundations of the first church were being laid. The well, which is covered, is in front of the altar. Its water is endowed with miraculous properties. The walls are lined with expressions of gratitude for favours obtained by praying to this tiny representative of the woman Mary.

It was within the walls of the upper church, when Pope Urban II. and Peter the Hermit were exhorting their hearers in 1096 to undertake the first crusade, that the whole assembly, as if impelled by an immediate inspiration, exclaimed with one voice, "It is the will of God!" which words became the signal of battle in all the future exploits of the Crusaders.

The open space behind the statue of General Desaix leads to the wide Rue Lagarlaye and to the Boulevard du Taureau, in which is situated the Académie or College of Clermont, containing, besides the class-rooms, the picture gallery, the museum of natural history, and the Public Library founded by Massillon when bishop of this diocese.

Behind the Academy are the Botanic Gardens, in which a considerable part is wisely devoted to the training, grafting, and pruning of fruit trees and vines. Attached is the École de Pisciculture, with tanks and a small aquarium. Near the Academy is the Hôtel Dieu.

372

PARIS
MILES FROM
ROMAGNAT. ISSOIRE.
MARSEILLES
MILES TO

Tolerable wine is made at Puy-de-Dome, but it is generally cold and flat, and does not sit easily on the stomach.

3¾ m. S. from Clermont is Romagnat, pop. 2000, at the foot of Mt. Rognon, 1875 ft., and 1½ m. more is Mt. Gergovia, 2240 ft., the site of the principal city of the Averni, which was successfully defended by Vercingetorix against a powerful army commanded by Cæsar, whom he compelled to retreat with great loss. The Roman headquarters are supposed to have been on a lower hill called Le Crest. (See also under Les Laumes, p. 19.)

Coach to the Puy-de-Dome from Clermont. The road from Royat up to the Puy-de-Dome passes by Fontanat and the poor village of Font-de-l'Arbre ; or, if preferred, the road to Fontgieve may be taken as far as the **Baraque**, and ascend by the S. side, which is easier.

The **Puy-de-Dome** is 4806 ft. above the level of the sea, has no crater, and is covered with a long tufted grass, with here and there a rough spongy rock cropping out, of volcanic origin, and called trachyte, of which the variety found here, and almost here alone, has been named domite. It is grayish-white, fine grained, compact, earthy, often friable, and with flakes of brown mica. It appears to be a decomposed trachyte, in which the feldspar has been affected, but not the mica. The most perfect craters here are the Puy-de-Pariou, 3970 ft. high, and the Nid de la Poule. On the top of the Puy-de-Dome is an observatory, connected with the keeper's house by an underground way. On the Puy are also the ruins of the chapel of St. Bernabé, 2d or 3d cent., and of a Gallo-Roman temple to Mercury.

For Clermont-Ferrand to Brive by Royat, Mont-Dore, and Bourboule, see p. 376. Junction at Clermont with rail to Lyons, 121 m. E. by Courty (where change for Thiers), Montbrison, St. Etienne, and Givors-Canal (see p. 349).

From Clermont-Ferrand the railway to Nîmes ascends the course of the Allier to La Bastide, 116 m. S. Some parts of the valley are very picturesque. The train after Clermont passes, 267 m., Le Cendre, 1145 ft. ; 270¼ m., Les Martres-de-Veyre, 1148 ft. ; 272 m., Vic-le-Comte, 1164 ft. ; 276½ m., Coudes. The station is near the Allier, 1173 ft., but the town is on the top of an adjoining hill, with the tower of Montpeyroux, 13th cent.

282½ ISSOIRE, pop. 6400, and 1200 ft. above the sea-level. *Hotels:* 247½ Poste ; Pezissat ; opposite each other in the principal street. It is a clean little town. The principal church, founded in the 10th cent., is a highly interesting specimen of the architecture of Auvergne. The

373

PARIS
MILES FROM
LE BREUIL. ARDES. ARVANT.
MARSEILLES
MILES TO

exterior is plain, but the plan admirable. The transepts are just suffi-ciently developed to give expression to the edifice ; while the elegant projection of the five apsidal chapels illustrates one of the characteristic beauties of the style. A mosaic decoration of differently-coloured lavas under a handsome cornice runs round the chancel, resembling what is seen on the south transept and tower of St. Amable at Riom. The interior is beautiful and harmonious, but the gaudy painting on the walls of an edifice of such a severe style surprises the eye on entering. The crypt (10th cent.), below the chancel, but not below the ground, consists of many short massive columns, bearing a complex series of arches around a central arch, under which is the altar.

287⅓
‒.‒ LE BREUIL, 1287 ft., pop. 1000. Opposite station, *Inn :* H. 242¼
Beranger. Coaches await passengers for St. Germain-Lembron, an agri-cultural town, 2 m. W., and Ardes. The road to Ardes from St. Germain ascends through a hilly and well-cultivated country, passing, at 4¼ m. from St. Germain, a bathing establishment, possessing a copious spring containing the carbonate of iron and a large quantity of free carbonic acid gas. 2½ m. farther is **Ardes** ; *Inns :* Paillardin ; Barreyre ; on an eminence rising from the Couze. In the low part of the village is the church, 11th cent., but restored and repaired. In the cemetery is a stone cross (1519) with Mary and Child against it, resting on a demure-looking figure holding an open book. The valley of the Couze, between high wooded mountains and great basaltic cliffs, offers an excellent field for geological and botanical rambles, while the river itself, which runs in a narrow bed at the foot of the mountains, through little meadows by the side of the road, contains excellent trout. High up are firs and forest trees, but below are apricot, apple, pear, quince, cherry, and walnut trees interspersed among small vineyards and meadows. The best display of the basaltic formation is between the first bridge and the village of Rentière, perched on a basalt cliff rising from the road. A little way beyond, on the right or opposite bank of the river, is an isolated cliff resembling a statue of Mary with the back towards the spectator. About 4½ m. up the valley are the ruins of a mill, La Gravière, destroyed by lightning in 1881. This is considered the commencement of the wildest and most imposing part of the valley, which extends to the Cantal. About 5 m. up, on the top of a hill on the right bank, is the chapel of St. Pesade.

2¼ m. S. from Le Breuil is Le Saut du Loup, a village with mineral waters, picturesquely situated on the Allier, 1277 ft. above the sea. Between Brassal, *Inn :* Chevalier, 3¾ m. farther S., 1322 ft. above the sea, and Arvant are valuable coal-fields and a bed of kaolin clay.

298
‒‒‒ ARVANT, 1400 ft., a dirty hamlet on the Vergonghéon, an 232
affluent of the Allier. The best of the inns is the H. Voyageurs.

Junction here with the line to Capdenac, 110 m. S.W., traversing the whole of the interesting geological region of the Cantal. (See Black's *South France*, West Half.)

From the hamlet of Neussargues, 30½ m. S.W. from Arvant, commences the loop-line of the Chemins de Fer du Midi, which traverses the lofty woodless highlands of Lozère, the coal-region of Aveyron, and the wine and olive department of Herault to Beziers on the Mediterranean line, between Cette and Narbonne. On this line, 11¾ m. S. from Neussargues, 7 m. S. from St. Flour, and 37½ m. N. from Marvejols, is the highest bridge in the world, the Pont de Garabit, which crosses the ravine of the Truyère 400 ft. above the river. The span of the great arch is 541½ ft., and the length of the viaduct 1851 ft.

$\frac{304}{\sim}$ BRIOUDE, 1430 ft. above the sea, pop. 5000. *Inns:* *Nord ; $\frac{226}{\sim}$ Commerce. A dirty town on a tableland, 1¼ m. from the Allier. The parish church St. Julien (restored) dates from the 11th and 12th cents. The W. façade, of red sandstone, is flat, with round-headed windows over the three portals. The largest, the centre one, is between two thick plain buttresses, over which rises a low square tower. On the S. side of the church is another portal, preceded by a massive portico on three large semicircular arches, resting on short square piers with attached columns bearing large foliaged capitals. On the N. side is a similar entrance, but plainer. From the choir rises a square tower, becoming octagonal in the two upper stages. From the apse, which is semicircular, radiate at a lower level five semicircular chapels, their roofs terminating in a cornice of tiny stone interlaced arches. The wall of the apse above the chapels is ornamented with a mosaic, chiefly stars, in black and white stones.

The interior of the church is surrounded by great, tall, square piers with attached columns and vaulting shafts bearing grotesque foliaged capitals. Over the arches, which are early pointed, run a built-up triforium and circular clerestory windows. The five chapels have a profusion of colonnettes, three round-headed windows each, and some beautiful sculpture in relief. Under the chancel is a crypt.

Behind the church is the covered market, and a little farther the Hôtel de Ville, with the town promenade on a terrace overlooking the plain.

$\frac{318½}{\sim}$ ST. GEORGES-D'AURAC, 1872 ft. above the sea. *Inn:* $\frac{211½}{\sim}$ Lombardin, near the station. Change carriages for Le Puy, 32 m. E., and for St. Etienne 54½ m. farther. (See p. 91, and map p. 46.)

$\overset{323}{\sim}$ LANGEAC, pop. 4800. *Inns:* H. Lombardin ; Pascon. (See $\overset{207}{\sim}$ p. 91, and map p. 46.) Between Langeac and Langogne the train passes through a most picturesque country. Rich vegetation amidst vast masses of basalt, either continuous or isolated, either rugged or grooved with pentagonal columns ; sometimes also rent into deep dark ravines, between vertical cliffs of which the eye just catches a glance while being hurried past in the train. 3¾ m. S. from Langeac is Chanteuges, 1800 ft., pop. 1000, on an eminence above the station. The fortified tower, the remains of the old abbey, is well seen from the rail. Just before arriving at the next station, Chazes, 8½ m. S. from Langeac, is an interesting church, 11th cent., against a rock. Then follow the stations of Monistrol-d'Allier, 2000 ft. (p. 91); Alleyras, 2195 ft. ; and Jonchure, 2238 ft.

$\overset{364½}{\sim}$ LANGOGNE, 2940 ft. above the sea, pop. 4000. *Inns:* $\overset{165½}{\sim}$ Cheval Blanc ; Chambon. Pleasantly situated on the Langouyrou. All the trains halt here. (See pp. 88 and 94, and map p. 46.) 7½ m. farther S. is Luc station, 2900 ft. ; and 4½ m. farther S., La Bastide, 3070 ft., the culminating point of the line. A few miles to the W. of the station is the source of the Allier. At Prevenchères, 6 m. S., the station is only 2580 ft. above the sea. The line now passes by immense rocks and cliffs of granite.

$\overset{390}{\sim}$ VILLEFORT, 1820 ft., pop. 2000. A poor village on the $\overset{140}{\sim}$ Devèze, in a deep valley at the foot of Mt. Lozère. Diligences at this station for Mende, passing through, at about half-way, Bagnols les Bains, 23½ m. W.

Bagnols les Bains, pop. 500. *Inns:* Lacombe ; Des Bains ; Midi. A poor village 3087 ft. above the sea, at the confluence of the Villaret and the Lot. It has a thermal establishment supplied by an unctuous and clear water, temperature 100° Fahr., efficacious in rheumatic affections, cutaneous diseases, bruises, etc. In the neighbourhood are pleasant excursions, good fishing in the Lot, and plenty of game on the mountains.

From Villefort to Alais the line penetrates a very mountainous country by numerous tunnels and viaducts. At La Grande Combe, with the two stations of La Levade and La Pise, the important coal, iron, and zinc mines commence which extend to Alais.

$\overset{419}{\sim}$ ALAIS, pop. 22,000, on the Gardon. *Hotels:* Commerce ; $\overset{111}{\sim}$ *Luxembourg ; Champagne. Situated, like Sainte Cecile, La Levade, La Pise, and Tamaris, among coal-fields, iron-works, and manufactories.

376

PARIS
MILES FROM

ROYAT. ST. MART.

MARSEILLES
MILES TO

This is the best station from which to enter the mountainous regions of Lozère, traversed easily by diligences corresponding with each other. Some very capital wine is made at Alais.

Junction at Alais with the branch line extending 62 m. N.E. to Teil (see p. 96, and map p. 56); also to Laudun, 35½ m. E. (see p. 99, and map p. 56).

450 NÎMES (see p. 101, and map p. 66).   80

467 TARASCON (see p. 66, and map p. 66).   63

470 ARLES (see p. 68, and map p. 66).   60

499½ ST. CHAMAS (see p. 76, and map p. 66).   30½

512½ ROGNAC (see p. 77, and map p. 66).   17½

518 PAS-DES-LANCIERS.   12

530 MARSEILLES (see p. 111, and map p. 123).

Clermont-Ferrand to Brive-la-Gaillard,

122 m. W. by rail, passing Royat 3¾ m., Durtol 5 m., Volvic 12¼ m., Vauriat 17½ m., St. Ours-les-Roches 20 m., Pont-Gibaud 24 m., La Miouze-Rochefort 28½ m., Bourgheade-Herment 35¼ m., Laqueuille 40¼ m., Meymac 73 m., and Tulle 105¾ m. S.W. from Clermont and 16¼ m. N.E. from Brive.

From Clermont station the train describes a semicircle as it ascends the highly-cultivated vineclad mountains rising from Clermont. The first station is Royat, with the hotels Univers; Monnet; Nice; St. Mart, adjoining the Casino; Grand Hotel; Continental Hotel. On the road up to Royat are H. Chabassière; Victoria; Paix; Paris; Europe; Lyons. Higher up beyond the hotels is the village of Royat. The parish church, founded in the 7th cent. and rebuilt in the 10th and 11th, was heightened and fortified in the 12th cent. In the centre of the transept is a low tower, square in the first stage and octagonal in the second. Under the small chancel, raised 5 ft. above the floor of the nave, is a crypt supported on six colonnettes.

In the "Place" is a crucifix of lava erected in 1486. At the back of J. C. is Mary with the child, and the apostles standing on consoles. The narrow steep road from in front of the Mary side leads

down to the Grotte des Sources, a cave in basalt, whence gush forth
sundry springs of crystal water. Only those, however, are seen which
are allowed to flow into the receptacle used by the washerwomen ; the
others are led to Clermont, where they supply the fountains. The
road, after crossing the Tirtaine, enters the territory of St. Mart. In
the lower part of the valley, in a small park on the right side of the
Tirtaine, is the bathing establishment, supplied by five springs, of
which the most important is the Eugénie, which rises in front of the
establishment ; temperature, 100° Fahr. The principal ingredients
are the chlorate of sodium, mixed with the bicarbonates of lime, soda,
and magnesia, and a little iron. The baths are made of volcanic tufa.
The charge is from 1½ fr. to 2½ frs. according to the season.

Besides the hotels already mentioned there are around the establishment the H. St. Mart; the H. Splendide ; Bains ; Bristol, all large
first-class houses. On the road up the left bank of the Tirtaine are
the Louvre ; Richelieu ; Belle Vue ; France et Angleterre ; Sources.
St. Mart is 1¼ m. from Clermont by omnibus, passing through
Chamalières. A great variety of excursions in the neighbourhood.

5⌇⌇ DURTOL, situated among high wooded mountains. 117⌇⌇

12½⌇⌇ VOLVIC. In the neighbourhood of the station are large 109½⌇⌇
quarries of lava, the produce of the extinct crater Puy de la Nugère,
3261 ft. Through the gap in the hill in front of the station is an
excellent view of Riom, 3½ m. E. from Volvic by coach. Volvic, pop.
4000, is partly on an eminence at the foot of Le Puy de la Bannière.
The parish church dates from the 13th cent. Quarrying, stonecutting,
and agriculture are the principal industries (see p. 369).

The train still ascending passes Vauriat 17½ m., St. Ours-les-Roches
20 m., and then arrives at the station for Pont-Gibaud, pop. 1300,
24 m. distant. *Inns:* H. Johannel ; H. Beraud. Their omnibuses
await passengers. Pont-Gibaud and its castle, 14th cent., are situated
on the Sioule, which traverses by a deep ravine a bed of lava from the
crater of Puy de Dome. Near the castle are the smelting-houses of the
important argentiferous mines in the neighbourhood.

40½⌇⌇ LAQUEUILLE, 3624 ft. above the sea. Change here for 81½⌇⌇
Mont-Dore-les-Bains 10½ m. S.E., and for Bourboule 8 m. S.W. The
beautiful mountain-road to Mont Dore passes through at about half-
way the village of Le Quaire, 3620 ft. above the sea. Immediately
below Le Quaire is Bourboule. The road to Bourboule passes through
the village of St. Sauves, 2838 ft. above the sea.

MONT-DORE-LES-BAINS

is situated among high mountains, in the narrow valley of the Dordogne, 3402 ft. above the sea. *Hotels.*—Considering the style of their furniture and of the meals, they are rather dear. The charge in the first-class houses is from 12 to 18 frs. per day, which includes coffee or tea in the morning, two meals with wine and service. The difference in the price is caused by the position of the room. Around the " Place " of the bathing establishment are the first-class houses, Chabaury ainé ; Paris ; Poste. By the side of the Casino, the H. du Parc and the Grand Hotel, which last charges from 16 to 21 frs. as it is rather better furnished. Around these hotels are what may be considered second-class houses, but if no agreement is made they are apt to charge as much as those of the first class : H. Bardet-Chanonat ; H. Boyer-Bertrand ; the Paix, open all the year ; H. Ramade ; H. Parisien ; France ; Nord ; Madeuf-Baraduc ; Thermes. The Casino is a handsome edifice, the greatest part being occupied by the theatre and the halls connected with it. The Mineral Bath Establishment and the Inhaling Establishment occupy two sides of the principal square ; the other two are occupied by the first-class hotels.

The bathing establishment is slightly lugubrious ; otherwise it is well adapted for the cure or alleviation of the diseases it professes to treat. The springs for drinking are arranged in the vestibule just within the entrance. In the right-hand corner is the Source de la Madeleine or Bertrand, temperature 113° Fahr. Besides containing the usual quantity of the arseniate of soda, about one-thousandth part in two pints, it contains more than any of the other springs of the bicarbonate of soda, lime, and magnesia. Next it is the Source Ramond, temperature 107°, containing the greatest quantity of iron. It rises in an octagonal basin built of large stones by the Romans. Then the Source César, temperature 113°, used chiefly for baths. Towards the left-hand end is the Source Sainte Marguerite, temperature 55°, used at table mixed with the wine.

Among the baths there are five upstairs supplied directly from some little springs which rise through the fissures of the rock. The flow in and out is constant. These baths are made of stone ; all the others are of iron. Besides the usual appliances for making the water act upon the more delicate parts of the body, there are also elaborate arrangements for foot-bathing and for douching the nose.

The tariffs of everything at Bourboule and Mont-Dore depend on the month. The hotels, baths, casinos, etc., are at their dearest during July, the height of the season. An ordinary bath with towels costs then 2 frs., at other times 1½ fr. ; a nose douche, 50 c. to 75 c. Baths from 92° to 100° should be continued from 30 to 40 minutes ; from 109° to 112°, from 10 to 15 minutes. The charge for drinking the water in July is 10 frs., in other months 5 frs. The men who carry the sedan-chairs between the hotels and the establishment are paid by tickets bought at the office of the baths.

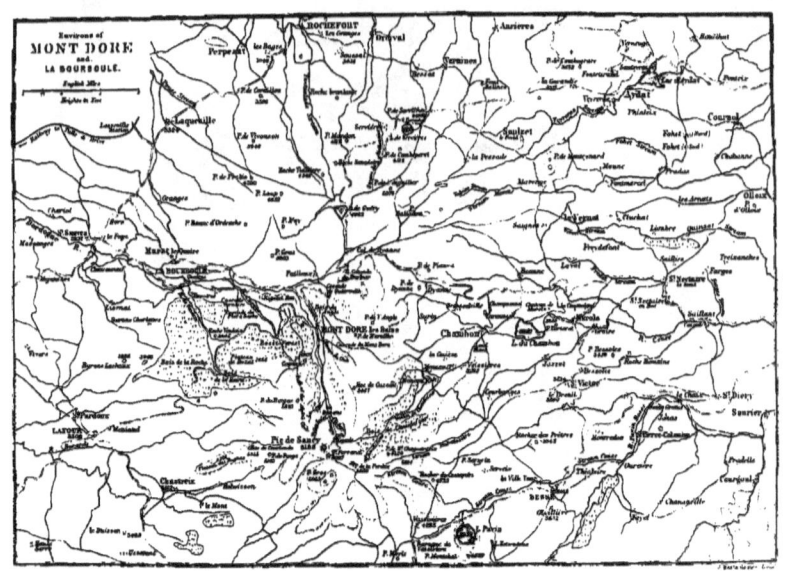

ANALYSIS OF THE WATER.   EXCURSIONS.

CONTENTS OF THE SPRINGS OF MONT-DORE AND BOURBOULE.

	Made-leine Spring.	Pavil-lon Spring.	Rigny Spring.	Caesar Spring.	Ramond Spring.	Bourboule, Perrière, and Choussy Springs.
Free carbonic acid gas	0·3552	0·3810	0·3644	0·5967	0·4997	0·0518
Bicarbonate of soda .	0·5362	0·5452	0·5375	0·5361	0·5362	2·8920
„ of potash	0·0309	0·0309	0·0232	0·0212	0·0212	....
„ of lime .	0·3423	0·3142	0·3092	0·3209	0·2720	0·1905
„ of magnesia .	0·1757	0·1676	0·1628	0·1676	0·1647	....
„ of protoxide of iron	0·0207	0·0235	0·025	0·0258	0·0317	0·0021
Chloride of sodium .	0·3685	0·3630	0·3599	0·3587	0·3578	2·8406
Sulphate of soda . .	0·0761	0·0761	0·0761	0·0756	0·0737	0·2084
Arseniate of soda .	0·00096	0·00096	0·00096	0·00096	0·00095	0·02347
Silicic acid . . .	0·1654	0·1686	0·1653	0·1552	0·1550	0·1200
Alumina . . .	0·0112	0·0094	0·0101	0·0083	0·0065	Traces.

Bourboule contains, besides what is given here, the chloride of potassium and magnesium. The active and special principle of both waters is the arseniate of soda, which, it will be observed, is 29 times more abundant in the Bourboule water than in that of Mont-Dore. The temperature of the two hottest Bourboule springs is 140° F., or 27° above the hottest of Mont-Dore.

These waters are recommended for certain forms of chronic bronchitis, asthma, and laryngeal complaints, gastro-enteric and uterine disorders marked by congestion, similar cases in which the liver is implicated, nervous maladies, and scrofulous diseases.—Madden's *Health Resorts.* Three or four glasses of the Madeleine water are taken daily by the majority of patients. It produces an increase of appetite, and is often attended with diarrhœa about the fifth or sixth day; this is mostly succeeded by a certain degree of constipation, which frequently lasts to the end of the course. About the twentieth day a disgust of the water is generally experienced, which is an indication that the saturation point has been obtained.—Lee's *Baths.*

As the weather of Mont-Dore is changeable, a supply of warm clothing is necessary. For excursions, a vehicle with 2 horses costs per day 20 to 25 frs.; saddle-horses, 5 to 10 frs. per day.

Excursions.—There are many pleasant and beautiful excursions around Mont-Dore, among the volcanic hills clothed with sombre pine forests and verdant meadows, rent at intervals by deep gullies with sullen waters or roaring torrents in the dark depths below, chafing against the jagged vertical cliffs of the ravines. Lakes sleep placidly in the craters which vomited forth these confused masses of rocks and knolls over which in many places now rush and tumble superb waterfalls. The Alpine Club have distributed over the district a liberal supply of finger-posts, which indicate the distance as well as the way to the different places.

One of the first excursions undertaken is to the **Cascade du Queureuilh**, about 2 m. N. by the village of Le Queureuilh, half-way between the falls and Mont-Dore. This cascade, one of the most beautiful in this region, is formed by the outlet of the Enfer from Lake Guéry (see below), 5 m. N. from Mont-Dore, or 3 from the falls. The stream, after rushing through the ravines of Blaise and Queue, tumbles over a hard basaltic precipice 98 ft. high. From the falls of Queureuilh tourists often return by what is incorrectly called the falls of the Rossignolet, a placid stream which enters the ravine of Enfer about half a mile below the falls of Queureuilh. This excursion may be made in a carriage. On foot it is easily walked in 4 hrs.

Excursions of much the same character, and in the same direction, are made to the Cascades de l'Angle 1¾ m., to the Saut-du-Loup 1¾ m., and to the Pré du Barbier.

The excursion to Lake Guéry, 5 m. N., commences by the new road to Randanne, cut in the flanks of the prettily-wooded Mt. Angle. At a turning of the road, just over the village of Queureuilh, there is a charming panoramic view of the valleys of Mont-Dore and of Sauves. To the W. are the towns of Le Quaire and Bourboule. Southwards are the Capucin, 4807 ft., the Aiguilles d'Enfer, and the giant peak De Sancy. Lake Guéry, one of the shallowest of the lakes, 4062 ft., is 1½ m. W. from the main road, in a desolate region, surrounded by arid rugged peaks. N. from the lake, at the entrance to a picturesque defile, stand like sentries, on the left the Roche Tuillière, 4246 ft., one side a vertical cliff, the other clothed with verdure ; on the right the Roche Sanadoire, with huge basaltic columns, resembling those of the Giant's Causeway.

4½ m. N. from Lake Guéry is the ancient village of **Orcival**, with an inn and a church of the 9th and 10th cents., containing a miraculous image found near it under the earth. 2½ m. W. from the Orcival road is the Pierre-Branlante, a slightly movable overhanging rock. From Orcival return by the Randanne road to Mont-Dore, 11 m. S.

N.E. from Lake Guéry, or 9½ m. N.E. from Mont-Dore by Mt. Aiguiller, 5076 ft., is Lake Servières, 3939 ft. above the sea, 75 ft. deep, in an extinct crater. On the N. margin are a tumulus and an ancient camp.

9 m. E., at the village of Fohet, S. from Lake Aydat, are some menhirs.

The village and lake of Chambon, 2881 ft. above the sea, are 12 m. E. from Mont-Dore by the valleys of Moneau and Chaudefour, and rather less by the highway passing Diane or Dyanne.

From Murols the road ascends 5¾ m. S. to Besse, whence it passes by Lake Pavin to Vassivières, 5¼ m. W. from Besse. At Vassivières a bridle-path diverges N. to the Pics of Ferrand and Sancy (see p. 381).

To the W. and S.W. of Mont-Dore are the Salon Mirabeau 2 m., the cascades of Vernière 3 m., and Plat-a-Barbe 3¼ m. (p. 385) ; and the top of the Puy Gros 3¾ m. (p. 385).

The most important excursion is to the summit of the Pic de

Pics de Sancy and Ferrand. Lake Pavin.

Sancy, 6188 ft. above the sea, or 2786 ft. above the village of Mont-Dore, and 5 m. S. from it by the valley of the Dordogne. Guide unnecessary. Good bridle-road till within 20 minutes of the top. Horse, 6 frs. From the Grande Rue enter the Pic de Sancy road, leave the Château-d'Eau on the left. At about a third of the way the Dordogne is crossed, and shortly afterwards is passed the ravine of the Egravats, formed by a landslip of the trachytic mountain, the Roc de Cuzeau, 5706 ft. ; and a little farther S. on the same (E.) side the Puy de Carcadogne, 5890 ft. To the right or W. side are the valleys of Lacour and Enfer, separated from each other by a dyke of dark porphyritic trachyte. Shortly after, the Dore is crossed where it joins the Dogne, 4420 ft. above the sea. A little farther is the cascade of the Serpent, where the Dogne, descending by a tortuous course, has been likened to a serpent. Opposite are the more noisy falls of the Dore. A path at the foot leads to an old alum mine.

The road, cut in the sides of the mountain, now ascends by the course of the Dogne, which rises between two large blocks. Then having crossed the infant Dore we arrive at the Buffet, 5863 ft., situated in the marshy meadow of the Dore. The horses are left here—25 c. charged for taking care of each. From this to the top on foot requires about 20 minutes. The view is splendid and of immense extent from this the highest mountain in central France and the culminating point of that great volcanic eruption called the Mounts Dore, 54 m. in circumference, which have broken their way through the early and solid granite rocks. A half-hour is sufficient to descend Sancy and mount the Puy Ferrand, 6066 ft. Return to Mont-Dore, 6 m. N., by the Chemin des Crètes.

3 m. S. from Sancy or 8 from Mont-Dore is Vassivières, a poor hamlet on a tableland, 4266 ft., with a church built in 1595, containing a miracle-working image, discovered while digging for water a little to the W. of the church. It spends four months of the year at Vassivières, and the rest in the church of Besse. It is carried between the two places with all the pomp possible ; the iron crosses on the road indicate the resting stations. 2¼ m. E. from Vassivières, or 10¼ m. from Mont-Dore, on the road to Besse, is the Lac-de-Pavin, 3928 ft. above the sea, in the crater of an extinct volcano, but not full to the brim. It is 2625 ft. long, 2462 ft. wide, and 315 ft. deep, completely surrounded, excepting at the outlet, by vertical cliffs from 300 to 500 ft. high. Boats are let for sailing and fishing on this singular lake. At the S. end rises the Puy Montchal, 4629 ft. At the foot of Montchal, S. side, is the Creux-de-Sancy, a circular cavity 55 ft. deep, at the bottom of which a stream of water is seen, supposed to come from Lake Pavin.

3 m. E., or 13 from Mont-Dore by an excellent road, is Besse-en-Chandesse, 3399 ft., on the slope of a mountain. *Inns:* Voyageurs ; Commerce ; pop. 2000, the wealthiest town in the neighbourhood, and excellent headquarters for visiting this region. It contains some 14th and 15th cent. houses and most of its old gates, one having the belfry or Tour du Belfroi built over it. In the centre of the town is

the house Queen Marguerite de Navarre inhabited ; now it is converted into shops and dwellings.

From Besse go 5¾ m. N. to Murols, 13 m. E. from Mont-Dore, on the highway between Mont-Dore and Issoire. The road to Murols discloses beautiful views of Limagne as it passes Montredon, Chomeilles, Breuil, St. Victor, and Bessoles. As most of the houses in Murols (*Inn :* Nierat, pop. 700) have been built of material taken from the castle, many have escutcheons and sculptured stones on their walls. On a cone of basalt, 3186 ft., overlooking the village, are the ruins of a formerly important castle, 12th or 13th cent., and favourite residence of the lords of Murols et d'Estaing. From the top of the repaired tower is a beautiful and extensive view, embracing Besse, St. Victor, Lake Pavin, the Chaudefour valley, Chambon with its lake, Varennes, the Dent-de-Marais, and Tartaret. 13 m. W. from Murols is Mont-Dore, passing on the left the Puy du Tartaret, 2953 ft., Lake Chambon, 2625 ft. above the sea, considered one of the prettiest lakes in Auvergne. A little farther W. is the village of Chambon, 40 ft. higher than the lake, pop. 1000, on the Couze and Surrain at the foot of a granite mountain.

The journey from Mont-Dore to the Pics de Sancy and Ferrand and back is 11 m. ; but if it be prolonged round by Vassivières, Besse, and Murols the entire distance is 32 m.

A very pleasant promenade is to the **Salon du Capucin**, recommended as well as the Salon de Mirabeau for the breathing of the air from the pine forest. If on foot, cross the suspension bridge, and having reached the Jubilee cross about 600 yards from Mont-Dore, take the road to the left which enters the forest, and after having ascended a few minutes, a stone to the right will be seen bearing the inscription : " Petit Chemin du Capucin," which take. Shortly after it divides, when take the left. At last the path enters a large open space surrounded by beeches, where several roads meet. The road to the left goes to the Vallée d'Enfer, to the right to the Rigolet, and the road in front to the Salon, which is quite near. The path which divides the Salon into two parts leads up to the top of the Rocher du Capucin, 4807 ft. above the sea, about 2 m. S. from Mont-Dore, commanding a charming view. It owes its name to the detached pinnacle, like a monk's hood, called the Aiguille du Capucin, which is rather difficult to ascend.

To go to the Vallée d'Enfer return to the open glade and take the Enfer path which leads to the valley by the Vallée Lacour, ⅔ m. long, near the top of which, at the Rocher de Courlande, 5325 ft., is the opening where those on foot climb over to the Vallée d'Enfer ; those on horseback have to pass round by Burens. The Vallée d'Enfer is an arid narrow gorge between naked volcanic cliffs traversed by vertical dykes. From the valley continue southwards to the Pic de Sancy, or return to Mont-Dore, 4¾ m. N.

BOURBOULE.

8 m. from Laqueuille, surrounded by wooded mountains, in the valley of the Dordogne, is Bourboule, pop. 1600, 2796 ft. above the sea, or 606 ft. lower than Mont-Dore. The rapid increase of Bourboule is due to the excellence of its mineral waters, of the same nature as those of Mont-Dore, but richer in the chief ingredient to which they owe their especial virtue—the arseniate of soda. The climate too is a little milder, and the valley of the Dordogne wider and more open than it is at Mont-Dore.

Hotels.—Around the principal establishment, called the Etablissement des Thermes, are the 'Grand Hotel; H. ¹Bellon ; ¹Univers ; Bains ; Europe ; Globe ; Étrangers ; H. de ¹l'Etablissement ; ¹Paris ; ¹Sources. On the other side of the Dordogne, by the side of the Parc de Fenestre, are the Angleterre ; France ; ¹Parc ; Beausejour ; and also the Casino, Theatre, and Gambling-rooms.

At the east end of the town, on the road to Mont-Dore, are the ¹l'oste ; Bourboule ; Helder ; ¹Louvre ; Nice ; ¹Ambassadeurs ; ¹Continental.

Abundance of furnished lodgings (Maisons Meublées) and villas to let.

The figure (¹) indicates that the hotel is first-class, with first-class prices, which vary according to the month and the story in which the room is situated. From the 25th of June to the 10th of August the charge is from 11 to 15 frs. the day, which includes room and two meals with wine. Coffee or tea in the morning, 1 fr. extra. Service, ½ to 1 fr. per day. Candles, 3 frs. at end of season. From the 25th of May to the 25th of June, and from the 10th of August to the 30th of September, the charges are less. Intending visitors should bear this in mind in their correspondence with the hotel-keepers.

The other hotels should charge less ; but unless the price be agreed upon beforehand it will be much the same.

The bath charges are rather complicated. There are three bathing-houses, of which the most important is the Etablissement des Thermes, a very large, well-arranged, and handsome building by the side of the Dordogne, opposite the park, near the springs Fenestre and Plage. Behind it, and more hidden among houses, are the Etablissement Chaussy and the Etablissement Mabru, both under the same roof. A part of the latter establishment is portioned off for the indigent.

In the Etablissement des Thermes a bath with linen, from 16th June to 31st August, 3 frs. ; from 25th May to 15th June, and from the 1st to the 30th September, 2½ frs.

In the Etablissement Choussy the charges are ½ fr. less than in the Thermes. In the Mabru they are ½ fr. less than in the Choussy.

The pump-rooms of the Thermes and Choussy cost the season 10 frs., and in the indigent department of Mabru 5 frs.

The duration of a bath, with or without a douche, and of an inhalation or pulverisation sitting bath, must never exceed one hour, including the time for dressing and undressing; whoever exceeds that time pays double. Chairmen to the baths and back, 1¼ fr.

The Springs.

Bourboule possesses seven mineral springs, of which five are on the right bank of the Dordogne, and two, the Sources Fenestre on the left, in the Park. The three most important, the Perrière, the Choussy, and Sédaiges, are within a few feet of each other, near the Mabru bath-house. They rise from the place where the trachytic rocks overlap the granite, and were obtained by boring to the depth of from 82 to 92 ft. The water pumped up by steam-engines has, above ground, a temperature of 140° F.

These three springs produce the strongest arsenical water as yet discovered. Near them, but still on the same side of the river, are the springs of the Puits de la Plage, 81°, and of the Puits Central, 104°, mineralised more feebly, but in the same proportions. The two springs Fenestre, on the opposite side of the river, are cold (64° F.), and as they contain more free carbonic acid gas than the others, are drunk with wine at dinner.

Their Constituents and Effects.

Of the springs, Perrière, Choussy, and Sédaiges, each litre (1¼ of a gallon) contains 82 grains of mineral substances, of which nearly one half is the bicarbonate of soda, and the other half the chloride of sodium; and every 28 ounces contains the third of a grain of the arseniate of soda (see p. 379). Besides the special uses of these waters arising from the arsenic, their composition, resembling that of the serum of the blood, makes them applicable to cases of arrested development, defective nutrition, cases of slow convalescence, and other forms of general debility. In all scrofulous affections, such as enlarged glands, scrofulous discharges from mucous membranes, diseases of the bones, etc., these waters produce great benefit. But it is more especially in the chronic forms of skin disease that La Bourboule claims to effect the most remarkable cures, and chiefly when they arise in connection with a rheumatic or scrofulous constitution, or as the result of simple debility. The scrofulous form of pulmonary consumption, nasal and pharyngeal catarrhs, asthma, and chronic bronchitis, are all alleviated by the use of the Bourboule waters.

Bourboule Excursions.

On the wall of the Etablissement des Thermes a notice indicates that it is 2¼ m. from the Cascade de la Vernière, 2½ m. from the Cascade du Plat-a-Barbe, 3⁷⁄₁₀ m. from Murat-le-Quaire, 5½ m. from Mont-Dore-les-Bains, 4⅓ m. from the Cascade du Queureuilh, 4½ m. from the Cascade de Rossignolet, 4¾ m. from the summit of the Puy Gros, 2¼ m. from the petrifying spring, 3½ m. from the village of St. Sauves, and 10¼ m. from Latour. The most of these places are between Mont-Dore and Bourboule.

The only promenade of interest which may be said to belong especially to Bourboule is to the top of the Roche-Vendeix, with splendid specimens of basaltic columns, 2¼ m. S. by a path following the right or east bank of the stream Vendeix. About ¼ m. beyond, the Vendeix path joins the high road between Latour and Mont-Dore, which traverses the forest of La Reine and the forest of Bozat. Near the point of junction, in a glade of the forest, are a large sawmill and Mont Bozat. About 1¼ m. E. from the junction the high road crosses the Clergue, where a path descends northwards by the stream passing the Cascade Plat-a-Barbe, about 4½ m. from Bourboule by this roundabout way, but only 2½ m. by the direct path. The falls, 60 ft. high, tumble into a cavity bearing some resemblance to a barber's shaving basin. A little way farther down through the woods the Clergue makes the cascade of La Vernière, consisting of a sheet of water 26 ft. high, 2¼ m. from Bourboule.

On the way between Bourboule and Mont-Dore, 1½ m. from Bourboule and 4 m. from Mont-Dore, a road extends 2½ m. N. to the summit of the Puy Gros, 5003 ft. above the sea.

Mont-Dore to Issoire,

31¾ m. E., by Saint Nectaire 15¼ m. E., and Champeix other 8¾ m. Diligence from St. Nectaire to Coudes railway station, 12½ m. E. The Mont-Dore coach, after having passed by the cascades of the Saut-du-Loup and of the Barbier, the village of Diane, the castle of Murols, and traversed the village of Sachapt and its narrow gorge, arrives at Saint-Nectaire-le-Bas, with a large bathing establishment. *Hotels:* Paris; Madeuf; Mandon, etc.

N. from St. Nectaire-le-Bas is Saint-Nectaire-le-Haut, also with a large bathing establishment, supplied with similar mineral waters. *Hotels:* Mont Cornadore; France. The waters are alkaline, ferruginous, and stimulant, temperature between 75° F. and 110° F., and are recommended for renal and hepatic diseases, amenorrhœa, leucorrhœa, and gout. The spécialité may be said to be baths and douches of carbonic acid gas. In Mont Cornadore are large caves.

The parish church, built on a rock, 11th cent., is a curious specimen of Auvergnian architecture. In the neighbourhood, at Pernay, is a dolmen, of which the horizontal surface is 13 ft. by 6½ ft.; and 2½ m. distant the cascade of the Granges. 8¾ m. beyond, towards Issoire, is Champeix, pop. 2100, most picturesquely situated in the valley of the Couze. From Champeix the plateau of Pardines, 1620 ft., may be ascended; whence continue to the Tour de Maurifolet, and descend by the stair in the cliff to Perrier, pop. 600, among rocks pierced with caves, 3 m. from Issoire (p. 372).

2 C

Continuation of Route—Clermont to Brive.

14 m. S.W. from Laqueuille by rail, 54 m. S.W. from Clermont, and 68 m. N.E. from Brive, is **Eyguirande**, pop. 1150. Junction here with loop-line to Largnac, 30 m. S. Coach daily to Murat 41 m. S., passing Mauriac 12 m. S. (see Black's *South France*, West Half).

31 m. S.W. from Eyguirande station is **Meymac**, pop. 3200, on the Lozege. Romanesque church, tower 15th cent. ; remains of fortifications. Junction here with loop-line to Puy-Imbert, 9½ m. N., and close to Limoges. (See *South France*, West Half.)

16¼ m. N.E. from Brive, and 105¾ m. S.W. from Clermont, is **Tulle**, pop. 15,500, on the Corrèze. *Hotels:* Notre Dame ; Lyon ; Charles. Firearms and coarse woollens are made here, but not an inch of the fabric called tulle.

122 m. S.W. from Clermont, 311 m. S. from Paris, 156 m. N. from Toulouse, and 45 m. E. from Perigueux, is **Brive-la-Gaillarde**, pop. 12,000, on the Corrèze. *Hotels:* Bordeaux ; Toulouse (see Black's *South France*, West Half).

. INDEX.

THE END.

Printed by R. & R. CLARK, *Edinburgh.*